Ann Radcliffe The Complete Novels

Ann Radcliffe

Published by

GRAPEVINE INDIA PUBLISHERS PVT LTD

www.grapevineindia.com
Delhi | Mumbai
email: grapevineindiapublishers@gmail.com

Ordering Information:
Quantity sales: Special discounts are available on quantity purchases by corporations, associations, and others.
For details, reach out to the publisher.

First published by Grapevine India 2023
Copyright © Grapevine 2023
All rights reserved

THE MYSTERIES OF THE UDOLFO CASTLE

VOL. ONE

... tore a handkerchief to bandage his wound...
Chap. IV

CHAPTER I

On the banks of the Garonne, in the province of Guienne, the castle of Sant'Aubert existed in the year 1584: from its windows one could discover the rich and fertile villages of Guienne, which extended along the river, crowned by woods, vineyards and olive groves. At noon, the perspective was circumscribed by the imposing mass of the Pyrenees, whose peaks, now hidden in the clouds, now revealingbizarreshapes sometimes showed themselves, naked and wild, in the midst of the blue vapors of the horizon, and sometimes they uncovered their slopes, along which large black fir trees swayed, tossed by the winds. Frightening precipices contrasted with the smiling greenery of the surrounding meadows and woods, and the tired gaze from the appearance of those chasms rested at the sight of the herds and the shepherds' huts. The plains of Languedoc extended as far as the eye could see to the north and east, and the horizon merged to the west with the waters of the gulf of Biscay.

Sant'Aubert, accompanied by his wife and daughter, often went for a walk on the banks of the Garonne; he delighted in listening to the harmonious murmur of her waters. He had at other times known another way of living quite different from this simple, country life; he had long lived in the vortex of the great world, and the flattering picture of the human species, formed by his young heart, had undergone the sad alterations of experience. Nevertheless, the loss of his illusions had neither shaken his principles, nor cooled his benevolence: he had abandoned society rather with pity than with anger, and had confined himself forever to the gentle enjoyment of nature, the innocent pleasures of study, and finally to the exercise of domestic virtues.

He was descended from a cadet of illustrious family; and his parents would have wished that, to make up for the injuries of fortune, he had had recourse to some rich party, or tried to raise himself by the intrigues of intrigue. For this last project, Sant'Aubert had too much honor and too much delicacy; and, as to the former, he had not enough ambition to sacrifice to the acquisition of wealth what he called happiness. After his father's death he married a lovely girl, equal to him by birth, no less than by fortune. The luxury and generosity of his father had so overloaded the inheritance received as a legacy, that he was forced to alienate a portion of it. A few years after his marriage, he sold it to Quesnel, his wife's brother, and retired to a small piece of Gascony,

For a long time this place had been dear to him; he had often come there in his childhood, and he still retained the impression of the pleasures enjoyed there; he hadn't forgotten the old farmer then in charge of keeping watch over him, nor his fruits, nor his cream, nor his caresses. Those green meadows, where, full of health, joy and youth, he had joked so much in the midst of flowers; the woods, whose cool shade had heard her first sighs, and held her reflective melancholy, which afterwards became the dominant trait of her character; the rural walks through the mountains, the rivers that he had crossed, the vast and immense plains like the hope of his youth! Sant'Aubert only remembered with enthusiasm and regret these places embellished by so many memories. Finally, released from the world, he came to fix his stay there and thus fulfill his lifelong vows.

The castle, in its then state, was very small; a stranger would no doubt have admired its elegant simplicity and outward beauty; but considerable work was needed to make it the home of a family. Sant'Aubert had a kind of affection for that part of the building which had known the past; and he never wanted a single stone to be altered, so that the new building, adapted to the style of the old one, made it a more comfortable than refined dwelling. The interior, abandoned to the care of Madame Sant'Aubert, afforded her the opportunity to show her taste; but the modesty which characterized her habits was always her guide in the embellishments she prescribed.

The library occupied the western part of the castle, and was filled with the best of ancient and modern works. This apartment overlooked a small wood which, planted along a gentle slope, led to the river, and whose tall and thick trees formed a thick and mysterious shade. From the windows one could discover, above the pergolas, the rich country which extended to the west, and one could see to the left the horrible precipices of the Pyrenees. Near the library there was a terrace with rare and precious plants. The study of botany was one of Sant'Aubert's amusements, and the nearby mountains, which offer so many treasures to naturalists, held him back. often full days. On his outings, he was sometimes accompanied by his wife, and sometimes by his daughter: a wicker basket to store the plants, another full of some food, which could not be found in the shepherds' huts, formed their crew; thus the wildest places flowed, the most picturesque views, and their attention was not totally concentrated on the study of the least works of nature, which did not allow them to equally admire their great and sublime beauties. Tired of climbing over cliffs, where they seemed to have been led by enthusiasm alone, and where no other footprints were seen on the moss except those of the shy chamois, they sought refuge in those beautiful temples of greenery, hidden in the heart of the mountains. In the shade of larches and tall pines,

To the left of the terrace, and towards the plains of Languedoc, was Emilia's cabinet, very well stocked with books, drawings, musical instruments, a few garrulous little birds and the most sought-after flowers; there, occupied in the study of the fine arts, she cultivated them with success, since they suited her taste and character very much. Her natural dispositions, followed by the instructions of her parents, had facilitated her rapid progress. The windows of this room opened to the ground on the garden which surrounded the house; and avenues of almond trees, figs, acacias and flowering myrtles led the view very far as far as the green margins irrigated by the Garonne.

The peasants of this beautiful climate, after the work, often came in the evening to dance on the banks of the river. The animated sound of music, the liveliness of their steps, the panache of their movements, the taste and the capricious attire of the villanelles gave the whole scene a very interesting character.

The facade of the castle, on the south side, was located facing the mountains. On the ground floor there was a large room and two comfortable sitting rooms. The upper floor, which was only one, was distributed in bedrooms, except for a single room, equipped with a large veranda, where breakfast was ordinarily taken.

In the external adjustment, St. Aubert's affection for the theater of his childhood had sometimes sacrificed taste for feeling. Two old larches shaded the castle, and somewhat impeded its view; but Saint Aubert sometimes said that if he saw them wither, he would perhaps have the weakness to mourn them. He planted near these larches a grove of beeches, pines and alpine ash; on a high terrace, above the river, there were several orange and lemon trees, whose fruits, ripening among the flowers, exhaled an admirable and sweet perfume in the air.

He joined them with some trees of another species, and there, under a thick plane tree whose fronds extended as far as the river, he loved to sit on the fine summer evenings between his wife and children. Through the foliage she saw the sun set on the distant horizon, she saw its last rays shine, fade and gradually confuse the purple reflections with the gray tints of the twilight. There too he loved to read and converse with his wife, to let his children play, to abandon himself to sweet affections, usual companions of simplicity and nature. He often thought, with tears in his eyes, how those moments were a hundred times sweeter than the noisy pleasures and tumultuous agitations of the world. His heart was content; for he had the rare advantage of not desiring greater happiness than that from which he enjoyed. manners, and, for such a spirit as his, gave a charm to happiness itself.

The total fall of the day did not take him away from his favorite plane tree; he loved that moment when the last lights go out, when the stars come to twinkle one after the other in space, and to be reflected in the mirror of the waters; pathetic and sweet instant, in which the delicate soul opens up to the most tender feelings, to the most sublime contemplations. When the moon, with its silvery rays, crossed the leafy foliage, Sant'Aubert still remained; and often he had the dairy products and fruits that made up his supper brought under that tree dear to him. When the night became darker, the nightingale sang, and his harmonious accents awakened a sweet melancholy in the depths of his soul.

The first interruption of the happiness which she had known in her retirement was caused by the loss of two boys: they died at that age in which infantile graces are so vague; and although, in order not to afflict his wife excessively, he had moderated the expression of her grief, and had endeavored to bear it steadfastly, he had no philosophy sufficient to withstand the test of such a misfortune. A daughter was now his only offspring. He carefully watched over the development of her character, and was continually concerned with keeping her in the most suitable dispositions to form her happiness. Since childhood she had announced a rare delicacy of spirit, lively affections and a docile benevolence; but she nonetheless showed too much susceptibility to enjoy lasting peace: advancing to puberty, this sensibility gave a reflective tone to her thoughts, and a sweetness to her manners, which, adding grace to beauty, rendered her much more interesting to those who approached her. But Saint Aubert had too much sense to prefer them attractions to virtue; they he was too shrewd not to know how dangerous these are to those who possess them, and he could not be very happy about them. So he tried to strengthen her character, to make her dominate her inclinations and know how to dominate her: he taught her not to give in so easily to the first impressions of her, and to calmly bear the infinite setbacks of life her. But to teach her to conquer herself and to acquire that level of tranquil dignity which alone can tame passions and raise us above accidents and misfortunes, he himself needed some courage, and not without great effort he seemed to see calmly the tears and the little disgusts, which his provident sagacity sometimes caused in Emilia.

This interesting girl resembled her mother; she had his elegant stature, her delicate features; of her he had, like her, blue eyes, languid and expressive; but however beautiful her features were, her expression, however, her physiognomy, as mobile as the objects that struck her, gave above all to her face an irresistible attraction.

Saint Aubert cultivated his spirit with extreme care. He imparted to her a tincture of the sciences, and an exact knowledge of the most exquisite literature. He taught her Latin and Italian, wishing he could read the sublime poems written in these two languages. She announced, from the earliest years, a strong taste for works of genius, to these principles increased the delight and satisfaction of Sant'Aubert. "A cultivated spirit," he said, "is the best preservative against the contagion of vice and follies: an empty spirit always needs entertainment, and plunges into error to avoid boredom. The movement of ideas, a form of reflection, a source of pleasures, and the observations supplied by the world itself, compensate for the dangers of the temptations it offers. how much in the city; in the country they prevent the languors of an indolent apathy, and supply new enjoyments for the taste and observation of great things; in the city, they make distraction less necessary, and consequently less dangerous. —

Her favorite walk was a fish-pond situated in a nearby grove, on the bank of a stream which, flowing down from the Pyrenees, foamed across the rocks, and escaped in silence under the shade of the trees; from this site the most beautiful sites of the surrounding villages were discovered among the leafy woods; the eye was lost in the midst of the sublime cliffs, the humble huts of the shepherds, and the smiling views along the river: in this delightful place also Sant'Aubert and his mother often went to enjoy the coolness in the summer heat, and towards evening, at the time of rest, the silence and the darkness came to greet us, and to listen to the querulous songs of the tender Filomela; she sometimes she still she brought the music; her echo woke up to the sound of the oboe,

One day, Emilia read in a corner of the table the following verses written in pencil:

Ingenuous children of the purest feelingYou so little explain my pain,My verses, if it will happen that in this darkSacred to peace taciturn horrorA gentle object never presents itself,Tell him about my love and my torments.That day that in my heart its semblanceThe first sparks aroused the amorous ones,Ah! fatal day! ah unfortunate lover!Against the bright light of his pupilsHelpless I was and without fearOf the beauty of their extreme power.And filled with angelic delightI already felt my soul palpitate in my breast:But the deception faded; the beloved objectFrom me he turned the plants in a flash,And let me leave all the strongestCrude transports of invincible love.

These verses were not addressed to anyone: Emilia could not apply them to herself, although she was, without any doubt, the nymph of those woods: she quickly scanned the narrow circle of her acquaintances, without being able to apply them, and remained in the uncertainty: uncertainty much less painful for her, than it would have been for a more idle spirit, not having the opportunity to occupy herself for long with a bauble, and to exaggerate its importance by thinking about it constantly. Her uncertainty, which did not allow her to suppose that those verses of hers were addressed to her, did not even oblige her to adopt the contrary idea of her; but the little vanity she felt did not last long, and she soon forgot it for her books, her studies, and her good works.

A short time later, her uneasiness was aroused by her father's indisposition; he was seized with fever, which, without being very dangerous, did not fail to give a sensitive jolt to his temper. Madame Sant'Aubert and her daughter assisted him with much concern, but his convalescence was slow, and while he was recovering his health, his wife lost hers. As soon as he was recovered, the first visit was to the fishpond: a basket of provisions, books, and Emilia's lute were first sent there; fishing was not mentioned, because Saint Aubert took no pleasure in the destruction of living beings.

After an hour of walking and botanical research, lunch was served: the satisfaction felt for the pleasure of seeing that favorite place again filled the diners with the sweetest sentiment: the dear family seemed to rediscover happiness under those blessed shadows. Sant'Aubert discoursed with singular joy: every object revived his senses; the amiable coolness, the delight one feels in the sight of nature after the sufferings of an illness and the stay of a bedroom, they can certainly neither understand nor describe themselves in a state of perfect health; the greenery of the woods and pastures, the variety of flowers, the blue vault of the skies, the smell of the air, the gentle murmuring of the waters, the buzzing of nocturnal insects, everything seems to enliven the soul and give value to existence. Saint Aubert, revived by the gaiety and convalescence of her husband, forgot her personal indisposition: she walked through the woods, and visited the delightful situations of that retreat: she conversed with her husband and daughter, and often looked at them with a degree of tenderness which made her cry. Saint Aubert, realizing it, tenderly reproached her for her emotion: she could only smile, shake his hand, hers, Emilia's, and cry for the benefit. the enthusiasmof feeling it became almost painful to her; a sad impression took possession of her senses, and sighs escaped him. - Perhaps, she said to herself, perhaps this moment is the end of my happiness, as it is its peak; but let us not cut it short with anticipated sorrows; Let's hope I haven't escaped death by having to mourn the only interesting beings that make me fear it. —

To get out of these gloomy thoughts, or perhaps rather to entertain them, he begged Emilia to fetch the lute and play him some beautiful pieces of tender music. As she approached the fishpond, she was surprised to feel the strings of her instrument touched by a master hand, and accompanied by a plaintive song, which captured her attention. She listened in profound silence, fearing that an indiscreet movement on her part would deprive her of a sound or interrupt the player. All was quiet in the pavilion, and as no one seemed to be there, she continued to listen; but finally surprise and delight gave way to her shyness; this increased by the remembrance of the verses written in pencil, which she had already seen, and she hesitated whether or not she should withdraw at once.

In the interval, the music ceased; Emilia regained her courage, and she advanced, albeit trembling, towards the fishpond, but she saw no one there: the lute was lying on the table, and everything else was as she had left it there. Emilia began to believe she had heard another instrument, but she remembered very well that, as she left, she had left her lute by the window; she felt agitated without knowing why; the darkness, the silence of that place, broken only by the slightest trembling of the leaves, increased her childish fear; she wanted to go out, but she found her weakening, and she was obliged to sit down; while she tried to recover, her eyes again met the verses written in pencil; she started as if she had seen a stranger, then struggling to overcome the terror, got up and she went to the window;

It was no longer possible for her to doubt that the homage was not meant for her, but it was no less impossible for her to guess its author: while she was thinking about it, she heard the sound of a few steps behind the building; frightened, she took the lute, ran away and met her parents in a small path along the clearing.

They all climbed together onto a knoll covered with figs, from which they enjoyed the most beautiful point of view of the plains and valleys of Gascony: they sat down on the grass, and while their eyes embraced the grandiose spectacle, they breathed in the sweet perfumes of the plants scattered in that enchanting place. Emilia repeated the songs most pleasing to her parents, and the expression with which she sang of her doubled their delight. Music and conversation kept them there until dusk: the candid veils that marked the rapid course of the Garonne below the mountains had ceased to be visible; it was a darkness more sad than sad. Sant'Aubert and his family got up and left that site regretfully. Alas! Madame Sant'Aubert was unaware of how she was never to return there again!

When she reached the fishpond, she realized that she had lost a bracelet, which she had taken off while having lunch, and had left on the table when going for a walk. She was looked for with great care, especially by Emilia, but in vain, and she agreed to give it up. Saint Aubert had this bracelet in great value, because it contained the portrait of her daughter; and this portrait, recently made, was of the most perfect likeness. When Emilia was certain of this loss, she blushed, and became thoughtful. A stranger had therefore entered the fishpond in their absence; the lute moved and the verses she read from her did not allow her to doubt it: she could therefore conclude with foundation, that the poet, the player and the thief were the same person. But though those lines, the music, and the theft of the portrait made a remarkable combination,

On returning home, the girl thought about what had happened to her; Saint Aubert abandoned himself to the sweetest enjoyment, contemplating the goods he possessed. His wife was disturbed and afflicted by the loss of the portrait; approaching the house, they distinguished a confused noise of voices and horses; several servants crossed the avenues, and a two-horse carriage arrived at the same point in front of the entrance door of the castle. Sant'Aubert recognized the livery of his brother-in-law, and in fact found ispousesQuesnel in the drawing room. They had been missing from Paris for a very few days, and were going to their lands ten leagues away from the valley, Sant'Aubert had sold them to them a few years ago. Quesnel was the only brother of Saint Aubert's wife; but the diversity of character having prevented their bonds from being strengthened, the correspondence between them had not been very sustained. Quesnel had entered the great world; he loved pomp, and aimed at becoming something important; his shrewdness, his insinuations almost got the job done. It is therefore not surprising if such a man did not know how to appreciate the pure taste, simplicity and moderation of Saint Aubert, and did not recognize in it anything other than pettiness of spirit and total incompetence. His sister's marriage had greatly mortified his ambition, for he flattered himself that she would form a kindred fitter to serve his designs. He had received proposals very suited to his hopes; but the sister, who at that time was requested by Saint Aubert, noticed, or thought she noticed, that happiness and splendor were not always synonymous, and his choice was soon made. Whatever Quesnel's ideas on the subject, he would gladly have sacrificed his sister's tranquility to the advancement of his own fortune; and when she married, he could not hide from her her contempt for her principles and for her union which they formed of her. The Saint Aubert hid the insult from her husband, but for the first time, perhaps, she conceived some resentment. She preserved her dignity, and conducted herself with prudence; but her reserved demeanor warned Quesnel enough of what she felt. raising one's fortune; and when she married, he could not hide from her her contempt for her principles and for the union which they formed in her. Saint Aubert hid the insult from her groom, but for the first time, perhaps, she conceived some resentment of her. She preserved her dignity, and conducted herself with prudence; but her reserved demeanor warned Quesnel enough of what she felt. raising one's fortune; and when she married, he could not hide from her her contempt for her principles and for the union which they formed in her. Saint Aubert hid the insult from her groom, but for the first time, perhaps, she conceived some resentment of her. She preserved her dignity, and conducted herself with prudence; but her reserved demeanor warned Quesnel enough of what she felt.

In marrying, he did not follow his sister's example; his wife was an Italian, a very rich heiress; but her naturalness and education made her as frivolous as she was vain.

They had resolved to spend the night in the house of Sant'Aubert, and as the castle was not large enough to house all the servants, they were sent to the neighboring village. After the first compliments and the necessary arrangements, Quesnel began to talk about the his relationships and friendships. Saint Aubert, who had lived long enough in retirement and solitude for this subject to seem new to him, listened to him with patience and attention, and his guest thought he recognized in it both humility and surprise. He vividly described the small number of parties which the turmoil of those times permitted at the court of Henry III, and his accuracy compensated for the arrogance: but when he came to speak of the Duke of Joyeuse, of a secret treaty, with which he knew the negotiations with the Porte, and the point of view under which Henry of Navarre was seen at the court, Saint Aubert recalled the ancient experience, and was easily convinced that at most the brother-in-law could hold the last place at the court; the imprudence of his speeches could not be reconciled with his alleged knowledge:

Madame Quesnel, meanwhile, was expressing her amazement à la Saint Aubert at the sad life she led, she said, in such a remote corner. Probably, to arouse envy, he then began to narrate the ball parties, the dinners, the vigils recently given at the court, and the magnificence of the parties held on the occasion of the wedding of the Duke of Joyeuse with Marguerite of Lorraine, sister of the queen ; she described with the same precision both what she had seen and what she had not been allowed to see. Emilia's fervid imagination received these tales with the ardent curiosity of her youth, and Saint Aubert, considering her daughter with tears in her eyes, understood that if splendor increases happiness, her only virtue but he can give birth to it.

Quesnel said to his brother-in-law: 'I have already bought your estate twelve years ago. "Approximately," answered Saint Aubert, repressing a sigh. "It's been five years since I've been there," he went on Quesnel; « Paris and its surroundings are the only place where one can live; but on the other hand, I am so busy, so well versed in business, I am so oppressed by it, that I have not been able without the greatest difficulty to get away for a month or two. Saint Aubert said nothing, and Quesnel went on: "I have often been amazed that you, accustomed to living in the capital, you, accustomed to the big world, can dwell elsewhere, especially in a country like this, where one does not hear of nothing, and where you hardly know you exist. "I live for my family and for myself," said Saint Aubert; « Today I am happy to know happiness, while I too have known the world in the past.

'I have decided to spend thirty or forty thousand livres in embellishments in my castle,' added Quesnel, ignoring his brother-in-law's reply; 'I have proposed to bring my friends here next summer. I hope the Duke of Durfort and the Marquis de Grammont will honor me with their presence for a month or two. »

Saint Aubert questioned him about his plans for embellishment; it involved demolishing the right wing of the castle to build the stables. "Later on," he added, "I'll make a dining room, a living room, a dining room, and quarters for all the servants, since I don't have to allocate a third part now."

"All my father's people lodged there comfortably," continued Saint Aubert, remembering the old house with displeasure, "and his entourage was also numerous."

"Our ideas have grown a little larger," said Quesnel; « what was decent in those times, now would no longer seem bearable. »

The phlegmatic Saint Aubert blushed at these words, but anger soon gave way tocontempt.

'The castle is cluttered with trees,' Quesnel added, 'but I intend to give it some air.

- Is that! would you like to cut down trees?

"Sure, and why not?" they block the view; there is an old chestnut tree which spreads its branches over a whole part of the castle, and covers the whole façade on the southern side; they say it is so old, that twelve men could fit comfortably in its hollowed out trunk: your enthusiasm will not go so far as to pretend that a very useless old tree has its beauty or its use.

— Good God! exclaimed Saint Aubert; « you will not destroy that majestic chestnut tree, which has existed for so many centuries, and adorns the earth! It was already big when the house was built; when I was young I often climbed his highest branches; hidden among his leaves, the rain could fall like a deluge, without a single drop of water touching me: how many hours have I spent there with a book in my hand! But forgive me," he continued, remembering that he didn't understand, "I speak of ancient times. My sentiments are no longer in fashion, and the conservation of a venerable tree is, like them, not up to par with today's times.

"I'll knock him down for sure," said Quesnel, "but in his place I'll be able to plant some fine Italian poplars among the chestnuts I'll leave in the avenue." Madame Quesnel is very fond of poplars, and she often tells me of her uncle's house on the outskirts of Venice, where this plantation makes a superb effect.

"On the banks of the Brenta," answered Sant'Aubert, "where its tall and straight stem marries pines and cypresses, and pumps around elegant porticoes and slender colonnades, it must actually adorn those delightful places, but among the giants of our forests, next to a gothic and pedantic architecture!

'That may be it, my dear sir,' said Quesnel, 'I don't want to dispute it. It must you return to Paris, before our ideas can have any connection. But speaking of Venice, I almost want to go there next summer. It may be that I will become the owner of the house of which he spoke to you, and which they say is very beautiful. In that case I'll postpone my embellishment plans to next year, and let myself be drawn into spending a few more months in Italy. »

Emilia was somewhat surprised to hear him speak in those terms. A man so needed in Paris, a man who could scarcely get away for a month or two, think of going to a foreign country, and live there for some time! Saint Aubert knew his vanity too well to marvel at such language, and seeing the possibility of an extension for the planned embellishments, he conceived the hope of a total abandonment.

Before parting, Quesnel wanted to speak in particular with his brother-in-law; they both entered another room and stayed there for a long time. The subject of their conversation remained unknown; but Saint Aubert on his return seemed very thoughtful, and the sadness painted on his face greatly alarmed his wife. When they were alone, she came in to ask him why; however, her delicacy held her back, reflecting that if her husband had thought it convenient to inform her, he would not have waited for her questions.

The next day, Quesnel left after having had another conference with Saint Aubert. This happened after lunch, and in the evening the new guests set off again for Epurville, where they urged their brothers-in-law to visit them, but more with the lure of showing off magnificence than out of a desire to make them enjoy its beauties.

Emilia returned with delight to the freedom of the state taken away by their presence. She found her books, her walks, her parents' instructive talks, ed they too enjoyed being freed from so much frivolity and arrogance.

Saint Aubert did not go for her usual walk, complaining of a little tiredness, and her husband went out with his daughter.

They took the road to the mountains. Their plan was to visit some old pensioners of Sant'Aubert. A modest income permitted him such a burden, while it is probable that Quesnel with all his treasures could not have borne it.

St. Aubert distributed the usual boons to his humble friends; he listened to some, consoled others; he satisfied them all with sweet glances of sympathy and a smile of affability, and crossing the shady paths of the forest with Emilia, he returned with her to the castle.

His wife had already retired to her rooms; the languor and despondency which had oppressed her, and which the arrival of the strangers had suspended, seized her again, but with more alarming symptoms. The following day she developed a fever; the doctor recognized in it the same character of the one in which Saint Aubert was healed; she had received the contagion by assisting her husband: her too weak complexion had not been able to resist: her disease, insinuated into her blood, had plunged her into languor. Sant'Aubert, driven by restlessness, kept the doctor in the house; he remembered the feelings and reflections which had disturbed his ideas the last time they had been together at the fishpond; he believed in the foreboding, and feared everything for the patient: he succeeded nevertheless in concealing her perturbation, and revived her daughter, raising their hopes. The doctor, questioned by him, replied that, before making a decision, he had to wait for a certainty, which he had not yet acquired. The sick woman seemed to have a less doubtful one, but her eyes alone could indicate it; she often stared at her with an expression mixed with pity and tenderness, as if she had anticipated their condolences, and seemed not to be attached to life except because of them and their pain. The seventh day was that of the crisis; the doctor took on a graver accent; she noticed it, and taking advantage of a moment that they were alone, she ascertained that she was very convinced of her imminent death. "Don't try to fool me," she told him; « I feel that I have little left to live, and for some time I have been preparing to die; but as it is, let not false pity lead you to flatter my family; if you did, their affliction would be too violent at the time of my death; I will make an effort, by example, to teach them resignation to supreme wishes. »

The doctor relented, promised to obey, and said somewhat rudely to Saint Aubert that there was no need to hope. The philosophy of this unfortunate man was not such as could withstand the test of so fatal a blow; but reflecting that an increase of affliction, in the excess of her grief, might have aggravated her wife more, he gathered strength enough to moderate it in her presence. Emilia fell unconscious, but as soon as she regained the use of her senses, deceived by the vivacity of her desires for her, she retained to the last moment the hope of her mother's recovery.

The disease was making rapid progress; the resignation and calm of the sick woman seemed to grow with her the tranquility with which she awaited death, born of a pure conscience, of a life without remorse, and as much as human frailty could entail, spent constantly in the presence of God and in the hopes of a better world; but her pity could not wipe out the pain she felt, leaving friends so dear to her heart. In the last moments, she talked a lot with her husband and with Emilia about her future life and other religious subjects; her resignation, the firm hope of finding in eternity the dear objects that he abandoned in this world; the effort he made to hide the pain caused by the momentary separation all contributed to such afflicting of Saint Aubert, who was forced to leave the room. He wept bitter tears, but in the end he forced himself, and returned with a restraint which could only increase his torment.

At no time had Emilia known better how prudent she was to moderate her sensibilities, nor had she ever dealt with it so courageously; but she, after the terrible and fatal moment, had to give in to the weight of her pain, and she understood how hope, like her strength, had contributed to sustaining her. Saint Aubert was too afflicted himself to be able to console his daughter.

CHAPTER II

The mortal remains of Sant'Aubert were buried in the church of the nearby village; husband and daughter accompanied the funeral train, and were followed by a prodigious number of inhabitants, all of whom sincerely mourned the loss of the excellent woman.

Returning from the church, Sant'Aubert shut himself up in his room, and came out with the serenity of courage and with the pallor of despair; he ordered all the people who made up his family to gather near him. Emilia alone did not appear: subdued by the lugubrious scene on which she had witnessed her, she had shut herself up in her closet to weep there in freedom. Saint Aubert went to look for him; he took her hand in silence, and her tears continued: he himself had great difficulty in regaining his voice and the ability to express himself; finally he said trembling: «Dear Emilia, we are going to pray for the soul of your good mother; won't you join us? We will implore the help of the Almighty: from whom can we wait for it if not from heaven? »

Emilia held back her tears, and followed her father into the drawing room where the servants were gathered. Saint Aubert read the office of the dead in a low voice, and added prayers for the souls of the dead. As he read, his voice failed him, and tears flooded the book; he halted, but the sublime emotions of pure devotion successively lifted his ideas above this world, and at last poured the balm of consolation into his heart.

The office finished, and the servants withdrawn, he embraced his Emilia tenderly. 'I have endeavored,' she said to her, 'from your earliest years to give you real control over yourself, and I have represented to you its importance in all the conduct of your life; this sublime quality sustains us against the most dangerous temptations of vice, calls us back to virtue, and likewise moderates the excess of the most virtuous emotions. There is a point at which they cease to deserve this name, if their consequence is an evil; any excess is vicious; displeasure itself, though amiable in its beginnings, becomes an unjust passion when one indulges in it at the expense of one's duties. By duty I mean to speak of what one owes to oneself, like what one owes to others, an immoderate pain weakens the soul, and deprives it of those sweet enjoyments which a beneficent God allocates to the ornament of our life. Emilia dear, invoke, make use of all the precepts that you have received from me, and of which experience has so often shown you the wisdom... Your pain is useless; do not regard this truth as a common expression of consolation, but as a real reason for courage. I would not stifle your sensitivity, my daughter, but only moderate its intensity. Of whatever nature the evils may be, but as a real reason for courage. I would not stifle your sensitivity, my daughter, but only moderate its intensity. Of whatever nature the evils may be, but as a real reason for courage. I would not stifle your sensitivity, my daughter, but only moderate its intensity. Of whatever nature the evils may be, wherefore a heart that is too tender is afflicted, one ought to hope for nothing from that which is not. You know my pain, you know if my words are those light speeches made at random to arrest sensitivity in its source, and whose sole purpose is to give pomp of a pretended philosophy. I will show you, dear daughter, that I can put the advice I am giving into practice. I speak to you thus, because I cannot see you, without pain, consume you in superfluous tears and make no effort to console you; I didn't talk to you before, because you are starting a moment in which any reasoning must yield to nature. This moment has passed, and when it is prolonged to excess, the sad habit that contracts, oppresses the spirit to the point of taking away its elasticity, you hit this rock, but I am convinced that you will try me by wanting to avoid it. »

Emilia, crying, smiled at her parent. "O father! » she exclaimed, and her voice failed her. No doubt she would have added: I want to prove myself worthy of your daughter's name. But a mixed movement of gratitude, tenderness and pain oppressed her again: Saint Aubert let her cry without interrupting her, and spoke of other things.

The first person who came to share in his affliction was a certain Barreaux, an austere man, and who seemed insensitive; the taste for botany had bound them in friendship, having often met in the mountains. Barreaux had withdrawn from the world, and almost from society, to live in a beautiful castle, at the entrance to the woods, and very close to the valley. Like Saint Aubert, he had been cruelly disillusioned by the opinion he had had of men, but, like him, he did not limit himself to afflicting himself with them and pitying them; he felt more disdain for their vices than pity for their weaknesses.

Saint Aubert was surprised to see him. She had often invited him to come and visit his family, without ever having been able to decide; that day he came without reserve, and entered the house as one of the closest friends of the family. The needs of misfortune seemed to have softened its harshness and tamed its prejudices. The desolation of Sant'Aubert seemed his sole occupation; manners, more than words, expressed their emotion: he spoke little of the subject of their affliction, but her delicate attentions, the sound of her voice, and the interest of his looks expressed the feeling of his heart; and this language was well understood.

At that painful time, Saint Aubert was visited by his only sister, Madame Cheron, a widow for some years, who was then living on her own land near Toulouse. Their correspondence had been inactive: her expressions were not lacking, however; she didn't mean that magic of the look, which speaks so well to the soul, and that sweetness of accents, which pours a salutary balm into afflicted and desolate hearts. She assured her brother that he took the most sincere interest in her grief, praised the virtues of his wife, and added what she fancied most consoling. Emilia did not stop crying until she spoke. Saint Aubert was calmer, listened in silence, and changed the tenor of the conversation.

As they left, Mrs. Cheron begged them to visit her soon. "The change of residence will distract you quite a bit," she said; « You do very badly to worry so much. Her brother understood the truth of these words, but he felt more repugnance than before to leave an asylum consecrated to her happiness. The presence of his wife had made those places so interesting to him that every day, calming the bitterness of her pain, he increased the vagueness of his recollections.

Nevertheless he had duties to perform, and of this kind was a visit to his brother-in-law Quesnel; an important business did not allow her to be deferred any longer, and wanting moreover to shake Emilia off her despondency, he took the road to Epurville with her.

When the carriage entered the wood that surrounded its ancient patrimony, and which discovered the avenue of chestnut trees and the turrets of the castle, in thinking of the events that had taken place in that interval, and how the current owner could neither appreciate nor respect so much well, Saint Aubert sighed deeply; finally, he entered the avenue, he saw those big trees again, delights of his childhood and confidants of his youth. Gradually the castle showed its massive grandeur. He saw again the big tower, the vaulted entrance door, the drawbridge, and the dry ditch that surrounded the whole building.

The noise of the carriage called a crowd of servants to the gate. Saint Aubert got out and led Emilia into a Gothic room; but the coats of arms, the ancient insignia of her family no longer decorated it. The beams, and all the oak lumber in the ceiling, had been stained white. The great table, where the feudal lord displayed his magnificence and hospitality every day, where laughter and happy songs had so often resounded, this table no longer existed; the very benches which surrounded the room had been removed. The thick walls were covered with nothing but frivolous ornaments, which showed how petty and petty was the taste and feeling of the present owner.

Saint Aubert was ushered into the drawing room by an elegant Parisian servant. Mr and Mrs Quesnel received him with cold politeness, with a few fashionable compliments, and seemed to have totally forgotten that they had ever had a sister.

Emilia was about to shed tears, but was held back by a just resentment. Saint Aubert, frank and tranquil, he preserved his dignity without seeming to notice it, and put Quesnel in awe; who could not explain why.

After a general conversation, Saint Aubert showed a desire to speak to him alone. Emilia stayed with Madame Quesnel, and was soon informed that a large company had been invited for that very day: she was forced to be told that an irreparable loss must not deprive one of any pleasure.

When Saint Aubert heard of this invitation, he felt a mixture of disgust and indignation at the insensitivity of Quesnel, and was almost tempted to return for the moment to his castle; but hearing that, with regard to her, Signora Cheron had also been invited to come, and considering that Emilia might one day experience the consequences of the enmity of such an uncle, he did not want to expose her to you; on the other hand, her instantaneous departure would undoubtedly have seemed inconvenient to people who none the less showed such a feeble sense of propriety.

Among the guests were two Italian gentlemen, one called Montoni, a distant relative of Signora Quesnel, aged about forty, of admirable stature; he had a virile and expressive countenance, but in general he expressed boldness and arrogance, rather than any other disposition.

Signor Cavignì, his friend, looked no more than thirty years old. He was inferior to it in birth, but not in penetration, and surpassed it in the talent for insinuating. Emilia was piqued by the way Cheron spoke to her father. 'My brother,' she said to him, 'I am sorry to see you looking so bad; you should consult some doctor. Saint Aubert answered her, with a melancholy smile, that she was almost as usual; and Emilia's fears made her find her father changed much more than he really was hers. If Emilia had been less oppressed, she would have amused, the diversity of the characters of the conversation during dinner, and the very magnificence with which it was served, far above anything she had hitherto beheld, would doubtless have failed to amuse her. Montoni, recently arrived from Italy, recounted the turmoil and factions that agitated that country. He painted the different parties with vivacity; he deplored the probable consequences of those horrible riots. His friend spoke with equal ardor of the politics of his country; he praised the government and prosperity of Venice, and boasted of her decided superiority over all the other states of Italy; he then turned to the ladies, and spoke with the same eloquence of the fashions, of the spectacles, of the affable manners of the French, and was shrewdness to drop his speech on everything that could flatter the taste of that nation: flattery was not known by those to whom it was addressed, but the effect it produced on their attention did not escape his perspicacity. When he could disengage himself from the other ladies, he turned to Emilia; but she knew neither the fashions nor the Parisian theaters, and her modesty and simplicity, and her beautiful manners contrasted sharply with the thunder of her companions. After lunch, St. Aubert went out only to visit once more the old chestnut tree, which Quesnel intended to destroy. Resting under that shade, he looked through its thick fronds, and glimpsed the blue vault of the heavens among the trembling leaves; the events of his youth all presented themselves to his imagination. He remembered his old friends, their character, and even their features. For a long time they no longer existed; he too seemed to be an almost isolated entity, and only his Emilia could make him love life again.

Lost in the crowd of images that his memory presented to him, he came to the painting of the dying bride; she gasped, and wanting to forget her, if he could, she returned to society.

Sant'Aubert had the carriage made up very early; Emilia realized on the way that he was more taciturn and more dejected than usual; she attributed the cause to her memories remembered to him from that place, nor did she suspect the real reason for a pain that he did not communicate to her.

Returning to the castle, her affliction was renewed, and she experienced more than ever the effects of the deprivation of such a dear mother, who always welcomed her with a smile and the most affable caresses, after even a momentary absence. Now everything was gloomy and deserted.

But what neither reason nor effort can obtain, time obtains. The weeks went by, and the horror of despair gradually transformed into a sweet feeling that the heart keeps, and becomes sacred to it. Saint Aubert, on the other hand, weakened appreciably, although Emilia, the only person who never abandoned him, was the last to notice it. His complexion had not recovered from the impact received in the illness, and the shock he felt at the death of his wife caused his extreme languor: his doctor advised him to travel. It was visible to him how strongly his nerves had been attacked by the access of pain; and it was believed that the change in the air and the motion, by calming its spirit, could succeed in restoring its former vigor.

Emilia then took care of the preparations, and Sant'Aubert of the calculations on the expenses of the trip. The servants had to be dismissed. Emilia, who rarely allowed herself to oppose questions or observations to her father's wishes, would have liked nonetheless to know why, in her infirm state, he did not reserve at least one servant for himself. But when, on the eve of their departure, she realized that Giacomo, Francesco and Maria had been fired, and she kept only Teresa, his former governess, was extremely surprised, and ventured to ask him why... "I do it for economy," he replied; 'We are embarking on a very expensive journey. The doctor had prescribed the air of Languedoc and Provence: Saint Aubert therefore resolved to walk slowly towards those provinces, skirting the Mediterranean.

They retired early to their rooms the evening before their departure. Emilia had to arrange some books and something else; she struck midnight before she had finished; she remembered her drawings of hers, which she wanted to take with her, and which she had left in the living room. She went there, and, passing by her father's room, she found the door ajar, and she thought it was in her cabinet, as she used to do every evening after her wife's death. Agitated by cruel insomniacs, he left his bed and went into that room to try to find rest there. When she was at the bottom of the stairs, he looked into the lavatory, but did not see it. As he went back up, he knocked lightly on the door, received no answer, and slowly advanced to find out where he was.

The room was dark, but through the glass door a light could be seen at the end of an adjoining room. Emilia was convinced that her father was there inside her; but fearing that he might be inconvenienced at that hour, she wanted to go and make sure of it. Considering, however, that so sudden an appearance of hers might perhaps frighten him, she left the lamp outside, and advanced slowly towards the room. There, she saw her father sitting in front of a table, and leafing through several papers, some of which absorbed her attention, and drew sighs and even sobs from him. Emilia, who had not approached the door except to make sure of her father's health, was detained at that moment by a mixture of curiosity and tenderness. She couldn't it discovers its pains, without desiring to know even the cause. She continued to observe him in silence, no longer doubting that those papers were letters. Suddenly, she and she knelt in a more solemn attitude than she had hitherto seen; and in a kind of bewilderment which closely resembled horror, she made a very long prayer. His face was covered in deathly pallor as she stood up. Emilia thought about withdrawing, but she saw him approach the cards again, and she checked herself. He took a small case, and took out a miniature: her light, which reflected above her, made her distinguish a woman, and this woman was not her mother!

Saint Aubert looked at the portrait with a lively expression of tenderness, brought it to his lips, to his heart, and sent out convulsive sighs. Emilia could not believe her own eyes, unaware that he possessed the portrait of another woman besides her of her mother, and especially then that she was so dear to him. She looked at it again for a long time to find the effigy of her parent, but her attention only served to convince her that hers was a portrait of another woman. Finally, her father put it back in her case, and Emilia, reflecting that she had indiscreetly observed his secrets, withdrew as slowly as possible.

CHAPTER III

St. Aubert, instead of taking the direct road which led to Languedoc, following the foothills of the Pyrenees, preferred a route on the heights, because it offered more extensive and more picturesque views. He went off the road a little to say goodbye to Barreaux; he found him herbalizing near his castle, and when he disclosed the subject of his visit and his resolution, the friend showed him a sensitive of which up to that point Saint Aubert had not believed him capable. They parted with mutual regret.

"If anything could have taken me away from my retreat," said Barreaux, "it would have been the pleasure of accompanying you on this journey; I don't give compliments, and you can believe me: I will await your return with great impatience. »

The travelers continued on their way: as they got into the carriage, Sant'Aubert turned around and saw his castle in the plain. Gloomy ideas invaded his spirit, and his melancholy imagination told him that he must never return. He dismissed this thought, but kept looking at her asylum until the distance no longer allowed him to distinguish it.

Emilia remained, like him, in profound silence, but after a few miles, her imagination, struck by the majesty of the surrounding objects, yielded to the most delicious impressions. The road passed, now along horrid precipices, now over the most delightful sites.

Emilia was unable to hold back her transports when, from the midst of the mountains and fir woods, she discovered in the distance immense plains, scattered with villas, vineyards and plantations of every kind. The majestic waves of the Garonne flowed into that rich valley, and from the summit of the Pyrenees, from which it originates, they led towards the ocean.

The difficulty of such an unfrequented road often forced travelers to walk; but they found themselves amply rewarded by the effort for the vagueness of the spectacle offered by nature. While the muleteer was slowly driving the carriage, they had all the comfort of traveling through the solitudes and abandoning themselves to sublime reflections which relieve the soul, soothe it, and finally fill it with that consoling certainty that God, it is present everywhere. The enjoyments of St. Aubert bore the imprint of his brooding melancholy. This arrangement adds a secret charm to the objects, and inspires a religious feeling for the contemplation of nature.

Our travelers had secured themselves against the lack of hotels, bringing provisions with them; they could therefore make their lunches in a clear sky, and rest for the night in any place they found a habitable hut. They had also made provisions for the spirit, bringing with them a botanical work written by Barreaux, and some Latin or Italian poet. Emilia, on the other hand, had her pencils with her, and every now and then she drew the points of view that struck her most.

The solitude of the street increased the effect of the scene; as soon as they met from time to time a farmer with mules, or some boy joking among the rocks. St. Aubert, enchanted by that way of travelling, decided to keep advancing into the mountains until he found a way, and not to leave it until Roussillon, near the sea, to then pass into Languedoc.

A little after noon they reached the top of a high peak which commanded parts of Gascony and Languedoc. There he enjoyed a thick shade. A spring gushed from it, which, fleeing under the trees among grassy margins, ran to fall downwards in brilliant cascades. Its soft murmur was finally lost in the underlying abyss, and the candid mist of its foam served only to distinguish its course among the black fir trees.

The place invited to rest. Lunch was prepared; the mules were detached, and the grass which grew thick around them, supplied them with copious nourishment.

When the meal was over, Saint Aubert took Emilia's hand and squeezed it tenderly without saying a word. A little while later, he called the muleteer and asked him if knew a road in the mountains that could lead to Roussillon. Michele replied to find many, but not being very practical. Sant'Aubert, not wanting to travel until sunset, asked for the name of various nearby hamlets, and informed him of the time it would take to get there. The muleteer calculated that it was possible to go to Mateau, but that, if one wanted to move towards the south, on the Roussillon side, there was a village which one would reach well before sunset.

Sant'Aubert took the latter course. Michele finished his meal, harnessed the mules, retired in the street, and stopped shortly. Saint Aubert saw him praying at the foot of a cross planted on the tip of a cliff at the edge of the road; when the oration was over, he cracked his whip and, without any regard for the difficulty of the road, or for the life of the poor mules, drove them at full gallop on the edge of a frightful precipice. Emilia's terror almost deprived her of the use of her senses. His father, who feared even more the danger of stopping suddenly, was forced to sit down again, and leave everything at the mercy of the mules, who seemed wiser than their conductor. The travelers arrived safely in the valley, and stopped at the edge of a stream.

Forgetting by now the magnificence of the grandiose views, they entered the narrow roomValley. Everything here was lonely or barren; not a living soul was seen there except the mountain roe deer, which, talfiata, suddenly showed itself on the steep summit of some inaccessible cliff. It was a site which Salvator Rosa would have chosen if he had lived. Then Sant'Aubert, struck by this aspect, almost expected to see a group of robbers emerge from some cave nearby, and held his weapons in his hand.

Meanwhile they advanced, and the valley widened, assuming a less frightening character. Towards evening, they found themselves in the mountains, in the midst of broom trees. From a long time, around them, the cowbell of the herds, the voice of the herdsmen were the only sound that was heard; and the residence of the shepherds the only dwelling that was discovered there. Sant'Aubert noticed that the lecce, the sovero and the fir grew last on the surrounding peaks. Smiling greenery carpeted the bottom of the valley. In the depths, in the shade of chestnut and oak trees, grazing and hopping large herds, dispersed or grouped with grace; some animals slept near the cool stream, others quenched their thirst, and others bathed in it.

The sun was beginning to leave the valley; its last rays shone upon the stream, enlivening the rich colors of the broom and flowering heather. Sant'Aubert asked Michele how far away was the farmhouse he had told him about, but he could not answer him exactly. Emilia began to fear she had lost her way; there was no human entity that could help them or guide them. By a long hand they had left behind them both the shepherd and the hut, the twilight diminished more and more, the eye could discern nothing amidst the darkness, and did not distinguish either farmhouse or hovel; a colored line marked only the horizon, forming the travellers' only resource. Michele strove to build up his courage by singing ariettas, which really didn't do much to dispel the lugubrious ideas with which the travelers were occupied.

They continued to walk absorbed in those profound thoughts which solitude and night bring with them. Michele no longer sang, and only the murmur of the breeze could be heard in the woods, nor did he feel anything but the coolness. Suddenly they were shaken by the explosion of a firearm; Saint Aubert made the carriage stop, and sat down to listen. The noise is not repeated, but is heard running through the bush. Sant'Aubert takes up his pistols, and orders Michael to quicken his pace. The sound of a hunting horn makes the mountains rumble; Saint Aubert observes, and sees a young man rushing into the street, followed by two dogs; the stranger was dressed as a hunter; a musket in the neck, a horn in his belt, and a kind of pike in his hand, gave a particular grace to his person, following the agility of his steps.

After a moment's reflection, Saint Aubert wanted to wait for him to question him about the farmhouse he was looking for: the stranger replied that the village was only half a league away, that he went there himself, and would serve as his guide; Saint Aubert thanked him, and struck by his simple and frank manners, offered him a seat in the carriage. The stranger refused, assuring him that he would follow the mules without difficulty. "But you will be badly lodged," he added; "These mountaineers are very poor people; not only do they not know luxury, but they also lack the things considered most indispensable. "I realize that you are not from this country," said Saint Aubert. "No, sir, I'm a traveller. »

The carriage advanced, and the growing darkness made better known the usefulness of a guide; then the paths that often met, would have increased their uncertainty. Finally they saw the lights of the village: some farmhouses could be distinguished, or rather they could be discerned thanks to the stream which still reverberates the feeble light of the twilight. The stranger advanced, and Sant'Aubert understood from him that no hotel existed in that place, but he offered to look for a refuge. Saint Aubert thanked him, and as the village was very close, he got out to accompany him, while Emilia followed them in a carriage.

Along the way, Saint Aubert asked his companion if he had had a good hunt. 'No, sir,' he replied, 'and neither was it my plan; I love this country and I intend to scroll through it for a few more weeks; I have dogs with me rather for pleasure than for utility; this dress then as a hunter it serves me as a pretext, and makes me enjoy the consideration, which would undoubtedly be refused to a foreigner with no apparent occupation. "I admire your taste," replied Saint Aubert, "and if I were younger, I too would like to spend a few weeks there; we too are travellers, but our aim is not the same. I seek health even more than pleasure. »Here he sighed and was silent for a moment; then, recollecting himself, he added: «I would like to find a somewhat good road, which would lead me to Roussillon, to then pass into Languedoc. You, who seem to know the country, could you point me to one? »

The stranger assured him that it would be a pleasure to serve him, and spoke to him of a road further east, which should lead to a city, and from there easily to Roussillon.

Once in the village, they began to look for an asylum that could offer them shelter for the night; they found in most houses nothing but ignorance, poverty, and panache; Sant'Aubert was looked at with a shy and curious air; one should not expect a good bed. Emilia arrived, and observing the tired and afflicted physiognomy of the poor father, she complained that he had chosen such an uncomfortable path for a sick person. The best dwellings consisted of two rooms; one for the mules and the cattle, and the other for the family, made up almost everywhere of seven or eight children, and all, with their father and mother, slept on skins or dry leaves; and as the only opening that was in those chambers was in the roof, there was such a smoke and a nauseating smell, that it almost took one's breath away on entering them. Emilia averted her gaze, and he stared at his father with tender disquiet, whose expression the young stranger seemed to understand; he drew Saint Aubert aside, and offered him his bed. "Compared to all the others, it's comfortable enough," he told him, "but elsewhere II would be ashamedto offer it to you. »

Saint Aubert attested his gratitude and refused the offer; but the stranger persisted. « Do not refuse; I should be too sorry, sir,' resumed he, 'if you lay upon a skin while I lay in bed; your refusals would offend my self-respect, and I might think my proposal displeases you; I'll show you the way, and my landlady will find a way to accommodate the young lady too. »

St. Aubert finally consented; and he was surprised that the stranger was so ungallant as to prefer the rest of a man to that of a charming young girl, not having offered Emilia his room; but she was not of the same opinion, and with an expressive smile she showed him how sensitive she was to the attention he had paid to her father.

The stranger, whose name was Valancourt, stopped first to say something to his landlady. The lodging she opened bore no resemblance to all those she had seen so far. The good woman employed all her attentions in welcoming the travellers, and they were forced to accept the only two beds that were found in that house. Eggs and milk were the only food she could afford, but Saint Aubert had provisions, and he begged Valancourt to dine with them; the invitation was very well received, and the conversation became animated. The frankness, simplicity, grandiose ideas and taste for nature that the young man showed, enchanted Sant'Aubert. He had often said that this interest in nature could not exist in a soul that did not have great purity of heart and

The conversations were interrupted by a violent tumult, in which the muleteer's voice drowned out all the others. Valancourt got up to find out the reason, and the dispute lasted so long that Saint Aubert lost his patience and left anyway. Michele argued with the landlady because she forbade him to bring in the mules in the stable, which he had allowed him to share with his three sons; the site wasn't very nice to tell the truth, but there was nothing better, and, more delicate than the countrymen, she didn't want her children to sleep in the same room with the mules. Valancourt finally managed to pacify everyone. She begged the innkeeper to leave the stable to the muleteer and his mules; he gave her sons the skins that had been prepared for him to rest on, and assured her that, wrapped in his cloak, he would spend the night very well on a bench near the door. The good woman did not want to accept such an arrangement, but Valancourt insisted so much that this great affair ended thus.

It was late when Sant'Aubert and Emilia retired to their rooms; Valancourt remained before the door. In that summer he preferred such a place to a small room and a bed of hides. Sant'Aubert was a little surprised to find Homer, Horace and Petrarch in the room, but the name of Valancourt written on those volumes let him know the owner.

CHAPTER IV

Saint Aubert awoke very early; sleep had refreshed him, and he wanted to leave at once. Valancourt lunched with him, and related that a few months earlier he had been as far as Beaujeu, a large city in Roussillon, and Saint Aubert, on his advice, decided to take that direction.

'The shortcut, and the road which leads to Beaujeu,' said the young man, 'join at the distance of a league and a half from here: if you will allow it, I can direct your mule track to you; I must go for walks, and the walk I will take with you will be more pleasing to you than any other. »

Sant'Aubert accepted the proposal with grateful heart; they left together, but the young man did not want to consent to enter the carriage. The road at the foot of the mountains ran through a charming valley, splendid for greenery and scattered with groves. Numerous herds rested there in the shade of oaks, beeches and sycamores; the ash and the aspen dropped the leafy tips of the branches on the arid rocks; a little earth barely covered its roots, and the slightest breath stirred all its branches.

People met there at every hour of the day. The sun had not yet appeared, and the shepherds were already leading an immense herd to graze on the mountains. Sant'Aubert had left very early to enjoy the view of the sunrise and breathe the pure morning air, so beneficial to the sick, and which must have been especially so in those regions where the abundance and variety of aromatic plants impregnated it with the sweetest fragrance.

The light mist that veiled the surrounding objects gradually disappeared, and allowed Emilia to contemplate the progress of the day.

The uncertain reflections of the dawn, gilding the tops of the cliffs, clothed them successively with vivid light, while their base and the bottom of the valley remained covered by black vapour. Meanwhile, the tints of the eastern clouds brightened, turned purple, and finally shone with a thousand splendid colors.

The transparency of the atmosphere left uncovered streams of pure gold, the brilliant rays dispelled the darkness, and penetrated the fondure of the valley reverberating in the silvery streams: nature awoke from death to life. Saint Aubert felt revived; his heart was moved; he shed tears and raised thoughts to the Creator of all things.

Emilia wanted to go down and trample on that grass all dewy with fresh dew; she wanted to taste that freedom which the chamois seemed to enjoy on the brown peaks of the mountains. Valancourt stopped with the travellers, feelingly showing them particular objects of his admiration. Saint Aubert was fond of him. - The young man is fiery, but good; he said to himself; "It is evident that he has never lived in Paris. He arrived at the point where the two roads joined, much to his displeasure; and he took his leave with more cordiality than a new acquaintance ordinarily permits. Valancourt continued to talk a good deal near the carriage; it was time to part ways, and he nevertheless always remained putting forward arguments to excuse him for this prolongation. At last he took leave, and when he left, Saint Aubert observed how he contemplated Emilia with an attentive and expressive gaze; she greeted him with shy sweetness; the carriage set off, but Saint Aubert a little later, sticking out his head, observed Valancourt motionless on the road, with his arms crossed on his cane, and eyes fixed on the carriage; she waved at him, and Valancourt, shaken by his ecstasy, saluted him and went away.

The appearance of the country changed in a short time: the travellers, then found themselves in the midst of very high mountains covered up to the top by black fir woods. Various granite peaks, rising from the valley itself, went to hide the snowy peaks in the bosom of the clouds. The brook, having become a river, flowed in sweet silence, and those dark woods reflected their shadow in its clear waters. For intervals a steep precipice raised its bold front above the woods and vapors which served as a girdle to the mountains; sometimes a marble needlefish supported itself perpendicularly to the flowery margin of the waters; a colossal larch embraced her with strong arms, and her forehead, furrowed by lightning, was still crowned with green vine leaves.

When the carriage was moving slowly, Sant'Aubert would get out, and take pleasure in going in search of curious plants, where those places were scattered; Emilia, in the exaltation of her enthusiasm, went into confinement in the thick woods, listening silently to their imposing murmur.

For the space of many leagues they met neither villages nor hamlets of any kind; a few hunters' huts here and there were the only traces of human habitation. The travelers dined in a clear sky, in a beautiful spot in the valley, seated in the shade of the beech trees; after which they immediately set out for Beaujeu.

The road rose sensibly, and leaving the pines below them, they found themselves in the midst of precipices. The twilight of the evening increases the horror of the place, and the travelers were unaware of the distance from Beaujeu. Sant'Aubert nonetheless believed he was not very far from it, and rejoiced that he was therefore no longer beyond that city, to cross such deserts. The woods, the cliffs, the surrounding ridges were gradually confused in the darkness, and in a short time it was no longer possible to discern those indistinct images. Michele proceeded cautiously, barely perceiving the road, but his mules, more expert, still walked with a frank step.

At the bend of a mountain, they saw a light; the cliffs and the horizon were illuminated at a great distance. It was certainly a great fire, but there was no indication whether it was accidental or prepared. Saint Aubert thought it kindled by some gang of those bandits who infested the Pyrenees; he was very careful, and he wanted to know if the road passed by that fire. He had weapons that he could defend himself in case of need; but what was the use of such a weak resource against a gang of determined killers? He was reflecting on this circumstance, when he heard a voice behind them, ordering the muleteer to stop. Sant'Aubert ordered him to walk faster, but whether it was due to the stubbornness of Michele, or of the mules, they didn't change their pace; the gallop of a horse was heard; a man reached the carriage, and again ordered a halt. Sant'Aubert, no longer doubting this design, unloaded a pistol from the door; the incognito staggered on his horse, and the sound of the blow was followed by a groan of pain. It will be easy to imagine the fright of Saint Aubert, who thought he recognized then the sorrowful voice of Valancourt. He stopped the carriage himself, pronounced the young man's name, and could no longer have any doubts. He got out immediately, and ran to help him; the young man was still on horseback, his blood was flowing copiously, and he seemed to be in great pain, though he tried to console Saint Aubert, assuring him that it was nothing, and felt only lightly hurt in his arm. Sant'Aubert and the muleteer helped him to dismount and laid him on the ground; the first wanted to bandage his wound, but his hands were shaking so much that he could not do it. Meanwhile Michele ran after the horse which had fled while the master got off it; he called Emilia, and receiving no answer, ran to the carriage, and found her in a faint. In this terrible situation, and impelled by the pain of leaving Valancourt to bleed, he endeavored to relieve her, and called to Michael for water from the nearby stream. Michele had gone too far, but Valancourt, hearing Emilia's name, understood what it was all about, and forgetting himself, went to his aid; she was already revived when he was near her; he learned that the swoon had been caused by fear of the accident, and in a voice disturbed by a feeling quite different from that of pain, he assured her that his wound was of very little consequence. saint Aubert then perceived that the blood had not yet stagnated; his fears changed subject; he tore a handkerchief to bandage his wound: the bleeding stopped, but he, fearing the consequences, asked several times if Beaujeu was still very far away, and having understood that he was two leagues away, his fear grew. She did not know whether Valancourt could have resisted the movement of the carriage, and saw him on the verge of fainting. As soon as the latter became aware of his disquietude, he hastened to cheer him up, and spoke of his adventure as if it were a bagatelle. Michele had led the horse back; Valancourt, got into the carriage; Emilia had recovered, and they continued along the road to Beaujeu.

Saint Aubert, revived by terror, expressed his surprise at the meeting at Valancourt; but he stopped it. "You have renewed my taste for society," he told him; 'After your departure, my cottage seemed a desert to me. And since my only aim is to travel for pleasure, I have decided to leave immediately. I took this road, because I knew it was more beautiful than any other; and besides," he added, hesitating a little, "I'll confess it (and why shouldn't I confess it?), I had some hope of joining you. "And I have cruelly returned your kindness," resumed Saint Aubert, who reproached himself for his haste, and explained the reason. But Valancourt, careful to avoid any uneasiness on his behalf, hid the anguish he felt, and continued to converse cheerfully. Emilia was silent, unless Valancourt spoke to her, and the moved tone with which she did so was in itself enough to express a great deal.

They then found themselves near that fire which stood out so brightly in the darkness of the night: it then illuminated the whole street, and it was easy to distinguish the figures that surrounded it. Approaching, they recognized a band of gypsies who, especially at that time frequented the Pyrenees, burglarizing travellers. Emilia noticed with fright the grim aspect of that company, and the fire that illuminated them, spreading a purple cloud over the trees, rocks and foliage, increased the bizarre effect of the picture.

All those gypsies were preparing dinner. A large cauldron stood on the fire, and several people were busy filling it. The brightness of the flame revealed a kind of rough tent, around which boys and dogs were frolicking in confusion. The whole formed a truly grotesque complex. Travelers felt danger. Valancourt was silent, but put his hand on one of Sant'Aubert's pistols, who, having done the same, made the muleteer advance. Nevertheless, they passed without receiving any insults. The thieves were probably not expecting such a meeting, and were too busy with dinner to then feel a completely different interest.

After an hour and a half's journey in the deepest darkness, the travelers arrived at Beaujeu and dismounted at the only inn there was, and which, although much superior to the huts, nevertheless did not cease to be bad.

The surgeon of the city was summoned immediately, if at any rate this name can be given to a kind of farrier, who treated men and horses, and who, in case of need, also acted as a barber. He examined Valancourt's arm, and having recognized that the ball had not penetrated his flesh, he treated him and advised him to rest; but the patient was in no way disposed to obey him. The pleasure of being better had succeeded the restlessness of the disease; because every enjoyment becomes positive when it contrasts with a danger. Valancourt had recovered his strength, and he wanted to take part in the conversation. Saint Aubert and Emilia, free from any fear, were of a singular joy. It was already late, and Sant'Aubert was forced to go out with the innkeeper to go find something for supper. Emilia, in the interval, he found the accommodation better disposed than he believed and then returned to join Valancourt. They spoke of the views discovered that day, of natural history, of poetry, and finally of Emilia's father who could not speak or hear speak, except with joy, of a subject so dear to her heart.

The evening passed pleasantly, but as Saint Aubert was tired, and Valancourt was still in pain, they parted soon after supper.

The following morning, Valancourt was feverish, had not slept, and his wound was inflamed: the surgeon, who came to see him early, advised him to remain calm at Beaujeu. St. Aubert had very little faith in his talents; but having heard that no more skilful one could be found, he changed his plan, and resolved to wait for the sick man to recover. Valancourt seemed to try to dissuade him, but with more politeness than good faith. His indisposition kept the travelers there for several days. Saint Aubert happened to know his talents and his character, with that philosophical precaution, which he knew so well to employ in all circumstances. He knew a frank and generous natural, full of ardor, susceptible to all that is great and good, but impetuous, almost wild and somewhat romantic. Valancourt knew little of the world; he had sensible ideas, right feelings; his indignation and his esteem were expressed without measure or consideration. Saint Aubert smiled at his vehemence, but seldom repressed it, and said to himself: "This young man, without a doubt, has never been to Paris." A sigh followed these reflections: he was determined not to leave Valancourt before his full recovery, and as he was then in a state to travel, but not on horseback, Saint Aubert invited him to take advantage of a few days in the carriage of he. Having learned that the young man was of a distinguished family of but he seldom repressed it, and said to himself: 'This young man has certainly never been to Paris. A sigh followed these reflections: he was determined not to leave Valancourt until he was fully recovered, and as he was then in a state to travel, but not on horseback, Saint Aubert invited him to take advantage of his carriage for a few days. Having learned that the young man was of a distinguished family of but he seldom repressed it, and said to himself: 'This young man has certainly never been to Paris. A sigh followed these reflections: he was determined not to leave Valancourt until he was fully recovered, and as he was then in a state to travel, but not on horseback, Saint Aubert invited him to take advantage of his carriage for a few days. Having learned that the young man was of a distinguished family of Gascony, whose rank and consideration were well known to him, his reserve was less great, and Valancourt having accepted the offer with pleasure, they all resumed the road which led to Roussillon.

They traveled without prompting, stopping when the site deserved attention; they often climbed high ground which the mules could not reach; they lost themselves among those cliffs, covered with lavender, thyme, juniper and tamarind, and protected by ancient shadows; a beautiful sight thrilled Emilia, surpassing the marvels of her wildest imagination. Sant'Aubert sometimes enjoyed herbalizing, while Emilia and Valancourt awaited some discovery of her: the young man made her observe the particular objects of her admiration, and recited the most beautiful passages of the Italian or Latin poets to whom she favored. In the interval of the conversation, and when he was not observed, he fixed his gaze on that graceful countenance, whose animated features indicated so much wit and intelligence: when he next spoke, the softness of her voice revealed a feeling which she tried in vain to hide. Gradually, his pauses and his silence became more frequent: Emilia showed great haste to interrupt them: until then so reserved, she spoke continuously, now of the woods, now of the valleys, now of the mountains, instead of exposing herself to the danger of certain moments of silence and sympathy.

The road to Beaujeu climbed very rapidly: and they found themselves in the midst of the loftiest mountains; the serenity and purity of the air in those high regions thrilled the three travellers; their souls seemed lightened by it, and their spirits became more penetrating. He had no words to express such sublime emotions, those of Sant'Aubert received a more solemn expression: the tears irrigated his cheeks, and he walked aside. Valancourt spoke from time to time to attract Emilia's attention; the clarity of the atmosphere which allowed her to distinguish all objects, she deceived her sometimes, and always with pleasure. She could not believe that what seemed so close was so far from her; the profound silence of solitude was only interrupted by the cry of the eagles fluttering in the air, and by the deaf roaring of the torrents at the bottom of the abyss. Above them the splendid vault of the heavens was not obscured by any cloud, the whirlwinds of vapor stopped in the bosom of the mountains, their rapid movement sometimes veiled the whole country, and sometimes uncovering part of it, left the eye with a few moments of observation. Emilia, ecstatic, contemplated the greatness of those clouds which varied in shape and colour; she admired the

After thus traveling several leagues, they began to descend into Roussillon, and the scene which unfolded exhibited a less harsh beauty. The travelers regretted the imposing objects they were about to abandon. Although tired by those vast aspects, the eye rested pleasantly on the green of the woods and meadows; the river that irrigated the hut under the shade of the beech trees, the joyful flocks of the shepherds, the flowers that adorned the slopes, together formed an enchanting spectacle.

Descending, they recognized one of the great gates of the Pyrenees in Spain: the fortresses, the towers, the walls, then received the rays of the sun at sunset; the surrounding woods no longer had anything but a yellowish reflection, while the tips of the cliffs were still tinged with pink.

Saint Aubert looked attentively without discovering the small city indicated to him. Valancourt could not inform him of the distance, having never gone so far; yet they saw a road, and they had to believe it direct, since after Beaujeu they had not been able to get lost anywhere.

The sun was nearing sunset, and St. Aubert urged the muleteer; he felt very weak, and longed for rest; after such a tiring day his restlessness did not calm down, observing a large train of men, mules and loaded horses, which paraded along the paths of the opposite mountain, and since the woods often hid their path, it was not possible to specify the number: something brilliant, like weapons, shone in the last rays of the sun and the military uniform stood out on the first ones, and on a few individuals scattered among the group. As soon as they were in the valley, another band came out of the woods, and Saint Aubert's fears increased, not doubting that they were many smugglers arrested in the Pyrenees, and escorted by soldiers.

The travelers had gone so far in the mountains that they were deceived in their calculations, and could not reach Montignì before nightfall. They crossed the valley, and noticed on a rustic bridge that joined two coasts, a group of children who amused themselves by throwing stones into the stream; as the stones fell, they caused columns of water to spray, sending a dull crash reverberated in the distance by the echoes of the mountains. Under the bridge the whole valley was revealed in perspective, a cataract in the middle of the cliffs, and a hut on a peak protected by age-old fir trees. That house seemed to be close to a small town. Sant'Aubert made them stop: he called the boys and asked them if Montignì was very far away; but the distance, the noise of the waters did not allow him to be heard, and the steepness of the mountains which supported the bridge was too steep for anyone other than a practical mountaineer to ascend them. Sant'Aubert therefore had to decide to continue the road under cover of twilight, which was so uncomfortable that it seemed better advice to go down of car. The moon was beginning to rise, but it gave off too little light; and they walked at random in the midst of dangers. At that point the bell of a convent was heard; the thick darkness blocked the view of the building, but the sound seemed to come from the woods that covered the mountain on the right. Valancourt proposed to go in search of them. 'If we don't find shelter in that convent,' he said, 'at least they'll show us the distance or position of Montignì. And he ran off without waiting for an answer; but Saint Aubert called him back saying: «I am horribly tired, I need prompt rest; we all go to the convent; your sturdy appearance would foil our designs; but when my exhaustion and Emilia's weariness are seen, shelter will not be denied.»

Saying so, he took Emilia's arm, and urging Michele to wait for him, he followed the sound of the bell and went up towards the woods, but with faltering steps. Valancourt offered him his arm which he accepted. The moon came to illuminate the path, and soon allowed them to see towers that rose on the hill. The bell continued to guide them; they entered the wood, and the dim light of the moon became more uncertain from the shadow and the trembling of the leaves. The darkness, the gloomy silence, when the bell did not ring, the sort of horror inspired by so wild a place, all filled Emilia with a fear which Valancourt's voice and conversation could only diminish. After some time of climbing, Sant'Aubert complained, and they all stopped on a grassy hillock, where the trees, more sparse, let them enjoy the moonlight. Saint Aubert sat down on the grass between the two young men. The bell no longer rang, and the nocturnal stillness was not interrupted by any noise, although the dull roar of some distant stream seemed to accompany rather than disturb the silence.

They then had the valley they had just left in sight. The silvery light that uncovered its foundations, reflecting on the cliffs and woods on the left, contrasted with the darkness, by which the woods on the right were as if enveloped. The peaks alone were lighted in flashes; the rest of the valley was lost in the bosom of a fog, of which the moonlight itself served only to increase its thickness. The travelers stopped for some time to contemplate this beautiful effect.

'Such scenes,' said Valancourt, 'delight the heart like the concerts of delightful music; whoever has once tasted the melancholy they inspire would not want to change the impression for that of the most exquisite pleasures. Hellene arouse our purest feelings; they dispose to benevolence, to piety, to friendship. Those whom I love, I always seemed to love them much more in this solemn hour. His voice trembled, and he paused.

Saint Aubert said nothing. Emilia saw a tear fall on her hand which she held in hers. She guessed well the thought of her; even hers had run to the compassionate memory of the mother. But Saint Aubert, reviving her: "Oh yes," she said repressing a sigh, "the memory of those we love, of a time gone by forever, it is in this instant that settles on our souls! It is like a distant melody in the silence of the nights, like the softened colors of this landscape. Then, after a pause, he continued: "I've always believed that ideas are more lucid at this hour than at any other, and the heart that doesn't recognize their influence is certainly a distorted heart." There are so many..."

Valancourt sighed.

"So there are many of them?" Emilia said. "Perhaps in a few years, dear daughter," answered Saint Aubert, "you will smile as you remember this question, if nevertheless this memory does not rob you of the tears. But come, I feel a little better. Let's go ahead. »

Finally they came out of the wood, and above an eminence they saw the convent they had been looking for so much. A very high wall that surrounded him led them to an ancient door; they knocked, and the layman who opened the door led them into a nearby room, asking them to wait until the superior was notified. In the interval, several friars appeared to observe them with curiosity; a little while later the layman returned and escorted them before the superior. He sat in a high chair; he had a large book in front of him, supported by a large lectern. He received the travelers politely without getting up, asked them a few questions, and consented to their request. After a very brief conference, with due compliments, they were led into a room, where supper was being prepared, and Valancourt, accompanied by a friar, went to look for Michele, the carriage and the mules. As soon as he had gone halfway down the road, he heard the voice of the muleteer, calling our travelers by name. Convinced, not without difficulty, that both he and his master had nothing more to fear, he let himself be led to a hut near the wood. Valancourt hurried back to dine with his friends, but Saint Aubert was in too much pain to eat heartily. Emilia, very worried about her father, did not know how to think of herself, and Aubert was in too much pain to eat heartily. Emilia, very worried about her father, did not know how to think of herself, and Aubert was in too much pain to eat heartily. Emilia, very worried about her father, did not know how to think of herself, and Valancourt sad and thoughtful, but always occupied with them, he thought of nothing else but to comfort and encourage Saint Aubert. Parting soon, they retired to their rooms. Emilia slept in an outhouse adjoining her father's room; she sad, thoughtful and occupied only by the state of languor in which she saw him, lying down without hope of rest.

Two hours later a bell rang, and hurried footsteps traveled the corridors. Little expert in cloistered customs, Emilia was appalling; her fears, still alive for her father, they made her suppose that he was worse off; she got up hastily to run to him, but having stopped for a moment at the door to let the friars pass, she had time to recover, to put her thoughts in order, and to understand that the bell had rung matins. This bell rang no more, all was quiet, and it went no further; but she, she could not sleep, and lured on the other hand by the splendor of a splendid moon, she opened the window and she began to gaze at the town.

The night was placid and beautiful, the firmament without clouds, and a light zephyr barely disturbed the trees of the valley. She was attentive, when the nocturnal hymn of the religious arose softly from the chapel, situated in a lower place, so that the sacred canticle seemed to rise to heaven through the silence of the nights. Her thoughts followed; from the admiration of her works, her soul passed to the adoration of their almighty and good author. Filled with a pure pity and free from profane feelings, her soul was raised above the universe; her eyes shed tears; she adored the Infinite Power in her works, and her goodness in her benefits.

The canticle of the friars again gave way to silence; but Emilia did not leave the window until the moon, the darkness having set, seemed to invite her to rest.

CHAPTER V

Saint Aubert found himself the following morning strong enough to continue his journey, and hoping to arrive in Roussillon the same day, he set out very early. The road that the travelers then traveled offered views as wild and picturesque as the previous ones; only now and then did the scenes, less severe, unfold a more pleasant and laughing beauty.

When Sant'Aubert seemed busy with the plants, he contemplated with transport Emilia and Valancourt, who were walking together; these with the demeanor and the emotion of pleasure indicated a beautiful view in the scene that was offered to them; she listened and watched with an expression of serious sensitivity indicating the elevation of her spirit. They resembled two lovers, who had never left their native mountains, that their situation had preserved them from the contagion of frivolity; whose ideas, simple and grandiose like the landscape they traversed, did not include happiness except in the tender union of pure hearts. Saint Aubert smiled and sighed at the same time, thinking of the romantic happiness with which his imagination offered him the picture;

"The world," he said, following his own thought, "the world makes fun of a passion it hardly knows; its movements and interests distract the spirit, deprave the tastes, corrupt the heart; and love cannot exist in a heart when it no longer has the dear dignity of innocence. Virtue and sympathy are almost the same thing; virtue is sympathy put into action, and the most delicate affections of two hearts together form true love. How is it possible to look for love in big cities? Frivolity, interest, dissipation, falsehood continuously substitute for you simplicity, tenderness and frankness. —

It was almost noon when the travelers reached a pass so dangerous that they had to get out of the carriage; the road was surrounded by woods, and instead of continuing on, they began to look for shade. A humid breeze was widespread in the air; the splendid emerald of the grass, the beautiful mixture of flowers, balms, thymes and lavenders that they glazed; the height of the pines, ash trees and chestnut trees that protected its existence, all combine to make it a truly delightful place. Sometimes the thicker foliage blocks the view of the landscape; elsewhere, some mysterious opening allowed the imagination to glimpse much more graceful pictures than it had hitherto observed, and the travelers willingly abandoned themselves to those almost ideal enjoyments.

The pauses and silence which had already interrupted the talks of Valancourt and d'Emilia were much more frequent that day. The young man, with the most expressive vivacity, fell into a fit of languor, and his melancholy was painted artlessly even in his smile. The girl could no longer deceive herself: her own heart shared the same sentiment.

When Sant'Aubert was refreshed, they continued to walk through the wood, always believing they were walking along the road; but they finally realized that they had completely lost it. They had followed the slope where the beauty of the places held them back, and the road instead went up the steep coast. Valancourt called to Michele, but only an echo answered his cries, and his efforts were likewise in vain to find his way back. In this state, they saw among the trees at some distance the hut of a shepherd. Valancourt ran there to ask for some directions; arrived there, he found only two boys playing on the grass. He looked into the house, and saw no one. The eldest of the boys told him that his father was in the fields, his mother in the valley, and would not be late in returning. The young man thought about what was best to do, when Michele's voice suddenly echoed on the surrounding cliffs. Valancourt answered immediately and tried to go and join him; after a tiring work among the bushes and boulders, he finally reached him and barely managed to silence him. The road was very far from the place where his father and daughter rested. It was difficult to drive the carriage there; it would have been too painful for Saint Aubert to climb through the woods, as he himself had done, and the young man was very distressed to find a more practicable path.

Meanwhile, Sant'Aubert and Emilia had approached the hut and were resting on a country bench located between two pine trees and shaded by their fronds; they had looked at Valancourt, and expected him to join them.

The eldest of the boys had left the game to admire the travellers; but the little one continued his leaps and pestered his brother so that he would come back to help him. Saint Aubert looked with pleasure on his childish simplicity, when suddenly this spectacle, reminding him of the children lost in that fresh age, and especially of their beloved mother, made him fall back into sadness. Realizing this, Emilia began one of those moving arias which he so much favored, and which she knew how to sing with the greatest grace and expression of hers. The father smiled at her through her tears, took her hand, squeezed it tenderly and tried to banish the melancholy thoughts of her. She was still singing when Valancourt returned; he did not want to interrupt her, and stopped to listen. When he had finished, he approached and told of having found Michael and also a way to ascend the cliff. Saint Aubert, at these words, measured its tremendous height with his eye; he felt oppressed, and the ascent seemed frightening to him. However, the party seemed to him preferable to a long and rough road at all; he resolved to tempt him, but Emilia, always solicitous, suggested that they dine first, in order to restore his strength somewhat, and Valancourt returned to the carriage to seek provisions.

On his return, he proposed to place himself a little higher up, as there was the most beautiful and extensive view. They were about to go there when they saw a young girl approach the boys, caress them, and weep bitterly.

The travellers, interested in her misfortune, stopped to better observe her. She took the youngest of her children in her arms, and having escorted the strangers, she hastily wiped her tears and approached the hut. Saint Aubert asked her the cause of her affliction. She told him that her husband was a poor shepherd, who every year spent the summer in that hut to take a herd to graze in the mountains. Last night she had lost everything; a band of gypsies, who had been infesting the country for some time, had kidnapped all his master's sheep. «Jacopo», added the woman, «having accumulated some peculiarities, he had bought a few sheep for us; but now it will be necessary to give them to replace the flock taken away from the master; the worst is that when he finds out about it, he will no longer want to entrust us with his rams; he is a bad man; and then, what will become of our children? »

The attitude of that woman, the simplicity of her story and her sincere pain led Saint

Aubert to believe her sad story. Valancourt, convinced that she was real, immediately asked how much she was worth the stolen herd; when he heard about it, he was baffled. Saint Aubert gave the woman some coins; Emilia contributed her purse, and then set off for the agreed place. Valancourt remained behind talking to the pastor's wife, who was then weeping for her gratitude and surprise; he asked her how much more she needed to restore the kidnapped herd. He found that the sum was almost all of what he carried with him. He was uncertain and afflicted. - This sum, he said to himself, would be enough for the happiness of this poor family; it is in my power to give it, and make them happy and contented; but how will I do it then? How will I get home with the little I have left? He hesitated for some time; he found a singular pleasure in saving a family from ruin, but he felt the difficulty of continuing on his way with the little money he would have reserved for himself.

He was so perplexed, when the same pastor appeared. The children ran to meet him; he took one in his arms, and with the other attached to his belt, he forwarded with slow steps. His dejected, dismayed appearance, Valancourt decided; he threw all the money he had, except for a few scudi, and ran after Saint Aubert, who, supported by Emilia, was walking towards the slope. The young man had never felt so lighthearted; his heart leapt with joy, and all the objects around him seemed more beautiful and interesting. Saint Aubert observed his transports, and said to him:

"What is it about you that so enchants you?"

— Oh! the beautiful day! exclaimed Valancourt; « how the sun shines, how pure is the aura what a magical site!

- Is gorgeous! said Saint Aubert, whose happy experience easily explained Valancourt's emotion; "It's a pity that so many rich people, who could get themselves a splendid sun at will, let their days wither in the mists of selfishness!" For you, my young friend, may the sun always seem as beautiful to you as today; may you, in your active charity, always unite goodness and wisdom! »

Valancourt, honored by this compliment, could only reply with a smile, and it was that of gratitude.

They continued to cross the wood between the fertile gorges of the mountains. As soon as they reached the site where they wanted to go, all together they broke into an exclamation; behind them, the perpendicular cliff rose to a prodigious height and then divided into two equally high peaks. Their gray tints contrasted with the enamel of the flowers peeling among the crevices; the ravines over which the eye runs rapidly to push itself down into the valley, were also scattered with shrubs; further down, a green carpet indicated the chestnut groves, in the midst of which the hut of the poor shepherd can be seen. On every side, the Pyrenees raise their majestic peaks; some, laden with immense boulders of marble, changed color and appearance at the same time as the sun; others, even higher, showed only the snowy peaks, and the colossal bases, uniformly upholstered, were covered all the way down into the valley with pines, larches and green oaks. This valley, though narrow, was the one which led to the Roussillon; the fresh pastures, the rich cultivation contrasted stupendously with the grandeur of the surrounding masses. The low Roussillon was discovered between the extended chains of mountains, and the great distance, confusing all the gradations, seemed to unite the coast with the candid waves of the Mediterranean. A promontory on which a lighthouse stood indicated only the separation and the beach; flocks of seabirds flew around. Further off, however, some white sails could be distinguished; the sun increased their whiteness, and their distance from the lighthouse made them judge their speed; but they were so distant that they only served to separate the sky and the sea.

On the other side of the valley, directly in front of the travellers, was a passage between the rocks, which led into Gascony. Costa, no vestiges of culture; the granite rocks rose spontaneously from the bases, piercing the skies with sterile needles; there, neither forests, nor hunters, nor hovels: sometimes, however, a gigantic larch threw its immense shadow over an immeasurable precipice, and a talfiata cross on a cliff hinted to the traveler the terrible fate of some imprudent. The loco seemed destined to become a shelter for bandits; Emilia at every moment expected to see them emerge; a little later, a no less terrible object struck her vision. A gallows, erected at the entrance to the passage, and just above a cross, sufficiently explained some tragic fact. She avoided talking about it to Sant'Aubert, but the sight made her uneasy; she would have liked to quicken the pace to arrive with certainty before sunset. But the father needed refreshment, and, sitting on the grass, the travelers voted for the basket.

Sant'Aubert was revived by the rest and the serene air of that esplanade. Valancourt was so ecstatic, so in need of conversation, that he seemed to have forgotten all the way that remained to be done. The meal over, they bid a long farewell to that wondrous site, and climbed again. Saint Aubert found the carriage with pleasure; Emilia went up there with him: but wanting to know more in detail the delightful country where they were about to descend, Valancourt untied his dogs and followed them on foot; he sometimes stopped on the heights that offered him a beautiful point of view; the pace of the mules afforded him such distractions. If some place displayed a rare magnificence, he returned to the carriage, and Saint Aubert, too tired to go and enjoy it himself, sent his daughter there and waited for her.

It was late when they descended from the beautiful heights which crown the Roussillon. This magnificent province is enclosed in their majestic barriers, remaining open only on the side of the sea. The aspect of culture basically embellished the landscape, and the plain was tinged with the most vivid colors, and which the luxuriant climate and the industry of the inhabitants could give birth to anywhere. Groves of orange and lemon embalmed the air; their already ripe fruits swayed among the fronds, and the slopes with an easy slope displayed the most beautiful grapes. Further, woods, pastures, cities, farmhouses, the sea, on whose refulgent surfacemany scattered sails flowed, a purple glittering sunset; this pass, in the midst of the mountains that dominated it, formed the perfect union of the pleasant with the sublime; it was the sleeping beauty within the horror.

The travellers, having reached the bottom, forwarded between hedges of myrtle and flowering pomegranate trees as far as the small city of Arles, where they intended to spend the night. They found simple but clean lodgings; they would have passed a delightful evening, after the toils and enjoyments of the day, if the moment of separation which was approaching had not cast a cloud over their hearts. Saint Aubert wanted to leave tomorrow, skirt the Mediterranean and thus reach Languedoc. Valancourt, recovered too soon, now without a pretext for following his new friends, had to part with them in that same place. Saint Aubert, who loved him, proposed that he go further; but he did not reiterate the invitation, and Valancourt had the courage not to accept, to show that he was worthy of it. So they had to leave the question: Sant' Aubert to leave for Languedoc, and Valancourt to take the mountain road again to get back home. All the evening he did not utter a syllable, and remained in thought: Saint Aubert was affectionate with him, but grave at the same time; Emilia was serious, though she tried to appear cheerful; and after one of the most melancholy evenings they had ever spent together, they parted for the night.

CHAPTER VI

The next day, Valancourt breakfasted with his companions, but none of them seemed to have slept. Saint Aubert bore the stamp of oppression and languor. Emilia found his health very weakened, and her anxieties grew continuously: she observed all his glances with timid concern, and their expression was immediately found faithfully repeated on hers.

From the very beginning of their acquaintance, Valancourt had indicated his name and family. Saint Aubert knew both, no less that the estates of his house, then possessed by an elder brother of Valancourt, which were distant about eight leagues from his castle; and had met this brother somewhere in the neighborhood. These preliminaries had facilitated his admission; his demeanor, manners and exterior had earned him the esteem of Saint Aubert, who willingly trusted his own judgment, but respected propriety; and all the good qualities she recognized in him would not have seemed sufficient reasons to bring him so close to his daughter.

Breakfast was almost as silent as supper had been the evening before; but their meditation was interrupted by the noise of the carriage which was to take Sant'Aubert and Emilia away. Valancourt got up, ran to the window, recognized the carriage, and returned to his chair without speaking. The time to part had now arrived. Saint Aubert told the young man that he hoped to see him again in the valley, and that he certainly would not have passed there without honoring them with a visit. Valancourt thanked him affectionately, and assured her that he would never fail us: as he said he timidly looked at Emilia, who was making an effort to smile in the midst of her profound sadness; they spent a few minutes in a very animated conversation; Saint Aubert went to the carriage, Emilia and Valancourt followed him in silence: the young man remained stationary at the door, and when they had gone up it seemed that no one had the courage to say good-bye. In the end Saint Aubert pronounced the sad word; Emilia did the same to Valancourt, who repeated it with a forced smile, and the carriage started off.

The travelers were silent for a long time. Saint Aubert finally said: «You are an interesting young man; it has been many years since such a brief acquaintance has not struck me so affectionately. He reminds me of the days of my youth, that time in in which everything seemed admirable and new to me. She sighed, and fell back into his meditation. Emilia looked out the door, and saw Valancourt motionless at the door again, following them with her eyes; he saw her, and greeted her with her hand; she returned her greeting, but at a turn in the road she was no longer able to see him.

"I remember what I was like at that age," added Saint Aubert; "I thought and felt exactly like him. The world then opened before me, and now it closes.

"Dear papa, don't abandon yourself to such gloomy thoughts," said Emilia in a trembling voice; 'You have, I hope, many years to live, for your happiness and mine.

Oh Emily! exclaimed Saint Aubert; « for yours! yes, I hope that is the case. He wiped away a tear that ran down his cheeks, and smiling at his emotion, he added in a tender voice: "Do you sense something in the ardor and ingenuity of that young man, which above all must move an old man, whose feelings the poison of the world has not altered." ; yes, I discover in him something insinuating, life-giving, like the sight of spring when one is sick. The patient's spirit absorbs something of the renewing juice, and his eyes revive in the meridian rays; Valancourt is for me this happy spring. »

Emilia, who lovingly shook her father's hand, had never heard from his mouth such praise that she found so welcome, not even when she herself had been the object of it.

They traveled in the midst of vineyards, woods and meadows, enthusiastic at every step of that magnificent landscape limited by the Pyrenees and the immense sea. After noon they reached Calliure, situated on the Mediterranean. They had lunch there, and once the heat had passed, they resumed following the magical shores that stretched out as far as the Languedoc. Emilia enthusiastically considered the vast empire of the waves, whose surface lights and shadows varied so singularly, and whose shores, adorned with woods, already covered the first sessions of autumn.

Saint Aubert was impatient to be in Perpignan, where he was expecting letters from Quesnel, and for this reason he had left Calliure quickly, despite the urgent need for some rest. After a few leagues of road, he fell asleep; and Emilia, who had put two or three books in the carriage starting from the valley, was able to make use of them. She looked for what Valancourt had read the day before: she wanted to go over the pages on which the eyes of so dear a friend had just fixed themselves. She wanted to go over the passages that he admired, pronounce them as he did, and bring him back, so to speak, to her presence. Looking for this book which she could not find, she saw instead of her a volume of Petrarch, belonging to the young man, whose name appeared written above it. She often and she read him some excerpts,

They arrived in Perpignan just after sunset. Saint Aubert found there the letters he expected from Quesnel. He was so painfully moved by it that Emilia, frightened, begged him, as far as her delicacy would allow, to explain its contents to him. He didn't answer her except with tears, and soon spoke of something else altogether. Emilia thought it best not to solicit him further, but the state of her father occupied her strongly, and she was unable to sleep all night.

The following day they continued along the coast to reach Leucate, a Mediterranean port situated on the frontiers of Roussillon and Languedoc. As they walked along, Emilia renewed the instances of the day before, and she seemed so disturbed by the silence and the despair of Sant'Aubert, that he finally banished any regard. 'I didn't want, dear Emilia,' he said to her, 'to poison your pleasures, and I would have liked, at least during the journey, to hide from you circumstances which unfortunately I would have had to reveal to you one day; your affliction prevents me, and you suffer perhaps more from uncertainty than you would from the truth. Mr. Quesnel's visit was a fateful time for me; and then he told me some of the displeasing news which is now confirmed to me by his letters. You must have heard me speak of such a manMottevilleof Paris, but you were unaware that the greater portion of what I possess was placed in his hands; I trusted him blindly, and I still don't want to believe him unworthy of my esteem: several circumstances have concurred in his ruin, and I am ruined with him. »

Here he paused to temper his emotion.

'The letters I received from Monsieur Quesnel,' he continued, becoming firmly excited, 'contained others from Motteville himself, and all my fears are confirmed.

"Will he have to abandon our castle?" Emilia said after a long silence.

"It's not quite certain yet," said Saint Aubert; "That will depend on the agreement Motteville can make with his creditors. My assets, you know, weren't very fat, and now they're almost nothing. I am most afflicted for you alone, dear daughter. »

His voice failed him at these words. Emilia, all tearful, smiled tenderly at him, and trying to overcome her agitation, she replied: "Do not grieve for yourself or for me, my good father. We can still be happy. Yes, if we have the castle in the valley left, we certainly will be; we'll keep one maid, and you won't notice the change in your fortune. take comfort, dear papa, we will feel no deprivation, since we have never tasted the vain superfluities of luxury, and poverty can never deprive us of our sweetest enjoyments; it will neither diminish our tenderness, nor degrade us in our eyes or in those of the people who esteem us. »

Sant'Aubert hid his face in his handkerchief, unable to speak; but Emilia continued to tell her father the truths that he himself had been able to inculcate in her. "Poverty," she said to him, "will not be able to deprive us of any of the delights of the soul; you can always be an example of courage and goodness, and I the consolation of a beloved parent. »

Saint Aubert could not answer: he pressed Emilia to his heart: their tears became confused, but they were no longer tears of sadness. After this language of feeling, any other would have been too weak, and both were silent. Saint Aubert spoke afterward in the usual way, and if the spirit was not in his ordinary tranquility, he had at least recovered its appearance.

They reached Leucate very early, but Sant'Aubert was very tired and wanted to spend the night there. In the evening he went for a walk with his daughter to visit its surroundings. He discovered the lake of Leucate, theMediterranean, a part of Roussillon surrounded by the Pyrenees, and a very considerable portion of Languedoc and its very fertile countryside. The grapes, already ripe, turned red on the open hills, and the harvest had begun. The two passers-by saw the happy crowds, heard the songs brought to them on the light zephyr walls and enjoyed in advance all the pleasures that the road promised them. Nonetheless, Saint Aubert did not want to leave the sea: he was often tempted to return to the valley, but the pleasure Emilia took in this journey always counterbalanced this desire; and besides, he wanted to test whether the sea air would lift him a little.

The following day they set off again. The Pyrenees, though very distant, afforded a most picturesque view; on their right they had the sea, and on their left immense plains, which merged with the horizon. Saint Aubert rejoiced at it, and spoke of it with Emilia; but her cheerfulness was more feigned than natural, and shadows of sadness often veiled her physiognomy well: a smile, however, from Emilia was enough to dispel them; but she herself was heartbroken, and she saw very well that the troubles of her father were visibly weakening her health every day.

They came very late to a small town in Languedoc; they had intended to sleep there, but it was impossible; the harvest kept all the places occupied, and it was advisable to go to a more distant village; the weariness and sufferings of Sant'Aubert required a prompt rest, and the night was already advanced; but necessity has no law, and Michele continued on his way.

The fertile plains of the Languedoc, in the fervor of the grape harvest, reverberated with French frizzies and noisy gaiety. Sant'Aubert could no longer enjoy them; his state contrasted too sadly with the vivacity, youth, and pleasures which surrounded him. When he turned his languid eyes upon that scene, he thought that soon he would never see it again. "Those distant and lofty mountains," she said to herself, considering the Pyrenees and the sunset, "these beautiful plains, that blue vault, the dear light of the day, will forever be closed to my eyes; soon the peasant's song, the consoling voice of man will no longer reach my ear... -

Emilia's eyes seemed to read everything that was passing in her father's soul: she fixed them on his face with an expression of tender pity. Forgetting then the arguments of a vain regret, he no longer saw anything but her, and the horrible idea of leaving his daughter without a protector, changed his pain into a real torment; she sighed from the bottom of her heart, and didn't move her lip. Emilia understood that sigh; she squeezed his hands tenderly, and she turned away from the door to hide her tears. The sun then projected a last ray on the Mediterranean, the vapors of which all seemed golden; gradually the twilight shadows relaxed; a discolored area appeared only to the west, marking the point where the sun was lost in the mists of an autumn evening. A cool breeze rose from the beach. Emilia dropped the crystals; but the coolness, so pleasant in her state of health, was unnecessary for an infirm one, and her father begged her to raise them up. As her indisposition grows, he thought then more than ever of putting an end to the day's march; Michele stopped to find out how far they were from the first village. "Four leagues," said the muleteer. "I won't be able to do them," said Saint Aubert; 'Seek, as you go on, if there is not a house on the road where they can receive us for the night. »

He threw himself back into the carriage; Michael cracked the whip, and galloped until Sant'Aubert, almost unconscious, signaled him to stop. Emilia looked at the door: she finally saw a farmer at some distance: they waited for him and asked him if there was no lodgings for travelers around. She replied that she did not know any. "There is a castle in the middle of the woods," she added, "but I believe that nobody is received there, and I cannot show you the way, being almost a stranger myself. »

Saint Aubert was about to renew his questions about the castle; but the man cried there and went away. After a moment's reflection, Saint Aubert ordered Michael to go slowly towards the woods. With every moment the twilight became more dark, and the difficulty of guiding oneself increased. Another villager passed.

"Which is the road to the castle in the woods?" Michele shouted.

"The castle in the woods!" the villager exclaimed. "Do you want to talk about those turrets?"

"I don't know if they're turrets," Michele said. "I'm talking about that white building that we see from afar among all those trees."

Yes, they are turrets. But what! would you consider going there? the man replied with surprise.

St. Aubert, hearing that strange question struck especially by the accent with which it was made, got out of the carriage and said to him: "We are travellers, and we are looking for a house to spend the night there: do you know one nearby here?"

'No, sir,' replied the man, 'unless you wish to try your luck in those woods: but I wouldn't recommend it myself.

Who owns that castle?

"I don't know, sir.

"So it's uninhabited?"

"No, it's not uninhabited; the steward and the governess are there, I believe. »

Upon hearing this, Sant'Aubert decided to risk a refusal by presenting himself at the castle. He begged the farmer to serve as Michele's guide, and promised him a reward. The man reflected for a while, and said that he had other matters, but that they could not go wrong following the path he indicated. Saint Aubert was about to answer when the villager, wishing him good night, left him without adding anything else.

The carriage headed for the avenue, where it found itself barred by a pole; Michele dismounted and went to take it off. Then they penetrated among ancient chestnut trees and age-old oaks, whose entangled branches formed a very high vault: there was something deserted and wild in the aspect of that avenue, and the silence was so imposing, that Emilia felt seized by an involuntary tremor. She remembered the villager's accent in speaking of that castle: she gave his words a more mysterious interpretation than she had not done before: she tried none the less to calm her fear; he thought that a disturbed imagination had made her susceptible to it, and that her father's state and his own situation must no doubt contribute to it.

They advanced slowly; the darkness was almost complete: the uneven ground and the roots of the trees which embarrassed him at every stretch obliged much caution. Suddenly, Michael stopped: Saint Aubert looked to find out the cause. At some distance he saw a figure crossing the avenue; it was too dark to make out any more, and he ordered them forward.

"It seems to me a strange place," said Michele; 'I see no houses, and we'd better go back.

"Go a little farther, and if we don't see buildings, we'll go back to the high road. »

Michele advanced, but with repugnance; and the excessive slowness of his march made Saint Aubert reappear at the door, and he saw the same figure again. This time he jumped. Probably the darkness makes him more prone to fear than usual; but, whatever it might be, he stopped Michele and told him to call the individual who was crossing the avenue in this way.

"With your permission," Michele said, "he could well be a thief."

" I certainly won't," resumed Saint Aubert, unable to refrain from smiling at that phrase; "Come on, let's get back on the road, for I don't see any appearance of finding here what we're looking for." »

Michele turned briskly and quickly went back up the avenue; a voice then left from among the trees a left; it was not a command, not a cry of pain, but a hoarse and prolonged sound that was in no way human. Michele spurred the mules on without thinking of the darkness, or of the hitches, or of the potholes, or even of the carriage; he nor he stopped until he was out of the avenue, and finally reaching the road, he slackened his pace.

"I'm very ill," said Saint Aubert, shaking his daughter's hand, who, frightened by the thunder of her father's voice, exclaimed: "Great God! you are more ill, and we are without help; how will we do? He leaned his head on her shoulder; she supported him in her arms, and brought the carriage to a halt. As soon as the noise of the wheels had ceased, they heard music in the distance, which was the voice of hope for Emilia, who said: 'Oh! we are close to some dwelling, and we will be able to find help.»She listened attentively: the sound was very distant, and it seemed to come from the depths of a wood, a part of which bordered the road. She looked towards where the sounds came from, and she saw in the moonlight something that looked like a castle, but it was difficult to get to. saint Aubert was too ill to bear the slightest movement: Michele could not leave the mules; Emilia, who still supported her father, did not want to abandon him, and she was even afraid of venturing alone at such a distance, without knowing where and to whom to turn: in the meantime, a decision had to be made, and without delay. Saint Aubert therefore told Michael to advance as slowly as possible, and after a moment he fainted. Therecarriagestopped again; he was completely devoid of the use of the senses. « Ah! my father, my dear father! cried Emilia in despair; and believing him on the verge of death, she exclaimed: «Speak, say a single word to me; let me once again hear the sound of your voice. »He didn't answer anything: she, more and more frightened, ordered Michele to go to draw water in the nearby stream; he brought some into her hat, which she sprinkled on her parent's face. The rays of the moon, then reflecting upon him, showed the impression of death. All movements of personal terror at that point gave way to a dominant fear, and, confiding Saint Aubert to Michael, who left the mules with great difficulty, Emilia leapt out of the carriage to look for the castle which she had seen from afar, and the music that directed her steps, made her enter a path that led into the interior of the wood. Her mind, occupied solely with her father and her own restlessness, had at first lost all fear; but the thickness of the trees, under which she passed, intercepted the rays of the moon; L' horror of that place reminded her of her peril; the music had ceased, and she was left with no other guide than her case. She stopped a little with inexpressible terror; but the image of her father overcame all other feelings, and she set off again. She saw no habitation, no creature, and she heard no sound; she always walked without knowing where, she avoided the thick of the wood and stayed in the middle as much as she could; she finally saw a kind of untidy avenue that led to a point illuminated by the moon; the state of that avenue reminded her of the castle of turrets, and she no longer doubted that she was near it. She hesitated to proceed, when a murmur of voices and bursts of laughter suddenly struck her hearing; it was not a laugh of joy, but that of an immoderate joy, and her embarrassment increased greatly. As she listened, a voice from a great distance made itself heard from the side of the road from which she had started; imagining it was Michele, her first thought was to go back, but then she couldn't make up her mind. The last extremity could only have decided Michele to leave her mules: believed the dying father, and ran with greater speed, in the weak flattery of receiving some help from the guests of the wood. His heart fluttered with terrible uncertainty; and the more she advanced, the more the rustling of the dry leaves made her tremble at every step. She came to an open moonlit place; she stopped, and saw between the trees a grassy bank formed in a circle on which several people were seated. As they approached, she judged from their clothing that they must be peasants, and she distinguished various huts scattered throughout the wood. While she was watching and trying to overcome the fear that made her motionless, some villanelles came out of a hut; the music continued and they began to dance again; it was the grape harvest festival, and the same music heard from afar. Her heart, too torn, he could not feel the contrast which all those pleasures formed with his own situation; he went before a group of old men seated near the hut, set forth his circumstance, and implored his assistance. Several of them got up lively, offered all their services, and followed Emilia, who seemed to have wings as she ran towards the main road.

When they reached the carriage, it found the father recovered. Recovering her senses, she had heard from Michele the departure of her daughter; her concern for her, going beyond her sense of her needs, had sent Michele to look for her; not therefore he was still in a state of languor, and feeling unable to go further, he renewed his questions about a hotel, or about the castle in the woods. 'The castle cannot receive you,' said a venerable peasant, who had followed Emilia, 'it has hardly been inhabited; but if you will do me the honor of accepting my hovel, I will give you my best bed. »

Saint Aubert was French: therefore he was not surprised by the courtesy of a Frenchman. Sick as he was, he felt how much value the offer made him, by the way he did it which one was made. She had too much delicacy to apologize, or to hesitate a single moment in receiving that peasant hospitality; he therefore accepted it with as much frankness as had been used in the offer.

The carriage moved slowly, following the peasants along the road Emilia had already taken, and they reached the hut. The affability of his host, and the certainty of a speedy rest, restored St. Aubert's strength; he saw with sweet complacency that interesting picture; the woods, made darker by contrast, surrounded the illuminated site; but thinning out at intervals, a white light made a hut stand out or was reflected in a trickle; he listened with pleasure to the merry sounds of the guitar and the tambourine, but he could not see the dancing of these peasants without emotion. The same thing did not happen to Emilia: the excess of her fear had changed into a profound sadness, and the accents of her joy, giving rise to unpleasant comparisons with her, still served to redouble her.

The dancing ceased as the carriage approached: she was a phenomenon in those remote woods, and everyone surrounded her with extraordinary curiosity. As soon as they heard that there was a sick stranger, many girls crossed the meadow, returned immediately with wine and baskets of fruit, and offered them to the travellers, disputing their preference. The carriage finally stopped near a very decent cottage, which belonged to the venerable leader; he helped Saint Aubert down, and led him with Emilia to a small room on the ground floor lit only by the moon. Sant'Aubert, happy to find the desired rest, lay down on aspeciesof armchair. The fresh balmy air, impregnated with sweet scents, penetrated the room through the open windows and revived his weakened faculties. His host who was called Voisin, immediately returned with fruit, cream, and all the country luxuries his retreat could provide. He offered everything with a smile of cordiality, and stood up behind the chair of Saint Aubert, who insisted on letting him take a seat at the table; when the fruits had quenched his burning thirst, he felt a little relieved, and began to talk. The guest communicated to him all the particularities relating to him and his family. This domestic picture, painted with heartfelt feeling, could not fail to excite the keenest interest. Emilia, sitting next to her father, holding one hand between hers, listened attentively to the good old man. Her heart was filled with sadness and she shed tears, thinking that sooner than she would no longer possess the precious possession that she still enjoyed. The dim ray of the autumn moon, and the music that was still being heard from afar matched his melancholy. The old man spoke of his family, and Saint Aubert was silent.

"I have only one daughter left," said Voisin, "but fortunately she is married and takes the place of everything for me. When my wife died," he added with a sigh, "I went to reunite with Agnese and her family. She has several children, whom you see dancing over there, merry and fat like so many finches. May they always be so! I hope to die among them, sir: now I am old, and I have little left to live; but it is a great consolation to die among her children.

"My good friend," said Saint Aubert in a trembling voice, "you will, I hope, live long among them."

"Oh, sir! in my age, I don't have much place to hope for it. The old man paused. "Besides, I hardly want it," he resumed then. « I trust that if I die, I will go straight to heaven; my poor wife is there before me. In the evening, in the moonlight, I think I see her wandering among these woods he loved so much. Do you think, sir, that we can visit the earth, when we have left our bodies?

"Do not doubt it," answered Saint Aubert; « Separations would be too painful if we believed them to be eternal. Yes, Emilia dear, we will meet again one day. »

He raised his eyes to heaven, and the rays of the moon, which fell upon him, showed all the peace and resignation of his soul, in spite of the expression of sadness.

Voisin understood that he had prolonged the theme too much, and interrupted him by saying: 'But we are in the dark; we need a light.

"No," said Saint Aubert to him, "I prefer the light of the moon: don't bother yourself, dear friend." Emilia, my love, I am much better now than I have been all day. This air refreshes me; I enjoy this rest, and I am pleased to listen to this beautiful music that is heard in the distance. Let me see your smile. Who plays the guitar so well? he said afterwards; "Are they two instruments or an echo?"

"It is an echo, sir, at least I think so. I have often heard this instrument at night, when all is calm: but nobody knows who plays it. Sometimes it is accompanied by a voice, but so sweet and so sad that one might believe that spirits appear in the wood.

"They will certainly appear there," said Saint Aubert smiling, "but in the flesh.

"Sometimes, at midnight, when I can't sleep," continued Voisin, who paid no attention to that observation, "I have heard it almost under my windows, nor have I ever heard such pleasant music: it made me think of my poor wife, and cried. Talfiata opened the window to try to see someone, but at the same instant it ceased harmony, and no one was to be seen. She listened with such recollection that the noise of a leaf or the slightest wind ended up frightening me. This music was said to be an announcement of death; but I have been listening to it for many years and I still survive this sad omen. »

Emilia smiled at such a ridiculous superstition, and not therefore, in the position of her spirit, she could not quite resist its contagious impression.

« All right, my friend, said Saint Aubert; but if anyone had the courage to go after the sound, the musician would have been known. Has anyone done this?

"Yes, sir, it was attempted several times, the music was followed as far as the wood, but it receded as we advanced, and always seemed to be at the same distance: our peasants were afraid, and did not want to go any further. It is seldom heard so early as tonight; usually this happens about midnight when that bright star which is now above those turrets sets on the left of the wood.

"What turrets?" asked Saint Aubert; "I don't see any.

"Pardon me, sir, there is one there, on which the moon reflects; do you see that avenue? the castle is almost entirely hidden by trees.

"Yes, papa," said Emilia, looking; "Don't you see something shining above the wood?" I believe it is a weather vane, on which the rays of the moon reflect.

Yes, now I see what you mention. Whose castle is that?

"The Marquis de Villeroy was its owner," replied Voisin with importance.

— Ah! said Saint Aubert in great agitation: "are we then so close to Blangy?"

"It was the Marquis's favorite residence," added Voisin; 'But he took a dislike to her, and hasn't been there for many years: I was told that he died recently, and that this fiefdom passed into other hands. »

Saint Aubert, who had fallen into thoughts, came out of his meditation at these last words exclaiming: « Dead! great God! and for how long? »

"I was told it had already been four weeks," replied Voisin; "Did you perhaps know him?"

"It is an extraordinary thing," answered Saint Aubert, without stopping at the question.

- And why? Emilia said with shy curiosity. He made no reply, and fell back into meditation on her; she came out shortly afterwards, and asked who was her heir.

"I forgot the name," said Voisin; «But I know that this gentleman lives in Paris, and that he does not think even for the shadow of coming to his castle.

"Is the castle still closed?"

"About a good deal, sir; the old castalda and her husband take care of them, but live in a little house not far away.

"The castle is spacious," said Emilia, "and it must be very deserted if it has only two inhabitants."

— Desert! oh yes, miss," answered Voisin; « I would not like to spend the night there for all the treasures in the world.

- What do you say? » added Saint Aubert, coming out of his meditation; and Voisin repeated the same protest. Saint Aubert could not hold back a kind of sob; but as if he wanted to avoid the observations, he promptly asked Voisin how long he had been living in that country.

"Almost from childhood," replied the visitor.

"Do you remember the late marquise?" said Sant'Aubert in an altered voice.

— Ah! sir, if I remember; there are many others who have not forgotten it either.

"Yes," answered Saint Aubert, "and I am one of them."

- So you will remember a beautiful and excellent lady: she deserved a better fate. »

Saint Aubert shed a few tears.

'Enough,' he said in an almost choked voice, 'enough, my friend. »

Emilia, although very surprised, did not allow herself to express her feelings with any question. Voisin wanted to apologize, but Saint Aubert interrupted him. "Apology is useless," he told him; "Let's rather change the subject of conversation. You were talking about the music we heard.

"Yes, sir, but be quiet, it begins again; listen to this voice. »

In fact, they heard a soft, tender and harmonious voice, but whose sounds, weakly articulated, did not allow them to distinguish anything resembling words. Soon it ceased, and the accompanying instrument intoned tender concerts. Saint Aubert observed that the thunders were fuller and more melodious than those of a guitar, and also more melancholy than those of a lute. They continued to listen, and heard nothing more.

"This is strange," said Saint Aubert, finally breaking the silence.

"Very strange," said Emilia.

"It is true," added Voisin; and everyone was silent.

After a long pause, Voisin resumed:

« It has been about eighteen years since I heard this music for the first time on a beautiful summer night, I remember less; but it was later. I walked alone in the woods; I still remember that he was very afflicted; she had a sick son, and was afraid of losing him; she had stayed up all evening at her bed, while her mother slept, having assisted him all the previous night. I went out to get some air; the day had been very hot, and I was walking thoughtfully under the trees; I heard music in the distance, and I thought it was Claudio playing his bagpipe; he was very fond of this instrument. When the evening was fine, she stood for a while at his door to play; but when I came to a place where the trees were less thick (I shall never forget that for the rest of my life), as I looked up at the northern stars, which were very high at that moment, all of a sudden I heard sounds, but sounds which 'I can't describe: it looked like a concert of angels; I looked carefully, and I always thought I saw them ascending to heaven. When I got home, I related what I had heard; they all made fun of me, and told me that they were shepherds, who had played their flute; I could never persuade them otherwise. A few nights later, my wife heard the same harmony, and was as surprised as I was. Her father Dionigi frightened her very much, telling her that heaven sent this warning to announce the death of her son, and that this music was around her houses, containing some dying. »

Emilia, hearing those words, felt struck by a superstitious fear quite new to her, and she had great difficulty in hiding her disturbance from her father.

'But our son lived, sir, in spite of his father Dionigi.

"Father Dionigi?" said Saint Aubert, who listened attentively to all the stories of the good old man; "So we are close to a convent?"

— Yes, sir, the convent of Santa Chiara is not far from us; it is on the seashore.

— Oh heavens! cried Saint Aubert, as if struck by a sudden recollection; « the convent of Santa Chiara! »

Emilia observed that the signs of pain scattered on his forehead were mixed with a feeling of horror. It remained motionless; the silvery light of the moon struck his face then; it resembled one of those marble statues which, placed on a mausoleum, seem to watch over the cold ashes and afflict themselves without hope.

'But, dear papa,' said Emilia, wanting to distract him from sad thoughts, 'you forget how much you need rest; if our good host permits me, I will go and make your bed, for I know how you wish it to be made. »

Saint Aubert collected himself somewhat, and smiling at her sweetly, begged her not to increase her fatigue with this new concern. Voisin, whose courtesy had been suspended by the interest which her stories had excited, excused himself for not having sent Agnese yet again, and went out to fetch her.

A little later he returned, bringing his daughter, a very amiable young girl. Emilia understood from her what she had not yet suspected, namely that, in order to shelter them, part of her family had to give up her beds. She grieved at this circumstance; but Agnes, in her reply, exhibited the same good grace and the same hospitality of her father. It was therefore decided that some of her and Michele's children should go to sleep in a nearby house.

"If tomorrow I am better, my dear Emilia," said Saint Aubert, "we will leave early to be able to rest during the heat of the day, and we will return home. In the state of my health and my ideas, I can think only with pain of a longer journey, and I feel the need to return to the valley. »

Emilia also longed for this return, but was disturbed by feeling such a sudden resolution. Her father, no doubt, was much worse off than he led us to believe. Saint Aubert withdrew to get some rest. Emilia closed her room, and being unable to sleep, her thoughts led her back to the last conversation concerning the state of souls after death. This subject affected her sensibly, as she could no longer flatter herself that she was keeping her father for long. She leaned thoughtfully against an open window. Absorbed in her reflections of her, she rolled her eyes; she saw the firmament strewn with innumerable stars, inhabited perhaps by incorporeal spirits; her eyes roamed in the immense ethereal spaces: her thoughts of her rose, as before her, to the sublimity of a God, and the contemplation of the future. The dancing had ceased, the huts were silent, the air just seemed to stir the tops of the trees a little; the bleating of some lost sheep, sometimes the distant sound of a bell, the sound of a door closing alone broke the silence of the night. Indeed at last these various sounds, which reminded her of the earth and its occupations, ceased altogether: with tearful eyes, filled with respectful devotion, she remained at the window till, about midnight, darkness had spread over the earth, and that the star indicated by Voisin disappeared behind the wood. She then remembered what he had said about it, and remembered the mysterious music; she stood at the window, hoping and darkness had spread over the earth, and that the star indicated by Voisin disappeared behind the wood. He then remembered what he had said about it, and remembered the mysterious music; he stood at the window, hoping and darkness had spread over the earth, and that the star indicated by Voisin disappeared behind the wood. He then remembered what he had said about it, and remembered the mysterious music; he stood at the window, hoping andfearingin the very time of hearing her return; she was occupied with her father's strong emotion when Voisin had announced the death of the Marquis de Villeroy and recalled the fate of the marquise, and she felt keenly interested in knowing her cause. Her curiosity about this subject was all the more lively, as her father had never mentioned the name of Villeroy in her presence. Her music was not heard: Emilia realized that her hours led her back to new toils; she thought she must get up early in the morning, and she made up her mind to go to bed.

CHAPTER VII

Emilia was awakened early, as she had foreseen. Sleep had refreshed her a little; she had been invaded by painful dreams, and the sweetest consolation of her unhappy ones had not helped them in the least. She opened the window, looked at the woods, breathed in the pure air of the dawn, and she felt calmer. The whole country breathed that coolness which seems to bring health. Only sweet and agreeable sounds were heard, such as the bell of a distant convent, the murmur of the waves, the song of the birds and the lowing of the cattle, which she saw walking slowly among the scrub and trees.

Emilia heard a movement in the room, and recognized the voice of Michele, who was speaking to his mules and went out with them from a nearby hut: she too went out, and found her father, who had gotten up at that moment, and was standing no better than Before. She led him into the little room where they had dined the previous evening: there they found a very good breakfast, and her host and daughter, who were waiting for them to wish them good morning.

"I envy you this beautiful house, my friends," said Saint Aubert on seeing them; « it is so pleasant, so placid, so decent! And the air you breathe! I'm sure this could perhaps restore my health. »

Voisin greeted him courteously, and replied with exquisite civility: 'My home has become enviable, since you and this young lady have honored her with your presence. »

Saint Auberthe smiled amicably at this compliment, and sat down at the table, which was covered with fruit, butter and fresh cheese. Emilia, who had carefully examined her father, and found him in a deplorable state, earnestly undertook him to prolong his departure until evening; but he seemed impatient to get home, and expressed this impatience with truly extraordinary warmth. He assured him that he hadn't felt so well for a long time, and that he would travel with less pain in the cool of the morning than at any other time of day. But while he was talking to her respectable guest, and she thanked him for the courteous welcome shown to him, she Emilia she saw him change color and fall into his chair before she could support him. In a few moments he recovered from his sudden swoon, but he was so ill that he recognized himself incapable of travelling; and after having struggled a little against the violence of his ailments, he asked to be helped up the ladder, and back into bed. This prayer renewed all the terrors Emilia had felt the day before,

As soon as he was in bed, he sent for Emilia, who was weeping outside the room, and asked to be left alone with her. He then took her hand, and fixed his eyes on her daughter with such tenderness and pain, that her courage left her, and she broke down into bitter tears. Saint Aubert tried to keep his firmness, and he could not speak; he could only squeeze her hand, and with difficulty hold back his tears; finally he spoke.

"My dear daughter," he said, forcing himself to smile amidst the impression of his pain, "my dear Emilia! He paused, raised his eyes to heaven, as if to implore his assistance, and then with a firmer tone of voice, with a look in which paternal tenderness was united with dignity to the pious solemnity of a saint, "Daughter, he said to her, "I'd like to sweeten the sad truths I'm forced to reveal to you, but I can't hide anything from you." Alas! I wish I could, but it would be too cruel to prolong your mistake: our parting is imminent; it is therefore advisable to talk about it, and prepare ourselves to bear it with our reflections and prayers. »She His voice failed him; Emilia, still crying, pressed his hand to her breast, and oppressed by convulsive sighs, she didn't even have the strength to raise her eyes.

"Let's not lose a single moment," said Saint Aubert, returning to himself; "I have many things to tell you. I must reveal to you a secret of the highest importance, and obtain from you a solemn promise; when this is done, I will be calmer. You must have already observed, my dear, how much I long to be at home; you ignore the reason: listen to what they are to tell you. But wait, I need this promise, made to your dying father! »

Emilia struck by these last words, as if for the first time she had known her father's danger, raised her head; her tears stopped, and she looking at him a moment with an expression of unbearable affliction, she was seized with convulsions, and she fainted. The cries of Sant'Aubert attracted Voisin and Agnes, who provided her with all possible help, but for a long time in vain of her. When Emilia came to, Saint Aubert was so exhausted by all that scene that he remained a few minutes without being able to speak. A cordial presented to him by Emilia revived his strength. When for the second time they were alone with her, he made an effort to calm her down, and lavished her with all the consolations compatible with the circumstance. She threw herself into her arms, wept bitterly, and her pain made her so insensitive to her talk, that he ceased to speak, being able only to soften and mix his tears with those of the girl. Called at last to a feeling of duty, she wished to spare her father a longer spectacle of her grief; she yes she released from his arms, wiped away her tears, and articulated a few words of consolation.

"Dear Emilia," resumed Saint Aubert, "my daughter, let us submit with humble resignation to the Institution which has protected and consoled us in dangers and afflictions. Every instant of our life is known by him; he has never abandoned us, and he will not want to abandon us even now. I feel this consolation in my heart; I will leave you, my daughter, I will leave you in his arms, and although I leave this world, I will always be in your presence. Yes; Emilia dear, don't cry: death in itself has nothing new or surprising, since we all know we were born to die; it has nothing terrible for those who trust in an almighty God. Had my life been prolonged, the course of nature would have taken it from me in a few years. Old age, and all that it brings with it infirmities, deprivations and troubles, would soon have been my legacy; death would finally come, and it would cost you those tears you shed right now. Rather rejoice, dear daughter, to see me freed from so many evils. I die with a free spirit, susceptible to the consolations of faith, and with perfect resignation. »

He stopped tired of talking. She Emilia forced herself to compose herself, and in answering what she had said to her, she tried to persuade him that she had not spoken in vain.

After a little rest, he resumed. « But let's go back to the subject that interests me so much. I told you that he had to ask you for a solemn promise; I must receive it, before explaining to you the main circumstance I have to tell you about; There are others that, for your rest, it matters that you ignore forever. So promise me that you will do exactly what I command you. »

Emilia, struck by the seriousness of these expressions, wiped away the tears, which she could not help shedding; and looking eloquently at her father, she bound herself by oath to do what he would require of her, not knowing what it was about her. Then he continued: "I know you too much, Emilia dear, to fear that you will ever fail in your commitments, but above all in such a respectable commitment." Your word calms me, and your loyalty becomes of an inconceivable importance for the tranquility of your days. Now listen to what I have to tell you. The lavatory adjoining my room in our castle in the valley contains a sort of trapdoor, which opens under a floorboard; you will recognize it by a remarkable knot in the wood; on the other hand, it is the penultimate board on the side of the wall, and facing the bedroom door. About an arm's length from the window, you will perceive a joint, as if the table had been changed by it; stamp your foot on that line, the plank will go down, and you can easily slide it under the other; below you will find a void. He stopped to take a breath, and Emilia remained in the deepest attention. "Do you understand these instructions, my dear?" he told her. Emilia, barely able to utter an accent, assured her that she understood it very well. and Emilia remained in the deepest attention. "Do you understand these instructions, my dear?" he told her. Emilia, barely able to utter an accent, assured her that she understood it very well. and Emilia remained in the deepest attention. "Do you understand these instructions, my dear?" he told her. Emilia, barely able to utter an accent, assured her that she understood it very well.

"When you get home..." And he sighed deeply.

As soon as she heard him speak of this return, all the circumstances which must have attended it presented themselves to her imagination; she had a new access of pain, and Saint Aubert, still more afflicted by the effort and the restraint he had made, could not hold back his tears. After a few moments, he recovered and continued: «Dear daughter, take comfort; when I no longer exist you will not be abandoned. I leave you under the immediate protection of Providence, which has never denied me her assistance. Do not afflict me with the access of your despair; teach me rather, by your example, to moderate what I resent. »

The sick man, who spoke only with difficulty, resumed his speech after a pause. « That lavatory, my dear ..... when you get home, go there, and under the table I have described, you will find a sheaf of papers; be careful now. The promise I received from you relates to this one object; you must burn those papers without observing or reading them; I absolutely command you. »

Emilia's surprise, overcoming her pain for an instant, asked the reason for that precaution. The father replied that if he could explain it to her, the promise she asked for would no longer be necessary. « It is enough for you, my daughter, to understand this reason well: it is of extreme importance. Under that same board you will find about two hundred doubles in a silk purse. This secret was already imagined to save the money that was in the castle, when the province was flooded by troops, who, taking advantage of the circumstance, indulged in all sorts of depredations and looting. I still have yet to receive one more promise from you, and that is, that in whatever critical position I may find you, you will never sell our possession of the valley. »

Sant'Aubert added that if she got married, she should have specified in the marriage contract that the castle would remain her absolute property. He later told her about her estate in more detail than she had done up to that point.

« The two hundred doubles, and the little money you'll find in my purse, are all the cash I have to leave you. I have already told you in what state our affairs are with M. Motteville of Paris. Ah my daughter, I leave you poor, but not in misery. »

Emilia could answer nothing; kneeling beside her bed, she wet her beloved hand with tears, which she still held in hers.

After this discourse, Saint Aubert's spirit seemed much calmer; but, exhausted by the effort made, he fell into a drowsiness. Emilia continued to assist him and weep next to him, until a light knock on her bedroom door forced her to get up. Voisin came to tell her that downstairs there was a confessor from the convent near her, ready to assist her father; but she did not want him to wake up, and she made the priest beg him not to leave. When Saint Aubert awoke from his slumber, all his senses were confused; and it was some time before he recognized Emilia. She then moved her lips, stretched out her hand, and she was painfully struck by the impression of death that she observed in all her features. After a few minutes she recovered her voice, and she Emilia asked him if she wanted to see a confessor. He answered yes, and as soon as the reverend father was ushered in, she withdrew. They stayed together for about half an hour: then Emilia was called back, who found her father more agitated than her, and she then looked at the confessor with some resentment, as if he had been the cause. The good religious looked at her gently, and Saint Aubert, in a trembling voice, begged her to join her prayers to those of the others, and asked if her guest did not want to join. The good old man and Agnese both arrived weeping, and knelt down by the bed. The reverend father, in a majestic voice, slowly recited the prayers of the dying. St. Aubert, with a serene countenance, fervently joined their devotion; a few tears sometimes escaped his half-closed pupils, and Emilia's sobs often interrupted the office. When it was finished, and the extreme unction was administered, the religious went away. Saint Aubert he signaled to Voisin to approach him, held out his hand, and was silent for some time. Finally he said to him in a weak voice:

'My good friend, our acquaintance was brief, but it was enough to show me your good heart; I have no doubt that you convey all this goodwill to my daughter: when I am no more, she will need it. I entrust him to your care, for the few days he has to spend here: I won't tell you more. You have children, you know the feelings of a father: mine would become very painful if I had less faith in you. »

Voisin reassured him, and his tears attested to his sincerity, that he would neglect nothing to alleviate Emilia's distress, and that, if he wanted it, he would take her back to Gascony. The offer pleased the dying man so much that he could not find words to express his gratitude, or rather that he accepted it.

'Above all, Emilia dear,' resumed the dying man, 'don't give in to the magic of good feelings: that is the mistake of an amiable spirit; but those who have real sensitivity must know early on how dangerous it is; it is she who derives an excess of trouble or pleasure from the slightest circumstance. In our passage through this world we encounter far more evils than enjoyments; and since the feeling of pain is always more alive than that of well-being, our sensitivity makes us a victim when we don't know how to moderate and contain it. »

Emilia repeated how precious his advice was to her, and promised to never forget it and to try to take advantage of it. Saint Aubert smiled at her with affection and sadness at the same time. "I repeat," he said to her, "I wouldn't want to numb you, even if I had the power; I would just like to heal you from the excesses of sensitivity and teach you to avoid them. That pretended humanity that she is content to pity, nor thinks of comforting, is very contemptible! ... »

Saint Aubert, some time later, spoke of Madame Cheron his sister.

"I must inform you," he added, "of a circumstance of interest to you. You know, we have had very few relations with her, but she is the only relative you have: I thought it convenient, as you will see in my will, to entrust you to her care until you come of age: she is not really the person to whom I would I wanted to restore my dear Emilia, but she had no other alternative, and I believe her basically a good woman; I need not, daughter, recommend that you use her prudence to reconcile her good graces: you will certainly do so in memory of one who has attempted it so many times for you. »

Emilia protested that what he recommended would be religiously carried out. « Alas! »She added, drowned in sobs; « here is in brief what will remain for me; it will be my only consolation to fulfill all your wishes exactly. »

The girl could only listen and cry, but her father's extreme calm, the faith, the hope he showed, somewhat soothed herdespair. Nonetheless, she saw that disorganized figure, those precursory signs of death, those sunken eyes of hers, and always fixed on her, those heavy pupils quick to close: her heart was lacerated, and she could not express herself. He wanted to give her blessing again. "Where are you, my dear?" he said, weakly stretching out his hands towards her.

Emilia was turned towards the window to hide her inexpressible grief; but she understood then that he was no longer able to see her: she imparted her blessing of her, which seemed the last effort of her life of her breathing of her, and she fell back on her pillow; she kissed him on the forehead; the cold sweat of death flooded his temples; and forgetting all her courage, she showered them with tears. The dying man opened his eyes; he still existed, but they were the last efforts of nature afflicted, and in a short time his soul flew before the Supreme Mover.

Emilia was forcibly snatched from that room by Voisin and her daughter, who tried to calm her pain; the old man cried with her, but Agnese's help was more timely.

CHAPTER VIII

The good religious in the morning returned in the evening to console Emilia, and brought her the invitation of the abbess of a convent near hers to go to her. The girl did not accept the offer, but she replied with great gratitude. The confessor's pious conversation, the sweetness of his manners, which resembled those of his late father, somewhat calmed the violence of his transports: he raised his heart to the Supreme Being, present everywhere. 'Relative to God,' thought Emilia, 'my most beloved father exists as yesterday he existed for me: he died only for me; for God, for him, it truly exists. —

Withdrawn to her bedroom, her melancholy thoughts still wandered about her father. Immersed in a kind of sleep, gloomy images clouded her imagination. She dreamed of seeing her parent approach her with benevolent demeanor. Suddenly she smiled sadly, raised her eyes, parted her lips; but instead of her words, she heard soft music, carried through the air at a very great distance. She then saw all her features come alive in the blessed ecstasy of a superior being: the harmony became stronger; she awoke. The dream was over, but the music still lasted, and it was celestial music.

She listened, and felt chilled by superstitious respect: the tears ceased, she got up, and looked out the window. Everything was dark, but she Emilia, averting her eyes from the gloomy woods that were jagged the horizon, he saw on his left that brilliant star about which the old man had spoken, and which was above the wood. I remembered what he had said, and as the music stirred the air at intervals, he opened the window to listen to the sweet harmony, which soon faded away, and she tried in vain to discover whence he came. The night did not allow her to make out anything on the underlying lawn, and her sounds, becoming successively more faint and soft, finally gave way to absolute silence ...

The next day she received a new invitation from the abbess; Emilia, who could not bring herself to abandon her cottage while the body of her father lay there, agreed with reluctance to go that same evening to pay her respect. About an hour before sunset, Voisin acted as her guide, and led her through the woods to the convent. This convent was located, like that of the friars we have mentioned, at the end of a small gulf in the Mediterranean. If Emilia had been less unhappy, she would have admired the beautiful view of an immense sea, which was discovered from a hill on which the building stood; she would have contemplated those rich beaches covered with trees and pastures, but her ideas were fixed in a single thought, and nature had neither shape nor color in her eyes. As she passed through the ancient door of the convent the bell rang at vespers, and it seemed to her the first chime of her father's funeral. The slightest accidents are enough to alter a spirit weakened by pain. Emilia overcame the painful crisis from which she was agitated, and she let herself be led by the abbess, who received her with maternal kindness. Her interesting physiognomy, her benign looks, filled Emilia with gratitude; her eyes were filled with tears, and she could not speak. The abbess sat him next to her and watched in silence as she tried to dry her tears. "Calm down, and she let herself be led by the abbess, who received her with maternal kindness. Her interesting physiognomy, her benign looks, filled Emilia with gratitude; her eyes were filled with tears, and she could not speak. The abbess sat him next to her and watched in silence as she tried to dry her tears. "Calm down, and she let herself be led by the abbess, who received her with maternal kindness. Her interesting physiognomy, her benign looks, filled Emilia with gratitude; her eyes were filled with tears, and she could not speak. The abbess sat him next to her and watched in silence as she tried to dry her tears. "Calm down, daughter," she said in an affectionate voice; « Don't talk, I understand you, you need rest. We go to prayer; do you want to accompany us? it is a consolation, dear girl, to be able to place one's worries in the bosom of our heavenly Father: he sees us, he pities us, and he chastises us in his mercy. »

Emilia shed new tears, but the sweetest emotions mitigated the bitterness. The abbess let her cry without interrupting her, looking at her with that good-natured air which seemed to indicate the attitude of a guardian angel; Emilia became calmer, speaking frankly, she explained her reasons for not leaving Voisin's home.

The abbess approved of her sentiments and her filial respect, but invited her to spend a few days at the convent before returning to her castle. "Try to distract yourselves, my daughter," she told her, "to recover a little from this shock, before risking a second one; I will not dissimulate how much your heart will feel torn at the sight of the theater of your past happiness; here you will find all the consolations that peace, friendship and religion can offer; but come," she added, seeing that her eyes filled with tears, "come, let's go down to the chapel. »

Emilia followed her into a room where all the nuns were already gathered; the abbess introduced her saying: «she is a young woman for whom I have great consideration; treat her like your sister. They all went to the chapel together, and the edifying devotion with which the divine office was recited lifted Emilia's spirit to the consolations of faith and perfect resignation.

The hour was already advanced, when the abbess agreed to leave her start. She came out of the convent less oppressed than she was when she entered it, and was brought home by Voisin. She followed him thoughtfully in a little beaten path, when suddenly his guide stopped, looked around, threw himself off the path into the broom, saying he had lost his way; he walked very fast. Emilia, who could not follow him on lewd ground and in the dark, remained at a great distance from her, and she was forced to call him: he did not want to stop, and roughly invited her to speed up her pace.

"If you're not sure of your way," Emilia said, "wouldn't it be better to direct you to that great castle I see there among the trees?"

"No," said Voisin, "it's not worth it: when we're at that stream where you see a light shining beyond the wood, we'll be home." I don't understand how I managed to get lost: perhaps it will be because I rarely come here after sunset.

"It's a very lonely place," Emilia said. "But aren't there any assassins?"

"No, miss, there are none.

"So what is it that frightens you so much, my friend?" Would you ever be superstitious?

"No, I'm not; but, to tell you the truth, miss, no one likes to be in the neighborhood of that castle at night.

— So who is it inhabited by to think it so formidable?

— Oh! miss, if at least it was inhabited! The marquis is dead, as I told you; he hadn't been there for many years, and his servants retired to a little house not far away. »

Emilia then understood that the castle was the one Voisin had already mentioned, and that it had belonged to the Marquis de Villeroy, whose death had so surprised her father.

"Ah," said Voisin; « how desolate it is! It was also a beautiful house; what a beautiful situation! when I remember..."

Emilia asked him the reason for that terrible change. The old man was silent, and she, struck by the fright he showed, occupied above all by the interest shown by her father, repeated the question and added: If it's not the inhabitants who frighten you, and if you're not superstitious, why so, my friend, don't you dare approach that castle in the evening?

'Well then, miss, I may be a little superstitious, but if you knew the real cause, you might too. Very strange things have happened there; your good father seemed to have known the marquise.

"Tell me, please, what happened?" Emilia told him very moved.

— Alas! answered Voisin; « ask me no more; my master's domestic secrets must always be sacred to me. »

Emilia, surprised by this last expression, and above all by the thunder of voice with which she had pronounced it, did not want to ask further questions. A more lively interest, the image of Saint Aubert, then occupied all her thoughts, she remembered the previous night's music, and spoke of it to Voisin. "You weren't the only one," he told her; « I heard it too; but this happens to me so often at that hour that I pay no more attention to it.

'You certainly believe,' said Emilia, 'that this music has some connection with the castle, and that's why you aresuperstitious, isn't it true?

"It may be Miss; but there are other circumstances relating to that castle, and of which I sadly keep the memory. »

These words were accompanied by a deep sigh, and Emilia's delicacy held back the curiosity which those mysterious sayings had aroused in her.

Back home, her despair began again: it seemed that he had only suspended its course by momentarily losing sight of the one who formed its subject; he immediately went to contemplate his father's body, and succumbed to all the transports of hopeless pain. Voisin having finally decided to leave her, he returned to her room. Overwhelmed by the day's labours, she fell asleep immediately, and when she awoke she found herself much more relieved.

Sant'Aubert had asked to be buried in the church of the nuns of Santa Chiara; he had chosen the northern chapel, next to the burial place of the Marquises de Villeroy, and had indicated its place. The superior agreed, and the funeral procession set off for that vault. The venerable father, followed by many priests, came to receive her at the door. The song of the Miserere, the sound of the organ, which resounded in the church when the coffin entered, the faltering steps, and Emilia's dejected air, would have wrested tears from the hardest hearts; but she did not pour a single one. With her face half covered by a black veil, she walked between two people who supported her; the abbess preceded her, the nuns followed her, and their plaintive song echoed the lugubrious one of the choir. When the procession had reached her tomb, Emilia lowered her veil, and in the interlude of her songs her sobs were easily distinguished. The reverend priest began mass, and Emilia managed to restrain herself somewhat, but when her body was deposed in the tomb, when she heard the earth being thrown that was to cover it, a feeble moan escaped her, and she fell into the arms of the person who supported her; but she quickly recovered, and she was able to understand those sublime words: - Her body rests in peace, and her soul has returned to the One who gave it to her. Her despair was then relieved by a deluge of tears.

The abbess took her out of the church, took her to her apartment, and offered her all the help of holy religion and tender piety. The girl made efforts to overcome her weakness; but her superior, who was observing her attentively, made her prepare a bed and induced her to rest. She kindly reclaimed her promise to spend a few days at the convent. Emilia, who was no longer reminded of the hut, the scene of her misfortune, then had the opportunity to consider her position, and felt incapable of leaving immediately.

Meanwhile the maternal goodness of the abbess and the sweet attentions of the nuns spared no effort to calm her spirit and restore her to health; but she had tried too much shock violent to recover quickly: she was therefore seized for several weeks by a slow fever, and fell into a state of languor. She grieved to leave the tomb where her father's ashes rested; she flattered herself that if she died there, she would be reunited with him. Meanwhile, Emilia wrote to Signora Cheron about her aunt and her old housekeeper to tell them what had happened, and to inform them of her situation. While the orphan was in the convent, the internal peace of that asylum, the beauty of the surroundings, the attentions of the superior and the nuns had such an attractive effect on her, that she was almost tempted to separate herself from the world; she had lost her dearest friends, she wanted to shut herself up in that cloister, in a living room that the sepulcher of her father makes sacred to her forever. The enthusiasm of the thought of her, which was almost natural to her, he had spread such pathetic varnish on the holy retreat of a nun, that he had almost lost sight of the real selfishness that produces it. But the colors which a melancholy imagination, slightly imbued with superstition, lent to the monastic life faded little by little, as her strength returned, and brought back an image which had only been temporarily banished. This memory tacitly calls one to hope, to consolation, to the sweetest sentiments; flashes of happiness showed themselves from afar, and although he was not ignorant to what point they could be deceptive, he did not want to deprive himself of them. After several days, she received a reply from her aunt, swollen with ordinary expressions of condolence, but no real grief; she announced that a person appointed by her would go to get her to bring her back to the castle in the valley, since her occupations did not allow her to undertake such a long journey. Although she Emilia preferred her valley to Toulouse, she was nonetheless struck by such indelicate and inappropriate conduct. Her aunt allowed her to return to her castle without relatives and without friends to console and defend her; and this conduct became all the more guilty,

A few days passed from the arrival of Signora Cheron's envoy to the time Emilia was able to leave. The evening before his departure, he went to the house of Voisin to say goodbye to that good family, and to express his gratitude: he found the good old man seated at the door, between his daughter and son-in-law, who, resting at that moment from the day's work , he played a kind of flute resembling a bagpipe. They had a small table laid out before them, well stocked with bread, fruit and wine; the boys, all handsome and in good health, enjoyed the lunch around the table which was distributed to them with unspeakable affection from their parents. Emilia stopped a moment before approaching, contemplating the interesting picture of these good people; she looked intently at that respectable old man, of his situation. She bade farewell to all the family with the most tender and sensitive expression; Voisin loved her as her daughter and shed tears. Emilia was crying; she avoided going into the little house, which would have renewed too painful impressions on her, and she left.

Back at the convent, she decided to visit her father's grave once more. Having understood that an underground passage led to those tombs, she waited until everyone was in bed, except for a nun who had promised her the key to the church. Emilia remained in the room until the clock struck midnight, and then the nun arrived with the promised key. They went down a spiral staircase together; the nun offered to accompany her to her tomb, adding that she was sorry to let her go alone at that hour; but she Emilia thanked her, and she could not consent to having a witness of her grief. The good nun opened a small door and handed her the light. Emilia thanked her, advanced into the church, and Sister Maria withdrew. Suddenly terrified, the girl went back to the door, and was tempted to call her back, but at the same moment, ashamed of his fear, he advanced again. The cold damp air of that place, the gloomy silence which reigned there, and a feeble moonbeam passing through a Gothic window, would no doubt have awakened superstition in anyone; but at that point she had no other thought than her pain. All of a sudden she thought she saw a shadow between the columns; she stopped, but having heard no one's footsteps, she knew it was the effect of her altered imagination of her. Saint Aubert was buried in a very simple urn, which bore no other inscription except his first and last name, the date of his birth and that of his death, and was situated at the foot of the pompous mausoleum de 'Villeroy. Emilia stayed there in prayer until the the cold damp air of that place, the gloomy silence which reigned there, and a feeble moonbeam passing through a Gothic window, would no doubt have awakened superstition in anyone; but at that point she had no other thought than her pain. All of a sudden she thought she saw a shadow between the columns; she stopped, but having heard no one's footsteps, she knew it was the effect of her altered imagination of her. Saint Aubert was buried in a very simple urn, which bore no other inscription except his name and surname, the date of his birth and that of his death, and was situated at the foot of the pompous mausoleum de 'Villeroy. Emilia stayed there in prayer until the the cold damp air of that place, the gloomy silence which reigned there, and a feeble moonbeam passing through a Gothic window, would no doubt have awakened superstition in anyone; but at that point she had no other thought than her pain. All of a sudden she thought she saw a shadow between the columns; she stopped, but having heard no one's footsteps, she knew it was the effect of her altered imagination of her. Saint Aubert was buried in a very simple urn, which bore no other inscription except his name and surname, the date of his birth and that of his death, and was situated at the foot of the pompous mausoleum de 'Villeroy. Emilia stayed there in prayer until the they would no doubt awaken superstition in anyone; but at that point she had no other thought than her pain. All of a sudden she thought she saw a shadow between the columns; she stopped, but having heard no one's footsteps, she knew it was the effect of her altered imagination of her. Saint Aubert was buried in a very simple urn, which bore no other inscription except his first and last name, the date of his birth and that of his death, and was situated at the foot of the pompous mausoleum de 'Villeroy. Emilia stayed there in prayer until the they would no doubt awaken superstition in anyone; but at that point she had no other thought than her pain. All of a sudden she thought she saw a shadow between the columns; she stopped, but having heard no one's footsteps, she knew it was the effect of her altered imagination of her. Saint Aubert was buried in a very simple urn, which bore no other inscription except his first and last name, the date of his birth and that of his death, and was situated at the foot of the pompous mausoleum de 'Villeroy. Emilia stayed there in prayer until the Saint Aubert was buried in a very simple urn, which bore no other inscription except his name and surname, the date of his birth and that of his death, and was located at the foot of the pompous mausoleum de' Villeroy. Emilia stayed there in prayer until the Saint Aubert was buried in a very simple urn, which bore no other inscription except his name and surname, the date of his birth and that of his death, and was located at the foot of the pompous mausoleum de' Villeroy. Emilia stayed there in prayer until the matins bell warned him it was time to retire. She shed a few more tears, kissed the precious sarcophagus, and went back to her room, leaving such a sad place. After that moment of effusion she relished a peaceful sleep; waking up, she felt her spirit calmer than her, and she seemed more resigned than she had been after her father's death.

When the moment of departure arrived, all her pain was renewed; the father's memory of him in the tomb, and the goodness of so many living people, attached him to that abode; she seemed to feel, for the place where Saint Aubert rested, that tender affection which is felt for her country. The abbess, in parting with her, gave her all the most sensitive evidence of attachment, and promised her to return, if elsewhere he did not encounter that consideration of her which he was to expect of her. The other nuns expressed her warmest regrets to her; at thefinally he left the convent with tears in his eyes, taking with him the affection and votes of all the people who remained there.

She had already covered a long stretch of country before the magnificent spectacle that offered her sight could distract her. She absorbed in her melancholy, she didn't notice so many enchanting objects except to better remember her lost father. Saint Aubert was with her when she had first seen them, and his observations of them came back to her memory. That day she passed in languor and despondency; that night she slept on the Languedoc frontier, and the next day she entered Gascony.

As the sun set, Emilia found herself in the vicinity of the valley all those places she knew so well, calling her back to recollections that tormented her heart, reawakened all her tenderness and her pain; she looked weeping at the peaks of the Pyrenees then colored by the most beautiful and vague hues of the sunset. "There," she exclaimed, "there they are those same caves; here is the same fir forest that he looked upon with such pleasure when we passed through those places together! There was that hut on the pleasant hill of which he had made me draw the view. Oh! my father, I will never see you again. »

The road at a turn let her see the castle in the midst of that magnificent landscape; the funnels, reddened by the sunset, rose behind the favorite plantings of Sant'Aubert, whose foliage hid the lower parts of the edifice. Emilia could not repress a deep sigh. This hour, she thought, was also her favorite hour. And seeing the country over which the shadows stretched out: "What quiet!" » she exclaimed; "What a delightful scene! all is calm, all is lovable, alas! as before! »

She was still resisting the terrible weight of her grief when she heard the music of the country dances which she had so often observed walking with her father on the flowering banks of the Garonne. She then she wept bitterly until the moment she stopped the carriage. She looked up, and recognized her old housekeeper as she opened the door to the house. Her father's dog came joyfully to meet her, and when she was gone from her he showered her with caresses; which increased her intense pain.

"My dear mistress..." Teresa said to her, and then stopped; Emilia's tears prevented her from replying; her dog skipped around her; she suddenly ran to the carriage. « Ah! Signora Emilia, my poor master! cried Teresa; "His dog went looking for him. »

Emilia sobbed as she saw that amorous animal jump into the carriage, get out, sniff, and search anxiously.

'Come, my dear young lady,' said Teresa, 'let's go; what can I give you to refresh you? »

Emilia took the governess's hand, making an effort to moderate her pain, with questions about the state of her health. She walked slowly to the door, stopped, took a step, and stopped again. What silence! What abandonment, what death in that castle! Afraid to go back inside, and reproaching herself for her hesitations, she quickly crossed the room, as if she were afraid to look around her, and opened the lavatory which at other times called hers .. The dusk of evening gave something solemn to the disorder of that place: the chairs, the tables, and all the other furniture, which in happier times he scarcely observed, then spoke too eloquently to his heart; she sat by a window looking upon the garden, whence she, in company with her father, had often contemplated the marvelous effect of the setting sun. She couldn't contain herself any longer and she found herself relieved by that outburst.

"I've prepared the green bed for you," Teresa said, bringing her the coffee; 'I thought you would now prefer it to yours. I never thought you'd come back alone. What day, great God! Her news, when I received it, pierced my heart: who would have said, when my poor master left, that she was never to return? »

Emilia covered her face with her handkerchief and motioned for her to be silent and go away.

The girl stayed some time immersed in high sadness; she did not see a single object that did not revive her pain: the favorite plants of Saint Aubert, the books chosen for her, and which they often read together, the musical instruments whose harmony she loved so much and which he played himself. Eventually, plucking up her courage, she wanted to see the abandoned flat; she felt her pain would be increased if she differed.

She crossed the courtyard, but her courage failed her as she opened the library; perhaps the darkness that evening and the foliage they spread around increased the religious effect of that place, where everything spoke to her of her father. Of her He saw the chair in which she sat: she was dumbfounded at this sight, and almost imagined she had seen him in person in front of her. She tried to dispel the illusions of a troubled imagination, but she could not refrain from a certain respectful terror mingling with her emotions. She moved slowly to the chair and sat down; she had near a lectern, on which was a book that her father had not closed; recognizing the open page, I remembered that on the eve of her departure Saint Aubert had read her something: it was her author, her favorite. She looked at the paper, wept, and looked at it again: that book was sacred to her; it would not have closed the page open to all the treasures of the world; she stood before the lectern,

In the midst of her sad thoughts, she saw the door slowly open; a sound which she heard in the back of the room made her jump; she thought she saw some movement. The subject of her meditation, the despondency of her spirits, the agitation of her senses, caused her a sudden terror; she expected something supernatural. But her reason overcoming her fear: «What am I to fear?» she said she; « if the souls of those we love appear, it can only be for our best.»

The silence that reigned made her ashamed of her fear; meanwhile the same sound began again; making out something around her, which came to bump her chair slightly, she let out a cry, but could not at the same time refrain from smiling a little confusedly, recognizing the good dog crouching beside her, and licking her hands. Emilia, not finding herself able to visit the whole castle that evening, went out and went for a walk in the garden, on the terrace overlooking the river. The sun had set, but under the leafy branches of the almond trees the streaks of fire that gilded the twilight could be distinguished. The maiden approached her favorite plane tree, where Saint Aubert often sat beside her, and where her tender mother had so often spoken to her of the delights of her future life; how many times had her father also found comfort in the idea of an eternal reunion! Overwhelmed by this recollection, she left the plane tree, and leaning against the wall of the terrace, she saw a group of peasants dancing merrily on the banks of the Garonne, whose vast expanse reflected the last rays of the day. What a painful contrast for poor Emilia, unhappy and desolate! She turned away, but alas! where could she go without encountering at every step objects made to aggravate her pain? she was walking slowly home when she met Teresa,

"Please, Teresa, leave me in peace," said Emilia; 'Your intention is excellent, but eloquence is ill-adapted at the moment.

"Meanwhile dinner is being prepared," replied the housekeeper.

"I can't eat," Emilia said.

"You are doing very badly, my dear mistress, we must feed ourselves. I have prepared a pheasant for you, which Monsieur Barreaux sent me this morning: having met him yesterday, I told him that he was expecting you; I swear I never saw a man more afflicted than he, when I gave him the sad news..."

Emilia, in spite of all Teresa's attentions, did not want to eat, and retired to her room.

A few days later she received letters from her aunt. Madame Cheron, after some expressions of consolation and advice from her, invited her to go to Toulouse, adding that her deceased brother, having entrusted her with her education, believed himself obliged to watch over her. Emilia would have preferred to stay in the valley; being it the asylum of her childhood and the abode of those she had lost forever, she could mourn them freely without being molested by anyone; but she equally wished not to displease her only remaining kinswoman.

Although her tenderness did not allow her to doubt for an instant the reasons which had determined Saint Aubert to make this choice, Emilia understood very well that her happiness was going to be exposed to the whims of her aunt. Answering her, she asked permission to remain a little longer in the valley, alleging her extreme despondency, and the need she had for rest and solitude, to recover from the sorrows she had suffered; she knew very well that her tastes differed greatly from those of her aunt, who loved dissipation, and her wealth enabled her to enjoy it. After writing this letter, Emilia felt more relieved.

He was visited by Barreaux, who sincerely mourned the loss of his friend.

"I can't recall it without the keenest interest," he said; "I won't find anyone like him. If I had met a lonely man like him in the world, I would not have given up. »

Barreaux's affection for Sant'Aubert endeared him extremely dear to Emilia; her greatest consolation consisted in talking about her and her parents to a man who held her very much in esteem, and who, under an unpleasant exterior, hid such a sensitive heart and such a cultivated spirit.

Several weeks elapsed, and Emilia in her peaceful retirement gradually passed from grief to a sweet melancholy; she could already read, and even read the books she had traveled with her father, sit in her place in her library, water the flowers at his planted, play the piano, and sing from time to time some of his favorite tunes.

When her spirits were somewhat relieved by this first jolt, she understood the danger of yielding to indolence, and thinking that sustained activity might restore her strength, she scrupulously adhered to methodically employing all the hours of the day. Then she knew more than ever the value of the education received. By cultivating her mind, Saint Aubert had secured her a refuge from idleness and boredom. The dissipation, the brilliant amusements and distractions of society from which she separated her present position from her, were not at all necessary. But, at the same time, her father had developed the precious qualities of her spirit; scattering charities around him, with his goodness and compassion he softened the evils of those whom he could not alleviate with help; in a word,

Not receiving any response from Cheron, Emilia began to flatter herself that she could extend her stay in the valley; and feeling sufficiently in her power, she ventured to visit those places where her past represented itself most vividly in her mind; I therefore went to the fishpond, and to increase the melancholy, which pleased her so much, she brought her lute with her, and she went there in one of those hours of the evening that so arouse the imagination and the heart: when the girl was in the woods and near that delightful place, she stopped, leaned against a tree, and cried a few minutes before advancing. The little road that led to the pavilion was then all overgrown with grass; the flowers his father had planted on the margins seemed almost to be smothered by them; nettles and honeysuckle grew in tufts; and she sadly watched that neglected walk; where everything announced disorder and carelessness, he opened the door shaking. « Ah! »said he; "Everything is in her place as I left it there when she was there in the company of whom I will never see again. She stood thoughtful, without reflecting that night was imminent, and that the last rays of the sun were already gilding the tops of the mountains; she would no doubt have remained in that situation longer had she not been roused by the sound of footsteps behind the building. A little later the door was opened, a stranger appeared, and amazed to see Emilia, begged her to excuse her indiscretion. At the sound of that voice, her fear vanished, but her emotion grew. Hers was familiar, and though she could not recognize her object, her memory served her too well for her to retain fear of her.

The unknown repeated his apologies. Emilia replied a few words, and then advancing with vivacity, she exclaimed: «Great God! is it ever possible? Of course, I'm not mistaken, it's Mademoiselle Sant'Aubert.

"That's true," said Emilia, recognizing Valancourt, whose physiognomy seemed very animated. A thousand painful recollections renewed her sad afflictions, and the effort she made of her to contain herself served only to agitate her to her advantage. Valancourt, meanwhile, eagerly inquired about the health of Sant'Aubert. A torrent of tears sadly let him know the fatal news. He led her to a chair, and sat next to her as she continued to cry, while the young man held his hand tightly between hers.

"I know," he finally said, "how useless consolations are in such cases: after such a great misfortune, I can only grieve with you." »

When Valancourt learned that Saint Aubert had died en route, and had left Emilia in the hands of strangers, he exclaimed involuntarily: 'Where was I? »So he changed the subject, and spoke of himself. He told her that, after their separation, he had wandered a few days on the seashore, and had returned to Gascony by way of the Languedoc.

After this brief narration, he was silent: Emilia was not prepared to speak again, and they walked towards the castle. When they reached the door, he stopped as if he thought he must go no further; he told Emilia that as he planned to go to Estuvière the following day, he asked permission to come and say goodbye to her, and she did not have the courage to deny him.

When night came, she could not sleep, being more than ever occupied by the memory of her father. Recalling in what precise and solemn manner she had ordered her to burn her papers, she reproached herself for not having obeyed sooner, and she resolved to make amends for this negligence.

CHAPTER IX

The following morning, Emilia had a fire lit in her father's bedroom, and went there to scrupulously carry out his orders: she closed the door so as not to be surprised, and opened the closet where the manuscripts were; there, in one corner, by a high chair, was the same table where she had seen her father seated the night before their departure, and she no longer doubted that the papers he had spoken to her about were not the very ones whose reading caused him to so much excitement. The solitary life lived by Emilia, her melancholy subjects of her usual thoughts, had made her susceptible to believing in ghosts and ghosts. She was especially strolling in the evening in a deserted house, which she had shivered several times at alleged apparitions, which would never have struck her when she was happy: when, raising his eyes for the second time on the chair placed in a dark corner, he saw the image of his parent. She was seized with terror, and rushed out. Presently I reproached his weakness in performing so serious a duty, and he reopened the lavatory. In accordance with the instructions received, she soon found the knot that was to serve as a guide: she pressed down with her foot, and the table ran by itself under the contiguous one. Emilia found there the sheaf of papers, the louis bag, and a few other scattered sheets; she took everything with a trembling hand, closed the secret again, and was about to get up, when she again saw before her the image of her which had frightened her: she rushed into her room, and fell over on a chair in a faint; presently she revived her, and she soon overcame that dreadful but pitiful surprise of her imagination. She went back to the cards, but his mind was so little at home that he fixed his eyes almost involuntarily on the open pages, without thinking that he was transgressing his father's formal orders; a sentence of extreme importance awakened her attention and memory. She abandoned the papers, but she could not erase from her spirit her words which so keenly revived his terror and her curiosity; they were extremely moved by it. The more she meditated, the more her imagination flared up. Driven by her most imperious reasons, she wanted to know the mystery that was hidden in that sentence; she repented of the oath she had sworn, and even came to doubt whether she was obliged to keep it; but her mistake was not of long duration. a sentence of extreme importance awakened her attention and memory. She abandoned the papers, but she could not erase from her spirit her words which so keenly revived his terror and her curiosity; they were extremely moved by it. The more she meditated, the more her imagination flared up. Driven by her most imperious reasons, she wanted to know the mystery that was hidden in that sentence; she repented of the oath she had sworn, and even came to doubt whether she was obliged to keep it; but her mistake was not of long duration. a sentence of extreme importance awakened her attention and memory. She abandoned the papers, but she could not erase from her spirit her words which so keenly revived his terror and her curiosity; they were extremely moved by it. The more she meditated, the more her imagination flared up. Driven by her most imperious reasons, she wanted to know the mystery that was hidden in that sentence; she repented of the oath she had sworn, and even came to doubt whether she was obliged to keep it; but her mistake was not of long duration. Driven by the most imperious reasons, she wanted to know the mystery that was hidden in that sentence; she repented of the oath she had sworn, and even came to doubt whether she was obliged to keep it; but her mistake was not of long duration. Driven by the most imperious reasons, she wanted to know the mystery that was hidden in that sentence; she repented of the oath she had sworn, and even came to doubt whether she was obliged to keep it; but her mistake was not of long duration.

"I promised," she said, "and I mustn't argue, but obey: let's avert a temptation that would make me guilty, since I feel strong enough to resist. And instantly everything was burned.

She had left her purse on the coffee table without opening it; but perceiving that it contained something larger than doubloons, she began to examine it.

"His hand placed them there," she said, kissing each coin and showering it with tears; "Her hand, which is now nothing but cold dust! »

At the bottom he found a small package containing a small ivory box in which there was a portrait of a lady. She was astonished and exclaimed: «It is the same one in front of which my father cried! »Carefully as he considered her, he could not pinpoint her resemblance: she was of strange beauty. Her particular expression was sweetness, but there reigned a shadow of sadness and resignation.

Saint Aubert had not prescribed anything about this painting. She emilia she believed she could keep it, and remembering how she had spoken to her of the Marquise de Villeroy, she easily imagined that this was her portrait: she too could not understand why he had kept it .

The girl observed the miniature, without understanding the interest she took in contemplating it, and the movement of affection and pity she felt within herself. Curls of brown hair carelessly played over her a broad forehead: her nose was almost aquiline. Her lips smiled, but with melancholy: she raised her blue eyes to heaven with amiable languor, and the kind of cloud scattered over her entire physiognomy of her seemed to express her most lively sensitivity.

Emilia was shaken by the profound meditation into which that portrait had plunged her, on hearing the garden door open: she knew that Valancourt was returning to the castle, and it took her a few moments to recover. When she met him in her living room, she was struck by the change in her physiognomy after their parting in Roussillon: pain and darkness had prevented her from noticing it the previous evening; but the despondency of Valancourt yielded to the joy of seeing her.

"You see," he said to her, "that I make use of the permission granted by you. I come to bid you farewell, though I have had thefortuneto meet you only yesterday. »

Emilia smiled faintly, and, as if embarrassed of what she should say, asked him how long it had been since he had been back in Gascony. 'I've been there since...' said Valancourt, blushing, 'after I had the misfortune to part with friends who had made my journey through the Pyrenees so delightful; I took a long ride. »

A tear fell from Emilia's eyes as Valancourt spoke; he saw it and spoke of quite another thing; he praised the castle, its beautiful situation and the viewpoints it offered. Emilia, very embarrassed by that interview, gladly chose an indifferent subject. They went onto the terrace, and Valancourt was enchanted by the view of the river, the meadows, and the many paintings that Guienne presented.

He leaned against the parapet, contemplating the rapid flow of the Garonne. 'It is not a long time,' he said, 'that I went up to its source; I did not then have the good fortune to know you, for in that case I would have felt your absence painfully. »

The young man was silent, and sat beside her, mute and trembling; he finally said in a broken voice: «This delightful place .... I will have to abandon it, and I will abandon you too, perhaps forever.

These moments may never come back; I don't want to lose them: suffer while, without offending your delicacy and your pain, I express once and for all the admiration and gratitude that your goodness inspires in me. Oh! if one day I could have the right to call love the lively feeling that..."

Emilia's emotion did not allow her to answer, and Valancourt, having cast his eyes on her, he saw her turn pale and on the verge of fainting: he made an involuntary movement to support her, and this movement was enough to bring her to her senses with certain fright. When Valancourt spoke again, everything in him, and even her voice, manifested the tenderest love.

"I would not dare," he added, "to speak to you at length about myself: but this cruel moment would have less bitterness, if I could bring hope with me, that the confession, which I have just escaped from me, will not exclude me in the future from your presence. »

Emilia made a new effort to overcome the confusion of her ideas. She was afraid of betraying her heart, and of revealing the preference she accorded to Valancourt. She hesitated to express her feelings with which she was animated, in spite of the fact that her heart urged her towards them with great vivacity. Nonetheless, she regained courage to tell him that she was honored by the kindness of a person for whom her father had had such esteem.

"He therefore judged me worthy of his esteem?" said Valancourt with dubious shyness; Then, recovering, he added: 'Pardon this question; I hardly know what he wants to tell me. If I dared to flatter myself with your indulgence, if you allowed me the hope of having your news sometime, I would part with you more calmly. »

After a moment's silence, Emilia replied: 'I'll be honest with you; you see my situation, and I am sure you will adapt to it. I live in this house, which was my father's, but I live there alone. Alas! I no longer have parents, whose presence can authorize your visits...

"I will not pretend not to hear this truth," said the young man. Then he added sadly: "But who will indemnify me for the sacrifice my frankness costs me? At least you will allow me to introduce myself to your relatives. »

The confused girl didn't know what to answer knowing the difficulty. Her isolation and her position left her no friend whose advice she could take. Her Cheron, her only relative, was occupied only with her own pleasures, and was so offended by Emilia's reluctance to leave her valley that she seemed to think no more of her.

« Ah! I see it,' said Valancourt, after a long silence, 'I know I flattered myself too much. You think me unworthy of your esteem. Most fatal journey! I regarded it as the most fortunate time of my life: those delicious days will poison my future. »

Here he stood up abruptly, and as he strode along the terrace, one could see despair painted on his face. Emilia was deeply moved. The movements of her heart triumphed over her shyness, and when he was close to her, she said to him in a voice that betrayed her: 'You are wrong both of us when you say that I believe you are unworthy of my esteem; I must confess that you have owned it for a long time, and that… »

Valancourt waited impatiently for the end of the sentence, but the words breathed on her lip: her eyes nevertheless manifested all the emotions of her heart; Valancourt quickly went from embarrassment to joy. 'Emilia,' he exclaimed, 'my dear Emilia. O heaven! how can you resist so much happiness! »

He brought the girl's hand to his mouth; she was cold and shivering, and Valancourt saw her grow pale; however, she quickly recovered and said to him with a smile: «It seems to me that I have not yet recovered from the terrible blow that my poor heart has received.

'Forgive me,' the young man answered, 'I won't speak any more of what can excite your sensibilities. » Then, forgetting his resolution, he began to talk about himself again.

"You don't know," he said to her, "how many torments I have suffered near you, when without a doubt, if you honored me with a thought, you must have believed me very far from here." I have not ceased to roam every night around this castle wrapped in profound darkness; how delightful it was to know that I was near you! She reveled in the idea that she watched over your retreat, and that you enjoyed peaceful sleep. These gardens are not new to me. One evening I climbed over the hedge, and spent one of the happiest hours of my life under the window, which believed yours. »

Emilia inquired how long Valancourt had been in the neighborhood. "Many days," he replied; « I wanted to take advantage of the permission granted me by Saint Aubert. I do not understand how he had this kindness, but though I earnestly desired it, when the moment approached, I lost courage, and postponed my visit. He was lodged in a nearby village, and he ran around the surroundings of this beautiful country with my dogs, longing for the good fortune to meet you, without having the audacity to come and see you. »

About two hours passed in this conversation; finally Valancourt, getting up: 'I must leave,' he said sadly, 'but with the hope of seeing you again, and with that of offering my respect and my servitude to your relatives. Your mouth confirm me in this hope.

- My relatives will be very fortunate to make the acquaintance of an old friend of my father's. »

Valancourt kissed her hand, and they remained motionless without being able to move away. Emilia was silent, she kept her eyes downcast, and those of Valancourt were fixed on her. At that point, they heard walking hastily behind the plane tree.

The girl, turning around, saw Signora Cheron; she blushed, and was seized with a sudden trembling; she got up too, and she ran to meet her aunt.

"Good morning, my niece," said la Cheron, throwing a look of surprise and curiosity at Valancourt, "good morning, my niece, how are you?" But the question is useless; your face indicates enough that you have already consoled yourself for your loss.

"My face does me wrong in that case, madam; the loss I made can never be repaired.

- Well!... Well!... I don't want to afflict you. You are very much like your father ... and certainly it would have been fortunate for the poor man if he had had a different character. »

Emilia did not want to reply, and introduced her to the afflicted Valancourt; the young man respectfully greeted Signora Cheron, who returned him a cold reverence, looking at him with disdain. After a few moments he took leave of Emilia with an air which sufficiently made her know the pain of leaving her, and leaving her in the company of her aunt.

"Who is that young man?" she said harshly; "I suppose he will be one of your worshippers; but I believed, my niece, that you had a little more respect for propriety, to receive the visits of a young boy in the state of solitude in which you are. The world watches these fouls; they will talk about it, believe me, I have more experience than you. »

Emilia, stung by such a violent reproach, would have liked to interrupt her, but her aunt continued: 'It is absolutely necessary that you find yourself under the direction of a person capable of guiding you more than you can do it yourself. Indeed, I have little time for such a task; nevertheless, since your poor father, in the last moments of his life, he asked me to watch over your conduct, I am obliged to take charge of it; but know, dear niece, that if you don't settle for the utmost docility, I won't worry too much about you. »

Emilia didn't even try to answer. The pain, the pride and the feeling of her innocence contained her until the moment in which the aunt added: «I have come to take you to take you to Toulouse; I am sorry, however, that your father died with such a small substance: in spite of this, I will take you into my house. That blessed father of yours was always more generous than provident; otherwise he would not have left his daughter to the discretion of her relatives.

"And that's exactly what he didn't do," said Emilia coldly; 'The disorder of his fortune does not proceed entirely from that noble generosity which distinguished him: Mr. Motteville's affairs may be arranged, as I hope, without ruining the creditors, and until then I consider myself very fortunate to reside in the valley.

"I don't doubt it," Cheron replied, with a smile full of irony. "Oh! I don't doubt it; and I see how salutary tranquility and retirement have been to the restoration of your spirit. She did not believe you capable, my niece, of such duplicity. When you attached this apology to me, I believed it in good faith, and I certainly didn't expect to find you in such amiable company as Signor La's.... Go... I've forgotten his name. It is clear that you observe the conveniences carefully!... »

Emilia burst into flames, related the report of Valancourt and her father, the circumstances of the pistol shot, and the continuation of their journeys; she added the chance encounter of the previous day, and she finally confessed that Valancourt had shown some interest in her, and asked permission to address her relatives.

"And who is that young adventurer?" » said Cheron; "What are his claims?

"He will explain them to you himself, madame; my father knew him, and I think him blameless.

"He will be a cadet," cried the aunt, "and consequently a beggar." So then my brother fell in love with this young man in a few days! it was always like this; in his youth he took a liking or an aversion, unable to guess the reason; and I have observed several times that the people from whom he distanced himself were always more amiable than those who interested him; but tastes cannot be disputed. He was accustomed to trust his physiognomy very much; what ridiculous enthusiasm! What does a man's face have in common with his character? Can't a good man sometimes have an unpleasant countenance? »

Cheron pronounced this sentence with the triumphant thunder of a person who, believing she has made a great discovery, is applauded by it, and thinks it cannot be contradicted.

Emilia, wishing to finish this conversation, asked her aunt to accept some refreshments.

As soon as she got home, she ordered her to make her preparations for leaving for Toulouse in two or three hours. She begged her to defer until at least the following day, and she obtained it with some difficulty.

The remainder of the day was spent in pedantic tyranny on the part of the aunt, and in disgust and grief on the part of the niece. As soon as hers had retired, Emilia bade a last farewell to her house, which had been her cradle. She left her without knowing the time of her absence, and for a new kind of life which she was utterly ignorant of; but she could not overcome her presentiment that she would never return to the valley. While she was in her father's library, and that she was choosing a few books to bring with him, Teresa opened the door to check, as usual, if everything was in order, and was surprised to find the mistress there. Emilia gave her the appropriate instructions for maintaining the castle.

« Alas! Teresa told her; "So you're leaving? If I am not mistaken, however, it seems to me that you would be happier here than where they want to take you. »

Emilia didn't answer her, and went back to her room. When she arrived there, she went to the window, and saw the garden dimly lit by the moon that was then rising above the fig trees. The placid beauty of the night increased her desire to taste a sad pleasure, even making greetings to the favorite places of her childhood. She was impelled to descend, and throwing on the light veil in which she used to walk, stepped cautiously into the garden, and made haste towards the distant groves, glad to still breathe a free aura and sigh without being observed by anyone. . The deep repose of nature, the sweet scents diffused by the nocturnal zephyr, the vast expanse of the horizon and the starry blue firmament enraptured her soul and her in sweet ecstasy.they carried gradually to those sublime heights from which the footsteps of this world vanish.

Emilia fixed her eyes on the plane tree, and rested there for the last time. There, just a few hours before, she was talking with Valancourt. I remembered his confession of her that she often wandered around her house at night, that he climbed over its fence; and she suddenly thought that at that very moment he might be in the garden perhaps. The fear of meeting him, fearlikewiseher aunt's censures induced her to retire to the house. She often stopped to examine the thickets before crossing them; she passed by without seeing anyone; but she came to a clump of almond trees nearer the house, and having turned to see the garden again, she thought she saw a person coming out of the darkest pergolas and walking slowly along an avenue of linden trees, then illuminated by the moon. The distance, the too dim light, did not allow her to ascertain whether it was illusion or reality. She continued to watch for some time, and presently she thought she heard walking near her. She rushed back, and back in her room, she opened the window at the moment when someone was entering under the almond trees, in the very place she had just left. She closed the window, and, though very agitated, she was able to enjoy a few hours of sleep.

CHAPTER X

The carriage that was to take Emilia and her aunt to Toulouse was at the door very early in the day. Mrs. Cheron appeared at breakfast before her niece arrived, and she piqued by the despondency in which she saw her when she appeared, she reproached him in a way incapable of stopping him. Not without great difficulty, Emilia managed to bring her dog so loved by her father with her. The aunt, eager to leave, moved the carriage forward; old Teresa stood at the door to take leave of her mistress. "God be with you, miss," she told her.

Emilia could only answer tenderly by squeezing her hand.

Many of the unhappy people who received help from her father were in front of the garden door, and came to greet the very afflicted Emilia. She distributed all the money she had in her pocket, and retired to the carriage with a deep sigh. The precipices, the gigantic height of the Pyrenees, and all the other magnificent sights, brought Emilia to mind a thousand interesting recollections; but these objects of enthusiastic admiration excited in her then only her pain and sorrows.

Meanwhile Valancourt had returned to Estuvière with his heart completely full of Emilia. He sometimes abandoned himself to dreams of a happy future, more often he gave in to anxieties, and quivered at the opposition he might find in Emilia's relatives. He was the last son of an old Gascony family. Having lost his parents in infancy, his education and his tenuous legitimacy had been entrusted to the Earl Duverney, his elder brother by twenty years. He had an elevation of spirit and a greatness of soul which made him shine in the exercises then called heroic. His substance was still diminished by the expense of his education; but the elder brother seemed to think perhaps that his genius and his talents would compensate for the injuries of fortune; they afforded Valancourt a bright prospect in a military career, only then could he be reasonably embraced by a gentleman; and in consequence he entered the service.

He had obtained a discharge from the regiment when he undertook the journey of the Pyrenees, at the time he had met Sant'Aubert. His permission being about to inspire, he therefore had greater haste to introduce himself to Emilia's relatives: he was afraid of finding them contrary to her vows. His patrimony, with the modest supplement of Emilia's, would have been sufficient for both, but it could not satisfy either vanity or ambition.

Meanwhile our female travelers advanced: Emilia made an effort to appear happy, and fell back into silence and dejection. Cheron attributed her melancholy to the displeasure of being away from her lover; she convinced that her niece's grief over her father's death was nothing more than an affectation of sensitivity, she did everything to ridicule him.

Finally they arrived in Toulouse. Emilia being there been many years ago, he had a very faint recollection of it left. She was surprised by the splendor of the house and the furniture; perhaps the modest elegance to which she was accustomed was the cause of her astonishment. She followed Cheron through a vast antechamber filled with servants dressed in rich liveries, she entered a handsome parlor decorated with more magnificence than taste, and her aunt ordered dinner to be served.

"I'm glad to be in my castle," she said, abandoning herself on a large sofa; « I have all my people around me; I hate travel, although I must have loved them, because everything I see outside here always makes me find everything more beautiful in my building. Well! don't you say anything? Why is she mute, Emilia? »

She held back the tears that escaped her, and pretended to smile. Her aunt spread much about the splendor of the house, about the conversations, and finally about what she expected of Emilia, whose reserve and shyness passed in her eyes for pride and ignorance. He took occasion to reproach her, not knowing what is necessary to guide a spirit who, distrusting his own strength, possessing a delicate discernment, and imagining that others are more enlightened, fears exposing himself to criticism, and seeks refuge in darkness of silence.

The supper interrupted Signora Cheron's haughty speech, and the humiliating reflections which she mixed into it for her niece. After dinner, Cheron retired to her apartment, and a maid brought Emilia to hers; they ascended a large stairway, traversed several corridors, descended a few steps, and passed through a narrow passage into a remote part of the house; finally the maid opened the door of a small room, and said it was the one intended for Signora Emilia: the girl, left alone, gave herself in the grip of all the excess of pain that he could no longer contain. Those who know by experience to what extent the heart becomes attached to even inanimate objects when it has become accustomed to them, how hard it is to leave them, with what tenderness it finds them again, with what sweet illusion it believes to see its former friends, these alone will understand the the abandonment in which Emilia found herself then, abruptly removed from the only shelter she recognized from childhood, and thrown onto a theater and among people who displeased her even more for their character than for their novelty. Her father's faithful dog was with her in her bedroom, petting her, and licking her hands as she cried. "Poor beast," she said; « I no longer have anyone else but you as a friend. »

CHAPTER XI

Madame Cheron's castle was very close to Toulouse, and surrounded by immense gardens; Emilia, having risen early, walked through them before breakfast. From a terrace which extended to the edge of these gardens, one could discover the whole of Lower Languedoc. Emilia recognized the high peaks of the Pyrenees; and her imagination soon painted for her the greenery and the pastures that are at the foot of them. Her heart flew to her placid abode. She took an inexpressible pleasure in supposing she saw its situation, though she could scarcely make out its mountains. Little concerned with the country in which she found herself, she fixed her eyes on Gascony, and her spirit fed on her with the interesting recollections of her aroused in her by this sight.

A servant came to tell her that breakfast was ready.

"Where have you been so early?" » Cheron said when her niece entered. 'I do not approve of these solitary walks. I don't want you to go out so early in the morning without being accompanied. A girl who made appointments in the moonlight at the castle in the valley needs a little supervision. »

The feeling of her own innocence did not prevent Emilia's blushing. She trembled, and lowered her eyes in confusion, while her aunt gave her bold glances, and blushed herself: but her blush was that of her satisfied pride, that of a person who takes pleasure in his own penetration.

Emilia, not doubting that her aunt meant to talk about her nocturnal walk before leaving the valley, thought she had to explain the reasons for it; but she, with a smile of her contempt, refused to listen to her.

'I don't trust,' he told her, 'anyone's protests; I judge people by their deeds, and I will test your conduct for the future. »

Emilia, less surprised by her aunt's moderation and mysterious silence than by the accusation, reflected deeply on it, and no longer doubted it was Valancourt whom she had seen at night in the gardens of the valley, and who aunt he might well have recognized. Meanwhile she, leaving no painful subject except to treat another which was no less so, spoke of Motteville and of the enormous loss which her niece made of her in her failure. While she was discussing with sumptuous pity the accidents that oppressed Emilia, she insisted on the duties of humanity and gratitude, making the poor girl devour the most cruel mortifications, and obliging her to consider herself not only under her dependence, but under that good also of all the servitude.

He then warned her that a lot of people were expected for dinner that day, and he repeated all the previous evening's lessons on social conduct: he added that he wanted to see her dressed in taste and elegance, and then he deigned to show her all the splendor of his castle, to make her observe everything that shone with a particular magnificence, and which was distinguished in the various apartments; whereupon she retired to her toilet room. Emilia shut herself up in her room, took out her books, and recreated her spirit by reading, until it was time to get dressed.

When the guests were assembled, Emilia entered the room with an air of shyness which she could not overcome, however hard she tried. The idea that her aunt was observing her with a stern eye disturbed her even more. Her mourning dress, her sweetness, the despondency of her beautiful countenance, no less than the modesty of her demeanor, made her most interesting to nearly all society. She recognized Montoni and his friend Cavignì, whom she had found in Quesnel's house; they had all the familiarity of old acquaintances in Cheron's house, and she too seemed to welcome them with great pleasure.

Montoni carried in his behavior the feeling of superiority: the spirit and the talents with which he was able to support it forced all the others to yield to him. The delicacy of his touch was strongly expressed in his countenance; but he knew how to dissemble when necessary, and one could often see in him the triumph of art over nature. His face was long and thin, yet they called him handsome; praise perhaps more to be attributed to the strength and vigor of the soul, which were outlined in all his features. Emilia conceived a kind of admiration for him, but not that admiration which she could lead to her esteem; it united a kind of fear, the reason for which she could not guess.

Cavignì was as cheerful and insinuating as the first time. Although almost always occupied with Signora Cheron, he found the means of talking to Emilia. He addressed some witticisms at first, e afterwards he assumed an air of tenderness of which she was very well aware, and which did not frighten her. She spoke little, but the grace and sweetness of her manners encouraged him to continue; she was not interrupted until a young lady of the club, who always talked, and about everything, came to mingle in their conversation; this lady, who displayed all the French vivacity and coquetry, affected to understand everything, or rather she did not even affect it. Never having come out of perfect ignorance, she supposed she had nothing to learn; she forced everyone to take care of her, sometimes entertained, tired after a moment, and then was abandoned.

Emilia, though refreshed by all that she had seen, withdrew without regret, and willingly abandoned herself again to the recollections which pleased her so much.

A fortnight passed in a throng of visits and dissipations; Emilia accompanied Cheron everywhere, she rarely enjoyed herself, and was often bored. She was struck by the apparent education and knowledge which the persons composing the conversation around her exhibited; it wasn't until much later that she recognized the fraud of all her supposed talents. What deceived her the most was that air of continual vivacity, and above all of goodness, which she observed in each character. She imagined that a usual and always ready affability was the real foundation. Finally, the exaggeration of someone, less skilled than the others, made her suspect that, if contentment and goodness are the only principles of a sweet pleasantness,

Emilia spent the most welcome moments in the pavilion on the terrace. She retired there with a book, to enjoy her melancholy, or with her lute, to overcome it. Seated with her eyes fixed on the Pyrenees and Gascony, she sang the most interesting little songs of her country, learned in childhood.

One evening, Emilia played the lute in the pavilion with an expression that came from the heart. The sun in the west still illuminated the Garonne, which fled to some distance, and whose waters had passed in front of the valley. Emilia was thinking of Valancourt; she had never heard of him since her stay in Toulouse; and now she, away from him, she felt all the impression she had made on his heart. She before havingknownValancourt, he had not met anyone whose spirit and taste so agreed with his own. Cheron had spoken to her of dissimulation, of tricks; she pretended that the delicacy she admired in her lover was nothing more than a snare to please her, yet she believed in his sincerity. A doubt nevertheless, weak as she was of hers, was enough to oppress her heart.

The noise of a horse on the street, under her window, roused her from these thoughts: she saw a knight whose staff and bearing reminded her of Valancourt, since the darkness did not allow her to distinguish his features. She drew back fearing to be seen, and at the same time wanting to observe. Her incognito passed without looking, and when she went to the window, she saw him in the avenue leading to Toulouse. This slight incident put her in a bad mood, and she, after a few rounds on the terrace, was soon back at the chateau.

Cheron came back rougher than usual; and Emilia was not happy until she was allowed to retire to her room.

The next day she was called by her aunt, who was burning with anger, and who, as soon as she saw her, presented her with a letter.

« Do you know this character? »He said to her in a severe voice, and looking at her fixedly, while Emilia examined the letter attentively.

"No, ma'am, I don'ti know, » he answered her.

"Don't make me lose my patience," said the aunt; "You know him, confess him immediately, I demand that you tell the truth. »

Emilia kept silent and was about to leave. Cheron called her back.

"Oh! you are guilty: I see now that you know the character.

"But if you doubted it, Signora," said Emilia with dignity, "why accuse me of having told a lie?"

"It's useless to deny it," said Signora Cheron; 'I see from your demeanor that you are not ignorant of the contents of this letter. I am quite sure that in my house, and without my knowledge, you have received letters from that insolent young man. »

Emilia, annoyed by the rudeness of that accusation, broke her silence and tried to justify herself, but without convincing her aunt.

'I cannot suppose that the young man would have dared to write to me if you had not encouraged him.

"Will you allow me to remind you, madame," said Emilia in a timid voice, "some particularities of a conversation we had together at my house: I then told you frankly that I did not object to M. Valancourt addressing my family.

"I don't want to be interrupted," said Mrs. Cheron; "I ... I ... why didn't you forbid him?" Emilia didn't answer. « A man unknown to all, absolutely foreign; an adventurer chasing after a rich girl! But at least, in this respect, it can be said that he was greatly deceived.

"I've already told you, ma'am, his family was known to my father," Emilia said modestly, and pretending not to have heard the last sentence.

— Oh! I don't trust his judgment at all favourable,' replied the aunt with her usual lightness. « He had such bad ideas! He judged people by physiognomy.

"Lady, a little while ago you believed me guilty, and yet you judged it by my physiognomy." »

Emilia allowed herself this reproach to somehow respond to the disrespectful tone with which Cheron spoke of her father.

'I sent for you,' added the aunt, 'to tell you that I don't intend to be bothered by letters or by visits from all the youngsters who will pretend to adore you. This Signor di Valla ... I don't know what you call him, has the impertinence to ask me to allow him to pay his respects to me; but she will answer him how it goes. As for you, Emilia, I repeat it once and for all, if you don't conform to my will, I will no longer worry about your education, and I will put you in a convent.

— Ah! madame,' said Emilia, melting away in tears, 'how can I have deserved this treatment? »

At that instant, Cheron could have obtained from her the promise to renounce Valancourt forever. Seized with terror, she would no longer consent to see him again; she was afraid of being mistaken, and finally she feared that she had not been reserved enough in the conference she had at the valley. She knew perfectly well that she did not deserve the odious suspicions formed by her aunt, but she was tormented by infinite scruples. She growing timid, and doubting that she would hurt her, she resolved to obey any command of hers, and she let him know her intention; but Cheron did not believe her, and saw in her nothing but her artifice, or her fear.

'Promise me,' she said to her niece, 'that you won't see that young man, and you won't write to him without my permission.

— Ah! madame,' replied Emilia, 'can you suppose that I was capable of doing it?

"I don't know what to suppose; youth is incomprehensible, for it lacks too much common sense to desire to be respected.

"I respect myself," Emilia replied; 'My father always taught me the need for it. He told me that, with my own esteem, I will always obtain that of others.

"My brother was a good man," Cheron added, "but he didn't know the world. But... in short, you haven't made me the promise I demand of you. »

Emilia made her promise, and went for a walk in the garden. Arriving at her favorite pavilion, she sat by the window looking out into a grove. The calm of that solitude enabled him to collect her thoughts and to judge for himself her conduct. She remembered the conversation she had at the castle, and she happily convinced herself that nothing could alarm her pride, nor her delicacy; she confirmed herself in the esteem of herself, and of which she felt so much need. In any case, she resolved not to entertain a secret correspondence, and to observe the same reservation with Valancourt whenever she would meet him. While she was making these reflections, she shed a few tears, but she quickly wiped them away, when she heard him walk, open the pavilion, and, turning her head, she recognized Valancourt. A mix of pleasure, of surprise and terror took such possession of her heart, that she was greatly moved. She turned pale, blushed, and was unable to speak or get up from her chair for a few moments. Valancourt's face was the faithful mirror of what she must express about her: his joy was suspended when she became aware of Emilia's agitation. Revived by her first surprise, she answered with a sweet smile; but a throng of contrary affections again assailed her heart, and strove mightily to subjugate her resolution. It was hard to know his joy was suspended when he became aware of Emilia's agitation. Revived by her first surprise, she answered with a sweet smile; but a throng of contrary affections again assailed her heart, and strove mightily to subjugate her resolve. It was hard to know his joy was suspended when he became aware of Emilia's agitation. Revived by her first surprise, she answered with a sweet smile; but a throng of contrary affections again assailed her heart, and strove mightily to subjugate her resolution. It was hard to know if she was overcome by either the joy of seeing Valancourt, or the fear of the transports to which her aunt would abandon herself when she learned of this meeting. After a few words that were as laconic as they were embarrassed, she led him into the garden and asked him if she had seen Mrs. Cheron.

'No,' he said, 'I haven't seen it, I was told it was busy, and when I heard you were in the garden, I hastened to come and see you. Then he added: "May I venture to tell you the subject of my visit without incurring your indignation?" Can I hope that you will not accuse me of haste, using the permission you granted me, to address me to your relatives? »

Emilia did not know what to answer, but her perplexity did not last long, and she was once again attacked by terror when, at the bend in the avenue, she saw Signora Cheron. She had regained the feeling of her own innocence, and her fear was so weakened that, instead of avoiding her aunt, she went very calmly to meet her with Valancourt. However, the discontent and impatient arrogance with which she observed them disconcerted Emilia: she understood that that meeting would have been believed premeditated; she introduced the young man, and, too agitated to stay with them, she ran to shut herself up in the house, where she waited a long time and with extreme disquiet for the result of the conference. She could not imagine how her lover could have broken into her aunt's house before having obtained her permission, which she asked for. It was unaware of a circumstance which must have rendered this step useless, even if Cheron had accepted it. Valancourt, in the agitation of her mind, had forgotten to date her letter; consequently, she could not have answered him.

Madame Cheron had a long conversation with Valancourt, and when she returned to the house, her demeanor it expressed more bad humor than that excessive severity with which Emilia had trembled.

"Finally," said the aunt, "I have dismissed that young man, and I hope I will never receive such visits again," she assured me that your meeting was not concerted.

"Madam," said Emilia moved, "did you ask him?"

"Of course I did!" you ought not to have thought me so imprudent as to think I should have neglected it.

"Heavens," cried the girl; "What idea will he have of me, madame, if you yourself show him such suspicions?"

"The opinion that people will form of you," resumed the aunt, "from now on is of very little consequence. I have put an end to this business, and I think you will have some opinion of my prudence. I let him see that she was not stupid, and above all not complacent enough to suffer a clandestine trade in my house. How indiscreet was your father,' she continued, 'in having left me in charge of your conduct! I would like to see you married; should I find myself bothered any longer by that M. Valancourt, or by others equal to him, I will certainly put you in a cloister. So remember the alternative. That audacious had the impertinence to confess to me that his substance is very tenuous, that he depends on his older brother, and that this substance depends on his advancement in a military career. Fool! he should have at least kept it from me if he was going to persuade me. He therefore had the presumption of supposing that I would have married my niece to a man with no property, to a wretch who confesses it himself..."

Emilia was sensitive to Valancourt's sincere confession; and though her poverty upset their hopes, her frankness conduct caused her a pleasure which momentarily surpassed all her troubles.

Cheron continued: « He also thought it best to tell me that he would not receive his leave except from you, which I positively denied. Thus he will know that it will be very sufficient that I do not like him, and I take this opportunity to repeat it: if you arrange the slightest conversation with him without my knowledge, get ready to leave my house at once.

"How little you know me, if you think such an order is necessary!" »

Mrs. Cheron went to her dressing table, being invited for a conversation that evening. Emilia would have liked to dispense with accompanying her, but she didn't dare ask for fear of a false interpretation. When she was in her room, he gave free rein to his grief: he remembered that Valancourt, ever more amiable to her, was banished from her presence, and perhaps forever. She spent the time her aunt dedicated to getting dressed in tears. When they met again at table, her eyes betrayed tears, and she was severely rebuked for it. She made great efforts to appear happy, and they were not entirely fruitless.

He went with his aunt to see Madame Clairval, a widow of a certain age, who had recently settled in Toulouse in her husband's villa. She had lived several years in Paris with great elegance: she was naturally cheerful, and after her arrival in Toulouse, she had given the most beautiful parties ever seen there.

All this excited not only the envy but also the frivolous ambition of Mrs. Cheron, and as she could not compete in pomp and expense, she wished at least to be believed to be Clairval's intimate friend.

To that end, he was most courteous to her; and when it came to being invited by her, he kept silent about any other commitment. She talked about it everywhere, and she gave herself great airs of importance, making one believe they were intrinsic friends.

The entertainment that evening consisted of a dance party and dinner. The dance was of an entirely new kind. We danced in different groups in very extensive gardens. The large and beautiful trees under which the party was held were illuminated by an infinite number of street lamps arranged with all possible variety. The different shapes increased the charm of that scene. While some danced, others, seated on the grassy turf, spoke freely, criticized the hairstyles, took refreshments or sang ariettas to the accompaniment of the guitar. The gallantry of the men, the coquetry of the women, the lightness and vivacity of the dances, the lute, the flute, the harpsichord, and the country air, which the woods gave to the whole scene, made this party a very piquant model of the French pleasures and taste. Emilia regarded this laughing picture with a kind of melancholy delight. It will be easy to understand his surprise when, throwing his eyes at random on a country dance, he recognized the lover who was dancing with a beautiful young lady, and seemed to have the most solicitous attention for her: he immediately turned away, wanting to take his aunt elsewhere, who was talking to Cavigni without having seen Valancourt. A sudden weakness in her compelled her to sit up, and the extreme pallor which appeared on her face, made those around her believe that she was inconvenienced. Cheron continued to talk to Cavigni, and the Count of Beauvillers, who had taken care of Emilia, made some malicious observations about the ball, to which she answered almost incoherently, so much did the idea of Valancourt torment her, she was so uneasy about staying so long near him. The count's remarks on her contradictory compelled him meanwhile to fix her eyes on it, which at the same moment met those of Valancourt. She shivered and turned the looks away quickly, but not without having distinguished his alteration on seeing her. He would have gladly moved away from that place at the same instant, if he hadn't thought that this conduct would have made him too aware of the impetus he had over her heart. She tried to continue the conversation with the count, who spoke to her about the lady who danced with Valancourt: the fear of letting the lively interest she took in it show, would undoubtedly have betrayed her, if the count's gazes had not fixed then about the couple he was talking about.

'That young knight,' he said, 'seems to be a perfect man in everything except dancing: his companion is one of the beauties of Toulouse, and she will be very rich. I want to hope that he will know how to make a better choice for the happiness of his life than he did for the country; I realize that he cheats all the others. However, I am surprised that that young man, with his beautiful bearing, has not learned to dance.»

Emilia, whose heart beat strongly at every word, wanted to cut short the conversation by inquiring the name of that lady: before the count could answer her, the contradanza ended; and Emilia, seeing Valancourt advancing towards her, immediately got up, and went beside her aunt.

"Here is the Chevalier Valancourt, madame," he said to her in a low voice; "Pray, let's retire. The aunt got up, but the young man had joined them; he greeted Mrs. Cheron with respect, and her nephew with grief. Since the presence of the latter prevented him from staying, she passed her with a demeanor whose sadness reproached Emilia for having been able to decide to increase it: she was standing in thought, when Count Beauvillers returned to her side.

'I beg your pardon, young lady,' he said to her, 'for an involuntary incivility. When she so freely criticized the gentleman in the dance, she was unaware that he was were of your knowledge. Emilia blushed and smiled. However, Cheron answered him: «If you talk about the young man who passed just now, I can assure you that he is neither my acquaintance nor that of Signorina Sant'Aubert.

"It's the Chevalier Valancourt," Cavignì said indifferently.

"Do you know him?" Mrs. Cheron resumed.

"I have no relation to him," answered Cavignì.

"Don't you know the reasons I have for describing him as impertinent?" It has the presumption to admire my niece.

"If, to deserve the epithet of impertinent, it is enough to admire Mademoiselle Emilia," added Cavignì, "I'm afraid there are many, and I'm joining the list."

— Oh! sir,' said Cheron with a forced smile, 'I realize you learned the art of compliments after your stay in France; but you shouldn't flatter girls, because they take flattery for truth. »

Cavignì turned his head for a moment and said in a studied voice: "So who can one compliment, then, lady?" Because it would be absurd to address a woman whose taste is already formed: she issuperiorto any praise. »

As he finished this sentence, he glanced stealthily at Emilia, and irony shone in his eyes. She understood him, and blushed for her aunt; but Cheron replied: 'You are perfectly right, sir; a woman of taste cannot, nor should she, suffer a compliment.

"I wanted to tell Signor Montoni," added Cavignì, "that a single woman deserved it.

"Really," Cheron exclaimed with a smile full of confidence; "And who will it be?"

— Oh! he replied: 'it is easy to know her. Not there is certainly more than one woman in the world who has both the merit of inspiring praise and the spirit of refusing it. And her eyes turned again to Emilia, who blushed more and more for her aunt.

"But good sir," said la Cheron, "I protest that you are French." I have never heard a foreigner express himself with such gallantry.

"It is very true, madame," replied the count, ceasing from his mute side; « but the gallantry of compliments would have been lost, without the ingenuity which discovers its application. »

Cheron did not know the satirical meaning of this sentence, and did not feel the pity that Emilia felt for her.

"Oh! here is Signor Montoni himself,' said the aunt; "I want to tell him all the nice things you've said to me. But the Italian passed into another avenue. 'Pray tell me what can occupy your friend so much tonight?' He never let himself be seen for a moment, Madame Cheron said spitefully.

"He has," said Cavignì, "a particular affair with the Marquis Larivière, who, from what I see, has occupied it up to now, because he certainly would not fail to come and offer his respects." »

From all that she heard, Emilia thought she perceived that Montoni was seriously courting her aunt, and that not only did she please him, but she was jealous of his slightest negligences. That Mrs. Cheron, at her age, should want to choose a second husband seemed ridiculous; yet her vanity did not make it impossible; but that, with his spirit, his face and his pretensions, Montoni could choose his aunt, that was what surprised Emilia. Her thoughts, however, were not long fixed on this object; it was plagued by multiple interests pressing. Valancourt, rejected by his aunt, Valancourt had danced with a beautiful young lady... Crossing the garden, she looked everywhere, hoping and fearing to see him appear in the crowd. She did not see him, and the pain that she suffered made her realize that she had hoped more than feared.

Montoni joined them shortly thereafter, and stammered a few words about his regret at having been so busy elsewhere. The aunt received this apology with the spiteful air of a child, and affected to speak only to Cavignì, who, looking at Montoni ironically, seemed to want to say: 'I will not abuse my triumph, and I will support my glory with all humility. »

Dinner was served in the various pavilions of the garden and in a large hall of the castle; Cheron and her party dined there with Madame Clairval, and Emilia could hardly repress her emotion, when she saw Valancourt take his place at the same table as herself. The aunt saw him anyway, and she asked her neighbor: "Who is that young man?

"It is the Chevalier Valancourt," she was answered.

" I too know his name," she added; "but who is this knight Valancourt who is introduced to this table?" »

The attention of the person she questioned was distracted before getting an answer. The table was very long; Valancourt was towards the middle with her companion, and Emilia, who was in a corner of the same, had not yet seen her; this gave her reason to make a thousand reflections, all equally disgusting to her.

Remarks on this subject formed the subject of an indifferent conversation, and someone took pleasure in addressing them to Madame Cheron, who was always intent on demeaning Valancourt.

"I admire that beautiful lady," she said, "but I condemn her choice.

— Oh! the Chevalier Valancourt is the most amiable young man I know,' replied the lady to whom the speech had been addressed; "It is even said that Mrs. Demery will marry him as soon as possible, and bring him his wealth as a dowry.

"That's impossible," exclaimed Cheron, bursting into flames; 'He has so little the air of a man of quality, that if I did not see him at Mrs. Clairval's table, I should never have persuaded myself that he could be such; on the other hand, I have strong reasons to doubt the rumor.

"And I can't doubt it," said the other lady, somewhat annoyed at this contradiction.

"May I ask you," said Clairval, "ladies, what is the subject of your question?"

"Do you see," Cheron said to her, "that young man almost in the middle of the table, talking to Signora Demery?" Well! that man, who is not known by anyone, has pretensionspresumptuouson my niece, and this circumstance, at least I fear, gave rise to the belief that he passed himself off as my adorer; consider now how offensive such talk is to me.

'I agree, my good friend,' replied Clairval, 'and you may be sure I will deny it everywhere. »And she turned away. Cavignì, who up to that point had been a cold spectator of that scene, was on the point of breaking into laughter, and abruptly left the place.

"I can see that you are unaware," the lady sitting next to her said to Cheron, "that the young man you spoke of to Madame Clairval is her nephew!....

- It's impossible! »Claimed Cheron, realizing her gross mistake; and from that moment she began to praise Valancourt as basely as malignantly she had hitherto employed to denigrate him.

Emilia had been absorbed during the greater part of the speech, and was thus preserved from the displeasure of hearing it; she was therefore very surprised to hear the praises with which her aunt showered Valancourt, and she still did not know that he was Clairval's nephew; however, without regret she saw her aunt, more embarrassed than she wanted to appear, trying to retire immediately after dinner. Montoni then came to give her hand to lead her to her carriage, and Cavignì, with ironic gravity, followed her, accompanying her Emilia. As she greeted them and lifted the door, she saw her lover among the people at the door. He disappeared before the departure of the carriage; the aunt said nothing to Emilia, and they separated on their way home.

The following morning, Emilia being at breakfast with her aunt, she was presented with a letter, of which, by the mere address, she recognized the character; she received it with a trembling hand, and her aunt immediately asked where she came from. Emilia unsealed it with her permission, and seeing Valancourt's signature, she handed it to him without reading it. Cheron took it impatiently, and as she read it, Emilia tried to guess its content in her eyes; she returned it to him almost at once, and as her niece's looks asked if she could read: "Yes, read, read, daughter," she said to her with less severity than she expected of her. Emilia had never obeyed so willingly. In his letter Valancourt spoke little of the meeting of the day before; he declared that he would not receive leave except from her alone,

— Heh! you have to see that young man, yes certainly,' said the aunt; "We have to see what he can say in favor of him; tell him to come. »

Emilia hardly dared to believe her own ears.

"No, no, stay, I'll write to him myself," added the aunt; and she asked for paper and an inkwell.

Emilia did not dare to trust the sweet sayings that animated her; her surprise would have been less great had she understood the previous evening what her aunt had not forgotten, namely, that Valancourt was Madame Clairval's nephew.

She did not know her aunt's secret motives; but the result was a visit, the same evening, from Valancourt, which Cheron received alone in her office. They had a long talk together before Emilia was called: when she entered, the aunt spoke sweetly, and the eyes of the young man, who promptly looked up, sparkled with joy and hope.

"We were talking about business," said the aunt; "The Chevalier was telling me here that the late Mr. Clairval was the brother of the Countess Duverney, his mother: I wish he had told me sooner of his relation to Mrs. Clairval; I would have regarded it as more than enough reason to receive it in my home. »

Valancourt bowed and wanted to introduce himself to Emilia, but Cheron prevented him.

"I have consented to your visits, and although I do not intend to commit myself to any promises, nor to say that I will regard him as my nephew, I will allow your report and will regard the union which he desires, as a fact which may take place between a few years, if the knight advances in rank, and if his circumstances permit him to marry; but M. Valancourt will observe, and you too, Emilia, that, up to that point, I positively forbid you any idea of marriage. »

Emilia's figure changed at every moment during this brusque speech; and, towards the end, her confusion was such that she was about to retire. Valancourt, meanwhile, almost as embarrassed as she is, doesn't he dared to look at her. When the aunt had finished, he replied: 'However flattering your approval may be for me, however honored I am by your esteem, nevertheless I fear so much, that I scarcely dare to hope.

"Explain yourself," Cheron said. The unexpected answer disturbed the young man so much that if he had been a spectator of that scene, he could not have helped laughing.

"Until Signora Emilia allows me to take advantage of your kindness," he said in a subdued voice, "until she allows me to hope...

If there is no other difficulty, I undertake to answer for you. Know, sir, that she is in my custody, and I expect her to comply in everything with my will. »

Saying this, she got up and retired to her room, leaving Emilia and Valancourt equally embarrassed: finally the young man, whose hope was greater than his fear, spoke to her with the vivacity and frankness natural to him: but Emilia did not recover until after a few time before understanding his questions and prayers.

Mrs. Cheron's conduct had been directed by her personal vanity. Valancourt, in his first conversation with her, had ingenuously confessed her present position and her hopes for the future; and with more prudence than humanity, she had severely and absolutely rejected her request: she wanted her niece to make a great marriage, not because he wished her the happiness that is supposed to be associated with rank and opulence, but to want to share the importance that an illustrious relative could give her. When she learned that Valancourt was the grandson of such a person as Madame Clairval, she longed for a union whose splendor would surely envelop her in her halo. Founding his hopes on Clairval's wealth, he forgot that she had a daughter. Valancourt, however, had not forgotten it, and counted so little on his aunt's inheritance that he had not even mentioned her in her first conversation with Cheron; but however she might in the future be Emilia's fortune, the distinction which this kinship afforded her was certain, for Clairval's brilliant situation formed the envy of all, and was an object of emulation for those who could support it. the competition. She had therefore agreed to leave her niece to the uncertainty of an engagement whose conclusion was doubtful and distant; and in this way her happiness was little combined either with her consent or with her opposition: however, she could have made this marriage safe and advantageous at the same time,

From that point, Valancourt paid frequent visits to Madame Cheron, and Emilia passed in her company the happiest moments she had enjoyed since her father's death. They were both too sweetly occupied with the present to be much interested in the future: they loved, they were loved in return, and they did not suspect that that same attachment, which formed their happiness, could one day cause the misfortune of their lives. In this interval, Cheron's relationship with Clairval became more and more intimate, and the former's vanity was already fed sufficiently, publishing everywhere the passion of her friend's nephew for Emilia.

Montoni also became the castle's daily guest, and Emilia realized, with the utmost displeasure, that he was her aunt's lover, and her favorite lover.

Thus our two young men passed the winter, not only in peace, but also in happiness. Valancourt's regiment was garrisoned near Toulouse, so they could see each other frequently. The terrace pavilion was their favorite conference venue; the aunt and Emilia went to work there, and Valancourt read to them witty works. He observed Emilia's enthusiasm, expressed his own, and finally convinced himself, every day more, that their souls were made for each other, and that with the same taste, the same goodness and nobility of feelings , they alone could make each other happy.

END OF THE FIRST VOLUME

HE MYSTERIES OF THE UDOLFO CASTLE

VOL. II

CHAPTER XII

Aunt Emilia's avarice finally yielded to her vanity. A few splendid dinners given by Clairval, and the general flattery with which she was the object of hers, increased Cheron's eagerness to secure a kinship which would so illustrate her to her own eyes and to those of the world. She proposed the forthcoming marriage of Emilia, and offered to secure her dowry, provided Clairval would do the same for her nephew. She pondered her proposal, and considering that Emilia was the closest heir to Cheron, she accepted it without difficulty. Emilia was unaware of these instructions when her aunt warned her to prepare for the wedding which was to take place without delay. The surprised girl did not understand the reason for such an instantaneous conclusion, in no way solicited by Valancourt. And in fact, not knowing the conventions of the two aunts, he was far from hoping for so great a happiness. Emilia showed some opposition, but Cheron, always jealous of her authority, insisted on her prompt marriage, with the same vehemence as hers, with which she had initially rejected her slightest appearances. All Emilia's scruples vanished, when Valancourt, then informed of her happiness, came to beg her to confirm it. the certainty.

While the preparations for this wedding were being made, Montoni became the declared lover of Cheron. Clairval was very discontented when she heard of their imminent marriage, and she wanted to prevent Valancourt's marriage to Emilia; but her conscience represented to her, that she had no right to punish them for the wrongs of others. Although a woman of the great world, she was nevertheless less familiar than her friend with the method of making happiness depend on the fortune and homage she attracts, rather than on her own heart.

Emilia anxiously observed the influence Montoni had acquired over her aunt, as well as the greater frequency of her visits. Her opinion of this Italian was confirmed by that of Valancourt, who had always expressed extreme aversion to him. One morning when she was working in the pavilion, enjoying the sweet spring freshness, Valancourt was reading beside her, and every now and then she put down the book to converse. She was advised that her aunt wanted to see her at once; she went into her lavatory, and compared Mrs. Cheron's dejected look with surprise with the refined kind of her attire.

"My niece..." she said, and stopped a little embarrassed. « I had you looked for... I... I... wanted to see you. I have some news to tell you... from now on you must consider Signor Montoni as your uncle; we got married this morning. »

Confused, not so much about the marriage as about the secret with which it had been done, the agitation with which it was announced to her, Emilia attributed this mystery to Montoni's will rather than to that of her aunt; but she this she didn't want her to think so.

"You see," she added, "that I wanted to avoid publicity; but now that the ceremony is done, I no longer care whether it is known. I'm going to tell my people right away that Signor Montoni is their master.»

Emilia did what she could to congratulate her aunt for such an imprudent marriage.

"I want to celebrate my wedding with all the splendour," continued Signora Montoni, "and in order not to waste time, I will make use of the preparations that have been made for yours, which will be delayed a little; but I want you to wear clothes made for your wedding to honor the party. I also wish you to make my change of name known to M. Valancourt, who will inform Mme. Clairval accordingly. In a few days I want to give a magnificent lunch, and I'm counting on them.»

Emilia was so amazed that she was barely able to reply to her aunt, and, in accordance with her wish, returned to the pavilion to inform her lover of what had happened. Surprise was not Valancourt's first feeling on hearing of this hasty nuptials; but when he learned that hers had been postponed, and that the ornaments prepared to embellish the hymene of her Emilia were about to be degraded by serving for Signora Montoni, pain and indignation agitated one another in her spirit. He could not hide it from the girl; her efforts to distract him and joke about these sudden fears were in vain. When he at length parted from her, he was oppressed by a tender uneasiness which struck her keenly, and he wept without knowing why, when she came to the garden-entrance.

Montoni took possession of the castle with the ease of a man who for a long time regarded it as his own. His friend Cavigni had singularly served him by lavishing on Cheron the attention and flattery she demanded, and to which Montoni seemed to lend himself with difficulty; he had an apartment in the castle, and was obeyed by the servants as the master himself.

A few days later, Signora Montoni, as she had promised, gave a magnificent dinner to one numerous companies. Valancourt intervened, but Clairval apologized for it. There was a music academy and dance party. Valancourt, as was right, danced with Emilia; he could not examine the party decorations without remembering that they were meant for her wedding. Nevertheless he tried to console himself, thinking that soon his wishes would be fulfilled. Signora Montoni danced, laughed and chatted continuously all evening. Montoni however, taciturn and reserved, seemed bored with that amusement, and with the frivolous society which formed its object.

It was the first and last banquet given on the occasion of that wedding. Montoni, whose severe character and taciturn pride prevented him from animating these celebrations, was nonetheless very disposed to provoke them. He seldom found in conversation a man who could rival him in wit or talent. All the advantage, in this sort of meeting, was therefore always on his side. Knowing how selfishly one attends society, he feared being defeated in simulation, or in consideration, wherever he was. But Mrs. Cheron, when it came to her own interest, had more discernment than vanity. She knew her inferiority to other women in all her personal qualities. The natural jealousy resulting from this knowledge therefore penchant for meetings that Toulouse offered. His politics had changed; she vigorously objected to her husband's taste for her great world, and did not doubt that he was not of hers to be so well received by all the women as he had been when he paid court to her.

A few weeks had passed since this marriage, when Signora Montoni shared with Emilia the plan of going to Italy, as soon as all the preparations for the trip had been completed.

"We will go to Venice," she said; «Montoni owns a beautiful palace there, and therefore we will move on to his castle in Tuscany. Why do you look so serious, daughter? You who love beautiful views so much, you should be delighted with this trip.

"Should I come too?" Emilia said with emotion and surprise at the same time.

"Yes, of course," replied the aunt; "How can you suppose we want to leave you here?" Ah! I see you think of the knight. I think he doesn't know anything, but he will surely know as soon as possible. Montoni has gone out to share it with Signora Clairval, and to announce to her that the knots proposed between our families have been irrevocably resolved. »

The insensitivity with which Montoni let her niece know that she was separated, perhaps forever, from the man with whom she was to unite for the rest of her life, increased the despair of the unfortunate woman even more at this news. When she was able to speak, she asked the reason for this change with respect to Valancourt; and the only answer she got was that Montoni had forbidden this marriage, given that Emilia could aspire to much more advantageous matches.

"I'm currently leaving this whole matter to my husband," added la Montoni; 'but I must agree that I never liked Monsieur Valancourt, and that I should never have given my consent. I am very weak; well often I am so good, that the pains of others sadden me, and your affliction won it over my opinion. However, Signor Montoni demonstrated very clearly to me the folly I was committing, but he certainly won't have to reproach me for it a second time. I absolutely demand your submission to those who know your interests better than you, and you must obey us in everything. »

Emilia would have been surprised by the assertions e from the eloquence of this speech, if all her faculties, annihilated by the shock received, had allowed her to understand a single word of it. Whatever was Signora Montoni's weakness, she could have avoided the reproach of excessive compassion and a prodigious sensitivity to the misfortunes of others, and above all to those of Emilia. That same ambition which had led her to brigade Clairval's relationship was now the subject of the break. Her marriage to Montoni exalted his own importance in her eyes, and consequently changed her aims for Emilia.

This interesting girl was too distressed to make her case, or go down to prayers. When she finally wished to make use of this last means, she failed for her word, and she retired to her own room to reflect, if it were possible, on so unexpected and tremendous a blow.

A great deal passed before she was well enough to think; but the thought of her that came upon her was sad and terrible. She believed that Montoni wanted to dispose of her for his own advantage, and she thought that Cavigni was the person who made him interested in her. The prospect of a trip to Italy became all the more disgusting when she considered the turbulent situation of that country torn by civil wars, a prey to all factions, and where every castle was open to invasion by the opposing party. She considered to whom her fate rested, and how far she would be from Valancourt. At this idea, all other images vanished, and her pain plunged all thoughts of her into her confusion.

Some hours passed in this painful state; when she was warned about lunch, she wanted to apologize for it. However, Montoni, who was alone, did not want to consent, and she agreed to obey. They spoke very little during lunch. One was oppressed by her pain, and the other annoyance at Montoni's unexpected absence. Her vanity was offended by such negligence, and her jealousy alarmed him chiefly at what she called a mysterious engagement. In spite of this, Emilia tried to speak again of Valancourt, but her aunt, insensitive to her pity and remorse, became almost furious at being allowed to remark on her authority and on that of Montoni; consequently poor Emilia retired weeping.

As he crossed the vestibule, he heard someone enter through the large door; she thought she saw Montoni and she doubled her pace; but she immediately recognized Valancourt's beloved voice.

« Emilia, my dear Emilia! he exclaimed in the thunder of her impatience as he advanced on her and discovered the traces of despair on her face. 'Emilia, I must speak to you; I have a thousand things to tell you; take me somewhere where we can talk freely. But! you tremble, you feel bad; let me lead you to a chair. »

He saw an open door, and tried to take Emilia there; but she, withdrawing her hand, said to him, smiling languidly:

"I'm already better. If you want to talk to my aunt, she's in the drawing room.

"I want to speak to you alone , my dear Emilia," replied Valancourt. "Great God! Have you already reached this point? Do you so easily consent to forget me? this place does not suit us, we can be understood. I only want a quarter of an hour of attention from you.

"Yes, when you have seen my aunt," said Emilia.

'I was already unhappy coming here,' exclaimed Valancourt; « do not increase my anguish with this coldness and with this cruel refusal. »

The energy with which he pronounced these words moved her to tears, but she persisted in the negativity of listening to him until she saw Signora Montoni.

"Where is your husband, where is this Montoni?" Valancourt said in an altered voice; "I must speak to him properly. »

Emilia, frightened of the consequences of the indignation that flashed in his eyes, assured him in a trembling voice that Montoni was not at home, and begged him to moderate his resentment. At the interrupted accents of her voice, Valancourt's glances immediately changed from fury to her tenderness.

"You feel bad, Emilia," he said, "and they want to lose us both." Forgive me if I dared to doubt your tenderness. »

Emilia no longer objected to granting him an interview in the next room. The manner in which you had named Montoni had caused him the most well-founded fears about the danger he himself might run; she thought no more than to prevent the terrible consequences of his revenge. He listened attentively to her prayers, and only answered them with looks of despair and tenderness. She hid her resentment for Montoni as best she could, and made an effort to allay her terrors; but Emilia, not very happy with that apparent tranquillity, was further disturbed by the advantage, and she tried to make Valancourt aware of the drawback of an altercation with Montoni, which could have made their separation irremediable. She yielded to her tender entreaties, and promised her that, however great Montoni's obstinacy might be,

Emilia made an effort to calm him with the assurance of an inviolable attachment. She made him observe that in about a year she would be of age, and that consequently she would then be released from guardianship. These assurances, however, consoled Valancourt little: he considered that then she would be in Italy, and at the mercy of those whose power over her would not have ceased so easily with their rights. Emilia, somewhat calmed by the promise obtained and by the tranquility he affected, was about to leave him, when her aunt entered her room. She cast a reproachful glance at her niece, who immediately withdrew, and a look of discontent and haughtiness at the unhappy youth.

" This is not the conduct I expected of you," she said, " sir; I didn't think I'd see you again in my house after having warned you that your visits were no longer welcome to me. She believed even less that you were trying to see my niece clandestinely, and that she had the imprudence to consent to receive you. »

Valancourt, seeing it necessary to justify Emilia, protested that the only purpose of his visit had been to ask Montoni to meet, and explained the reasons with moderation that the sex, more than the character of that superb woman, could only demand of him.

His prayers were harshly received. The aunt complained that her prudence had yielded to what she called her compassion for her, adding finally that knowing very well the folly of her first compliance, and wanting to avoid falling back into it, she forgave this matter entirely and exclusively to her husband.

The sentimental eloquence of the young man at last made her understand the unworthiness of his conduct; she knew shame, but not remorse. She was vexed that Valancourt had reduced her to that painful situation, and her hatred of her grew with the awareness of her own wrongs. The antipathy which he inspired in her was all the stronger than her in that, without accusing her of her, he compelled her to convince herself of herself. He left her no excuse for the violence of resentment with which she regarded him. At thefinally, his anger became so violent, that Valancourt decided to leave at the moment, in order not to lose his esteem in an ill-measured reply, and he was fully convinced that he should expect neither pity nor justice from a person who felt the burden of evil deeds, and not the humility of repentance.

The same idea as Montoni had formed, it being clear that the plan for the separation came directly from him. It was not likely that he would abandon his design for prayers or reasons which he must have foreseen, and against which he was prepared. Meanwhile, faithful to the promises made to Emilia, more occupied with his love for him than jealous of his own dignity, Valancourt took good care of irritating Montoni without necessity. He wrote to him, not to ask him for an interview, but to solicit his favour, and waited for his reply with some tranquillity.

CHAPTER XIII

Madame Clairval kept aloof from all this intrigue: when she had consented to the marriage of Valancourt, it was in the belief that Emilia would inherit from her aunt. When the marriage of the latter had disillusioned her in this respect, her conscience prevented her from breaking off a union almost formed; but her benevolence did not go so far as to push her to take a step that she had to decide entirely. She rejoiced that Valancourt was released from a commitment that she believed to be so beneath him because of her wealth, as she Montoni judged this relationship humiliating because of Emilia's beauty. Clairval could be offended that a member of her family should have been like that discharged; but he did not deign to express his resentment in any other way than silence.

Montoni, in his reply, assured Valancourt that a meeting, since it could neither change the resolution of one nor overcome the desires of the other, would only end in a quite useless dispute, and that for this reason he thought it best not to grant it to him.

The moderation so much recommended to him by Emilia, and the promises made to her, could only hold back the impetuosity of Valancourt, who wanted to run to Montoni to ask firmly what was being refused to his prayers. He therefore confined himself to renewing his requests, and supported them with all the reasons that he could give his position. A few days passed in questioning on one side and inflexibility on the other. Whether out of fear, or out of shame, or out of the hatred that resulted from these two feelings, Montoni carefully avoided the one he had so offended; he was neither softened by the pain expressed in Valancourt's letters, nor struck by repentance for the solid reasons contained in them. Finally, the unfortunate young man's letters were rejected without being opened. In her first despair, he forgot all the promises except that of avoiding violence, and ran to the castle, determined to see Montoni, and to do everything to succeed. The Italian let it be said that he was not at home, and when Valancourt asked to speak to the lady or to Emilia, he was positively denied entry. Not wanting to engage in altercations with the servants, he left and returned home in a state of frenzy: he wrote what had happened to Emilia, expressing without reserve the anguish of her soul; and he begged her, since only this expedient remained, to grant him a secret meeting. he was positively denied entry. Not wanting to engage in altercations with the servants, he left and returned home in a state of frenzy: he wrote what had happened to Emilia, expressing without reserve the anguish of her soul; and he begged her, since only this reserve remained of hers, to grant him a secret interview. he was positively denied entry. Not wanting to engage in altercations with the servants, he left and returned home in a state of frenzy: he wrote what had happened to Emilia, expressing without reserve the anguish of her soul; and he begged her, since only this reserve remained of hers, to grant him a secret interview.

As soon as that letter was sent, his anger calmed down: he recognized the fault he had committed, increasing Emilia's pains with the description too much sincere about her troubles. She would have given half the world to recover that imprudent letter. Emilia, however, was preserved from the pain she would have felt on receiving it. Signora Montoni had ordered that all her letters addressed to her niece be brought to her: she read them, and being furious at the way in which Valancourt treated Montoni in them, she burned them.

Montoni, in the meantime, increasingly impatient to leave France, pressed the preparations for departure, and hastily finished what remained for him to do. He observed the profoundest silence over the letters in which Valancourt, despairing of obtaining more, and tempering the passion which had caused him to transcend, solicited permission only to say adieu to Emilia. But when the young man learned that she was leaving in a few days, and that it had been decided that he would never see her again, he lost all prudence, and in a second letter he proposed a secret marriage. This letter went, like the other, into the hands of Signora Montoni, and the eve of the departure came without Valancourt having received a single line of consolation, or the slightest hope of a last conversation.

Meanwhile Emilia was plunged into amazement produced by so many unexpected and irremediable misfortunes. She loved Valancourt with the tenderest affection of her own; she had long been accustomed to regard him as her lifelong friend and companion; she had not a thought of happiness to which her idea of her was not united. So what must have been his pain at the moment of such an unexpected, and perhaps eternal, separation and at such a distance, where the news of their existence could hardly arrive, and all this to obey the wishes of a foreigner, those of a person who provoked hasn't healed their marriage yet? In vain did she try to overcome her pain and resign herself to an inevitable misfortune. Valancourt's silence still afflicted her more, because he could not attribute it to his real reason; but when, on the eve of leaving Toulouse, she learned that she was not allowed to say goodbye to him, grief oppressed her even more, and she could not refrain from asking her aunt if she had positively been denied this consolation, which was barbarously confirmed.

"If the knight had wanted to obtain this favor from us," she said, "he would have had to act differently. He had to wait patiently for us to be willing to grant it to him; he wouldn't have reproached me for persisting in denying him my niece, and he wouldn't have molested Signor Montoni, who didn't think it advisable to enter into discussions about this prank. His conduct in this affair was wholly presumptuous and importunate; I wish never to hear of him again, and that you be freed from this ridiculous sadness, from these sighs, from this gloomy air, which would make one believe you were always inclined to whine; do like everyone else; your silence is not enough to hide your uneasiness at my penetration; I see that you are willing to weep at this moment, yes at this very moment, in spite of my prohibition. »

Emilia, who had turned away to hide her tears, hastily withdrew to shed a copy. Her agitation was so great at reflecting on her condition and at the idea of not seeing Valancourt any more, that I felt faint of her. As soon as she had recovered a little, she looked out the window, and the cool night air revived her somewhat. The moonlight, falling upon a long avenue of elms below her, invites her to try, if not her movement and the open air would soothe the irritation of all her nerves. Everyone they slept in the castle: Emilia descended the grand staircase, and crossing the vestibule, cautiously entered the garden by a solitary passage. She walked more or less swiftly, according as the shadows deceived her, believing she saw someone from afar, and fearing it was not some spy of her aunt's. Meanwhile, the desire to see again the pavilion, in which she had spent so many happy moments with Valancourt, where she had admired with him the beautiful plains of Languedoc, and Gascony, her dear homeland, this desire overcame her fear of being observed, and she went towards the terrace, which extended up to the entrance to the garden, dominating a large part of the underlying prairie, to which one descended via a marble stairway. When she was at the staircase, she paused for a moment to look around. The distance from the castle increased the kind of fright that the silence, the hour and the darkness caused her; but seeing nothing that could justify her fears of her, she climbed onto the terrace, whereby the moonlight uncovered the breadth, and showed the pavilion at the back. She advanced towards it, and entered it; the darkness of the place was not enough to lessen his shyness. The jalousies were open, but the plants of flowers cluttered up the outside of the windows, barely allowing the country dimly lit by the moon to be seen through the branches. As she approached a window, she did not enjoy the sight except in so far as it could serve to recall the image of Valancourt more vividly to her imagination. barely allowing the country dimly lit by the moon to be seen through the branches. As she approached a window, she did not enjoy the sight except in so far as it could serve to recall the image of Valancourt more vividly to her imagination. barely allowing the country dimly lit by the moon to be seen through the branches. As she approached a window, she did not enjoy the sight except in so far as it could serve to recall the image of Valancourt more vividly to her imagination.

« Ah! »She exclaimed with a great sigh, throwing herself on a chair; « how many times have we sat in this place! How many times have we contemplated this beautiful view! Will we no longer admire it together? never, maybe we will never see each other again! »

Suddenly, fear suspended her tears: having heard a voice close to her in the pavilion, she let out a cry, but the noise repeating itself distinguished the beloved voice of Valancourt. It was himself, it was the young man who held her in his arms. In that instant her emotion deprived her of the use of words.

'Emilia,' Valancourt said at last, holding her hand tightly between his, 'my dear Emilia! She was silent again, and the accent with which she had pronounced this name expressed both her tenderness and her pain.

"Oh my Emilia! he added after a long pause; « I see you again, and I still hear the sound of your voice! I wandered about these places and this garden for so many nights, and had only the faintest hope of seeing you again! This was the only resource I had left; thank goodness I didn't miss it. »

Emilia uttered a few words, hardly knowing what she was saying, expressed her inviolable affection, and strove to calm Valancourt's agitation. When he had recovered a little, she said to her:

« I came here immediately after sunset, nor did I stop walking through the gardens and the pavilion afterwards. She had given up all hope of seeing you; but he could not resolve me to detach myself from a place where he knew there so close to me, and I would probably have stayed all night in these surroundings. But when you opened the pavilion, the darkness prevented me from distinguishing with certainty whether it was my dear Emilia: my heart beat so strongly with hope and fear that I could not speak. As soon as I heard the plaintive accents of your voice, all doubts vanished, but not my fears, until you mentioned my name. In the excess of joy, I didn't think of the fear I would have caused you; but she could no longer be silent. Oh! Emilia, in such precious moments, consolation and pain fight so hard, that the heart can hardly bear the duel. »

Emilia's heart felt this truth; but the joy of seeing her lover again at the moment when she realized she was separated from him for good, soon mingled with her grief, as her reflection guided his imagination about the future. She made every effort to recover the calm and dignity so necessary to hold this last interview. Valancourt could not restrain himself; the transports of joy suddenly changed into those of despair; and he expressed in the most impassioned language the horror of separation, and the little likelihood of a possible reunion. Emilia endeavored to contain her own sadness, and to sweeten that of her lover.

"You leave me," he said to her, "you are going to a foreign land!" And at what distance! You go to find new societies, new friends, new admirers; they will try to make you forget me, and new knots will be prepared for you. How can I know all this, and not feel that you will never come back for me, that you will never be mine again? »His voice was choked with sobs.

"Do you believe then," said Emilia, "that my affliction arises from a slight and momentary affection?" Can you believe it?

- Suffer! Valancourt interrupted; « suffer for me! My Emilia, how sweet and how bitter these words are at the same time! I must not doubt your constancy; yet, such is the inconsequence of true love; it is always ready to suspect; and even when reason proves it again, he would always want a new insurance. Now I see you, I hold you in my arms: a few more moments, and it will be nothing more than a dream: I will look, and I will never see you again... I am reborn from death to life, when you tell me that I am dear to you; but as soon as I no longer listen to you, I fall back into doubt, and I abandon myself to distrust. »Then, seeming to collect himself, he exclaimed: «How guilty am I of tormenting you thus in these moments when I should console you, and support your courage! »

This reflection moved him singularly. Her voice and his words were so passionate, that Emilia, no longer able to contain her own, ceased to repress the pain of Valancourt, who in these terrible moments of love and pity almost lost the power and the will to dominate her agitation.

'No,' he exclaimed, 'I can't, I mustn't leave you. Why shall we entrust the happiness of our life to the wills of those who have no right to destroy it, and who cannot contribute to it except by conceding yourself to me? O Emilia! dare to trust your heart! Dare to be mine forever! »His voice trembled, and he said no more. Emilia wept and was silent. Valancourt proposed to her to marry secretly. « At the tip of the day you will leave Signora Montoni's house, and you will follow me to the church of Sant'Agostino, where a priest is waiting to join us. »

The silence with which the girl listened to a proposal dictated by love and desperation, at a time when she was barely able to reject it, when her heart was softened by the pain of a separation, which could be eternal, when her reason he was in the grip of illusions of love and terror; this silence encouraged the hopes of Valancourt. "Speak, my dear Emilia," he said ardently; « let me hear the sound of your sweet voice; let me hear confirmation of my fate from you.» She remained silent, a cold shiver came over her, and she fainted. Valancourt's troubled imagination pictured her as moribund. He called her by name, and got up to go to the castle to ask for help; but thinking of her situation, he shivered at the idea of going out and leaving her in that state.

After a few moments she sighed and came to. The contrast she suffered between love and her duty, submission to her father's sister, repugnance to a clandestine marriage, fear of an indissoluble bond, misery and repentance in into which she could immerse the object of her affections, were too strong motives for a spirit distressed by disasters, and her reason was somewhat suspended. But her duty and wisdom, painful though they might be, finally triumphed over her tenderness and sad forebodings. She was especially afraid of plunging Valancourt into obscurity, and into those vain remorse which would, or seemed to her ought to be, the necessary consequence of a marriage in their position. No doubt she conducted herself with an uncommon greatness of spirit, when she resolved to experience a present evil, rather than to cause a future misfortune.

She explained herself with a candor that fully justified the extent to which she esteemed him edloved, and therefore became to him, if it were possible, even more dear. She explained to him all the reasons which decided her to reject her offer. He refuted, or rather contradicted, all that concerned him alone; but the others called upon him to hold considerations about her, which the fury of her passion and despair had forced him to forget. That same love which made him propose a secret and immediate marriage, then obliged him to renounce it. Victory cost her heart too much; he forced himself to calm down so as not to afflict her further, but he could not hide everything he felt. 'O Emilia,' he said, 'I must leave you, and I am sure I will leave you forever.»

Convulsive sobs interrupted him, and they both wept hot tears. Finally remembering the danger of being discovered, and the inconvenience of prolonging an interview which would expose her to the censure of others, Emilia plucked up courage, and she bade her last farewell.

'Stay,' said Valancourt, 'stay a moment longer, I beg you; I have a thousand things to tell you. The agitation of my spirit did not allow me to tell you about a very important suspicion; I feared appearing indiscreet, and appearing to have the sole aim of alarming you, to make you accept my proposal.»

Emilia, perturbed, did not let him go, but made him leave the pavilion, and as they strolled on the terrace, Valancourt continued:

"That Montoni! I have heard very strange rumors about him. Are you quite sure that he is really of Mrs Quesnel's family, and that his fortune is such as it appears to be?

"I have no reason to doubt it," replied Emilia with surprise; « I am certain of the first point, but I have no means of judging the second; and please tell me everything you know about it.

"I certainly will, but this information is very imperfect and unsatisfactory. By chance I met an Italian who was talking to someone about this Montoni, they were talking about his marriage, and the Italian said that if it was what he imagined, Signora Cheron would not be too happy. He continued to speak of him with very little consideration, but in general terms, and said certain things about his character, which excited my curiosity. I asked him a few questions, but he was reserved in his answers; and after some time hesitating, he confessed that Montoni, according to public rumor, was a man lost in possessions and in reputation. He added something about a castle he owns in the middle of the Apennines, and some other circumstance relating to his first kind of life: I squeezed him tighter, but the keen interest in my questions was, as far as I believe, too visible, and made him suspicious. No prayer was able to bring him to explain to me the circumstances to which he had alluded, or to say more: I remarked to him that if Montoni possessed a castle in the Apennines, this seemed to indicate a distinguished birth, and to contradict the assumption of his downfall. The incognito shook his head and made a very significant gesture, but did not answer.

« The hope of knowing something more positive kept me close to him for a long time; I repeated my questions several times, but the Italian kept in perfect confidentiality, telling me that everything he had stated was nothing but the result of a vague rumor; that hatred and malice often invented such stories, and little was needed to believe them. I was therefore forced to renounce having any advantage, since the Italian seemed alarmed at the consequences of his indiscretion. I therefore remained uncertain about an object in which it is almost unbearable. Think, dear Emilia, of how much I must suffer; I see you leaving for foreign lands with a man of such a suspicious character as that of this Montoni, but I don't want to alarm you unnecessarily; it is probable, as the Italian said, that this Montoni is not the one he was talking about; nevertheless, reflect, my dear, before you entrust yourself to him. But by now she had forgotten all the reasons which a little while ago made me abandon my hopes and give up the desire to possess you right away. »

Valancourt was striding along the terrace, while Emilia, leaning on the parapet, was immersed in profound meditation. The news she had just received alarmed her greatly, and renewed her inner conflict. She had never loved Montoni. The fire in her eyes, the fierceness of her glances, his pride, her audacity, the depth of her resentment, which some occasions, however slight, had set themselves in the event of developing, were so many circumstances which she always had watched with some astonishment; and the ordinary expression of her features had always inspired antipathy in her. He believed it more every moment that it was the Montoni of whom the Italian had spoken. The idea of being under her absolute sway in a foreign country seemed terrifying to her; but fear of her was not the only reason he should induce her to hasty marriage. Her tenderest love had already spoken to her in favor of her lover, and in her opinion of hers had not been able to win her over her duty, over the interest of Valancourt as well, and over her delicacy which made her oppose a clandestine marriage. It was therefore not advisable to wait for terror to work more than pain and love could not; but this terror restored all their energy to motives already fought, and necessitated a second victory. Valancourt, whose fears for Emilia grew stronger and stronger as reasons weighed, he could not adjust to this second win. He was more than convinced that the trip to Italy would immerse his Emilia in a labyrinth of evils. He was therefore resolved to stubbornly oppose her, and to obtain a title from her, to become her legitimate protector.

'Emilia,' he said with the keenest ardor, 'this is not the time for scruples; this is no time to calculate the frivolous and incidental incidents relating to our future happiness. I see now, more than ever, what are the dangers you are facing with a man of Montoni's character. The speech of the Italian makes me fear a lot, but less so than his physiognomy, and the idea that it has formed in me of him; I implore you, for your interest, and for mine, to prevent the misfortunes that make me tremble to foresee them only.... Dear Emilia! suffer that my tenderness and my arms take you away from it; give me the right to defend you. I am torn with pain at the idea of our separation, and of the evils that can result from it. There are no dangers that I am not able to face to save you. No, Emilia, no, you don't love me.

"We have few moments to lose in recriminations and oaths," she said, trying to hide her emotion; 'if you doubt how dear you are to me, and how eternally you will be, then no expression on my part is capable of convincing it.»These last words expired on her lips, and she burst into tears. After a few moments, she recovered from that state of sadness, and she said to him: «I must leave you: it's late, and in the castle they might notice my absence. Think of me, love me, when I'm far from here. My confidence in this regard will form all my consolation.

— Thinking of you, loving you! cried Valancourt.

"Try to moderate such transports for my sake, try it!

"For your sake!"

"Yes, for my sake," said the girl in a trembling voice; "I can't leave you in this state.

'Well, don't leave me,' replied Valancourt; « why leave us, or at least leave us before dawn?

"It's impossible," added Emilia; « you are tearing my heart apart; but I will never consent to this imprudent and hasty proposition.

- If we had the time, dear Emilia, it wouldn't have fallen so much. We have to submit to the circumstances.

"Yes, of course, you have to submit to it. I have already opened my heart to you: now I feel exhausted.

- Forgive me, Emilia; think of the disarray in my spirit at this moment when I am about to leave all that I hold most dear in the world. When you are gone, I will remember with remorse all that I made you suffer; then I will wish in vain to see you, if only for an instant, to soothe your pain. »

Tears interrupted him; Emilia wept with him.

'I will prove myself more worthy of your love,' said Valancourt at last; « I will not prolong these cruel moments, my Emilia, my only good, never forget me: God knows when we will meet again. I entrust you to Providence. O God, my God, protect her, bless her! »

He pressed her hand to his heart: Emilia almost fell from himlifelesson the breast. They no longer cried, they did not speak to each other. Valancourt, then repressed her despair, tried to console and cheer her up. But she seemed incapable of understanding him, and a sigh which she exhaled at intervals proved only that she had not fainted.

He supported her walking with slow steps towards the castle, crying and always talking to her. She answered only with sighs. At last having reached the head of the avenue, she seemed to revive, and looking around:

"Here we must separate," she said, pausing. « Why prolong these moments? Give me that courage I need so much. Goodbye,' she added in a languid voice; 'When you leave, I will remember a thousand things I was supposed to tell you.

- And me! of many and many others,' answered Valancourt; « I have never left you without immediately remembering a question, a prayer, and a circumstance relating to our love, which I was burning with the desire to communicate to you, but which escaped my imagination as soon as I saw you. O Emilia! those features that I contemplate at this moment will soon be far from my eyes, and all the efforts of the imagination will not be able to delineate them with sufficient precision..."

Having said that, he pressed her again to his breast, where he held her in silence, wetting her with his tears, which also relieved the girl's distress. They said goodbye, and parted ways. Valancourt seemed to be making every effort to walk away. He rushed across the avenue; and Emilia, who was walking slowly towards the castle, listened to her quick steps. The melancholy calm of the night finally ceased to be broken. She hurried back to her room to seek rest, but, alas! it had fled from her, and her misfortune no longer allowed her to taste it.

CHAPTER XIV

The carriages were at the door early: the noise of the servants who came and went through the galleries woke Emilia from a troubled sleep. Her agitated spirit had represented to her all night the most frightening images and the saddest future. She made every effort to banish these sinister impressions, but she went from imaginary evil to the certainty of real evil. Recalling that she had left Valancourt, and perhaps for ever, her heart failed her in proportion as her imagination of her represented him far away; these efforts spread an expression of resignation over her physiognomy, as a light veil makes beauty more interesting than her by hiding only a few faint features. But Signora Montoni noticed her extraordinary pallor, and reproached her severely; he told his niece that it was ill-advised that she had indulged in childish anxieties, that she begged her to observe decorum a little more, and not to let it appear that she was incapable of renouncing an inappropriate affection. Breakfast was served: Montoni spoke very little, and seemed impatient to leave. The windows of the room overlooked the garden, and as she passed by, Emilia could not help but glance at that place where, on the previous night, she had separated from Valancourt. The Emilia could not help but glance at that place where, on the previous night, she had separated from Valancourt. The Emilia could not help but glance at that place where, on the previous night, she had separated from Valancourt. The crews were already in order, and the travelers got into the carriage and set off. Emilia would have left the castle without regrets if Valancourt had not lived nearby.

From a small eminence, she observed the immense plains of Gascony, and the rugged peaks of the Pyrenees which rose far on the horizon, already illuminated by the rising sun. "Dear mountains," she said to herself, "how long it will be before I see you again!" how many misfortunes in this interval will be able to aggravate my misery! Oh! if I could be sure of never returning, but that Valancourt lived one day for me, I would leave in peace! He will see you, he will contemplate you, while I will be far from here. »

The trees of the road, which formed a line of perspective to the immense distances, were about to block his sight; but the blue mountains could still be distinguished through the foliage, and Emilia did not leave the door until she had completely lost sight of them.

Another object quickly aroused his attention. She had just observed a man walking along the street with his hat pulled down over his eyes, but adorned with a military plume. At the sound of the wheels he turned, and she recognized Valancourt. He signaled to her, went over to the carriage, and from the door thrust a letter into her hand. She forced a smile through the despair she saw painted on her face; this smile remained imprinted forever in Emilia's soul: she looked out her door, and she saw him on a small hill, leaning against one of the trees that shaded her; she followed the carriage with her eyes, and stretched out her arms; she continued to look at him until the distance had erased his features, and the road, turning, did not make them disappear at all.

They stopped at a castle not far away for take Cavigni there, and the travelers traveled over the plains of Languedoc. Emilia was recklessly relegated to the second carriage with her aunt's maid. Her presence prevented her from reading Valancourt's letter, not wanting to expose herself to her probable observations on her emotion that would have caused her reading it. Nevertheless, such was her curiosity, that her trembling hand was a thousand times on the verge of breaking the seal. At lunchtime, Emilia was able to open it: she had never doubted Valancourt's feelings; but the new assurance which she received of it, restored some calm to her heart. She wetted the letter with tears of tenderness, and set it aside to read when she would be greatly afflicted, and to deal with him less painfully than their parting would have done. After many details which interested her greatly, because they expressed her love for her, he begged her to always think of him at sunset. "Our thoughts will then unite," he said; « I will wait for the sunset with the greatest impatience, and I will rejoice in the idea that your eyes will fix themselves at that moment on the same objects as mine, and that our hearts will understand each other. You don't know, Emilia, the consolation I promise myself, but I flatter myself that you will feel it too. » « I will wait for the sunset with the greatest impatience, and I will rejoice in the idea that your eyes will fix themselves at that moment on the same objects as mine, and that our hearts will understand each other. You don't know, Emilia, the consolation I promise myself, but I flatter myself that you will feel it too. » « I will wait for the sunset with the greatest impatience, and I will rejoice in the idea that your eyes will fix themselves at that moment on the same objects as mine, and that our hearts will understand each other. You don't know, Emilia, the consolation I promise myself, but I flatter myself that you will feel it too. »

It is needless to say with what emotion Emilia waited all day for the sun to set: finally she saw it decline over the immense plains, she saw it descend and lower on the side where Valancourt lived. From that moment her spirit was calmer and more resigned than it had been after the marriage of Montoni and her aunt.

For several days the travelers traversed the Languedoc, and then entered the Dauphiné. After a few journeys through the mountains of that picturesque province, they got out of their carriages and began to climb the Alps. Here scenes so sublime were offered to their eyes that the pen could not undertake to describe them in any way. These new and surprising images so occupied Emilia that they drove her away from the constant idea of Valancourt. More often they reminded her of the Pyrenees, which she had admired together, and of which she then believed that nothing surpassed her beauty. How many times did she wish to communicate to him the new sensations which animated her in this spectacle: how many times she delighted in guessing the observations he would make, and she always imagined him close by: these noble and grandiose ideas gave her soul, to her affections a new life.

With what lively and tender emotions did she join Valancourt's thoughts at sunset! Wandering in the middle of the Alps, she contemplated that marvelous star which was lost behind their peaks, whose last colors died on the snow-covered peaks, and this theater was enveloped in a majestic darkness. When that moment passed, Emilia turned her eyes away from the west with the displeasure she feels at the departure of a friend. The singular impression that spreads the veil of night, as it unfolded, was increased more and more by those muffled noises which are never heard except with the progressive fall of darkness, and which make the general calm much more impressive: it is the light rustling of the leaves, the last breath of the breeze that rises at sunset, the murmur of the nearby streams.....

In the early days of this journey across the Alps, the scene represented a surprising alternation of deserts and dwellings, cultured and barren lands. On the edge of frightening precipices, in the hollows of the cliffs, beneath which a thick fog could be seen, villages, bell towers and monasteries were discovered. Green pastures, fertile vineyards, formed an interesting contrast with the superimposed perpendicular boulders, whose tips of marble or granite crowned themselves with heather, and showed nothing but massive rocks piled one upon the other, terminated by mounds of snow, from which cascaded the roaring streams at the bottom of the valley.

The snow had not yet melted on the heights of the Cenisio, which the travelers crossed with some difficulty; but Emilia, observing the lake of ice and the vast plain surrounded by those steep cliffs, easily imagined the beauty with which they would be adorned when the snow disappeared.

Descending on the Italian side, the precipices became more frightening, the views more alpine and majestic. Emilia never tired of looking at the snowy peaks of the mountains at different hours of the day: they reddened at sunrise, they flared up at noon, and in the evening they covered themselves in purple; the traces of man could only be recognized in the shepherd's bagpipes, the hunter's horn, or in the appearance of a bold bridge thrown over the stream to serve as a passage for the hunter following in the footsteps of the fugitive chamois.

Traveling above the clouds, Emilia observed with respectful silence their immense surface, which quite often covered the whole scene subjected, and resembled a world in chaos; at other times, as they thinned out, they gave a glimpse of some village or part of that impetuous stream, the noise of which made the caves rumble; one could see the cliffs, their peaks of ice, and the dark fir forests that reached halfway up the mountains. But who could describe Emilia's ecstasy when she first discovered Italy! From the edge, one of the terrifying precipices of the Cenisio, which stand at the entrance to this beautiful country, cast his gaze at the foot of those horrid mountains, and saw the fruitful valleys of Piedmont and the immense plains of Lombardy. The greatness of the objects that suddenly faced it, the region of the mountains, which seemed to accumulate, the deep precipices subjected, that dark greenery of firs and oaks which covered the deep chasms, the thunderous torrents, whose rapid waterfalls raised a kind of fog, and formed seas of ice, everything took on a sublime character and opposed to the peace and beauty of Italy; this beautiful plain which had the horizon as its limits increased its splendor more and more with the blue hues which blended into the horizon itself.

Signora Montoni was terrified as she observed the precipices, along the edge of which the porters ran as lightly as they could, and leapt like chamois. Emilia was trembling all the same, but her fears were a mixture of surprise, admiration, astonishment and respect, so that she had never felt anything like it.

The porters stopped to catch their breath, and the travelers sat down on the top of a cliff. Montoni and Cavignì argued about Hannibal's passage across the Alps: the latter claimed that he had entered from the Cenisio, and the latter maintained that he had descended from the San Bernardo. This controversy presented to Emilia's imagination all that that famous warrior had had to suffer in so daring and perilous an enterprise.

Signora Montoni meanwhile looked at Italy; she contemplated with her imagination the magnificence of the palaces and the majesty of the castles of which she went to be mistress in Venice and in the Apennines, and of which she believed she had become the princess. Far from the anxieties that had prevented her in Toulouse from receiving all the beauties, of which her husband spoke with greater complacency for her vanity than for their honor and respect for the truth, Signora Montoni planned academies, although he did not like music; conversations, though he had no talent for appearing in society; in short, she wanted to surpass all the nobility of Venice with the splendor of her feasts and the richness of her liveries. This flattering idea was nevertheless a little disturbed by the reflection that her husband, although he indulged in all sorts of amusements when they presented themselves to him, nevertheless affected the greatest contempt for the frivolous ostentation which usually accompanies them. But thinking that his pride in her would perhaps be more satisfied with explaining her pomp among her fellow citizens and friends than it had been in France, she continued to feed on these illusions, which never ceased to enrapture her. .

As the travelers descended, they saw winter give way to spring, and the sky began to take on that beautiful serenity which belongs only to the climate of Italy. The river Dora, which springs from the top of the Cenisio, and rushes from waterfall to waterfall through the deep ravines, slowed down, without ceasing to be picturesque, as it approached the valleys of Piedmont. The travelers descended there before sunset, and Emilia once again found the placid beauty of a pastoral scene: she saw herds, verdant hills of woods, and graceful shrubs such as she had seen in the Alps themselves: the meadows were enamelled with flowers spring flowers, buttercups and violets that do not transmit such a sweet smell in any other country. Emilia would have liked to become a Piedmontese peasant,

The current site often depicted Valancourt's image to her; she saw him on the tip of a rock observing with ecstasy the beautiful nature that surrounded him; he saw him wandering in the valley, stopping often to admire that interesting scene, and in the fire of poetic enthusiasm, throwing himself on some boulder. But when she thought afterwards of the time and the distance that must separate them, when she thought that each of her steps increased this distance, her heart ached, and the town lost all its charm.

After crossing the Novalese, they arrived in the evening at the ancient and small city of Susa, which had previously closed the passage of the Alps into Piedmont. After the invention of artillery, the heights that dominate it made its fortifications useless; but, in the moonlight, those picturesque heights, the underlying city, its walls, its towers and the lights that illuminated portions of it, formed a very interesting picture for Emilia. They spent the night in a hotel that offered few resources; but the appetite of travelers gave a delicious taste to coarser dishes, and weariness ensured their sleep. In this place, Emilia understood the first piece of Italian music on Italian territory. Seated after supper near an open window, she watched the effect of moonlight on rugged mountain peaks. He remembered that on a similar night he had rested on a rock in the Pyrenees with his father and Valancourt. He heard the harmonious sounds of a violin below her; the expression of that instrument, in perfect harmony with the tender feelings in which she was immersed, surprised and enchanted her at the same time. Cavignì, who approached the window, smiled at her surprise.

« Eh! huh! he said to her; "You'll hear the same thing, perhaps in all hotels: it must be the innkeeper's son who plays like that, I don't doubt it." »

Emilia always attentive, she thought she was hearing an artist: a melodious and querulous song plunged her into meditation step by step; Cavignì's banter made it unpleasant. At the same time Montoni ordered the crews to be prepared early, because she wanted to dine in Turin.

Signora Montoni rejoiced at last being on a flat street: she recounted at length all the fears she experienced, doubtless forgetting that she was describing her dangers to her companions; she and she added that she hoped soon to lose sight of those horrible mountains. "For all the money in the world," she said, "I wouldn't make the same trip again." She »she Complained of weariness, and she retired early. Emilia did the same, and learned from Annetta, her aunt's maid, that Cavignì had not been deceived about the violinist. He was the son of a peasant living in the nearby valley, who was going to spend the carnival in Venice, and who was thought to be very amiable. "As for me," said Annetta, "I'd rather live in these woods, and on these beautiful hills, than go to a city." It is said that we will no longer see woods, mountains or meadows, and that Venice is built in the middle of the sea. »

Emilia agreed with Annetta that the young man lost a lot in the exchange, since he left the innocence and country beauty for the voluptuousness of a corrupt city.

When she was alone, she could not sleep. The meeting at Valancourt, and the circumstances of their separation, never ceased to occupy her spirit, retracing for her the picture of a fortunate union in the bosom of nature, and of the happiness from which she feared she would be far away forever.

CHAPTER XV

The following day, very early in the day, the travelers left for Turin. The rich plain which extends from the Alps to that magnificent city was not then, as it is now, shaded by large trees. Plantations of olive trees, mulberry trees, fig trees, mixed with vines, formed a magnificent landscape, through which the impetuous Eridanus rushes from the mountains, and joins Turin with the waters of the humble Dora. As the travelers advanced, the Alps took on all the majesty of their appearance. The yokes rose one above the other in a long succession. The highest peaks, covered with clouds, were sometimes lost in their undulations, and often leapt above them. The slopes of those mountains, whose irregular cavities had all sorts of shapes, they were tinged with purple and blue with the movement of light and shadows, varying the scene at every moment. To the east the plains of Lombardy spread out; The towers of Turin were already revealed, and, at a greater distance, the Apennines circumscribed an immense horizon.

The magnificence of that city, the sight of its churches, palaces and grandiose squares, surpassed not only all that Emilia had seen in France, but all that had yet been imagined.

Montoni, who already knew Turin, and was not surprised by this, did not give in to his wife's prayers, who would have liked to see some palace; he only stayed long enough to rest, and he hastened to leave for Venice. During the journey, he showed himself haughty and very reserved, especially with his wife; but this reservation, however, was less that of respect than of pride and discontent. He paid little attention to Emilia. His talks with Cavignì always had war or politics as their subject, which the convulsive state of Italy at the time made very interesting. Emilia observed that, in recounting some illustrious event, Montoni's eyes lost their dull hardness, and seemed to sparkle with joy. Though she might sometimes doubt that this instantaneous change was rather the effect of malice than proof of valour, yet this seemed very well suited to his character, and to his superb and chivalrous manners; and Cavignì, with all his ease and good grace, was unable to compare with him.

Entering the Milanese, they left their French hat for the scarlet Italian cap, embroidered in gold. Emilia was surprised to see Montoni add the military plume, and Cavignì content himself with the feathers usually worn. Finally, he believed that Montoni would take the soldiers' crew in order to cross with more safety a district inundated with troops and sacked on all sides. The devastation of war could be seen in those fertile plains. Where the lands did not remain uncultivated, the traces of the robbery could be recognized. The vines were torn from the trees that were to support them; the olives lay trampled; the mulberry groves had been cut to light the devastating fire of the farmhouses and villages. Emilia turned her gaze, sighing, to the north, on the Helvetic Alps:

Travelers often observed detachments of troops marching some distance, and in the inns where they stayed they experienced the effects of extreme famine, and all the other inconveniences which are the consequences of internecine warfare. Yet they never had any reason to fear for their safety. Once in Milan, they did not stop either to consider the grandeur of that metropolis, or to visit its magnificent temple, which was still under construction.

Past Milan, the country bore the character of a more frightening devastation. All then seemed calm; but like the repose of death upon a face which still bears the horrible imprint of the last convulsions. Leaving the Milanese, they again encountered troops. The evening was advanced; they saw an army marching from afar across the plain, and whose spears and helmets still gleamed in the last rays of the sun. The column advanced over a part of the road closed between two knolls. The leaders directing the march could easily be distinguished. Several officers galloped on the flanks, transmitting the orders received from their superiors; others, separated from the vanguard, circled the plain to the right.

As he approached, Montoni, from the plumes, flags and colors of the uniforms of the various corps, thought he recognized the small innkeeper commanded by the famous leader Utaldo. He was a friend of him and of the chieftains. He made the carriages stop to wait for them, and let the way clear. A warrior music was soon heard; it kept growing, and Montoni, convinced that it was really the band of the famous Utaldo, stuck his head out of the carriage, and saluted the general by waving his cap in the air. The leader saluted with his sword, and various officers, approaching the carriage, welcomed Montoni as an old acquaintance: the captain himself arrived shortly after; the troop halted, and the leader spoke to Montoni, whom he seemed delighted to see again. Emilia understood, from their speeches, to be that a victorious army returning to its country; the numerous carriages that accompanied it were laden with the rich spoils of the enemies, as well as with the wounded and captives who would be ransomed to peace. The leaders had to separate the following day, divide the booty, and retire, with their own bands, in their respective castles. That evening was therefore to be consecrated to pleasures, in memory of the common victory, and of the farewell which they mutually took.

Utaldo told Montoni that his hosts would encamp that night in a village half a mile away; he bade her come back, and take part in the banquet, assuring him that the ladies would be well treated. Montoni excused himself by alleging that he wanted to arrive in Verona that same evening, and after a few questions about the state of the surroundings of that city, he took his leave and left, but could not reach Verona until very late at night.

Emilia could not see the delicious situation until the following day. They left that beautiful city early, and when they reached Padua, they embarked on the Brenta for Venice. Here, the scene was entirely changed. They were no longer the vestiges of war scattered across the plains of Milan, but on the contrary everything breathed luxury and elegance. The verdant banks of the Brenta offered nothing but beauty, delights and opulence. Emilia looked with astonishment at the villas of the Venetian nobility, their cool porticoes, the beautiful colonnades shaded by majestically tall poplars and cypresses; the orange trees, whose fragrant flowers embalmed the air, and the thick willows that bathed their long foliage in the river, forming shady shelters. The Venice carnival seemed to have been transported to those enchanting shores. The gondolas, in perpetual motion, they increased their life. All the extravagance of the masquerade formed a superb decoration; and towards evening, many groups went to dance under the big trees.

Cavignì instructed Emilia on the name of gentlemen to whom the villas belonged; and to amuse her she would add a slight sketch of their characters to it, she sometimes delighted in listening to it; but her vivacity no longer had the same effect on Signora Montoni as it did before her: she almost always seemed serious, and Montoni was constantly reserved.

The wonder of the girl when she discovered Venice, its islets, its palaces and its towers that all together rose from the sea reflecting their various colors on the clear and flickering surface is indescribable. The sunset gave the distant waters and mountains of Friuli, which surround the Adriatic to the north, a yellowish tint with a most admirable effect. The marble porticoes and columns of San Marco were clad in rich hues and the stately shade of evening. As they advanced, the magnificence of the city became more detailed. Its terraces, surmounted by aerial yet majestic buildings, illuminated, as they were then, by the last rays of the sun, seemed rather to have been brought out of the waves by a magician's wand than built by a mortal hand.

The sun having finally disappeared, the shadow gradually invaded the waters and the mountains, extinguishing the last fires that gilded their summits; and the melancholic purplish of the evening spread like a veil everywhere. How profound and beautiful was the tranquility that enveloped the scene! Nature seemed immersed in rest. The sweetest emotions of the soul were the only ones that awoke. Emilia's eyes filled with tears: she felt the transports of sublime devotion, raising her gaze to the celestial vault, while delightful music accompanied the murmur of the waters. She listened in silent ecstasy, and no one dared break the silence. The sounds seemed to float in the air. The boat moved forward with such a placid movement that it could scarcely be distinguished; and the brilliant city seemed to move towards them himself to receive strangers. Then they distinguished a woman's voice which, accompanied by some instrument, sang a sweet and languid tune. Her pathetic expression, which seemed now that of passionate love, and now the plaintive accent of hopeless pain, announced well that the feeling he was dictating to her was not feigned. « Ah! said Emilia, sighing and remembering Valancourt; « that song certainly comes from the heart! »

She looked around with attentive curiosity. The twilight left only imperfect images visible. Meanwhile, at some distance away, she thought she saw a gondola, and in the same tempo she heard a harmonious chorus of voices and instruments. It was so sweet, so sweet! It was like the hymn of angels descending into the silence of the night. The music ended, and it seemed to her that the sacred choir ascended to the sky. The profound calm that followed was as expressive as the harmony that had just ceased. Finally, a general sigh seemed to awaken everyone from a kind of ecstasy. Emilia, however, remained for a long time abandoned to the amiable sadness that she had taken possession of her senses; but the laughing and tumultuous spectacle of the Piazza di San Marco dispelled her meditations. The moon, which then rose above the horizon,

The music, which the travelers had already heard, passed close to Montoni's boat, in one of those gondolas which one saw wandering on the sea, full of people who went to enjoy the cool of the evening. Most of them had musicians. The murmur of the water, the measured strokes of the oars on the sparkling waves, added a special charm. Emilia watched, she listened, and she felt as though she were in the temple of the fairies. The aunt also felt some pleasure. Rams he was happy to have finally returned to Venice, which he called the first city in the world ; and Cavignì was more cheerful and animated than usual.

The boat passed through the Grand Canal where Montoni's house was located. The palaces of Sansovino and Palladio displayed in Emilia's eyes such a kind of beauty and magnificence that her imagination could not form an idea. The air was agitated by sweet sounds repeated by the echo of the canal, and groups of masks dancing in the light of the moon performed the most brilliant functions of the phantasmagoria.

The boat stopped in front of the portico of a large house, and the travelers disembarked on a terrace which, via a marble staircase, led them to a sitting room, the magnificence of which amazed Emilia. The walls and ceiling were decorated with frescoes. Silver lamps, suspended from silver chains, lit up the room. The floor was covered with colorfully painted Indian mats. The tapestry of the windows was of light green silk, embroidered in gold, enriched with green and gold fringes. The balcony overlooked the Grand Canal. Emilia, struck by Montoni's gloomy character, observed the luxury and elegance of that furniture with surprise. She remembered with astonishment that they had described him as a ruined man. — Ah! she said to herself; "If Valancourt saw this house, he wouldn't talk like that anymore! How convinced he would be of the falsehood of the gossip. —

Signora Montoni assumed the airs of a princess; Montoni, impatient and annoyed with her, didn't even have the civility to greet her and compliment her on her entry into her house. As soon as he arrived he ordered the gondola and went out with Cavignì to take part in the pleasures of the evening. Montoni then became serious and thoughtful: Emilia, who was surprised by everything, made an effort to cheer her up, but her reflection did not diminish. neither the whims nor the bad mood of her aunt, whose replies were so rude that Emilia, giving up the plan of distracting her, went to a window, at least to enjoy such a new and interesting spectacle. The first object that struck her was a group of people dancing to the sound of a guitar and other instruments. The woman holding the guitar and the one playing the tambourine also danced with great grace, panache and agility. After these came the masks: some were dressed up as gondoliers, others as minstrels and they all sang verses accompanied by a few instruments. They stopped at some distance from the portico, and in these songs Emilia recognized the octaves of Ariosto. They sang of the wars of the Moors against Charlemagne, and the misfortunes of the paladin Orlando. She changed the music's thunder, and heard the melancholy rooms of Petrarch; the magic of those painful accents was supported by a truly Italian expression and music. The moonlight worked the spell.

Emilia was thrilled; she shed tears of tenderness, and his imagination of her carried itself to France near Valancourt; she regretfully saw that enchanted scene vanish, and she remained for some time absorbed in thoughtful tranquillity. Other sounds soon awakened her attention: it was a majestic harmony of horns. She observed that many gondolas lined up at the banks; she recognized in the distant perspective of the canal a sort of procession furrowing the surface of the water; as she approached, the horns and other instruments made the air echo the sweetest concerts .... Shortly afterwards the fabulous deities of the city seemed to rise from the bosom of the waters. Neptune, with Venice as his wife, advanced on the liquid element, surrounded by the Tritons and the naiads. to have suddenly realized all the poets' visions; the vague images of her, with which Emilia's soul was filled, remained impressed on her long after the appearance of her masquerade.

After dinner, her aunt stayed up for a long time, but Montoni didn't come home. If Emilia had admired the magnificence of the living room, she was none the less surprised to observe the bare and miserable state of all the rooms, which she had to cross to reach her room: she saw a long succession of large apartments, the dilapidation of which sufficiently indicated as if they had not been inhabited for a long time. On some walls there were faded pieces of very ancient wallpaper, on some others some frescoes almost destroyed by humidity. Finally she reached her room, spacious, elevated, unfurnished like the others, and with large windows; this room recalled her darkest ideas to her imagination, but the view of the sea dispelled them.

CHAPTER XVI

Montoni and his companion had not yet returned home at dawn: the groups of masks or dancers dispersed at daybreak, like so many chimeras. Montoni had been occupied elsewhere; his soul little susceptible to frivolous voluptuousness, fed on the development of energetic passions, the difficulties, the storms of life which overturn the happiness of others, revived all the elasticity of his soul, procuring him the only enjoyments of which he could to be capable; without extreme interest life was but a sleep to him. When he lacked real interest, he formed artificial ones for himself, until habit, coming to distort them, ceased to be fictitious: such was the love of play. He had abandoned himself in the beginning only to get rid of inertia and languor, and had persisted in it with all the ardor of obstinate passion. She had spent the night with Cavignì playing in a society of young men who had a lot to spend and many vices to satisfy. Montoni despised the greater part of these people, more for the weakness of their talents than for the baseness of their inclinations, and he did not associate with them except to make them instruments of his designs. Among these, however, there were the most capable, and Montoni admitted them to his intimacy, while maintaining over them that decisive arrogance which commands submission to cowardly or timid spirits, and arouses hatred and pride in superior spirits. He therefore had numerous and mortal enemies; but the antiquity of their hatred was the sure proof of his power; and since power was his only aim, he gloried more than this I hate that of all the esteem they could have paid him. He therefore despised such a moderate sentiment as that of esteem, and would have despised himself if he had believed himself capable of contenting himself with it. In the small number of those whom he distinguished, there were the lords Bertolini, Orsino and Verrezzi. The former had a cheerful character and lively passions; he was of unparalleled dissipation and extravagance, but otherwise generous, bold and forthright. Orsino, proud and reserved, loved power more than ostentation: he had a cruel and suspicious nature; he felt the insults keenly, and the thirst for revenge gave him no rest. Shrewd, fruitful in his expedients, patient, constant in his perseverance, he knew how to dominate actions and passions. Pride, vengeance and avarice were almost the only he knew: few reflexes that could stop him, and few obstacles that could elude the depth of his stratagems. He was Montoni's favourite.

Verrezzi was not lacking in talent; but the violence of his imagination enslaved him to opposite passions. He was cheerful, voluptuous, enterprising, but he had neither firmness nor true courage, and the vilest selfishness was the only principle of his actions. He is ready in projects, petulant in hopes, the first to undertake and to abandon not only his own enterprises, but also those of others; proud, impetuous and insubordinate: such Verrezzi; but whoever knew his character thoroughly, and knew how to direct his passions, guided him like a child.

These were the friends Montoni introduced into his house, and admitted to table, the day after his arrival in Venice. There was likewise among them a Venetian noble named Count Morano, and a lady from Livona, whom Montoni presented to his wife as a person of distinguished merit; she had come in the morning to congratulate him on his arrival, and had been invited to dinner.

Signora Montoni received the compliments of those gentlemen with ill grace. It was enough, to displease her, that they were friends of her husband; and she hated them because they accused them of having helped him spend the night out of the house. Finally, she envied her, who, though convinced of her little influence over Montoni, supposed that she preferred their society to hers. The rank of Count Morano earned him a welcome that he refused to all the others: her bearing, contemptuous manners, and her extravagant and refined clothing (she had not yet adopted the Venetian style), contrasted strongly with the beauty, modesty, sweetness and simplicity of the granddaughter. This she observed with more attention than pleasure the society that surrounded her: her beauty however, and the seductive graces of Signora Livona interested him involuntarily;

To take advantage of the cool evening, the whole company embarked on Montoni's gondola. The splendid radiance of the sunset still colored the waves, going to die to the west; the last hues seemed to fade little by little, while the dark blue of the firmament began to sparkle with stars. Emilia abandoned herself to sweet and serious emotions at the same time; the stillness of the lagoon on which he rowed, the images that came to hang there, a new sky, the stars reflected in the waters, the gloomy profile of the towers and porticoes, finally the silence in that solemn hour, interrupted only by the gurgling of the wave and indistinct sounds of distant music, everything sublimated his thoughts. tears welled up; the rays of the moon, always brighter than the spreading shadows, then cast their silver splendor upon her. Semi-covered with a black veil, her figure receives an unspeakable softness. Count Morano, seated next to Emilia, and who had been considering her in silence, suddenly took up a lute, and playing it with great agility, sang an aria full of melancholy in an insinuating voice. When he had finished, he gave the lute to Emilia, who, accompanying herself on that instrument, sang a romance with great gusto and simplicity, then a popular song from her town; but this song of hers brought back to her thoughts painful remembrances: her trembling voice breathed on her lip, and the strings of her lute sounded no more of hers under her hand. Ashamed at last of her emotion that she had betrayed her, she promptly passed on to a song so gay and pretty, that the whole conversation broke into applause, and she was obliged to repeat it.

The count, Emilia, Cavigni and Signora Livona sang then songs accompanied by two lutes, and some other instrument. Sometimes the instruments were silent, and the voices, in perfect accord, were weakening to the last degree; after a short pause they rose again, the instruments regained strength, and the general chorus echoed through the air.

Meanwhile, Montoni, bored with that music, was thinking about the means of disengaging himself to follow those who wanted to go and play in a casino. He proposed returning to land: Orsino supported it with pleasure, but the count and all the others vigorously opposed it.

Montoni was again pondering how to get rid of that embarrassment; an empty gondola returning to Venice passed by his. Without tormenting himself any longer for an excuse, he took advantage of the opportunity, and entrusting the ladies to his friends, left with Orsino. Emilia, for the first time, saw him go with regret, for she regarded his presence as a protection for her, without quite knowing what she had to fear. He landed in the Piazza San Marco, and running to the casino, he got lost in the crowd of gamblers.

The count had secretly sent one of his servants away in Montoni's boat to send for his players and his own gondola. Emilia, unaware of all this, heard the cheerful little songs of the gondoliers who, disturbing the silvery waves with their oars, where the moon reverberated, approached, and shortly afterwards she distinguished the sound of the instruments, and a truly harmonious symphony; at the same instant the boats approached, the count explained everything, and they passed into his gondola paraded with the most exquisite taste.

While the company enjoyed refreshments of fruit and ice cream, the players in the other boat played delicious melodies: the count, seated next to Emilia, he attended to her alone, and lavished her with a sweet and passionate voice on compliments, the meaning of which could not be doubted; to avoid them, she spoke to Signora Livona, and she spoke with him in a reserved and imposing tone, but too soft to contain his concern. He could see or hear anyone but Emilia, and he could only speak of her to her. Cavignì observed her with a bad mood, and the girl with embarrassment.

They all disembarked in Piazza San Marco; the serenity of the night determined Montoni to accept the count's proposals, that is, to spend some time before going to dinner, in his casino with the rest of the company. If anything could have dispelled Emilia's anxieties, it would certainly have been the novelty of everything that surrounded her, the ornaments of the rich palaces and the tumult of the masks.

Finally they went to the casino, decorated with the best taste: a splendid dinner was prepared for you; but here Emilia's reserved demeanor made the count understand how much he needed Montoni's favor; the condescension she had already shown prevented him from judging the undertaking very difficult; she then directed part of his attentions to her aunt, who was so flattered by this distinction, that she could not disguise her joy, and before the end of the dinner the count possessed his full esteem. When he turned to her, her frowning face calmed down, and she smiled at all her words, she appreciated all his proposals: Morano invited her in company to have coffee in her box at the theater to the evening after; Emilia, having understood that she accepted,

It was already late when they embarked; Emilia's surprise was extreme when, leaving the casino, she saw the sun rising from the Adriatic, and the Piazza San Marco still full of people. Sleep for a long time the patch aggravated her eyelids; the coolness of the sea wind revived her, and she would have left there with regret, had it not been for the presence of the count, who absolutely wanted to accompany the ladies up to her house. Montoni had not yet returned: his wife went into her own rooms and freed Emilia from the boredom of her company.

Montoni returned late and was furious: he had made a big loss; before going to bed, he wanted to have a private conversation with Cavignì, and the latter's attitude made it known enough the following day that the subject of the conference had found him not very pleasant.

La Montoni, who had been taciturn and thoughtful all day, received some Venetians towards evening, whose affability greatly pleased Emilia. These ladies had an air of fluency and cordiality inexpressible with strangers; they seemed to have known them for a long time; their conversation was mutually tender, sentimental, and spirited. Montoni herself, who had no attraction for that kind of entertainment, and whose dryness and selfishness often contrasted excessively with their exquisite courtesy, herself could not be insensitive to their graces.

Cavignì went to see the ladies in the evening: Montoni had other commitments. They embarked in the gondola to go to Piazza San Marco, where the crowd was numerous. After a short walk, they sat down at the door of a casino; and while Cavignì had coffee and ice cream brought, Count Morano arrived. She approached Emilia with an air of impatience and pleasure which, combined with his attentions of the previous evening, obliged her to receive him with timid reserve.

It was almost midnight when they went to the theatre. Emilia entering it, she remembered all that she had seen, and she was less dazzled. All of it splendor of art seemed to her inferior to the simplicity of nature. Her heart was not moved by admiration as at the sight of the immense ocean and the grandeur of the skies, at the roar of the tumultuous waves, at the melodies of country music. Such memories of her must have rendered the affected scene which offered itself to her gaze insipid.

Thus several weeks passed, in which Emilia was pleased to consider a theater the customs so opposed to the French; but Count Morano was there too frequently for her tranquillity. Her charms, her figure, her beautiful gifts, which made her universal admiration, would perhaps have interested Emilia too, if her heart had not been biased towards Valancourt. Perhaps she, too, would have done better to put less persistence in her attentions. Some trait of her character which she revealed about her annoyed Emilia, and prevented her against her by his better qualities.

Shortly after his arrival in Venice, Montoni received a letter from Quesnel, announcing the death of his wife's uncle at his villa on the Brenta, and his plan to come quickly and take possession of this house and other property. touch him. This uncle was Mrs Quesnel's mother's brother. Montoni was his father's kinsman, and although he had nothing to claim from this rich inheritance, he could not hide all the envy that this news aroused in his heart.

Emilia had observed that, after her departure from France, Montoni had retained no regard for her aunt: at first she had neglected her, and now she showed her only aversion and bad temper. She had never supposed that her aunt's defects had escaped Montoni's discernment, and that her spirit and figure had deserved her attention. The surprise caused by this marriage had been extreme; but the choice was made, and she could not imagine how he could so soon show his open contempt for her. Montoni, enticed by Cheron's apparent wealth, found himself singularly disappointed in her hopes. Seduced by the ruses she put into practice as long as he had deemed it necessary, he found himself caught in the snare into which he would have wanted to make her herself fall. He had been played upon by the shrewdness of a woman, whose intelligence he thought very little, and he found himself having sacrificed her pride and freedom, without preserving himself from the disastrous ruin hanging over his head. Mrs. Cheron had got most of her stuff into her own head. Montoni had taken possession of the rest of her, and although the sum obtained was less than his expectations and her needs,

The rumors reported to Valancourt about Montoni's character and situation were unfortunately too accurate. It was up to time and circumstances to unravel the mystery.

Montoni did not have the character to suffer an insult with kindness, much less to resent it with dignity. Her exacerbated pride was explained by all the violence, all the bitterness of a limited or at least badly regulated mind. She didn't even want to acknowledge having somehow provoked such contempt with her duplicity. She persisted in believing she alone was to be pitied and Montoni to blame. Unable to conceive of any moral idea of obligation, he did not feel its strength except when he violated it against her. Her vanity was already suffering cruelly from the open contempt of her husband; it remained for her to suffer the advantage, discovering the state of fortune. The disorder of his house let dispassionate people know part of the truth; but the ones that don't they decidedly wanted to believe if not according to their wishes, they were quite blind. Montoni thought of herself as nothing less than a princess, since she was the mistress of a palace in Venice and a castle in the Apennines. Sometimes Montoni spoke of going to his castle at Udolfo for a few weeks to examine its state and collect its income. It seemed that he had not been there for two years, and that the castle was abandoned in the care of an old servant, whom he called her steward.

Emilia heard talk of this trip with pleasure, as it promised her new ideas and some respite from Morano's assiduity. On the other hand, in the countryside, she would have been more at ease dealing with Valancourt, and with the melancholy memory of her native places.

Count Morano did not take long for the silent language of kindness. He declared her passion to Emilia, and made proposals to his uncle, who accepted in spite of her refusal. Encouraged by Montoni, and especially by blind vanity, the count did not despair of succeeding. Emilia was surprised and sensibly offended by his persistence. Morano spent all his time at Montoni's house, ate lunch there, and followed Emilia and her aunt everywhere.

Montoni no longer spoke of going to Udolfo, and he was not at home until the count and Orsino were there. Some coldness was noted between him and Cavignì, although the latter still lived in the building. Emilia noticed that her uncle often shut himself up in his rooms with Orsino for whole hours, and whatever the theme of their conversations, it must be said that it was very interesting, because Montoni even neglected his favorite passion for gambling, and spent the night in home. There was something mysterious in Orsino's visits; Emilia was more uneasy than surprised, having involuntarily discovered what he was trying to hide. Montoni, after visits from his friend, he was sometimes more thoughtful than usual; at other times, his profound meditations removed her from what surrounded him, and spread over his physiognomy such an alteration as to make it terrible. At other times his eyes sparkled, and all the energy of his soul seemed to gain strength in the idea of a formidable surprise. Emilia tried to follow his changes with interest, but she was careful not to let the outcome of her observations be known to her aunt, who did not see her husband's strange ways as anything other than the consequence of an ordinary severity of her.

A second letter from Quesnel announced the arrival of him and his wife in Miarenti: it also contained details of the fortunate event which led them to Italy, and ended with a very pressing invitation for Montoni, his wife and niece, to go and see him in his new possessions.

Emilia received, almost at the same time, a much more interesting letter, and which for some time soothed the bitterness of her heart. Valancourt, hoping that she was still in Venice, had risked a letter by post; he spoke to her of her love, of his anxieties and of her constancy. He had languished for some time in Toulouse after her departure, having enjoyed the pleasure of visiting those places every day, where she was as usual, and they had left to go to her brother's castle, near the valley. After the tenderest expressions and lengthy details, he added:

' You must observe that my letter is dated several different days. Look at the first lines, and you will know that I wrote them immediately after your departure from France. Writing to you is the only occupation that has been able to make your absence bearable for me. When I converse with you on paper, and I express each of my sentiments, and all the affections of my heart, it seems to me that you are always present: up to now I have had no other consolation. I have deferred sending the envelope solely for the pleasure of increasing it. When any circumstance had interested my heart and instilled a ray of joy in my soul, I hastened to communicate it to you, and I seemed to see you enjoying such a description.

« I must point out to you a circumstance which destroys all my illusions in one single point. I am forced to go and join my regiment, and I can no longer wander under those pleasant shadows, where I imagined seeing you at my side. The valley is rented. I have reason to believe that this happened without your knowledge, from what Teresa told me this morning, and that is precisely why I am telling you about it. She wept as she told me that she was leaving the service of her dear mistress, and the castle in which she spent so many happy years. And what's worse, she added , without a letter from Signora Emilia to ease my pain. This is Mr. Quesnel's work; and I dare to say that she is ignorant of all that is done in this place.

' Teresa told me she had received a letter from him, announcing to her that the castle was rented, that there was no longer any need for her service, and that she had to move out within a week. Some days before receiving this letter, she had been surprised by the arrival of Monsieur Quesnel and a stranger, who had examined the castle in detail. »

Towards the end of the letter dated a week after this last sentence, Valancourt adds:

' Before leaving for the regiment, I went to the valley this morning. I learned that the tenant has already lodged there, and that Teresa has left. I tried to have news of this gentleman's character, but in vain. The fishpond was always open. I went there and spent an hour feeding on the image of my dear Emilia. Oh my Emilia! surely we are not separated forever, yes I hope so, and we will live for each other. »

This letter made her shed many tears, but tears of tenderness and satisfaction, on feeling that Valancourt was in good health, and that his affection for her was not weakened either by time or by distance. As for the news of her which he gave about her castle, she was astonished and offended that Quesnel had rented it without even deigning to consult her. This proceeding evidently proved to what extent he believed her authority to be absolute and her powers unlimited in the administration of her estate. It is true that before her departure he had proposed to rent those properties, and out of concern for economy she had not made any objection; but to entrust her possessions and her paternal house to the whim of a stranger, to deprive her of a safe haven in case some unfortunate circumstance might make it necessary; that's what she had decided to oppose it strongly. Saint Aubert, in the last moments of her life, had received from her a solemn promise never to dispose of the castle, and, in suffering its tenancy, this promise was violated. It was too evident that Quesnel had paid no attention to her objections, and that he regarded as indifferent anything opposed to pecuniary advantages alone. It also seemed that he had not deigned to inform Montoni of this operation, since the latter would have had no reason to hide it from him, if she had been known to him. This conduct greatly displeased Emilia and surprised her; but what the most afflicted was the dismissal of his father's old and faithful servant. "Poor Teresa," Emilia said, "you can't have accumulated any of your salary; you were charitable to the unhappy, and thought you were dying in that house where you spent your prime! Poor Theresa! Now they have driven you out in your old age, and you will be forced to go begging for a loaf of bread! »

And he wept bitterly as he made these reflections, thinking of what he might have done for Teresa, and how to explain himself to Quesnel about it. She greatly feared that his insensitive soul was incapable of pity. He wanted to inquire if in his letters to Montoni he made mention of his affairs; In a little while her uncle made her beg to go to her office, and imagining that he wanted to communicate to her some passage from Quesnel's letter relating to the valley affair, she went at once and found him alone.

'I am writing to Monsieur Quesnel,' he said to her, when he saw her enter, 'in reply to a letter which I have lately received. He wished to speak to you about an article of this letter.

"I too wanted to talk to you about this subject," replied Emilia.

"It's a very interesting thing for you," added Montoni; « you will certainly see her under the same aspect as me, since she cannot be seen otherwise; You will therefore agree that any objection founded on sentiment , as they say, must yield to considerations of a more positive advantage.

"According to this," Emilia said modestly, "it seems to me that considerations of humanity should also enter into the calculation; but I am afraid it is not too late to deliberate on that point, and I am sorry that it is no longer in my power to reject it.

"It's too late," said Montoni; 'but I like to see you submit to reason and necessity, without abandoning yourself to useless complaints. I very much applaud such conduct, which heralds a fortitude of which your sex is hardly capable. When you are a few years older, you will recognize the service your friends are doing you by moving away from the romantic illusions of feeling . I have not closed the letter yet, and you may add a few lines informing my uncle of your consent: you will see shortly, being my intention to take you to Miarenti in a few days with my wife; so you can talk about this business. »

Emilia wrote the following lines:

' It is useless now, sir, to comment on the matter which Signor Montoni tells me he wrote to you about. I could have wished it had ended less hastily; that would have given me time to overcome what he calls prejudices, the weight of which oppresses my heart. Since the matter is done, I submit to you, but notwithstanding my submission, I have much to say on other points relating to the same subject, and I reserve them for the time when I have the honor of seeing you. In the meantime, I beg you, sir, to take care of poor Teresa, in consideration of your very affectionate niece.

Emilia Saint-Aubert . »

Montoni smiled ironically at what Emilia had written, but made no objection. She retired to her apartment, and began a letter for Valancourt; she related to it the peculiarities of her journey, and her arrival in Venice. She described the most interesting scenes of her passage in the Alps, her emotions at the first sight of Italy, the customs and character of the people around her, and some details on Montoni's conduct. She was careful not to mention Count Morano, and still less of his declaration, knowing how easy true love is to get alarmed.

CHAPTER XVII

The next day the count dined at the Montoni house; he was extraordinarily cheerful. Emilia observed in her manners with her an air of confidence and joy which she had never known; she tried to suppress it by doubling down the usual coldness, but it didn't succeed. He seemed to be looking for an opportunity to speak to her without witnesses, but she Emilia never wanted to listen to things that couldn't be said aloud. Towards evening, Signor Montoni and the whole company went to enjoy themselves on the sea; the count, leading Emilia to the zendaletto[1] , he brought her hand to his lips, and thanked her for the condescension she had deigned to show. The girl, surprised and discontented, hastened to withdraw her hand, and she thought she was joking; but when at the bottom of the stairs she learned, by his livery, that he was the count's zendaletto, and that the rest of the company, having already entered other gondolas, were about to leave, she resolved not to suffer a particular conversation; she bade him good evening, and she returned to the porch. The count followed her, praying and imploring, when Montoni arrived, who took her by the hand and led her to the zendaletto; Emilia begged him in a low voice to consider the impropriety of that step.

"This caprice is intolerable," he said; "I don't see any inconvenience here. »

From that point, Emilia's aversion to the count became a kind of horror; the inconceivable audacity with which he continued to persecute her in spite of her refusal, the indifference he showed towards her particular opinion, as long as Montoni favored her claims, all combined to increase the excessive repugnance which she never had stopped feeling for him. However, she was somewhat reassured when she heard that Montoni would come with them. He stood on one side and Morano on the other. Everyone was silent while the gondoliers readied the oars; but Emilia, trembling at the conversation that would follow that silence, finally had enough courage to break it with a few indifferent words, to prevent the solicitations of one and the reproaches of the other.

'I was impatient,' the count told her, 'to express my gratitude to your kindness: but I must also thank Signor Montoni, who gave me a much desired opportunity. »

Emilia looked at the count with a mixture of surprise and discontent.

" As! he added; "Would you like to diminish the satisfaction of this delicious moment?" Why plunge me back into the perplexity of doubt, and deny, with your looks, the favor of your last declarations? You cannot doubt my sincerity and all the ardor of my passion. It is useless, charming Emilia, no doubt, it is absolutely useless for you to try to hide your feelings any longer.

"If you had ever hidden them, sir," replied Emilia, "it would no doubt be useless to conceal them even more. She had hoped you would spare me the need to declare them again; but since you oblige me to do so, I protest to you, and for the last time, that your perseverance deprives you even of the esteem with which I was disposed to believe you worthy.

— By God! cried Montoni; « this exceeds my expectation; he had known whims in women, but ... Observe, Mademoiselle Emilia, that if the count is your lover, I am not, and he will not serve as a toy for your capricious uncertainties. We propose a marriage that would honor any family: remember that yours is not noble; you resisted my reasons for a long time; my honor is now engaged, and I don't mean to look sad. You will persist, if you like, in the declaration you instructed me to make to the count.

"It must be certain that you have fallen into error, sir," said Emilia; 'My replies on this subject were constantly the same; it is worthy of you to accuse me of caprice. If you agree to take charge of my answers, it is an honor that I did not solicit. I myself declared to Count Morano, and to you, sir, that noi will acceptnever the honor he wants to do me, and I repeat. »

The count looked at Montoni with amazement; the demeanor of the latter also showed surprise, but a surprise mixed with indignation.

« Here there is audacity and caprice together. Will you deny your own expressions, miss?

"Such a question deserves no answer," said Emilia, blushing; 'You will remember it, and you will regret having done it.

"Answer categorically," Montoni replied vehemently. "So you dare to rescind your words?" Would you like to deny that you recognized just now that it was too late to release yourselves from your engagements, and that you accepted the hand of the count? will you deny it?

"I will deny everything, because none of my words ever expressed anything like it.

"Will you deny what you wrote to Monsieur Quesnel your uncle?" If you dare to do so, your character will testify against you. What can you say now? Montoni continued, making use of Emilia's silence and confusion.

"I realize, sir, that you are in a great mistake, and that I myself was deceived.

"No more pretending, please. Be frank and sincere if possible.

'I've always been like that, sir, and I certainly don't deserve any credit. I have no reason to pretend.

"What does all this mean?" exclaimed Morano somewhat moved.

"Suspend your judgement, Count," replied Montoni; "A woman's ideas are impenetrable. Now, let's get to the explanation....

'Excuse me, sir, if I suspend this explanation until such time as you seem more inclined to trust; everything I could say now would only serve to expose me to insults.

"Please explain," said Morano.

"Speak," added Montoni, "I place all my trust in you; we feel.

"Let me enlighten you by asking a question.

"A thousand if you like," said Montoni disdainfully.

"What was the subject of your letter to Mr. Quesnel?"

— Heh! what could it be? The honorary offering of Count Morano.

"Then, sir, we were both strangely deceived.

- We explained ourselves badly, I suppose, in the conversation preceding the letter. I must do you justice; you are very ingenious in giving rise to a misunderstanding. »

Emilia tried to hold back her tears and you will answer firmly. 'Permit me, sir, to explain myself fully, or to keep silent altogether.

'Montoni,' cried the count, 'let me plead my own cause; it is clear that you can do nothing about it.

"Any talk on the subject," said Emilia, "is useless; if you will pardon me, do not prolong it.

- It is impossible, madame, for me to stifle a passion which forms the charm and torment of my life. I will always love you, and I will persecute you with tireless ardor; when you are convinced of the strength and constancy of my passion, your heart will give way to pity, and perhaps to repentance. »

A ray of moon, falling on Morano's face, he discovered the disturbance and agitation of his soul. Suddenly he exclaimed: "It's too much, Signor Montoni, you deceived me, and I ask you for satisfaction.

"To me, sir?" you will have it,' he stammered.

"You have deceived me," continued Morano, "and you want to punish the innocence of the bad success of your projects. »

Montoni smiled disdainfully. Emilia, frightened by the consequences that this quarrel could have, she could not keep silent any longer. She explained the reason for the mistake, and declared that she had not intended to consult Montoni except for the lease of the valley, she concluded, and begged him to write to Quesnel immediately in order to make up for this mistake.

The count could hardly contain himself; nevertheless, while she spoke, they both paid attention to what she was saying. A little calmed her fright,Rams he begged the count to order the gondoliers to go back, promising them a particular interview; Morano joined without difficulty.

Emilia, consoled by the prospect of some repose, employed her conciliatory attentions to prevent a rupture between two persons who had persecuted her, and even insulted her without regard.

The zendaletto stopped at Montoni's house; the count led Emilia into a room, where his uncle took her by the arm and said something to her in a low voice. Morano kissed her hand despite all her efforts to withdraw it, wished her good night with her most tender expression, and returned to the zendaletto, accompanied by her other.

Emilia, in her room, considered with extreme disquiet the unjust and tyrannical conduct of Montoni, the impudent pertinacity of Morano and her own very sad situation, far from friends and from her country. In vain did she think of Valancourt, as her protector: he was kept away from her service, but she consoled herself at least in knowing that there existed in the world a person who shared her pains, and whose vows aimed only to free her.

Nonetheless, she resolved not to cause him unnecessary pain by informing him how she was sorry for having rejected her judgment on Montoni, although she did not regret having listened to the voice of indifference and delicacy, refusing the proposal of a clandestine marriage. She harbored some hopes in the forthcoming interview with her uncle; she was determined to picture to him her plight, and to beg him to allow her to accompany him on his return to France; when I suddenly remembered that her valley, her favorite place to stay, her only asylum, would no longer be at her disposal for a long time. She wept then, fearing to find little pity in a man like Quesnel, who disposed of her property without even deigning to consult her, and dismissed an old and faithful servant of hers, thus putting her in the street. But although certain that she no longer had a home in her country, and few friends, she wanted to return there, to escape the dominion of Montoni, whose tyranny towards her and harshness towards others seemed unbearable to her. Nor did she wish to live with her uncle, whose progress in her regard was enough to convince her likewise that she would have done nothing but change her oppressor.

Montoni's conduct seemed singularly suspicious to her in connection with the letter to Quesnel. He might, at first, have been deceived; but she feared that he might not voluntarily persist in her mistake in order to frighten her, bend her to her wishes, and compel her to marry her count. In any event, however, she was most eager to tell Quesnel of it, and she regarded her imminent visit with a mixture of impatience, hope, and fear.

The following day, Montoni, finding herself alone with Emilia, spoke to her about Count Morano. She looked surprised that the evening before he had not caught up with the other gondolas, and so soon resumed the turn of Venice. Emilia recounted everything that had happened, expressing her condolences for the misunderstanding that had arisen between her and Montoni, and begged her aunt to interpose her good offices, so that the latter would give the count a decisive and formal refusal; but she soon realized that she already knew everything.

'You mustn't expect any condescension from me,' he said to her: 'I have already given my vote, and Signor Montoni is right to extract your consent with all the means in his power. When youth blind themselves to his true interests, and stubbornly turn away from them, the best luck he can have is in finding friends who oppose their follies. Please tell me if, for your birth, you could have aspired to such an advantageous match as the one offered to you?

"No, ma'am," replied Emilia; "I don't have the pride to claim...

"There's no denying you don't have a good deal of it. My poor brother, your father, was also very proud; but, in truth, it must be confessed, fortune did not favor him too much. »

Indignant at this malicious allusion to her father, and unable to answer with sufficient moderation, Emilia hesitated a moment in confusion; the aunt triumphed; at last she said to her: 'My father's pride, madam, had a very noble object; the only happiness he knew came from her goodness, education and charity towards her neighbour. He never made her consist in surpassing others in wealth, nor was he humbled by her inferiority in that regard. He did not reject the miserable and the unfortunate. He sometimes despised those people who, in the midst of prosperity, made themselves hated by force of vanity, ignorance and cruelty. So I will make my glory consist in imitating him.

"I have no pretension, my niece, of understanding this hodgepodge of good feelings; I leave all the glory to you; but I would like to teach you a little common sense, and not see in you the wonderful wisdom of despising your happiness. I do not boast of an education as refined as the one your father was pleased to give you, but I am content with a little common sense. It would have been very lucky, for your father and for you, if he had taught you how to use it. »

Emilia, sensitively offended by such reflections on her father's memory, despising this speech, suddenly left her and retired to her room.

In the few days which elapsed between this interview and his departure for Miarenti, Montoni never addressed a word to his niece; his looks expressed his resentment; but Emilia was very surprised how he could refrain from renewing the subject. She was even more so when she saw that, in the last three days, the count did not appear, and that Montoni did not even mention his name. Several conjectures occurred to her mind; at times she feared that the quarrel had renewed itself and proved fatal to the count; sometimes inclined to believe that her weariness and disgust had resulted from her refusal of her, and that he had abandoned her plans; lastly, she imagined that the count resorted to the ruse of suspending her visits, obtaining from Montoni not to mention him, in the hope that gratitude and generosity would work a lot on her, and would bring about a consent that he no longer expected from love. Time passed in these vain conjectures, yielding time after time to hope and love: finally they left for Miarenti, and that day, like the others, the count did not appear, nor was he mentioned in the least.

Montoni having decided not to leave Venice before evening, to avoid the heat and enjoy the cool of the night, embarked to reach the Brenta an hour before sunset. Emilia, sitting alone at the stern, silently contemplated the objects that fled as the boat moved forward: she saw the palaces disappear little by little confused with the waves; soon the stars succeeded the last rays of the sun, and one cool and calm night she invited him to sweet meditations, disturbed only by the momentary noise of the oars, and by the light murmur of the waters.

Once they reached the mouths of the Brenta, they harnessed the horses to the boat, and made it advance quickly between two banks mutually decorated with very tall trees, rich palaces, delightful gardens, and groves fragrant with myrtle and orange trees. Then tender memories appeared to the girl; she thought of her beautiful evenings spent in her valley, and of those she spent with Valancourt near Toulouse in her aunt's gardens. Lost in sad reflections, and often with tears in her eyes, she was suddenly shaken by the voice of Montoni, who invited her to have some refreshments. Going to the cabin, she found her aunt there alone. The latter's physiognomy of hers was ablaze with anger, produced, apparently, by a conversation he had with her husband. He looked at her with an air of anger and contempt, and for some time they both remained in perfect silence.

'I flatter myself, you will not persist in maintaining that you were ignorant of the subject of my letter.

'After your silence I imagined, sir, that it was no longer necessary to insist, and that you would have recognized your mistake.

"You had hoped for the impossible," cried Montoni; « I should have expected from your sex a sincerity and a more reflective conduct, glue as easily as you could imagine convincing me of error. »

Emilia blushed, and spoke no more. She knew then too clearly that she had in fact hoped for the impossible, and that where there had been willful error, she could not be hoped to convince; it was evident that Montoni's conduct had not been the result of a misunderstanding, but that of a concerted plan.

Impatient to escape an interview so unpleasant and humiliating for her, Emilia sat back out in the stern. There, at least, her nature granted her that quiet that Montoni denied her.

When, awakened by the voice of a guide or by some movement in the boat, she fell back into her reflections, she thought of the welcome Mr and Mrs Quesnel would give her, and what she would say about the valley. Then she tried to distract the spirit from such an annoying subject, amusing herself by contemplating the features of the beautiful country illuminated by the moon. While her imagination was thus distracted, she discovered a building rising above the trees. As the boat went on, she heard the sound of voices; she shortly made out the high porch of a handsome house shaded by pines and poplars, and recognized it by the same state house already shown as the property of Mrs. Quesnel's kinsman.

The boat stopped near a marble staircase that led to the porch, which was lighted. Montoni disembarked with his family, and they found Mr and Mrs Quesnel among their friends, seated on sofas, enjoying the cool of the night eating fruit and ice cream, while some musicians, in some distance, made a beautiful serenade. Emilia was already accustomed to the customs of hot countries, and she was not surprised to find these gentlemen outside their porch at two hours after midnight.

Without the usual compliments, the company took place under the porch, and from a nearby room she was served the most exquisite refreshments. The little tumult of the arrival had ceased, and when Emilia had recovered from the disturbance felt on the boat, she was surprised by the singular beauty of that place, and by the comforts it offered to heal herself from the annoyances of the season. It was a rotunda with an open dome of white marble, supported by colonnades of the same material. The two wings overlooked long courtyards, leaving immense terraces visible on the banks of the river. A fountain in her midst, with her jets, formed a pleasant murmur as it fell, and the sweet smell of the flowers perfumed that delightful place.

Quesnel spoke of his business in his ordinary tone of importance. He boasted of the new acquisitions, and affectedly pitied Montoni for the recent losses he had made. The latter, whose pride at least was capable of scorning such an ostentation, easily discovered, beneath a feigned compassion, Quesnel's true malignity. He listened to him with disdainful silence, when he mentioned his niece, they both got up and went for a walk in the garden.

Meanwhile Emilia approached Signora Quesnel, who was speaking of France. The only name of her homeland was dear to her: she took great pleasure in considering a person who came from it. Moreover, that village was inhabited by Valancourt, and she listened attentively in the slight flattery of hearing his name. La Quesnel who, during her stay in France, spoke with ecstasy of Italy, she spoke in Italy only of the delights of France, endeavoring to excite the curiosity of others by relating all the beautiful things which she had had the good fortune to see there.

Emilia waited in vain for Valancourt's name. Signora Montoni spoke to her of the beauties of Venice, and of her pleasure which she hoped to enjoy by visiting the castle of Montoni in the Apennines. The latter article was treated only out of vanity. Emilia was well aware that her aunt had little appreciation for solitary grandeurs, and especially those that Udolfo's castle could present. The conversation went on, maligning each other, as far as civilization would permit, with mutual ostentation. Seated on soft sofas, under an elegant portico, surrounded by the prodigies of nature and art, the less sensitive beings should have felt transports of cordiality, good dispositions, and surrendered with transport to all the sweetness of those enchanted places.

Soon it dawned; the sun rose, and he allowed the astonished gaze to contemplate the magnificent spectacle that the snow-covered mountains, the verdant slopes and the fertile plains that extended at their bases offered from afar.

Peasants going to market passed by boat. Umbrellas of colored canvas, which most wore to protect themselves from the sun's rays; the baskets of fruit and flowers that they arranged along the way; the simple and picturesque attire of the villanelles, all formed one of the most surprising eye-catchers. The rapidity of the current, the liveliness of the rowers, the songs of those peasants in the shade of the sails, and the sound of some rustic instrument, gave the whole scene the character of a country festival.

When Montoni and Quesnel had joined the ladies, they all strolled together in the gardens, the elegant distribution of which did much to distract Emilia. The majestic shape and the rich greenery of the cypresses, which she found here in their perfection, the immeasurable height of the pines and poplars, the thick branches of the plane trees, contrasted with her art in those marvelous gardens; the groves of myrtle and other flowering plants confused the aromatic scents with those of a thousand flowers which glazed the ground, and the air it was refreshed by the clear streams, meandering among the green pergolas.

Meanwhile the sun was rising above the horizon, and the heat was beginning to be felt. The company left the gardens to seek rest.

CHAPTER XVIII

Emilia took advantage of the first propitious opportunity to tell Quesnel about the castle of the valley. Her replies were concise, and in the tone of one who, not ignorant of her absolute power, is impatient to see him questioned. She declared to her that the disposition taken was a necessary measure, and that she owed to his prudence the advantages that would accrue to her.

"After all," she added, "when the Venetian count, whose name I don't remember, has married you, the annoyances of your dependence will cease. As your kinsman, I rejoice for you at such a happy occasion, and, I dare to say, so little expected by your friends. »

For a few moments, Emilia was silent and cold; then she tried to disabuse him about the postscript she added to Montoni's letter; Quesnel seemed to have particular reasons for not believing her, and persisted for a long time in accusing her of caprice. Convinced at last of her aversion to Morano, and of the positive rejection she had given him of her, he indulged in the extravagance of her resentment, expressing himself with the greatest harshness. Secretly flattered by the kinship of a nobleman, by whom he had pretended to forget the family line, he was incapable of being moved by the sufferings he could meet her niece in the path that marked her ambition.

Emilia soon saw all the difficulties that threatened her; and though no persecution could make her give up Valancourt for Morano, she quivered at the idea of his uncle's violence. To so much anger and so much indignation of her she opposed only the sweet dignity of a superior spirit; but the measured firmness of her conduct served only to exacerbate Quesnel's anger, by forcing him to acknowledge her inferiority. She finished by declaring to her that if she persisted in her folly for her, he and Montoni would abandon her to universal contempt.

The calm in which Emilia had maintained herself in the presence of her uncle abandoned her when she was alone: she wept bitterly; more than once she repeated the name of her father, of that tender father whom she no longer saw than she did, and whose warnings she had given her on her deathbed she remembered. « Alas! she said; « I know well now that the strength of courage is preferable to the graces of sensitivity. I will make every effort to fulfill my promise; I will not abandon myself to useless lamentations, and I will try to suffer with fortitude the oppression that I cannot avoid. »

Relieved in some way by her firm intention to partially fulfill her father's last wishes, she wiped away her tears, and appeared at the table with her usual serenity.

Towards evening, the ladies went to get some fresh air in Quesnel's carriage on the banks of the Brenta. Emilia's situation formed a melancholy contrast with the gaiety of the brilliant societies assembled under the trees along the delightful river. Some danced in the shade, others, lying on the grass, drank ice creams, ate fruit and savored in peace the sweetness of a beautiful evening in the sight of the most beautiful country in the world.

The girl, considering the distant snowy peaks of the Apennines, thought of the castle of

Montoni, and trembled at the idea that he would lead her there, and would know how to compel her to obey. This fear, however, vanished when he reflected that he was in his power in Venice, as it would be in any other part.

They returned to Miarenti very late; dinner was prepared in the magnificent rotunda already so much admired by Emilia: the ladies rested under the portico, until Quesnel, Montoni and other gentlemen came to join them. Emilia was making every effort to calm down when a boat suddenly stopped at the garden steps, and she heard Morano's voice, who appeared shortly after. She received his compliments in silence, and his coldness seemed at first to disconcert him, but afterwards he recovered, regained his vivacity, and the girl observed that the kind of flattery with which her uncles oppressed her, and with which she marveled strongly, it only excited his disgust.

As soon as she was able to retire, her reflections almost involuntarily wandered about the possible means of inducing the count to desist from his pretensions; her delicacy did not find more effective than that of confessing to him a bond already formed, and relying on his generosity for it. Nevertheless, when her question renewed her attention, Emilia abandoned that project: it would be too repugnant to her pride to reveal the secret of her heart to a man like Morano, and ask him for a sacrifice; so that she impatiently rejected the already conceived plan. She repeated her refusal in more decisive terms than she, and severely reproached her conduct towards her. The count seemed mortified, but continued to persist in his usual assurances of tenderness; the arrival of the Quesnel interrupted her, and it was a great relief for Emilia.

In this way, Emilia spent the most unhappy days in that delightful house because of the stubborn assiduity of Morano, and the cruel tyranny exercised over her by Quesnel and Montoni, who seemed, like their aunt, more resolute than ever to such a marriage. Quesnel, finally seeing that speeches and threats were equally useless to come to a prompt decision, he renounced it, and everything was left to the time and power of Montoni. Meanwhile Emilia wanted to return to Venice, hoping there to partially escape Morano's persecutions; on the other hand, Montoni, distracted by his occupations, would not always be at home. In the midst of her misfortunes, he too thought of strongly recommending poor Teresa to Quesnel who flattered her by promising that he would not forget her.

Montoni, in a long conversation, agreed with Quesnel the plan to be carried out with regard to his niece, and the latter promised to be in Venice soon after the celebration of the wedding.

Emilia for the first time felt no regret at separating from her relatives. Morano returned to Venice in the same boat as Montoni. The girl, who was gradually observing the approach of that superb city, saw herself close by the only person who could diminish her pleasure. They arrived about midnight; Emilia was freed from the presence of the count, who followed Montoni into a casino, and she was finally able to retire to her room.

The following day, in a brief conversation, the uncle declared to Emilia that he did not intend to be dragged out any longer; her marriage to her count was of such a prodigious advantage to her, that it would be madness to oppose it, and an inconceivable madness, and which would be celebrated without delay, and, if necessary, without her consent. The young woman, who until then had used her reasons, had recourse to her prayers: her pain prevented her from considering that, with a man of Montoni's character, her pleas would produce no better effect than her reasons. She then asked him by what right he exercised that unlimited authority over her. In a calmer state, she would not have risked this question which was of no use to her, and made Montoni triumph over her weakness and her isolation.

"By what right?" he exclaimed with a malicious smile; « with the right of my will; if you can escape from it, I will not ask you by what right you did so. I remind you for the last time: you are a foreigner, far from your homeland; you must be interested in having me as a friend, and you know the means; if you compel me to become your enemy, I will venture to say that the punishment will exceed your expectation; you should well know that I am not made to be mocked. »

Emilia remained motionless after Montoni had left her: she was desperate, or rather amazed; her feeling of her misery was the only one she had kept of her: Montoni found her in that state. Her maid raised her eyes, and the pain expressed by her whole person having no doubt moved her aunt, spoke to her with unusual goodness; Emilia's heart was moved by this, and after weeping a little for her, he mustered enough strength in her to tell her the subject of her grief, and to endeavor to interest her for her. The aunt's compassion had been surprised, but her ambition could not be restrained, and she believed she was already the aunt of a countess. The girl's attempts did not succeed better with her than with Montoni of hers: she returned to her room, and began to cry again, very determined to defy Montoni's revenge at all costs,

A little later a matter arose which suspended Montoni's attention for a few days; Orsino's mysterious visits had been renewed more frequently after Montoni's return. Cavignì, Verrezzi, and someone else, besides Orsino, were admitted to these councils nocturnal: Montoni became more reserved and severe than ever. If her own interests hadn't made her indifferent to everything else, Emilia would have noticed that she was meditating on some project.

One evening when there was no meeting to be held, Orsino arrived very agitated and sent a confidant of his to the casino in search of Montoni: he begged him to return home immediately, urging the messenger not to mention his name. Montoni returned instantly, found Orsino, and immediately learned the reason for his visit and agitation, already knowing a part of it.

A Venetian gentleman, who had recently provoked Orsino's hatred, had been stabbed by the latter's hired thugs. The deceased belonged to the first families, and the Senate had taken that matter to heart. One of the assassins was arrested, and confessed, Orsino was the offender. Upon hearing of his danger, he came to see Montoni to facilitate his escape, knowing that at that moment all the police officials were looking for him throughout the city, so that it was impossible for him to get out. Montoni agreed to hide him for a few days until vigilance was eased, and he could safely leave Venice. He knew the danger he was incurring by granting asylum to Orsino; but such was the nature of his obligations to this man, that he did not think it prudent to deny them.

Such was the person admitted by him into his confidence, and for whom he felt as much friendship as his character could carry.

For the entire time that Orsino remained hidden in the house, Montoni did not want to attract public attention by celebrating the count's wedding; but when the flight of the criminal had removed this obstacle, he informed Emilia that her wedding was to take place the following morning. She protested that she would never consent, and he replied with a malicious smile, assuring her that the count and a priest would be in her house very soon, and advising her not to challenge his resentment by an opposition contrary to her wishes. and to her own good.

"I'm going out all evening," he added: "remember that tomorrow I'll give your hand to Count Morano." »

Emilia, who, after his last threats, flattered herself that the crisis would come to an end, was little shaken by this declaration; she therefore studied the means of gaining courage considering that the marriage could not be valid as long as in the presence of the priest she would refuse to take part in the ceremony. The moment of the test was approaching, and she was equally agitated by the idea of revenge and by that of the hymene. Absolutely uncertain of the consequences of her refusal at the altar, she feared more than ever Montoni's unlimited power, and was convinced that she would ruthlessly transgress all the laws to succeed in her plans.

While she was immersed in this sea of worries, she was warned that Morano wanted to speak to her. As soon as the servant had gone out with her apologies, she regretted it, called him back, and wanting to test whether prayers and trust would produce a better effect than refusal and contempt, she made him say that she would go and see him herself.

The dignity and noble demeanor with which she moved towards the count, the resigned and thoughtful air which softened her physiognomy, were not capable means of making him renounce her, nor did they serve anything other than to increase a passion which had already intoxicated him. He listened to what she said with apparent complacency and a great desire to please him, but her resolve was invariable. He put the finest art and insinuation to work with her. She persuaded Emilia that she had nothing to hope from his justice, she solemnly repeated her protests of opposition, and she left him with the formal assurance that she would be able to remain negative even in spite of the violence. A just pride had held back the tears in Morano's presence, but as soon as she found herself alone, she wept bitterly, invoking her father, and attaching herself with inexpressible grief to the idea of Valancourt.

The evening was well advanced when Montoni entered her room with the wedding ornaments that the count had sent her. She had avoided her niece all day, fearing to give in to an unusual sensitivity of hers: she did not dare expose herself to Emilia's despair; and perhaps her conscience, whose language was so infrequent, reproached her for such harsh conduct towards her, an orphaned daughter of her brother, and whose happiness a dying father had entrusted her with.

Emilia did not want to see those presents, and tried, though without hope, a new and last effort to interest her aunt's sympathy. Moved perhaps alternately by her pity or remorse, she knew how to hide both, and she reproached her niece for the folly of afflicting herself with a marriage which could not fail to make her happy. "Of course," she said to her, "if I weren't married, and if the count were to offer me his hand, I'd be very flattered by this distinction. If I think I must think so, you, my niece, who are not rich, must undoubtedly find yourself very honored by it, and show gratitude and humility towards Morano, such as to correspond to her condescension. I am surprised, I confess, to see him so subdued and you so proud. I marvel at his patience, and, if I were him, I would certainly make you remember your duties a little better. I will not flatter you, I tell you frankly; it is this ridiculous flattery which gives you such and such an opinion of yourself, which makes you believe that there is no one who can deserve you. I have often told the count this; I paid no attention to the extravagance of his compliments, and you took them literally.

"Your patience, madame," said Emilia, "suffered much less then than mine."

"All this is pure affectation, nothing else," replied the aunt; « I know that flattery makes you proud and makes you so vain, that you naively believe that you see all men at your feet; but you are mistaken. I can assure you, my niece, that you will not find many adorers like the earl; anyone else would have turned their backs on you, and left you in belated repentance.

— Oh! why doesn't the count do what the others would do? Emilia said with a sigh.

"It is fortunate for you that it is not so," replied the aunt.

"I am not ambitious; I just want to stay in the state I'm in.

"It's not about that," added the aunt; 'I see you always think of that Valancourt. Drive away, I pray you, these lusts of love and this ridiculous pride; become reasonable. On the other hand, it's all useless chatter; you will be married tomorrow, whether you like it or not, you already know it: the count does not want to be your laughing stock any longer. »

The girl did not try to answer such a singular herring, feeling its uselessness. The aunt placed the count's presents on a table where Emilia was leaning, and wished her good evening. The orphan girl fixed her eyes on the door from which her aunt had come out; she listened attentively if any sound came to raise the dreadful despondency of her spirits. It was past midnight; everyone was asleep, except the servant who was waiting for the master. Her mind, prostrated by her sorrows, then yielded to imaginary terrors; she trembled considering the darkness of the large room in which she found herself; she feared without knowing why. She lasted in such a state for so long that she would have called Annetta, her aunt's maid, if her fear had allowed her to get up from her chair and cross the rooms. The gloomy illusions gradually vanished; she and she went to bed, try to calm the disorder of the heated imagination and gather the strength that would have been necessary for the following morning.

CHAPTER XIX

A knock on Emilia's door roused her from the kind of sleep she had fallen prey to. She jumped: Montoni and Morano immediately came to mind. She listened for a few moments, and recognizing Annetta's voice she risked opening the door.

"What brings you here so early?" »she asked her all trembling.

"Please, miss, don't be frightened; you are so pale that you frighten me too. Downstairs they make a great noise; all the servants come and go in fury, and no one can guess why.

"Who's with them?" Emilia said; "Annetta, don't deceive me.

- Heaven help me, for all the money in the world I wouldn't deceive you. I only saw that Signor Montoni shows extraordinary impatience, and he gave me the order to make you get up at the moment.

— Heavens! help me,' Emilia cried in despair. "So Count Morano has come?"

"No, miss, as far as I know he is not here. His Excellency sent me to tell you that in a moment the gondolas will be here, and we will leave Venice. I must hurry to get back to her mistress, who is so confused that she no longer knows what to do.

"But what does all this mean anyway?"

— Oh! Signora Emilia, all I know is that Signor Montoni returned home very agitated, and he made us all get up, declaring that we must leave at once.

"Is Count Morano coming with us?" and where do we go?

"I don't know. I understood that Lodovico was talking about a castle that the master has in certain mountains.

"In the Apennines?"

"Exactly, miss; but urge yourselves, and think of Signor Montoni's impatience. Good God! I can already hear the oars of the gondolas arriving. »

Annetta rushed out. Emilia prepared herself for this unexpected journey, and as soon as she had thrown her books and clothes into the trunk, she received a second notice; she went down to her aunt's lavatory, where Montoni reproached her for her slowness. He then went out to give some orders, and Emilia asked the reason for that sudden departure. The aunt seemed to be as ignorant of it as she was, and that she did not undertake that journey except with extreme repugnance.

Finally the whole family embarked, but neither Morano nor Cavignì showed up. This circumstance revived a little the dejected spirits of Emilia, who resembled a man condemned to death, who is granted a short reprieve: her heart lightened even more when they had gone round San Marco without stopping to pick up the Count .

Dawn was just beginning to whiten the horizon and the beach. Emilia did not dare to ask Montoni any questions, who remained for some time in gloomy silence, and then wrapped herself up in her cloak, as if she wanted to sleep. His wife did the same. Emilia, unable to sleep, raised a curtain and began to look at the sea. The dawn greatly illuminated the tops of the Friulian mountains; but their coasts and the waves that bathed them were nevertheless buried in the shadows: the girl, immersed in sweet melancholy, observed the progress of the day, which spread over the sea, illuminating Venice, its islets, and finally the Italian beaches, along which the boats were already starting to move. Gondoliers were often called by those who brought provisions to the Venice market. An infinite number of small boats covered the lagoon in a short time. Emilia cast her last gaze upon that magnificent city; but her mind then was occupied only with a thousand conjectures about the events that awaited her, about the country where she was being transported, and about the reason for that sudden journey.

After mature reflections, it seemed to her that Montoni was leading her to his isolated castle in order to compel her obedience more securely by means of terror. If the gloomy and solitary scenes which unfolded thereresortedthe longed-for outcome, his wedding would necessarily be celebrated there, and perhaps with greater mystery and less humiliation for Montoni's honour. The little courage rendered in her by her reprieve vanished at this dreadful idea, and when she hit shore, she was relapsed into the most pitiful dejection.

Montoni did not go back up the Brenta, but continued in the carriage to go to the Apennines. During this trip he was so severe with Emilia that this alone would have served to confirm his alarming conjectures about him.

Travelers began to climb the Apennines: at that time those mountains were covered by immense fir forests. The road passed through the middle of these woods, and left only terrifying cliffs hanging over their heads, unless some clearing allowed the underlying plain to be distinguished momentarily. The darkness of those places, their gloomy silence, when not even the slightest wind stirred the tops of the trees, the horror of the precipices that followed each other, each object, in a word, made Emilia's sad reflections more impressive. She saw around her only images of frightening grandeur and gloomy sublimity.

As the travelers climbed through the woods, the rocks piled up, the mountains seemed to multiply, and the top of an eminence seemed serve as a basis for another. Finally they found themselves on a small plain, where the muleteers stopped. The vast and magnificent scene which presented itself in the valley excited universal admiration, and even interested Signora Montoni. Emilia forgot her woes for a moment in the immensity of nature. Beyond an amphitheater of mountains, whose masses seemed as numerous as the waves of the sea, and whose slopes were covered with thick woods, the Italian countryside was revealed, where rivers, cities, olive groves, vineyards and all the prosperity of the crop mixed in rich confusion. The Adriatic circumscribed the horizon. The Po and the Brenta, after having fertilized the entire extension of the beautiful country, came to discharge their fertile waters. Emilia contemplated for a long time the splendor of those delightful places which she abandoned, and whose magnificence seemed to unfold before her except to cause her greater regret. For her, the whole world contained only Valancourt, her heart turned to him alone, and for him alone she shed so many tears.

From that sublime point of view the travelers continued to climb entering a narrow gorge that showed only menacing cliffs hanging over the road. No human vestige, no sign of vegetation appeared there. This gorge led into the heart of the Apennines. Finally it widened, discovering a chain of extremely sterile mountains, through which it was necessary to travel for several hours.

Toward evening, the road turned into a deeper valley, surrounded almost entirely by craggy mountains. The sun then set behind the same mountain that the travelers descended, extending its shadow towards the valley; but its horizontal rays, traversing some cleft, gilded the summits of the opposite forest, and glittered on the lofty towers and chimneys of a castle, whose vast ramparts extended down a terrifying precipice. The splendor of so many well-lit objects was enhanced by the contrast of the shadows that already enveloped the valley.

"Here is Udolfo's castle," Montoni said, speaking for the first time in several hours.

Emilia looked at the castle with a kind of terror when she learned that it was Montoni's; though illuminated at that moment by the setting sun, the gothic magnificence of that architecture, the ancient walls of gray stone, formed an imposing and sinister object. The light faded imperceptibly, shedding a purplish hue which gradually died out, and left the mountains, the castle, and all the surrounding objects in gloomy darkness.

Isolated, vast and massive, it seemed to dominate the country. The darker the night became, the more imposing its tall towers seemed. The extension and the darkness of those immense woods were considered by Emilia as suitable only to serve as a hideout for robbers. Finally, the carriages arrived at the castle gates. The long swing of the bell that was rung at the front door increased Emilia's terror. While she waited for someone to arrive to open those formidable shutters, she considered the majestic edifice. The darkness that enveloped it did not allow her to discern its enclosure, the thick walls, the crenellated ramparts and to realize that it was vast, ancient and frightening. The front door led into the courtyards, and was of gigantic proportions. Two very strong towers defended the passage. Instead of banners were seen fluttering up the uneven stones, very long grasses and wild plants clinging to the ruins, and which seemed to grow with difficulty in the midst of the desolation that surrounded them. The towers were joined by a curtain wall equipped with merlons and casemates. A heavy portcullis was falling from the top of the vault. From this gate, the walls of the ramparts communicated with other towers projecting over the precipice; but these nearly ruined walls showed the ravages of war. As Emilia watched so intently, she heard the heavy bolts open. An old servant appeared, and pushed the shutters open leaveenter his lord. While her wheels turned with a crash under those impenetrable shutters, Emilia felt her heart fail, believing she was entering her prison. The gloomy courtyard which they passed through confirmed their dismal idea of her; and her imagination of hers, always active, suggested to her a terror greater than her reason could justify it.

Another door introduced him into the second courtyard, even sadder than the first. She Emilia judged it in the dim light of twilight, seeing its high walls covered with ivy and moss, and its gigantic crenellated towers. The idea of her long sufferings and murder struck her imagination with sudden horror. This feeling did not diminish when she entered a Gothic hall, immense, dark. A face shining from afar through a long row of archways only served to make its darkness more perceptible.

Montoni's unexpected arrival had not allowed any preparations to receive him. The servant sent by him from Venice had preceded him by a few moments, and this circumstance in some way excused the state of nudity and disorder in the castle.

The servant who came to get some light greeted his master in silence, and his physiognomy was not animated by any appearance of pleasure. Montoni returned the greeting with a slight wave of his hand and passed. His wife followed him, looking around her with a surprise and a discontent which she seemed afraid to express. Emilia, seeing the immense extent of that building, with timid astonishment, approached a marble staircase. Here the arches formed a very high vault, from the center of which hung a lamp with three spouts, which the servant hurried to light. The richness of the frames, the size of a gallery that led to many apartments, and the colored glass of a Gothic window, were the objects that were subsequently discovered.

After having rounded the foot of the staircase and crossed an antechamber, they entered a very vast room. The black larch boarding increased the darkness.

"Bring some more lights," Montoni said as he entered. The servant put down the lamp and went out to obey. The mistress observed that the evening air was damp in that climate, and that she would like some fire: Montoni ordered some to be lit.

While he strolled thoughtfully about the room, Signora Montoni was resting silently on a sofa, awaiting the return of the servant. Emilia observed the imposing singularity and abandonment of that place, illuminated by a single lamp placed in front of itto the great mirror of Venice, which reflected the scene darkly, and the tall stature of Montoni, who passed and repassed with his arms crossed, and his face shaded by the feathers of his large hat. The old servant soon returned loaded with a bundle of wood and followed by two other servants with lights.

"Your Excellency is welcome," said the old man, after setting down the wood. « This castle has long been deserted. You'll excuse us knowing we had very little time. It will be two years on Saint Mark's day next, that your Excellency has not come here.

"Precisely," said Montoni, "you have a good memory, Carlo; how did you manage to live so long?

— Ah! sir, very hardly. The cold winds that blow in these places in the winter are bad for me. He had more than once thought of asking Your Excellency's permission to let me leave the mountains to withdraw into the valley; but I don't know how it is, I can't resolve to abandon these old walls where I have lived for so many years.

"Good," said Montoni; « What did you do in this castle after my departure?

'More or less as usual; but all is ruined here: there is the north tower which needs to be compensated; many fortifications are in a bad state; part of the roof of the great hall collapsed, and nearly fell on my poor wife's head (God rest her). All the winds went down there last winter. We nearly died of cold.

— Are there any other repairs to be made? said Montoni impatiently.

— Oh! yes, excellency. The bastion is ruined in three places. The stairs of the north-facing gallery are filled with so much rubble that it is dangerous to pass through them. The corridor leading to the oak room is in the same state. One evening I ventured there; And...

"Enough, enough," said Montoni earnestly; "We'll talk about it tomorrow morning. »

The fire was already lit. Carlo swept the fireplace, arranged the chairs, dusted a nearby marble table and went out.

Our characters approached the fire. Montoni tried to strike up a conversation, but her husband's brusque replies distracted her. Emilia tried to cheer up, and in a trembling voice she said: 'May I ask you, sir, the reason for this sudden departure? »After a long pause she had enough courage to repeat her question.

"I don't like answering questions," said Montoni, "just as you don't want to. Time will explain everything. I now wish not to be bothered any longer. I advise you to adopt a more reasonable course. All these ideas of alleged sensitivity are, to put it bluntly, nothing but weaknesses. »

Emilia got up to leave. "Good night," she said to her aunt, hiding her emotion with difficulty.

"Good night, my dear," she replied with an accent of extraordinary goodness in her. Her unexpected tenderness made the girl cry, and, having said goodbye to Montoni, she set off. "But you don't know where your room is?" the aunt added. Montoni called the servant who was waiting in the antechamber and ordered him to bring in his wife's maid, who arrived shortly after and followed Emilia.

"Do you know where my room is?" she said to Annetta as she crossed the hall.

"I think I do, miss, but it is a very extravagant room; it is situated on the southern bastion, and you go there from the grand staircase: the lady's room is at the other end of the castle. »

Emilia climbed the ladder and entered the corridor. Walking through it, Annetta resumed the chatter.

« This castle is a lonely and sad place; I tremble all over to think that I must sojourn there. Oh! how many times have I regretted having abandoned France! I never expected, when I followed the lady around the world, to be imprisoned in such a place. Oh! I would not have left my country, even if they covered me with gold.

"This way, miss, turn left. Indeed, I am almost tempted to believe in giants. This castle seems to have been made especially for them. We'll see some goblins some night; some must appear in that great hall, which, in its heavy pillars, looks more like a church than anything else.

"Yes," said Emilia, smiling, glad to escape more serious thoughts, "if we came here at midnight and looked into the vestibule, we would certainly see it illuminated by more than a thousand lamps." All the spirits would dance around to delightful music; it is customary always to keep their congregations in similar places. I'm afraid, Annetta, you don't have enough courage toassistyeah nice show. If you spoke, everything would instantly vanish.

"And therefore I think that if I live here for a while, I too will become a shadow."

'I hope you won't confide your fears to Signor Montoni; they would be very sorry.

- As! So you know everything, miss? Oh! ninth. I know what I have to do, and if the master can sleep in peace, certainly everyone here can do the same... For this passage, young lady; it leads to a ladder. Oh! if I see something, I will definitely pass out.

"It's not possible," said Emilia, smiling, and turning the passage that led to another tunnel. Annetta then realized that she had taken the wrong road, and she became more and more lost along other corridors: she finally frightened by their rounds and their loneliness, she cried out asking for help; but the servants were on the other side of the castle, and could not hear her. Emilia opened the door of a room on the left. The waitress exclaimed:

"Don't go in there, lady, we'll get lost even more."

— Bring the light: we will find our way through all these rooms. »

Annetta stood hesitating at the door; she held out the lamp to let the room be seen, but her rays did not penetrate halfway through it. "Why don't you come in?" Emilia said; « let me see where it goes from here. »

The other advanced reluctantly. The room overlooked access to an escape of ancient and spacious rooms. The furniture that adorned them was as old as the walls, and retained an appearance of grandeur, though worn by time and dust.

"How cold it is here," said Annetta; 'it is said that no one has lived there for many centuries. Let's go away.

"Perhaps we can get to the grand staircase this way," replied Emilia, and continuing on, they found themselves in a room decorated with paintings; she took the lamp to examine that of a soldier on horseback on the battlefield. He pointed his sword at a man lying at the feet of his steed, and who seemed to beg his mercy. The soldier, with his visor up, looked at him with an air of vengeance.

This expression and the whole complex surprised Emilia by its resemblance to Montoni; she shivered and looked away. As she passed her other paintings with the lamp, she saw one covered by a black veil; this singularity struck her; stopped with the intention of lifting the veil and considering what was so carefully hidden therein; she too hesitated. « Madonna! cried Annetta; what does this even mean? It is certainly painting, the painting that was talked about in Venice.

- What painting? Emilia said. "What painting?"

"A picture," answered Annetta, trembling and pale. 'I never knew what it was.

"Lift that veil, Annetta.

- Who? I, miss, I? No, for all the gold in the world.

"But what did you learn about this painting, which frightens you so much?

"Nothing, miss, I was told nothing. Let's go away.

"Sure, but I want to see the picture first; take the light, Annetta, I will lift the veil. »

The maid took the lamp and fled hastily, without wanting to listen to Emilia, who, not wanting to remain in the dark, was forced to follow her.

"But what's wrong, Annetta?" What were you told about that picture, that you run away when I beg you to stay?

"I don't know why, and they haven't told me anything." All I know is that there was something scary about it; that afterwards he was always kept covered in a black veil, and that no one has seen him for a long time. This is said to have some connection with the person who owned the castle before it belonged to the master; And...

"Very well, Annetta, I realize that in fact you know nothing about the picture."

"No, not really, miss; because they made me promise never to talk about it. But...

"In that case," added Emilia, seeing her torn by the desire to reveal a secret, and by the fear of the consequences, "in that case, I don't want to know more."

"No, miss; don't ask me.

"You would say everything. »

Annetta blushed, Emilia smiled; they finished traversing those rooms, and finally found themselves at the top of the staircase. The maid left the mistress to call a servant of the castle, and be led to the room in vain sought.

Meanwhile Emilia was thinking about the painting. Her curiosity prompted her to go back to examine it; but the hour, the place, the gloomy silence that reigned around her, all turned her away. She too resolved to return with the new day to the mysterious painting and lift its veil.

The servant finally appeared, and took Emilia to her room, located at the end of the castle and at the end of the corridor, onto which the row of rooms that had crossings opened. The deserted aspect of that room made the girl want to that Annetta did not leave immediately. The damp cold that was felt there chilled her as much as the fear of her; she begged Catherine, the castle's servant, to light her some fire.

"Oh! Signorina, it has been many years since a fire has been lit in this room,' said the maid.

"There was no need to tell us, good woman," added Annetta; "All the rooms of this castle are as cool as wells in summer time: I wonder you can live in such a place." For me, I would like to be in Venice, or rather France. »

Emilia nodded to Caterina to go get some wood.

"I don't understand," said the maid, "why this is called the double room." »

Meanwhile the mistress was observing her in silence, and found her tall and spacious like all the others she had already seen. Her walls were larch-boarded; the bed and other furniture seemed very old, and had that air of gloomy grandeur which was observed throughout the building. She opened a large window; but the darkness did not allow her to make out anything.

In Annetta's presence, Emilia tried to contain herself and hold back her tears. She anxiously wanted to know when she was expecting Count Morano at the castle; but she feared making a useless inquiry, and divulging family interests in the presence of her servants. Meanwhile, Annetta's thoughts were occupied with very different objects: she was very fond of the marvellous; he had heard of a circumstance relating to the castle, which greatly aroused her curiosity about her. They had recommended her secret to her and her desire to talk about her was so violent that she was about to tell everything at any moment. It was such a strange circumstance! Not being able to talk about it was a severe punishment for her; but Montoni could impose stricter ones on her and she was afraid of provoking him.

Caterina brought the wood, and the sparkling flame somewhat dispelled the lugubrious mist of the room; the maid told Annetta that her mistress was looking for her: Emilia was left alone, prey to her sad reflections. To escape it, she got up to take a closer look at the room and the furniture. She saw a loosely closed door; but realizing that she was not the one through whom she had entered, she took the light to find out where she was leading her. She opened it, and saw the steps of a secret stairway. She wanted to see where she put her, especially as she communicated with her room; but in the present state of her spirit she lacked the courage to go further than her. She closed the door, and tried to free it, having observed that on the inside it had no bolt, while on the outside there were as many as two. By propping up a heavy chair, she partly remedied the danger; but she was very afraid of being forced to sleep in that isolated room, alone and with a door of which she didn't know the outcome. She almost wanted to go and beg Signora Montoni to allow Annetta to spend the night with her, but she rejected this idea, convinced that her fears would be called childish, and so as not to shock too much the young girl's already disturbed imagination. These afflicting reflections were interrupted by the sound of footsteps in the corridor: it was Annetta and her servant who were bringing her dinner from her aunt. He sat down at the table by the fire, and made the maid eat with her. Encouraged by this condescension, and by the splendor and warmth of the fire, the good girl drew her chair up to Emilia's, and said to her: She almost wanted to go and beg Signora Montoni to allow Annetta to spend the night with her, but she rejected this idea, convinced that her fears would be called childish, and so as not to shock too much the young girl's already disturbed imagination. These afflicting reflections were interrupted by the sound of footsteps in the corridor: it was Annetta and her servant who were bringing her dinner from her aunt. He sat down at the table by the fire, and made the maid eat with her. Encouraged by this condescension, and by the splendor and warmth of the fire, the good girl drew her chair up to Emilia's, and said to her: She almost wanted to go and beg Signora Montoni to allow Annetta to spend the night with her, but she rejected this idea, convinced that her fears would be called childish, and so as not to shock too much the young girl's already disturbed imagination. These afflicting reflections were interrupted by the sound of footsteps in the corridor: it was Annetta and her servant who were bringing her dinner from her aunt. He sat down at the table by the fire, and made the maid eat with her. Encouraged by this condescension, and by the splendor and warmth of the fire, the good girl drew her chair up to Emilia's, and said to her: and so as not to shake the young girl's already altered imagination even too much. These afflicting reflections were interrupted by the sound of footsteps in the corridor: it was Annetta and her servant who were bringing her dinner from her aunt. He sat down at the table by the fire, and made the maid eat with her. Encouraged by this condescension, and by the brightness and warmth of the fire, the good girl drew her chair up to Emilia's, and said to her: and so as not to shake the young girl's already altered imagination even too much. These afflicting reflections were interrupted by the sound of footsteps in the corridor: it was Annetta and her servant who were bringing her dinner from her aunt. He sat down at the table by the fire, and made the maid eat with her. Encouraged by this condescension, and by the brightness and warmth of the fire, the good girl drew her chair up to Emilia's, and said to her:

'Have you ever heard, miss, of the strange chance which put the master in possession of this castle?'

"What wonderful story was ever told to you? replied Emilia, trying to hide the keen curiosity that tormented her.

"I know everything," added Annetta, looking around and drawing them closer and closer; 'Benedetto told me everything on the way. "Annetta," he said to me, "don't you know anything about that castle we're going to?" "No," I answered him, Signor Benedetto; and what do you know? "But I flatter myself you'll be able to keep a secret, or I wouldn't tell you anything for all the gold in the world. "I promised not to talk about it, and he assures himself that the master would be very sorry if he talked about it.

"If you promised the secret," said Emilia, "you do wrong to reveal it." »

Annetta was silent for a while, then added: "Oh! but for you, young lady, I know very well that I can confide everything to you. »

Emilia began to laugh, saying: 'I will keep silent as faithfully as you. »

Annetta replied gravely, that it was indispensable, and continued: 'You must know that this castle is very old and well fortified; it is said that it has already sustained several sieges, and it did not always belong to Signor Montoni, nor to his father; but by any disposition he was bound to take possession of it if the lady died without marrying.

"What lady?" Emilia said.

"Slowly," added Annetta; "She is the lady I will come to tell you about. She lived in the castle, and had, as you can imagine, a large train. Her master often came to visit her; he fell in love with her and offered to marry her; they were distantly related, but that didn't matter. The lady loved another man, and she would have nothing to do with him, so they say he was furious with her; and you well know what a man he is when he is angry. Perhaps she saw him in one of these transports, and she refused him. But, as she told you, she seemed sad, unhappy, and that for a long time. Hate! What noise is this? Don't you hear, miss?

"It's the wind," said Emilia; "Continue your story.

'As she told you, she was afflicted and unhappy, she walked alone on the terrace, under the windows, and there she wept bitterly... I heard all of this in Venice; but what follows, I only learned today: the case happened many years ago, when Signor Montoni was still young; the lady's name was Signora Laurentini; she was beautiful, but she often got angry, like her master. Realizing that she didn't want to listen to him, what does she do? she leaves the castle, and she never returns; but that mattered little to her, since he too was unhappy when he was absent. Finally one evening,' the girl added, lowering her voice, and looking around uneasily, 'according to what they say, towards the end of the year, that is, in mid-September, or in early October, I suppose, or perhaps even mid-November... it doesn't matter, it's always towards the end of the year: but I can't specify the moment, because they didn't tell me either. In addition, towards the end of the year, this lady went for a walk outside the castle in the nearby wood, as she usually did. She was alone, with her maid: she was cold; and the wind, sweeping away the leaves, blew sadly through those big chestnut trees we passed yesterday: Benedetto showed me the trees while he told them. The wind was therefore very cold, and the maid begged her to go back, but she would not agree to it, as she enjoyed walking through the woods in any season, especially in the evening; and if dry leaves fell around her, she was more pleased. Well! she was seen descending towards the wood; evening came, and it did not appear. Ten o'clock struck, eleven o'clock, midnight, and was not seen to return; the servants, thinking that some misfortune had befallen her, went in search of her; they searched all night, but found none, and could have none no clues. They have heard nothing more since that day.

- It's really true? Emilia said in surprise.

"Very true, madame," answered Annetta in horror; " Unfortunately it's true. But it is said,' she added in a low voice, 'that for some time now Signora Laurentini had been seen several times at night in the woods and on the outskirts of the castle; some of the old servants, who remained here after her sad case, assure that they have seen her. The old farmer could tell very strange things, it is said.

What a contradiction! Emilia added; "You say that she was never heard of again, and then you assert that she was seen.

"All this was told to me in the utmost secrecy," continued Annetta, paying no attention to the observation; "I'm sure you won't do us an injustice to Benedetto and me by talking about this fact."

"Don't be afraid of my indiscretion," replied Emilia; « but allow me to advise you to be a little more prudent, and not to reveal to anyone what you have said to me. Mr. Montoni, as you say, could very well get angry if he heard of it. But what research was done about this unfortunate woman?

— Oh! endless, because the master had rights to the castle, being the closest relative of Signora Laurentini; and it is said that the judges, senators, and others declared that he could not take possession of it until after many years, and that if after this period of time the lady had not been found, then the castle would have belonged to him. as if she were dead. But the fact spread, and so many strange rumors spread about it, that I dare not even mention them to you...

"It's strange," said Emilia; «But when Signora Laurentini then reappeared in the castle, did she not speak to anyone?»

- Spoke! talk to her! cried Annetta with fright. 'No, no, and then no, rest assured.

- Why not? Emilia said, longing to know more.

- Holy Mother! Talk to a spirit!

"But what reason is there to believe she was a spirit, if no one approached her, and if no one spoke to her?"

— Oh! Miss, I can't tell you that. How can you ask me such extravagant questions? But no one saw her come and go in the castle. Now they were seeing her on one site, and a little later she was on another. She did not speak, and if she had been alive, what would she have done in this castle without speaking? there are even several places where no one has dared to go, and always for the same reason.

Why didn't she speak? Emilia said, forcing herself to laugh, despite her fear that he was beginning to possess her.

"No," replied Annetta annoyed; 'but because we could see something. There is also said to be an old chapel in the western part of the castle, where groans are sometimes heard at midnight. I cringe just thinking about it! very extraordinary things have been seen there.

"End it once with these fairy tales.

- Tales! young lady, I can tell you about a story that Caterina told me. It was a cold winter evening, and Caterina was sitting in the living room with old Carlo and his wife. Carlo wanted to eat figs, and he instructed the maid to go and look for some in the pantry, which was at the end of the northern gallery. Caterina took the lamp... Shut up, lady, I hear a crash!... »

Emilia, in whom Annetta had then made her fear pass, listened attentively; but she heard nothing. The maid continued: 'Caterina went to the gallery ... she is the one we passed through before coming here. She went with the lamp in her hand without any fear... Again! »she exclaimed suddenly; « I have heard again: now I am not deceived.

- Shut up! said Emilia all trembling. They listened, and stood still. A knock was heard in the wall. Annetta let out a loud cry, the door opened slowly, and they saw Caterina enter, who had come to tell the maid that her mistress was looking for her. Annetta, laughing and crying, reproached Caterina for having frightened her so much: she was afraid she had heard what she had said. Emilia, deeply struck by the main circumstance of Annetta's story, would not have wanted to remain alone in the present situation; but she, in order to avoid Signora Montoni's sarcasm and not betray her own weakness, fought against the illusions of her fear, and dismissed Annetta for the whole night.

When she was alone, she thought of Signora Laurentini's strange story, and then of the situation in which she found herself in that terrible castle, in the middle of deserts and mountains, in a foreign country, under the dominion of a man she hadn't known a few months before. , and whose character he regarded with a horror justified by the general terror which he inspired. Then, remembering the prophetic fears of Valancourt, her heart was painfully tightened, giving way to vain regrets.

The wind, whistling loudly outside in the corridor, increased her melancholy. Emilia remained fixed in front of the cold ashes of the extinguished hearth, when an impetuous gust, penetrating those corridors with a frightening noise, shook doors and windows, and frightened her all the more as it moved, in the shock, the chair which she had used to free the door of the ladder, which was ajar. Frozen with terror of her, she stood still, she then plucked up courage, and she ran to secure him as best she could; then I went to bed, leaving the lamp on the table; but that gloomy light doubled his fear. In the trembling of the uncertain rays she always seemed to see shadows moving in the dark background of the room, and appearing right up to the curtains of the bed. The castle clock struck an hour before she could fall asleep.

CHAPTER XX

The daylight dispelled the vapors of superstition, but not those of fear. She got up, and to distract herself from the importunate ideas, she tried to deal with external objects. She gazed from the window at the wild grandeur that offered her; the mountains stacked one on top of the other, only allowed to see narrow valleys shaded by thick woods. The vast ramparts, the various buildings of the castle, extended along a steep rock at the foot of which a torrent roared as it rushed under age-old fir trees into a deep ravine. A light mist filled the distant fondure, and gradually fading in the rays of the sun, she discovered the trees, the coasts, the herds and the shepherds.

Observing these admirable views, Emilia found herself somewhat relieved.

The fresh morning air did a great deal to revive her. She lifted her thoughts to heaven, as she felt more and more peaceful when she tasted the sublimities of nature. As she withdrew from the window, she turned her eyes to the door she had so carefully secured the previous night. She was determined to examine the success of it, when, as she approached to remove her chair, she realized that she had already been pushed back a little. It is impossible to describe her surprise at finding the door closed afterwards. She was astonished as if she had seen a ghost. The door to the corridor was closed as she had left it; but the other, which could only be closed from the outside, it had necessarily been during the night. She was frightened at the idea of having to sleep again in a room which was so easy to get into, and so far from any assistance: she therefore decided to tell Signora Montoni, and ask her to change the room.

After some difficulty, she managed to find the room from the previous evening, where breakfast was already being prepared. Her aunt was alone, Montoni having gone to visit the surroundings of the castle, to examine the state of the fortifications in the company of Carlo. Emilia noticed that her aunt had been crying, and her heart was moved for her with a feeling that showed itself more in her manners than in her words. In spite of this, she plucked up courage, and taking advantage of Montoni's absence, she asked for another room, and informed him of the reason for that trip. On her first article, her aunt sent her back to Montoni, refusing to mix with her; and on the second, she protested the utterest ignorance of her. They then spoke of the castle and the country that surrounded it; and the aunt could not resist the pleasure of making fun of the good Emilia about her taste for the beauties of nature.

Emilia, who was silently observing him, saw in his physiognomy an expression more gloomy and severe than usual. — Oh! if I could guess,' she said to herself, 'the thoughts and plans of that head, I would not be condemned to this cruel state of uncertainty! Before the end of breakfast, which passed in silence, Emilia ventured the question of changing rooms, attaching the reasons which led her to do so.

"I don't have time to occupy myself with these trifles," said Montoni; 'that is the room that was intended for you, and you must be content with it. It is not presumable that no one has taken the trouble to climb a ladder to close a door; if it wasn't when you entered, it is highly probable that the wind has blown a latch. But I don't know why I should concern myself with such a frivolous circumstance. »

This answer did not satisfy Emilia at all, who had noticed how rusty the bolts were, and consequently not so easy to move. She didn't make this remark of hers known, but she asked again.

"If you want to be a slave to such fears," Montoni said severely, "at least refrain from molesting the others. Know how to overcome all these frivolities, and occupy yourself with fortifying your spirit. You do not start a more despicable existence than one poisoned by fear.» Saying yes, he looked fixedly at his wife, who blushed and did not utter a word. Emilia, disconcerted and offended, then found her fears too justified to deserve such sarcasms; but seeing that any remark on the subject would be quite useless, she changed the subject.

Carlo entered shortly thereafter bearing fruit. "Your Excellency must be tired from that long walk," said he, placing the fruit on the table; "but after breakfast we have much more to see: there is a place, in the underground road, which leads to..."

Montoni frowned and motioned for him to withdraw. Carlo broke off the conversation and lowered his eyes; then, approaching the table, he added: "I have taken the liberty, Your Excellency, of bringing some cherries for my mistresses: deign to taste them," he said, presenting the basket to the women; « they are very good; I picked them myself; you see, they're as big as plums.»

"Let's go, let's go," said Montoni impatiently, "that's enough. Go out and wait for me, as I will need you.» When the two spouses were retired, Emilia tried to distract herself by examining the castle. She opened a large door and passed over the ramparts, surrounded on three sides by precipices. The breadth of them and the varied country they dominated excited her admiration. Walking through them, she often stopped to contemplate the Gothic magnificence of Udolfo, his proud irregularity, the high towers, the fortifications, the narrow windows, the numerous loopholes in the turrets. Leaning over the parapet, she measured with her eyes the frightful abyss of the underlying precipice, whose depth was still hidden by the black tops of the woods. Wherever she looked, she saw only steep peaks, gloomy fir trees and narrow gorges, which entered the Apennines and disappeared from sight among those inaccessible regions. She was so intent when she saw Montoni accompanied by two men who were climbing a path dug in the rock. He stopped on a hillock looking at the rampart, and turning to the escort, he expressed himself with a very energetic air and gestures. Emilia realized that one of them was Carlo, and that Montoni's orders were directed only to the other, dressed as a peasant. She withdrew from the wall at the sudden crash of several carriages and the tinkling of the entrance bell, and the idea immediately occurred to her that Count Morano had arrived. She hastily returned to her room, agitated by a thousand fears; she ran to the window, and on the bastion she saw Montoni strolling with Cavignì: they seemed to be having a very animated conversation. and turning to the escort, he expressed himself with a very energetic air and gestures. Emilia realized that one of them was Carlo, and that Montoni's orders were directed only to the other, dressed as a peasant. She withdrew from the wall at the sudden crash of several carriages and the tinkling of the entrance bell, and she immediately got the idea that Count Morano had arrived. She hastily returned to her room, agitated by a thousand fears; she ran to the window, and on the bastion she saw Montoni strolling with Cavignì: they seemed to be having a very animated conversation. and turning to the escort, he expressed himself with a very energetic air and gestures. Emilia realized that one of them was Carlo, and that Montoni's orders were directed only to the other, dressed as a peasant. She withdrew from the wall at the sudden crash of several carriages and the tinkling of the entrance bell, and she immediately got the idea that Count Morano had arrived. She hastily returned to her room, agitated by a thousand fears; she ran to the window, and on the bastion she saw Montoni strolling with Cavignì: they seemed to be having a very animated conversation. entrance, and the idea immediately occurred to her that Count Morano had arrived. She hastily returned to her room, agitated by a thousand fears; she ran to the window, and on the bastion she saw Montoni strolling with Cavignì: they seemed to be having a very animated conversation. entrance, and the idea immediately occurred to her that Count Morano had arrived. She hastily returned to her room, agitated by a thousand fears; she ran to the window, and on the bastion she saw Montoni strolling with Cavignì: they seemed to be having a very animated conversation.

While she was flustered and perplexed, she heard footsteps in the corridor, and Annetta entered.

« Ah! Signorina,' she said, 'Signor Cavignì has arrived: I am delighted to finally see a Christian face in this place. He is so good, he has always shown me so much interest .... There is also Signor Verrezzi, and another whom you would never guess.

"Count Morano perhaps, I suppose..." And giving in to emotion, she almost fainted on the chair.

"The count?" But who tells you? No, miss, he is not here, take heart.

"Are you quite sure of that?"

'Praise God,' Annetta added, 'that you recovered quickly. In truth, she thought you were dying.

--But are you quite sure that the count isn't here?

— Oh! very sure. I was looking out of a window in the north turret when the carriages arrived: such a dear sight certainly did not await me in this dreadful citadel. But now there are masters, servants, and there is a bit of movement. We'll be merry: we'll go dance and sing in the living room, which is far from the master's apartment. But, by the way, Lodovico came with them. You must remember Lodovico, Signora Emilia: that handsome young man who steered the knight's gondola in the last regatta, and won the prize! The one who sang such beautiful poems, always under my window, in the moonlight, in Venice! Oh! as I listened to it!

— I fear those verses have not won your heart, my Annetta. But if that's the case, remember not to let them figure it out. Now I'm back, and you can leave me.

"I forgot to ask you how you were able to rest in this ancient and dreadful chamber last night.

"As usual.

"So you heard no noise?"

- No.

"Have you seen anything?"

- Not at all.

- It is surprising.

"But tell me, why are you asking me these questions?"

— Oh! miss, I wouldn't tell you for all the gold in the world, much less what I was told about this room... You'd be too frightened.

"If so, you've already scared me. So you can tell me everything you know about it without aggravating your conscience.

— Lord God! spirits are said to appear in this room, and for quite some time.

"If it's true, he's got a spirit who knows how to close the bolts very well," said Emilia, forcing herself to laugh, despite her fear. 'Yesterday evening I left that door open, and this morning I found it closed. »

Annetta turned pale and was silent.

"Did you hear that some servant closed this door this morning before I got up?"

"No, Signora Emilia, I swear I don't know, but I'll go and ask," said Annetta, running to the corridor door.

"Stop, Annetta, I have more questions for you." Tell me what you know about this chamber and the secret stairway.

"I'll go and ask right away, miss; and besides, I'm convinced that the mistress will need me, and I can't stay any longer. »And she left quickly, without waiting for an answer. Emilia, relieved by the certainty that Morano had not arrived, could not help laughing at Annetta's sudden superstitious terror, though she too resented it.

Montoni had denied Emilia another room, and she resolved to bear in resignation the evil she could not avoid. She endeavored to make her habitation as comfortable as she could; she placed her little library of hers on a large wardrobe, delight of happy days, and consolation in her melancholy of hers, she prepared the pencils, having decided to draw the sublime point of view that was seen from the window; but remembering how many times she had undertaken a distraction of that kind elsewhere too, and how many times she had been prevented by new unforeseen misfortunes, she hesitated to get ready for work, disturbed by the presumed imminent arrival of the count.

To avoid these painful reflections, he began to read; but his attention, unable to fix itself on the book in his hand, threw it on the table, and resolved to visit the castle. Recalling the strange story of the former owner, he remembered the picture covered by the veil, and resolved to go and discover it. Crossing the rooms that led to it, she felt strongly agitated: the relations of that picture with the lady of the castle, Annetta's speech, the circumstance of the veil, the mystery of that affair, aroused in her soul a slight feeling of terror, but of that terror which takes possession of the spirit, it raises it to grandiose ideas, and, for one species of magic, to the object itself, which is its cause.

Emilia walked trembling, and stopped a moment at the door before resolving to open it. She advanced towards the picture, which seemed to be of extraordinary size and was located in a corner; she stopped again; in the end, with a timid hand she lifted the veil, but quickly let it fall. It wasn't a painting she had seen, and before she could escape, she passed out on the floor.

When she had recovered the use of her senses, the memory of what she had seen almost made her faint a second time, and she had scarcely the strength to leave that place and return to her chamber. When she returned, she did not have the courage to remain alone. Her horror possessed her entirely, and when she was somewhat recovered, she could not decide whether to inform Signora Montoni of what she had seen; but the fear of being mocked again, determined her to keep silent. She sat at the window to gather courage. Montoni and Verrezzi passed shortly thereafter; they talked and laughed, and their voices cheered her somewhat. Bertolini and Cavigni joined them on the terrace. Emilia, then assuming that Signora Montoni was alone, went out to go to her. Her aunt was dressing for lunch. The pallor and consternation of her niece surprised her greatly, but the girl had strength enough to keep silent, though her lip was at every moment about to betray her. She stayed in her aunt's flat until lunchtime; she found there the strangers, who had an unusual air of concern, and seemed distracted by interests too important to pay attention to Emilia or her aunt: they spoke little, and Montoni even less: Emilia trembled to see him. The horror of that room was always before her, and she changed color fearing she could not contain the emotion; but she was able to overcome herself, taking an interest in speeches and affecting a hilarity that did not agree with the sadness of the heart. Montoni evidently seemed to be thinking about some great operation. The meal was silent. The sadness of that stay even influenced Cavigni's cheerful character.

Count Morano was not named. The conversation turned entirely to the wars that were tearing Italy apart in those times, to the strength of the Venetian militias and the skill of the generals. After lunch, Emilia understood that the knight on whom Orsino had satiated his vengeance had died as a result of the wounds he had received, and that the murderer was being sought with care. This news seemed to alarm Montoni; but he knew how to dissemble, and inquired where Orsino was hidden. The guests, with the exception of Cavigni, unaware that Montoni in Venice had aided his escape, replied that he had escaped that same night in such haste and secrecy that not even his closest friends had heard anything about it.

Emilia withdrew shortly afterwards with Signora Montoni, leaving those gentlemen occupied in their councils secrets. Montoni had already warned his wife, with expressive nods, to withdraw. This she went to the ramparts to walk, nor opened her mouth: Emilia did not interrupt the course of her thoughts. It needed all her firmness to refrain from communicating to her aunt the terrible subject of the picture. She felt all convulsed, and was tempted to tell her everything in order to relieve her heart; but she, considering that an imprudence of her aunt could lose them both, she preferred to suffer a present malady rather than submit to a greater one in the future. She had strange premonitions that day. It seemed to her that her fate chained her to that gloomy place. Nevertheless, the remembrance of Valancourt, the perfect trust which she had in her, her constant love for her, were enough to pour the balm of consolation into her bosom.

As he leaned against the parapet of the rampart, he saw several workmen and a pile of stones which seemed destined to fill a breach. He also saw an ancient cannon disassembled. The aunt stopped to talk to the workers, asking them what they were doing. "We want to compensate for the fortifications, madame," said one of them. She was surprised that Montoni was thinking of those jobs, especially since he had never expressed his intention of staying there for a long time. She advanced towards a high arch which led to the south rampart, and which, being joined on one side to the castle, supported a watchtower which commanded the whole valley. As she approached that archway, she saw a large troop of horses and men descending from the woods in the distance, whom he recognized as soldiers only by the splendor of the spears and other weapons, since the distance did not allow him to judge the colors exactly. As he watched, the vanguard moved out of the woods, but the troop continued to spread out to the edge of the mountain. The military uniform stood out in the front rows, at the head of which forwarded the commander, who seemed to direct the march of the ranks, gradually approaching the castle.

Such a spectacle, in those solitary districts, singularly surprised and alarmed Montoni, who ran hurriedly to some peasants who worked on the other bastion, to ask them what that troop was. Queglino could not give her any satisfactory answer; and, also surprised, stupidly watched the ride. The lady, thinking it necessary to communicate to her husband the subject of her surprise at her, sent Emilia to warn him that she wished to speak to him. The niece did not approve of the embassy, fearing her uncle's bad mood; she too obeyed without opening her mouth.

As she approached the rooms where Montoni was with the guests, Emilia heard a violent argument. She stopped fearing the anger her unexpected arrival might produce. A little later everyone fell silent; then she dared to open the door. Montoni turned quickly and looked at her without speaking; she carried out the commission. "Tell the lady I'm busy," she answered.

The girl thought it best to tell him the reason for the embassy. Montoni and the others got up quickly and ran to the windows; but, not seeing the troops, they went to the bastion, and Cavignì conjectured it must be a legion of leaders marching for Modena. Part of that soldiery was then in the valley, the other was going up the mountains to the west, and the rearguard was still on the edge of the precipices whence they had come. While Montoni and the others watched that military march, the ringing of trumpets and timpani was heard, the sharp sounds of which were repeated by the echoes. Montoni explained the signals, of which he seemed to be an expert, and concluded that there was nothing hostile about them. The uniform of the soldiers and the quality of weapons confirmed this in the opinion of Cavigni; he had the satisfaction of seeing them dismissed, nor retired until they had entirely disappeared.

Emilia, not feeling sufficiently recovered to bear the solitude of her room, remained on the rampart until evening. The men dined among themselves. Signora Montoni did not leave her rooms: Emilia went to her before retiring, and found her weeping and agitated. The tenderness of her niece was naturally so insinuating, that she almost always succeeded in consoling her grieving ones; but her sweetest expressions were useless with her aunt. She pretended, with her usual delicacy, not to observe her pain, but in her manners she used such exquisite grace, such affectionate attention, that her proud one was offended. To excite her niece's pity was such a cruel affront to her pride in her that she hastened to dismiss her. Emilia did not tell her of her extreme repugnance at being isolated; she only asked in favor that Annetta could stay with her until it was time to go to bed. She barely got it; and since Annetta was then with her servants, she had to retire alone. She traversed the long tunnels quickly. The faint glow of the lamp served only to make the darkness more sensitive, and the wind threatened to extinguish it at every moment. Passing in front of the series of rooms visited in the morning, she thought she heard some sound, but I was careful not to stop to make sure of it. When she reached her room, she didn't find even a spark of fire there. He took a book to occupy himself, until Annetta came; but solitude and almost darkness plunged her back into desolation, especially since she was close to the horrible place she had discovered in the morning. Not knowing how to make up his mind to sleep in that room where someone had certainly entered the night before, he waited for Annetta with painful impatience, wanting to know an infinite number of circumstances from her. He still wanted to question her on that object of horror, of which he believed her informed, though inaccurately. However, she was amazed that the chamber that contained it remained open so imprudently. The faint light spread on the walls by the light about to go out increased her terror. She got up to go back to the inhabited part of the castle before the oil was completely used up.

As he opened the door, he heard some voices, and saw a light at the end of the corridor. It was Annetta with another servant. "I'm glad you came," said Emilia; "What reason has kept you so long? Favorite to light the fire.

"The landlady needed me," answered Annetta a little embarrassed. "I'll go get some wood right away."

"No," said Caterina, "it's my duty." »And she went out. Annetta wanted to follow her; but Emilia called her back, and she began to talk loudly and laugh, as if she were afraid to keep silent.

Caterina returned with wood, and as soon as the fire was lighted and the servant had gone, the girl asked Annetta if she had taken the information ordered.

'Yes, ma'am,' replied the girl, 'but nobody knows anything. I have observed Carlo carefully, because they say he knows strange things; that old man has a certain air that I can't express: he asked me several times if she was quite sure that the door to the secret stairway wasn't closed. "Sure," I replied. In truth, miss, I am so amazed, that I do not know what to tell me. I would rather sleep in this room than on the cannon of the bulwark over there.

"And why less on that cannon than in any other part of the castle?" Emilia said, smiling. 'I think the bed would be hard.

"Yes, but you can't find a worse one. The fact is that last night something was seen near that cannon, which was there as a guard.

"And you believe in all the fairy tales that they pretend to be you?"

"Miss, I will show you the cannon in question. You can see it here from the window.

"That's true, but is it evidence that a ghost is watching him?"

- As! If I show you the cannon, won't you believe it even then?

- No, I believe nothing but what I see with my own eyes.

"Well, you'll see, if you'll just go to the window. »

Emilia could not hold back her laughter, and Annetta looked disconcerted. Seeing her facility in believing her marvelousness, the girl thought it best to refrain from speaking to her on the subject of her terror, lest she succumb to ideal fears. So you spoke of the Venice regattas.

"Oh! yes, Signorina," said Annetta, "those beautiful lampposts and those beautiful nights in the moonlight: that is what is magnificent about Venice; I'm sure the moon is more beautiful in that city than elsewhere. What delightful music was heard! Lodovico sang so often near my window, on the porch! It was Lodovico who told me about that painting you were so eager to see yesterday.

- What painting? Emilia said, wanting to get Annetta to talk.

— That terrible picture with the black veil.

"Have you seen it?"

- Who? I? never; but this morning,' continued the maid, speaking in a low voice, and looking around, 'this morning, when it was light day, 'you know I was longing to see him, and had heard strange things about it,' I went as far as the door, determined to enter it, but I found it closed. »

Emilia shuddered, and fearing that she had been observed, since the door had been closed for so little time after her visit, she feared her curiosity might not attract Montoni's vengeance; and realizing that the subject was too dreadful to deal with at this hour, she changed the subject. It was nearly midnight, and Annetta was about to leave, when they heard the bell at the front door ring; they stood frightened: after a long pause they heard the sound of a carriage in the courtyard; Emilia leaned back in her chair, exclaiming: 'It's definitely the count.

- At this time! oh no! it seems to me impossible that he chose this moment to arrive at a house.

"My dear, let's not waste time in vain talk," said Emilia, frightened; "Go, please, go and see who it could be. »

Annetta went out, taking the lamp away and leaving her in the dark: this would have frightened her a few minutes earlier, but at that moment she paid no attention to it: she waited and listened almost without breathing. Finally she Annetta reappeared.

"Yes," she said, "you were right; he is the count.

— Good heavens! cried Emilia; "But is it really him? did you really recognize him?

Yes, I saw it distinctly; I went to the window of the western court which, as you know, looks into the surrounding courtyard. I saw his carriage, where he was waiting for someone: there were many riders with lighted torches. When Carlo introduced himself to him, he said a few words that I couldn't understand, and went downstairs in the company of another gentleman. Thinking that the master was already in bed, I ran to the mistress's room to find out something; I met Lodovico, from whom I learned that Signor Montoni was still watching, and held council with the other gentlemen at the end of the east gallery. Lodovico signaled me to shut up, and I came right back here. »

Emilia asked who the count's companion was, and how Montoni had received them; but Annetta was unable to tell her anything.

'Lodovico,' she added, 'was just going to call the master's valet to inform him of this arrival, when I found him. »

Emilia remained uncertain for some time; finally she begged Annetta to go and find out, if it were possible, the count's intention by coming to the castle.

"Willingly," replied the other; "but how will I be able to find the ladder if I leave you the lamp?" »

Emilia offered to light her up. When they reached the top of the stairs, she reflected that she might be seen by the count, and, to avoid going through the drawing-room, Annetta led her through several passageways to a secret staircase which led to the dining room.

Turning back, Emilia was afraid of getting lost, and being frightened again by some mysterious sight, and she trembled at the idea of opening a single door. While she was perplexed and thoughtful, she thought she heard a sob; she stopped, and she distinctly heard another: she had several doors to the right; she pricked up her ear; when she was on her second, she heard a plaintive voice, but she could not make up her mind to open the door, or to walk away. She knew convulsive sighs and a heart's grievance at her despair: she grew pale, and she looked anxiously upon the darkness which surrounded her: her lamentations went on; her pity conquered terror. In the probability that her attentions could console him, she put down the lamp, and opened the door slowly: everything was darkness, except a lavatory at the end of which leaked a dim light. Seeming to recognize her voice,

A man was seated near the fireplace, but she could not distinguish him, because his back was to her; From time to time he said a few words in a low voice, which could not be understood, and then the aunt cried no more strong. Emilia would have liked to guess the reason for that scene, and to recognize the man who was there at that hour: however, not wanting to increase her aunt's yearnings by discovering her secrets, she withdrew cautiously, and, although with difficulty, she managed to find her room, where soon other interests made her forget her surprise.

Annetta returned without a satisfactory answer. The servants with whom she had spoken were ignorant of how long the count was to remain in the castle: they spoke only of the bad roads traversed, of the dangers overcome, and they were amazed that their master had taken that road so late in the night. She ended up asking permission to go and rest.

Emilia, knowing it would be cruel to detain her, dismissed her. She was left alone, thinking of her own situation and that of her aunt; and her eyes finally stopped on the portrait found in the papers that her father had forced her to burn, and which was on the table with various drawings taken from a little box a few hours before: this sight plunged her into sad reflections, but the moving expression of the portrait soothed his bitterness. She looked tenderly at those graceful features; suddenly, I recalled, disturbed, the words of the manuscript found with the miniature, and which then had filled her with uncertainty and horror. Finally, she roused herself, and she resolved to lie down; but the silence, the solitude in which she found herself at that late hour, the impression left on her by the subject on which she was meditating, they took away her courage. Annetta's stories, though frivolous, had nevertheless disturbed her, all the more after the frightening circumstance she had witnessed not far from her room.

The door to the secret stairway was perhaps the subject of a better founded fear. Determined not to undress, she threw herself fully dressed on the bed; her father's dog, her good Fido, lying at her feet, served as sentry.

Thus prepared, she endeavored to banish sad ideas; but her mind still wandered on the points that most interested him, and the clock struck two before she could sleep a wink. She finally succumbed to a light sleep, and was awakened by a noise she seemed to hear in her bedroom. Trembling she raised her head, she listened attentively: everything was in silence; thinking she was mistaken, she leaned back on the pillow.

A little later the noise began again: it seemed to come from the side of the ladder. Then he remembered the disgusting incident of last night, in which an unknown hand had opened that door. Her terror froze her heart. She got up on the bed, and lightly stretching the curtain, she looked at the door to the staircase. The lamp that burned on the fireplace gave off a very dim light. The noise she believed to be coming from the door continued to be heard. It seemed to her that they loosened the bolts; then they would stop, and then slowly begin again, as if they were afraid of being overheard. While Emilia fixed her eyes on that side, she saw the shutter move, slowly open and something enter her room, without the darkness allowing her to make out anything. She nearly died of fright, she was self-possessed enough not to cry out and let the curtain fall. She silently observed that mysterious object, which seemed to hunt itself in the darkest parts of the room, then sometimes stop; but when she approached the fireplace, she Emilia she could distinguish a human figure. A gloomy recollection was almost to make her succumb. Despite her, she continued to observe that figure, which remained motionless for a long time, and she then slowly approached the foot of the bed. Her curtains, somewhat ajar, permitted the girl to see her; but her terror deprived her even of the strength to make a movement. After an instant, the figure returned to the fireplace, took the lamp, considered the room, and slowly went back to the bed. The rays of the lamp awakened which seemed to hunt itself in the darkest parts of the room, then sometimes stop; but when she approached the fireplace, she Emilia she could distinguish a human figure. A gloomy recollection was almost to make her succumb. Despite her, she continued to observe that figure, which remained motionless for a long time, and she then slowly approached the foot of the bed. Her curtains, somewhat ajar, permitted the girl to see her; but her terror deprived her even of the strength to make a movement. After an instant, the figure returned to the fireplace, took the lamp, considered the room, and slowly went back to the bed. The rays of the lamp awakened which seemed to hunt itself in the darkest parts of the room, then sometimes stop; but when she approached the fireplace, she Emilia she could distinguish a human figure. A gloomy recollection was almost to make her succumb. Despite her, she continued to observe that figure, which remained motionless for a long time, and she then slowly approached the foot of the bed. Her curtains, somewhat ajar, permitted the girl to see her; but her terror deprived her even of the strength to make a movement. After an instant, the figure returned to the fireplace, took the lamp, considered the room, and slowly went back to the bed. The rays of the lamp awakened which remained motionless for a good while, and then slowly approached the foot of the bed. Her curtains, somewhat ajar, permitted the girl to see her; but her terror deprived her even of the strength to make a movement. After an instant, the figure returned to the fireplace, took the lamp, considered the room, and slowly went back to the bed. The rays of the lamp awakened which remained motionless for a good while, and then slowly approached the foot of the bed. Her curtains, somewhat ajar, permitted the girl to see her; but her terror deprived her even of the strength to make a movement. After an instant, the figure returned to the fireplace, took the lamp, considered the room, and slowly went back to the bed. The rays of the lamp awakened then the dog, which jumped to the ground, barked loudly, and ran on the unknown, who pushed him back with the sword covered by the sheath. Emilia recognized Count Morano. She looked at him silently with fear. He fell to his knees, begging her not to be afraid, and throwing away her shoe, he wanted to take her hand. But recovering then the strength paralyzed by her terror, Emilia jumped out of bed, Morano got up, followed her to the door of the ladder, and stopped her as she touched the first rung; but already by the brightness of a lamp, she had seen another man halfway up the same staircase. She let out a cry of despair, and believing herself betrayed by Montoni, she gave herself up for lost.

The count dragged her into the room. "Why so frightened?" he said in a trembling voice. « Listen to me, Emilia, I don't come to do you any harm; no, I swear to heaven, I love you too much, no doubt for my rest. »

Emilia looked at him for a moment with the uncertainty of fear. 'Leave me, sir,' she said to him, 'leave me then at the moment.

"Listen, Emilia," Morano added, "listen to me: I love you, and I'm desperate, yes, desperate. How can I look at you, perhaps for the last time, and not feel all the fury of despair? But no, you will be mine in spite of Montoni, in spite of all his cowardice.

"In spite of Montoni!" Emilia exclaimed vivaciously. "Oh heavens! what do I hear?

"That Montoni is a villain," cried Morano vehemently, "a villain who was selling you to my love, who...

— And what he bought me was less? she said, throwing a contemptuous glance at the count. 'Get out, sir, get out immediately. She Then she added in a voice moved by hope and fear, though she knew she could be understood by no one: "Oh I'll turn the whole castle upside down, and I will obtain from Signor Montoni's resentment what I implored in vain from his pity.

"Do not expect anything from his pity; he betrayed me unworthily: my vengeance will pursue him everywhere; and as for you, Emilia, he undoubtedly has more lucrative plans than the first. »

The ray of hope which the count's first words had given back to Emilia was almost extinguished by these last expressions. Her physiognomy was disturbed by it, and Morano tried to take advantage of it. He said:

'I'm wasting my time, I didn't come to declaim against Montoni, I came to solicit, to beg Emilia; I came to tell her all that I suffer from her, to conjure her to save us both: me from her despair and she from her ruin. Emilia, Montoni's projects are such that you cannot conceive them; they are terrible, I swear. Escape, escape from this horrid prison with the man who adores you. A servant, earned by dint of gold, will open the gates of the castle for me, and you will soon be free from this scoundrel. »

Emilia was oppressed by the terrible blow she received while hope was reviving in her heart. She saw herself lost without shelter. Incapable of answering and almost unable to reflect, she sank into a chair, pale and taciturn; it was highly probable that in the beginning Montoni had sold her to Morano, but it was clear that later he had retracted her promise, and the count's conduct proved it. It also appeared that a more advantageous project could only decide the selfish Montoni to abandon that plan, which he had so earnestly solicited. These reflections of hers made her tremble at Morano's words, which she did not hesitate to believe. But while she trembled at the idea of the misfortunes that awaited her in Udolfo's castle, she considered that the only way out was the protection of a man, with which more certain and no less terrible disasters could not be lacking; evils in the end, of which she could not bear the thought.

Her silence encouraged the count's hopes, and he watched her impatiently; he took her hand and implored her to make up her mind. 'All the moments of delay,' he told her, 'make the departure more dangerous; the few moments we miss can give Montoni time to surprise us.

"For pity's sake, sir, don't bother me," said Emilia feebly; « I am unhappy, and I must continue to be so. Leave me, please, leave me to my fate.

"Never," cried the count impetuously; « I will rather perish... but forgive this violence: the idea of losing you alters my reason. You cannot ignore Montoni's character; but you can ignore his plans, yes, you certainly ignore them, otherwise you would not hesitate between my love and his power.

"I don't hesitate at all," said Emilia.

"Let's go, then," Morano added, kissing her hand and getting up quickly. « My carriage awaits us under the castle walls.

"You are mistaken, sir; I thank you for the interest you take in my fate, but I will remain under the protection of Signor Montoni.

"Under your protection!" Morano exclaimed violently; « his protection Of him! Emilia, oh! do not let yourselves be deceived... I have already told you what his protection of her would be.

"Excuse me if at this moment I do not believe a simple assertion, and if I demand some proof.

"I don't have the time or the means to produce any.

"And I won't have any will to listen to them.

"You mock my patience and pains mine,' continued Morano; "Is a marriage with the man who adores you so terrible in your eyes?" Do you prefer this cruel captivity? Oh! there is certainly someone who robs me of the affections that should belong to me, otherwise you would not be able to refuse a party that can save you from the most barbarous tyranny. »And he ran lost up and down the room.

"Your speech, Count Morano, proves enough that my affections could not belong to you," said Emilia gently. 'This conduct proves enough that I would be equally tyrannized if I were in your power. If you want to persuade me otherwise, stop bothering me with your presence; if you denied it to me, you would oblige me to expose you to Signor Montoni's wrath.

- But let him come! exclaimed Morano furiously; « let him come! Dare to provoke mine! dare to look in the face of the man who has so insolently outraged! I'll teach him what morality is, justice, and especially revenge! come, and I will plunge my sword into his bosom. »

The vehemence with which she expressed herself became a new cause for concern for Emilia. She got up from the chair, but her legs were shaking, and she fell back. She looked intently at the closed door to the corridor, convincing herself that she could not escape without being impeded.

'Count Morano,' she finally said, 'calm down, I beg you, and listen to reason, if not pity. You are equally deceived in love and hate. I will never be able to match the affection with which you are pleased to honor me, and certainly I have never encouraged it. Signor Montoni cannot have outraged you: know that he has no right to dispose of my hand, even if he also had the power. Leave me, leave this castle, as long as you can do it safely. Spare yourself the terrible consequences of an unjust revenge, and the sure remorse of having prolonged my sufferings.

"An unjust revenge!" the count exclaimed, suddenly recovering the fury of passion. « And who will ever be able to see this angelic face, and believe any punishment whatsoever proportionate to the offense that was done to me? Yes, I will leave this castle, but I won't leave alone. My people await me, and will take you to my carriage; your cries will be useless; no one can hear them in this remote place. So give in to necessity, and let yourself be led.

"Count Morano," she said, getting up, and pushing him away as he advanced, "I am now in your power, but bear in mind that such conduct cannot win you the esteem you claim to be worthy of. »

Here she was interrupted by the grumbling of her dog, who jumped out of bed for the second time; Morano looked towards the stairway and, seeing no one, called aloud to Cesario .

"Emilia," he said to her afterwards, "why do you force me to use this method?" Oh! how much I would like to persuade you, rather than force you to be my wife! But I swear to heaven that Montoni won't sell you to another. In the meantime you will come with me. Caesarius, Caesarius!..."

A man appeared. Emilia let out a loud shriek as the count dragged her along. At that point a noise was heard at the corridor door. The count stopped, as if hesitating between love and revenge; the door opened, and Montoni, followed by the old superintendent and several others, rushed into the room saying: 'Ah traitor! you will pay the penalty for your infamous attempt; beware! »

The count did not wait for a second challenge; he handed Emilia over to Cesario, and turning round proudly: «I'm from you, infamous one,' he cried, giving him a desperate blow. Montoni defended himself valiantly, but they were separated from his followers, while Carlo took Emilia away from the people of Morano.

"Is that why," Montoni said ironically, "is that why I received you in my roof, and allowed you to spend the night there?" Did you come, then, to reward my hospitality with an unworthy betrayal, and to steal my niece from me?

"That anyone who speaks of treason," replied Morano with concentrated anger, "dares to show himself without blushing. Montoni, you are a villain; if there is treason here, you alone are the author.

- Oh coward! shouted the other, freeing himself from whoever was holding him and running towards the count. They went out the corridor door. The fighting was so furious that no one dared approach. Montoni, on the other hand, swore to pierce the first one who got in the way. Jealousy and revenge increased Morano's rage and blindness. Montoni, more master of himself and very skilful, had the advantage and wounded his adversary; but the latter, appearing insensitive to the pain and loss of blood, continued to fight, and bruised Montoni slightly in his arm, but at the same moment he touched a large wound, and fell into Cesario's arms. Montoni, leaning his sword against his chest, wanted to force him to ask for his life. Morano could barely reply with a gesture and a negative word, and he fainted. The other was about to pierce him,

Emilia, who had not been able to leave the room during the frightful tumult, entered the corridor, and courageously defending the cause of humanity, begged Montoni to grant Morano, in the castle, the assistance that his condition demanded. Rams, who almost never listened to pity, seemed at that moment thirsty for revenge. With the cruelty of a monster he ordered for the second time that his vanquished enemy be transported immediately outside the castle in the state in which he was. Those surroundings, covered with woods, hardly offered a solitary hut to spend the night. The count's servants declared that they would not move him from there until he gave at least some sign of life. Those of Montoni remained motionless, and Cavignì remonstrated in vain: Emilia alone, paying no attention to threats, brought water to Morano, and ordered the bystanders to bandage his wounds. Montoni, finally feeling some pain in him, withdrew to be treated.

In that interval, the count came to his senses. The first object that struck him, when he opened his eyes, was Emilia bending over him with an expression of the greatest disquiet. He looked at her painfully.

"I deserved it," he said, "but not from Montoni." I deserved to be punished by you, and instead I receive pity. After a few pauses he added: "I must abandon you, but not to Montoni." Forgive me the sorrows I caused you. The betrayal of that villain will not go unpunished.... I'm not in a state to walk, but it doesn't matter: take me to the nearest hut. I would not spend the night in this place, even if I were certain of dying on the short journey I have to make. »

Cavignì proposed to go and conform if there were any dwellings nearby, before removing him from there, but the count was too impatient to leave. The anguish of his spirit seemed even more violent than the suffering of the wound. He indignantly rejected Cavignì's proposal, nor did he want permission to be obtained for him to spend the night in the castle. Cesario wanted to bring the carriage forward, but Morano forbade him. "I couldn't bear it," said he; « Call my servants: they will carry me on their arms. »

Finally, calming down somewhat, he agreed that Cesario should go first in search of a shelter. Emilia, seeing that he had regained his senses, was preparing to go out when Montoni ordered it through a servant, adding that if the count had not left, she was to leave immediately. Morano's eyes flashed with indignation, and he flared up.

'Tell Montoni,' he added, 'that I will leave when it suits me. I will leave this castle which he calls his , as one leaves a snake's nest; but it won't be the last time he will hear of me. Tell him that, as much as I can, I won't leave another murder on his conscience.

"Count Morano, do you know exactly what you are saying?" Cavigni said.

"Yes, I know very well, and he will understand what I mean. His conscience, on this point, will second his intelligence.

"Count Morano," said Verrezzi, who had kept silent until then, "if you dare to insult my friend again, I'll plunge my sword into your heart."

"It would be an action worthy of a friend of an infamous man," said Morano, and the violence of his indignation made him lift from the arms of the servants; but his energy was momentary, and he fell back exhausted. Montoni's people detained Verrezzi, who seemed willing to carry out his threat. Cavignì, less irritated than he, tried to get him out, Emilia, restrained until then by her compassion, was about to withdraw when Morano's voice stopped her. She waved her over. She advanced timidly, but the languor which disfigured the wounded man's face excited her pity.

"I leave you forever," he said to her; "Maybe I won't see you again. I would like to take your pardon with me, and, if I were not too intrusive, I dare to ask for your kindness.

"Receive this pardon," said Emilia, "with the most sincere wishes for your speedy recovery. »

So begged him to leave the castle quickly, collected by his uncle. He was in the cedar parlor on a sofa, suffering greatly from his wound, but bearing it with great courage.

Emilia trembled as she approached him; and he rebuked her loudly for not having obeyed immediately, and capriciously attributed her pity for her wounded man.

The girl, stung by those outrageous words, did not answer.

At that Lodovico entered the room, reporting that they were carrying Morano on a mattress to a nearby hut. Montoni seemed to calm down, and told Emilia that he could go back to her room. She went away willingly; but the idea of spending the night in a room which might be open to all frightened her then more than ever. He resolved to go to his aunt and ask her permission to take Annetta with him.

As he approached the gallery, he heard voices of people who seemed to be quarreling; he recognized that they were Cavigni and Verrezzi; the latter protested that he wanted to go and inform Montoni of the insult done to him by Morano. Cavigni seemed to try to calm him down.

'One must pay no attention,' he said, 'to the injuries of an angry man; your obstinacy will be fatal to the count and to Montoni; we now have much more serious interests to discuss. »

Emilia united her prayers with Cavigni's arguments, and they succeeded in the end in dissuading Verrezzi from his project.

When she went to her aunt's, her calmness made her believe that she was unaware of what had happened; she wanted to tell him carefully; but her aunt interrupted her by saying that she knew all about her. Although Emilia knew perfectly well that she had little reason to love her husband, she still did not believe her capable of such indifference. She obtained permission to take Annetta with her, and she immediately withdrew. A streak of blood, lining the corridor, leads to to his room, and in the place of the fight the ground was completely covered with it. The girl trembled, and leaned on the maid as she passed. When she arrived in the room, she wanted to examine where she put the ladder, her safety depending a lot on this circumstance. Annetta, both curious and frightened, agreed to the project; but as they approached the door, they found it closed on the outside, so that they had to content themselves with securing it inside, placing the heaviest furniture they could dislodge. Emilia went to bed, and the maid sat down on a chair near the fireplace, where a few embers were still smoking.

CHAPTER XXI

It is necessary now to refer to some circumstances which the sudden departure from Venice and the rapid succession of cases that followed in the castle did not allow us to deal with.

The very morning of that departure, Morano, at the agreed time, went to the Montoni house to receive his bride. He was not a little surprised by the silence and solitude of the arcades, full of servants as usual; but surprise immediately gave place to the height of astonishment and anger, when an old woman opened the door, and said that her master and all her family had left Venice very early on for the mainland. Not being able to believe it, he disembarked from the gondola and ran into the hall to inquire more minutely from the old woman, who persisted in her assertion, and the solitude of the palace convinced him of the truth. He grabbed her by her arm, and seemed to want to vent the bile that was burning her on the poor thing. She asked her a thousand questions at once, accompanied by gestures so furious that she, terrified, she was unable to answer him. He released her, and started pacing the porch and courtyards like a senseless, cursing Montoni and his own gullibility.

When the woman had recovered from her terror, she told him what she knew; in truth it was little, but it was enough to make Morano understand how Montoni had gone to his castle in the Apennines. He followed him as soon as his people had made the necessary preparations, accompanied by a friend and numerous servants. He was determined to get Emilia, or sacrifice Montoni to his revenge. When he had calmed down somewhat, his conscience reminded him of some circumstances which sufficiently explained Montoni's conduct. But how could the latter ever have suspected an intention which he alone knew, and which he could not guess? On this point, however, he had been betrayed by the sympathetic intelligence which exists, so to speak, among insensitive souls, and makes one man judge what another should do in a given circumstance. In fact, this was what had happened to Montoni. He had finally acquired the certainty of what he already suspected: that the substance of Count Morano, that is, instead of being considerable, as he had believed it at the beginning, was, on the contrary, in a very bad state. Montoni had favored his claims alone for personal reasons, out of pride, out of avarice. The kinship of a Venetian noble would certainly have satisfied the former, and the latter speculated on the assets of Emilia of Gascony, which were to be handed over to him on the very day of the wedding. He had already conceived some suspicions about the count's excesses, but he hadn't acquired the certainty of his ruin until the eve of the wedding. He therefore did not hesitate to conclude that Morano was deceiving him for certain on the article of Emilia's assets, and this doubt was confirmed, when, after agreeing to sign the contract that same night, the count broke his word. A man so unreflective, so absent-minded as Morano, in the when he was attending to his wedding, he could easily have failed without malice; but Montoni interpreted the incident according to his own ideas. After waiting a while, he ordered his whole family to be ready at the first sign. Hurrying to get to Udolfo's castle, he wanted to rescue Emilia from all Morano's searches, and release himself from the engagement without exposing himself to altercations. If the count, on the contrary, had had only honorable claims, as he called them, he would certainly have followed Emilia and signed the concerted cession. On this pact Montoni would have sacrificed her without scruple to a ruined man, for the sole purpose of enriching himself. Nonetheless, he refrained from saying a single word to her about the reasons for that departure, fearing that a

It was for such considerations that he had suddenly left Venice; and, for opposite reasons, Morano had run after him across the precipices of the Apennines. When he learned of his arrival, Montoni, convinced that he was coming to fulfill his promise, hastened to receive him; but Morano's anger, expressions and demeanor soon disillusioned him. Montoni partially explained the reasons for his sudden departure; and the count, persisting in asking for Emilia, filled up withreproachesnot to mention the old covenant.

Finally, the castellan, tired of the dispute, deferred the conclusion to the question, and Morano withdrew with some hope on his apparent perplexity; but when, in the silence of the night, she remembered their conversation, his character, and examples of his duplicity, the little hope she retained left her, and she resolved not to lose the opportunity of possessing Emilia in another way. He called his confidant, communicated his plan, and instructed him to discover among the servants of the castle someone who wanted to lend themselves to seconding Emilia's kidnapping: he deferred entirely to the choice and prudence of his agent, and not wrongly, since the latter did not take long to find a man who had recently been treated rigorously by Montoni, and who thought only of betraying him. He led Cesario out of the castle, and by a secret passage introduced him to the staircase, showed him a shorter way, and gave him the keys which could facilitate his retreat; he was well rewarded in advance, and we have seen what success the count's attempt had.

Meanwhile, old Carlo had surprised two of Morano's servants, who, having been ordered to wait with the carriage outside the castle, communicated their amazement at the sudden and secret departure of their master. The valet had confided to them about Morano's project only what they had to do; but suspicions were aroused, and Carlo made the best of it. Before running to Montoni, he tried to gather more news, and for this purpose, accompanied by another servant, he placed himself in ambush at the corridor door of Emilia's room; nor did he remain in vain, since, shortly after, he heard Morano arrive, and having ascertained his plans, he ran to warn the master, thus helping to prevent the kidnapping.

Montoni, the next day, with his arm in a sling, made the usual tour of the walls, visited the workmen, increased their number, and returned to the castle, where he was awaited by new guests. He had them come to a separate apartment, and Montoni remained shut up with them for almost two hours. After calling Carlo, he ordered him to lead the strangers to the rooms intended for the officials of the house, and to have them immediately refreshed.

Meanwhile the count lay in a hut in the forest, oppressed by double suffering, and meditating a terrible revenge. His servant, sent to the nearest village, did not return until the following day with a surgeon, who did not want to explain the nature of the wound, and wishing first to examine the progress of the inflammation, administered a sedative, and remained with him. to judge its effects.

Emilia was able to rest a little for the rest of that night. Waking up, she remembered that she had finally been freed from Morano's persecutions, and she felt largely relieved of the evils that had oppressed her for so long. However, the count's suspicions about Montoni's designs still afflicted her: he had said that her plans were impenetrable, but terrible. To drive away the thought, she looked for her pencils, looked out the window, and contemplated the town to choose a beautiful view.

So busy, she recognized on the ramparts the men who had just arrived at the castle. The sight of those foreigners surprised her, but even more their exterior: they had a singularity of clothing, a pride of looks, which captured her attention. She withdrew from the window as they passed beneath her, but she quickly reappeared to get a better look at them. So well did their physiognomies accord with the harshness of the whole scene, that she, as they surveyed the castle, drew them like highwaymen in her view of her.

Carlo, having provided them with the necessary refreshments, returned to Montoni, who wanted to discover the traitor from whom Morano had received the keys the previous night; but Carlo, too faithful to his master to suffer harm, would not have denounced the comrade, not even to justice. He ascertained that he was ignorant of it, and that the conversation of the count's servants had revealed to him nothing but the plot. Montoni's suspicions fell naturally on the porter, and he made him come. Bernardino denied it with such boldness that Montoni himself doubted his guilt, without being able to believe him innocent; finally he sent him back, so that although he was the real author of the conspiracy, he had the art of escaping a severe punishment.

Montoni was taken away by his wife, and Emilia did not delay in joining them; she found them in a violent quarrel and wanted to retire, but her aunt called her back.

"You will be a witness," she said, "of my resistance. Now repeat, sir, the command which I have so often refused to obey. »

He sternly ordered his granddaughter to retire. The aunt insisted that she stay. Emilia wished to escape the scene of that altercation; she wanted to serve her aunt, but she despaired of calming Montoni, in whose gaze the storm of his soul was depicted in strokes of fire.

"Get out," he finally shouted in a thunderous voice. Emilia obeyed and went to the bastion, where the foreigners were no longer there. Meditating on the unhappy union made by her father's sister, and on the horror of her own situation, caused by her aunt's ridiculous imprudence, she would have liked to respect her as much as she was attached to her; but Ms. Montoni's conduct had always made it impossible for her. The pity for her, however, which she felt for the condolences of her unhappy one, made her forget the wrongs of which she could accuse her.

While she was thus walking on the rampart, Annetta appeared, who, looking around cautiously, said to her:

« My dear mistress, I look for you everywhere; if you want to follow me, I'll show you a picture.

- A framework! she exclaimed trembling.

"Yes, the portrait of the former mistress of the castle. Old Carlo has just told me that it was she, and I thought to thank you for her by taking you to see her: as for the lady, you know that she cannot be told of her.

And so you talk about it with everyone.

- Yes Madam; What would I do here if I couldn't speak? If I were in prison and they let me chat, it would at least be a consolation: yes, I would like to talk, even if I were against the walls. But come, let's not waste time: I need to show you the picture.

Is it perhaps covered by a veil? Emilia said after a pause; "I have no desire to see him.

- As! Signora Emilia, don't you want to see the mistress of the castle, that lady who disappeared so strangely? As for me, I would have traversed all the mountains to see the portrait. To tell you the truth, this singular tale makes me shudder to think of it, yet it is all that interests me.

"Are you sure it's a painting?" have you seen it? Is it covered by a veil?

— Good God! yes, no and yes: I'm sure it's a painting. I have seen it, and it is not covered by any veil. »

The accent and the air of surprise with which Annetta replied reminded Emilia of her prudence, and with a forced smile, concealing her emotion, she agreed to go and see the portrait placed in a dark room adjoining the dining room.

"Here it is," Annetta said softly, showing her the picture. Emilia looked at him, and she saw that she represented a lady in the prime of her age and beauty. Her features were noble, regular, and filled with a strong expression, but not with that seductive sweetness that she would have liked to find in Emilia, nor with that tender melancholy that so interested her.

"How many years has it been," said Emilia, "since this lady disappeared?"

"About twenty years, they say. »

The girl continued to examine the portrait.

'I think,' resumed Annetta, 'that Signor Montoni ought to put him in a more beautiful room. In my opinion, the portrait of the lady, of which has inherited the riches, he should stay in the noble apartment. In truth, she was a beautiful woman, and the master could, without shame, have her taken to the large apartment where the veiled picture is. (Emilia turns around). It is true that one would not see it better: I always find the door closed.

"Let's go out," said Emilia; 'Let me, Annetta, come back and recommend him to you; she tries to be very reserved in your talks, and not to let anyone suspect that you know the slightest thing about that picture.

"Good God, it's not a secret already: all the servants have seen it many times.

"But how can that be?" Emilia said with a start; " saw! when? as?

- There is nothing surprising: already we are all a little curious.

"But what if you told me the door was closed?"

"If so, how could we get in?" »And she looked everywhere.

— Ah! you're talking about this picture here,' Emilia said, calming down. « Come, Annette. I don't see anything else worthy of attention. Let's go away. »

Going to her room, she saw Montoni go downstairs, and went back to her aunt's bathroom, finding her alone and weeping. Her pain and resentment fought over her countenance. Her pride had hitherto held back her grievances. Judging Emilia for herself, and being unable to dissimulate what the unworthiness of her treatment deserved from her, she believed that her troubles would excite her niece's joy rather than any sympathy from her. She believed that he would despise her, nor would he have the slightest pity for her; but she knew very little of Emilia's kindness.

The pains finally won the proud character. When Emilia had entered her rooms in the morning, she would have revealed everything to her, if her husband had not had prevented it; and now that his presence did not prevent her, she broke into bitter lamentations.

"O Emilia," she exclaimed, "I am the most unhappy woman!" I am treated in a barbaric way! Who would have foreseen, when she had such a beautiful prospect before me, that I would experience such a terrible fate? Who would have believed, when I married a man like Montoni, that I would have poisoned my life? There is no means of guessing the best side to take; there is none to recognize the true good. The most flattering hopes deceive us, thus deceiving even the wisest. Who would have foreseen, when I married Montoni, that I would regret my generosity so quickly? »

Emilia was well aware that she should have foreseen all these inconveniences, but as this was not the time to reproach her uselessly, she sat down with her aunt, took her hand, and with that pitying air which made her look like a guardian angel, spoke to her with infinite sweetness. All her talk, however, was not enough to calm Signora Montoni, who did not want to hear anything; she needed to let off steam even before being consoled.

"Ungrateful! »said she, «she deceived me in every way. She knew how to tear me away from my homeland, from her friends; he shut me up in this ancient castle, and he believes to force me to yield to all his wishes; but he will see that he is deceived, he will see that no threat will suffice to induce me to ... But who would have believed it? Who would have guessed that, with his name, his apparent wealth, he had nothing at all? No, not even a sequin of his! I thought he was doing well: he thought he was a man of importance and very opulent, otherwise I wouldn't have married him. Ungrateful! Perfidious! Monster!...

"Dear aunt, calm down; Signor Montoni may be less rich than you thought, but he's not that poor after all. The home of Venice and this castle they are his. May I ask you what are the circumstances which particularly afflict you?

What circumstances! cried the furious aunt. " That! it is not enough? For a long time ruined at the game, he has also lost all that I have given him, and now he demands that I give him all my possessions. Luckily most of them are in my head: he would like to squander these too and throw himself into an infernal project of which only he can understand the idea; and... is all this not enough?

"Of course," said Emilia, "but remember, Signora, that I was absolutely ignorant of it."

"And isn't it enough that his ruin be accomplished, that he is full of debts of all sorts to the point that, if he were to pay them, he would have neither the castle nor the house in Venice?"

- I am very saddened by what you tell me...

"And it's not enough," interrupted the aunt, "that he treated me with such negligence and cruelty, because I refused him the assignment; why, instead of trembling at his threats, did I resolutely challenge him, reproaching him, for his shameful conduct? I suffered it with all possible sweetness. You know well, nephew, if a word of complaint has ever escaped me till now; I, whose only fault is too great a kindness and too easy condescension! And to my misfortune I see myself chained for life to this vile, cruel and perfidious monster! »

Emilia, realizing that her ills admitted no real consolation, and despising common phrases, thought it better to keep silent; However, Signora Montoni, jealous of her superiority, interpreted that silence as indifference or contempt, and reproached her for forgetting her duties and her lack of sensitivity.

"Oh! how I distrusted that vaunted sensibility, when she was to be tested! » she added; 'I knew very well that it would teach you neither tenderness nor affection for relatives who have treated you as their daughter.

'Forgive me, aunt,' said Emilia gently, 'I boast little, and if I did, I wouldn't already boast of my sensitivity, which is a gift perhaps more to be feared than to be desired.

"Amazingly, nephew, I don't want to argue with you; but, as I said, Montoni threatens me with violence if I persist any longer in denying him the assignment; he was just the subject of our contention when you entered this morning. Now I am decided; there is no force on earth that can compel me to do so, and I will not suffer so many ill treatments calmly; he will tell him everything he deserves, in spite of her threats and his ferocity. »

Emilia took advantage of a moment's silence to say to her: 'Dear aunt, you would only irritate him unnecessarily; please do not provoke the cruel evils you fear.

'Never mind, but I'll never satisfy him; would you perhaps advise me to strip myself of all mine?

"No, aunt, I don't mean that.

"So what do you mean?"

"You were talking about reproaching Signor Montoni..." Emilia said hesitantly.

- That! Maybe he doesn't deserve them?

- Certain; but I don't think it's prudent to do them to him in the current situation.

- Caution! caution with a man who ruthlessly tramples even the laws of humanity! and will I be careful with him? No, I won't be cowardly like that.

"For your own interest alone, and not for Montoni's," said Emilia modestly, "I would consider it wise to consult prudence." Your reproaches, however just, would be in vain, and would only push him to terrible excesses.

- As! Shall I then blindly submit to all that he commands me? Would you expect me to throw myself at his feet to thank him for his cruelty? Would you expect me to donate all my possessions to him?

— Dear aunt, perhaps I am explaining myself badly! I am not in the position to advise you on such a delicate point; but suffer if I tell you: if you love your rest, try to calm Signor Montoni rather than irritate him.

- Calm him down! it's impossible, I repeat, I don't even want to try. »

Emilia, though annoyed by her aunt's obstinacy and false ideas, felt pity for her misfortunes, and did everything possible to calm and console her, saying:

'Your situation is perhaps less desperate than you think. Signor Montoni can paint you his business in a worse state than it really is, to exaggerate and demonstrate the need he has for your assignment; on the other hand, as long as you keep your assets, they will offer you a resource, if the future conduct of your husband obliges you to separate from him....

'You cruel and insensitive nephew,' the aunt interrupted her impatiently, 'are you trying to persuade me that I have no reason to complain? That my husband is in a brilliant position? that my future is comforting, and that my troubles are puerile and romantic like yours? Strange consolations! Persuade me that I am devoid of judgment and feeling, because you feel nothing, and you are very indifferent to the misfortunes of others! I thought I was opening my heart to a compassionate person who sympathized with my pains; but unfortunately I realize that sentimental people can only feel for themselves. Go away. »

Emilia, without answering her, came out with a mix of pity and contempt. As soon as she was alone, she succumbed to painful thoughts of her who gave birth to her aunt's unhappy position. Her own observations, Morano's equivocal words, had convinced her that Montoni's assets did not correspond to her appearances. She saw his magnificence, the number of servants, his new expenses for the fortifications, and reflection increased her uncertainty about the fate of her aunt and her own, thinking of her uncle's grim character which was increasingly unfolding in his ferocity .

While she was thinking these afflicting thoughts, Annetta brought her lunch to her room. Surprised by this novelty, she asked who had ordered it. "My mistress," Annetta replied. «The gentleman has ordered that she dine in her apartment and she sends you lunch in yours. There have been strong discussions between them, and it seems to me that things are getting serious.»

Emilia, paying little attention to her chatter, sat down to table, but Annetta was not so easily silent: she spoke of the arrival of the men she had already seen on the bastion, and of their strange figure, no less than of the good welcome given them by Montoni. "Do they dine with him?" Emilia said.

"No, miss; they have already eaten in their rooms at the end of the northern gallery. I don't know when they will leave. The master has ordered Carlo to bring them what they need. They have already toured the whole castle, and he directed many questions to the unskilled workers. Never in my life have I seen such ugly mugs; they are scary to see.»

The girl asked her if she had heard of Count Morano again, and if there was any hope of recovery for him. Annetta only knew that she was in a hut, and very aggravated. Emilia could not hide her emotion.

"Miss," said the chatterbox, "how well women know how to hide love!" I thought you hated the count, and I was mistaken.

"I don't think I hate anyone," replied Emilia, forcing a smile; 'but I'm certainly not in love with Count Morano; and I would be equally very sorry for anyone's violent death.»

Annetta went back to talking about the disagreements between the Montoni couple. «It is nothing new,» she said, «since we have heard and seen everything as far as Venice, although she has never told you about it.

"And you did very well, and you would have done better to keep silent; So be careful, I don't like this speech.

— Ah! dear Signora Emilia, I see what respect you have for people who care so little about you! I cannot bear to see you thus deluded; I must tell you this solely for your own interest, and without any design of harming my mistress, though, to tell the truth, I have little reason to love her.

"You certainly aren't talking about my aunt," said Emilia gravely.

- Yes Madam; but I'm beside myself. If you knew all that I know, you wouldn't be angry. Often, very often, I heard her and the master talking of marrying you off to the count: she always told him not to let you give in to your ridiculous whims, but to know how to force you to obey. My heart ached to hear such cruelty; it seemed to me that being herself unhappy, she would have to pity the misfortunes of others and ....

'Thank you for your pity, Annetta; but my aunt was unhappy, and perhaps her ideas were altered. Otherwise I think... I'm convinced that... Come on, leave me alone, Annetta, I've finished lunch.

"You have eaten almost nothing; take another bite ... Do you alter his ideas? affè! I think they always are. In Toulouse I have often heard the landlady speak of you and M. Valancourt to Mme Marville and Mme Vaison in an unkind way: she told them it was hard to contain you. within the bounds of duty, that you were a great burden to her, and that if she hadn't kept a close watch on you, you would have gone off to run around the countryside with Monsieur Valancourt; that you made him come at night, and....

— Great God! exclaimed Emilia, bursting into flames; 'It is impossible that my aunt painted me like this.

"Yes, ma'am, that is the plain truth, though I don't tell it all. It seemed to me that she could have spoken of her niece in a different way, even if you had committed some foul play. But rest assured that I have never believed a single syllable of all of her speeches. The mistress never looks at what she says when she talks about others.

'In any case, Annetta,' said Emilia, recovering herself with dignity, 'you are doing very badly to accuse my aunt against me; I know your intention is good, but let's not talk about it anymore; clear the table. »

The waitress blushed, lowered her eyes and hastened to leave.

"So is this the reward of my honesty?" »Emilia said when she was alone. "Is this the treatment I should receive from a relative, from an aunt, who was supposed to defend my reputation instead of slandering it?" Oh! my tender and most affectionate father, what would you say if you were still in the world? What would you think of your sister's unworthy conduct towards me?... But come on, no useless recriminations, and let us only think that she is unhappy. »

To digress somewhat, she took the veil, and descended on the ramparts, the only walk that was permitted to her. Yes, she would have wanted to walk through the woods below, and contemplate the sublime pictures of nature; but Montoni, not wanting her to leave the castle, tried to be satisfied with the picturesque views which she observed from the walls. No one was there then; the sky was gloomy and sad like her. However, leaking the sun from the clouds, Emilia wanted to see its effect on the north tower: turning around, she saw the three strangers from the morning, and felt an involuntary tremor. They approached her as she hesitated. She wanted to withdraw, and lowered her veil, which badly hid her beauty. They looked at her attentively, talking to each other: the pride of her physiognomies struck her even more than her singular clothing. The figure especially the one in her midst exhaled a savage, grim and malignant ferocity that terrified her. She passed quickly: when she was at the end of the terrace, she turned around, and saw the strangers in the shadow of the turret, intent on considering her, and talking fieryly among themselves. She hastened to retire to her room.

Montoni dined late, and sat for a while at the table with the guests in the cedar parlor. Swollen with his recent triumph over Morano, he emptied the goblet often, and indulged unrestrainedly in the pleasures of table and conversation. Cavignì's vivacity, on the contrary, seemed to have diminished: he looked at Verrezzi, whom he had had great difficulty containing until then, and who always wanted to show Montoni the count's latest insults.

A guest brought up last night's cases, and Verrezzi's eyes sparkled: then they spoke of

Emilia, and it was a concert of praise. Montoni was silent only. When the servants had gone, the conversation became freer; Verrezzi's irascible temper sometimes mixed a little bitterness into what he said, but Montoni explained his superiority even in looks and manners. One of them imprudently nominated Morano again; Verrezzi warmed by wine, and without paying attention to the repeated signsOf Cavignì, mysteriously gave some hints about the incident the day before. Montoni didn't seem to notice it and continued to keep silent, showing no alteration. That apparent insensitivity increased the wrath of Verrezzi, who ended up manifesting the sayings of Morano, that is, that the castle did not legitimately belong to him, and that he would not voluntarily leave another murder on his soul.

"Would I be insulted at my table, and would I be insulted by a friend?" shouted Montoni, pale with fury. "Why repeat to me the mottos of a fool?" Verrezzi, who expected to see Montoni's anger turn against the count, looked at Cavignì with surprise, and the latter enjoyed his confusion. "Would you have the weakness to believe the talk of a man led astray by the delirium of revenge?"

"Lord," said Verrezzi, we only believe what we know.

- As! Montoni interrupted gravely; "Where's your evidence?"

"We only believe what we know, and we know nothing of what Morano told us. »

Montoni seemed to recover, and said: 'I'm always ready, friends, when it comes to my honor; no one could doubt it with impunity. Come on, let's drink."

"Yes, let's drink to Signora Emilia's health," Cavignì said.

"With your permission, first to that of the lady of the castle," Bertolini added. Montoni was silent.

"Cheers to the chatelaine," said the guests, and Montoni nodded slightly as a sign of approval.

'I'm surprised, sir,' Bertolini told him, 'that you have neglected this castle so much: it's a beautiful building.

"It's very suitable for our designs," replied Montoni. "You don't know, I think, by what chance I have it?"

"But," said Bertolini, laughing, "it's a very fortunate case, and I would like something like this to happen to me."

"If you'd like to listen to me," Montoni continued, "I'll tell you the story." »

The physiognomies of Bertolini and Verrezzi expressed anxious curiosity. Cavignì, who didn't mention it, probably already knew the story.

« I have owned this castle for almost twenty years. The lady who owned it before me was a distant relative of mine. I am the least of the family: she was beautiful and rich, and I offered her my hand, but as she loved another, she rejected me herself. It is probable that her favorite rejected her, who was assailed by a constant melancholy, and I have every reason to believe that she ended her days herself. I was not then in the castle: it is a case full of strange and mysterious circumstances which I want to repeat to you.

"Repeat them," said a voice.

Montoni was silent, and his guests, looking at each other, wondered who had spoken, and they realized that everyone was asking the same question.

"We are listened to," said Montoni; "We'll talk about it another time: let's drink. »

The guests looked all over the room.

"We're alone," said Verrezzi, "please do us the favor to continue."

"Didn't you hear something?" Montoni exclaimed.

"I think so," replied Bertolini.

"Pure illusion," said Verrezzi, looking again. « We are alone. Please continue. »

Montoni resumed in a low voice, while the guests gathered around him.

'You should know that for some months Signora Laurentini had been showing the symptoms of a great passion and an altered imagination. She sometimes lost herself in placid meditation, but she often raved. One evening in October, after one of these attacks, she retired alone to her room, forbidding her to be disturbed. It was the room at the end of the corridor, which was the scene of last night's scene: from that moment they never saw it again.

- As! Was she never seen again? Bertolini said. "Wasn't her body found in her room?"

Wasn't his body found? they all exclaimed unanimously.

"Never," replied Montoni.

- What reasons were there for supposing that she had killed herself? Bertolini said. - Yes, what reasons? Verrezzi said. Montoni gave him a disdainful look. 'Forgive me, sir,' added the other; he did not think the lady was your relation, when I spoke of her so lightly. »

Montoni, receiving this excuse, continued: 'I'll explain everything to you right away: listen.

— Listen! a voice repeated.

Everyone was silent, and Montoni changed colour.

"This is not an illusion," Cavignì finally said. "No," said Bertolini; "I understood it too.

"This is becoming extraordinary," added Montoni, standing up hastily. All the guests got up in disorder: the servants were called, searches were made, but no one was found. Surprise and consternation grew. Montoni was baffled. "Let us leave this room," he said, "and the subject of our discourse; it's too serious. »The guests, willing to go out, begged Montoni to go elsewhere to continue his story, but in vain; despite all his efforts to appear calm, he was visibly agitated.

" As! Verrezzi said; « Would you be superstitious, you who make fun of other people's credulity?

"I'm not superstitious," replied Montoni, "but it's good to know what that means. »He went out, and they all withdrew.

END OF THE SECOND VOLUME

THE MYSTERIES OF THE UDOLFO CASTLE

VOL. III

THE CORPSE
... his face, disfigured by death, was disgusting and covered with livid wounds.

CHAPTER XXII

Montoni made the most exact searches in vain about the strange circumstance which had alarmed him, and having been unable to discover anything, he was forced to believe that one of his people was the author of such an ill-timed hoax. Her quarrels with his wife, regarding her sale, becoming more frequent than her, he thought to confine her to her room, threatening her with greater severity if she persisted in refusing her.

If Signora Montoni had been more reasonable, she would have understood the danger of irritating, with that long resistance, a man like the husband in whom she was the nurse. Nor had she forgotten how important it was for her to maintain her possession of her property, which would have rendered her independent, had she been able to escape the despotism of Montoni. But at that moment she had a more decisive guide than reason, that is the spirit of revenge, which made her oppose the negative to the threat, and obstinacy to arrogance.

Reduced to not being able to leave the room, she finally felt the need and the value of the already despised company of her niece, because Emilia, after Annetta, was the only person she was allowed to have. see.

The girl often inquired about Count Morano. She annexed knew very little about it, except that the surgeon thought his recovery impossible. Emilia grieved at being the involuntary cause of his death. Annetta, who observed her emotion, interpreted it in her own way. One day, she came into her room panting and weeping. "For heaven's sake, let's find a way out of this hellish place. Know," she said, "that we are on the eve of some bad scene in this accursed castle. Those gentlemen hold council meetings every night, where they are expected to discuss important business: moreover, what do all the preparations that are made on the ramparts and walls mean? And then, how many people enter the castle every day with horses! and it seems that they must stay there, because the master has ordered to give them what they need. I learned everything from Lodovico, who advised me to keep quiet; but as I love you as much as myself, I could not help but tell you as well. Ah! someday they'll kill us all for sure.

"Don't you know anything else, Annetta?"

- As! Isn't all this enough?

"Yes, but that's not enough to persuade me that they want to kill us all." »

Emilia refrained from expressing her fears so as not to increase the maid's fear. The current state of the castle surprised and disturbed her. As soon as Annetta had finished, she left her alone, to go on to new discoveries.

That evening the girl spent a few very sad hours in the company of her aunt. She was about to go to bed when she heard a loud knock at the bedroom door, produced by the fall of some object. She called to find out what it was she was, and she was not answered. She called a second time with no better success: she thought it was some of the recently arrived strangers in the castle had discovered his room, and went there with bad intentions. She restless, she stayed attentive, always trembling that the noise would be renewed. Instead she steeled herself; she approached the door of the corridor all trembling, and heard a slight sigh so close to her, that she was convinced that there was someone behind her door. As she still listened, the same sigh made itself heard more distinctly, and her terror increased. She didn't know what to solve, and she always heard sighs. Her anxiety grew so strong that she resolved to open the window and call people. As she was preparing for it, she thought she heard someone's footsteps in the secret stairway, and overcoming all other fears she ran towards the corridor. Eager to escape, she opened the door, and tripped over a body lying on the ground. She cried out, and looking at the unconscious person, she recognized her as Annetta. Greatly surprised, she made every effort to help the unfortunate. When she had regained the use of her senses, Emilia helped her into the room, and when she was able to speak of her, the girl assured her, with a firmness that shook even the incredulity of the other, that she had saw a shadow in the corridor.

"I had heard strange things about the adjoining room," said Annetta; "But as she is close to yours, Mademoiselle, she did not want to tell you so as not to frighten you. Every time I passed by, she ran as fast as she could; and I also assure you that I often thought I heard noise. But tonight, walking in the corridor, without thinking of anything, I see a light appear, and looking back I see a large larva. I saw it, young lady, as distinctly as you do at this moment. A great figure entered the room which was always closed, of which none other than the master holds the key, and the door shut immediately.

"It must have been Signor Montoni," said Emilia.

— Oh! no, it wasn't him, having left him quarreling with the mistress in his room.

— You tell me very strange stories, Annetta; this morning you scared me with fear of murder, and now you would have me believe...

"I won't tell you anything more; but still if I hadn't been terribly afraid, I wouldn't have fainted, as I did.

Was it perhaps the room with the picture of the black veil?

— No, ma'am, it's the one closest to yours: how am I going to get back to my room? For all the gold in the world I would never cross the aisle again. »

Emilia, moved by this incident, and by the idea of having to be alone all night, replied that he could stay with her.

"Oh! no, really," said Annetta, "I wouldn't sleep in this room right now, not even for a thousand sequins. »

Emilia, remembering having heard people on the stairs, insisted that she spend the night for centuries, and she obtained it with great difficulty, and after the fear of repassing the corridor had persuaded her.

The next day, Emilia, crossing the hall to go to the walls, heard noise in the courtyard and the stamping of many horses. The tumult piqued her curiosity. Without going any further, she looked out a window, and saw a troop of horsemen in the courtyard; they had bizarre uniforms and complete, albeit varied, armament. They wore a short jacket striped in black and scarlet; they wrapped themselves in large ironworkers, under one of which she saw daggers of various sizes dangling from the waist; she then observed that almost all were well equipped with them, and several added the pike and the javelin; they wore Italian caps trimmed with black plumes; she didn't remember ever having seen so many ugly thugs gathered together. Seeing them, she thought she was surrounded by bandits, and it immediately occurred to her that Montoni was the leader of these rascals, [9] and the castle their meeting place. This strange assumption, however, was fleeting. As she watched, she saw Cavignì, Verrezzi and Bertolini come out dressed like the others; they had only hats adorned with large red and black plumes; when they mounted the horse, Verrezzi shone with joy; Cavignì seemed cheerful, but his demeanor was reflective, and he handled the horse with extreme grace. The figure of him amiable of him, and which seemed that of a hero, had never appeared with so much advantage. Emilia, considering him, thought that he resembled Valancourt, and indeed had all the fire and dignity of him; but she sought in vain the sweetness of physiognomy, and that frank expression of soul which characterized him.

Montoni then appeared, but without a uniform. He scrupulously examined the knights, conversed at length with the leaders, and when he had greeted them, the troop went around the courtyard and, commanded by Verrezzi, passed under the vault and went out.

Emilia withdrew from the window, and in the certainty of being calmer, went to the ramparts: she no longer saw any workers, and observed that the fortifications seemed completed. As she strolled absorbed in her reflections of her, she heard footsteps beneath the castle walls, and saw several men, whose exterior matched the troops which had departed shortly before her.

Assuming her aunt was up, she went to wish her good morning, and told her what she had seen; but she didn't want to, and she couldn't give her account of anything. Montoni's reservation towards his wife, in this regard, was by no means extraordinary. However, in Emilia's eyes, she added some shadow to her mystery, and made her suspect a great danger or great horrors in the project he conceived.

Annetta returned panting, as usual; her mistress solicitously asked her what was new, and she replied, "Ah! ma'am,[10] no one understands anything about it. Carlo knows everything, but he is reserved like his master. Someone says that Signor Montoni wants to frighten the enemy; others claim that he wants to storm some castle, but he has so much place in him that he certainly doesn't need to go and steal those of others. Lodovico seems to see better than anyone else, because he says he can guess all his master's projects.

"And what did he tell you?"

— He told me that the master .... that Signor Montoni is ..... is .....

"What in short?" said Signora Montoni, growing impatient.

- That the master has made himself the head of assassins, and sends to steal on his behalf.

- You are crazy. How come you can believe?...

In that Montoni appeared; Annetta ran away trembling. Emilia wanted to retire, but her aunt held her back, since her husband had made her so many times a witness of their quarrels, that they were no longer in awe of them.

"What does all this mean?" his wife asked him; « Who are those armed parties who have just left and why did you have the castle fortified? I want to know it.

"Come on, I've got something else to think about," replied Montoni; "You'd better obey me. Give me the cession of your property without many arguments.

"Never!" But what are your projects? Do you fear an attack? Will I be killed in a siege?

"Sign this paper, and you will know.

— What enemy comes? the woman interrupted him: "are you in the service of the state?" Am I a prisoner until the hour of my death?

"It could be," added Montoni, "if you don't yield to my question; you will not leave the castle if you have not satisfied me. »

The lady uttered frightful cries, but then stopped them thinking that her husband's speeches were not what tricks to extort the donation. And he told her shortly afterwards, adding that his purpose was certainly not as glorious as that of serving the State; that he had probably made himself the leader of bandits, to join the enemies of Venice and devastate the country.

Montoni looked at her grimly for a moment; Emilia was trembling, and her aunt, for the first time, thought she had said too much. 'This very night,' he said, 'you will be dragged to the eastern tower, where perhaps you will understand the danger of offending a man whose power over you is unlimited. »

The girl threw herself at his feet and begged him, weeping, to forgive her aunt. This she, frightened and indignant, now wanted to burst into imprecations, now join the prayers of her niece. Montoni, interrupting them with a horrible curse, broke away harshly from Emilia, who was holding him by the cloak: she fell on the floor with such violence that she hurt her forehead, and he went out without deigning to lift her up. She started at her aunt's tears, ran to help her, and found her all convulsive. She spoke to her without receiving an answer, but her convulsions redoubling, she was forced to go for help. Crossing the hall, she met Montoni, and begged him to go back and console her, her wife. He walked away with the utmost indifference; finally, she found old Carlo who was coming with Annetta. Go into the toilet, they carried Montoni into the adjoining room. They put her on the bed, and could hardly prevent her from getting hurt. Annetta was shaking and crying. Carlo was silent, and he seemed to pity her.

When the convulsions had somewhat ceased, Emilia, seeing that her aunt was in need of rest, said: 'Go, Carlo, if we need help I will send for you; but in the meantime, if the opportunity presents itself, speak to Signor Montoni on behalf of your mistress.

— Alas! replied Carlo; "I've seen too many!" I have little influence over my master's heart. But you, young lady, take care of yourself; I think you are not doing too well. »

And he left shaking his head. Emilia continued to look after her aunt, who, after a long sigh, came to her senses; but her eyes were wild, and she scarcely recognized her niece. Her first question concerned Montoni. Emilia begged her to calm down and rest, adding: 'If you want him to say something, I'll take care of it. "No," she replied languidly. "Does he still persist in snatching me from my room?" »

The girl replied that she had said nothing more, and made every effort to distract her; but her aunt did not listen to her, and she seemed oppressed by thoughts of her. Emilia, leaving her in the custody of her maid, ran to look for Montoni, and found him on the walls in the midst of a group of frightening-looking men. He spoke with vivacity. Finally some expression of his was repeated by the troop, and when they separated, the girl heard the following words: Tonight the watch begins at sunset. " At sunset ," they replied, and they withdrew.

Emilia joined Montoni, although he seemed to want to avoid her, and she had the courage to pray for her aunt, and to tell her of her condition and the danger to which her health would be exposed in an apartment that was too cold. "She Suffers because of her," replied he, "and she deserves no sympathy. You know very well what you must do to prevent the evils that await you. Obey, sign, and I won't think about it anymore. »

By dint of prayers, she obtained that the aunt would not be removed until the following day. Montoni left them all night to reflect. Emilia ran to announce the postponement. She didn't answer, but she looked very thoughtful. Meanwhile, her resolution on the disputed point seemed to give way in something. Her niece urged her, as an indispensable measure of security, to submit. "You don't know what you're suggesting," the woman replied. « Remember that my property belongs to you after my death, if I persist in the refusal.

'I was unaware of it, dear aunt; but this news will certainly not prevent me from recommending a step on which your rest depends, and I dare say even your life. No consideration for such a feeble interest, I beg you, do not make you hesitate for a moment to give him everything.

"Are you sincere, nephew?"

"And could you doubt it?" »

Signora Montoni seemed moved. "You deserve these possessions, dear niece, and I would like to be able to keep them for you: you have a virtue of which he didn't believe you capable. But Monsieur Valancourt?

"Madam," Emilia interrupted, "let's change the subject, please, and don't think that my heart is capable of selfishness." » The dialogue ended like this.

Emilia remained with her aunt, and did not leave her until very late.

At that moment, all was quiet, and the house seemed buried in sleep. Traversing the long and deserted galleries of the castle, Emilia was afraid without knowing why; but when, entering the corridor, she recalled the event of the other night, she was seized with sudden terror, and trembled lest an object such as that seen by Annetta should not present itself before her, and that ideal or well-founded fear should not produce the same effect on her senses. She did not know exactly which room the damsel had spoken of, but she was not unaware that she had to pass in front of it. Her restless gaze made it possible to distinguish in the darkness: she walked slowly and with an uncertain step. Reaching a door, she heard a small noise; she hesitated, but soon feared her became such that he no longer had the strength to walk. Suddenly the door opened, a person who looked to her like Montoni appeared, promptly re-entered the room and closed it. By the light that was in it, he thought he made out a person near the fire, in a melancholy attitude. Her terror vanished, and gave way to surprise: the mystery of Montoni, the discovery of an individual whom he visited at midnight in a forbidden apartment, and of whom many things were told, strongly excited her curiosity.

While she was perplexed, wishing to spy on Montoni's movements, but fearing to irritate him if she saw any, the door opened again and closed again for the second time. Then Emilia went straight into the adjoining room, and placing the lamp there, she hid in a dark vault of the corridor, to see if the person coming out was really Montoni. After a few minutes the door opened for the third time; the same person reappeared: it was Montoni; he looked around, closed it and went away. After a while he felt closed inside. She returned to her room in complete surprise. It was already midnight: having approached the window, she intended to walk on the terrace below, and she saw several people moving in the shade; she was struck by a noise of arms, and a password said in a low voice: then she remembered Montoni's orders, and she understood that for the first time they were mounting guard in the castle; when all was quiet, she went off to rest.

CHAPTER XXIII

The following morning, Emilia went to see her aunt very early in the morning; she had slept well, and recovered her spirits and strength, but her resolution to resist her husband was checked by [15] fear of her. The girl, fearing the consequences of her stubbornness, did everything to persuade her, but Signora Montoni, as we have seen, had the spirit of her contradiction; and when disgusting circumstances presented themselves, she sought less truth than arguments to fight. A long habit of hers had so confirmed this natural disposition in her that he was no longer aware of it. Emilia's reasons only awakened her pride rather than convinced her; and she thought only of evading the necessity of obedience on the point in question. If she managed to escape from the castle, she already counted on separating legally, and living in comfort with her remaining possessions. Emilia would have wanted it as much as she did, but she didn't flatter herself about a favorable outcome; she showed her the impossibility of going out the door, secured and watched with such caution; the extreme danger of confiding to the discretion of a servant of hers, who could betray her through malice or imprudence; and finally the revenge of Montoni, if she had discovered the plot ...

This struggle of contrary affections was tearing the heart of the aunt, when suddenly her husband entered, and without speaking of her indisposition, he declared to come and remind her how vainly she tried to resist her wishes. He gave her all day to grant her request, protesting that, in case of refusal, that the same evening he would bind her in the eastern tower; she added that many knights having to dine that same day in the castle, she would do the honors of the table with her niece. Signora Montoni did not want to accept, but reflecting that during lunch, her freedom, albeit restricted, could have favored her plans, she consented; the husband retired quickly. The order received filled Emilia with amazement and fear; she trembled at the idea of being exposed to such looks, and Count Morano's words were not meant to calm her. So he agreed to get ready to appear at dinner, but she too dressed more simply than usual, to avoid being distinguished. This policy did not succeed, since, when she returned to her aunt, Montoni di lei, reproaching her for making her resigned, prescribed her a more refined dress, using for this purpose the ornaments intended for her marriage to Morano. Adorned with her best taste and greatest magnificence, Emilia's beauty had never shone so brightly. Her only hope at that point was that Montoni planned less some extraordinary event than the triumph of ostentation, explaining the opulence of her family to the eyes of the guests. When she entered the hall, where a lavish dinner was being prepared, the castellan and his guests were already at table; she was going to take her place with her aunt, but Montoni motioned to her with her hand; two horsemen arose, and seated her between them.

The most advanced in age of these was large, had characteristic features, an aquiline nose, deeply penetrating sunken eyes; his face was thin and haggard as after a long illness.

The other, aged about forty, had a different physiognomy; oblique but vulpine look, brown eyes, small and sunken, almost oval face, irregular and ugly.

Eight other characters sat at the same table, all in uniform, and all wore a more or less strong expression of ferocity, cunning or libertinism. Emilia looked at them timidly, remembering the troop she had seen the previous day, and she thought she was surrounded by bandits. The place for the supper was an immense ancient and dark room, lit by a single very high Gothic window, from which one could see the western bastion and the Apennines. She observed that Montoni treated the guests with great authority, who reciprocated with dignity deference. During lunch time, all they spoke was of war and politics, of Venice, of his dangers, of the character of the reigning doge and of the primary senators. After lunch, the guests got up and all drank to Montoni's health and to the glory of his exploits. As he raised the goblet to his mouth, the wine bubbled over and broke the crystal into a thousand pieces. He made use of that kind of Venetian glass which has the property of breaking when it receives poisoned liquor. Suspecting that one of the guests had made an attempt on his life, he had the doors closed, and drawing his sword, he cast furious glances at everyone without distinction, shouting: «Here is a traitor! may all those who are innocent help me find the culprit. The knights broke into cries of indignation, and they drew their swords. Signora Montoni wanted to flee, but her husband forced her to stay, adding something else that she didn't understand because of her tumult and cries. Then all the servants appeared before him, and declared their ignorance. However, the protest could not be admitted, it being undeniable that only the wine of the castellan had been poisoned, so that at least the steward had to have been conniving. This man, with another, whose physiognomy betrayed the conviction of the crime, or the fear of punishment, was put in chains and dragged into a gloomy prison; Montoni would have treated all the guests in the same way if he hadn't feared the consequences of such a daring step: he therefore contented himself with swearing that not a single one of them would leave before this matter was cleared up.

Half an hour later he appeared in her toilet; Emilia shuddered at the sight of her grimness, her eyes flashing with rage and livid lips. " It's useless keep you on the negative side,' he cried furiously to his wife, 'since I have proof of your crime: you have no hope of pardon except in a sincere confession; your accomplice has revealed everything. »

Emilia was struck by the atrocious accusation. Her aunt's agitation did not allow her to speak; her face went from extreme pallor to a fiery red.

"Save the useless talk," said Montoni, seeing her disposed to speak; 'Your demeanor is enough to betray you; now you will be taken to the eastern tower.

'This accusation,' replied his wife, who could scarcely articulate a word, 'is a pretext for your cruelty; disdain to answer you.

'Sir,' said Emilia earnestly, 'this horrible accusation is false; I dare to make myself surety about my life. Yes, sir,' she added, 'this is not the time to show respect. You seek to deceive yourselves willfully, for the sole purpose of losing my poor aunt.

- If your life is dear to you, be silent. »

Emilia, rolling her eyes, exclaimed: 'There's no more hope. »

He turned to his wife, who, recovered from her surprise, rejected his suspicions with vehement bitterness. Montoni's anger increased; Emilia, foreseeing her consequences, rushed to his feet, embracing his knees and begging him, weeping, to calm her fury; but deaf to the prayers of his niece and the justifications of her wife, he fiercely threatened both, when she was called. He went out, closing the door and taking the key with him. So they found themselves captives. Montoni looked around her looking for a means of escape. But how to do it? She knew too well how strong the castle was, and with what vigilance watched. He was afraid of entrusting his fate to the whim of a servant whose assistance he had to beg.

Meanwhile they heard a great tumult and confusion in the gallery; at times the clash of swords could be heard. Montoni's provocation, his impetuosity, his violence, made Emilia suppose that weapons alone could end the horrible contest. Her aunt had exhausted all her expressions of indignation, and her niece all her consoling phrases. They were both silent in that sort of calm which occurs in nature after the conflict of the elements. The circumstances of which Emilia had witnessed her represented a thousand confused fears, and her ideas succeeded each other in tumultuous disorder; she was jolted out of her meditation of hers by hearing a knock at the door, and she recognized Annetta's voice.

"My dear lady, open up: I have many things to tell you," said the poor girl in a low voice. "The door is closed," answered the landlady. "Yes, I see it, ma'am, but please open it. "The master has brought the key with him. — O Blessed Virgin! what will become of us? "Help us out," said la Montoni. "Where's Lodovico?" - In the great hall with the others, fighting valiantly. — Fight! and who are the others? "The master, all those gentlemen, and many others. - Is there anyone injured? Emilia said in a trembling voice. "Yes, ma'am, there are some lying on the ground soaked in blood. Great God! let me enter, madam; ha! here they come; they definitely kill me. "Flee," said Emilia, "flee; we can't open you. »

Annetta repeated that they were coming, and fled.

'Calm down, aunt,' said Emilia, 'for pity's sake, calm down; perhaps they come to free us. Who knows if Mr. Montoni hasn't already won.

'Here they are,' cried the aunt, 'I hear them coming. »

Emilia raised her languid eyes to the door, scared togreatestsign. The key was put in the lock; the door opened, and Montoni entered, followed by three satellites. "Do my orders," he said to them, pointing to his wife; she gave a cry and was dragged away on the spot. Emilia fell senseless on a chair: when she revived, she saw herself alone, and looking around the whole room with bewildered eyes, she seemed to question everything about her aunt's fate. Finally, she rose to examine, albeit with little hope, whether the door was free, and she found it unlocked. She stepped timidly into the gallery, unsure where she should go. Her first wish was to obtain some news of her aunt's fate. She went down to the dining room. As she advanced, she heard angry voices from a distance: the faces of hers that she met in the numerous passages and the confusion that reigned in her increased her fear. Finally he came to the room he was looking for, but there was none. Unable to stand any longer, she rested for a moment. He reflected that she would have looked in vain for her aunt in the immense labyrinth of that castle, which seemed to be besieged by brigands. So he thought of going back to his room, but he was afraid of meeting those fierce men, when a dull murmur broke the gloomy silence; the noise increased: he made out a few voices and heard footsteps approaching. She got up to leave but they were coming precisely by the only route she could follow: so she thought of waiting for them to enter. She heard moans, and shortly afterwards saw a man appear carried by four. Terrified at this sight, she barely had enough strength to go back to her room without being able to know who the wretch surrounded by those people was.

His affection for his aunt grew ever greater; she remembered that Montoni had threatened to lock her in the eastern tower, and it was probable that this punishment had satisfied his vengeance on her.[21] So he resolved, during the night, to look for a way to go to that tower. He knew well that he could not have effectively helped his aunt, but he believed that in her sad prison it would always be a consolation for her to hear the voice of her niece. A few hours passed thus in solitude and silence, and it seemed that Montoni had completely forgotten her. As soon as night fell, sentries were posted.

The darkness of the room revived Emilia's terror. Leaning against the window, she was attacked by a thousand disgusting ideas. " Is that! she said; "If one of these bandits, under the cover of darkness, were to enter my room, what would happen to me?" Then, remembering the mysterious inhabitant of the adjoining chamber, her terror changed its object. "He is not a prisoner, though he remains hidden in that room; it is not Montoni who shuts it up from the outside, but it is the unknown itself which takes care of this. »Making all these reflections, she withdrew from the window, and lit the lamp. So she hurried to secure the stairway door as best she could. This work occupied him until midnight. All was quiet, and only the footsteps of the sentry on the rampart could be heard. She opened the door carefully, and seeing and hearing a most perfect calm, she went out; but as soon as she had taken a few steps, she saw a faint glow on the walls of the gallery. She went back to her room and closed the door, imagining that maybe Montoni was going to pay her visit incognito. After about half an hour she went out again, and seeing no one, she took the direction of the Scala di Tramontana, imagining that she could more easily find the tower there. She stopped often, listening fearfully to the howl of the wind, and looking from afar through the darkness of the long halls. Finally he came to the stairway he was looking for, which led to two different passages. She hesitated a little, and she chose the one that led into a vast gallery.

The solitude of that place froze her with fear, and she even trembled at the echo of her own footsteps. Suddenly she thought she heard a voice, and fearing equally to advance or retreat, she remained motionless, scarcely daring to raise her eyes. It seemed to her that the voice uttered lamentations, and she was confirmed in this idea by a long moan. She believed she might be her aunt, and she stepped towards that part. Nonetheless, before speaking about her, she was afraid to confide in some indiscreet person that she might report her to Montoni. The person, whoever she was, looked very distressed. While she hesitated, that voice called Lodovico. Emilia then recognized Annetta, and she happily approached to answer her.

"Lodovico! cried Annetta in tears; "Lodovico!

"It's me," Emilia said, trying to open the door, "But how are you here? Who locked you up?

- Lodovico! Lodovico!

It's not Lodovico; it's me, it's Emilia. »

Annetta stopped crying and was silent.

"If you can open the door, I'll go in," said Emilia; « do not be afraid of anything.

- Lodovico! oh Lodovico! cried Annetta.

Emilia lost her patience, and fearing being discovered, wanted to leave; but she reflected that the girl might have some news of her aunt, or at least she could show her the way to the tower. She finally got an answer, albeit an unsatisfactory one. Annetta knew nothing of her mistress, and she begged her only to tell her what had become of Lodovico. She Emilia replied that she didn't know, and asked her why she was locked up there inside her.

'Lodovico put me here. After escaping from the mistress's toilet, I ran without knowing where: I met him in the gallery, and he confined me to this room, taking away the key, so that no harm would happen to me. He promised me to come back when everything is quiet. But it's already late, and I don't see him coming; who knows they didn't kill him? »

Emilia then remembered the wounded man she had seen carried into the room, and she no longer doubted that it was Lodovico, but she said no. Eager to know something about her aunt, she begged her to show her the way to the tower.

"Oh! don't go, miss, for God's sake, don't leave me here alone.

'But, dear Annetta,' replied Emilia, 'don't think I can stay here all night. Teach me the way to the tower, and in the morning I will see to your deliverance.

- Blessed Mary! said Annetta; "Do I have to stay here all night?" I will die of fear and hunger, having eaten nothing since lunch. »

Emilia could hardly contain her laughter at these expressions. She finally got some sort of direction to the eastern tower. After much searching, she reached the tower stairway, and paused a moment to fortify her courage with the feeling of duty. As she examined the place, she saw a door opposite the stairway. Not sure if this would lead her to her aunt, she pulled the latch and opened it. She saw that she was standing on the rampart, and the wind almost put out the light. The clouds stirred by the winds were struggling to show a few stars, redoubling the horrors of the night. She closed the door and went up.

The image of her aunt, perhaps stabbed by her husband's own hand, frightened her; and she regretted having dared to go to that place. But her duty triumphed over her fear, and she kept walking. All was calm. Finally she caught her eyes a streak of blood on her stairway; the walls and all the steps were sprinkled with it. She stopped struggling to steady herself, and her trembling hand nearly dropped the lamp. She felt nothing; that tower not it seemed inhabited by a living soul. She reproached herself a thousand times for having gone out; she was always afraid of discovering some new object of horror; yet she, close to the end of her research, she could not bring herself to lose the fruit. She regained her courage, and when she reached the tower, she saw another door and opened it. The dim rays of her lamp let her see only damp, bare walls. Entering that room, and in the dreadful expectation of finding her aunt's body there, she saw something in a corner, and struck by a horrible conviction, she remained motionless for some time. Animated therefore by a kind of desperation, she approached the object of her terror, and she recognized an old military implement, under which weapons were piled up. As she made her way to the stairway to exit, she saw another door bolted to the outside, and in front of which other footprints of blood could be seen: the aunt called aloud, but no one answered. « She is dead! » she exclaimed then; "they killed her; her blood reddens these steps. »She lost all strength, she put down the lamp, and sat down on the ladder. After new useless efforts to open it, she went downstairs to go back to her room. As soon as she was in the corridor, she saw Montoni, and she, more frightened than ever, threw herself into a corner so as not to meet him. She heard him close a door, the same one she had already noticed. She heard his steps go away from her, and when her extreme distance no longer allowed her to distinguish him, she went into her room and lay down. he put down the lamp, and sat down on the ladder. After new useless efforts to open it, she went downstairs to go back to her room. As soon as she was in the corridor, she saw Montoni, and more frightened than ever, she threw herself into a corner so as not to meet him. She heard him close a door, the same one she had already noticed. She heard his steps go away from her, and when her extreme distance no longer allowed her to distinguish him, she went into her room and lay down. he put down the lamp, and sat down on the ladder. After new useless efforts to open it, she went downstairs to go back to her room. As soon as she was in the corridor, she saw Montoni, and more frightened than ever, she threw herself into a corner so as not to meet him. She heard him close a door, the same one she had already noticed. She heard his steps go away from her, and when her extreme distance no longer allowed her to distinguish him, she went into her room and lay down.

The dawn was already glistening and Emilia's eyelids had not yet closed in sleep; but finally exhausted nature gave some respite to his pains.

CHAPTER XXIV

Emilia remained in her room all morning, without receiving any orders from Montoni, nor seeing anything other than the armed men walking on the bastion. Anxiety about her aunt's fate finally overcame her horror at speaking to that barbarian, and she decided to go to him to obtain permission to see her.

Annetta's too prolonged absence further proved that some misfortune had befallen Lodovico, and that she was nevertheless locked up. Emilia therefore resolved to go and see if she was still in the room, and to inform Montoni: she was striking midday. The lamentations of the poor woman could be heard at the end of the gallery: she deplored her own fate and that of Lodovico; when he heard Emilia, he begged her to release her at once, because she was starving. Her mistress replied that she would go immediately to ask for her release; then the fear of her hunger yielded for the moment to that of her master; and when the girl left her, she warmly begged her not to discover the asylum where she was hiding: Emilia approached the great hall, and the tumult she heard, the individuals she met renewed their fears. But they seemed peaceful: they looked at her avidly, sometimes they spoke to her. Crossing the room to go to the cedar drawing room, where Montoni usually lived, he saw broken swords and drops of blood on the floor: he almost believed he saw a corpse. As she advanced, she made out a murmur of voices, which made her wonder whether or not she should advance. She looked in vain for some servant to be announced, but none appeared. Her accents, which she meant for her, no longer expressed her anger, and she recognized the voices of several of the previous evening's guests. While she was preparing to knock, Montoni himself appeared; surprised, he let all the various movements of his soul be seen in his physiognomy. Emilia, trembling, remained mute. Montoni asked her sternly what he had understood of their conversation. he secrets, but to beg his clemency for his aunt and for Annetta. Montoni seemed to doubt it, stared at her with an inquiring eye, and the disquiet he felt could not have arisen from frivolous reasons. Emilia begged him to let her go and visit her aunt: he replied with a bitter smile, which confirmed her fears, and made her lose the courage to renew her prayer to him.

"For Annetta," he said, "go and find Carlo, who will open them." The fool who locked her up no longer exists. »

Emilia, trembling, replied: "But my poor aunt, sir, please tell me about my aunt...

"He's taking care of it," Montoni added. "I don't have time to answer your vain questions. »And he wanted to leave her. Emilia detained him begging him to let her know where she was her wife; suddenly they heard the trumpet, and a confused noise of men and horses in the courtyard. Montoni immediately ran out. Emilia, in the uncertainty of following him, looking out the window, seemed to distinguish the same knights she had seen leaving a few days before her, and, seeing people flocking from all sides, she thought it best to take refuge in her room. Montoni's manner and expressions when he spoke of her wife partially confirmed her suspicions of her. She was absorbed in those dark thoughts, when she saw old Carlo enter.

'Dear young lady,' he said to her, 'I haven't been able to take care of you until now. I bring you fruit and wine, because you must need it.

"Thank you, Carlo," she said; "Have you perhaps received this order from Signor Montoni?"

"No ma'am," replied the old man; 'His Excellency has too many occupations. »

The girl renewed her questions about her aunt's fate: but while they were dragging her away, Carlo was on the other side of the castle, and from that moment he no longer knew anything about it. While he was saying this, she Emilia looked at him attentively, and she could not understand whether she was speaking out of ignorance, or dissimulation, or fear of offending her master. He replied laconically about her fight the night before, assuring her at the same time that the altercations were over, and that the castellan believed he had been deceived in suspecting the guests. "The fight had no other origin," Carlo added, "but I flatter myself that I will never see such a spectacle again in this castle, even though strange things are being prepared there. She begged him to explain. « Ah! Madame," he said, "I cannot betray the secret, nor express all my thoughts on the subject; but time will reveal all. »

She begged him to open to Annetta, showing him the room where the poor woman was confined; Carlo promised to satisfy her; as she was leaving, she asked him who the new arrivals were: her conjecture came true: it was Verrezzi with his troops.

More than an hour passed before Annetta appeared. She finally came in crying and moaning.

"Who would have predicted that, miss?" Oh! terrible case! Oh! poor Lodovico!"

"Did they actually kill him?" Emilia asked, moved.

- No; but he was badly wounded. That's why he couldn't come and open me; but now he begins to feel better.

— Dear Annetta, I am very happy to hear that he exists. »

As soon as the girl had calmed down somewhat, Emilia sent her to inquire about her aunt, but was unable to get any news of her.

The next two days passed without any notable incident, and without her being able to know anything about her aunt. On the evening of the second day, prey to her grief and assailed by baleful images, to drive them away, she looked out the window, considering the so many very bright and sparkling stars in the empyrean blue, that all follow a specific path without getting confused in space. He remembered how many times with his beloved father he had observed its course. These reflections ended up causing her pain and surprise almost equally. She thought of the sad events that had followed the first sweets of life, of the last shocks, of her present situation in a foreign land, in an isolated castle, surrounded by all vices, exposed to all violence, and she seemed to be deluded by a dream produced by the distorted imagination, nor could he persuade himself that so many evils were not ideal. She wept at the thought of how much her parents would have suffered if they could have foreseen the misfortunes that awaited them.

He raised his eyes to heaven, and saw the same planet observed in Languedoc the night before his father's death; now it was above the eastern towers. He remembered the speeches relating to the state of souls, and the understood melody, and of which his tenderness, in spite of reason, had admitted the superstitious sense. Suddenly the sounds of sweet harmony seemed to pass through the air; he shivered, listened for a few minutes in painful expectation, making an effort to gather his thoughts and resort to reason. But human reason has no dominion over the ghosts of the imagination, any more than the senses have the means to judge the shape of luminous bodies, which shine and are soon extinguished in the darkness of the night.

Her surprise at that music so sweet and delightful was at least excusable, since it had already been a long time since she had heard the slightest melody. The sharp sound of the fife and the trumpet was the only music known in Udolfo's castle.

When she had recovered a little, she tried to ascertain from which direction the sound came. It seemed to her that she was starting from the bottom of the castle, but she could not specify it. Fear and surprise soon gave way to the pleasure of harmony, which the nocturnal silence made even more interesting. The music ceased, and Emilia's ideas wandered for a long time about this strange circumstance; it was singular to hear music after midnight, when everyone must have been at rest, and in a castle where for so many years nothing resembling it had been heard. Her long sufferings had rendered her sensitive to terror, and susceptible to superstition. It seemed to her that her father could have spoken to her with that music, to inspire her consolation and confidence on her subject with which she was then occupied. Her reason, however, suggested this conjecture to be ridiculous, and she rejected it; but she, by a natural inconsequence of heated imagination, she indulged in ideas more bizarre than her: he recalled the singular case that had placed Montoni in possession of the castle; he considered the mysterious manner of the disappearance of the former owner; she was never heard from again, and her spirit was struck with fear. There was no apparent connection between that event and the melody, yet he believed that these two things were linked by some secret bond.

Finally she withdrew from the window, but her legs trembled as she approached the bed. The light was about to go out, and she trembled at having to remain in the dark in that vast room; but soon ashamed of her weakness, she went to bed thinking of the new incident, and she resolved to wait until the following night for the same hour to watch for the return of the music.

CHAPTER XXV

Annetta came to her in the morning out of breath. "Oh! young lady," she said in truncated words, "how many things I have to tell you! I found out who the prisoner is, but he wasn't the prisoner; he is the closed one in that room, of which I told you, and I had taken him for a shadow!

"Who was that prisoner?" Emilia asked, thinking back to last night's case.

"You are mistaken, madame, he wasn't a prisoner at all.

"So who is it?"

- Blessed Virgin! how did I stay! I just met him on the rampart below! Ah! Signora Emilia, this place is really strange. If we lived there for a thousand years, I would never cease to be amazed. But, as he told you, I met him on the rampart, and he was certainly thinking of anything but him.

'This talk is unbearable; please, Annetta, do not abuse my patience.

"Yes, miss, guess what? who was mo; he is someone you know very well.

"I can't guess," Emilia replied impatiently.

"Well, I'll put you on the road. A large man, with a long face, who walks gravely, who wears a great plume on his hat, who lowers his eyes when spoken to, and looks at people from under thick black eyelashes! You have seen it a thousand times in Venice; he was a close friend of the master. And now, when I think about it, what was he afraid of in this wild old castle to shut himself up so cautiously? But now he's taking off, and I just found him on the bastion. He trembled to see him; he always scared me; but he didn't want him to notice. As he passed me, I made him a curtsey, and said: Welcome to the castle, Signor Orsino.

— Ah! so it was Orsino?

- Yes Madam; himself, the one who had that Venetian gentleman killed.

— Great God! cried Emilia; "He has come to Udolfo!" He did well to stay hidden.

"But what need is there for so many precautions?" Who could ever imagine finding it here?

"It's very true," said Emilia, and she might have concluded that nocturnal music came from Orsino, if she hadn't been certain he had neither taste nor talent for that art. Not wishing to augment Annetta's fears by speaking of what caused her pain, she asked her if there was anyone in the castle who could play any instrument.

"Oh, yes, miss, Benedetto plays the drum well, Lancellotto is good on the trumpet, and Lodovico plays the trumpet well too." But he is sick now. I remember once...

"Hadn't you heard a piece of music," said Emilia interrupting her, "after our arrival in this place, and especially last night?

"No, ma'am; I have never heard any other music than that of drums and trumpets. And as for last night, all I've done is dream of my late mistress's shadow.

"Your late mistress?" said the girl trembling; "So you know something? Tell me everything you know, please.

'But, young lady, you are aware that no one knows what has happened to her: it is therefore clear that she has taken the same path as the former mistress of the castle, of whom no one has heard anything since. »

Emilia, deeply afflicted, dismissed the maid, whose speeches had revived her terrible suspicions about her aunt's fate, which determined her to make a second effort to obtain some certainty on the subject, heading once more to Montoni.

Annetta returned a few hours later and told Emilia that the porter of the castle wished to speak to her as he had a secret to reveal. This embassy surprised her, and made her wonder if there was any danger; she was already hesitant to consent; but a brief reflection he demonstrated the improbability of it, and blushed at his weakness.

"Tell him to come into the corridor," she replied, "and I'll talk to him." »

Annetta left, and returned shortly after saying:

« Bernardino doesn't dare come into the corridor, fearing to be seen. He would stray too far from his seat, and he can't do it right now. But if you please come and see him at the gate, we will go through a secret road that he has taught me, without crossing the courtyard, and he will tell you things that will surprise you very much. »

Emilia, not approving of that project, positively denied going. 'Tell him,' she added, 'that if he has any confidences to share with me, I will listen to him in the corridor when he has time to come. »

Annetta went to bring the answer, and when she returned she said to Emilia: 'I haven't concluded anything, young lady; Bernardino cannot in any way leave the door at this moment; but if tonight, as soon as night falls, you wish to come to the eastern rampart, he may perhaps be able to withdraw for a minute and reveal his secret to you. »

Emilia, surprised and alarmed at the same time by the mystery he demanded, hesitated about which course to take; but considering that perhaps she would warn him of some misfortune, she or she would have to give her news of her aunt; she resolved to accept the invitation. 'After sunset,' she said, 'I will be at the bottom of the east rampart; but then the sentry will be posted; how will Bernardino not be seen?

That is precisely what I told him, and he replied that he had the key to the communicating door between the courtyard and the bastion, through which he proposes to pass; that as for the sentinels, they do not put any at the end of the rampart, because the very high walls and the east tower are sufficient from that side to watch the castle, and that when it is dark, it cannot be seen at the other end.[33]

"Well," said Emilia, "I'll hear what you want to tell me, and I beg you to accompany me to the bastion tonight: in the meantime, tell Bernardino to be punctual at the indicated time, since I could still be seen by Signor Montoni." Where is he? I'd like to talk to him.

— He It is he in the cedar parlor, in parliament with other gentlemen. I think he wants to give a banquet to make up for last night's mess: everyone in the kitchen is very busy. »

The landlady asked her if they were expecting new guests. Annetta didn't believe it. "Poor Lodovico! she said; "He'd be as cheerful as the others if he got better! However, the case is not desperate: Count Morano was more wounded than him, and in the meantime he recovered and returned to Venice.

"How did you know that?"

"They told me last night, miss; I forgot to tell you. »

Emilia begged her to warn her when Montoni was alone. Annetta went to take the answer to Bernardino, who was waiting impatiently for her. Meanwhile the castellan was so busy all day that Emilia did not have the opportunity to allay her fears about her aunt's fate. She turned her thoughts to the caretaker's errand: she lost herself in a thousand conjectures, and as the hour of the mysterious interview approached, her impatience with her grew. The sun finally set: she heard the sentries posted, and as soon as Annetta arrived, who was to accompany her, they went down together. Emilia feared meeting Montoni, or someone of hers. "Reassure yourself," said Annetta, "they're all still at the table, and Bernardino knows it." »

When they reached the first terrace, the sentry shouted: Who goes there? Emilia answered, and they walked to the eastern rampart, where they were stopped by another sentry, and after a second reply, they were able to continue. Emilia did not like exposing herself so late to the [34] discretion of those people, impatient to retire, she quickened her pace to reach Bernardino, but not finding him, she leaned thoughtfully on the parapet. The wood and the valley were buried in darkness, a light breeze disturbed only the tops of the trees, and from time to time voices were heard inside the vast building.

"What are these rumors?" Emilia said trembling.

"Those of the master and his guests who revel," replied Annetta.

— Great God! how is it possible for a man to be so cheerful when he forms the unhappiness of his fellow man!... And the girl looked with horror at the eastern tower where she was standing: she saw a dim light through the ironwork of the lower room: a a person passed by with the lamp in his hand; this circumstance did not revive her hopes in relation to Signora Montoni, since, having looked for her precisely there, she had found there only an old uniform and some weapons. Nonetheless, she decided to try to open the tower outside her as soon as Bernardino had left her.

Time passed, and he did not appear. Emilia, restless, hesitated whether she should wait for him again; she would have sent Annetta to look for him, if she hadn't been afraid of being left alone.

While she was talking with the follower of lateness, she saw him appear. She emilia lei hurried to ask him what she wanted to tell her, begging him not to waste time, as the night air made her uncomfortable.

"Fire the maid, young lady," Bernardino said to her in a sepulchral voice, which made her tremble, "I can only reveal my secret to you alone." Emilia hesitated, but she finished by begging Annetta to go away a few steps; she then said to him: «Now, my friend, I'm alone, what do you want to tell me?»

He was silent for a moment, as if to reflect, then he replied: « I would certainly lose my job if [35] the boss knew. Promise me, miss, that you won't tell anyone a syllable of what I'm about to tell you. Whoever trusted me in this business would make me pay the penalty if he came to understand that I had betrayed him. But I was interested for you, and I want to tell you everything. »Emilia thanked him assuring him of her secrecy, and she begged him to continue. "Annetta told me in the dining room how much you feel sorry for Signora Montoni, and how much you want to be informed of her fate.

- It's true, if you know it, tell me immediately what is most terrible about it; I am saved from everything.

"I can tell you, but I see you so afflicted that I don't know how to begin.

"I am parried against everything, friend," Emilia repeated in a firm and imposing voice, "and I prefer the most terrible certainty to this cruel doubt.

"If so, I'll tell you everything. You already know that his master and his wife did not get along; it is not for me to know the reason, but I think you will know the result.

"Well," said Emilia, "and so?"

- It seems the master has lately had a strong altercation with her: I saw everything, understood everything, and more than they can suppose; but as this did not concern me, I said nothing. A few days ago he sent for me and said: Bernardino, you are a good man, and I think I can trust you... I assured him of my fidelity. Then, as far as I remember, he said to me: I need you to serve me in an important business. He ordered me what he was to do; but of this I will say nothing, as it concerns only the mistress.

— Heavens! what did you do? what fury could drive you both to such a detestable act?

"It was a fury," replied Bernardino in a dark voice, and they both fell silent. Emilia didn't have the courage to ask for help. Bernardino seemed afraid to explain himself more specifically; finally[36] he added: « It is useless to go back to the past. The master was too cruel, yes, but he wanted to be obeyed. If I had refused, he would have found another less scrupulous than me.

"Did you kill her?" stammered Emilia; "So I'm talking to an assassin?" Bernardino was silent, and the girl took a step to leave him.

"Stay, miss," he said to her; 'You deserve to let yourself believe it, since you thought me capable of it.

"If you're innocent, say it quickly," added Emilia, almost dying; « I don't have enough strength to listen to you longer.

Well, Signora Montoni is alive only for me; she is my prisoner: her excellency confined her to the room above the door, and she entrusted me with her custody. She wanted to tell you that you could talk to her; but now... "

Emilia, relieved by these words from inexpressible anguish, implored him to let her see her aunt. He consented without asking her much, and told her that the following night, when Montoni was in bed, if she wanted to go to the gate of the castle, she could perhaps introduce her to the prisoner.

In the midst of her gratitude that such a favor from her inspired in her, she seemed to perceive in his glances a certain malignant satisfaction as she pronounced these last words. She dismissed the idea at first, she thanked him again, and she commended her aunt to his pity, assuring him that she would reward him, and she would be exact at the appointed appointment; she then she wished him good evening, and went away.

A few hours passed before the joy excited in her by Bernardino's story allowed her to judge accurately the dangers that still threatened her aunt and herself. When her agitation subsided, she reflected that her aunt was the prisoner of a man, who could sacrifice her to her vengeance or avarice. When she thought of the atrocious physiognomy [37] of her porter, she believed that the decree of her death was already signed; imagining the one capable of consuming any barbaric act. These ideas of hers reminded her of her accent in which she had promised to show her the prisoner. It occurred to her a thousand times that her aunt might already be dead, and that the scoundrel was perhaps in charge of sacrificing her too to the avarice of Montoni, who in this way would come into possession of her properties in Languedoc, which they had formed the theme of such a hateful contestation. The enormity of this double crime made him at last dismiss the likelihood of her; but she did not lose all the fears, nor all the doubts inspired by Bernardino's manners.

The night was already far advanced, and she was almost distressed at not hearing the music, whose return she awaited with a feeling stronger than her curiosity. She made out for a long time the immoderate laughter of Montoni and his guests, the lewd songs, and she heard their noisy conversations finish very late. There followed a deep silence broken only by the footsteps of those retiring to their respective lodgings. Emilia, remembering that the previous evening she had heard the music at about the same hour, slowly opened the window, listening to her sweet harmony.

The planet she observed at the first hearing of the music was not yet seen, and yielding to a superstitious impression, she watched attentively the part of the sky in which she was to appear, waiting for the melody at the same moment. Finally it appeared, shining above the eastern towers. Emilia listened, but in vain. The hours passed in anxious expectation; no sound disturbed the solemn calm of nature. She remained at the window until dawn began to whiten the peaks of the mountains, and then persuaded that the music would not be heard otherwise, she went to bed.

CHAPTER XXVI

Emilia was surprised the following day to hear that Annetta knew of her aunt's detention in the room above the entrance door to the castle, and was not even unaware of the plan for a nocturnal visit; that Bernardino could have confided such an important mystery to the maid was hardly probable, but in the meantime he sent her a message relating to their conversation, inviting her to be alone, an hour after midnight, on the rampart, and adding that he would act according to his promise. Emilia shuddered at this proposal, and she was assailed by a thousand fears similar to those which had agitated her during the night. She did not know what side to take with her: it was often imagined that Bernardino had deceived her; that perhaps he had already murdered his aunt; that at that moment he was Montoni's assassin, who wanted to sacrifice her for the execution of her plans. The suspicion that the unhappy woman was no longer alive joined his personal fears. In fact, the uncle knew that, in the event of his wife's death without having given him her assets, Emilia would inherit them; nor was it improbable that he would think of getting rid of her too in order to enter into tranquil possession of her much coveted substances. Finally, her desire to free herself from so many cruel uncertainties made her decide not to miss her meeting.

"But how can I," she said, "cross the bastion so late?" The sentries will stop me, and Signor Montoni will know about it.

"Bernardino has thought of everything," answered Annetta; « he gave me this key, putting me in charge to inform you that it opens a door at the end of the vaulted gallery, which leads to the eastern bastion; so you won't be afraid to meet the men on watch. She also instructed me to tell you that she makes you go on the terrace alone to lead you to the place agreed, in order not to open the great hall, whose gate creaks. This natural explanation soothed Emilia.

"But why does he want me to go alone?"

- Why? I just asked him. Why, I told him, couldn't I come too? what's wrong with that? But she said no. I wanted to persist: he was inflexible. But I assume you'll know who you're going to see.

"Did Bernardino perhaps tell you that?"

"No, ma'am, he didn't tell me anything. »

For the rest of the day, Emilia was prey to constant uncertainty. She heard midnight strike and was still hesitating. Pity for her aunt finally overcame all repugnance: she begged Annetta to follow her to the gallery door, and there to wait for her return. Once there, she opened the door, trembling, and entered the bastion alone and without light, advanced cautiously and attentively towards the agreed place, looking for Bernardino through the darkness. She was horrified at the sound of a hoarse voice speaking close to her, and she immediately recognized the porter, who was waiting for her leaning on the parapet. And he reproached her for being late, telling her that he had missed more than half an hour. He told her to follow him, and approached the place where he had entered the terrace. When the door was opened, the gloomy gloom of the passage, illuminated by a single torch that burned fixed in the ground, it made her tremble; he refused to enter it, unless he allowed Annetta to accompany her. Bernardino opposed it, but skilfully combined her refusal with many peculiarities peculiar to her to excite Emilia's curious pity for her aunt, who managed to persuade her to follow him to the front door. He took the torch and went on. At the end of the corridor he opened another door, and after going down a few steps they found themselves in a ruined chapel. The girl remembered some of Annetta's speeches on this subject. She gazed in terror at those vaultless walls who managed to persuade her to follow him to the door. He took the torch and went on. At the end of the corridor he opened another door, and after going down a few steps they found themselves in a ruined chapel. The girl remembered some of Annetta's speeches on this subject. She gazed in terror at those vaultless walls who managed to persuade her to follow him to the door. He took the torch and went on. At the end of the corridor he opened another door, and after going down a few steps they found themselves in a ruined chapel. The girl remembered some of Annetta's speeches on this subject. She gazed in terror at those vaultless walls and covered with moss; those Gothic windows where the ella and brionia made up for a long piece of glass, and whose festoons mingled with the broken capitals. Bernardino struck a stone and burst into a horrible curse, made more terrible by the lugubrious echo. Her heart froze, but he kept following him, and he turned right. "This way, miss," he said to her, descending a stairway that seemed to lead to deep dungeons. Emilia stopped asking him in a trembling voice where she wanted to take her.

"At the door," replied Bernardino.

"Can't we go through the chapel?"

"No, madame, it would lead us to the second courtyard, which I want to avoid." »

Emilia still hesitated, fearing equally to go ahead, and to irritate him by refusing to follow him.

"Come, young lady," he said, having already reached the bottom of the stairs, "make haste: I can't stay here all night; I don't wait for you anymore. »Saying yes, he went ahead, always carrying the torch. Emilia, fearing to remain in the dark, followed him reluctantly. They reached a cellar, where the damp, thick air and the thick vapors obscured the torch so much that Bernardino, for fear it might go out, stopped for a moment to kindle it; in the interval, Emilia observed near her a double iron gate, and, further away from her, some mounds of earth which seemed to surround a grave for the dead. Such a sight in that place would have struck her violently at any other time, but then she believed that this was the tomb of her aunt, and that the perfidious Bernardino was also leading to her death. The dark and terrible place where they found themselves almost justified his thought, which seemed adapted to the crime, and a murder could be committed there with impunity. She overcome by terror, she didn't know what to solve, thinking how vain was the escape, impeded by the darkness and the long journey, as well as by his weakness. Pale and restless, she waited for Bernardino to light the torch, and since the sight of her always called to mind the grave, she could not help but ask him for whom she was prepared. The man turned her gaze towards her without answering. She repeated the question; he, shaking his face, went further, nor opened his mouth. The girl walked trembling as far as another staircase, climbing which they found themselves in the first courtyard. In crossing it, the flame let us see the high black walls covered with long grasses protruding from the joints, and crowned by turrets contrasting with the enormous towers of the gate. In that painting the stocky figure of Bernardino stood out. He was wrapped in a long dark cloak, under which his buskins, or sandals, and the tip of the long saber which he constantly wore at his side were barely exposed. On his head was a low cap of black velvet trimmed with a small feather. His hard features expressed a gruff, cunning and impatient mood. The sight of the courtyard revived the despondent Emilia, and as she approached the gate she began to hope that she had deceived herself in her fearful conjectures about her; looking restlessly at the first window above the vault, and seeing it dark, she asked if that was the place where her aunt was locked up. She spoke slowly, and Bernardino did not seem to understand her because he did not answer her. They entered the building, and found themselves at the foot of the stairway of one of the towers. On his head was a low cap of black velvet trimmed with a small feather. His hard features expressed a gruff, cunning and impatient mood. The sight of the courtyard revived the despondent Emilia, and as she approached the gate she began to hope that she had deceived herself in her fearful conjectures about her; looking restlessly at the first window above the vault, and seeing it dark, she asked if that was the place where her aunt was locked up. She spoke slowly, and Bernardino did not seem to understand her because he did not answer her. They entered the building, and found themselves at the foot of the stairway of one of the towers. On his head was a low cap of black velvet trimmed with a small feather. His hard features expressed a gruff, cunning and impatient mood. The sight of the courtyard revived the despondent Emilia, and as she approached the gate she began to hope that she had deceived herself in her fearful conjectures about her; looking restlessly at the first window above the vault, and seeing it dark, she asked if that was the place where her aunt was locked up. She spoke slowly, and Bernardino did not seem to understand her because he did not answer her. They entered the building, and found themselves at the foot of the stairway of one of the towers. approaching the door she began to hope that she had been deceived in her fearful conjectures; looking restlessly at the first window above the vault, and seeing it dark, she asked if that was the place where her aunt was locked up. She spoke slowly, and Bernardino did not seem to understand her because he did not answer her. They entered the building, and found themselves at the foot of the stairway of one of the towers. approaching the door she began to hope that she had been deceived in her fearful conjectures; looking restlessly at the first window above the vault, and seeing it dark, she asked if that was the place where her aunt was locked up. She spoke slowly, and Bernardino did not seem to understand her because he did not answer her. They entered the building, and found themselves at the foot of the stairway of one of the towers.

"Signora Montoni sleeps up there," said Bernardino.

- He is sleeping! Emilia answered as she climbed up.

"He sleeps in that room up there," the man added.

The wind that blew through those deep hollows increased the flame of the torch, which brightened better the atrocious figure of Bernardino, the ancient walls, the spiral staircase blackened by time, and the remains of old armor that look like the trophy of ancient victories.

When they reached the landing, the guide put a key in the lock of a room, "You can enter here," he said, "and wait for me: in the meantime, I'm going to tell the landlady that you've arrived."

"It's a useless precaution, since my aunt will see me willingly."

"I'm not quite sure," added Bernardino, pointing to the room. 'Come in, miss, I'll go warn you. »

Emilia, surprised and offended in a certain way, didn't dare resist; but as he was taking away her torch, she begged him not to leave it in the dark. He looked around, and seeing a lamp on the staircase, he lit it and gave it to the girl, who entered, and he closed the door on the outside; she listened attentively, and it seemed to her that, instead of going up, she was going down the stairs, but the impetuous wind that blew under the door did not allow her to distinguish any sound; finally, not hearing any movement in the upper room she had told the caretaker that Montoni was staying, she became more and more perplexed. A little later, in a lull, she thought she heard Bernardino come down into the courtyard, and even heard her voice. All her former fears came back to strike her harder than she was, she persuaded she was no more a mistake than her imagination, but a warning of the fate she was to suffer: she had no doubt that her aunt had not been immolated, and perhaps in that same room where she too had been treated for the same object. Bernardino's demeanor and words about his aunt confirmed his lugubrious ideas. She was attentive, and she heard no noise either on the staircase or in the upper room; she approached the window equipped with iron bars, she heard some voices in the breath of the wind, and by the light of a torch that seemed to be under the vault, he saw on the ground the shadow of several men, including a colossal one, which he recognized as that of the fierce guardian.

As soon as her spirit had calmed down, she took the light to see if it was possible for her to escape. The room was spacious, and had no other openings than the window and the door by which she had entered: there was no furniture, except for a bronze high chair fixed in the middle of the room, and on which hung a large iron chain. , fixed to the vault. She looked at him for a long time in horror and surprise; she observed various circles also of iron to close the legs, and other similar rings on the armrests of the chair. She became convinced that that odious machine was an instrument of torture, and that more than one unfortunate man chained there must have died of starvation. Her hair stood on end at the thought of being in such a place, and rushed to the other end of her to look for a footstool; but she saw only a dark curtain, which entirely covered part of the room. Astonished, she stood looking upon it with awe: she longed and dreaded to lift it to see what it covered: twice was she detained by the remembrance of the horrible sight which her rash hand had uncovered in the closed apartment; but she thinking that maybe she was hiding the corpse of her murdered aunt she, driven by her desperation, she raised it. Behind her was a corpse stretched out on a low, bloodstained cot; got up. Behind it was a corpse stretched out on a low bed stained with blood; got up. Behind it was a corpse stretched out on a low bed stained with blood;his face, disfigured by death, was disgusting and covered with livid wounds. Emilia contemplated him with a greedy and bewildered eye: but her light fell from her hand; and she herself fell in a faint at the foot of the horrible object.

When she regained her senses, she found herself in the arms of Bernardino, and surrounded by people who were carrying her outside: she realized what it was; but her extreme weakness did not permit her to raise her voice, nor to make any movement, and went down the stairs. They stopped under the vault: one of them, taking away Bernardino's torch, opened a side door, and going out onto the platform, he let us distinguish a large number of people on horseback. Whether her open air had revived her a little, or whether those strange objects restored her to the feeling of danger, the girl let out a few cries and made vain efforts to free herself from those brigands.

Meanwhile Bernardino asked for the torch, some distant voices answered, several people approached, and a light appeared in the courtyard; Emilia was dragged out of the door: she saw the same man who held the porter's torch, busy giving light to another, who was saddling a horse in haste, surrounded by other grim-looking horsemen.

"Why waste so much time?" said Bernardino, cursing and approaching; "Hurry up, hurry up, by God!"

"The saddle is almost ready," replied the man who was buckling it up, and Bernardino cursed again for such negligence. Emilia, who was crying out for help in a faint voice, was dragged towards the horses, and the brigands argued among themselves which one should mount her. At that many people came out with lights, and Emilia distinctly recognized, among all the others, Annetta's screaming voice: then she saw Montoni and Cavignì followed by soldiers. She no longer saw them with fear, but with hope, and she no longer thought of the dangers of the castle, from which she had longed so much before to escape.

After a short fight, Montoni and his men defeated the enemies, who, in fewer numbers, and perhaps not very interested in the enterprise they were in charge of, fled at a gallop. Bernardino disappeared in the darkness, and Emilia was taken back to the castle. Passing back from the courtyard, the memory of what she had seen in her doorway room renewed her terrors. primeval; and when she heard the portcullis that still enclosed her within those formidable walls fall, she shuddered, and almost forgetting the new danger from which she had escaped, she could not understand how life and freedom were not found beyond those barriers.

Montoni ordered Emilia to wait for him in the cedar room. She went there shortly after, and severely questioned him about the mysterious event. Though she regarded him then as her aunt's murderer, and could scarcely answer her questions, yet her answers could convince him that she had voluntarily had no part in the plot, and he dismissed her as soon as he saw her people appear, which she had done round up to discover the accomplices.

Emilia was agitated for a while before she could reflect on what had happened. The corpse seen behind her curtain was always before her eyes, and she broke down in bitter tears. Annetta asked her why, but she didn't want to tell him, for fear of irritating Montoni.

Forced to concentrate all the horror of that secret within herself, her reason was to succumb to the unbearable weight. When Annetta spoke to her, she did not hear him, or answered out of purpose; she sighed, but she shed no tears. Frightened by her situation, Annetta ran to inform Montoni: he had then dismissed her servants, without having discovered anything about her. The touching story that the maid told him about Emilia's state induced him to go to her. At the sound of her voice, the girl raised her eyes, a ray of light seemed to revive her spirits: she got up to retire slowly to the back of her room. Montoni spoke to her gently: she looked at him with a curious and frightened air, always answering yes to all her questions. Her spirit seemed to have received only one impression, that of fear. this disorder, and Montoni, after useless efforts to make her speak, ordered the damsel to stay there all night, and inform him of her condition the next day.

Having left, Emilia approached and asked who it was who had come to disturb her, Annetta replied that it was Signor Montoni, and she, repeating this name repeatedly, allowed herself to be led to the bed, and examined him with an eye. lost; turning then trembling to her follower, she begged her not to leave her, saying that after her father's death she had been forsaken by all. Annetta had the prudence not to interrupt her, and when she, after much weeping, finally saw her succumb to sleep, the affectionate girl, forgetting all her fears, remained alone to assist Emilia all night.

CHAPTER XXVII

Rest restored the girl's strength. Waking up she saw to her surprise Annetta asleep in a nearby chair and tried to recall the circumstances of the evening which had come so far out of her memory that no trace of her remained.

« Ah, dear mistress, do you recognize me? she exclaimed.

"If I recognize you!" Surely; you are Annetta; but how are you here?

— Oh! you have been very bad, in truth, and I thought...

"It's singular," said Emilia, trying to recall the past; 'But it seems to me that you were tormented by a horrible dream! Good God! »She added horrified; 'certainly it could only be a dream. »And she fixed frightened looks on Annetta, who, wanting to reassure her, replied: «It wasn't a dream, no, but now it's all over.

"So she was killed?" Emilia said trembling. Annetta cried out; she ignored the circumstance that the girl remembered, and attributed the phrase to her delirium. When she had clearly explained what she had meant to tell her, Emilia remembered her attempt to kidnap her, and she asked if the perpetrator of the plan had been discovered. Her other answered no, though it was easy to guess, and said he owed her deliverance to her. "That's right, Signora Emilia," continued Annetta; «I was determined to be more shrewd than Bernardino, who hadn't wanted to confide his secret to me; but I was piqued to find out. She kept watch on the terrace; and as soon as he had opened the door, I went out to try to follow you, very convinced that nothing good could be planned with so much mystery. Assuring me that he had not closed the door inward, I opened it, and followed it from afar, aided by the light of the torch, right up to the vault of the chapel. I was afraid to go on, having heard strange things about that place, but she was equally afraid to go back alone; and while Bernardino poked the torch, I overcame all fear, followed you to the courtyard, and when you climbed the stairs, I slipped very slowly under the door, where I heard a trampling of horses outside, and various men cursing against Bernardino, because he was late to lead you; but there I was almost surprised: the caretaker got out, and I just had time to dodge him. He had heard enough to know what it was about, and I no longer doubted that Count Morano had anything to do with that project, even though he had left. I ran back in the dark, forgetting all fears; yet I would not make the same journey again for all the gold in the world. Fortunately Signor Cavignì and the master were still up; in the twinkling of an eye we gathered people, and drove the brigands away. »

The maid had stopped speaking, and Emilia seemed to be listening again. Finally, breaking the silence, she said: 'I think it's best to go and see him myself. Where? »

Annetta asked who he was talking about.

« From Mr. Montoni; i need to see it. Annetta, then remembering the order received in the evening, got up immediately, saying that she would take it upon herself to go and look for him.

The good girl's suspicions about the count were well founded; and Montoni, himself not doubting it, began to assume that the poison mixed with the wine had been put there by order of Morano.

The protests of repentance which he made to Emilia when he was wounded were sincere when he made them, but he too was deceived. He had thought she disapproved of his plans, and only grieved at their baleful result; but when he was healed, his hopes for him revived, and he found himself willing to undertake new attempts. The porter of the castle, the same one he had already used, gladly accepted a second gift, and when they had agreed on Emilia's abduction, the count publicly left the abode where he had been for treatment, and withdrew with his people to a few miles away. Annetta's reckless chatter having given Bernardino an almost sure means of deceiving Emilia, the count on the agreed night sent all his servants to the castle gate, remaining at the I dwell there to wait for the girl whom he proposed to take to Venice. We have already seen how unsuccessful her plan was; bad violentand various passions by which his jealous soul was agitated are difficult to express.

Annetta sent the message to Montoni and asked him for an interview for her niece: he replied that in an hour he would be in the cedar drawing room. Emilia did not know what outcome she should expect from the interview, and she shuddered with horror at the mere idea of her presence; she wanted to tell him about the baleful fate of his aunt, and beg him for a favor that he scarcely dared to hope for, that is, to return to his homeland, since his aunt no longer existed.

While, torn by a thousand fears, she reflected on the forthcoming conference, and on the probable consequences that could ensue from it, Montoni made her say that he could not see her until the next day: Emilia didn't know what to think of this delay. Annetta told her that Verrezzi and his troop were certainly returning to war: the courtyard was full of horses, and she learned that the rest of the band was expected to take another direction all together. When it was night, Emilia remembered the mysterious music she had already heard; she nevertheless took a kind of interest in it, hoping to find some relief from it. The influence of superstition was daily growing more active upon her enfeebled fancy; she dismissed Annetta, and she resolved to stay alone to wait for the music. She went several times to the window in vain; she seemed to have heard a voice,

Thus the time passed until midnight, and then all the distant noises that made themselves heard in the inhabited area ceased almost at the same moment, and sleep seemed to reign everywhere. She went back to the window, and was startled by extraordinary sounds: it was not a harmony, but the low moan of a desolate person. Terrified, she listened: the feeble moans had ceased: she bent out of the window to discover some light: perfect darkness enveloped the rooms below, but she thought she saw a short distance away, on the rampart, some object moving. The faint light of the stars did not allow her to distinguish well: she imagined she was a sentry, and she hid the light to better observe without being seen.

The same object reappeared almost below the window: she made out a human figure; but the silence with which she advanced made her believe it was not a sentry; her figure approached: Emilia wanted to withdraw, but her curiosity drove her to stay, and in that uncertainty her unknown placed itself in her face and remained motionless. The profound silence, the mysterious shadow so struck her, that she was about to recoil, when she saw her figure move along the parapet and disappear. Emilia thought for some time about this strange circumstance, not doubting that she had seen a supernatural apparition. When she was calmer, she remembered what they had told her about Montoni's rash exploits, and it occurred to her that she had seen one of those unfortunates stripped by bandits, who had become their prisoner, and that he was the author of the music. mysterious.

She later believed that Morano had found a means of getting into the castle, but the difficulties and dangers of such an enterprise soon presented themselves to her, especially since if he had succeeded in reaching there, he would not have contented himself with remaining silent at midnight under the window, since he knew the secret staircase perfectly, and he certainly would not have made those lamentations intended by her. He even came to suppose, it was someone who wanted to take over the castle; but his painful sighs destroyed even this conjecture. So she resolved to stay awake the following night to try to elucidate the mystery, determined to interrogate the figureself had shown itself again.

CHAPTER XXVIII

The following day Montoni sent Emilia a second apology, which surprised her quite a bit.

Towards evening, the detachment that had made the first raid into the mountains returned to the castle: from her remote chamber, Emilia heard the frantic cries and songs of victory. Annetta came a little later to tell her that they rejoiced at the sight of an immense booty. This circumstance confirmed her idea that Montoni was really a leader of robbers, and had set out to restore her opulence by assaulting the travellers. In truth, when she reflected on the position of that very strong castle, almost inaccessible, isolated in the midst of those wild and lonely mountains, far from cities, hamlets and villages, on the passage of the richest travellers; it seemed to her that this situation was very suitable for robbery projects, and she did not doubt that Montoni was not really a leader of assassins. His unbridled nature, daring, cruel, and enterprising, he was very much suited to such a profession; he loved tumult, and stormy life; he was numb to pity and fear; his courage resembled animal ferocity: it was not that noble impulse which excites the generous against the oppressor for the benefit of the oppressed; but a simple physical disposition that does not allow the soul to feel fear, because it feels nothing else.

Emilia's supposition, although plausible, was not however exact enough: she was ignorant of the situation in Italy, and of the respective interests of many belligerent districts. Since the incomes of several states were not sufficient to maintain armies, not even in the short period in which the turbulent genius of governments and peoples allowed them to enjoy the benefits of peace, an order was formed at that time of unknown men in our century, and badly painted in the history of that. Of the soldiers dismissed at the end of each war, only a very small number returned to the unprofitable arts of peace and rest. The others sometimes passed into the service of the potentates in war; at other times they formed into bands of brigands, and masters of some forts, their desperate character, the weakness of the governments, and the certainty that at the first signal they would run under the flags, put them covered from any civil persecution. They often attached themselves to the fortune of a popular leader, who led them into the service of some state, and bargained the price of their courage. This use gave them the epithet of leaders, a formidable name in Italy for a very long period. Its end is fixed at the beginning of the seventeenth century; but it would be almost impossible to pinpoint its origin precisely.

When not hired, the chief-of-ordinary resided in his castle; and there, or in the surrounding places, they all enjoyed idleness and rest. Sometimes they satisfied the wants at the expense of the villages, but sometimes their prodigality, when dividing the booty, paid usury for their tortures, and their hosts assumed in the long run some tint of the warlike character. Montoni, driven by the great losses in gambling, had ended up making himself the leader of one of these gangs; Orsino and others joined him, and the surplus of their possessions had served to form a fund for the enterprise.

As soon as night fell, Emilia returned to the window, determined to observe the figure more exactly, in case it ever reappeared. Meanwhile he lost himself in a thousand conjectures. She felt almost irresistibly driven to try and talk to her; but terror held her back. 'If you were a person,' she thought, 'that you had designs on this castle, my curiosity might perhaps become fatal to me; yet those laments, that music heard by me are certain of her, nor can they come from an enemy. »

The moon went down, the darkness became deep; she heard it strike midnight without seeing or hearing anything, and she began to form some doubts about the reality of her previous vision, whereupon, tired of waiting in vain, she went to bed.

Montoni did not even think the following day of having her called for the requested interview. More interested than ever to see him, she made him ask, through Annetta, at what time she could see her; he assigned her eleven hours. Emilia was punctual, she plucked up courage to bear the sight of her aunt's murderer, and found him in the cedar parlor surrounded by all her guests, some of whom turned as soon as they saw her, making a ' exclamation of surprise. Emilia, seeing that Montoni paid no attention to her, wanted to withdraw, when he called her back.

'I would like to speak to you alone, sir, if you had the time.

"I am in the company of good friends from whom I have no secrets; speak freely, then,' replied Montoni.

Emilia, without opening her mouth, walked towards the door, and then Montoni got up and led her into a lavatory, closing the door spitefully. She raised her eyes to his barbarous countenance, and thinking that she was contemplating her aunt's murderer, including her with her horror, she lost the memory of the purpose of her visit, and she dared no longer mention Signora Montoni. He finally impatiently asked her what she wanted of him. Emilia then told him that, wishing to return to France, she was coming to ask his permission. He looked at her in surprise, asking her the reason for this request. Emilia hesitated, trembled, turned pale, and felt his heart go down. He saw her emotion with indifference, and broke the silence to tell her that she was anxious to return to the living room; Emilia steeling herself, she then repeated her question, and Montoni gave her an absolute negative. She then emboldened: "I can no longer, sir," said she, "remain here conveniently, and I could ask you by what right you want to prevent me from leaving.

"By my will," he replied, walking towards the door, "that's enough for you." »

Emilia, seeing that such a decision admitted no appeal, made no attempt to uphold her rights, and made only a feeble effort to demonstrate its justice. "As long as my aunt lived," she said in a trembling voice, "my residence here could have been decent, but now that she is no longer, I must be allowed to leave. My presence, sir, cannot be welcome to you, and a longer stay here would only serve to afflict me.

"Who told you that Signora Montoni is dead?" he said, staring at her with an inquiring eye. She hesitated; no one had told her, and she didn't dare confess to him how she had seen in the room by the door the horrible spectacle that she had led him to believe.

"Who told you that?" Montoni repeated with impatient severity.

'I know too badly for myself; for pity's sake, don't tell me about it anymore. And she felt faint.

"If you want to see her," said Montoni, "you can; it is in the east tower. »And he left her without waiting for an answer. Several of the knights, who had never seen Emilia, began to make fun of this discovery, but Montoni, having accepted such jests with serious demeanor, changed the subject.

Emilia, meanwhile, confused by his last words, thought only of seeing her unhappy aunt again, spurred on by from imperious duty. As soon as he saw Annetta, he begged her to accompany him and obtained it with great difficulty. Leaving the corridor, they reached the foot of the bloody staircase; Annetta did not want to go any further. Emilia went up alone; but when she saw her streaks of blood again, she felt faint, and stopped. A few minutes of pause refreshed her. When she reached the landing, she was afraid of finding the door closed; but she was mistaken: the door opened easily, introducing her into a dark and deserted room. She considered her fearful: she advanced slowly, and heard a faint voice. Unable to speak or make any movement, she stood still: the voice made itself heard again, and then, thinking she recognized that of her aunt, she gathered courage, went up to a bed which she saw at the end of the vast room, opened the curtains, and he found there a gaunt, pale figure; she shivered, and took her hand, which resembled that of a skeleton, and looking at it attentively, she recognized Madame Montoni, but so disfigured that her present features scarcely reminded her of what she had been. She still lived, and opening her eyes, she turned them to her niece. "Where have you been for a long time?" »He asked her with the same sound of voice; "She thought you had abandoned me.

"Do you live," Emilia spoke at last, "or are you a shadow?"

— I live, but I feel that I am about to die. »

Emilia tried to console her, and asked her who had reduced her to that state.

By having her transported there on the improbable suspicion that she had made an attempt on his life, Montoni had made his agents swear to the deepest secret. There were two reasons for this rigor: to deprive her of Emilia's consolations, and to procure the opportunity of having her die without a fuss, if some circumstance should confirm her suspicions. The perfect knowledge of the hate she had deserved by his wife had naturally led him to accuse her of the attack. She had no other reason to assume she was guilty, and she still believed it. She abandoned her in that tower to her harshest captivity, where, without remorse and without mercy, she left her to languish in the grip of a burning fever, which had finally reduced her to the brink of her sepulchre.

The streaks of blood seen by Emilia on the stairs came from a wound touched, in the fight, by one of the satellites carrying her, and which fell apart while walking. For that night they contented themselves with locking up the prisoner well, not thinking of guarding her. This is why, on the first search, Emilia found the tower deserted and silent. When she tried to open the door to the room, her aunt was asleep. But if her terror hadn't prevented her from calling her again, she would have woken her at last, and thus spared her much trouble. The corpse observed in the room by the door was that of the wounded man she had seen carried into the room where he had sought asylum, who died on the roof a few days later, and who was to be buried the following morning in the grave dug under the chapel where

Emilia, after a thousand interrogations, left her aunt for an instant to go in search of Montoni. The keen interest he felt for her made her forget the resentment to which her remonstrances would expose him, and the little semblance of getting what she wanted to ask of him.

"Your wife is dying, sir," she said to him as soon as she saw him; « Your wrath certainly won't want to persecute her until the last moments. Therefore allow her to be transported to her rooms, and the necessary aids to be prepared for her.

"What will this do if she dies?" Montoni said indifferently.

"It will help, sir, to spare you some of the gods remorse that will tear you apart when you are in her situation. »

The audacious answer did not shake him at all; he resisted for a long time to prayers and tears; in the end the pity, which had assumed the expressive forms of Emilia, managed to move that heart of stone. He turned away, ashamed of a good feeling, and at times inflexible and moved, he agreed to let her go back to her bed, and to assist his niece, fearing at the same time that the rescue would not be too late, and that Montoni would not retract himself. Emilia thanked him as soon as He hurried to make his aunt's bed, helped by Annetta, and brought her a refreshment which would enable her to bear the transport.

As soon as he arrived in her rooms, Montoni revoked the order; but Emilia, glad to have acted with such solicitude, ran to see him, explained to him that a new journey would prove fatal, and obtained that she leave her where she was.

Throughout the day she did not abandon her aunt, except to prepare the necessary food for her. Signora Montoni took it out of complacency, convinced that she was soon to die. The girl nursed her with tender disquiet: now she was no longer dealing with an imperious aunt, but with the sister of an adored father, whose situation was pitiful. When night came, he wanted to spend it with her, but she absolutely opposed it, demanding that he go and rest, and contented herself with Annetta's company. In truth, rest was necessary for Emilia, after the jolts and motions of that day, but she did not want to leave her aunt before midnight, a time regarded by the doctors as critical. Then, after advising Annetta carefully to assist her carefully and to warn her at the slightest sign of danger, she wished her good night and withdrew from her. She was heartbroken by the horrible state of her aunt, from whom she scarcely dared to hope for her recovery. She saw herself shut up in an isolated ancient castle, far from all aid, and in the hands of a capable man who could dictate her interest and pride to him.

Occupied by these sad reflections, Emilia did not go to bed, and she leaned against the sill of the open window. The woods and mountains, dimly lit by the nocturnal star, formed a painful contrast to the state of her mind; but the slight rustling of the fronds and the sleep of nature ended up gradually sweetening the tumult of her affections, and lifting her heart to the point of making her cry. Thus she remained in that position without having any other idea than the vague feeling of the misfortunes which oppressed her; when at last she removed the handkerchief from her eyes, he saw on her rampart, in front of her, motionless and mute, her figure already observed of her: he examined it carefully, trembling, but he could not speak to her as it was. proposed.

The moon shone, and the agitation of her spirit was perhaps the only obstacle that prevented her from clearly distinguishing that figure, which, making no movement, seemed inanimate. She then collected her lost ideas and wanted to withdraw, when her figure seemed to extend a hand as if to greet her, and while she stood motionless in her surprise and fear, the gesture was repeated. She tried to speak of her, but the words breathed on her lip, and as she retired from the window to get the lamp, she heard a dull groan; she listened without daring to reappear, and she heard another.

"Great God! she exclaimed; "What does this mean? She »she He listened again, but she no longer understood anything. After a long interval, recovering, she returned to the window, and saw the figure again. She received a new greeting, and she heard new sighs.

« This moan is certainly human! I want to talk,' she said. " Who is there? »She then cried under her breath; who's walking around at this hour? The figure raised its head, and walked towards the parapet. Emilia followed her with her eyes, and saw her disappear in the moonlight. The sentry then advanced with slow steps under the window, where she stopped by her, called her by her name, and respectfully asked her if she had seen anything go by. She replied that she thought she had seen a shadow. The sentry said no more; and she came back; but since that man was on her watch, Emilia knew that she could not leave her post, and she waited for his return. She shortly after she heard him scream aloud. Another distant voice answered her. Soldiers came out of the guardhouse, and the whole detachment crossed the rampart. Emilia asked what it was; but the soldiers passed without heeding her.

Meanwhile she was lost in a thousand conjectures. Had she been more vain, she might have supposed that some inhabitant of the castle was strolling under her window in the hope of gazing at her and declaring her feelings for her; but the idea did not occur to her, and when it had, she would have dismissed it as improbable, for that person, who might have spoken to her, had been silent, and when she herself had said a word, the figure had abruptly moved away. . While she was reflecting, two soldiers passed on the bastion, and talking to each other, they made Emilia understand that one of their comrades had fallen stunned. A little later she saw three other soldiers advancing slowly, and a faint voice; when they were under the window, he could distinguish that the speaker was being supported by his companions. She called them to ask what had happened;

"Is he subject to these swoons?" the young woman asked.

"Yes, Signorina, yes," replied Roberto: "but even if I weren't there, what I saw would have frightened even the Pope."

"And what did you see?"

"I can't say what it was, or what I saw, or how it disappeared," replied the soldier, still shivering with fright. 'When I left you, miss, you could see me going onto the terrace; but I saw nothing until I was on the east rampart. The moon was shining, and I saw a shadow flee a little way before me; I stopped at the corner of the tower where I had seen that figure: it had disappeared; I looked under the ancient arch: nothing. Suddenly I heard a noise, but it wasn't a moan, a cry, an accent, in short, something I had ever heard in my life. I only heard it once, but that was enough; I no longer know what happened to me until the moment I found myself surrounded by my companions.

"Come, friends," said Sebastiano, "let's go back to our places. Good night Miss."

"Good night," replied Emilia, closing the window, and withdrawing to reflect on that strange circumstance which coincided with the events of the other nights; she tried to draw from it some more certain result than a conjecture; but her imagination was still too heated, her judgment too dulled, and the terrors of superstition still mastered her ideas.

CHAPTER XXIX

Emilia went very early to see her aunt, and found her in almost the same state: she had slept very little, and the fever hadn't stopped. She smiled at her niece, and seemed to perk up at her sight: she spoke little of her, and never mentioned Montoni. A little later he entered himself; his wife was greatly agitated and she did not say a word; but as she rose from her chair beside her bed, she pleaded in a low voice not to abandon her.

Montoni did not come to console his wife, whom she knew she was dying, or to obtain her forgiveness; he came solely to make a last-ditch effort to extract her signature, so that after her death she might remain the owner of all her possessions which belonged to Emilia. It was an atrocious scene, in which one demonstrated impudent barbarism, the other a pertinacity that even survived his physical strength. Emilia declared a thousand times that she preferred to renounce all her rights, rather than see the last moments of her unhappy aunt embittered by her cruel argument. Montoni nevertheless did not go out until her wife, exhausted by her frantic quarrel, finally lost the use of her senses, Emilia thought she saw her expire in her arms; she too recovered her speech, and after taking a cordial, she spoke to her niece for a long time with precision and clarity about her possessions in France. She taught her where some important papers taken away from her husband's research were, and she expressly ordered her never to take them away.

After this conversation, Montoni dozed off and dozed off until evening: when she awoke, she seemed to feel better, but Emilia did not leave her until long after midnight, and when she was absolutely ordered to; she complied willingly, as the patient appeared somewhat relieved. She was then the second guard and the hour the figure had already appeared. The girl heard the sentries change, and when all was quiet again, she leaned out the window, and she hid the lamp so as not to be seen. The moon cast a dim and uncertain light; thick vapors obscured it, sometimes plunging it into darkness. In one of these intervals, she noticed a small flame hovering over the terrace; as she stared at it, it vanished. A gleam made her head look up; lightning flickered in a black cloud,

Lowering his eyes again, he saw the flame again: it seemed to be in motion. A little while later she heard the sound of footsteps: the blaze showed and disappeared time after time. Suddenly, in the flash of lightning, he saw someone on the terrace. All former anxieties were renewed; the person forwarded, and the little flame, which seemed to be joking, appeared and vanished at intervals. Emilia, wishing to put an end to her doubts, when she saw the light just under the window, asked in a languid voice who she was.

"Friends: I'm Antonio, the soldier on guard duty," they replied.

"What's that flame?" see how it shines and then disappears!

'She appeared at my spearhead last night, when I was on patrol; but I don't know what that means.

"It's strange," Emilia said.

"My comrade," continued the soldier, "also has a similar flame on the tip of his pike, and he says he has already observed the same prodigy.

And how does he explain it?

"Make sure it's a bad omen, and nothing else. Ah! but I must go to my place. Good night Miss. »And she walked away.

She closed the window, and threw herself on the bed. Meanwhile the storm, which menaced on the horizon, had broken out with unspeakable violence; the awful rumble of thunder prevented her from sleeping. After some time, she thought she heard a voice amidst the dreadful din of the unleashed elements; I got up to make sure of it, and approaching her door, she recognized Annetta, who, when it was opened to her, cried out:

'She dies, miss, my mistress dies. »

The girl gave a start and ran to her aunt; when she came in, Signora Montoni seemed to have fainted: she was calm and insensitive. Emilia, with a courage that did not give in to pain when her duty required her activity, spared no means to call her back to her life, but the last effort had already been made, her wretchedness had ceased to suffer.

When Emilia realized the futility of her attentions, she questioned the trembling Annetta, and learned that her aunt, who fell into a kind of stupor immediately after her departure, had remained in that state until the moment of agony. After a brief reflection, she decided not to inform Montoni of the unfortunate case until the morning, thinking that he would end up making some inhuman expression, that she would not be able to suffer. In the company of Annetta alone, encouraged by her example, she watched over the deceased all night, reciting the office of the dead.

CAPITOLO XXX

When Montoni was informed of his wife's death, considering that she had expired without making him the cession so necessary to the fulfillment of his wishes, nothing could stop the expression of his resentment. Emilia carefully avoided his presence in her, and in the course of thirty-six hours she never left her aunt's corpse. Deeply distressed by her sad fate, she forgot all her faults, injustices and hardness, only remembering her sufferings.

Montoni did not disturb her prayers: he avoided the room where his wife's body was, and even that part of her castle, as if he feared the contagion of her death. He appeared to have given no orders relating to her funeral; so that Emilia feared it was an insult to her aunt's memory; but she got out of her uncertainty when, on the evening of the second day, Annetta came to inform her [64] that her deceased would be buried that same night. Figuring that Montoni would not have witnessed it, she was torn by the idea that the poor aunt's corpse would go to her burial without a relative or friend rendering her last duties: she therefore decided to go there herself; without this reason, he would have trembled to accompany the procession, made up of people who had all the demeanor and figure of assassins, under the horrid vault of the chapel, and at midnight, that is, at the time of silence and mystery, chosen by Montoni to abandon to oblivion the ashes of a bride, whose barbaric conduct had at least hastened the end.

Seconded by Annetta, she arranged the body for her burial. At midnight, the men appeared who were to carry her to her grave. Emilia could hardly contain her agitation seeing those horrid figures: two of them, without saying a word, took the corpse on her shoulders, and the third, preceding them with a torch, all descended together into the basement of the chapel. They had to cross the two courtyards of the eastern part of the castle, which was almost completely ruined. The silence and darkness of the places had little effect on the spirit of Emilia, who was occupied with far more lugubrious ideas. When they reached the edge of the cellar, she stopped, overwhelmed by an inexpressible emotion of pain and fear, and she turned to lean on Annetta, silent and trembling like her. After a few pauses, she went on, and glimpsed, between the arches, the men placing the coffin on the edge of a grave. There were another servant of Montoni and a priest whom she did not notice until she began her prayers. She then raised her eyes, and saw the venerable face of a religious, who in a low and solemn voice recited the office of the dead. At the instant in which the corpse was lowered into the tomb, the picture was such that the most skilful brush would not have disdained to paint. The ferocious features, the[65] bizarre shapes of those thugs, leaning with their torches over the grave, the venerable aspect of the friar, wrapped in long white woolen robes, whose hood, lowered back, brought out a pale face, overshadowed by a few white hairs, whereby the light of the torches showed the affliction softened by pity; the interesting attitude of Emilia leaning against Annetta with her face half-covered by a black veil, the sweetness and beauty of her physiognomy, and her intense pain, which did not allow her to cry, while she entrusted the last to the earth relative that she had of her; the flickering reflections of light under the vaults, the unevenness of the ground, where other bodies had recently been buried, the lugubrious darkness of the place, so many circumstances brought together, would have drawn the imagination of the spectator to some event perhaps more horrible than the funeral of the senseless and unhappy Signora Montoni.

After the function, the friar looked at Emilia with attention and surprise; he seemed to want to talk to her, but the presence of the robbers held him back. As they left the chapel, they indulged in unworthy jokes about the ceremony and his state, much to Emilia's horror. He suffered them in silence, limiting himself to asking to be brought back safe and sound to his convent, from which he had come at the express request of the castellan, induced to do so by the requests of his niece. Once in the second courtyard, the friar imparted her blessing to the girl, staring at her with a pitying eye, then walked towards the door. The two women retired to their rooms.

Emilia spent several days in absolute solitude, in terror for herself and in regret at the loss of her aunt. She finally determined to try a new effort to get Montoni to let her go to France. She could not form any conjecture as to the reasons she might have for preventing him; she was too convinced that he wanted to keep her [66] with him, and her first refusal left her little hope. Her horror inspired by his presence made her postpone the interview from day to day. However, a message from Montoni himself relieved her of this uncertainty; he wished to see her at the time he indicated. It was almost to flatter himself that, her aunt being dead, he would consent to relinquish her usurped authority; but then remembering that the goods so contested had now become hers, she feared that Montoni wanted to use some stratagem to get them to be handed over to her, and would not keep her prisoner until then. This idea, instead of depressing her, revived all the powers of her soul, and gave her new courage. She would have given up everything to ensure her aunt's rest, but she resolved that any personal persecution of her would have the power to make her withdraw from her rights. She was keenly interested in preserving her legacy concerning her especially Valancourt, with whom she flattered herself thus to spend a happy life. At this idea of her he felt how dear he was to her, and he imagined in advance the moment in which her generous friendship could tell him that it brought him all her possessions as a dowry; he imagined seeing the smile that would animate her features, and the affectionate glances that would express all her joy and gratitude. At that moment she believed she could face all the evils that Montoni's infernal malice would have prepared for her. She then remembered, for the first time after her aunt's death, that she had papers relating to these properties, and she resolved to search for them as soon as she had spoken to Montoni.

With this idea, he went to see him at the prescribed time: he was in the company of Orsino and another officer, and he seemed to be diligently examining many papers placed on a table.

'I've sent for you,' he said, raising his head, 'because I want you to be witnesses to a deal I have to complete with my friend Orsino. All what is required of you is that you sign this charter. »He took it, muttered a few lines from it, placed it on the table, and gave her a pen. She was about to sign when she suddenly remembered his drawing; she dropped the pen from her hand, and she denied signing without reading the contents: Montoni affected a smile, and taking up the paper, he pretended to read it again as he had already done. Emilia, trembling with the danger and excess of credulity which had almost betrayed her, she positively refused to sign. Montoni continued the jokes for a while; but when, by her persistence, he realized that he had guessed her plan, he changed his tongue and ordered her to follow him. As soon as they were alone, he told her that he had wanted, for her and for himself, to prevent a useless quarrel in a matter in which his will for her formed justice, and it would become a law; that he would rather persuade her than coerce her, and that in consequence she fulfilled his duty to him.

'I, as husband of the late Signora Cheron,' he added, 'become the heir to everything she owned; her possessions, which she did not want to give me while she lived, must not now pass into other hands. I would like, for your sake, to disabuse you of the ridiculous idea that she gave you in my presence, that her possessions, that is, hers, would be yours if she died without giving them to me. I think you are too reasonable to provoke my just resentment; I do not flatter, and you may regard my praise as sincere. You possess a higher criterion than your sex; and you have none of those weaknesses which distinguish the character of women in general, that is, avarice and the desire to dominate. »

Montoni stopped; Emily didn't answer.

'Judging by how I do it,' he resumed, 'I can't believe you'll want to field one useless dispute. Nor do I believe that you are thinking of acquiring or possessing property to which justice grants you no right. So choose the alternative that I propose. If you form a correct opinion of the subject we are dealing with, you will soon be brought back to France. And if you are so wretched as to persist in the error into which your aunt led you, you will remain my prisoner until you open your eyes. »

Emilia replied calmly: 'I am not so poorly educated in the laws relating to this subject, to be deceived by any assertion whatsoever; the law grants me possession of the goods in question, and my hand will not betray my rights.

"It seems I was deceived in the opinion that I had of you," said Montoni severely; 'You speak boldly and presumptuously on a subject you do not understand. I would like, for once, to forgive the stubbornness of ignorance; the weakness of your sex, from which you do not seem exempt, also demands this indulgence. But if you persist, you will have to fear everything from my justice.

"From your justice, sir," replied Emilia, "I have nothing to fear, but everything to hope for." »

Montoni looked at her impatiently, and seemed to be pondering what he had to say to her.

'I see you are weak enough to believe a ridiculous assertion. I'm sorry for you; as for me, it matters little to me; your credulity will find its punishment in the consequences, and I pity the weakness of spirit which exposes you to the pains which you force me to prepare for you.

"You will find, sir," replied Emilia with gentleness and dignity, "the strength of my spirit equal to the justice of my cause; and I can suffer bravely when I resist tyranny.

"You talk like a heroine," said Montoni contemptuously; "We'll see if you know how to suffer just the same. »

Emilia didn't answer, and left. Remembering that she was thus resisting for Valancourt's sake, she smiled with pleasure at the thought of her threatened ill-treatment. She went to look for the place indicated to her by her aunt, as a deposit for the papers relating to her possessions, and she found them there; but not knowing a safer place to keep them, she put them away without examination, fearing surprise.

As she returned to her solitude, she reflected on Montoni's words and the dangers she was incurring by opposing his will, she heard peals of laughter on the rampart; she went to the window, and was surprised to see three women, dressed in Venetian style, walking with some gentlemen. As they passed under the window, one of the strangers raised her head. Emilia recognized in her that Signora Livona, whose affable manners had so seduced her the day after her arrival in Venice, and who on that same day had been admitted to Montoni's table: this discovery caused her a joy mixed with some uncertainty ; it was a subject of satisfaction for her to see a person as amiable as Signora Livona seemed, in the very place she inhabited. Nonetheless, her arrival at the castle under similar circumstances, her attire, that she indicated that she had not been forced to do so, made her suspect her principles and character; but the idea of her displeased Emilia so much, already won over by the seductive manners of the beautiful Venetian, that she preferred to think only of her graces, and she banished almost entirely any other reflection.

When Annetta entered, he asked her several questions about the arrival of the strangers, and found that she was more anxious to answer than she was to question.

'They came from Venice,' said the maid, 'with two gentlemen, and I was delighted to see some other Christian face in this horrid living room. But what do they expect by coming here? You have to be really mad to come to this place, or else they came freely, as they are cheerful.

"Perhaps they may have been taken prisoner," Emilia added.

"Prisoners! Oh! no, miss: no, I'm not. I well remember seeing one in Venice; she came two or three times to our house. She even told herself, although I never believed it, that her master loved her madly. »

Emilia begged Annetta to inquire in detail about all that concerned those ladies, and, therefore changing the subject, spoke of France, giving her the glimpse of the hope of returning there shortly.

The girl went out to gather information, and Emilia tried to forget her anxieties by feeding on the fantastic imaginations created by poets.

Towards evening, not wanting to expose himself to the greedy gazes of Montoni's associates on the walls, he went for a walk in the gallery adjoining his room. Reaching the bottom of it he heard repeated peals of laughter. They were the transports of debauchery, and not the moderate outbursts of a sweet and honest joy. They seemed to come from the gate of the Montoni quarter. Such an uproar at that moment in which the unhappy aunt had just expired, irritated her to the utmost, and she recognized in it the consequence of Montoni's bad conduct. Listening, he thought he recognized some female voices; this discovery confirmed her suspicions conceived about Signora Livona and her companions: it was evident that they were not necessarily in the castle. Thus Emilia saw herself in the alpine recesses of the Apennines, surrounded by men whom she regarded as brigands, vices, which horrified her. The image of Valancourt lost all influence, and fear of her made her change her plans, reflecting on all the horrors which Montoni was preparing against her; trembling with vengeance, to which he could have abandoned himself without remorse, she almost resolved to cede to him the contested goods, if he still persisted in it, and thus redeem her security and freedom; but, a little later, the memory of her lover returned to tear her soul apart and plunge her back into the anguish of doubt about her. She continued walking until the evening shadows invaded the arches. Nevertheless, the girl, not wanting to return to her isolated room before Annetta's return, still strolled through the gallery. As she passed the apartment where she had once dared to lift the veil of the picture, she was reminded of that horrid spectacle, and feeling horrified, urged to leave the gallery while he still had the strength. Suddenly he heard footsteps behind her. She might have been Annetta, but she, fearfully turning her eyes, saw through the darkness a great figure following her, and presently she found herself clasped in the arms of a person and heard a voice whispering in her ear her. When she had somewhat recovered from her surprise, she asked who could possibly detain her thus? a person and heard a voice whispering in his ear. When she had somewhat recovered from her surprise, she asked who could possibly detain her thus? a person and heard a voice whispering in his ear. When she had somewhat recovered from her surprise, she asked who could possibly detain her thus?

"It's me," replied the voice; « don't be afraid. »

Emilia watched the figure who spoke of her, but the dim light of the Gothic window did not allow her to distinguish who she was.

'Whoever you are,' she said in a tremulous voice, 'for the love of God, leave me.

"Charming Emilia," she added, "why sequester you like this in this gloomy place, while so much merriment reigns down below?" Follow me into the cedar living room: you will form the best ornament, and you won't mind the change. »

Emilia disdained to answer, but she tried to let go.

'Promise me you will come, and I will leave you at once; but grant me the reward first.

- Who are you? Emilia asked with indignation and fear, trying to escape; "Who are you who has the cruelty to insult me like this?"

"Why call me cruel?" he replied. « I would like to take you away from this horrible solitude, and lead you into a brilliant society. Don't you know me? »

Emilia then vaguely remembered that he was one of the strangers who surrounded Montoni the morning she went to see him. 'Thank you for your good intention,' she replied without seeming to understand, 'but all I want for now is that you let me go.

'Charming Emilia,' he added, 'abandon this taste for solitude. Follow me to the conversation, and come to eclipse all the beauties that compose it; you alone deserve my love. »And she wanted to kiss her hand; but the strength of her indignation gave her the power to free herself, and fleeing into her room, she closed the door before he reached it, and she collapsed exhausted on a chair. She heard his voice and the attempts she made to open, without having the strength to ask for help. Finally she realized that he had gone away, but he thought of the door to the secret stairway, which he could easily have penetrated, and he immediately set about securing it as best he could. It seemed to her that Montoni was already carrying out her plans for revenge, depriving her of her protection, and she almost regretted having rashly provoked him. She now thought it impossible to retain her possessions. To preserve her life and perhaps her honour, she made her resolution that, if she escaped the horrors of the next night, she would make her surrender the following morning, provided Montoni would permit her to leave Udolfo.

Taking this approach, she calmed down: she remained like this for some hours in absolute darkness; Annetta did not arrive, and she began to fear for her; but not daring to risk going out, he was forced to remain uncertain as to the reason for her absence. She often approached the stairs to hear if someone was going up, and not hearing any noise, but determined to stay awake all night, she threw herself fully dressed on the sad bed and wet it with her innocent tears. She thought of her loss of her relatives, she thought of Valancourt away from her. She called them by her name, and her profound calm, broken only by her lamentations, increased their sombre meditations.

In this state, she suddenly heard the chords of distant music; she listened, and immediately recognizing the instrument already heard at midnight, she slowly went to open the window. The sound seemed to come from the rooms below. A little later the interesting melody was accompanied by a voice, but so expressive, that it cannot be supposed that she sang imaginary evils. She thought she already knew those tender and extraordinary accents; but she scarcely remembered it as something far away. That music penetrated her heart, in her current anguish, like a celestial harmony that comforts and encourages. But who could describe her emotion when she heard a popular aria from her native country sing, with the taste and simplicity of true feeling; one of those little songs of hers learned in her childhood, and so often made to be repeated by her father? At that well-known song, hitherto never heard outside her dear homeland, her heart dilated to the remembrance of the past. The vague and placid solitudes of Gascony, the tenderness and goodness of the parents, the simplicity and happiness of the first years, all leap into the imagination, forming a picture so graceful, brilliant and strongly opposed to the scenes, characters and dangers waves was currently surrounded, that her spirit no longer had the strength to go back to the past and she no longer felt anything but the weight of her worries.

Suddenly, the music changed, and the astonished girl recognized the same tune already intended for her fishpond. Then an idea presented itself to her with lightning speed, and a chain of hopes electrified her; she could scarcely breathe, and she vacillated between hoping and fearing her: she pronounced Valancourt's name softly. It was possible that the young man was close to her, and remembering having heard him say several times that the fishpond, where he had heard that song, and found the verses written for it, was his favorite walk even before they met, she was persuaded that it was his voice.

As her reflections consolidated, joy, fear and tenderness fought in her: she leaned out the window to listen better to those accents, which could confirm or destroy her hope, Valancourt having never sung to her presence; her voice and instrument ceased presently, and she pondered for a moment whether she should venture to speak. Unwilling, if it was Valancourt, to commit the imprudence of naming him, and too interested in the weather itself to neglect an opportunity of clarifying herself, she cried from the window: 'Is this a song of Gascony? »She Restless, attentive, she waited for an answer, but in vain. She repeated the question, but she heard no more noise but the whistling of the wind across the battlements of the walls. She tried to console herself by persuading herself that her unknown had left before she spoke to him.

Had Valancourt heard and recognized her voice, she certainly would have answered. She then reflected that perhaps her prudence had forced him to keep silent. 'If he is in the castle,' she said, 'he must be there as a prisoner; so he must have been afraid to answer me so close to the sentries. »

Perplexed, restless, she stayed at the window until dawn, then she went back to bed, but she couldn't sleep a wink; joy, her tenderness, doubt, fear of her occupied all the hours of sleep, hours that did not seem as long as that time. She hoped to see Annetta return, and to receive from her some certainty which would put an end to her present torments.

CAPITOLO XXXI

Annetta came to see her early.

"I was very uneasy not seeing you come back last night," Emilia told her. "What ever happened to you?"

— Ah! young lady, who would have dared to cross the long corridors of the house last night in the midst of all those drunken people? Imagine that they have been drinking all night with the ladies who recently came. What a racket, Lord God!... what a racket!... Lodovico, fearing for me, locked me in a room with Caterina.

"Oh what a horror!...." exclaimed Emilia; "but tell me: would you know, by any chance, if there are prisoners in the castle, and if they are shut up in this vicinity?"

- I was not downstairs when the first troop returned from the raid, and the last has not yet returned: therefore I do not know if there are prisoners; but they expect you tonight or tomorrow, and then I'll know something for sure. »

Emilia asked her if her servants had spoken of prisoners.

« Ah! Mademoiselle,' said Annetta, laughing, 'now I perceive that you are thinking of Monsieur Valancourt. You certainly believe that he came with troops who say they arrived from France to wage war in these regions. Do you believe that, having met us, he was taken prisoner. O Lord! as I would be delighted if that were the case.

"Would you like it?" Emilia said in a tone of painful reproach.

"Yes, miss, and why not? Wouldn't you be glad to see M. Valancourt again? I know of no more reputable knight; I really have a lot of consideration for him.

"And in probation," replied Emilia, "you wish to see him prisoner." »

"Not to see him taken prisoner, but I'd be delighted to see him again. I dreamed about it the other night too... But by the way, I forgot to tell you what I was told about those pretended ladies who arrived at Udolfo. One of them is Signora Livona, whom the master introduced to your aunt in Venice: now she is her lover, and then, I dare to say, it was much the same thing. Lodovico told me (but please, miss, don't talk about it) that your Excellency hadn't introduced her except to save her appearances. He was already beginning to murmur about it; but when they saw that the mistress received her in her house, all those rumors about her were believed to be slanders. The other two are the mistresses of Signori Bertolini and Verrezzi. Signor Montoni invited them all, and yesterday he gave a magnificent dinner: there were wines of all sorts; the laughter, the songs and toasts echoed. When they were drunk, they scattered about the castle; it was then that Lodovico prevented me from coming here. It was a real indecency! so shortly after the death of the poor mistress! what would she have said, if she could have understood that noise? »

Emilia turned her head to hide her emotion, and begged Annetta to make exact inquiries about the prisoners who might be in the castle, begging her to use prudence, and never to mention either her name or that of Valancourt.

"Now that I think about it, Signorina," said Annetta, "I think there are some prisoners." I heard yesterday in the antechamber a soldier was talking about ransom: he said that his Excellency did very well to take the people, and that that was the best booty because of the ransoms. His comrade murmured, saying that it was advantageous for the captain, but not for the soldiers. "We the rest of us," said that ugly thug, "get nothing in the ransoms." »

This news increased Emilia's impatience, and she sent Annetta out to find out.

The resolution taken by the girl to cede everything to Montoni at that moment succumbed to new reflections. The possibility of Valancourt being near her revived her courage, and she resolved to face outrages and threats, at least until she could ascertain whether the young man was really in the castle. She was just thinking about it when Montoni sent to look for her.

He was alone. 'I sent for you,' he said to her, 'to hear if you would finally decide to give up your ridiculous claims on Languedoc property. For now I will limit myself to giving you advice, although I could impose orders. If you really were in error, if you really believed that those assets belonged to you, at least don't persist in this error which could become fatal for you. Do not provoke my wrath, and sign this paper.

"If I have no right, sir," replied Emilia, "what need do you have of my renunciation?" If the goods are yours, you can possess them in complete safety without my intervention and without my consent.

"I won't argue any more," Montoni said, giving her a look that made her tremble. "I should have seen that there's no use reasoning with boys." The memory of how much your aunt suffered as a result of her mad obstinacy serves as a lesson to you now ... Sign this paper. »

Emilia remained somewhat undecided; he shivered with remembrance and the threats that came before her; but the image of Valancourt, which had animated her for so long, who was perhaps close to her, united with her strong indignation from the first years conceived at her injustice, administered to her at that moment an imprudent, but noble courage.

"Sign this paper," Montoni repeated with greater impatience.

"No, never," replied Emilia; "Your proceeding would prove to me the injustice of your claims, if I had ignored my rights. »

Montoni turned pale with fury; His lips trembled, and his flaming eyes made Emilia almost regret her bold reply.

" Tremble at my imminent vengeance," he exclaimed, with a horrendous blasphemy; "You will have neither the possessions of Languedoc nor those of Gascony. You dared to question my rights; now you dare to doubt my power. I have ready a punishment which you do not expect; it's terrible. Tonight, yes, tonight itself...

— Tonight! a voice repeated.

Montoni was dumbfounded and turned away, then, seeming to collect himself, said softly: 'Lately you have seen a terrible example of obstinacy and madness; but I think it was not enough to frighten you. I could mention others to you, and make you tremble just by telling you about them. »

He was interrupted by a moan that seemed to come from downstairs. I looked around: his eyes sparkled with anger and impatience; a shadow of fear nevertheless seemed to alter his physiognomy. Emilia sat down near the door, because the different movements tried had, so to speak, annihilated her strength; Montoni paused briefly, then resumed in a lower but more severe voice:

'I told you I could give you other examples of my power and character. If you conceived it, you would not dare challenge him. I could prove to you that when I made up my mind... But I'm talking to a little girl; I repeat, the terrible examples I could cite would be of no use to you; and even when repentance ended your opposition, she would not appease me. I will be avenged; I will do justice. »

Another groan followed Montoni's speech.

"Go out," he said, without seeming to notice the strange incident.

Out of the state of imploring his mercy, Emilia got up to go out, but being unable to stand up, and succumbing to terror, fell back on her chair.

"Get out of my presence," continued Montoni; 'This pretense of fear is ill suited to a heroine who dared to face all my indignation.

"Have you heard nothing, sir?" Emilia said trembling.

"I hear only my own voice," replied Montoni severely.

"Anything else?" the girl added, expressing herself with difficulty. "Still... don't you hear anything now?"

"Obey," repeated Montoni. 'Then I'll be able to discover the author of these indecent jokes. »

Emilia got up with difficulty and went out. Montoni followed her, but instead of calling the servants to search the living room, as on the other time, she went to the walls.

From a window in the corridor, the girl saw a detachment of Montoni's troops descending from the mountains. She paid no attention to it except to reflect on the unhappy prisoners they perhaps led to the castle. Finally arriving in the room, she slumped a chair over her, oppressed by new anxieties which made her situation worse. She could neither repent nor praise herself for her conduct: she only remembered that she was in the power of a man who knew no other rule than his own will. Sad thoughts shook her as she heard a mixture of voices and neighing [80] in the courtyards. A sudden hope of some fortunate change was offered to her; but she, thinking of the troops seen from the window, she believed were the same as hers, of which she Annetta had told her that she expected her return.

A little later she heard many voices in the halls. The noise of the horses ceased, and was followed by perfect silence. Emilia listened attentively, trying to know Annetta's footsteps in the corridor; all was quiet. Suddenly, the castle seemed plunged into utter confusion. It was a scurrying, a coming and going in halls and galleries and courtyards, and vehement talk on the rampart. Running to the window, she saw Montoni and the other officers leaning against the parapet, or busy in entrenchments, while the soldiers were setting up their cannons. The new show amazed her.

Finally Annetta arrived, but she knew nothing of Valancourt. "Everyone makes me understand," she said, "that they know nothing about prisoners; but here's some good news! The troop returned to gallop, and at the risk of being crushed, they competed to enter under the vault. They have brought the news that a party of enemies, as they say, are following them to attack the castle. Sky! what a fright!

"Good God, thank you," said Emilia fervently. 'Now I have some hope left.

"What do you say, miss?" would you like to fall into the hands of enemies?

"We can't be worse off than here," replied Emilia.

"Listen, listen, the whole castle is upside down. The cannons are loaded, the gates and walls are examined, they bang, knock, shut up, they come and go as if the enemy were about to give the climb. But what will become of me, of you, of Lodovico? Oh! if I hear the cannon fire, I will die[81] of fear. If I could find the door open for half a minute, I'd quickly run away from here, and they'd never see me again.

"If I too could find it open for just an instant, I'd be saved. »And she briefly told the waitress the substance of her conversation with Montoni, then she added: «Run to Lodovico immediately; tell him what I have to fear, and what I have suffered: beg him to find a means of escape without delay, and for this I trust entirely in his prudence. If he wants to take charge of our liberation, he will be well rewarded. I cannot speak to him myself: we would be observed and our escape would be prevented. But be quick, Annetta, and try to act with circumspection. I will wait for you here. »

The good girl, whose sensitive soul had been penetrated by this story, was then as eager to obey, as her mistress was to employ her, and she immediately went out.

Reflecting Emilia on the reasons for the unexpected assault, she concluded that Montoni had devastated the town, and that the inhabitants came to attack it to take revenge.

Montoni, without being precisely, as Emilia assumed, a leader of robbers, had employed his troops in expeditions that were both audacious and atrocious. Not only had they despoiled all the unarmed travellers, if necessary, but also sacked all the houses located in the middle of the mountains. In these expeditions, the leaders never showed up: the soldiers, partly disguised, were sometimes taken for ordinary robbers, other times for foreign bands, which at that time flooded Italy. So they had plundered houses, and carried away immense treasures; but having attacked a castle with auxiliaries of their kind, they had been repulsed, pursued by the allies of their adversaries. Montoni's troops retreated hastily towards Udolfo, but were pursued so closely in the gorges, that having just reached the heights surrounding the fort, they saw the enemy in the valley, a little more than a league away. Then they quickened their pace to warn Montoni to prepare for defense; and it was their sudden arrival which had plunged the castle into such confusion.

While Emilia anxiously awaited the return of her faithful handmaid, she saw from the window a body of militia descending from the heights. Annetta had just left; she had to perform a delicate and dangerous mission, yet she was already racked with impatience. She listened, opened the door, and moved towards them as far as the end of the corridor. Finally she heard walking, and saw, not Annetta, but old Carlo. She was assailed by new fears. He told her that her master had sent him to warn her to prepare to leave immediately, as the castle was about to be besieged, adding that her mules were being prepared to take her, under good escort, to a place of safety.

" Safety! Emilia exclaimed without thinking. "So Signor Montoni has so much consideration for me?" Carlo didn't answer. The girl was alternately fought over by a thousand contrary affections: it seemed impossible to her that Montoni would take measures for her safety. So strange was it to drive her out of her castle, that she did not attribute this conduct to anything other than the design of carrying out some new plan of vengeance, as she had threatened it; shortly afterwards he rejoiced at the idea of leaving those sad places; but afterwards, thinking of the probability that Valancourt was a prisoner there, he felt it keenly.

Charles reminded her that there was no time to lose, the enemy being in sight. Emilia begged him to tell her where they were to take her. He hesitated, but she repeated her question, and then she replied: 'I think you must go to Tuscany.

- In Tuscany! cried the girl; "And why in that country?" »

Carlo said he knew nothing else, except that she would be taken to the Tuscan borders, to a little house at the foot of the Apennines, a few days' walk away.

Emilia dismissed him. Trembling, she was preparing a small suitcase when Annetta appeared.

"Oh! miss, there is no escape; Lodovico assures that the new porter is even more vigilant than Bernardino. The poor young man is desperate for me, and he says that he will die of fright at the first cannon shot. »

She began to cry, and hearing that Emilia was leaving, she begged her to take her with her.

'Very willingly,' she replied, 'if Signor Montoni agrees. »

Annetta did not answer her, and ran to find the castellan, who was on the walls surrounded by officers. She prayed, wept and tore her hair, but all was in vain, and Montoni drove her away harshly with a rebuff.

In her desperation, she returned to Emilia, who wished ill for that refusal. They immediately came to warn her to go down into the large courtyard, where the guides and the mules were waiting for her. She tried in vain to console Annetta, who, yearning in tears, kept repeating about her that she would never see her dear little mistress again. This she thought to herself, that her fears could unfortunately be too well founded, yet she tried to calm her down, and she said goodbye with apparent tranquility. Annetta accompanied her into the courtyard, saw her get on a mule and leave with her guides, then she went back to her room to weep freely.

Emilia meanwhile, as she went out, observed the castle, which was no longer immersed in gloomy silence, as when she had entered it; everywhere was one a clamor of arms, a bustle with preparations for defence. When she was out of the door, when she had left behind that formidable portcullis, those gloomy ramparts, she felt a sudden joy, like a slave recovering her freedom. This sentiment of hers did not allow her to reflect on the new dangers that could threaten her: the mountains infested with bag addicts, a journey begun with guides, whose physiognomy alone was worth frightening her. At first, however, she rejoiced, finding herself outside those walls, where she had entered with such sad omens. She remembered what superstitious presentiments she had then seized, and she smiled at the impression she received from her heart.

He observed the towers of the castle with such sentiments, and thinking that the stranger whom he believed held there might be Valancourt, his joy was of little duration. He gathered all the circumstances related to the unknown, since the night he had heard him sing a song of his country about him. She had often remembered them, without drawing any conviction from them, and she only believed that Valancourt might be a prisoner in Udolfo. It was probable that, along the way, he would collect more detailed information from his conductors; but fearing to question them too soon, lest a mutual diffidence prevent them from explaining themselves in each other's presence, he waited for a favorable opportunity to question them separately.

Shortly after, they heard the sound of a trumpet in the distance. The two guides stopped looking back. The very thick wood by which they were surrounded left nothing to be seen. One of them climbed a hillock to observe whether the enemy was advancing, for the bugle no doubt belonged to his vanguard. While the other was left alone with Emilia, she ventured to question him about the supposed Valancourt. Ugo, such was the name of the man, replied that the castle contained several prisoners, but that, not remembering either the figure or the time of arrival, he could not give her precise information. She asked him what prisoners had been taken since the time he indicated, that is, since he had first heard music. 'I've been out with the troops all week,' replied Ugo, 'and I don't know anything about what happened in the castle. »

Bertrando, the other guide, returned to inform his companion of what he had seen, and Emilia asked no more. The travelers left the wood, and descended into a valley in a direction opposite to that which the enemy was to take. Emilia saw the whole castle, and she contemplated with tears in her eyes those walls where Valancourt was perhaps enclosed. They began to hear the cannon fire; they electrified Ugo, who burned with impatience to find himself in battle, cursing Montoni for sending him so far away. The feelings of her companion seemed very different, and more adapted to cruelty than to the pleasures of war.

Emilia made frequent inquiries about the place of her fate; but she was unable to know anything else, except that she was going to Tuscany; and every time she spoke of it, she seemed to discover in the faces of those two men an expression of malice and pride which made her tremble.

They traveled for some hours in profound solitude; towards evening they engulfed among precipices shaded by cypresses, pines and firs; it was a desert so rough and wild that if melancholy had to choose an asylum, that would have been her favorite stay. The guides decided to rest there. "Evening is coming on," Ugo said, "and going further we'd be exposed to being devoured by wolves." This was bad news for Emilia, finding herself so late in those wild places, at their discretion. The horrific suspects conceived on Montoni's drawings they appeared more forcefully; he did everything to prevent us from stopping, and asked uneasily how far there was still to go.

"Many miles yet," Bertrando said; « if you don't want to eat, good mistress, but we want to dine, because we need it. The sun has already set: let's stop under this cliff. His comrade consented, they made Emilia get off the mule, and they all sat down on the grass and began to eat some food taken from a suitcase.

Uncertainty had so increased Emilia's anxiety about the prisoner that, unable to converse with Bertrando alone, she interrogated him in Ugo's presence; in vain: he said he knew nothing at all. Chatting about various things, they came to talk about Orsino and why he had fled from Venice. What was Emilia's horror when Bertrando told the story of another murder committed on behalf of the knight, and in which the bravo had played a leading part! At this discovery, a thousand terrible assumptions assailed her: she believed she was falling victim to the greed of Montoni, who had decided to get rid of her in silence, and through those thugs, to appropriate her goods in peace.

The sun had set in thick clouds, and Emilia ventured trembling to remind the guides that it was beginning to get late, but they were too busy with their talk to pay any attention to her. After they had finished supper, they resumed the valley road in silence. Emilia kept thinking about her own situation, and about the reasons Montoni might have for treating her like this. He was sure he had bad designs on her. If he did not make her perish in order to instantaneously appropriate her possessions, he did not make her hide for a time, except to reserve her for sadder projects, worthy of her than her greed, and better suited to his revenge. As she recalled the insult to her in the gallery, his horrible supposition gained strength. To what end, however, did he remove her from the castle, where so many crimes had probably already been committed in secrecy?

Her terror then became so excessive that she burst into tears. He thought at the same time of her beloved father, and of what he would suffer if he could foresee her strange and painful adventures. With what care would he have taken care not to entrust his orphan daughter to a woman as weak as Signora Montoni! Her present position seemed to her so romantic, that, recalling the calm and serenity of her early years, she almost fancied herself the victim of some dreadful dream, or of a delirious imagination. The reserve imposed on her by the presence of the guides changed her terror to grim despair. The frightening prospect of what might happen to her next made her almost indifferent to the dangers around her. The night was already so far advanced that the travelers could scarcely see the road.

After many hours of painful walking, even interrupted by a violent storm, they found themselves outside those woods. Emilia felt as if she had been reborn, reflecting that if those two men had had orders to kill her, they would certainly have carried it out in the horrid desert from whence they had come, and where could she ever find traces of her. Enlivened by this reflection, and by the tranquility of her guides, she descended in silence along a path made only for herds, contemplating with interest the underlying valley crowned to the east and north by the Apennines; to the west and south, the view extended over the beautiful plains of Tuscany.

"The sea is there," said Bertrando, as if he had guessed that Emilia was examining those objects which [88] the moonlight allowed her to see; 'now lies in the west, though we cannot tell it apart. »

Emilia immediately found a difference in climate, much more temperate than that of the alpine places, crossed a little before. The country now contrasted so much with the terrifying grandeur of those where it had been confined, and with the customs of those who lived there, that Emilia believed herself transported to her dear valley of Gascony. She was amazed how Montoni had sent her to that delightful country, and she could not believe she had been chosen by him to serve as a theater for a crime.

The girl ventured to ask if their destination was still very far away. Ugo replied that they weren't far away. "To that chestnut wood at the bottom of the valley," he said, "near the stream, where the moon is reflected. I can't wait to rest there with a flask of good wine and a slice of ham. »Emilia exulted when she heard that her journey was coming to an end. In a few moments they reached the entrance to the wood. They saw a light from a distance: they advanced along the stream, and soon arrived at a hut. Bertrand hammered hard. A man looked out of a small window, and having recognized him, immediately went down to open the door. The dwelling was rustic, but decent; he ordered his wife to bring some refreshments to the travellers, and meanwhile spoke to one side with Bertrando: Emilia observed him; he was a large peasant, but not robust, pale, and with penetrating eyes. His exterior did not announce a character capable of inspiring confidence, and he had no manners that could reconcile him with benevolence.

Ugo grew impatient, asked after supper, and even assumed an authoritative manner, which did not seem to admit of a reply. "He was expecting you an hour ago," said the farmer, "having already received a letter from Signor Montoni.

- Hurry up, please, we're hungry; and above all bring lots of wine. The farmer immediately handed them lard, wine, figs, bread and delicious grapes. After Emilia had refreshed herself somewhat, the farmer's wife showed her to her room. The girl asked her some questions about Montoni: Dorina, that was the woman's name, answered with great discretion, pretending to ignore her Excellency's intentions. Convinced then that she would receive no explanation of her new fate, she dismissed her, and went to bed; but the marvelous scenes which had taken place, all those which she foresaw of her, presented themselves at the same time to her uneasy imagination, and combined with the feeling of the new situation to deprive her of all sleep.

CHAPTER XXXII

When, at daybreak, Emilia opened the window, she was surprised as she contemplated the beauties that surrounded her. The house was shaded by chestnut trees mixed with cypresses and larches. To the north and east the Apennines, covered with woods, formed a superb and majestic amphitheater. Their slopes were green with vineyards and olive groves. The very elegant villas of the Tuscan nobility, scattered here and there on the hills, formed a surprising view. Grapes hung in festoons from the branches of poplars and mulberries. Immense meadows bordered the stream that descended from the mountains; to the west and to the south, the sea could be seen at a great distance. The house faced south, and was surrounded by figs, jasmine, and vines with ruddy clusters, which hung around the windows: the little lawn in front of the house was glazed with flowers and fragrant herbs.

She was called at breakfast time by the farmer's daughter, a girl of interesting physiognomy, about seventeen years of age. She Emilia saw with pleasure that she seemed animated by the purest affections of nature: all those around her announced more or less bad dispositions: cruelty, malice, ferocity and duplicity; this last character especially distinguished the physiognomy of Dorina and her husband. Maddalena spoke little, but with a soft voice and a modest and complacent air that interested Emilia. The women had breakfast at home while Ugo, Bertrando and their host ate ham and cheese on the lawn, washed down with Tuscan wines. As soon as they had finished, Ugo hurried off to look for his mule. Emilia learned then that he had to go back to Udolfo, while Bertrando would remain at the hut.

When Ugo had left, Emilia suggested a walk in the woods; but having been told that she could not go out except in the company of Bertrando, she thought it best to retire to her room.

Preferring solitude to the company of the villain and his guests, Emilia dined in her room, and Maddalena was allowed to wait on her. Her ingenuous conversation let her know that the peasants had lived in that house for a long time, which was a gift from Montoni in reward for a service rendered to him by Marco, a close relative of the old Carlo. "It's been so many years, madame," said Maddalena, "that I know very little; but certainly my father must have done a great deal of good to you, His Excellency, because my mother said very often that this house was the least gift she could give him. »

Emilia listened with pain to this story, which gave an unfavorable color to Marco's character. A service that Montoni rewarded in this way could only be criminal; and she was always convinced more than not having been sent to that place except for a desperate blow.

"Do you know how long it will be," Emilia said, thinking of the time when Signora Laurentini had disappeared from the castle, "do you know how long it has been since your father rendered Signor Montoni the service you tell me about?"

"It was some time before he came to live in this house; it will be about eighteen years old. »

It was the time when it was said that Signora Laurentini had almost disappeared. It occurred to Emilia that Marco could have served Montoni in that mysterious affair, perhaps supporting a murder. The horrible thought of her plunged her into anguished reflections. She remained alone until evening, she saw the sun set, and at her twilight time her ideas of her were all occupied with Valancourt. She brought together the circumstances relating to the nocturnal music, and all that supported her conjectures of his imprisonment in the castle, and she confirmed herself in the opinion that she had heard her voice. Tired of toiling, she finally threw herself on the bed, and succumbed to sleep. A knock on her door did not take long to wake her up. The image of Bertrando with her easy-going style presented itself to her distorted imagination. She asked who she was. "It's me,

"What brings you so late?" Emilia said making her enter.

"Shut up, lady, for God's sake, let's not make any noise. If they heard us, they wouldn't forgive me. My father, my mother and Bertrando are asleep,' she added, closing the door. « Since you haven't had supper, I have brought you grapes, figs, bread and a glass of wine. »She Emilia thanked her, but she let her know that she exposed herself to Dorina's resentment, when she noticed the lack of her fruits. "Take them back, Lena," she told her, "I'll suffer less not to eat, than if you knew you were to be scolded by your mother tomorrow.

— Oh! Lady! there's no danger,' added la Lena; 'my mother can't notice anything, as it is my share of dinner; you would displease me by refusing. Emilia was so moved by the generosity of the good girl that tears came to her eyes. "Don't worry," Lena told her; "My mom is a little alive, but she gets over it quickly. So don't worry. She often scolds me, but I have learned to suffer for her; and if she manages to escape into the woods, when she's done, I forget everything. »

Emilia smiled despite her tears, told Lena that she had a good heart, and accepted the gift. She very much wanted to know if Bertrando, Dorina and Marco had spoken about Montoni and her orders from him in Maddalena's presence; but she did not want to seduce the innocent girl, making her betray her parents' speeches. When she was gone, she Emilia begged her to come and see her as often as she could, but without failing in the duties of her daughter; Lena promised it, and wished her good night.

Emilia never left her room for a few days, and Lena came to visit her only during her mealtimes. Her sweet countenance and interesting manners consoled our lonely heroine. In this interval her spirit, having received no fresh jolt of pain or fear, was able to avail itself of the amusement of reading her. She found some sketches, paper and pencils, and she felt willing to recreate herself by drawing some part of the magnificent perspective that she had before her eyes.

One day in the evening when it was very hot, Emilia wanted to try going for a walk, although Bertrando had to accompany her. She took the Lena and went out followed by her goon, who left her free to choose the road. The weather was clear and cool: [93] Emilia enthusiastically admired that beautiful district.

The western sun still gilded the tops of the trees and the highest peaks. Emilia followed the course of the stream along the trees that bordered it. On the opposite bank some white sheep stood out among the greenery. Suddenly, she heard a chorus of voices. She stops, listens attentively, but she fears being seen. It was the first time she regarded Bertrando as her protector; she and followed her closely talking with a shepherd. Reassured by this certainty, she advances behind a small hill; the music stopped, and presently she heard a woman's voice singing alone. Emilia, redoubling her pace, turned behind the hill, and saw a small meadow crowned with very tall trees. She observed two groups of peasants standing around a young girl, who was singing, holding a garland of flowers in her hand.

When the song was over, some shepherdesses approached Emilia and Lena, made them sit among them, and presented them with grapes and figs. That placid country scene moved her beyond measure, and when she returned home, she felt her spirit calmer than hers.

After that evening she often walked in Lena's company, but always accompanied by Bertrando. The tranquility in which she lived about her made her believe that there were no bad designs about her; and without the probable idea that Valancourt was at that moment a prisoner in the castle, she would have preferred to remain there until the time of her return to her country. However, reflecting on the reasons which might have decided Montoni to let her pass through Tuscany, her concern did not diminish, not being convinced that the sole interest of her safety had decided him to behave in this manner.

Emilia spent some time in the hut before remembering that, in her hasty departure, she had left her aunt's papers relating to the property to Udolfo of the Languedoc. This made her feel sorry for her, but then she hoped that her hiding place would escape Montoni's searches.

CHAPTER XXXIII

Let us go back to Venice for a moment, where Count Morano is groaning under the weight of new disasters. As soon as he arrived there, he had been arrested by order of the Senate, and placed in such a rigorous dungeon, that all the efforts of his friends failed to hear the news. He had not been able to guess to which enemy he owed his imprisonment, unless it was Montoni, on whom his suspicions were fixed.

They were not only probable but also well founded. In the matter of the poisoned cup, Montoni had suspected Morano; but, unable to acquire the degree of proof necessary for the conviction of the crime, he had recourse to other ways of revenge. From a trusted person he had a letter of accusation thrown into the lion's mouth, intended to receive secret denunciations against political conspirators.

The count had attracted the rancor of the principal senators; his haughty ways, his immoderate ambition made him hated by others; therefore he should expect no mercy from his enemies.

Montoni meanwhile faced other dangers. His castle was besieged by people determined to conquer. The strength of the square resisted the violent attack, the garrison defended itself strenuously and the lack of food forced the assailants to leave. When Montoni saw himself once again the peaceful owner of Udolfo, impatient to still have Emilia in his hands, he sent to look for her. Forced to leave, the girl bid a tender farewell to sweet Lena. Climbing the Apennines, she fixed a single gaze of regret upon the delightful country which she was abandoning; but the pain he felt at having to return to the scene of his sufferings was softened by the probable hope of finding Valancourt there, though a prisoner.

Arrived in the evening, and without sad encounters, near the castle, they were able to see in the moonlight the damage suffered by the walls during the siege. Even the woods had suffered: trees knocked down, crashed, stripped of fronds, burned, indicated the fury of war.

Profound silence had followed the uproar of arms. At the gate, a soldier equipped with a lamp came to recognize the travellers, and ushered them into the courtyard. Emilia was seized with almost desperation on hearing those formidable shutters close behind her, which seemed to separate her from the world forever.

Having crossed the second courtyard, they found themselves at the door of the vestibule; the soldier wished them good night and returned to his place. Meanwhile, Emilia was thinking of a way to retire to her old room without being seen, for fear of running into either Montoni or someone from her company so late. The joy that reigned in the castle at the time was so clamorous that Ugo knocked on the door without being able to make himself understood by the servants. This circumstance increased Emilia's fears, and she gave her time to reflect. She might perhaps have reached the staircase, but she could not go to her room without a light. Bertrando hardly had a torch, and she knew very well that the servants only accompanied by the light as far as the door, because the lamppost suspended from the vault sufficiently illuminated the vestibule.

Carlo finally opened the door: Emilia asked him to send Annetta immediately with a light into the large gallery where she was going to wait for her, and, having climbed the stairs, she sat down on the last step. The darkness of the tunnel dissuaded her from entering it. While she was listening to hear if Annetta was coming, she heard Montoni and his family comrades, who, talking tumultuously with drunken people, made their way with staggering steps towards the stairs. Forgetting her fear, she entered the gallery with her arms extended, always attentive to the voices she heard downstairs, and among which she distinguished those of Bertolini and Verrezzi. From the few words she was able to understand, she understood that they were talking about her: each of her was claiming some old promise from Montoni. After a few altercations, she heard people coming up, and she darted into the gallery with the rapidity of lightning. Thus she traversed several of these ancient passages by chance; she finally succeeded in one of them at the bottom of which she seemed to see a thread of light.

As she was making her way there, she saw Verrezzi staggering towards her. To get rid of him, she threw herself into a door she found on the left, hoping she hadn't been seen; a little later, she opened the door to try to leave, when a light came out at the end of that corridor, and she recognized Annetta; he ran to meet her, and she, seeing him, threw herself on her neck with a cry. Emilia was able to make her understand her danger, and they both went to Annetta's room at a somewhat distant distance. However, no fear could not silence her. "Oh! my dear mistress,' she said as she walked, 'how scared I was! Ah! I thought I'd die a thousand times, and she didn't know if I'd survive the thunder of the cannons to see you again. Never in my life have I felt more content than now that I find you again.

- Shut up! said Emilia; "We're being chased! »

But it was the echo of their footsteps.

"No," said Annetta, "they've closed a door."

- Let's be silent, for heaven's sake, and don't speak any more, until we reach your room. They finally arrived there without sinister encounters. The maid opened it, and Emilia sat up in bed to rest a little. Her first question is whether Valancourt was a prisoner. Annetta answered her not being able to tell him exactly, but be sure that there were many prisoners in the castle. Then he began in his own way to make the description of the siege, or rather the detail of all the fears suffered during the attack. 'But,' she added, 'when I heard the cries of victory on the walls, I believed that we had been taken, and I kept lost; instead we had driven out the enemies. I went into the northern gallery, and saw a large number of fugitives in the mountains. After all, it can be said that the ramparts are in ruins. It was frightening to see so many dead piled up on top of each other in the woods subjected to it!... During the siege, Signor Montoni ran here, there, he was everywhere, according to what Lodovico told me. For me, he didn't let me see anything. He locked me in a room in the center of the castle, he brought me food, and came to see me as often as he could. I must confess that, without Lodovico, I would certainly have died.

"And how are things after the siege?"

"There's a terrible noise," answered Annetta; 'Gentlemen do nothing but eat, drink and play. They sit at table all night and gamble with each other the nice and rich things they got when they went to plunder or something like that. They have very lively altercations about loss and gain; Signor Verrezzi always loses, according to what they say: Orsino wins, and they are always in dispute. All those beautiful ladies are still here, and I confess they disgust me when I meet them.

"Surely," Emilia said with a start, "I hear a noise, listen."

- Oibo! it's the wind. I often hear it when it blows harder than usual, and shakes the gallery doors. But why don't you want to go to bed? I don't think you want to stay like this all night. »

Emilia lay down on the bed begging her to leave the light on. Annetta lay down next to her; but [98] the girl could not sleep, and she always seemed to hear some noise. While Annetta was trying to persuade her that it was the wind, they heard footsteps near her door. The maid wanted to get out of bed, but Emilia held her back; she knocked lightly, and she called herself Annetta in a low voice.

"For heaven's sake, don't answer," Emilia said, "she's quiet. We would do well to put out the light, which could give us away.

- Madonna! cried the waitress; "I wouldn't stay in the dark now for all the gold in the world." »Annetta's name was repeated louder as she spoke. « Ah! it's Lodovico,' she cried then, and she got up to open the door; but Emilia prevented it by first wanting to make sure if she was alone. Annetta spoke to him for some time, and he told her that, having let her go to visit her mistress, she was coming to lock her up again. She fearing she'd be surprised if they kept talking like that, she agreed to let him in. The frank and good-natured physiognomy of the young man reassured Emilia, who implored his assistance if Verrezzi made it necessary. Lodovico promised to spend the night in an adjoining room to protect her from any insult, and, lighting a lamp, he went off in her place.

Emilia would have liked to rest, but too many interests occupied her mind: she saw herself in a place that had become the residence of vice and violence, outside the protection of the laws, in the power of a man tireless in persecution and revenge; and she recognized that to resist his bullying any longer would be madness. She therefore abandoned the hope of living comfortably with Valancourt, and she decided to surrender everything to Montoni the following morning, provided he would allow her to return to France soon. These reflections kept her awake all night.

As soon as it was day, Emilia had a long conversation with Lodovico, who told her various circumstances relating to the castle, and gave her some information on Montoni's projects, which increased her well-founded fears. He showed great surprise that, looking so moved by her sad situation in that castle, he didn't think of leaving. He assured her that it was not her intention to stay there, and then she risked asking him if she would assist her escape. Lodovico assured her that he was quite willing to try her, but he explained to her all the difficulties of the enterprise, since his loss would have been certain if Montoni reached them before they were out of the mountains. He promised nonetheless to seek the opportunity carefully, and to take care of a plan of escape. Emilia then confided to him the name of Valancourt, begging him to inquire whether he was among the prisoners. Her feeble hope, which arose from this conversation, dissuaded Emilia from dealing immediately with Montoni; if possible, she resolved to delay speaking to him until she heard something from Lodovico, and not to give her up until she found every means of escaping impossible. While she was thus daydreaming, Montoni, revived by her drunkenness, sent for her; she obeyed, and she found him alone. 'I hear,' said he, 'that you did not spend the night in your room; where have you been?»She Emilia detailed to him the circumstances which had prevented it, and asked her for her protection for the future. "You know the terms of my protection," he said; "if you really notice it, try to deserve it. » inquire whether it was in the number of prisoners. Her feeble hope, which arose from this conversation, dissuaded Emilia from dealing immediately with Montoni; if possible, she resolved to delay speaking to him until she heard something from Lodovico, and not to give her up until she found every means of escaping impossible. While she was dreaming like this, Montoni, revived from drunkenness, sent for her; she obeyed, and she found him alone. 'I hear,' said he, 'that you did not spend the night in your room; where have you been?»She Emilia detailed to him the circumstances which had prevented it, and asked her for her protection for the future. "You know the terms of my protection," he said; "if you really notice it, try to deserve it. » inquire whether it was in the number of prisoners. Her feeble hope, which arose from this conversation, dissuaded Emilia from dealing immediately with Montoni; if possible, she resolved to delay speaking to him until she heard something from Lodovico, and not to give her up until she found every means of escaping impossible. While she was dreaming like this, Montoni, revived from drunkenness, sent for her; she obeyed, and she found him alone. 'I hear,' said he, 'that you did not spend the night in your room; where have you been?»She Emilia detailed to him the circumstances which had prevented it, and asked her for her protection for the future. "You know the terms of my protection," he said; "if you really notice it, try to deserve it. » The feeble hope which arose from this interview dissuaded Emilia from dealing immediately with Montoni; if possible, she resolved to delay speaking to him until she heard something from Lodovico, and not to give her up until she found every means of escaping impossible. While she was thus daydreaming, Montoni, revived by her drunkenness, sent for her; she obeyed, and she found him alone. 'I hear,' said he, 'that you did not spend the night in your room; where have you been?»She Emilia detailed to him the circumstances which had prevented it, and asked her for her protection for the future. "You know the terms of my protection," he said; "if you really notice it, try to deserve it. » The feeble hope which arose from this interview dissuaded Emilia from dealing immediately with Montoni; if possible, she resolved to delay speaking to him until she heard something from Lodovico, and not to give her up until she found every means of escaping impossible. While she was thus daydreaming, Montoni, revived by her drunkenness, sent for her; she obeyed, and she found him alone. 'I hear,' said he, 'that you did not spend the night in your room; where have you been?»She Emilia detailed to him the circumstances which had prevented it, and asked her for her protection for the future. "You know the terms of my protection," he said; "if you really notice it, try to deserve it. » if possible, to delay speaking to him until she heard something from Lodovico, and not to make the assignment until every means of escape proved impossible for her. While she was thus daydreaming, Montoni, revived by her drunkenness, sent for her; she obeyed, and she found him alone. 'I hear,' said he, 'that you did not spend the night in your room; where have you been?»She Emilia detailed to him the circumstances which had prevented it, and asked her for her protection for the future. "You know the terms of my protection," he said; "if you really notice it, try to deserve it. » if possible, to delay speaking to him until she heard something from Lodovico, and not to make the assignment until every means of escape proved impossible for her. While she was thus daydreaming, Montoni, revived by her drunkenness, sent for her; she obeyed, and she found him alone. 'I hear,' said he, 'that you did not spend the night in your room; where have you been? »She Emilia detailed to him the circumstances which had prevented it, and asked her for her protection for the future. "You know the terms of my protection," he said; "if you really notice it, try to deserve it. » Montoni, revived from drunkenness, sent for her; she obeyed, and found him alone. 'I heard,' he said, 'that you did not spend the night in your room; where have you been? »She Emilia detailed to him the circumstances which had prevented it, and asked her for her protection for the future. "You know the terms of my protection," he said; "if you really notice it, try to deserve it. » Montoni, revived from drunkenness, sent for her; she obeyed, and found him alone. 'I heard,' he said, 'that you did not spend the night in your room; where have you been? »She Emilia detailed to him the circumstances which had prevented it, and asked her for her protection for the future. "You know the terms of my protection," he said; "if you really notice it, try to deserve it. »

That precise declaration, which would not have protected her except conditionally, during her captivity in the castle, convinced Emilia of the need to surrender; but she first asked him if she would allow her to leave immediately after signing her assignment; he made them solemn promised, and presented her with the charter, with which she transferred all her rights to him.

He was for some time unable to sign, having his heart torn by opposing affections; he was about to give up the happiness of his life, and the hope that he had sustained her through so long a course of adversity.

Montoni repeated her pacts of obedience, observing that all moments were precious. She took the pen and signed the assignment. As soon as she had finished, she begged him to order her departure and to let her take Annetta with her. Montoni then started laughing. "It was necessary to deceive you," he said; 'it was the only way to make you act reasonably: you will leave but not now. First I need to take possession of those goods; when this is done, you can go back to France. »

The cold villainy with which he violated the solemn commitment he had made reduced Emilia to despair, knowing that her sacrifice would do her no good and would remain a prisoner: she could not find words to express her feelings, and she well understood that any observation would have been fruitless; she looked at Montoni with a pleading air, but he turned her head away and begged her to withdraw. Unable to take even a step, she sank back into a chair, sighing heavily, unable to cry or speak.

« Why abandon yourselves to this inopportune pain? Montoni told her; « strive to courageously bear what you cannot now avoid. You have no real trouble to complain of; be patient, and you will be sent back to France. Meanwhile, go back to your room.

"I don't dare, sir," replied Emilia, "to go to a place where Signor Verrezzi can enter. "Didn't I promise to protect you?" Montoni said. — I promise! Emilia retorted hesitantly. — The Isn't my promise enough? he resumed severely. "Remember your first promise," said Emilia trembling, "and you will judge for yourself which case I should make of the others." "Beware of making me retract my words. Retreat, you have nothing to fear in your apartment. »

Emilia withdrew with slow steps, and when she had reached her room, carefully examined whether anyone was hidden there, closed the door, and sat down by the window. The poor wretch might have lost her reason if she hadn't struggled strongly against the weight of her misfortunes. She tried in vain to believe that Montoni would really have sent her back to France, as soon as he had secured her property, and that in the meantime he would have cured her of the insults. However, her main hope lay in Lodovico; nor did she doubt his zeal, despite his own lack of confidence in the projected escape.

This sad day he spent like so many others in his own room. Night fell, and Emilia would have retired to Annetta's room if a stronger interest had not detained her: she wanted to await the return of the music at the usual time, which, if it could not positively assure her of Valancourt's presence in the castle, was to confirm her in her idea and to provide her with a consolation so necessary in her present despondency.

The night was stormy: the wind was blowing vehemently; the hours passed: Emilia heard the sentinels posted. A little later, a faint melody crossed the air; she recognized the sound of a lute accompanied by the querulous accents of a man. She listened hoping and fearing; she found the harmonious sweetness of voice and lute, which she already knew. Convinced that the music was coming from one of the rooms below, she leaned out to discover no light, but in vain. She also called softly, but the wind prevented no doubt to hear it; the music continued. Suddenly, he heard a knock on her bedroom door, and having recognized Annetta's voice, he opened them, inviting her to approach the window slowly to listen.

"Great God! cried Annetta; 'I know this song: it is French, and one of the favorite arias of my dear country... It is a compatriot of ours who sings it and it must be Monsieur Valancourt. "Softly, Annetta," said Emilia, "don't speak so loudly; we could be understood. - From who? from the knight? "No, but someone could betray us. Why do you think it's Valancourt that he sings? But shut up: his voice gets louder. Do you recognize her? "Miss," answered Annetta, "I've never heard the knight sing." Emilia was very sorry that Annetta's only reason for believing it was Valancourt was that the singer was French. Shortly after she heard the romance intended at the fishpond, and her name was repeated so often, that Annetta cried aloud: 'Mr. Valancourt! Monsieur Valancourt! » Emilia tried to hold her back, but she cried louder and louder; the music stopped, and no one answered. "It doesn't matter, Signora Emilia," said the girl; "It's definitely the knight, and I want to talk to him." — No, no, Annetta; I want to talk to him myself. If it's him, she'll recognize my voice, and respond. Who is he, » she cried, « singing so late? »She A long silence ensued. She repeated the question, and heard faint accents, which seemed to come from so far away, that she could make out no words. She then she believed that her incognito was Valancourt without a doubt, for she had responded to her voice, and flattering herself that she had recognized her, she gave herself up to transports of joy. Meanwhile Annetta kept calling. Emilia, then fearing being betrayed in her search for her, silenced her, reserving the right to question

Lodovico the following morning. the music stopped, and no one answered. "It doesn't matter, Signora Emilia," said the girl; "It's definitely the knight, and I want to talk to him." — No, no, Annetta; I want to talk to him myself. If it's him, she'll recognize my voice, and respond. Who is he, » she cried, « singing so late? »She A long silence ensued. She repeated the question, and heard faint accents, which seemed to come from so far away, that she could make out no words. She then she believed that her incognito was Valancourt without a doubt, for she had responded to her voice, and flattering herself that she had recognized her, she gave herself up to transports of joy. Meanwhile Annetta kept calling. Emilia, then fearing being betrayed in her search, silenced her, reserving the right to question Lodovico the following morning. the music stopped, and no one answered. "It doesn't matter, Signora Emilia," said the girl; "It's definitely the knight, and I want to talk to him." — No, no, Annette; I want to talk to him myself. If it's him, she'll recognize my voice, and respond. Who is he, » she cried, « singing so late? »She A long silence ensued. She repeated the question, and heard faint accents, which seemed to come from so far away, that she could make out no words. She then she believed that her incognito was Valancourt without a doubt, for she had responded to her voice, and flattering herself that she recognized her, she gave herself up to transports of joy. Meanwhile Annetta kept calling. Emilia, then fearing being betrayed in her search, silenced her, reserving the right to question Lodovico the following morning. the girl said; "It's definitely the knight, and I want to talk to him." — No, no, Annette; I want to talk to him myself. If it's him, she'll recognize my voice, and respond. Who is he, » she cried, « singing so late? »She A long silence ensued. She repeated the question, and heard faint accents, which seemed to come from so far away, that she could make out no words. She then she believed that her incognito was Valancourt without a doubt, for she had responded to her voice, and flattering herself that she recognized her, she gave herself up to transports of joy. Meanwhile Annetta kept calling. Emilia, then fearing being betrayed in her search, silenced her, reserving the right to question Lodovico the following morning. the girl said; "It's definitely the knight, and I want to talk to him." — No, no, Annetta; I want to talk to him myself. If it's him, she'll recognize my voice, and respond. Who is he, » she cried, « singing so late? »She A long silence ensued. She repeated the question, and heard faint accents, which seemed to come from so far away, that she could make out no words. She then she believed that her incognito was Valancourt without a doubt, for she had responded to her voice, and flattering herself that she recognized her, she gave herself up to transports of joy. Meanwhile Annetta kept calling. Emilia, then fearing being betrayed in her search, silenced her, reserving the right to question Lodovico the following morning. he will recognize my voice, and he will answer. Who is she," she cried, "that sings so late? »She A long silence ensued. She repeated the question, and heard faint accents, which seemed to come from so far away, that she could make out no words. She then she believed that her incognito was Valancourt without a doubt, for she had responded to her voice, and flattering herself that she recognized her, she gave herself up to transports of joy. Meanwhile Annetta kept calling. Emilia, then fearing being betrayed in her search for her, silenced her, reserving the right to question Lodovico the following morning. he will recognize my voice, and he will answer. Who is she," she cried, "that sings so late? »She A long silence ensued. She repeated the question, and heard faint accents, which seemed to come from so far away, that she could make out no words. She then she believed that her incognito was Valancourt without a doubt, for she had responded to her voice, and flattering herself that she recognized her, she gave herself up to transports of joy. Meanwhile Annetta kept calling. Emilia, then fearing being betrayed in her search for her, silenced her, reserving the right to question Lodovico the following morning. incognito was Valancourt no doubt, for he had answered her voice, and flattering himself that he recognized her, gave himself up to transports of joy. Meanwhile Annetta kept calling. Emilia, then fearing being betrayed in her search for her, silenced her, reserving the right to question Lodovico the following morning. incognito was Valancourt no doubt, for he had answered her voice, and flattering himself that he recognized her, gave himself up to transports of joy. Meanwhile Annetta kept calling. Emilia, then fearing being betrayed in her search for her, silenced her, reserving the right to question Lodovico the following morning.

They both spent some time at the window, but everything remained calm. Emilia strode jubilantly about the room, calling softly to Valancourt, and she then returned to the window, where she heard nothing but the murmur of the wind in the fronds. Annetta was as impatient as she; but her prudence finally determined them to close the window, and go to bed.

CHAPTER XXXIV

A few days passed in uncertainty. Lodovico could only know that there was a prisoner in the place indicated by Emilia, a Frenchman, who had been caught in a skirmish. In the interval, Emilia escaped persecution by Verrezzi and Bertolini, confined herself to her room. She sometimes she walked in the corridor in the evening. Montoni seemed to respect his last promise, even though he had violated the first; and she could attribute her repose only to the favor of his protection. She was then so persuaded of it that she did not wish to leave the castle until she had obtained some certainty about Valancourt. So she waited for him, without it costing her any sacrifice, since up to then no propitious opportunity to flee had presented herself.

Finally, Lodovico came to warn her that he hoped to see the prisoner, since the latter must have a soldier with whom he had made friends for guard the following night. His hope was not in vain, since she was able to enter the prison under the pretext of bringing him water. Prudence, however, forced him not to confide to the sentry the real reason for that visit, which was very brief.

Emilia waited impatiently for the result; finally she saw the young man reappear with Annetta. "The prisoner, miss," said he, "he didn't want tell me his name. When I pronounced yours, he showed less surprise than I imagined.

- How is he? He must be very dejected after such a long captivity ... - Oh no! he seemed to me that he was fine, although I didn't ask him. "He didn't give you anything for me?" Emilia said. "He gave Me this, saying he would write to you if he had the means. Take.»And he handed her a thumbnail. Emilia recognized her own portrait, the same one that had lost her mother in such a singular way at the fishpond in the valley. She wept then with joy and tenderness, and Lodovico continued: «He begged me to get him an interview with you. I explained to him how difficult it seemed to me to get his keeper to agree to it; he replied that it was easier than I imagined, and that if I had brought him your answer, he would have explained himself better. "When you can see the knight again, tell him I agree to see him. "But when, madame, in what place?" "That will depend on the circumstances; they will fix the time and place.»

The young man wished her good night, and went away.

A week passed before Lodovico was able to return to the prison. In the interval, he communicated frightening reports to Emilia of what was happening in the castle: her name was often mentioned in the speeches of Bertolini and Verrezzi, and she always became the subject of altercations. Montoni had lost enormous sums in gambling with Verrezzi, and there was every probability that he was going to give it to her in marriage to get out of debt, despite Bertolini's opposition. At this news, the poor girl implored Lodovico to see the prisoner again quickly, and to facilitate their escape.

Finally Lodovico told her that he had seen the knight again, who had induced him to trust the jailer, whose condescension he had already experienced, and who had promised him to go out for half an hour the following night, when Montoni and his companions were carousing. "It is certainly a fine thing," added the young man; «But Sebastiano knows well that he doesn't run any risk, letting the prisoner out, because if he can escape from the iron doors he will be very dexterous. The knight sends me to you, madame, to beg you in his name to allow me to see you tonight, even if it were only for a moment, since I can no longer live under the same roof without seeing you; about the time, he can't specify it, since it depends on the circumstances, as you said, and he asks you to choose the place you think is the safest. »

Emilia was so agitated by the imminent hope of seeing Valancourt again that some minutes passed before she could reply. Finally, she couldn't point to a safer place than the corridor. It was therefore established that the knight would come that night in the corridor, and that Lodovico would think about choosing the hour. Emilia, as may be supposed, passed this interval in a tumult of hope, joy, and anxious impatience. Since her arrival at the castle she had never watched the sunset with such pleasure. She counted the hours, and it seemed to her that time never passed.

Finally midnight struck. He opened the corridor door to listen for noise in the castle, and heard only the echo of inordinate laughter from the great hall. He imagined that Montoni and his guests were at the table. 'They are busy all night,' he said to himself, 'and Valancourt will be here soon. He closed the door, and paced about the room with the agitation of impatience. He looked out the window, flattering himself to hear the lute playing; but all was silence, and hers emotion grew. Annetta, whom he had kept in her company, was chatting as usual; but Emilia did not understand the syllable of her speech. Returning to the window, she finally heard the usual voice singing accompanied by her lute. She could not refrain from weeping at her tenderness. The romance finished, she Emilia considered it as a signal indicating the exit of Valancourt. Presently she heard footsteps in the corridor, opened the door, ran to meet her lover, and found herself in the arms of a man she had never seen before. Her face and the sound of her incognito voice disillusioned her in the moment, and she fainted.

Allorchè risensò, trovossi sostenuta da quest'uomo, il quale la considerava con viva espressione di tenerezza e d'inquietudine. Non ebbe la forza per interrogare, nè per rispondere: proruppe in dirotto pianto, e si sciolse dalle di lui braccia. L'incognito impallidì. Sorpreso, guardava Lodovico come per domandargli qualche schiarimento; ma Annetta gli spiegò il mistero che non intendeva neppur Lodovico. « Signore, » gridò ella singhiozzando, « voi non siete l'altro cavaliere. Noi aspettavamo il signor Valancourt, e non siete voi quello. Ah! Lodovico, come avete potuto ingannarci così? la mia povera padrona se ne risentirà per molto tempo. » L'incognito, il quale pareva agitatissimo, voleva parlare, ma gli spirarono le parole sul labbro, e battendosi colla mano la fronte, come preso da improvvisa disperazione, si ritirò dalla parte opposta del corridoio.

Annetta wiped away her tears and said to Lodovico: 'It may be that the other knight, that is, Signor Valancourt, is still downstairs. Emilia raised her head. 'No,' replied Lodovico, 'Monsieur Valancourt has never been there, if this knight isn't him. If you had the kindness to confide your name to me, sir," he said to the unknown, "this misunderstanding it would not have taken place. "It's very true," he replied in bad Italian; 'but I was very concerned that Montoni ignored it. Madame," he then added, turning to Emilia in French, "allow me a few words. Suffer that I explain to you alone my name and the circumstances that led me into error. I am your compatriot, and we are both in a strange land. »

Emilia tried to calm down, and was hesitant to grant him her request; finally, she begged Lodovico to go and wait for her at the end of the corridor, detained Annetta, and told her incognito that the girl, understanding Italian very little, could speak to her in that language. They withdrew to a corner, and her incognito said to her, after a long sigh: 'Madam, my family must not be unknown to you. My name is Dupont; my relatives lived at some distance from your castle in the valley, and I was fortunate enough to meet you sometimes when visiting the neighbourhood. I will certainly not offend you by repeating how much you knew how to interest me, how much I enjoyed wandering in the places you frequented, how many times I visited your favorite fishpond, and how much she moaned at the time about the circumstances which prevented me from declaring my passion to you! I will not explain to you how I was able to give in to temptation, and how I became the owner of a treasure invaluable to me, which I entrusted to your messenger a few days ago, with a very different hope from the one I now have. I won't extend further. Let me beg your pardon, and as for that portrait which I returned so ill-timed, your generosity will excuse its theft, and will return it to me. My crime itself has become my punishment; and that portrait which I flew fed a passion which must ever be my torment. » I won't extend further. Let me beg your pardon, and as for that portrait which I returned so ill-timed, your generosity will excuse its theft, and will return it to me. My crime itself has become my punishment; and that portrait which I flew fed a passion which must ever be my torment. » I won't extend further. Let me beg your pardon, and as for that portrait which I returned so ill-timed, your generosity will excuse its theft, and will return it to me. My crime itself has become my punishment; and that portrait which I flew fed a passion which must ever be my torment. »

Emilia, interrupting him, said: 'I leave it to your conscience, sir, to decide whether, after all what happened with respect to M. Valancourt, I must return your portrait. It would not be a generous action: you must admit it yourself, and you will allow me to add that you would be doing me an insult by insisting on obtaining it. I am honored by the favorable opinion you conceived of me; but... this evening's misunderstanding dispenses me from telling you more.

— Yes, madam, alas! yes,' replied Dupont; « Allow me at least to let you know my disinterest, if not my love. Accept the services of a friend, who, though a prisoner, swears to make every effort to remove you from this horrible stay, and do not deny me the reward of having at least tried to deserve your gratitude.

"You already deserve it, sir," said Emilia, "and the vote you express deserves all my thanks." Excuse me if I remind you of the danger to which we are exposed by prolonging this meeting. It will be a great consolation for me, whether your attempts fail or have a happy outcome, to have a generous compatriot willing to protect me. »

Dupont took the hand of Emilia, who wanted to withdraw it, and brought it respectfully to his lips.

'Allow me,' he said to her, 'to sigh deeply for your happiness, and praise me with a passion which it is impossible for me to overcome. »At that point she Emilia she heard a noise in her room, and turning that way, she saw a man who, rushing down the corridor brandishing a stiletto, shouted: «I will teach you to overcome this passion! »And she ran to meet Dupont who was helpless. The latter dodged the blow, threw himself on him, in which Emilia recognized Verrezzi and disarmed him. During the fight, Emilia and Annetta ran to call Lodovico, but he had disappeared. Backing away, the noise of the struggle reminded her of danger. Annetta went to look for Lodovico; the girl hastened to where Dupont and Verrezzi were still grappling, and he begged them to separate. The first finally threw his opponent to the ground and left him stunned by the fall. Emilia begged him to flee before Montoni or someone else appeared: he refused to leave her thus without defence, and while she, more frightened for him than for herself, redoubled her solicitous requests, they heard the secret staircase ascend.

"You are lost," she said; "It's the people of Montoni. Dupont didn't answer, and supporting Emilia, who was struggling to keep up, waited for his adversaries on firm foot. A little later Lodovico entered alone, and glancing everywhere: 'Follow me,' he said to them, 'if your life is dear to you; we don't have a moment to lose. »

Emilia asked what had happened, and where to go.

"I don't have time to tell you," replied Lodovico. "Flee, flee. »

She followed instantly, supported by Dupont. They went down the stairs, and while they were crossing a secret passage, she remembered Annetta, and asked where she was. "She's waiting for us," Lodovico replied in a low voice. 'A little while ago the doors were opened for an arriving detachment, and I fear they will be closed again before we get there. »Emilia trembled more and more after knowing that her escape depended on a single instant. Dupont gave her his arm, and tried, by walking, to revive her courage.

Lodovico opened another door, behind which they found Annetta, and they went down a few steps. The young man said that this passage led to the second courtyard and communicated with the first. As they advanced, a confused tumult, which seemed to come from the second courtyard, frightened Emilia.

"Don't be afraid, madame," said Lodovico, "our only hope lies in this tumult: while the people of the castle are occupied with those that arrive, we may perhaps be able to leave the gates unnoticed. But shut up," he added, approaching a small door that led onto the first courtyard; "Stay here a moment: I'm going to see if the doors are open, and if there's anyone on the way." I beg you, sir, to put out the lamp if you hear me speaking," he added, handing the lamp to Dupont, "and in that case remain silent. »

He went out, and closed the door. "We will soon be outside these walls," said Dupont to Emilia; "Take courage, and everything will be fine. »

A little later they heard Lodovico speaking loudly, and they also distinguished another voice. Dupont immediately put out the light. "Great God! It's too late,' exclaimed Emilia; "What will become of us? They listened attentively, and realized that Lodovico was talking to the sentry. Emilia's dog, which had followed her, began to bark. Dupont took him in his arms to silence him, and they heard the young man say to the sentry: 'Meanwhile I'll keep watch for you. "Wait a moment," replied the sentry, "and you won't have this inconvenience." The horses must be sent to the nearby stables, the doors will close, and I will be able to leave for a minute — Oibò! He's not an inconvenience for me, dear comrade,' said Lodovico; 'You will do me the same service another time. Go, go and taste that wine, otherwise the troops that have arrived will drink it all, and there will be no more. »

The soldier hesitated, and called into the second courtyard, to ask if the horses should be led out, and if the doors could be closed. They were all too busy to answer him even if they heard.

"Yes, yes," said Lodovico, "they're not that stupid, they share everything among themselves." If you wait for the horses to leave, you will find the wine all gone. I had my share, but since you don't want any, I'll go in your stead.

'Up there, comrade,' added the sentry, 'take my place for a few minutes, I'll be right back.' »

And go running.

Lodovico, seeing himself free, hurried to open the door of the passage. Emilia almost succumbed to the anxiety caused by the long conversation. He told them that the courtyard was free: they followed him without wasting time, and led with them two horses which they found isolated.

Leaving unhindered through the formidable gates, they ran to the woods. Emilia, Dupont and Annetta were on foot; Lodovico on one horse, leading the other. Once in the forest, the two girls mounted on the back with their protectors. Lodovico served as guide, and they fled as quickly as the ruined road and the feeble moonlight through the trees allowed.

Emilia was so stunned by the unexpected departure that she hardly dared to believe she was awake: however, she very much doubted that the adventure could end well, and the doubt was unfortunately too reasonable. Before leaving the wood they heard loud cries, and saw many lights in the vicinity of the castle. Dupont spurred his horse, and with much pain forced it to run faster.

« Povera bestia, » disse Lodovico, « dev'essere ben stanca, essendo stata fuori tutto il giorno. Ma signore, andiamo da questa parte, perchè i lumi vengono per di qua. » E spronati i cavalli, si misero a galoppare. Dopo una lunga corsa, guardarono indietro: i lumi erano tanto lontani, che a mala pena potevano distinguersi; le grida avean fatto luogo a profondo silenzio. I viaggiatori allora moderarono il passo, e tennero consiglio sulla direzione da prendere. Decisero di andare in Toscana per guadagnare il Mediterraneo, e cercar d'imbarcarsi prontamente per la Francia. Dupont aveva progettato di accompagnarvi Emilia, se avesse potuto sapere che il suo reggimento vi fosse tornato.

Erano allora sulla strada già percorsa da Emilia con Ugo e Bertrando. Lodovico, il solo di essi che conoscesse i tortuosi sentieri di que' monti, assicurò che a poca distanza ne avrebbero trovato uno pel quale sarebbesi potuto scender facilmente in Toscana, e che alle falde degli Appennini c'era una piccola città, dove avrebbero potuto procacciarsi le cose necessarie pel viaggio.

Emilia pensava a Valancourt ed alla Francia con gioia; ma intanto essa sola era l'oggetto delle riflessioni malinconiche di Dupont. L'affanno però ch'ei provava pel suo equivoco, veniva addolcito dal piacere di vederla, Annetta pensava alla lor fuga sorprendente, e al susurro che avrebber fatto Montoni ed i suoi. Tornata in patria, voleva sposare il suo liberatore per gratitudine e per inclinazione. Lodovico, per parte sua, si compiaceva di avere strappato Annetta ed Emilia al pericolo che le minacciava, lieto di fuggire egli stesso da quella gente che gli faceva orrore. Aveva resa la libertà a Dupont, e sperava di viver felice coll'oggetto del suo amore.

Occupati dai loro pensieri, i viaggiatori restarono in silenzio per più di un'ora, meno qualche domanda che faceva tratto tratto Dupont sulla direzione della strada, o qualche esclamazione di Annetta sugli oggetti che il crepuscolo lasciava vedere imperfettamente. Infine scorsero lumi alle falde di un monte, e Lodovico non dubitò più non fosse la desiata città. Soddisfatti di questa certezza, i suoi compagni si abbandonarono di nuovo ai loro pensieri; Annetta fu quindi la prima a parlare.

« Dio buono, » diss'ella, « dove troveremo noi denaro? So che nè la mia padrona, nè io non abbiamo un soldo. Il signor Montoni ci provvedeva egli! » L'osservazione produsse un esame che terminò in un imbarazzo seriissimo. Dupont era stato spogliato di quasi tutti i suoi denari allorchè cadde prigioniero; il resto l'aveva regalato alla sentinella, che avevagli permesso di uscire dal carcere. Lodovico, che da molto tempo non poteva ottenere il pagamento del suo salario, aveva appena di che supplire al primo rinfresco nella città in cui dovean giungere.

La loro povertà li affliggeva tanto più, perchè poteva trattenerli in cammino, e, sebbene in una città, temevano sempre il potere di Montoni. I viaggiatori adunque non ebbero altro partito che quello di andare avanti a tentar la fortuna. Passarono per luoghi deserti; finalmente udirono da lontano i campanelli di un armento, e poco dopo il belato delle pecore, e riconobbero le tracce di qualche abitazione umana. I lumi veduti da Lodovico erano spariti da molto tempo, nascosti dagli alti monti. Rianimati da questa speranza, accelerarono il passo, e scopersero alfine una delle valli pastorali degli Appennini, fatta per dare l'idea della felice Arcadia. La sua freschezza e bella semplicità contrastavano maestosamente colle nevose montagne circostanti.

L'alba faceva biancheggiare l'orizzonte. A poca distanza, e sul fianco di un colle, i viaggiatori distinsero la città che cercavano, e vi giunsero in breve. Con molta difficoltà poterono trovarvi un asilo momentaneo. Emilia domandò di non fermarsi più del tempo strettamente necessario per rinfrescare i cavalli; la di lei vista eccitava sorpresa, essendo senza cappello, ed avendo appena avuto il tempo di prendere un velo. Le rincresceva perciò la mancanza di denaro, che non permettevale di procacciarsi quest'articolo essenziale.

Lodovico esaminò la sua borsa, e trovò che non bastava neppur a pagare il rinfresco. Dupont si arrischiò di confidarsi all'oste, che gli pareva umano ed onesto; gli narrò la loro posizione, pregandolo d'aiutarli a continuare il viaggio. Colui promise di far tutto il possibile, tanto più essendo essi prigionieri fuggiti dalle mani di Montoni, cui egli aveva ragioni personali per odiare: acconsentì a somministrar loro i cavalli freschi per partire immediatamente, ma non era ricco abbastanza per fornirli anche di denaro. Stavano lamentandosi, lorchè Lodovico, dopo aver condotto i cavalli in istalla, ritornò tutto allegro, e le mise tosto a parte della sua gioia: nel levare la sella ad un cavallo, vi avea trovata una borsa piena di monete d'oro, porzione senza dubbio del bottino fatto dai condottieri. Tornavano essi dal saccheggio allorchè Lodovico era fuggito, ed il cavallo essendo uscito dal secondo cortile, ove stava a bere il suo padrone, aveva portato via il tesoro, sul quale per certo contava quel birbante.

Dupont trovò questa somma sufficientissima per ricondurli tutti in Francia, e risolse allora di accompagnarvi Emilia. Si fidava di Lodovico quanto poteva permetterglielo una conoscenza sì breve, eppure non reggeva all'idea di confidargli Emilia per un sì lungo viaggio. D'altronde, non aveva forse il coraggio di privarsi del pericoloso piacere di vederla.

Tennero consiglio sulla direzione da prendere. Lodovico avendo assicurato che Livorno era il porto più vicino ed accreditato, decisero d'incamminarvisi.

Emilia comprò un cappello e qualche altro piccolo oggetto indispensabile. I viaggiatori cambiarono i cavalli stanchi con altri migliori, e si rimisero lietamente in cammino al sorger del sole. Dopo qualche ora di viaggio attraverso un paese pittoresco, cominciarono a scendere nella valle dell'Arno. Emilia contemplò tutte le bellezze di quei luoghi pastorali e montuosi, unite al lusso delle ville dei nobili fiorentini, e alle ricchezze di una svariata coltura. Verso mezzogiorno scoprirono Firenze, le cui torri s'innalzavano superbe sullo splendido orizzonte.

Il caldo era eccessivo, e la comitiva cercò riposo all'ombra. Fermatisi sotto alcuni alberi, i cui folti rami li difendevano dai raggi del sole, fecero una refezione frugale, contemplando il magnifico paese con entusiasmo.

Emilia e Dupont ridiventarono a poco a poco taciturni e pensierosi, Annetta era giuliva, e non si stancava mai di ciarlare, Lodovico era molto allegro, senza obliare però i riguardi dovuti ai suoi compagni di viaggio. Finito il pasto, Dupont persuase Emilia a procurare di gustar un'ora di sonno, mentre Lodovico avrebbe vegliato. Le due fanciulle, stanche dal viaggio, si addormentarono.

Quando Emilia svegliossi, trovò la sentinella addormentata al suo posto, e Dupont desto, ma immerso ne' suoi tristi pensieri. Il sole era ancora troppo alto per continuare il viaggio, e giustizia volea che Lodovico, stanco dalle tante fatiche, potesse finire in pace il suo sonno. Emilia profittò di questo momento onde sapere per qual caso Dupont fosse caduto prigioniero di Montoni. Lusingato dall'interesse che dimostravagli questa domanda, e dell'occasione che gli somministrava di parlare di sè medesimo, Dupont la soddisfece immediatamente.

« Io venni in Italia, signora, al servizio del mio paese. Una mischia ne' monti colle bande di Montoni mise in rotta il mio distaccamento, e fui preso con alcuni altri. Quando seppi d'essere prigioniero di Montoni, questo nome mi colpì. Mi rammentai che vostra zia aveva sposato un Italiano di tal nome, e che voi li avevate seguiti in Italia. Non potei però sapere con certezza, se non molto dopo, che costui era quello stesso, e che voi abitavate sotto il medesimo tetto con me. Non vi stancherò dipingendovi la mia emozione allorchè seppi questa nuova, la quale mi fu data da una sentinella che potei sedurre fino al punto di accordarmi qualche ricreazione, una delle quali m'interessava assai, ed era pericolosissima per lui. Ma non fu possibile indurlo ad incaricarsi d'una lettera, e di farmi conoscere a voi. Temeva di essere scoperto, e provare tutta la vendetta di Montoni. Mi somministrò però l'occasione di vedervi parecchie volte. Ciò vi sorprende, ma vi spiegherò meglio. La mia salute soffriva molto per mancanza d'aria e d'esercizio, e potei finalmente ottenere, dalla pietà o dall'avarizia sua, di passeggiare la notte sul bastione.» Emilia divenne attenta, e Dupont continuò:

« Accordandomi questo permesso, la mia guardia sapeva bene ch'io non poteva fuggire. Il castello era custodito con vigilanza, ed il bastione sorgea sopra una rupe perpendicolare. M'insegnò egualmente una porta nascosta nella parete della stanza, ov'io era detenuto, ed imparai ad aprirla. Questa porta metteva in un andito stretto praticato nella grossezza del muro, che girava per tutto il castello, e veniva a riuscire all'angolo del bastione orientale. Ho saputo in seguito che ve ne sono altri consimili nelle muraglie enormi di quel prodigioso edifizio, destinati senza dubbio a facilitare la fuga in tempo di guerra. Per tal mezzo adunque io andava la notte sul bastione, e vi passeggiava con cautela onde non essere scoperto. Le sentinelle erano molto lontane, perchè le alte mura da quella parte supplivano ai soldati. In una di queste passeggiate notturne, osservai un lume alla finestra d'una stanza superiore alla mia prigione: mi venne in idea che quella fosse la vostra camera, e, sperando di vedervi, mi fermai in faccia alla finestra.»

Emilia, rammentandosi allora la figura veduta sul bastione, che l'aveva tenuta in tanta perplessità, esclamò: « Eravate dunque voi, signor Dupont, che mi cagionaste un terrore così ridicolo? La mia fantasia era tanto indebolita dai lunghi patimenti, che il più lieve incidente bastava a farmi tremare.»

Dupont le manifestò il suo rammarico d'averla spaventata, poi soggiunse: « Appoggiato al parapetto in faccia alla vostra finestra, il pensiero della vostra situazione malinconica e della mia mi strappò alcuni gemiti involontari che vi attrassero alla finestra, almeno così supposi. Vidi una persona, e credetti foste voi. Non vi dirò nulla della mia emozione in quel momento. Voleva parlare ma la prudenza mi trattenne, e l'avanzarsi della sentinella mi obbligò a fuggire.

« Passarono alcuni giorni prima ch'io potessi tentare una seconda passeggiata, poichè non poteva uscire se non quando era di guardia il milite da me guadagnato coi doni. Intanto mi persuasi della realtà delle mie congetture sulla situazione della vostra camera. Appena potei uscire, tornai sotto la vostra finestra, e vi vidi senza ardir di parlarvi. Vi salutai colla mano, e voi spariste. Obliando la mia prudenza, esalai un lungo sospiro. Voi tornaste e diceste qualcosa. Intesi la vostra voce, e stava per abbandonare ogni riguardo, quando udii venire una sentinella, e mi ritirai prontamente; ma quel soldato mi aveva veduto. Egli mi seguì, e mi avrebbe raggiunto, senza un ridicolo stratagemma che formò in quel momento la mia salvezza. Conoscendo la superstizione di quella gente, gettai un grido lugubre, sperando che avrebbe cessato d'inseguirmi, e fortunatamente riuscii. Quell'uomo pativa di mal caduco: il timore ch'io gl'incussi lo fece cadere a terra tramortito, ed io m'involai prontamente. Il sentimento del pericolo incorso, e che il raddoppiamento delle guardie, per questo motivo, rendeva maggiore, mi dissuase dal tornar a passeggiare sul bastione. Nel silenzio delle notti però mi divertiva con un vecchio liuto procuratomi dal mio custode, e talvolta cantava, ve lo confesso, sperando d'essere inteso da voi. Infatti poche sere fa, parvemi udire una voce che mi chiamasse, ma non volli rispondere per timore della sentinella. Ditemi, in grazia, signora, eravate voi?

— Sì, » rispose Emilia, con un sospiro involontario, « avevate ragione. »

Dupont, osservando la penosa sensazione che tal soggetto le cagionava, cambiò discorso.

"On one of my trips to the passage I told you about, I heard," he said, "a singular conversation that came from a room adjoining the same. The wall was so thin in that place, that I could distinctly hear all the talks that were being made. Montoni was there with his companions. He began the story of the extraordinary story of the former mistress of the castle. He described strange circumstances; but her conscience must know to what extent they were credible. But you must know, young lady, the vague news that is being circulated about the mysterious fate of that lady.

"I know them, sir," said Emilia, "and I see that you don't believe them."

"I doubted it," replied Dupont, "before the time of which I speak to you; but Montoni's story aggravated my suspicions, and I remained almost convinced that he was a murderer. I trembled for you. He had heard your name pronounced by the guests in a disturbing way, and knowing that the most impious men tend to be the most superstitious, I decided to frighten them, to divert them from the new crime I feared. I listened carefully to Montoni, and in the most interesting place in the story, I repeated his last words several times.

Weren't you afraid of being discovered? Emilia asked.

"No," replied Dupont, "knowing that if Montoni had he known the secret of the corridor, he would not have locked me up in that room. The company, for a few moments, paid no attention to my voice, but finally the alarm was so great that they all fled. Montoni ordered the servants to make an active search, and I returned to my prison. »

Dupont and Emilia went on talking about Montoni, France, and the plan of their journey. She told him that she intended to retire to a convent in the Languedoc; she thought of writing to Quesnel, to inform him of her conduct, and wait for the lease of her chateau in the valley to expire before going and settling there. Dupont persuaded her that her possessions, of which Montoni had wished to strip her, were not lost forever, and she rejoiced that she had escaped from the hands of that barbarian, who would doubtless keep her a prisoner for life. The probability of claiming her aunt's possessions, not so much for herself as for Valancourt, made her feel a sense of joy in her with which she had been deprived for a long time.

Toward sunset, Dupont woke Lodovico to continue their journey. They arrived in Florence late in the night, and would have liked to stay there for a few days to admire the beauties of that famous metropolis, but impatience to return to their homeland made them give up this idea; and the following day, very early in the day, they set out for Pisa, which they crossed, stopping just long enough to refresh the horses, and reached Livorno towards the evening of the following day.

The sight of that flourishing city filled with people of many different nations, and their varied attire, reminded Emilia of the masquerades of Venice at carnival time; but the liveliness and cheerfulness of the Venetians did not reign there, being all people engaged in commerce.

Dupont ran to the port, and learned that a vessel he was to set sail shortly for Marseilles, where they could easily find embarkation to cross the Gulf of Lyons and reach Narbonne. The convent, to which Emilia wanted to retire, was located a short distance from this city. The girl was therefore delighted to hear that her journey to France would not suffer any obstacle. No longer fearing being pursued, and hoping to soon see her dear homeland and the country inhabited by Valancourt, she found herself so relieved that, after her father's death, she had never spent such tranquil moments. Dupont was informed at Livorno that his regiment had returned to France: this news filled him with joy, since otherwise he would not have been able to accompany Emilia there without exposing himself to the reproaches and perhaps even to the punishment of his colonel.

CHAPTER XXXV

Now let's go back to Languedoc, and let's take care of the Count of Villefort, the same one who had inherited the properties of the Marquis of Villeroy, near the monastery of Santa Chiara. Let us remember that that castle was uninhabited when Emilia was in that vicinity with her father, and that Saint Aubert seemed very moved when she learned that she was so close to the castle of Blangy. The good Voisin had made very alarming speeches because of Emilia's curiosity about that place.

In 1584, the year in which Saint Aubert died, Francis of Beauveau, count of Villefort, took possession of the immense estate called Blangy, located in Languedoc, on the shores of the sea. These lands had belonged to his for several centuries family, and they returned to him on the death of the Marquis de Villeroy, his relative, a man of austere character and very reserved manners. This circumstance, combined with the duties of his profession, which often called him to war, had prevented any sort of intrinsicities between him and the Count of Villefort. They knew each other little, and the count did not learn of his death until he received the will making him master of Blangy. He did not visit his new possessions until a year later, and spent the whole autumn there. Blangy was often remembered with the vivid colors which the imagination lends to the remembrance of youthful delights. In his early years, he had known the marquise, and visited that stay in the age in which pleasures remain sensitively impressed. The interval hereafter between the tumult of business,

The late Marquis had abandoned the castle many years ago, and his old agent had let it fall into disrepair. The count therefore took the decision to spend the autumn there to have it restored. Even the prayers and tears of the countess, who knew how to weep when necessary, had no power to make him change his mind. She therefore had to reconcile herself to allowing what she could not prevent, and to leave Paris. Her beauty caused her to be admired, but her wit was little fit to inspire esteem. The mysterious shadow of the woods, the wild grandeur of the mountains, and the imposing solitude of the Gothic halls, of the long galleries, offered her only a sad perspective. She tried to take courage thinking about the stories told about the beautiful vintage of Languedoc, to flatter a heart from which luxury and vanity had long banished the taste for simplicity and good inclinations.

The count had two sons from his first bed, and he wanted them to come with him. Enrico, at the age of twenty, was already in military service; Bianca, who was not yet eighteen, was still in her convent, where she had been placed at the time of her father's second wedding. The countess did not have enough talent to give her stepdaughter a good education, nor her courage to undertake it, and therefore she had advised her husband to remove her from her; fearing therefore that a nascent beauty would come to eclipse hers, she had subsequently employed all the art to prolong the imprisonment of the girl. The news that she was leaving the monastery was a great mortification for her, but she mitigated herself by considering that, if Bianca left the cloister, the darkness of the province would have buried her graces for some time.

On the day of departure, the count's carriage stopped at the convent. The girl's heart beat with pleasure at the ideas of novelty and freedom that were offered to her. As the time of the journey approached, her impatience with her grew to the point of even counting the minutes that remained to finish that night. As soon as dawn broke, Bianca had leapt out of bed to greet that beautiful day, in which she would be freed from the bonds of the cloister, to go and enjoy freedom in a world where pleasure always smiles, goodness never alters, and reigns with pleasure without any obstacle. When she heard the bell ring, she ran to the visiting room, heard the noise of the wheels and saw her father's carriage stop in the courtyard: drunk with joy, she ran along the corridors announcing her imminent departure to her friends. to lead her to the temple of happiness. The countess, however, on seeing her, was not animated by the same sentiments. Bianca had never seemed so amiable, and her cheerful smile gave her whole physiognomy the beauty of her happy innocence. After a brief conversation, the countess took her leave: it was the moment that Bianca was waiting for impatiently, like the moment in which she was about to begin her happiness with her; but she could not refrain from shedding tears, embracing her companions who also wept as they bid her farewell. The abbess, so serious, so imposing, saw her leave with a displeasure of which she would not have thought herself capable an hour before her. Bianca then came out crying from that living room, which she had imagined leaving her laughing.

The presence of his father, the distractions of the journey soon absorbed his ideas, and dispersed that shadow of sensitivity. She paid little attention to the countess and Mademoiselle Bearn's conversations about her friend who accompanied her; she lost herself in sweet meditations; she saw the silent clouds furrow the blue firmament veiling the sun, and thus obscuring sections of the country with a beautiful alternation of shadows and light. That trip was a continuation of pleasures for Bianca; her nature, in her eyes, varied every moment, showing her the most beautiful and enchanting views of herself.

Toward the evening of the seventh day, the travelers saw Blangy Castle in the distance. Its picturesque situation greatly impressed the maiden. As they approached, she admired the Gothic structure, the superb towers, the immense gate of the ancient building; she almost believed she was approaching one of those castles celebrated in ancient history, where the knights saw from the battlements a champion with his retinue, clad in black armour, come to snatch the lady of her thoughts from the oppression of a proud rival. She had read this novella in the monastery library, filled with ancient chronicles.

The carriages stopped at a door which led into the enclosure of the castle, and which was then closed. The large bell which served to announce foreigners had long since fallen off; a servant climbed a ruined wall to warn the agent of the master's arrival. Bianca, leaning against the door, considered the surrounding places with emotion. The sun had set, twilight enveloped the mountains; the distant sea still reflects a strip of light on the horizon. The monotonous roar of the waves that came to break on the shore was heard. Each of the company thought about the different objects that most interested him. The countess longed for the pleasures of Paris, seeing with pain what she called horrid woods and savage solitude; she penetrated by the only idea of having to be sequestered in that ancient castle, he regretted everything. Enrico's feelings were the same; sighing he thought of the delights of the capital and of a very lovely lady whom he loved; but the country, and a different kind of life, held for him the spell of novelty, and his regret was tempered by the cheerful illusions of youth.

The doors opened at last; the carriage slowly entered the thick chestnut trees which blocked the view. It was the avenue in which Saint Aubert and Emilia had already interned in the hope of finding an asylum nearby.

« What bad places! cried the countess; 'certainly, sir, you don't count on staying all autumn in this barbarous solitude. It would be necessary to have brought a bottle of Lethe's water, lest at least the remembrance of a less disagreeable country should not increase the sadness of this one.

"I will act according to the circumstances," replied the count; « This barbarous solitude was the home of my ancestors. »

The keeper of the castle together with the servants were sent from Paris in advance, they received the master at the entrance to the portico. Bianca recognized that the building was not entirely Gothic in style. The immense room they entered was not, however, of modern taste. A large window let us see an inclined plane of greenery, formed by the tops of the trees on the slope of the hill, where the castle stood. Beyond, the waves of the Mediterranean could be seen disappearing, to the south or to the east, in the horizon.

Bianca, as she crossed the room, stopped to observe such a beautiful glance, but was soon roused by the countess who, dissatisfied with everything, impatient to refresh herself and rest, hurried to reach a sitting room, adorned with very ancient furniture, but richly trimmed with velvet and gold fringes.

While the countess was waiting for some refreshments, the count, in the company of Enrico, toured the interior of the castle. Bianca witnessed her, in spite of her, the bad mood and discontent of her stepmother.

"How much time did you spend in this sad living room?" »Asked the countess of the keeper's wife when she came to offer her her homage.

"It must be thirty years, madame, on the day of San Lorenzo."

- How did you manage to stay there so long and almost alone? However, I was told that the castle has been closed for some time.

"Yes, madame, a few months after my late Marquis left for the war; my husband and I have been in his service for more than twenty years. This house is so large and deserted that at the end of some time we went to live near the village, and only came from time to time to visit the castle. When my master ended his campaigns, having taken a dislike to this stay, he never returned, and did not want us to leave our home. But alas! How much the castle has changed since that time! My poor mistress lived there with the greatest pleasure, and I will always remember that day when she arrived here after being married! How beautiful she was! Since then the castle has always been neglected, and I will never spend such happy days again. »

The countess seemed almost offended by that good woman's naive talk about past times, and Dorotea added: 'However, the castle will be inhabited again; but I wouldn't be there alone for all the money in the world. »

The count's arrival put an end to the old woman's chatter. He told her that he had visited a large part of the castle, which needed a lot of repairs before it was habitable.

"I'm sorry," said the countess.

"And why, ma'am?"

- Because this place will correspond badly to so many attentions. »

The count did not reply, and turned abruptly towards a window.

The countess's maid entered; she asked to be taken to her flat, and she withdrew with Mrs Bearn.

Bianca, taking advantage of the little daylight that still remained, went to make new discoveries. After going through various apartments, she found herself in a vast gallery adorned with very ancient paintings and statues representing, as it seemed to her, her ancestors. She was beginning to get dark, and she looked out of a window, where she contemplated with interest the imposing view of those marvelous places, hearing the dull and distant murmur of the sea, and thus abandoning herself to the enthusiasm of that completely new scene for her.

- So I have lived a long time in this world, she said to herself, without having seen this stupendous spectacle, without having tasted these delights! The humblest villain of my father's possessions, she must have seen nature's beautiful sight since her childhood, and traveled freely through these picturesque locations, and I, at the back of a cloister, was left without these marvels, which must enchant the eye and enrapture all hearts! How is it possible that those poor nuns, those poor friars can feel a violent fervour, if they do not see the sun rise or set? I have never known what devotion really is until tonight. Until this evening I had never seen the sun leave our hemisphere. Tomorrow I will see it arise for the first time. How is it possible to live in Paris, seeing only dark houses and muddy streets, when in the countryside one can see the blue vault of the sky and the enamel green of the earth? —

This soliloquy was interrupted by the slight sound of footsteps, and Bianca having asked who it was, she heard the answer: "It's me, Dorotea, who's coming to close the windows. »However, the thunder of voice with which she pronounced these words surprised Bianca somewhat. 'You seem frightened to me; »She told her; "Who scared you?

"No, no, I'm not frightened, miss," answered Dorotea hesitantly. « I am old and it doesn't take much to upset me. However, I am glad that the Count has come to live in this castle, which has been deserted for so many years; now he'll look a little like the time my poor mistress lived. Bianca asked her how long the marquise had been dead. 'So much has already passed that I'm tired of counting the years. Since that time the castle has always seemed to me in mourning, and I am sure that the vassals always have it in their hearts. But you are lost, miss. Do you want to go back to the other part of the house? »

The girl asked how long ago the neighborhood where they were meeting had been built. « Little after my master's wedding,' replied Dorotea. 'The castle was large enough without this addition. There are many apartments in the old building which have never been used. It is a princely residence; but my master thought it sad, as indeed it is. Bianca told her to take her to the inhabited area; Dorotea made her pass through a courtyard, opened the great hall, and found Mrs. Bearn there. "Where have you been up to now?" this one told her. "She was beginning to believe that some surprising adventure had happened to you, and that the giant of this enchanted castle, or the spirit that appears there, had thrown you through a trapdoor into some dungeon, never to let you out again.

"No," answered Bianca, laughing; "You seem so fond of adventures that I give them all to you."

- Well! I agree, provided that one day she can tell them.

'My dear Mrs. Bearn,' said Enrico, entering the room, 'the spirits of today would not be so rude to try to silence you. Our ghosts are too civilized to condemn a lady to a crueler purgatory than theirs, whatever it may be. »

Bearn laughed; she entered Villefort, and supper was served. The count spoke very little, seemed abstracted, and often made the observation that since he hadn't seen it, the castle had changed a great deal. "It's been many years," he said, "the sites are the same, but they make a very different impression on me from the one I felt at other times.

"Did this place seem more pleasant to you in the past than now?" Bianca said; "It seems impossible to me. »

The count looked at her with a melancholy smile. "It was formerly so delightful in my eyes, as it is now to yours. The country hasn't changed, but I've changed over time. The illusion of my spirit reveled in the sight of nature; now it is lost! If in the course of your life, dear Bianca, you return to these places after having been absent for many years, you will perhaps remember your father's feelings, and then you will understand them. »

Bianca was silent, afflicted by these words, and turned her ideas to the time of which the count was speaking. Considering that whoever spoke to her then she would probably no longer exist than her, she lowered her eyes, and hearing them filled with tears, she took her father's hand, smiled at him tenderly, and went to the window to hide her emotion her.

The weariness of the journey forced the company to part early. Bianca, crossing a long gallery, withdrew to her own apartment, a spacious place, with high windows, whose lugubrious appearance was not capable of compensating for the almost isolated position in which she found herself. The furniture was antique, the bed of blue damask trimmed with silver fringes. For young Bianca everything was an object of curiosity. She took the light of the woman who accompanied her to examine the paintings on the ceiling, and she recognized a fact of the siege of Troy. She amused herself a little by pointing out the absurdities of the composition, but when she reflected that the artist who had executed it, and the poet from whom he had drawn the subject were nothing more than cold ashes, she was seized with melancholy.

She gave orders to be awakened before sunrise, sent off the maid, and desiring to dispel that shadow of sadness, opened a window, and revived at the sight of nature. The earth, the air and the sea, all were still. The sky was clear: some light vapor slowly wavered in the highest regions, increasing the splendor of the stars, which glittered like so many suns. Bianca's thoughts involuntarily rose to the great Author of those sublime objects. She made a more fervent prayer than she had ever done under the sad vaults of the cloister; then at midnight she lay down, and she had but happy dreams. Sweet sleep, known only to health, contentedness, and innocence!

CHAPTER XXXVI

Bianca slept much more than the hour indicated so impatiently: her maid, tired from the journey, woke her only for breakfast time. This displeasure was quickly forgotten when, opening the window, she saw on one side the wide sea colored by the morning rays, the white sails of the boats and the oars cleaving the waves; on the other, the woods, their freshness, the vast plains, and the blue mountains that were tinged with the splendor of the day.

Breathing that pure air, her cheeks turned purple, and making her prayer: "Who could ever invent convents?" she said; "Who was the first to persuade mortals to go there, and under the pretext of religion, distance them from all the objects that inspire them?" The homage of a grateful heart is what God asks of us; and when you see her works, aren't you grateful? I have never felt such devotion, in all the boring hours spent in the convent, as in the few minutes I spent here. I look around and adore God from the bottom of my heart. »

Saying this, he withdrew from the window, and crossing the gallery, entered the dining room, where he found his father. The bright sun had dispelled his sadness; her laughter touched his lips: he spoke to her daughter with serenity, and her heart corresponded to hers sweet disposition. Henry, the Countess, and Mademoiselle Bearn appeared shortly afterwards, and the whole party seemed to be influenced by time and place.

They parted after breakfast. The count retired to his office with the intendant. Enrico ran to the shore to examine a boat, which they were to use that same evening, and had a small tent fitted in it. The Countess and Mademoiselle Bearn went to see an elegantly built modern flat. The windows looked onto a terrace facing the sea, thus avoiding the view of the wild Pyrenees.

Meanwhile, Bianca enjoyed seeing the parts of the building she didn't yet know. The oldest of hers quickly attracted her curiosity. She mounted the grand staircase, and traversing an immense gallery, she entered a row of rooms, the walls decorated with tapestries, or covered with colored inlaid cedar; the furniture seemed to date from the same date as the castle; the large fireplaces offered the cold image of abandonment: all those rooms bore the imprint of solitude and desolation so well that those whose portraits hung there seemed to have been the last inhabitants.

On leaving thence, he found himself in another gallery, one end of which led to a stairway, and the other to a closed door. Going down the stairs, she found herself in a small room in the west tower. Three windows presented three different and sublime points of view: to the north the Languedoc; to the west the Pyrenees, whose peaks crowned the country; at midday, the Mediterranean and part of the Roussillon coast. He left the tower, and going down a very narrow staircase, he found himself in a dark passage, where he got lost. Unable to find his way, and impatience giving way to fear, he cried out for help. He heard walking at the end of the corridor and saw a light shine held by a person who opened a small door with caution. Not daring to go forward, Bianca watched him in silence, but when she saw the door close, she called again, she ran to that vault, and recognized old Dorotea.

« Ah! is it you, dear mistress? » she said, « how come you could come to this place? »If Bianca had been less occupied with fear than her, she would probably have observed the strong expression of terror and surprise that altered Dorotea's physiognomy, which made her pass through an infinite number of rooms, which seemed uninhabited for a century. Finally arriving at the caretaker's residence, Dorotea asked her to sit down and freshen up. Bianca, accepting her invitation, spoke of the beautiful uncovered tower, and showed a desire to appropriate it. Whether Dorotea was less sensitive to the great beauties of nature, or whether her habit of hers had rendered them less interesting, did not encourage Bianca's enthusiasm, who, asked where she led the closed door at the end of the gallery . L'

'Our late mistress died there, and I never had the courage to enter again. »

Bianca, curious to see that place, refrained from asking Dorotea about it, seeing her eyes watering with tears: a little later she went to get dressed for dinner. All society assembled in good spirits, except the countess, whose spirit, absolutely empty, oppressed by idleness, could neither make her happy nor contribute to the happiness of others.

The joy Bianca felt in reuniting with her family was moderated when she was on the seashore, and looked fearfully at that great expanse of water. From a distance she had watched with enthusiasm; but she struggled to overcome her fear and follow her father by boat.

He silently contemplated the vast horizon, which he circumscribed only the sight of the sea, a sublime emotion fought in her against the feeling of danger. A light zephyr rippled the surface of the water, brushing the sails and shaking the fronds of the forests that crowned the coast for many miles.

At some distance in those woods there was a casino which was in other times the asylum of pleasures, and because of its position it was always interesting and picturesque. The count had had coffee and refreshments brought to you. The oarsmen made their way that way, skirting the winding shore, past the vast wooded promontory and the circumference of a bay, while in a second boat some players made the surrounding cliffs echo with beautiful melodies. Bianca was no longer afraid; a delicious tranquility had taken possession of her, and silenced her. She was too happy to remember the monastery, and the boredom she had felt there for so long.

After an hour's sailing, they landed and climbed a narrow path strewn with flowering turf. At a short distance, and at the tip of an eminence, the casino shaded by trees can be seen. Although hastily prepared, it was decent enough. While the company took their refreshments and ate their fruit, the musicians interrupted the delightful stillness of that isolated place. The casino even came to interest the countess, who, perhaps for the pleasure of talking about things belonging to luxury, spread at length about the need to embellish it.

After a very long walk, the family embarked again. The beauty of the evening induced him to prolong the trip and advance into the bay. A perfect calm had succeeded the wind, which until then had driven the boat, and the sailors took to the oars. Bianca was pleased to see rowing; she observed the concentric circles formed in the water by the blows, and the trembling they impressed on the picture of the town without disfiguring its harmony. Above the darkness from the wood he made out a group of turrets still illuminated by the rays of the sun, and in an interval of silence from the music he heard a chorus of voices.

"What voices are these?" said the count, listening attentively; but the singing stopped. "It's the hymn for vespers," said Bianca, "I heard it in the convent." "So we are close to a monastery?" said the count; and the boat having rounded a very high point, they saw the convent of Santa Chiara at the bottom of a small bay: the wood that surrounded it, let us see part of the building, the main door, the Gothic window of the atrium, the cloister and one side of the chapel; a majestic arch which formerly united the house to another portion of the buildings, then demolished, remained as a venerable ruin detached from the whole building.

All was in profound silence, and Bianca observed with admiration that majestic arch, the effect of which grew with the masses of light and shadow, which spread the sunset covered with clouds. In that the imposing hymn of vespers began again, accompanied by the grave sound of the organ; then the chorus gradually faded away, and then died out altogether. While they were all intent on listening with religious recollection, they saw a procession of nuns dressed in black with a white veil on their heads coming out of the cloister, passing through the woods, and going around the monastery. The countess was the first to break the silence. "This hymn and these nuns have a sadness that oppresses me," she said; 'it's starting to get late; we return to the castle, and it will already be night before we get there. The count raised his eyes, and he perceived that a menacing storm was anticipating darkness. The seabirds circled the waves, wet their feathers, and fled to some distant haven; the sailors worked their oars, but the roaring thunder from afar, and the rain, which was already beginning to fall, determined the count to seek refuge in the monastery. The boat changed direction, and as the storm approached to the west, the air grew darker, and frequent lightning set the tops of the trees and the chimneys of the convent aflame. The appearance of the skies alarmed the countess and Bearn, whose screams and cries disturbed the count and the rowers. Bianca kept silent, now agitated by her fear, now by her admiration: she observed the size of the clouds, their effect on the scene, and listened to the peals of lightning which shook the air.

The boat stopped in front of the monastery. The count sent a servant to announce her arrival to the superior and ask her for asylum. Although the order of Santa Chiara had not been austere since that time, single women could be received in the holy enclosure. The servant brought back an answer which was both hospitality and pride, but a pride hidden under the veil of submission. They disembarked, and having quickly crossed the meadow due to the pouring rain, they were received by the superior who extended her hand before her and imparted her blessing. They passed into a room where some nuns were all dressed in black and veiled in white. However, the abbess' veil was half-lifted, revealing a sweet dignity tempered by a courteous smile. She led the Countess, Bearn and Bianca into a sitting room,

The abbess asked for refreshments, and meanwhile spoke with the countess. Bianca, approaching a window, was able to consider the progress of the storm; the waves of the sea, which a few moments before seemed still asleep, swelled enormously, crashing without interruption against the coast. A sulphurous color surrounded the clouds, which were gathering in the west, while lightning illuminated the shores of the Languedoc from afar: everything the rest was shrouded in darkness. In some intervals, a lightning gilded the wings of a seabird flying in the highest regions, or alighting on the sails of a ship at the mercy of the billows. Bianca observed for some time the danger of that vessel, sighing over the fate of the crew and the passengers.

Finally, the darkness became complete. The vessel was scarcely distinguishable, and Bianca was forced to close the window by the force of the wind. The abbess, having exhausted all the civilized compliments with the countess, was able to turn to Bianca. Their conversation was soon interrupted by the sound of the bell inviting the nuns to prayer, as the storm was always growing. The count's servants had gone to the castle to bring the carriages, which arrived at the end of the prayer. The storm being less violent, the count returned to the castle with his family. Bianca was surprised to see how much she was mistaken about the distance from the monastery to the sinuosities of the beach.

As soon as she arrived, the countess retired to her apartment. The count, Enrico and Bianca went into the living room, but as soon as they got there, they heard a cannon shot. The count recognized the signal of a ship in distress asking for help; he opened a window, but the sea enveloped in darkness and the noise of the storm did not let us distinguish anything. Bianca remembered the ship she had already seen, and tremblingly warned her father. A little later they heard another cannon shot, and were able to see in the light of a flash a boat tossed about by the foamy waves, with only one sail, and which, now disappearing into the abyss, now rising up to the clouds, was trying to gain the it costs. Bianca clung to her father's neck with a painful look in which fear and compassion were depicted. You weren't needed of this means to soften the count: he looked at the sea with an expression of pity, but seeing that the boats could not withstand the storm, he forbade risking a sure loss, and had many lighted torches carried to the tops of the rocks, as a lighthouse.

Enrico went out to direct the servants, and Bianca remained with her father at the window, from where the wretched vessel could be seen in the light of the lightning. The servants responded to each cannon by raising and waving their torches, and in the faint light of the lightning Bianca once again thought she saw the ship very close to the shore. Then the count's servants were seen running from all sides, advancing on the tip of the rocks, bending down holding out their torches; others, whose direction could not be distinguished except by the movement of the lights, descended by dangerous paths as far as the beach, calling loudly to the sailors, whose whistles and faint voices they heard, which for intervals were confused with the noise of the storm. Those unexpected cries which issued from the rocks increased Bianca's terror to an unbearable degree; but her tender interest was shortly relieved, when Henry came running to give the news that the vessel had dropped anchor in the bottom of the bay, but in such a wretched state that it would perhaps submerge before the crew was landed. The count immediately made all the boats leave, announcing to the foreigners that he would receive them in the castle. Among them were Emilia Sant'Aubert, Dupont, Lodovico and Annetta, who embarked in Livorno, and arrived in Marseilles, were crossing the Gulf of Lyons when they were attacked by the storm. They were all received by the count with great cordiality. Emilia would have liked to go to the convent of Santa Chiara that same evening, but he would not allow it. still at the bottom of the bay, but in such a wretched state that it would perhaps have submerged before the crew had landed. The count immediately made all the boats leave, announcing to the foreigners that he would receive them in the castle. Among them were Emilia Sant'Aubert, Dupont, Lodovico and Annetta, who embarked in Livorno, and arrived in Marseilles, were crossing the Gulf of Lyons when they were attacked by the storm. They were all received by the count with great cordiality. Emilia would have liked to go to the convent of Santa Chiara that same evening, but he would not allow it. still at the bottom of the bay, but in such a wretched state that it would perhaps have submerged before the crew had landed. The count immediately made all the boats leave, announcing to the foreigners that he would receive them in the castle. Among them were Emilia Sant'Aubert, Dupont, Lodovico and Annetta, who embarked in Livorno, and arrived in Marseilles, were crossing the Gulf of Lyons when they were attacked by the storm. They were all received by the count with great cordiality. Emilia would have liked to go to the convent of Santa Chiara that same evening, but he would not allow it. Dupont, Lodovico and Annetta, who embarked in Livorno and arrived in Marseilles, were crossing the Gulf of Lyons when they were attacked by the storm. They were all received by the count with great cordiality. Emilia would have liked to go to the convent of Santa Chiara that same evening, but he would not allow it. Dupont, Lodovico and Annetta, who embarked in Livorno and arrived in Marseilles, were crossing the Gulf of Lyons when they were attacked by the storm. They were all received by the count with great cordiality. Emilia would have liked to go to the convent of Santa Chiara that same evening, but he would not allow it.

The count rediscovered an ancient knowledge in Dupont, and the warmest compliments were made. Emilia was received with the most courteous hospitality, and supper was served.

Bianca's natural affability, and the joy she expressed for the safety of the strangers, whom she had so sincerely mourned, gradually revived Emilia's spirits. Dupont, relieved of the fear he felt for her and for himself, felt the difference in his situation. Emerging from a stormy sea, about to swallow them up, he found himself in a beautiful house, where abundance and taste reigned, and in which he received a most courteous welcome.

Meanwhile Annetta told the servants about the dangers she had suffered, congratulating herself on her own safety and that of Lodovico. In a word, she awakened liveliness and gaiety in all those people. Lodovico was as happy as she was, but he knew how to contain himself, and he tried in vain to keep her silent. Finally, the immoderate laughter was heard even from the countess's apartment, which she sent to hear what that noise was, recommending her silence.

Emilia withdrew early to seek the rest she needed so badly; but she stayed for a while without being able to sleep, because her return to her homeland reawakened interesting memories in her. The cases that occurred to her, the sufferings suffered after her departure, confronted her with force, yielding only to the image of Valancourt. Knowing that she lived in the same land, after such a long separation, was a source of joy for her. She then passed on to her disquiet and anxiety, as she considered the space of time which had elapsed since the last letter received, and all the happenings which, in that interval, might have conspired against her repose and happiness of her; but the idea that Valancourt was no more, or that, if she lived, she had forgotten her, was so terrible to her heart, that she could not bear it. She resolved d' France with a letter. The hope finally of knowing in a short time that he was well, that he was not far from her, and especially that he still loved her, calmed her agitation: her spirit rallied, closed her eyes, and fell asleep.

CHAPTER XXXVII

Bianca had taken such an interest in Emilia that when she learned that she wanted to go and live in the nearby convent, she begged her father to engage her in extending her stay in the castle. "You understand very well," she added, "how happy I would be to have a such companion. Now I have no friend with whom I can read or walk. Mrs Bearn is friends only with her mother. »

The count smiled with that ingenuous simplicity which made his daughter give in to first impressions. He proposed to demonstrate to her the danger of her in her time; but at that point she applauded, with her silence, that cordiality of hers which led her to instantly trust a stranger.

He had observed Emilia attentively, and he had liked her, as much as such a brief acquaintance could entail. The manner in which Dupont had spoken to him of her confirmed his idea of her; but very vigilant about his daughter's relations, and understanding how Emilia was known at the convent of Santa Chiara, he resolved to go and visit the abbess, and if her information corresponded to his wishes, he wanted to invite Emilia to spend a few days at his house . He had in view, in this respect, more the pleasure of her daughter than the desire to please the orphan, but nevertheless he took a sincere interest in her.

The next day, Emilia was too tired, and couldn't go down to breakfast with the others. Dupont was asked by the count, as an old acquaintance, to extend his stay in the castle. He consented willingly, especially as this circumstance kept him with Emilia. In the depths of his heart he could not nurture the hope that she would ever correspond to her passion but he did not have the courage to try to overcome her.

When Emilia was somewhat rested, she went for a walk with the new friend, and was very sensitive to the beauties of those points of view. On seeing the bell tower of the monastery, she announced to Bianca that this was the place where she wanted to go and reside.

"Ouch," replied this surprise; "I've just left the convent, and you want to shut yourself up there!" If you knew how much pleasure I take in walking here with freedom, and in seeing the sky and fields and woods around me, I think you would abandon this idea. Emilia smiled at her eloquence with which she expressed herself, telling her how she had no intention of shutting herself up in a monastery for the rest of her life.

Returning to the house, Bianca led her to her favorite tower, and to the ancient rooms she had already visited. Emilia amused herself by examining the distribution, by considering the type and magnificence of the furniture and by comparing it with those of Udolfo's castle, which however were older and more extraordinary. She also considered Dorotea who accompanied them, and she seemed almost as ancient as the objects that surrounded her. It seemed that her old woman was looking at Emilia with interest, and indeed she was observing him with such attention, that she hardly understood what they were saying to her.

Emilia, looking out a window, turned her gaze to the countryside, and saw with surprise many objects, of which she still retained the memory: the fields, the woods and the stream that she had crossed with Voisin one evening, after the death of Saint Aubert, returning from the convent to that good old man's house. She recognized Blangy to be the castle which he had then avoided, and about which Voisin had made such strange speeches.

Surprised by this discovery, and intimidated without knowing why, she remained silent for some time, and remembered her father's emotion at being near that house. Even the music she had heard, and about which Voisin had told her such a ridiculous story, came back to her then. Curious to find out more, she asked Dorotea if she still heard music at midnight, and if she knew the author.

'Yes, madam,' replied the old woman, 'one still hears that music, but the composer is not known, and I believe it will never be known. Start someone guessing what it is.

- Really! cried Emilia; "And why don't they keep doing research?"

— Ah! miss, we have searched too much; but who can follow a spirit? »

Emilia smiled, and remembering how much she had recently suffered from superstition, she resolved to resist it, although in spite of herself she felt a certain fear mingling with her curiosity. Bianca, who until then she had listened to in silence, asked what this music was, and how long she had been hearing it.

"Always, after our mistress's death," answered Dorotea. «But that has nothing to do with what she wanted to tell you.

"Tell us, please, tell us everything," replied Bianca. « I took great interest in what Sister Concetta and Sister Teresa told me in the convent about the apparitions.

"Have you never known, Signorina, why we were forced to leave the castle to go and live in that cottage?" » continued Dorotea.

"Certainly not," answered Bianca impatiently.

"Nor the reason why the marquis ..." Here he hesitated, and changed the subject; but Bianca's curiosity was aroused; she urged the old woman to continue her story, but she could not persuade her. It was therefore evident that she was alarmed by her imprudence.

"I know very well," Emilia said, smiling, "that all old houses are haunted by spirits. I come from a theater of prodigies, but unfortunately, after I left it, I had an explanation. »

Bianca was silent, and Dorotea was serious and sighed. Emilia, remembering the spectacle seen in a room of Udolfo, and, for a bizarre report, the alarming words read accidentally in one of the papers burned in blind obedience to her father's orders, she trembled at the meaning they seemed to have, almost as much as at the horrible object she had discovered under the baleful veil.

Meanwhile Bianca, unable to induce Dorotea to explain herself further, asked her, passing by the closed door, to show her all the apartments.

'Dear young lady,' replied the caretaker, 'I have already given you my reasons for not opening that room. I have not entered it since the death of my dear mistress: that room would afflict me too much: for heaven's sake, excuse me.

"Yes, of course," replied Bianca, "if that is your real reason."

"Unfortunately he's the only one," said the old woman. « We loved her so much, and I will always mourn her. Time flies so fast! She has been dead for many years, yet I remember, as if she were today, all that happened then. Many new things escaped me from her memory; but the ancient ones I see as in a mirror. Then, advancing in the gallery, and looking at Emilia, she added: "This young lady reminds me of the Marchioness: I remember that she was fresh like her and had the same smile. Poor woman! She how merry she was when she brought her in here!

- That! maybe it wasn't even later? Bianca said.

Dorothea shook her head. Emilia watched her, and felt herself penetrated by lively interest. "If that doesn't afflict you," Bianca said, "do us the favor of telling something about the Marchesa."

"Madam," replied Dorotea, "if you knew as much as I do, you would find them too painful, and you would regret it. I would like to erase the idea from my memory, but it is impossible ... I always see my dear mistress of her at her deathbed, I see her looks and I remember her speeches. God! what a terrible scene!

"So what's so terrible about it?"

— Ah! Isn't death terrible enough? »

The old woman did not answer any of Bianca's questions. Emilia, observing that her tears were welling up, ceased to importune her, and endeavored to draw the attention of her young friend to some spot in her garden. The count, the countess and Dupont were strolling there, and they joined them.

When the count saw Emilia, he went to meet her, and introduced her to the countess in such a kind manner, which reminded her of her own parent's affability.

Before having finished her thanks for the hospitality received, and expressed the desire to go immediately to the convent, she was interrupted by a pressing invitation to extend her stay in the castle. The count and countess begged her so sincerely, that in spite of her longing to see her friends at the monastery again, and to sigh again at the grave of her beloved father, she agreed to stay for a few days. In the meantime, he wrote to her abbess to inform her of her arrival, and to ask her to receive her in the convent as a boarder. She wrote equally to Quesnel and to Valancourt, and as she did not knew exactly where to address this last letter, he sent it in Gascony to the knight's brother.

Towards evening, Bianca and Dupont accompanied Emilia to Voisin's house; as she approached it, she felt a kind of pleasure mingled with bitterness. Time had soothed her pain, but her loss to her could not cease to feel; she abandoned herself with sweet sadness to the memories of her reminding her of that place. Voisin still lived, and seemed to enjoy, as in the past, the placid evening of a life without remorse. He was sitting in front of the door of his house, enjoying the sight of his grandchildren joking around him, and whose laughter, now his words, excited emulation. He immediately recognized Emilia, and showed great joy in seeing her again, announcing to her that, after her departure, his family had not suffered any troubles or fatal losses.

Emilia did not have the courage to enter the room where Saint Aubert had died, and after an hour's conversation, she returned to the castle.

During the first few days that he stayed at Blangy, he observed with pain the deep melancholy which too often absorbed Dupont. Emilia lamented the blindness which kept him close to her, and resolved to retire to the convent as soon as he could. The dejection of his friend did not take long to disturb the count, and Dupont finally confided to him the secret of his hopeless love for him. Villefort confined himself to pitying him, but decided within himself not to neglect any opportunity to favor him. When she learned of Dupont's dangerous situation, she feebly objected to his expressed desire to leave Blangy the next day; but she made him promise to come and spend some time there, when her heart was at ease. Emilia, who despite not being able to encourage her love for her, esteemed her good qualities, and was very grateful to his services, when she saw him leave for Gascony. He separated from her with such an expression of pain that the count became even more interested in her friend.

A few days later, Emilia also left the castle, having however had to promise the count and countess to come and see them often. The abbess received her with her maternal goodness of which she had already shown her, and the nuns with new signs of friendship. That convent, so familiar to her, reawakened her sad ideas; she thanked the Supreme Mover for having made her escape from so many dangers, she felt the price of the goods that remained to her, and although she often bathed her father's grave with her tears, she no longer felt the same bitterness as hers .

Some time after her arrival at the monastery, Emilia received a letter from her uncle Quesnel in reply to hers, and to questions about her possessions, which he had assumed to administer in her absence. She had especially inquired about the rent of the castle in the valley, which she wished to live in, if her means allowed it. Quesnel's answer was dry and cold as he expected it; he expressed neither interest in her sufferings nor pleasure in her that he had escaped them. Quesnel did not miss the opportunity to reproach her for refusing the wedding of Count Morano, whom he sought to represent as a man of honor and wealth; he declaimed vehemently with that same Montoni, to whom until then he had recognized himself so much inferior; he was laconic about Emilia's pecuniary interests, warning her, however, that the the lease of the castle in the valley expired shortly; she did not invite her to go to him, and added that, in the mean state of her substance, she would have done very well to stay for some time in Santa Chiara. He answered nothing to her questions about the fate of poor Teresa, her father's old servant. In a postscript, Quesnel, speaking of Motteville, into whose hands Saint Aubert had placed most of his patrimony, announced to her that his business was about to settle down, and that she would receive more from it than she could have expected. The letter also contained a sight note to collect a modest sum from a merchant of Narbonne.

The tranquility of the monastery, the freedom granted by the state to walk on the beach and in the surrounding woods, gradually calmed Emilia's spirit, who, however, felt uneasy about Valancourt, and impatient to receive an answer.

END OF THIRD VOLUME

A Sicilian Romance

by Ann Radcliffe

On the northern shore of Sicily are still to be seen the magnificent remains of a castle, which formerly belonged to the noble house of Mazzini. It stands in the centre of a small bay, and upon a gentle acclivity, which, on one side, slopes towards the sea, and on the other rises into an eminence crowned by dark woods. The situation is admirably beautiful and picturesque, and the ruins have an air of ancient grandeur, which, contrasted with the present solitude of the scene, impresses the traveller with awe and curiosity. During my travels abroad I visited this spot. As I walked over the loose fragments of stone, which lay scattered through the immense area of the fabrick, and surveyed the sublimity and grandeur of the ruins, I recurred, by a natural association of ideas, to the times when these walls stood proudly in their original splendour, when the halls were the scenes of hospitality and festive magnificence, and when they resounded with the voices of those whom death had long since swept from the earth. 'Thus,' said I, 'shall the present generation—he who now sinks in misery—and he who now swims in pleasure, alike pass away and be forgotten.' My heart swelled with the reflection; and, as I turned from the scene with a sigh, I fixed my eyes upon a friar, whose venerable figure, gently bending towards the earth, formed no uninteresting object in the picture. He observed my emotion; and, as my eye met his, shook his head and pointed to the ruin. 'These walls,' said he, 'were once the seat of luxury and vice. They exhibited a singular instance of the retribution of Heaven, and were from that period forsaken, and abandoned to decay.' His words excited my curiosity, and I enquired further concerning their meaning.

'A solemn history belongs to this castle, said he, 'which is too long and intricate for me to relate. It is, however, contained in a manuscript in our library, of which I could, perhaps, procure you a sight. A brother of our order, a descendant of the noble house of Mazzini, collected and recorded the most striking incidents relating to his family, and the history thus formed, he left as a legacy to our convent. If you please, we will walk thither.'

I accompanied him to the convent, and the friar introduced me to his superior, a man of an intelligent mind and benevolent heart, with whom I passed some hours in interesting conversation. I believe my sentiments pleased him; for, by his indulgence, I was permitted to take abstracts of the history before me, which, with some further particulars obtained in conversation with the abate, I have arranged in the following pages.

CHAPTER I

Towards the close of the sixteenth century, this castle was in the possession of Ferdinand, fifth marquis of Mazzini, and was for some years the principal residence of his family. He was a man of a voluptuous and imperious character. To his first wife, he married Louisa Bernini, second daughter of the Count della Salario, a lady yet more distinguished for the sweetness of her manners and the gentleness of her disposition, than for her beauty. She brought the marquis one son and two daughters, who lost their amiable mother in early childhood. The arrogant and impetuous character of the marquis operated powerfully upon the mild and susceptible nature of his lady: and it was by many persons believed, that his unkindness and neglect put a period to her life. However this might be, he soon afterwards married Maria de Vellorno, a young lady eminently beautiful, but of a character very opposite to that of her predecessor. She was a woman of infinite art, devoted to pleasure, and of an unconquerable spirit. The marquis, whose heart was dead to paternal tenderness, and whose present lady was too volatile to attend to domestic concerns, committed the education of his daughters to the care of a lady, completely qualified for the undertaking, and who was distantly related to the late marchioness.

He quitted Mazzini soon after his second marriage, for the gaieties and splendour of Naples, whither his son accompanied him. Though naturally of a haughty and overbearing disposition, he was governed by his wife. His passions were vehement, and she had the address to bend them to her own purpose; and so well to conceal her influence, that he thought himself most independent when he was most enslaved. He paid an annual visit to the castle of Mazzini; but the marchioness seldom attended him, and he staid only to give such general directions concerning the education of his daughters, as his pride, rather than his affection, seemed to dictate.

Emilia, the elder, inherited much of her mother's disposition. She had a mild and sweet temper, united with a clear and comprehensive mind. Her younger sister, Julia, was of a more lively cast. An extreme sensibility subjected her to frequent uneasiness; her temper was warm, but generous; she was quickly irritated, and quickly appeased; and to a reproof, however gentle, she would often weep, but was never sullen. Her imagination was ardent, and her mind early exhibited symptoms of genius. It was the particular care of Madame de Menon to counteract those traits in the disposition of her young pupils, which appeared inimical to their future happiness; and for this task she had abilities which entitled her to hope for success. A series of early misfortunes had entendered her heart, without weakening the powers of her understanding. In retirement she had acquired tranquillity, and had almost lost the consciousness of those sorrows which yet threw a soft and not unpleasing shade over her character. She loved her young charge with maternal fondness, and their gradual improvement and respectful tenderness repaid all her anxiety. Madame excelled in music and drawing. She had often forgot her sorrows in these amusements, when her mind was too much occupied to derive consolation from books, and she was assiduous to impart to Emilia and Julia a power so valuable as that of beguiling the sense of affliction. Emilia's taste led her to drawing, and she soon made rapid advances in that art. Julia was uncommonly susceptible of the charms of harmony. She had feelings which trembled in unison to all its various and enchanting powers.

The instructions of madame she caught with astonishing quickness, and in a short time attained to a degree of excellence in her favorite study, which few persons have ever exceeded. Her manner was entirely her own. It was not in the rapid intricacies of execution, that she excelled so much in as in that delicacy of taste, and in those enchanting powers of expression, which seem to breathe a soul through the sound, and which take captive the heart of the hearer. The lute was her favorite instrument, and its tender notes accorded well with the sweet and melting tones of her voice.

The castle of Mazzini was a large irregular fabrick, and seemed suited to receive a numerous train of followers, such as, in those days, served the nobility, either in the splendour of peace, or the turbulence of war. Its present family inhabited only a small part of it; and even this part appeared forlorn and almost desolate from the spaciousness of the apartments, and the length of the galleries which led to them. A melancholy stillness reigned through the halls, and the silence of the courts, which were shaded by high turrets, was for many hours together undisturbed by the sound of any foot-step. Julia, who discovered an early taste for books, loved to retire in an evening to a small closet in which she had collected her favorite authors. This room formed the western angle of the castle: one of its windows looked upon the sea, beyond which was faintly seen, skirting the horizon, the dark rocky coast of Calabria; the other opened towards a part of the castle, and afforded a prospect of the neighbouring woods. Her musical instruments were here deposited, with whatever assisted her favorite amusements. This spot, which was at once elegant, pleasant, and retired, was embellished with many little ornaments of her own invention, and with some drawings executed by her sister. The cioset was adjoining her chamber, and was separated from the apartments of madame only by a short gallery. This gallery opened into another, long and winding, which led to the grand staircase, terminating in the north hall, with which the chief apartments of the north side of the edifice communicated.

Madame de Menon's apartment opened into both galleries. It was in one of these rooms that she usually spent the mornings, occupied in the improvement of her young charge. The windows looked towards the sea, and the room was light and pleasant. It was their custom to dine in one of the lower apartments, and at table they were always joined by a dependant of the marquis's, who had resided many years in the castle, and who instructed the young ladies in the Latin tongue, and in geography. During the fine evenings of summer, this little party frequently supped in a pavilion, which was built on an eminence in the woods belonging to the castle. From this spot the eye had an almost boundless range of sea and land. It commanded the straits of Messina, with the opposite shores of Calabria, and a great extent of the wild and picturesque scenery of Sicily. Mount Etna, crowned with eternal snows, and shooting from among the clouds, formed a grand and sublime picture in the background of the scene. The city of Palermo was also distinguishable; and Julia, as she gazed on its glittering spires; would endeavour in imagination to depicture its beauties, while she secretly sighed for a view of that world, from which she had hitherto been secluded by the mean jealousy of the marchioness, upon whose mind the dread of rival beauty operated strongly to the prejudice of Emilia and Julia. She employed all her influence over the marquis to detain them in retirement; and, though Emilia was now twenty, and her sister eighteen, they had never passed the boundaries of their father's domains.

Vanity often produces unreasonable alarm; but the marchioness had in this instance just grounds for apprehension; the beauty of her lord's daughters has seldom been exceeded. The person of Emilia was finely proportioned. Her complexion was fair, her hair flaxen, and her dark blue eyes were full of sweet expression. Her manners were dignified and elegant, and in her air was a feminine softness, a tender timidity which irresistibly attracted the heart of the beholder. The figure of Julia was light and graceful—her step was airy—her mien animated, and her smile enchanting. Her eyes were dark, and full of fire, but tempered with modest sweetness. Her features were finely turned—every laughing grace played round her mouth, and her countenance quickly discovered all the various emotions of her soul. The dark auburn hair, which curled in beautiful profusion in her neck, gave a finishing charm to her appearance.

Thus lovely, and thus veiled in obscurity, were the daughters of the noble Mazzini. But they were happy, for they knew not enough of the world seriously to regret the want of its enjoyments, though Julia would sometimes sigh for the airy image which her fancies painted, and a painful curiosity would arise concerning the busy scenes from which she was excluded. A return to her customary amusements, however, would chase the ideal image from her mind, and restore her usual happy complacency. Books, music, and painting, divided the hours of her leisure, and many beautiful summer-evenings were spent in the pavilion, where the refined conversation of madame, the poetry of Tasso, the lute of Julia, and the friendship of Emilia, combined to form a species of happiness, such as elevated and highly susceptible minds are alone capable of receiving or communicating. Madame understood and practised all the graces of conversation, and her young pupils perceived its value, and caught the spirit of its character.

Conversation may be divided into two classes—the familiar and the sentimental. It is the province of the familiar, to diffuse cheerfulness and ease—to open the heart of man to man, and to beam a temperate sunshine upon the mind.—Nature and art must conspire to render us susceptible of the charms, and to qualify us for the practice of the second class of conversation, here termed sentimental, and in which Madame de Menon particularly excelled. To good sense, lively feeling, and natural delicacy of taste, must be united an expansion of mind, and a refinement of thought, which is the result of high cultivation. To render this sort of conversation irresistibly attractive, a knowledge of the world is requisite, and that enchanting ease, that elegance of manner, which is to be acquired only by frequenting the higher circles of polished life. In sentimental conversation, subjects interesting to the heart, and to the imagination, are brought forward; they are discussed in a kind of sportive way, with animation and refinement, and are never continued longer than politeness allows. Here fancy flourishes,—the sensibilities expand—and wit, guided by delicacy and embellished by taste—points to the heart.

Such was the conversation of Madame de Menon; and the pleasant gaiety of the pavilion seemed peculiarly to adapt it for the scene of social delights. On the evening of a very sultry day, having supped in their favorite spot, the coolness of the hour, and the beauty of the night, tempted this happy party to remain there later than usual. Returning home, they were surprised by the appearance of a light through the broken window-shutters of an apartment, belonging to a division of the castle which had for many years been shut up. They stopped to observe it, when it suddenly disappeared, and was seen no more. Madame de Menon, disturbed at this phaenomenon, hastened into the castle, with a view of enquiring into the cause of it, when she was met in the north hall by Vincent. She related to him what she had seen, and ordered an immediate search to be made for the keys of those apartments. She apprehended that some person had penetrated that part of the edifice with an intention of plunder; and, disdaining a paltry fear where her duty was concerned, she summoned the servants of the castle, with an intention of accompanying them thither. Vincent smiled at her apprehensions, and imputed what she had seen to an illusion, which the solemnity of the hour had impressed upon her fancy. Madame, however, persevered in her purpose; and, after along and repeated search, a massey key, covered with rust, was produced. She then proceeded to the southern side of the edifice, accompanied by Vincent, and followed by the servants, who were agitated with impatient wonder. The key was applied to an iron gate, which opened into a court that separated this division from the other parts of the castle. They entered this court, which was overgrown with grass and weeds, and ascended some steps that led to a large door, which they vainly endeavoured to open. All the different keys of the castle were applied to the lock, without effect, and they were at length compelled to quit the place, without having either satisfied their curiosity, or quieted their fears. Everything, however, was still, and the light did not reappear. Madame concealed her apprehensions, and the family retired to rest.

This circumstance dwelt on the mind of Madame de Menon, and it was some time before she ventured again to spend an evening in the pavilion. After several months passed, without further disturbance or discovery, another occurrence renewed the alarm. Julia had one night remained in her closet later than usual. A favorite book had engaged her attention beyond the hour of customary repose, and every inhabitant of the castle, except herself, had long been lost in sleep. She was roused from her forgetfulness, by the sound of the castle clock, which struck one. Surprised at the lateness of the hour, she rose in haste, and was moving to her chamber, when the beauty of the night attracted her to the window. She opened it; and observing a fine effect of moonlight upon the dark woods, leaned forwards. In that situation she had not long remained, when she perceived a light faintly flash through a casement in the uninhabited part of the castle. A sudden tremor seized her, and she with difficulty supported herself. In a few moments it disappeared, and soon after a figure, bearing a lamp, proceeded from an obscure door belonging to the south tower; and stealing along the outside of the castle walls, turned round the southern angle, by which it was afterwards hid from the view. Astonished and terrified at what she had seen, she hurried to the apartment of Madame de Menon, and related the circumstance. The servants were immediately roused, and the alarm became general. Madame arose and descended into the north hall, where the domestics were already assembled. No one could be found of courage sufficient to enter into the courts; and the orders of madame were disregarded, when opposed to the effects of superstitious terror. She perceived that Vincent was absent, but as she was ordering him to be called, he entered the hall. Surprised to find the family thus assembled, he was told the occasion. He immediately ordered a party of the servants to attend him round the castle walls; and with some reluctance, and more fear, they obeyed him. They all returned to the hall, without having witnessed any extraordinary appearance; but though their fears were not confirmed, they were by no means dissipated. The appearance of a light in a part of the castle which had for several years been shut up, and to which time and circumstance had given an air of singular desolation, might reasonably be supposed to excite a strong degree of surprise and terror. In the minds of the vulgar, any species of the wonderful is received with avidity; and the servants did not hesitate in believing the southern division of the castle to be inhabited by a supernatural power. Too much agitated to sleep, they agreed to watch for the remainder of the night. For this purpose they arranged themselves in the east gallery, where they had a view of the south tower from which the light had issued. The night, however, passed without any further disturbance; and the morning dawn, which they beheld with inexpressible pleasure, dissipated for a while the glooms of apprehension. But the return of evening renewed the general fear, and for several successive nights the domestics watched the southern tower. Although nothing remarkable was seen, a report was soon raised, and believed, that the southern side of the castle was haunted. Madame de Menon, whose mind was superior to the effects of superstition, was yet disturbed and perplexed, and she determined, if the light reappeared, to inform the marquis of the circumstance, and request the keys of those apartments.

The marquis, immersed in the dissipations of Naples, seldom remembered the castle, or its inhabitants. His son, who had been educated under his immediate care, was the sole object of his pride, as the marchioness was that of his affection. He loved her with romantic fondness, which she repaid with seeming tenderness, and secret perfidy. She allowed herself a free indulgence in the most licentious pleasures, yet conducted herself with an art so exquisite as to elude discovery, and even suspicion. In her amours she was equally inconstant as ardent, till the young Count Hippolitus de Vereza attracted her attention. The natural fickleness of her disposition seemed then to cease, and upon him she centered all her desires.

The count Vereza lost his father in early childhood. He was now of age, and had just entered upon the possession of his estates. His person was graceful, yet manly; his mind accomplished, and his manners elegant; his countenance expressed a happy union of spirit, dignity, and benevolence, which formed the principal traits of his character. He had a sublimity of thought, which taught him to despise the voluptuous vices of the Neapolitans, and led him to higher pursuits. He was the chosen and early friend of young Ferdinand, the son of the marquis, and was a frequent visitor in the family. When the marchioness first saw him, she treated him with great distinction, and at length made such advances, as neither the honor nor the inclinations of the count permitted him to notice. He conducted himself toward her with frigid indifference, which served only to inflame the passion it was meant to chill. The favors of the marchioness had hitherto been sought with avidity, and accepted with rapture; and the repulsive insensibility which she now experienced, roused all her pride, and called into action every refinement of coquetry.

It was about this period that Vincent was seized with a disorder which increased so rapidly, as in a short time to assume the most alarming appearance. Despairing of life, he desired that a messenger might be dispatched to inform the marquis of his situation, and to signify his earnest wish to see him before he died. The progress of his disorder defied every art of medicine, and his visible distress of mind seemed to accelerate his fate. Perceiving his last hour approaching, he requested to have a confessor. The confessor was shut up with him a considerable time, and he had already received extreme unction, when Madame de Menon was summoned to his bedside. The hand of death was now upon him, cold damps hung upon his brows, and he, with difficulty, raised his heavy eyes to madame as she entered the apartment. He beckoned her towards him, and desiring that no person might be permitted to enter the room, was for a few moments silent. His mind appeared to labour under oppressive remembrances; he made several attempts to speak, but either resolution or strength failed him. At length, giving madame a look of unutterable anguish, 'Alas, madam,' said he, 'Heaven grants not the prayer of such a wretch as I am. I must expire long before the marquis can arrive. Since I shall see him no more, I would impart to you a secret which lies heavy at my heart, and which makes my last moments dreadful, as they are without hope.' 'Be comforted,' said madame, who was affected by the energy of his manner, 'we are taught to believe that forgiveness is never denied to sincere repentance.' 'You, madam, are ignorant of the enormity of my crime, and of the secret—the horrid secret which labours at my breast. My guilt is beyond remedy in this world, and I fear will be without pardon in the next; I therefore hope little from confession even to a priest. Yet some good it is still in my power to do; let me disclose to you that secret which is so mysteriously connected with the southern apartments of this castle.'—'What of them!' exclaimed madame, with impatience. Vincent returned no answer; exhausted by the effort of speaking, he had fainted. Madame rung for assistance, and by proper applications, his senses were recalled. He was, however, entirely speechless, and in this state he remained till he expired, which was about an hour after he had conversed with madame.

The perplexity and astonishment of madame, were by the late scene heightened to a very painful degree. She recollected the various particulars relative to the southern division of the castle, the many years it had stood uninhabited—the silence which had been observed concerning it—the appearance of the light and the figure—the fruitless search for the keys, and the reports so generally believed; and thus remembrance presented her with a combination of circumstances, which served only to increase her wonder, and heighten her curiosity. A veil of mystery enveloped that part of the castle, which it now seemed impossible should ever be penetrated, since the only person who could have removed it, was no more.

The marquis arrived on the day after that on which Vincent had expired. He came attended by servants only, and alighted at the gates of the castle with an air of impatience, and a countenance expressive of strong emotion. Madame, with the young ladies, received him in the hall. He hastily saluted his daughters, and passed on to the oak parlour, desiring madame to follow him. She obeyed, and the marquis enquired with great agitation after Vincent. When told of his death, he paced the room with hurried steps, and was for some time silent. At length seating himself, and surveying madame with a scrutinizing eye, he asked some questions concerning the particulars of Vincent's death. She mentioned his earnest desire to see the marquis, and repeated his last words. The marquis remained silent, and madame proceeded to mention those circumstances relative to the southern division of the castle, which she thought it of so much importance to discover. He treated the affair very lightly, laughed at her conjectures, represented the appearances she described as the illusions of a weak and timid mind, and broke up the conversation, by going to visit the chamber of Vincent, in which he remained a considerable time.

On the following day Emilia and Julia dined with the marquis. He was gloomy and silent; their efforts to amuse him seemed to excite displeasure rather than kindness; and when the repast was concluded, he withdrew to his own apartment, leaving his daughters in a state of sorrow and surprise.

Vincent was to be interred, according to his own desire, in the church belonging to the convent of St Nicholas. One of the servants, after receiving some necessary orders concerning the funeral, ventured to inform the marquis of the appearance of the lights in the south tower. He mentioned the superstitious reports that prevailed amongst the household, and complained that the servants would not cross the courts after it was dark. 'And who is he that has commissioned you with this story?' said the marquis, in a tone of displeasure; 'are the weak and ridiculous fancies of women and servants to be obtruded upon my notice? Away—appear no more before me, till you have learned to speak what it is proper for me to hear.' Robert withdrew abashed, and it was some time before any person ventured to renew the subject with the marquis.

The majority of young Ferdinand now drew near, and the marquis determined to celebrate the occasion with festive magnificence at the castle of Mazzini. He, therefore, summoned the marchioness and his son from Naples, and very splendid preparations were ordered to be made. Emilia and Julia dreaded the arrival of the marchioness, whose influence they had long been sensible of, and from whose presence they anticipated a painful restraint. Beneath the gentle guidance of Madame de Menon, their hours had passed in happy tranquillity, for they were ignorant alike of the sorrows and the pleasures of the world. Those did not oppress, and these did not inflame them. Engaged in the pursuits of knowledge, and in the attainment of elegant accomplishments, their moments flew lightly away, and the flight of time was marked only by improvement. In madame was united the tenderness of the mother, with the sympathy of a friend; and they loved her with a warm and inviolable affection.

The purposed visit of their brother, whom they had not seen for several years, gave them great pleasure. Although their minds retained no very distinct remembrance of him, they looked forward with eager and delightful expectation to his virtues and his talents; and hoped to find in his company, a consolation for the uneasiness which the presence of the marchioness would excite. Neither did Julia contemplate with indifference the approaching festival. A new scene was now opening to her, which her young imagination painted in the warm and glowing colours of delight. The near approach of pleasure frequently awakens the heart to emotions, which would fail to be excited by a more remote and abstracted observance. Julia, who, in the distance, had considered the splendid gaieties of life with tranquillity, now lingered with impatient hope through the moments which withheld her from their enjoyments. Emilia, whose feelings were less lively, and whose imagination was less powerful, beheld the approaching festival with calm consideration, and almost regretted the interruption of those tranquil pleasures, which she knew to be more congenial with her powers and disposition.

In a few days the marchioness arrived at the castle. She was followed by a numerous retinue, and accompanied by Ferdinand, and several of the Italian noblesse, whom pleasure attracted to her train. Her entrance was proclaimed by the sound of music, and those gates which had long rusted on their hinges, were thrown open to receive her. The courts and halls, whose aspect so lately expressed only gloom and desolation, now shone with sudden splendour, and echoed the sounds of gaiety and gladness. Julia surveyed the scene from an obscure window; and as the triumphal strains filled the air, her breast throbbed; her heart beat quick with joy, and she lost her apprehensions from the marchioness in a sort of wild delight hitherto unknown to her. The arrival of the marchioness seemed indeed the signal of universal and unlimited pleasure. When the marquis came out to receive her, the gloom that lately clouded his countenance, broke away in smiles of welcome, which the whole company appeared to consider as invitations to joy.

The tranquil heart of Emilia was not proof against a scene so alluring, and she sighed at the prospect, yet scarcely knew why. Julia pointed out to her sister, the graceful figure of a young man who followed the marchioness, and she expressed her wishes that he might be her brother. From the contemplation of the scene before them, they were summoned to meet the marchioness. Julia trembled with apprehension, and for a few moments wished the castle was in its former state. As they advanced through the saloon, in which they were presented, Julia was covered with blushes; but Emilia, tho' equally timid, preserved her graceful dignity. The marchioness received them with a mingled smile of condescension and politeness, and immediately the whole attention of the company was attracted by their elegance and beauty. The eager eyes of Julia sought in vain to discover her brother, of whose features she had no recollection in those of any of the persons then present. At length her father presented him, and she perceived, with a sigh of regret, that he was not the youth she had observed from the window. He advanced with a very engaging air, and she met him with an unfeigned welcome. His figure was tall and majestic; he had a very noble and spirited carriage; and his countenance expressed at once sweetness and dignity. Supper was served in the east hall, and the tables were spread with a profusion of delicacies. A band of music played during the repast, and the evening concluded with a concert in the saloon.

CHAPTER II

The day of the festival, so long and so impatiently looked for by Julia, was now arrived. All the neighbouring nobility were invited, and the gates of the castle were thrown open for a general rejoicing. A magnificent entertainment, consisting of the most luxurious and expensive dishes, was served in the halls. Soft music floated along the vaulted roofs, the walls were hung with decorations, and it seemed as if the hand of a magician had suddenly metamorphosed this once gloomy fabric into the palace of a fairy. The marquis, notwithstanding the gaiety of the scene, frequently appeared abstracted from its enjoyments, and in spite of all his efforts at cheerfulness, the melancholy of his heart was visible in his countenance.

In the evening there was a grand ball: the marchioness, who was still distinguished for her beauty, and for the winning elegance of her manners, appeared in the most splendid attire. Her hair was ornamented with a profusion of jewels, but was so disposed as to give an air rather of voluptuousness than of grace, to her figure. Although conscious of her charms, she beheld the beauty of Emilia and Julia with a jealous eye, and was compelled secretly to acknowledge, that the simple elegance with which they were adorned, was more enchanting than all the studied artifice of splendid decoration. They were dressed alike in light Sicilian habits, and the beautiful luxuriance of their flowing hair was restrained only by bandellets of pearl. The ball was opened by Ferdinand and the lady Matilda Constanza. Emilia danced with the young Marquis della Fazelli, and acquitted herself with the ease and dignity so natural to her. Julia experienced a various emotion of pleasure and fear when the Count de Vereza, in whom she recollected the cavalier she had observed from the window, led her forth. The grace of her step, and the elegant symmetry of her figure, raised in the assembly a gentle murmur of applause, and the soft blush which now stole over her cheek, gave an additional charm to her appearance. But when the music changed, and she danced to the soft Sicilian measure, the airy grace of her movement, and the unaffected tenderness of her air, sunk attention into silence, which continued for some time after the dance had ceased. The marchioness observed the general admiration with seeming pleasure, and secret uneasiness. She had suffered a very painful solicitude, when the Count de Vereza selected her for his partner in the dance, and she pursued him through the evening with an eye of jealous scrutiny. Her bosom, which before glowed only with love, was now torn by the agitation of other passions more violent and destructive. Her thoughts were restless, her mind wandered from the scene before her, and it required all her address to preserve an apparent ease. She saw, or fancied she saw, an impassioned air in the count, when he addressed himself to Julia, that corroded her heart with jealous fury.

At twelve the gates of the castle were thrown open, and the company quitted it for the woods, which were splendidly illuminated. Arcades of light lined the long vistas, which were terminated by pyramids of lamps that presented to the eye one bright column of flame. At irregular distances buildings were erected, hung with variegated lamps, disposed in the gayest and most fantastic forms. Collations were spread under the trees; and music, touched by unseen hands, breathed around. The musicians were placed in the most obscure and embowered spots, so as to elude the eye and strike the imagination. The scene appeared enchanting. Nothing met the eye but beauty and romantic splendour; the ear received no sounds but those of mirth and melody.

The younger part of the company formed themselves into groups, which at intervals glanced through the woods, and were again unseen. Julia seemed the magic queen of the place. Her heart dilated with pleasure, and diffused over her features an expression of pure and complacent delight. A generous, frank, and exalted sentiment sparkled in her eyes, and animated her manner. Her bosom glowed with benevolent affections; and she seemed anxious to impart to all around her, a happiness as unmixed as that she experienced. Wherever she moved, admiration followed her steps. Ferdinand was as gay as the scene around him. Emilia was pleased; and the marquis seemed to have left his melancholy in the castle. The marchioness alone was wretched. She supped with a select party, in a pavilion on the sea-shore, which was fitted up with peculiar elegance. It was hung with white silk, drawn up in festoons, and richly fringed with gold. The sofas were of the same materials, and alternate wreaths of lamps and of roses entwined the columns. A row of small lamps placed about the cornice, formed an edge of light round the roof which, with the other numerous lights, was reflected in a blaze of splendour from the large mirrors that adorned the room. The Count Muriani was of the party;—he complimented the marchioness on the beauty of her daughters; and after lamenting with gaiety the captives which their charms would enthral, he mentioned the Count de Vereza. 'He is certainly of all others the man most deserving the lady Julia. As they danced, I thought they exhibited a perfect model of the beauty of either sex; and if I mistake not, they are inspired with a mutual admiration.' The marchioness, endeavouring to conceal her uneasiness, said, 'Yes, my lord, I allow the count all the merit you adjudge him, but from the little I have seen of his disposition, he is too volatile for a serious attachment.' At that instant the count entered the pavilion: 'Ah,' said Muriani, laughingly, 'you was the subject of our conversation, and seem to be come in good time to receive the honors allotted you. I was interceding with the marchioness for her interest in your favor, with the lady Julia; but she absolutely refuses it; and though she allows you merit, alleges, that you are by nature fickle and inconstant. What say you—would not the beauty of lady Julia bind your unsteady heart?'.

'I know not how I have deserved that character of the marchioness,' said the count with a smile, 'but that heart must be either fickle or insensible in an uncommon degree, which can boast of freedom in the presence of lady Julia.' The marchioness, mortified by the whole conversation, now felt the full force of Vereza's reply, which she imagined he pointed with particular emphasis.

The entertainment concluded with a grand firework, which was exhibited on the margin of the sea, and the company did not part till the dawn of morning. Julia retired from the scene with regret. She was enchanted with the new world that was now exhibited to her, and she was not cool enough to distinguish the vivid glow of imagination from the colours of real bliss. The pleasure she now felt she believed would always be renewed, and in an equal degree, by the objects which first excited it. The weakness of humanity is never willingly perceived by young minds. It is painful to know, that we are operated upon by objects whose impressions are variable as they are indefinable— and that what yesterday affected us strongly, is to-day but imperfectly felt, and to-morrow perhaps shall be disregarded. When at length this unwelcome truth is received into the mind, we at first reject, with disgust, every appearance of good, we disdain to partake of a happiness which we cannot always command, and we not unfrequently sink into a temporary despair. Wisdom or accident, at length, recal us from our error, and offers to us some object capable of producing a pleasing, yet lasting effect, which effect, therefore, we call happiness. Happiness has this essential difference from what is commonly called pleasure, that virtue forms its basis, and virtue being the offspring of reason, may be expected to produce uniformity of effect.

The passions which had hitherto lain concealed in Julia's heart, touched by circumstance, dilated to its power, and afforded her a slight experience of the pain and delight which flow from their influence. The beauty and accomplishments of Vereza raised in her a new and various emotion, which reflection made her fear to encourage, but which was too pleasing to be wholly resisted. Tremblingly alive to a sense of delight, and unchilled by disappointment, the young heart welcomes every feeling, not simply painful, with a romantic expectation that it will expand into bliss.

Julia sought with eager anxiety to discover the sentiments of Vereza towards her; she revolved each circumstance of the day, but they afforded her little satisfaction; they reflected only a glimmering and uncertain light, which instead of guiding, served only to perplex her. Now she remembered some instance of particular attention, and then some mark of apparent indifference. She compared his conduct with that of the other young noblesse; and thought each appeared equally desirous of the favor of every lady present. All the ladies, however, appeared to her to court the admiration of Vereza, and she trembled lest he should be too sensible of the distinction. She drew from these reflections no positive inference; and though distrust rendered pain the predominate sensation, it was so exquisitely interwoven with delight, that she could not wish it exchanged for her former ease. Thoughtful and restless, sleep fled from her eyes, and she longed with impatience for the morning, which should again present Vereza, and enable her to pursue the enquiry. She rose early, and adorned herself with unusual care. In her favorite closet she awaited the hour of breakfast, and endeavoured to read, but her thoughts wandered from the subject. Her lute and favorite airs lost half their power to please; the day seemed to stand still—she became melancholy, and thought the breakfast-hour would never arrive. At length the clock struck the signal, the sound vibrated on every nerve, and trembling she quitted the closet for her sister's apartment. Love taught her disguise. Till then Emilia had shared all her thoughts; they now descended to the breakfast-room in silence, and Julia almost feared to meet her eye. In the breakfast-room they were alone. Julia found it impossible to support a conversation with Emilia, whose observations interrupting the course of her thoughts, became uninteresting and tiresome. She was therefore about to retire to her closet, when the marquis entered. His air was haughty, and his look severe. He coldly saluted his daughters, and they had scarcely time to reply to his general enquiries, when the marchioness entered, and the company soon after assembled. Julia, who had awaited with so painful an impatience for the moment which should present Vereza to her sight, now sighed that it was arrived. She scarcely dared to lift her timid eyes from the ground, and when by accident they met his, a soft tremour seized her; and apprehension lest he should discover her sentiments, served only to render her confusion conspicuous. At length, a glance from the marchioness recalled her bewildered thoughts; and other fears superseding those of love, her mind, by degrees, recovered its dignity. She could distinguish in the behaviour of Vereza no symptoms of particular admiration, and she resolved to conduct herself towards him with the most scrupulous care.

This day, like the preceding one, was devoted to joy. In the evening there was a concert, which was chiefly performed by the nobility. Ferdinand played the violoncello, Vereza the German flute, and Julia the piana-forte, which she touched with a delicacy and execution that engaged every auditor. The confusion of Julia may be easily imagined, when Ferdinand, selecting a beautiful duet, desired Vereza would accompany his sister. The pride of conscious excellence, however, quickly overcame her timidity, and enabled her to exert all her powers. The air was simple and pathetic, and she gave it those charms of expression so peculiarly her own. She struck the chords of her piana-forte in beautiful accompaniment, and towards the close of the second stanza, her voice resting on one note, swelled into a tone so exquisite, and from thence descended to a few simple notes, which she touched with such impassioned tenderness that every eye wept to the sounds. The breath of the flute trembled, and Hippolitus entranced, forgot to play. A pause of silence ensued at the conclusion of the piece, and continued till a general sigh seemed to awaken the audience from their enchantment. Amid the general applause, Hippolitus was silent. Julia observed his behaviour, and gently raising her eyes to his, there read the sentiments which she had inspired. An exquisite emotion thrilled her heart, and she experienced one of those rare moments which illuminate life with a ray of bliss, by which the darkness of its general shade is contrasted. Care, doubt, every disagreeable sensation vanished, and for the remainder of the evening she was conscious only of delight. A timid respect marked the manner of Hippolitus, more flattering to Julia than the most ardent professions. The evening concluded with a ball, and Julia was again the partner of the count.

When the ball broke up, she retired to her apartment, but not to sleep. Joy is as restless as anxiety or sorrow. She seemed to have entered upon a new state of existence;— those fine springs of affection which had hitherto lain concealed, were now touched, and yielded to her a happiness more exalted than any her imagination had ever painted. She reflected on the tranquillity of her past life, and comparing it with the emotions of the present hour, exulted in the difference. All her former pleasures now appeared insipid; she wondered that they ever had power to affect her, and that she had endured with content the dull uniformity to which she had been condemned. It was now only that she appeared to live. Absorbed in the single idea of being beloved, her imagination soared into the regions of romantic bliss, and bore her high above the possibility of evil. Since she was beloved by Hippolitus, she could only be happy.

From this state of entranced delight, she was awakened by the sound of music immediately under her window. It was a lute touched by a masterly hand. After a wild and melancholy symphony, a voice of more than magic expression swelled into an air so pathetic and tender, that it seemed to breathe the very soul of love. The chords of the lute were struck in low and sweet accompaniment. Julia listened, and distinguished the following words;

SONNET

Still is the night-breeze!—not a lonely sound
   Steals through the silence of this dreary hour;
O'er these high battlements Sleep reigns profound,
   And sheds on all, his sweet oblivious power.
On all but me—I vainly ask his dews

> To steep in short forgetfulness my cares.
> Th' affrighted god still flies when Love pursues,
>   Still—still denies the wretched lover's prayers.

An interval of silence followed, and the air was repeated; after which the music was heard no more. If before Julia believed that she was loved by Hippolitus, she was now confirmed in the sweet reality. But sleep at length fell upon her senses, and the airy forms of ideal bliss no longer fleeted before her imagination. Morning came, and she arose light and refreshed. How different were her present sensations from those of the preceding day. Her anxiety had now evaporated in joy, and she experienced that airy dance of spirits which accumulates delight from every object; and with a power like the touch of enchantment, can transform a gloomy desert into a smiling Eden. She flew to the breakfast-room, scarcely conscious of motion; but, as she entered it, a soft confusion overcame her; she blushed, and almost feared to meet the eyes of Vereza. She was presently relieved, however, for the Count was not there. The company assembled—Julia watched the entrance of every person with painful anxiety, but he for whom she looked did not appear. Surprised and uneasy, she fixed her eyes on the door, and whenever it opened, her heart beat with an expectation which was as often checked by disappointment. In spite of all her efforts, her vivacity sunk into languor, and she then perceived that love may produce other sensations than those of delight. She found it possible to be unhappy, though loved by Hippolitus; and acknowledged with a sigh of regret, which was yet new to her, how tremblingly her peace depended upon him. He neither appeared nor was mentioned at breakfast; but though delicacy prevented her enquiring after him, conversation soon became irksome to her, and she retired to the apartment of Madame de Menon. There she employed herself in painting, and endeavoured to beguile the time till the hour of dinner, when she hoped to see Hippolitus. Madame was, as usual, friendly and cheerful, but she perceived a reserve in the conduct of Julia, and penetrated without difficulty into its cause. She was, however, ignorant of the object of her pupil's admiration. The hour so eagerly desired by Julia at length arrived, and with a palpitating heart she entered the hall. The Count was not there, and in the course of conversation, she learned that he had that morning sailed for Naples. The scene which so lately appeared enchanting to her eyes, now changed its hue; and in the midst of society, and surrounded by gaiety, she was solitary and dejected. She accused herself of having suffered her wishes to mislead her judgment; and the present conduct of Hippolitus convinced her, that she had mistaken admiration for a sentiment more tender. She believed, too, that the musician who had addressed her in his sonnet, was not the Count; and thus at once was dissolved all the ideal fabric of her happiness. How short a period often reverses the character of our sentiments, rendering that which yesterday we despised, to-day desirable. The tranquil state which she had so lately delighted to quit, she now reflected upon with regret. She had, however, the consolation of believing that her sentiments towards the Count were unknown, and the sweet consciousness that her conduct had been governed by a nice sense of propriety.

The public rejoicings at the castle closed with the week; but the gay spirit of the marchioness forbade a return to tranquillity; and she substituted diversions more private, but in splendour scarcely inferior to the preceding ones. She had observed the behaviour of Hippolitus on the night of the concert with chagrin, and his departure with sorrow; yet, disdaining to perpetuate misfortune by reflection, she sought to lose the sense of disappointment in the hurry of dissipation. But her efforts to erase him from her remembrance were ineffectual. Unaccustomed to oppose the bent of her inclinations, they now maintained unbounded sway; and she found too late, that in order to have a due command of our passions, it is necessary to subject them to early obedience. Passion, in its undue influence, produces weakness as well as injustice. The pain which now recoiled upon her heart from disappointment, she had not strength of mind to endure, and she sought relief from its pressure in afflicting the innocent. Julia, whose beauty she imagined had captivated the count, and confirmed him in indifference towards herself, she incessantly tormented by the exercise of those various and splenetic little arts which elude the eye of the common observer, and are only to be known by those who have felt them. Arts, which individually are inconsiderable, but in the aggregate amount to a cruel and decisive effect.

From Julia's mind the idea of happiness was now faded. Pleasure had withdrawn her beam from the prospect, and the objects no longer illumined by her ray, became dark and colourless. As often as her situation would permit, she withdrew from society, and sought the freedom of solitude, where she could indulge in melancholy thoughts, and give a loose to that despair which is so apt to follow the disappointment of our first hopes.

Week after week elapsed, yet no mention was made of returning to Naples. The marquis at length declared it his intention to spend the remainder of the summer in the castle. To this determination the marchioness submitted with decent resignation, for she was here surrounded by a croud of flatterers, and her invention supplied her with continual diversions: that gaiety which rendered Naples so dear to her, glittered in the woods of Mazzini, and resounded through the castle.

The apartments of Madame de Menon were spacious and noble. The windows opened upon the sea, and commanded a view of the straits of Messina, bounded on one side by the beautiful shores of the isle of Sicily, and on the other by the high mountains of Calabria. The straits, filled with vessels whose gay streamers glittered to the sun-beam, presented to the eye an ever-moving scene. The principal room opened upon a gallery that overhung the grand terrace of the castle, and it commanded a prospect which for beauty and extent has seldom been equalled. These were formerly considered the chief apartments of the castle; and when the Marquis quitted them for Naples, were allotted for the residence of Madame de Menon, and her young charge. The marchioness, struck with the prospect which the windows afforded, and with the pleasantness of the gallery, determined to restore the rooms to their former splendour. She signified this intention to madame, for whom other apartments were provided. The chambers of Emilia and Julia forming part of the suite, they were also claimed by the marchioness, who left Julia only her favorite closet. The rooms to which they removed were spacious, but gloomy; they had been for some years uninhabited; and though preparations had been made for the reception of their new inhabitants, an air of desolation reigned within them that inspired melancholy sensations. Julia observed that her chamber, which opened beyond madame's, formed a part of the southern building, with which, however, there appeared no means of communication. The late mysterious circumstances relating to this part of the fabric, now arose to her imagination, and conjured up a terror which reason could not subdue. She told her emotions to madame, who, with more prudence than sincerity, laughed at her fears. The behaviour of the marquis, the dying words of Vincent, together with the preceding circumstances of alarm, had sunk deep in the mind of madame, but she saw the necessity of confining to her own breast doubts which time only could resolve.

Julia endeavoured to reconcile herself to the change, and a circumstance soon occurred which obliterated her present sensations, and excited others far more interesting. One day that she was arranging some papers in the small drawers of a cabinet that stood in her apartment, she found a picture which fixed all her attention. It was a miniature of a lady, whose countenance was touched with sorrow, and expressed an air of dignified resignation. The mournful sweetness of her eyes, raised towards Heaven with a look of supplication, and the melancholy languor that shaded her features, so deeply affected Julia, that her eyes were filled with involuntary tears. She sighed and wept, still gazing on the picture, which seemed to engage her by a kind of fascination. She almost fancied that the portrait breathed, and that the eyes were fixed on hers with a look of penetrating softness. Full of the emotions which the miniature had excited, she presented it to madame, whose mingled sorrow and surprise increased her curiosity. But what were the various sensations which pressed upon her heart, on learning that she had wept over the resemblance of her mother! Deprived of a mother's tenderness before she was sensible of its value, it was now only that she mourned the event which lamentation could not recall. Emilia, with an emotion as exquisite, mingled her tears with those of her sister. With eager impatience they pressed madame to disclose the cause of that sorrow which so emphatically marked the features of their mother.

'Alas! my dear children,' said madame, deeply sighing, 'you engage me in a task too severe, not only for your peace, but for mine; since in giving you the information you require, I must retrace scenes of my own life, which I wish for ever obliterated. It would, however, be both cruel and unjust to withhold an explanation so nearly interesting to you, and I will sacrifice my own ease to your wishes.

'Louisa de Bernini, your mother, was, as you well know, the only daughter of the Count de Bernini. Of the misfortunes of your family, I believe you are yet ignorant. The chief estates of the count were situated in the Val di Demona, a valley deriving its name from its vicinity to Mount AEtna, which vulgar tradition has peopled with devils. In one of those dreadful eruptions of AEtna, which deluged this valley with a flood of fire, a great part of your grandfather's domains in that quarter were laid waste. The count was at that time with a part of his family at Messina, but the countess and her son, who were in the country, were destroyed. The remaining property of the count was proportionably inconsiderable, and the loss of his wife and son deeply affected him. He retired with Louisa, his only surviving child, who was then near fifteen, to a small estate near Cattania. There was some degree of relationship between your grandfather and myself; and your mother was attached to me by the ties of sentiment, which, as we grew up, united us still more strongly than those of blood. Our pleasures and our tastes were the same; and a similarity of misfortunes might, perhaps, contribute to cement our early friendship. I, like herself, had lost a parent in the eruption of AEtna. My mother had died before I understood her value; but my father, whom I revered and tenderly loved, was destroyed by one of those terrible events; his lands were buried beneath the lava, and he left an only son and myself to mourn his fate, and encounter the evils of poverty. The count, who was our nearest surviving relation, generously took us home to his house, and declared that he considered us as his children. To amuse his leisure hours, he undertook to finish the education of my brother, who was then about seventeen, and whose rising genius promised to reward the labours of the count. Louisa and myself often shared the instruction of her father, and at those hours Orlando was generally of the party. The tranquil retirement of the count's situation, the rational employment of his time between his own studies, the education of those whom he called his children, and the conversation of a few select friends, anticipated the effect of time, and softened the asperities of his distress into a tender complacent melancholy. As for Louisa and myself, who were yet new in life, and whose spirits possessed the happy elasticity of youth, our minds gradually shifted from suffering to tranquillity, and from tranquillity to happiness. I have sometimes thought that when my brother has been reading to her a delightful passage, the countenance of Louisa discovered a tender interest, which seemed to be excited rather by the reader than by the author. These days, which were surely the most enviable of our lives, now passed in serene enjoyments, and in continual gradations of improvement.

'The count designed my brother for the army, and the time now drew nigh when he was to join the Sicilian regiment, in which he had a commission. The absent thoughts, and dejected spirits of my cousin, now discovered to me the secret which had long been concealed even from herself; for it was not till Orlando was about to depart, that she perceived how dear he was to her peace. On the eve of his departure, the count lamented, with fatherly yet manly tenderness, the distance which was soon to separate us. "But we shall meet again," said he, "when the honors of war shall have rewarded the bravery of my son." Louisa grew pale, a half suppressed sigh escaped her, and, to conceal her emotion, she turned to her harpsichord.

'My brother had a favorite dog, which, before he set off, he presented to Louisa, and committing it to her care, begged she would be kind to it, and sometimes remember its master. He checked his rising emotion, but as he turned from her, I perceived the tear that wetted his cheek. He departed, and with him the spirit of our happiness seemed to evaporate. The scenes which his presence had formerly enlivened, were now forlorn and melancholy, yet we loved to wander in what were once his favorite haunts. Louisa forbore to mention my brother even to me, but frequently, when she thought herself unobserved, she would steal to her harpsichord, and repeat the strain which she had played on the evening before his departure.

'We had the pleasure to hear from time to time that he was well: and though his own modesty threw a veil over his conduct, we could collect from other accounts that he had behaved with great bravery. At length the time of his return approached, and the enlivened spirits of Louisa declared the influence he retained in her heart. He returned, bearing public testimony of his valour in the honors which had been conferred upon him. He was received with universal joy; the count welcomed him with the pride and fondness of a father, and the villa became again the seat of happiness. His person and manners were much improved; the elegant beauty of the youth was now exchanged for the graceful dignity of manhood, and some knowledge of the world was added to that of the sciences. The joy which illumined his countenance when he met Louisa, spoke at once his admiration and his love; and the blush which her observation of it brought upon her cheek, would have discovered, even to an uninterested spectator, that this joy was mutual.

'Orlando brought with him a young Frenchman, a brother officer, who had rescued him from imminent danger in battle, and whom he introduced to the count as his preserver. The count received him with gratitude and distinction, and he was for a considerable time an inmate at the villa. His manners were singularly pleasing, and his understanding was cultivated and refined. He soon discovered a partiality for me, and he was indeed too pleasing to be seen with indifference. Gratitude for the valuable life he had preserved, was perhaps the groundwork of an esteem which soon increased into the most affectionate love. Our attachment grew stronger as our acquaintance increased; and at length the chevalier de Menon asked me of the count, who consulted my heart, and finding it favorable to the connection, proceeded to make the necessary enquiries concerning the family of the stranger. He obtained a satisfactory and pleasing account of it. The chevalier was the second son of a French gentleman of large estates in France, who had been some years deceased. He had left several sons; the family-estate, of course, devolved to the eldest, but to the two younger he had bequeathed considerable property. Our marriage was solemnized in a private manner at the villa, in the presence of the count, Louisa, and my brother. Soon after the nuptials, my husband and Orlando were remanded to their regiments. My brother's affections were now unalterably fixed upon Louisa, but a sentiment of delicacy and generosity still kept him silent. He thought, poor as he was, to solicit the hand of Louisa, would be to repay the kindness of the count with ingratitude. I have seen the inward struggles of his heart, and mine has bled for him. The count and Louisa so earnestly solicited me to remain at the villa during the campaign, that at length my husband consented. We parted—O! let me forget that period!—Had I accompanied him, all might have been well; and the long, long years of affliction which followed had been spared me.'

The horn now sounded the signal for dinner, and interrupted the narrative of Madame. Her beauteous auditors wiped the tears from their eyes, and with extreme reluctance descended to the hall. The day was occupied with company and diversions, and it was not till late in the evening that they were suffered to retire. They hastened to madame immediately upon their being released; and too much interested for sleep, and too importunate to be repulsed, solicited the sequel of her story. She objected the lateness of the hour, but at length yielded to their entreaties. They drew their chairs close to hers; and every sense being absorbed in the single one of hearing, followed her through the course of her narrative.

'My brother again departed without disclosing his sentiments; the effort it cost him was evident, but his sense of honor surmounted every opposing consideration. Louisa again drooped, and pined in silent sorrow. I lamented equally for my friend and my brother; and have a thousand times accused that delicacy as false, which withheld them from the happiness they might so easily and so innocently have obtained. The behaviour of the count, at least to my eye, seemed to indicate the satisfaction which this union would have given him. It was about this period that the marquis Mazzini first saw and became enamoured of Louisa. His proposals were very flattering, but the count forbore to exert the undue authority of a father; and he ceased to press the connection, when he perceived that Louisa was really averse to it. Louisa was sensible of the generosity of his conduct, and she could scarcely reject the alliance without a sigh, which her gratitude paid to the kindness of her father.

'But an event now happened which dissolved at once our happiness, and all our air-drawn schemes for futurity. A dispute, which it seems originated in a trifle, but soon increased to a serious degree, arose between the Chevalier de Menon and my brother. It was decided by the sword, and my dear brother fell by the hand of my husband. I shall pass over this period of my life. It is too painful for recollection. The effect of this event upon Louisa was such as may be imagined. The world was now become indifferent to her, and as she had no prospect of happiness for herself, she was unwilling to withhold it from the father who had deserved so much of her. After some time, when the marquis renewed his addresses, she gave him her hand. The characters of the marquis and his lady were in their nature too opposite to form a happy union. Of this Louisa was very soon sensible; and though the mildness of her disposition made her tamely submit to the unfeeling authority of her husband, his behaviour sunk deep in her heart, and she pined in secret. It was impossible for her to avoid opposing the character of the marquis to that of him upon whom her affections had been so fondly and so justly fixed. The comparison increased her sufferings, which soon preyed upon her constitution, and very visibly affected her health. Her situation deeply afflicted the count, and united with the infirmities of age to shorten his life.

'Upon his death, I bade adieu to my cousin, and quitted Sicily for Italy, where the Chevalier de Menon had for some time expected me. Our meeting was very affecting. My resentment towards him was done away, when I observed his pale and altered countenance, and perceived the melancholy which preyed upon his heart. All the airy vivacity of his former manner was fled, and he was devoured by unavailing grief and remorse. He deplored with unceasing sorrow the friend he had murdered, and my presence seemed to open afresh the wounds which time had begun to close. His affliction, united with my own, was almost more than I could support, but I was doomed to suffer, and endure yet more. In a subsequent engagement my husband, weary of existence, rushed into the heat of battle, and there obtained an honorable death. In a paper which he left behind him, he said it was his intention to die in that battle; that he had long wished for death, and waited for an opportunity of obtaining it without staining his own character by the cowardice of suicide, or distressing me by an act of butchery. This event gave the finishing stroke to my afflictions;—yet let me retract;—another misfortune awaited me when I least expected one. The Chevalier de Menon died without a will, and his brothers refused to give up his estate, unless I could produce a witness of my marriage. I returned to Sicily, and, to my inexpressible sorrow, found that your mother had died during my stay abroad, a prey, I fear, to grief. The priest who performed the ceremony of my marriage, having been threatened with punishment for some ecclesiastical offences, had secretly left the country; and thus was I deprived of those proofs which were necessary to authenticate my claims to the estates of my husband. His brothers, to whom I was an utter stranger, were either too prejudiced to believe, or believing, were too dishonorable to acknowledge the justice of my claims. I was therefore at once abandoned to sorrow and to poverty; a small legacy from the count de Bernini being all that now remained to me.

'When the marquis married Maria de Vellorno, which was about this period, he designed to quit Mazzini for Naples. His son was to accompany him, but it was his intention to leave you, who were both very young, to the care of some person qualified to superintend your education. My circumstances rendered the office acceptable, and my former friendship for your mother made the duty pleasing to me. The marquis was,

I believe, glad to be spared the trouble of searching further for what he had hitherto found it difficult to obtain—a person whom inclination as well as duty would bind to his interest.'

Madame ceased to speak, and Emilia and Julia wept to the memory of the mother, whose misfortunes this story recorded. The sufferings of madame, together with her former friendship for the late marchioness, endeared her to her pupils, who from this period endeavoured by every kind and delicate attention to obliterate the traces of her sorrows. Madame was sensible of this tenderness, and it was productive in some degree of the effect desired. But a subject soon after occurred, which drew off their minds from the consideration of their mother's fate to a subject more wonderful and equally interesting.

One night that Emilia and Julia had been detained by company, in ceremonial restraint, later than usual, they were induced, by the easy conversation of madame, and by the pleasure which a return to liberty naturally produces, to defer the hour of repose till the night was far advanced. They were engaged in interesting discourse, when madame, who was then speaking, was interrupted by a low hollow sound, which arose from beneath the apartment, and seemed like the closing of a door. Chilled into a silence, they listened and distinctly heard it repeated. Deadly ideas crowded upon their imaginations, and inspired a terror which scarcely allowed them to breathe. The noise lasted only for a moment, and a profound silence soon ensued. Their feelings at length relaxed, and suffered them to move to Emilia's apartment, when again they heard the same sounds. Almost distracted with fear, they rushed into madame's apartment, where Emilia sunk upon the bed and fainted. It was a considerable time ere the efforts of madame recalled her to sensation. When they were again tranquil, she employed all her endeavours to compose the spirits of the young ladies, and dissuade them from alarming the castle. Involved in dark and fearful doubts, she yet commanded her feelings, and endeavoured to assume an appearance of composure. The late behaviour of the marquis had convinced her that he was nearly connected with the mystery which hung over this part of the edifice; and she dreaded to excite his resentment by a further mention of alarms, which were perhaps only ideal, and whose reality she had certainly no means of proving.

Influenced by these considerations, she endeavoured to prevail on Emilia and Julia to await in silence some confirmation of their surmises; but their terror made this a very difficult task. They acquiesced, however, so far with her wishes, as to agree to conceal the preceding circumstances from every person but their brother, without whose protecting presence they declared it utterly impossible to pass another night in the apartments. For the remainder of this night they resolved to watch. To beguile the tediousness of the time they endeavoured to converse, but the minds of Emilia and Julia were too much affected by the late occurrence to wander from the subject. They compared this with the foregoing circumstance of the figure and the light which had appeared; their imaginations kindled wild conjectures, and they submitted their opinions to madame, entreating her to inform them sincerely, whether she believed that disembodied spirits were ever permitted to visit this earth.

'My children,' said she, 'I will not attempt to persuade you that the existence of such spirits is impossible. Who shall say that any thing is impossible to God? We know that he has made us, who are embodied spirits; he, therefore, can make unembodied spirits. If we cannot understand how such spirits exist, we should consider the limited powers of our minds, and that we cannot understand many things which are indisputably true. No one yet knows why the magnetic needle points to the north; yet you, who have never seen a magnet, do not hesitate to believe that it has this tendency, because you have been well assured of it, both from books and in conversation. Since, therefore, we are sure that nothing is impossible to God, and that such beings may exist, though we cannot tell how, we ought to consider by what evidence their existence is supported. I do not say that spirits have appeared; but if several discreet unprejudiced persons were to assure me that they had seen one, I should not be proud or bold enough to reply—'it is impossible.' Let not, however, such considerations disturb your minds. I have said thus much, because I was unwilling to impose upon your understandings; it is now your part to exercise your reason, and preserve the unmoved confidence of virtue. Such spirits, if indeed they have ever been seen, can have appeared only by the express permission of God, and for some very singular purposes; be assured that there are no beings who act unseen by him; and that, therefore, there are none from whom innocence can ever suffer harm.'

No further sounds disturbed them for that time; and before the morning dawned, weariness insensibly overcame apprehension, and sunk them in repose.

When Ferdinand learned the circumstances relative to the southern side of the castle, his imagination seized with avidity each appearance of mystery, and inspired him with an irresistible desire to penetrate the secrets of his desolate part of the fabric. He very readily consented to watch with his sisters in Julia's apartment; but as his chamber was in a remote part of the castle, there would be some difficulty in passing unobserved to her's. It was agreed, however, that when all was hushed, he should make the attempt. Having thus resolved, Emilia and Julia waited the return of night with restless and fearful impatience.

At length the family retired to rest. The castle clock had struck one, and Julia began to fear that Ferdinand had been discovered, when a knocking was heard at the door of the outer chamber.

Her heart beat with apprehensions, which reason could not justify. Madame rose, and enquiring who was there, was answered by the voice of Ferdinand. The door was cheerfully opened. They drew their chairs round him, and endeavoured to pass the time in conversation; but fear and expectation attracted all their thoughts to one subject, and madame alone preserved her composure. The hour was now come when the sounds had been heard the preceding night, and every ear was given to attention. All, however, remained quiet, and the night passed without any new alarm.

The greater part of several succeeding nights were spent in watching, but no sounds disturbed their silence. Ferdinand, in whose mind the late circumstances had excited a degree of astonishment and curiosity superior to common obstacles, determined, if possible, to gain admittance to those recesses of the castle, which had for so many years been hid from human eye. This, however, was a design which he saw little probability of accomplishing, for the keys of that part of the edifice were in the possession of the marquis, of whose late conduct he judged too well to believe he would suffer the apartments to be explored. He racked his invention for the means of getting access to them, and at length recollected that Julia's chamber formed a part of these buildings, it occurred to him, that according to the mode of building in old times, there might formerly have been a communication between them. This consideration suggested to him the possibility of a concealed door in her apartment, and he determined to survey it on the following night with great care.

CHAPTER III

The castle was buried in sleep when Ferdinand again joined his sisters in madame's apartment. With anxious curiosity they followed him to the chamber. The room was hung with tapestry. Ferdinand carefully sounded the wall which communicated with the southern buildings. From one part of it a sound was returned, which convinced him there was something less solid than stone. He removed the tapestry, and behind it appeared, to his inexpressible satisfaction, a small door. With a hand trembling through eagerness, he undrew the bolts, and was rushing forward, when he perceived that a lock withheld his passage. The keys of madame and his sisters were applied in vain, and he was compelled to submit to disappointment at the very moment when he congratulated himself on success, for he had with him no means of forcing the door.

He stood gazing on the door, and inwardly lamenting, when a low hollow sound was heard from beneath. Emilia and Julia seized his arm; and almost sinking with apprehension, listened in profound silence. A footstep was distinctly heard, as if passing through the apartment below, after which all was still. Ferdinand, fired by this confirmation of the late report, rushed on to the door, and again tried to burst his way, but it resisted all the efforts of his strength. The ladies now rejoiced in that circumstance which they so lately lamented; for the sounds had renewed their terror, and though the night passed without further disturbance, their fears were very little abated.

Ferdinand, whose mind was wholly occupied with wonder, could with difficulty await the return of night. Emilia and Julia were scarcely less impatient. They counted the minutes as they passed; and when the family retired to rest, hastened with palpitating hearts to the apartment of madame. They were soon after joined by Ferdinand, who brought with him tools for cutting away the lock of the door. They paused a few moments in the chamber in fearful silence, but no sound disturbed the stillness of night. Ferdinand applied a knife to the door, and in a short time separated the lock. The door yielded, and disclosed a large and gloomy gallery. He took a light. Emilia and Julia, fearful of remaining in the chamber, resolved to accompany him, and each seizing an arm of madame, they followed in silence. The gallery was in many parts falling to decay, the ceiling was broke, and the window-shutters shattered, which, together with the dampness of the walls, gave the place an air of wild desolation.

They passed lightly on, for their steps ran in whispering echoes through the gallery, and often did Julia cast a fearful glance around.

The gallery terminated in a large old stair-case, which led to a hall below; on the left appeared several doors which seemed to lead to separate apartments. While they hesitated which course to pursue, a light flashed faintly up the stair-case, and in a moment after passed away; at the same time was heard the sound of a distant footstep. Ferdinand drew his sword and sprang forward; his companions, screaming with terror, ran back to madame's apartment.

Ferdinand descended a large vaulted hall; he crossed it towards a low arched door, which was left half open, and through which streamed a ray of light. The door opened upon a narrow winding passage; he entered, and the light retiring, was quickly lost in the windings of the place. Still he went on. The passage grew narrower, and the frequent fragments of loose stone made it now difficult to proceed. A low door closed the avenue, resembling that by which he had entered. He opened it, and discovered a square room, from whence rose a winding stair-case, which led up the south tower of the castle. Ferdinand paused to listen; the sound of steps was ceased, and all was profoundly silent. A door on the right attracted his notice; he tried to open it, but it was fastened. He concluded, therefore, that the person, if indeed a human being it was that bore the light he had seen, had passed up the tower. After a momentary hesitation, he determined to ascend the stair-case, but its ruinous condition made this an adventure of some difficulty. The steps were decayed and broken, and the looseness of the stones rendered a footing very insecure. Impelled by an irresistible curiosity, he was undismayed, and began the ascent. He had not proceeded very far, when the stones of a step which his foot had just quitted, loosened by his weight, gave way; and dragging with them those adjoining, formed a chasm in the stair-case that terrified even Ferdinand, who was left tottering on the suspended half of the steps, in momentary expectation of falling to the bottom with the stone on which he rested. In the terror which this occasioned, he attempted to save himself by catching at a kind of beam which projected over the stairs, when the lamp dropped from his hand, and he was left in total darkness. Terror now usurped the place of every other interest, and he was utterly perplexed how to proceed. He feared to go on, lest the steps above, as infirm as those below, should yield to his weight;—to return was impracticable, for the darkness precluded the possibility of discovering a means. He determined, therefore, to remain in this situation till light should dawn through the narrow grates in the walls, and enable him to contrive some method of letting himself down to the ground.

He had remained here above an hour, when he suddenly heard a voice from below. It seemed to come from the passage leading to the tower, and perceptibly drew nearer. His agitation was now extreme, for he had no power of defending himself, and while he remained in this state of torturing expectation, a blaze of light burst upon the stair-case beneath him. In the succeeding moment he heard his own name sounded from below. His apprehensions instantly vanished, for he distinguished the voices of madame and his sisters.

They had awaited his return in all the horrors of apprehension, till at length all fear for themselves was lost in their concern for him; and they, who so lately had not dared to enter this part of the edifice, now undauntedly searched it in quest of Ferdinand. What were their emotions when they discovered his perilous situation!

The light now enabled him to take a more accurate survey of the place. He perceived that some few stones of the steps which had fallen still remained attached to the wall, but he feared to trust to their support only. He observed, however, that the wall itself was partly decayed, and consequently rugged with the corners of half-worn stones. On these small projections he contrived, with the assistance of the steps already mentioned, to suspend himself, and at length gained the unbroken part of the stairs in safety. It is difficult to determine which individual of the party rejoiced most at this escape. The morning now dawned, and Ferdinand desisted for the present from farther enquiry.

The interest which these mysterious circumstances excited in the mind of Julia, had withdrawn her attention from a subject more dangerous to its peace. The image of

Vereza, notwithstanding, would frequently intrude upon her fancy; and, awakening the recollection of happy emotions, would call forth a sigh which all her efforts could not suppress. She loved to indulge the melancholy of her heart in the solitude of the woods. One evening she took her lute to a favorite spot on the seashore, and resigning herself to a pleasing sadness, touched some sweet and plaintive airs. The purple flush of evening was diffused over the heavens. The sun, involved in clouds of splendid and innumerable hues, was setting o'er the distant waters, whose clear bosom glowed with rich reflection. The beauty of the scene, the soothing murmur of the high trees, waved by the light air which overshadowed her, and the soft shelling of the waves that flowed gently in upon the shores, insensibly sunk her mind into a state of repose. She touched the chords of her lute in sweet and wild melody, and sung the following ode:

EVENING

Evening veil'd in dewy shades,
    Slowly sinks upon the main;
See th'empurpled glory fades,
    Beneath her sober, chasten'd reign.

Around her car the pensive Hours,
    In sweet illapses meet the sight,
Crown'd their brows with closing flow'rs
    Rich with chrystal dews of night.

Her hands, the dusky hues arrange
    O'er the fine tints of parting day;
Insensibly the colours change,
    And languish into soft decay.

Wide o'er the waves her shadowy veil she draws.
    As faint they die along the distant shores;
Through the still air I mark each solemn pause,
    Each rising murmur which the wild wave pours.

A browner shadow spreads upon the air,
    And o'er the scene a pensive grandeur throws;
The rocks—the woods a wilder beauty wear,
    And the deep wave in softer music flows;

And now the distant view where vision fails,
    Twilight and grey obscurity pervade;
Tint following tint each dark'ning object veils,
    Till all the landscape sinks into the shade.

Oft from the airy steep of some lone hill,
    While sleeps the scene beneath the purple glow:
And evening lives o'er all serene and still,
    Wrapt let me view the magic world below!

And catch the dying gale that swells remote,

That steals the sweetness from the shepherd's flute:
The distant torrent's melancholy note
   And the soft warblings of the lover's lute.

Still through the deep'ning gloom of bow'ry shades
   To Fancy's eye fantastic forms appear;
Low whisp'ring echoes steal along the glades
   And thrill the ear with wildly-pleasing fear.

Parent of shades!—of silence!—dewy airs!
   Of solemn musing, and of vision wild!
To thee my soul her pensive tribute bears,
   And hails thy gradual step, thy influence mild.

Having ceased to sing, her fingers wandered over the lute in melancholy symphony, and for some moments she remained lost in the sweet sensations which the music and the scenery had inspired. She was awakened from her reverie, by a sigh that stole from among the trees, and directing her eyes whence it came, beheld—Hippolitus! A thousand sweet and mingled emotions pressed upon her heart, yet she scarcely dared to trust the evidence of sight. He advanced, and throwing himself at her feet: 'Suffer me,' said he, in a tremulous voice, 'to disclose to you the sentiments which you have inspired, and to offer you the effusions of a heart filled only with love and admiration.' 'Rise, my lord,' said Julia, moving from her seat with an air of dignity, 'that attitude is neither becoming you to use, or me to suffer. The evening is closing, and Ferdinand will be impatient to see you.'

'Never will I rise, madam,' replied the count, with an impassioned air, 'till'—He was interrupted by the marchioness, who at this moment entered the grove. On observing the position of the count she was retiring. 'Stay, madam,' said Julia, almost sinking under her confusion. 'By no means,' replied the marchioness, in a tone of irony, 'my presence would only interrupt a very agreeable scene. The count, I see, is willing to pay you his earliest respects.' Saying this she disappeared, leaving Julia distressed and offended, and the count provoked at the intrusion. He attempted to renew the subject, but Julia hastily followed the steps of the marchioness, and entered the castle.

The scene she had witnessed, raised in the marchioness a tumult of dreadful emotions. Love, hatred, and jealousy, raged by turns in her heart, and defied all power of controul. Subjected to their alternate violence, she experienced a misery more acute than any she had yet known. Her imagination, invigorated by opposition, heightened to her the graces of Hippolitus; her bosom glowed with more intense passion, and her brain was at length exasperated almost to madness.

In Julia this sudden and unexpected interview excited a mingled emotion of love and vexation, which did not soon subside. At length, however, the delightful consciousness of Vereza's love bore her high above every other sensation; again the scene more brightly glowed, and again her fancy overcame the possibility of evil.

During the evening a tender and timid respect distinguished the behaviour of the count towards Julia, who, contented with the certainty of being loved, resolved to conceal her sentiments till an explanation of his abrupt departure from Mazzini, and subsequent absence, should have dissipated the shadow of mystery which hung over this part of his conduct. She observed that the marchioness pursued her with steady and constant observation, and she carefully avoided affording the count an opportunity of renewing the subject of the preceding interview, which, whenever he approached her, seemed to tremble on his lips.

Night returned, and Ferdinand repaired to the chamber of Julia to pursue his enquiry. Here he had not long remained, when the strange and alarming sounds which had been heard on the preceding night were repeated. The circumstance that now sunk in terror the minds of Emilia and Julia, fired with new wonder that of Ferdinand, who seizing a light, darted through the discovered door, and almost instantly disappeared.

He descended into the same wild hall he had passed on the preceding night. He had scarcely reached the bottom of the stair-case, when a feeble light gleamed across the hall, and his eye caught the glimpse of a figure retiring through the low arched door which led to the south tower. He drew his sword and rushed on. A faint sound died away along the passage, the windings of which prevented his seeing the figure he pursued. Of this, indeed, he had obtained so slight a view, that he scarcely knew whether it bore the impression of a human form. The light quickly disappeared, and he heard the door that opened upon the tower suddenly close. He reached it, and forcing it open, sprang forward; but the place was dark and solitary, and there was no appearance of any person having passed along it. He looked up the tower, and the chasm which the stair-case exhibited, convinced him that no human being could have passed up. He stood silent and amazed; examining the place with an eye of strict enquiry, he perceived a door, which was partly concealed by hanging stairs, and which till now had escaped his notice. Hope invigorated curiosity, but his expectation was quickly disappointed, for this door also was fastened. He tried in vain to force it. He knocked, and a hollow sullen sound ran in echoes through the place, and died away at a distance. It was evident that beyond this door were chambers of considerable extent, but after long and various attempts to reach them, he was obliged to desist, and he quitted the tower as ignorant and more dissatisfied than he had entered it. He returned to the hall, which he now for the first time deliberately surveyed. It was a spacious and desolate apartment, whose lofty roof rose into arches supported by pillars of black marble. The same substance inlaid the floor, and formed the stair-case. The windows were high and gothic. An air of proud sublimity, united with singular wildness, characterized the place, at the extremity of which arose several gothic arches, whose dark shade veiled in obscurity the extent beyond. On the left hand appeared two doors, each of which was fastened, and on the right the grand entrance from the courts. Ferdinand determined to explore the dark recess which terminated his view, and as he traversed the hall, his imagination, affected by the surrounding scene, often multiplied the echoes of his footsteps into uncertain sounds of strange and fearful import.

He reached the arches, and discovered beyond a kind of inner hall, of considerable extent, which was closed at the farther end by a pair of massy folding-doors, heavily ornamented with carving. They were fastened by a lock, and defied his utmost strength.

As he surveyed the place in silent wonder, a sullen groan arose from beneath the spot where he stood. His blood ran cold at the sound, but silence returning, and continuing unbroken, he attributed his alarm to the illusion of a fancy, which terror had impregnated. He made another effort to force the door, when a groan was repeated more hollow, and more dreadful than the first. At this moment all his courage forsook him; he quitted the door, and hastened to the stair-case, which he ascended almost breathless with terror.

He found Madame de Menon and his sisters awaiting his return in the most painful anxiety; and, thus disappointed in all his endeavours to penetrate the secret of these buildings, and fatigued with fruitless search, he resolved to suspend farther enquiry.

When he related the circumstances of his late adventure, the terror of Emilia and Julia was heightened to a degree that overcame every prudent consideration. Their apprehension of the marquis's displeasure was lost in a stronger feeling, and they resolved no longer to remain in apartments which offered only terrific images to their fancy. Madame de Menon almost equally alarmed, and more perplexed, by this combination of strange and unaccountable circumstances, ceased to oppose their design. It was resolved, therefore, that on the following day madame should acquaint the marchioness with such particulars of the late occurrence as their purpose made it necessary she should know, concealing their knowledge of the hidden door, and the incidents immediately dependant on it; and that madame should entreat a change of apartments.

Madame accordingly waited on the marchioness. The marchioness having listened to the account at first with surprise, and afterwards with indifference, condescended to reprove madame for encouraging superstitious belief in the minds of her young charge. She concluded with ridiculing as fanciful the circumstances related, and with refusing, on account of the numerous visitants at the castle, the request preferred to her.

It is true the castle was crowded with visitors; the former apartments of Madame de Menon were the only ones unoccupied, and these were in magnificent preparation for the pleasure of the marchioness, who was unaccustomed to sacrifice her own wishes to the comfort of those around her. She therefore treated lightly the subject, which, seriously attended to, would have endangered her new plan of delight.

But Emilia and Julia were too seriously terrified to obey the scruples of delicacy, or to be easily repulsed. They prevailed on Ferdinand to represent their situation to the marquis.

Meanwhile Hippolitus, who had passed the night in a state of sleepless anxiety, watched, with busy impatience, an opportunity of more fully disclosing to Julia the passion which glowed in his heart. The first moment in which he beheld her, had awakened in him an admiration which had since ripened into a sentiment more tender. He had been prevented formally declaring his passion by the circumstance which so suddenly called him to Naples. This was the dangerous illness of the Marquis de Lomelli, his near and much-valued relation. But it was a task too painful to depart in silence, and he contrived to inform Julia of his sentiments in the air which she heard so sweetly sung beneath her window.

When Hippolitus reached Naples, the marquis was yet living, but expired a few days after his arrival, leaving the count heir to the small possessions which remained from the extravagance of their ancestors.

The business of adjusting his rights had till now detained him from Sicily, whither he came for the sole purpose of declaring his love. Here unexpected obstacles awaited him. The jealous vigilance of the marchioness conspired with the delicacy of Julia, to withhold from him the opportunity he so anxiously sought.

When Ferdinand entered upon the subject of the southern buildings to the marquis, he carefully avoided mentioning the hidden door. The marquis listened for some time to the relation in gloomy silence, but at length assuming an air of displeasure, reprehended Ferdinand for yielding his confidence to those idle alarms, which he said were the suggestions of a timid imagination. 'Alarms,' continued he, 'which will readily find admittance to the weak mind of a woman, but which the firmer nature of man should disdain.—Degenerate boy! Is it thus you reward my care? Do I live to see my son the sport of every idle tale a woman may repeat? Learn to trust reason and your senses, and you will then be worthy of my attention.'

The marquis was retiring, and Ferdinand now perceived it necessary to declare, that he had himself witnessed the sounds he mentioned. 'Pardon me, my lord,' said he, 'in the late instance I have been just to your command—my senses have been the only evidences I have trusted. I have heard those sounds which I cannot doubt.' The marquis appeared shocked. Ferdinand perceived the change, and urged the subject so vigorously, that the marquis, suddenly assuming a look of grave importance, commanded him to attend him in the evening in his closet.

Ferdinand in passing from the marquis met Hippolitus. He was pacing the gallery in much seeming agitation, but observing Ferdinand, he advanced to him. 'I am ill at heart,' said he, in a melancholy tone, 'assist me with your advice. We will step into this apartment, where we can converse without interruption.'

'You are not ignorant,' said he, throwing himself into a chair, 'of the tender sentiments which your sister Julia has inspired. I entreat you by that sacred friendship which has so long united us, to afford me an opportunity of pleading my passion. Her heart, which is so susceptible of other impressions, is, I fear, insensible to love. Procure me, however, the satisfaction of certainty upon a point where the tortures of suspence are surely the most intolerable.'

'Your penetration,' replied Ferdinand, 'has for once forsaken you, else you would now be spared the tortures of which you complain, for you would have discovered what I have long observed, that Julia regards you with a partial eye.'

'Do not,' said Hippolitus, 'make disappointment more terrible by flattery; neither suffer the partiality of friendship to mislead your judgment. Your perceptions are affected by the warmth of your feelings, and because you think I deserve her distinction, you believe I possess it. Alas! you deceive yourself, but not me!'

'The very reverse,' replied Ferdinand; 'tis you who deceive yourself, or rather it is the delicacy of the passion which animates you, and which will ever operate against your clear perception of a truth in which your happiness is so deeply involved. Believe me, I speak not without reason:—she loves you.'

At these words Hippolitus started from his seat, and clasping his hands in fervent joy,

'Enchanting sounds!' cried he, in a voice tenderly impassioned; 'could I but believe ye!—could I but believe ye-this world were paradise!'

During this exclamation, the emotions of Julia, who sat in her closet adjoining, can with difficulty be imagined. A door which opened into it from the apartment where this conversation was held, was only half closed. Agitated with the pleasure this declaration excited, she yet trembled with apprehension lest she should be discovered. She hardly dared to breathe, much less to move across the closet to the door, which opened upon the gallery, whence she might probably have escaped unnoticed, lest the sound of her step should betray her. Compelled, therefore, to remain where she was, she sat in a state of fearful distress, which no colour of language can paint.

'Alas!' resumed Hippolitus, 'I too eagerly admit the possibility of what I wish. If you mean that I should really believe you, confirm your assertion by some proof.'—'Readily,' rejoined Ferdinand.

The heart of Julia beat quick.

'When you was so suddenly called to Naples upon the illness of the Marquis Lomelli, I marked her conduct well, and in that read the sentiments of her heart. On the following morning, I observed in her countenance a restless anxiety which I had never seen before. She watched the entrance of every person with an eager expectation, which was as often succeeded by evident disappointment. At dinner your departure was mentioned:—she spilt the wine she was carrying to her lips, and for the remainder of the day was spiritless and melancholy. I saw her ineffectual struggles to conceal the oppression at her heart. Since that time she has seized every opportunity of withdrawing from company. The gaiety with which she was so lately charmed—charmed her no longer; she became pensive, retired, and I have often heard her singing in some lonely spot, the most moving and tender airs. Your return produced a visible and instantaneous alteration; she has now resumed her gaiety; and the soft confusion of her countenance, whenever you approach, might alone suffice to convince you of the truth of my assertion.'

'O! talk for ever thus!' sighed Hippolitus. 'These words are so sweet, so soothing to my soul, that I could listen till I forgot I had a wish beyond them. Yes!—Ferdinand, these circumstances are not to be doubted, and conviction opens upon my mind a flow of extacy I never knew till now. O! lead me to her, that I may speak the sentiments which swell my heart.'

They arose, when Julia, who with difficulty had supported herself, now impelled by an irresistible fear of instant discovery, rose also, and moved softly towards the gallery. The sound of her step alarmed the count, who, apprehensive lest his conversation had been overheard, was anxious to be satisfied whether any person was in the closet. He rushed in, and discovered Julia! She caught at a chair to support her trembling frame; and overwhelmed with mortifying sensations, sunk into it, and hid her face in her robe. Hippolitus threw himself at her feet, and seizing her hand, pressed it to his lips in expressive silence. Some moments passed before the confusion of either would suffer them to speak. At length recovering his voice, 'Can you, madam,' said he, 'forgive this intrusion, so unintentional? or will it deprive me of that esteem which I have but lately ventured to believe I possessed, and which I value more than existence itself. O! speak my pardon! Let me not believe that a single accident has destroyed my peace for ever.'—'If your peace, sir, depends upon a knowledge of my esteem,' said Julia, in a tremulous voice, 'that peace is already secure. If I wished even to deny the partiality I feel, it would now be useless; and since I no longer wish this, it would also be painful.' Hippolitus could only weep his thanks over the hand he still held. 'Be sensible, however, of the delicacy of my situation,' continued she, rising, 'and suffer me to withdraw.' Saying this she quitted the closet, leaving Hippolitus overcome with this sweet confirmation of his wishes, and Ferdinand not yet recovered from the painful surprize which the discovery of Julia had excited. He was deeply sensible of the confusion he had occasioned her, and knew that apologies would not restore the composure he had so cruelly yet unwarily disturbed.

Ferdinand awaited the hour appointed by the marquis in impatient curiosity. The solemn air which the marquis assumed when he commanded him to attend, had deeply impressed his mind. As the time drew nigh, expectation increased, and every moment seemed to linger into hours. At length he repaired to the closet, where he did not remain long before the marquis entered. The same chilling solemnity marked his manner. He locked the door of the closet, and seating himself, addressed Ferdinand as follows:—

'I am now going to repose in you a confidence which will severely prove the strength of your honour. But before I disclose a secret, hitherto so carefully concealed, and now reluctantly told, you must swear to preserve on this subject an eternal silence. If you doubt the steadiness of your discretion—now declare it, and save yourself from the infamy, and the fatal consequences, which may attend a breach of your oath;—if, on the contrary, you believe yourself capable of a strict integrity—now accept the terms, and receive the secret I offer.' Ferdinand was awed by this exordium—the impatience of curiosity was for a while suspended, and he hesitated whether he should receive the secret upon such terms. At length he signified his consent, and the marquis arising, drew his sword from the scabbard.—'Here,' said he, offering it to Ferdinand, 'seal your vows—swear by this sacred pledge of honor never to repeat what I shall now reveal.' Ferdinand vowed upon the sword, and raising his eyes to heaven, solemnly swore. The marquis then resumed his seat, and proceeded.

'You are now to learn that, about a century ago, this castle was in the possession of Vincent, third marquis of Mazzini, my grandfather. At that time there existed an inveterate hatred between our family and that of della Campo. I shall not now revert to the origin of the animosity, or relate the particulars of the consequent feuds—suffice it to observe, that by the power of our family, the della Campos were unable to preserve their former consequence in Sicily, and they have therefore quitted it for a foreign land to live in unmolested security. To return to my subject.—My grandfather, believing his life endangered by his enemy, planted spies upon him. He employed some of the numerous banditti who sought protection in his service, and after some weeks past in waiting for an opportunity, they seized Henry della Campo, and brought him secretly to this castle. He was for some time confined in a close chamber of the southern buildings, where he expired; by what means I shall forbear to mention. The plan had been so well conducted, and the secrecy so strictly preserved, that every endeavour of his family to trace the means of his disappearance proved ineffectual. Their conjectures, if they fell upon our family, were supported by no proof; and the della Campos are to this day ignorant of the mode of his death. A rumour had prevailed long before the death of my father, that the southern buildings of the castle were haunted. I disbelieved the fact, and treated it accordingly. One night, when every human being of the castle, except myself, was retired to rest, I had such strong and dreadful proofs of the general assertion, that even at this moment I cannot recollect them without horror. Let me, if possible, forget them. From that moment I forsook those buildings; they have ever since been shut up, and the circumstance I have mentioned, is the true reason why I have resided so little at the castle.'

Ferdinand listened to this narrative in silent horror. He remembered the temerity with which he had dared to penetrate those apartments—the light, and figure he had seen—and, above all, his situation in the stair-case of the tower. Every nerve thrilled at the recollection; and the terrors of remembrance almost equalled those of reality.

The marquis permitted his daughters to change their apartments, but he commanded Ferdinand to tell them, that, in granting their request, he consulted their ease only, and was himself by no means convinced of its propriety. They were accordingly reinstated in their former chambers, and the great room only of madame's apartments was reserved for the marchioness, who expressed her discontent to the marquis in terms of mingled censure and lamentation. The marquis privately reproved his daughters, for what he termed the idle fancies of a weak mind; and desired them no more to disturb the peace of the castle with the subject of their late fears. They received this reproof with silent submission—too much pleased with the success of their suit to be susceptible of any emotion but joy.

Ferdinand, reflecting on the late discovery, was shocked to learn, what was now forced upon his belief, that he was the descendant of a murderer. He now knew that innocent blood had been shed in the castle, and that the walls were still the haunt of an unquiet spirit, which seemed to call aloud for retribution on the posterity of him who had disturbed its eternal rest. Hippolitus perceived his dejection, and entreated that he might participate his uneasiness; but Ferdinand, who had hitherto been frank and ingenuous, was now inflexibly reserved. 'Forbear,' said he, 'to urge a discovery of what I am not permitted to reveal; this is the only point upon which I conjure you to be silent, and this even to you, I cannot explain.' Hippolitus was surprized, but pressed the subject no farther.

Julia, though she had been extremely mortified by the circumstances attendant on the discovery of her sentiments to Hippolitus, experienced, after the first shock had subsided, an emotion more pleasing than painful. The late conversation had painted in strong colours the attachment of her lover. His diffidence—his slowness to perceive the effect of his merit—his succeeding rapture, when conviction was at length forced upon his mind; and his conduct upon discovering Julia, proved to her at once the delicacy and the strength of his passion, and she yielded her heart to sensations of pure and unmixed delight. She was roused from this state of visionary happiness, by a summons from the marquis to attend him in the library. A circumstance so unusual surprized her, and she obeyed with trembling curiosity. She found him pacing the room in deep thought, and she had shut the door before he perceived her. The authoritative severity in his countenance alarmed her, and prepared her for a subject of importance. He seated himself by her, and continued a moment silent. At length, steadily observing her, 'I sent for you, my child,' said he, 'to declare the honor which awaits you. The Duke de Luovo has solicited your hand. An alliance so splendid was beyond my expectation. You will receive the distinction with the gratitude it claims, and prepare for the celebration of the nuptials.'

This speech fell like the dart of death upon the heart of Julia. She sat motionless—stupified and deprived of the power of utterance. The marquis observed her consternation; and mistaking its cause, 'I acknowledge,' said he, 'that there is somewhat abrupt in this affair; but the joy occasioned by a distinction so unmerited on your part, ought to overcome the little feminine weakness you might otherwise indulge. Retire and compose yourself; and observe,' continued he, in a stern voice, 'this is no time for finesse.' These words roused Julia from her state of horrid stupefaction. 'O! sir,' said she, throwing herself at his feet, 'forbear to enforce authority upon a point where to obey you would be worse than death; if, indeed, to obey you were possible.'—'Cease,' said the marquis, 'this affectation, and practice what becomes you.'—'Pardon me, my lord,' she replied, 'my distress is, alas! unfeigned. I cannot love the duke.'—'Away!' interrupted the marquis, 'nor tempt my rage with objections thus childish and absurd.'—'Yet hear me, my lord,' said Julia, tears swelling in her eyes, 'and pity the sufferings of a child, who never till this moment has dared to dispute your commands.'

'Nor shall she now,' said the marquis. 'What—when wealth, honor, and distinction, are laid at my feet, shall they be refused, because a foolish girl—a very baby, who knows not good from evil, cries, and says she cannot love! Let me not think of it—My just anger may, perhaps, out-run discretion, and tempt me to chastise your folly.—Attend to what I say—accept the duke, or quit this castle for ever, and wander where you will.' Saying this, he burst away, and Julia, who had hung weeping upon his knees, fell prostrate upon the floor. The violence of the fall completed the effect of her distress, and she fainted. In this state she remained a considerable time. When she recovered her senses, the recollection of her calamity burst upon her mind with a force that almost again overwhelmed her. She at length raised herself from the ground, and moved towards her own apartment, but had scarcely reached the great gallery, when Hippolitus entered it. Her trembling limbs would no longer support her; she caught at a bannister to save herself; and Hippolitus, with all his speed, was scarcely in time to prevent her falling. The pale distress exhibited in her countenance terrified him, and he anxiously enquired concerning it. She could answer him only with her tears, which she found it impossible to suppress; and gently disengaging herself, tottered to her closet. Hippolitus followed her to the door, but desisted from further importunity. He pressed her hand to his lips in tender silence, and withdrew, surprized and alarmed.

Julia, resigning herself to despair, indulged in solitude the excess of her grief. A calamity, so dreadful as the present, had never before presented itself to her imagination. The union proposed would have been hateful to her, even if she had no prior attachment; what then must have been her distress, when she had given her heart to him who deserved all her admiration, and returned all her affection.

The Duke de Luovo was of a character very similar to that of the marquis. The love of power was his ruling passion;—with him no gentle or generous sentiment meliorated the harshness of authority, or directed it to acts of beneficence. He delighted in simple undisguised tyranny. He had been twice married, and the unfortunate women subjected to his power, had fallen victims to the slow but corroding hand of sorrow. He had one son, who some years before had escaped the tyranny of his father, and had not been since heard of. At the late festival the duke had seen Julia; and her beauty made so strong an impression upon him, that he had been induced now to solicit her hand. The marquis, delighted with the prospect of a connection so flattering to his favorite passion, readily granted his consent, and immediately sealed it with a promise.

Julia remained for the rest of the day shut up in her closet, where the tender efforts of Madame and Emilia were exerted to soften her distress. Towards the close of evening Ferdinand entered. Hippolitus, shocked at her absence, had requested him to visit her, to alleviate her affliction, and, if possible, to discover its cause. Ferdinand, who tenderly loved his sister, was alarmed by the words of Hippolitus, and immediately sought her. Her eyes were swelled with weeping, and her countenance was but too expressive of the state of her mind. Ferdinand's distress, when told of his father's conduct, was scarcely less than her own. He had pleased himself with the hope of uniting the sister of his heart with the friend whom he loved. An act of cruel authority now dissolved the fairy dream of happiness which his fancy had formed, and destroyed the peace of those most dear to him. He sat for a long time silent and dejected; at length, starting from his melancholy reverie, he bad Julia good-night, and returned to Hippolitus, who was waiting for him with anxious impatience in the north hall.

Ferdinand dreaded the effect of that despair, which the intelligence he had to communicate would produce in the mind of Hippolitus. He revolved some means of softening the dreadful truth; but Hippolitus, quick to apprehend the evil which love taught him to fear, seized at once upon the reality. 'Tell me all,' said he, in a tone of assumed firmness. 'I am prepared for the worst.' Ferdinand related the decree of the marquis, and Hippolitus soon sunk into an excess of grief which defied, as much as it required, the powers of alleviation.

Julia, at length, retired to her chamber, but the sorrow which occupied her mind withheld the blessings of sleep. Distracted and restless she arose, and gently opened the window of her apartment. The night was still, and not a breath disturbed the surface of the waters. The moon shed a mild radiance over the waves, which in gentle undulations flowed upon the sands. The scene insensibly tranquilized her spirits. A tender and pleasing melancholy diffused itself over her mind; and as she mused, she heard the dashing of distant oars. Presently she perceived upon the light surface of the sea a small boat. The sound of the oars ceased, and a solemn strain of harmony (such as fancy wafts from the abodes of the blessed) stole upon the silence of night. A chorus of voices now swelled upon the air, and died away at a distance. In the strain Julia recollected the midnight hymn to the virgin, and holy enthusiasm filled her heart. The chorus was repeated, accompanied by a solemn striking of oars. A sigh of exstacy stole from her bosom. Silence returned. The divine melody she had heard calmed the tumult of her mind, and she sunk in sweet repose.

She arose in the morning refreshed by light slumbers; but the recollection of her sorrows soon returned with new force, and sickening faintness overcame her. In this situation she received a message from the marquis to attend him instantly. She obeyed, and he bade her prepare to receive the duke, who that morning purposed to visit the castle. He commanded her to attire herself richly, and to welcome him with smiles. Julia submitted in silence. She saw the marquis was inflexibly resolved, and she withdrew to indulge the anguish of her heart, and prepare for this detested interview.

The clock had struck twelve, when a flourish of trumpets announced the approach of the duke. The heart of Julia sunk at the sound, and she threw herself on a sopha, overwhelmed with bitter sensations. Here she was soon disturbed by a message from the marquis. She arose, and tenderly embracing Emilia, their tears for some moments flowed together. At length, summoning all her fortitude, she descended to the hall, where she was met by the marquis. He led her to the saloon in which the duke sat, with whom having conversed a short time, he withdrew. The emotion of Julia at this instant was beyond any thing she had before suffered; but by a sudden and strange exertion of fortitude, which the force of desperate calamity sometimes affords us, but which inferior sorrow toils after in vain, she recovered her composure, and resumed her natural dignity. For a moment she wondered at herself, and she formed the dangerous resolution of throwing herself upon the generosity of the duke, by acknowledging her reluctance to the engagement, and soliciting him to withdraw his suit.

The duke approached her with an air of proud condescension; and taking her hand, placed himself beside her. Having paid some formal and general compliments to her beauty, he proceeded to profess himself her admirer. She listened for some time to his professions, and when he appeared willing to hear her, she addressed him—'I am justly sensible, my lord, of the distinction you offer me, and must lament that respectful gratitude is the only sentiment I can return. Nothing can more strongly prove my confidence in your generosity, than when I confess to you, that parental authority urges me to give my hand whither my heart cannot accompany it.'

She paused—the duke continued silent.—''Tis you only, my lord, who can release me from a situation so distressing; and to your goodness and justice I appeal, certain that necessity will excuse the singularity of my conduct, and that I shall not appeal in vain.'

The duke was embarrassed—a flush of pride overspread his countenance, and he seemed endeavouring to stifle the feelings that swelled his heart. 'I had been prepared, madam,' said he, 'to expect a very different reception, and had certainly no reason to believe that the Duke de Luovo was likely to sue in vain. Since, however, madam, you acknowledge that you have already disposed of your affections, I shall certainly be very willing, if the marquis will release me from our mutual engagements, to resign you to a more favored lover.'

'Pardon me, my lord,' said Julia, blushing, 'suffer me to'—'I am not easily deceived, madam,' interrupted the duke,—'your conduct can be attributed only to the influence of a prior attachment; and though for so young a lady, such a circumstance is somewhat extraordinary, I have certainly no right to arraign your choice. Permit me to wish you a good morning.' He bowed low, and quitted the room. Julia now experienced a new distress; she dreaded the resentment of the marquis, when he should be informed of her conversation with the duke, of whose character she now judged too justly not to repent the confidence she had reposed in him.

The duke, on quitting Julia, went to the marquis, with whom he remained in conversation some hours. When he had left the castle, the marquis sent for his daughter, and poured forth his resentment with all the violence of threats, and all the acrimony of contempt. So severely did he ridicule the idea of her disposing of her heart, and so dreadfully did he denounce vengeance on her disobedience, that she scarcely thought herself safe in his presence. She stood trembling and confused, and heard his reproaches without the power to reply. At length the marquis informed her, that the nuptials would be solemnized on the third day from the present; and as he quitted the room, a flood of tears came to her relief, and saved her from fainting.

Julia passed the remainder of the day in her closet with Emilia. Night returned, but brought her no peace. She sat long after the departure of Emilia; and to beguile recollection, she selected a favorite author, endeavouring to revive those sensations his page had once excited. She opened to a passage, the tender sorrow of which was applicable to her own situation, and her tears flowed wean. Her grief was soon suspended by apprehension. Hitherto a deadly silence had reigned through the castle, interrupted only by the wind, whose low sound crept at intervals through the galleries. She now thought she heard a footstep near her door, but presently all was still, for she believed she had been deceived by the wind. The succeeding moment, however, convinced her of her error, for she distinguished the low whisperings of some persons in the gallery. Her spirits, already weakened by sorrow, deserted her: she was seized with an universal terror, and presently afterwards a low voice called her from without, and the door was opened by Ferdinand.

She shrieked, and fainted. On recovering, she found herself supported by Ferdinand and Hippolitus, who had stolen this moment of silence and security to gain admittance to her presence. Hippolitus came to urge a proposal which despair only could have suggested. 'Fly,' said he, 'from the authority of a father who abuses his power, and assert the liberty of choice, which nature assigned you. Let the desperate situation of my hopes plead excuse for the apparent boldness of this address, and let the man who exists but for you be the means of saving you from destruction. Alas! madam, you are silent, and perhaps I have forfeited, by this proposal, the confidence I so lately flattered myself I possessed. If so, I will submit to my fate in silence, and will to-morrow quit a scene which presents only images of distress to my mind.'

Julia could speak but with her tears. A variety of strong and contending emotions struggled at her breast, and suppressed the power of utterance. Ferdinand seconded the proposal of the count. 'It is unnecessary,' my sister, said he, 'to point out the misery which awaits you here. I love you too well tamely to suffer you to be sacrificed to ambition, and to a passion still more hateful. I now glory in calling Hippolitus my friend—let me ere long receive him as a brother. I can give no stronger testimony of my esteem for his character, than in the wish I now express. Believe me he has a heart worthy of your acceptance—a heart noble and expansive as your own.'—'Ah, cease,' said Julia, 'to dwell upon a character of whose worth I am fully sensible. Your kindness and his merit can never be forgotten by her whose misfortunes you have so generously suffered to interest you.' She paused in silent hesitation. A sense of delicacy made her hesitate upon the decision which her heart so warmly prompted. If she fled with Hippolitus, she would avoid one evil, and encounter another. She would escape the dreadful destiny awaiting her, but must, perhaps, sully the purity of that reputation, which was dearer to her than existence. In a mind like hers, exquisitely susceptible of the pride of honor, this fear was able to counteract every other consideration, and to keep her intentions in a state of painful suspense. She sighed deeply, and continued silent. Hippolitus was alarmed by the calm distress which her countenance exhibited. 'O! Julia,' said he, 'relieve me from this dreadful suspense!—speak to me—explain this silence.' She looked mournfully upon him—her lips moved, but no sounds were uttered. As he repeated his question, she waved her hand, and sunk back in her chair. She had not fainted, but continued some time in a state of stupor not less alarming. The importance of the present question, operating upon her mind, already harassed by distress, had produced a temporary suspension of reason. Hippolitus hung over her in an agony not to be described, and Ferdinand vainly repeated her name. At length uttering a deep sigh, she raised herself, and, like one awakened from a dream, gazed around her. Hippolitus thanked God fervently in his heart. 'Tell me but that you are well,' said he, 'and that I may dare to hope, and we will leave you to repose.'—'My sister,' said Ferdinand, 'consult only your own wishes, and leave the rest to me. Suffer a confidence in me to dissipate the doubts with which you are agitated.'—'Ferdinand,' said Julia, emphatically, 'how shall I express the gratitude your kindness has excited?'—'Your gratitude,' said he, 'will be best shown in consulting your own wishes; for be assured, that whatever procures your happiness, will most effectually establish mine. Do not suffer the prejudices of education to render you miserable. Believe me, that a choice which involves the happiness or misery of your whole life, ought to be decided only by yourself.'

'Let us forbear for the present,' said Hippolitus, 'to urge the subject. Repose is necessary for you,' addressing Julia, 'and I will not suffer a selfish consideration any longer to with-hold you from it.—Grant me but this request—that at this hour to-morrow night, I may return hither to receive my doom.' Julia having consented to receive Hippolitus and Ferdinand, they quitted the closet. In turning into the grand gallery, they were surprised by the appearance of a light, which gleamed upon the wall that terminated their view. It seemed to proceed from a door which opened upon a back stair-case. They pushed on, but it almost instantly disappeared, and upon the stair-case all was still. They then separated, and retired to their apartments, somewhat alarmed by this circumstance, which induced them to suspect that their visit to Julia had been observed.

Julia passed the night in broken slumbers, and anxious consideration. On her present decision hung the crisis of her fate. Her consciousness of the influence of Hippolitus over her heart, made her fear to indulge its predilection, by trusting to her own opinion of its fidelity. She shrunk from the disgraceful idea of an elopement; yet she saw no means of avoiding this, but by rushing upon the fate so dreadful to her imagination.

On the following night, when the inhabitants of the castle were retired to rest, Hippolitus, whose expectation had lengthened the hours into ages, accompanied by Ferdinand, revisited the closet. Julia, who had known no interval of rest since they last left her, received them with much agitation. The vivid glow of health had fled her cheek, and was succeeded by a languid delicacy, less beautiful, but more interesting. To the eager enquiries of Hippolitus, she returned no answer, but faintly smiling through her tears, presented him her hand, and covered her face with her robe. 'I receive it,' cried he, 'as the pledge of my happiness;—yet—yet let your voice ratify the gift.' 'If the present concession does not sink me in your esteem,' said Julia, in a low tone, 'this hand is yours.'—'The concession, my love, (for by that tender name I may now call you) would, if possible, raise you in my esteem; but since that has been long incapable of addition, it can only heighten my opinion of myself, and increase my gratitude to you: gratitude which I will endeavour to shew by an anxious care of your happiness, and by the tender attentions of a whole life. From this blessed moment,' continued he, in a voice of rapture, 'permit me, in thought, to hail you as my wife. From this moment let me banish every vestige of sorrow;—let me dry those tears,' gently pressing her cheek with his lips, 'never to spring again.'—The gratitude and joy which Ferdinand expressed upon this occasion, united with the tenderness of Hippolitus to soothe the agitated spirits of Julia, and she gradually recovered her complacency.

They now arranged their plan of escape; in the execution of which, no time was to be lost, since the nuptials with the duke were to be solemnized on the day after the morrow. Their scheme, whatever it was that should be adopted, they, therefore, resolved to execute on the following night. But when they descended from the first warmth of enterprize, to minuter examination, they soon found the difficulties of the undertaking. The keys of the castle were kept by Robert, the confidential servant of the marquis, who every night deposited them in an iron chest in his chamber. To obtain them by stratagem seemed impossible, and Ferdinand feared to tamper with the honesty of this man, who had been many years in the service of the marquis. Dangerous as was the attempt, no other alternative appeared, and they were therefore compelled to rest all their hopes upon the experiment. It was settled, that if the keys could be procured, Ferdinand and Hippolitus should meet Julia in the closet; that they should convey her to the seashore, from whence a boat, which was to be kept in waiting, would carry them to the opposite coast of Calabria, where the marriage might be solemnized without danger of interruption. But, as it was necessary that Ferdinand should not appear in the affair, it was agreed that he should return to the castle immediately upon the embarkation of his sister. Having thus arranged their plan of operation, they separated till the following night, which was to decide the fate of Hippolitus and Julia.

Julia, whose mind was soothed by the fraternal kindness of Ferdinand, and the tender assurances of Hippolitus, now experienced an interval of repose. At the return of day she awoke refreshed, and tolerably composed. She selected a few clothes which were necessary, and prepared them for her journey. A sentiment of generosity justified her in the reserve she preserved to Emilia and Madame de Menon, whose faithfulness and attachment she could not doubt, but whom she disdained to involve in the disgrace that must fall upon them, should their knowledge of her flight be discovered.

In the mean time the castle was a scene of confusion. The magnificent preparations which were making for the nuptials, engaged all eyes, and busied all hands. The marchioness had the direction of the whole; and the alacrity with which she acquitted herself, testified how much she was pleased with the alliance, and created a suspicion, that it had not been concerted without some exertion of her influence. Thus was Julia designed the joint victim of ambition and illicit love.

The composure of Julia declined with the day, whose hours had crept heavily along. As the night drew on, her anxiety for the success of Ferdinand's negociation with Robert increased to a painful degree. A variety of new emotions pressed at her heart, and subdued her spirits. When she bade Emilia good night, she thought she beheld her for the last time. The ideas of the distance which would separate them, of the dangers she was going to encounter, with a train of wild and fearful anticipations, crouded upon her mind, tears sprang in her eyes, and it was with difficulty she avoided betraying her emotions. Of madame, too, her heart took a tender farewell. At length she heard the marquis retire to his apartment, and the doors belonging to the several chambers of the guests successively close. She marked with trembling attention the gradual change from bustle to quiet, till all was still.

She now held herself in readiness to depart at the moment in which Ferdinand and Hippolitus, for whose steps in the gallery she eagerly listened, should appear. The castle clock struck twelve. The sound seemed to shake the pile. Julia felt it thrill upon her heart. 'I hear you,' sighed she, 'for the last time.' The stillness of death succeeded. She continued to listen; but no sound met her ear. For a considerable time she sat in a state of anxious expectation not to be described. The clock chimed the successive quarters; and her fear rose to each additional sound. At length she heard it strike one. Hollow was that sound, and dreadful to her hopes; for neither Hippolitus nor Ferdinand appeared. She grew faint with fear and disappointment. Her mind, which for two hours had been kept upon the stretch of expectation, now resigned itself to despair. She gently opened the door of her closet, and looked upon the gallery; but all was lonely and silent. It appeared that Robert had refused to be accessary to their scheme; and it was probable that he had betrayed it to the marquis. Overwhelmed with bitter reflections, she threw herself upon the sopha in the first distraction of despair. Suddenly she thought she heard a noise in the gallery; and as she started from her posture to listen to the sound, the door of her closet was gently opened by Ferdinand. 'Come, my love,' said he, 'the keys are ours, and we have not a moment to lose; our delay has been unavoidable; but this is no time for explanation.' Julia, almost fainting, gave her hand to Ferdinand, and Hippolitus, after some short expression of his thankfulness, followed. They passed the door of madame's chamber; and treading the gallery with slow and silent steps, descended to the hall. This they crossed towards a door, after opening which, they were to find their way, through various passages, to a remote part of the castle, where a private door opened upon the walls. Ferdinand carried the several keys. They fastened the hall door after them, and proceeded through a narrow passage terminating in a stair-case.

They descended, and had hardly reached the bottom, when they heard a loud noise at the door above, and presently the voices of several people. Julia scarcely felt the ground she trod on, and Ferdinand flew to unlock a door that obstructed their way. He applied the different keys, and at length found the proper one; but the lock was rusted, and refused to yield. Their distress was not now to be conceived. The noise above increased; and it seemed as if the people were forcing the door. Hippolitus and Ferdinand vainly tried to turn the key. A sudden crash from above convinced them that the door had yielded, when making another desperate effort, the key broke in the lock. Trembling and exhausted, Julia gave herself up for lost. As she hung upon Ferdinand, Hippolitus vainly endeavoured to sooth her—the noise suddenly ceased. They listened, dreading to hear the sounds renewed; but, to their utter astonishment, the silence of the place remained undisturbed. They had now time to breathe, and to consider the possibility of effecting their escape; for from the marquis they had no mercy to hope. Hippolitus, in order to ascertain whether the people had quitted the door above, began to ascend the passage, in which he had not gone many steps when the noise was renewed with increased violence. He instantly retreated; and making a desperate push at the door below, which obstructed their passage, it seemed to yield, and by another effort of Ferdinand, burst open. They had not an instant to lose; for they now heard the steps of persons descending the stairs. The avenue they were in opened into a kind of chamber, whence three passages branched, of which they immediately chose the first. Another door now obstructed their passage; and they were compelled to wait while Ferdinand applied the keys. 'Be quick,' said Julia, 'or we are lost. O! if this lock too is rusted!'—'Hark!' said Ferdinand. They now discovered what apprehension had before prevented them from perceiving, that the sounds of pursuit were ceased, and all again was silent. As this could happen only by the mistake of their pursuers, in taking the wrong route, they resolved to preserve their advantage, by concealing the light, which Ferdinand now covered with his cloak. The door was opened, and they passed on; but they were perplexed in the intricacies of the place, and wandered about in vain endeavour to find their way. Often did they pause to listen, and often did fancy give them sounds of fearful import. At length they entered on the passage which Ferdinand knew led directly to a door that opened on the woods. Rejoiced at this certainty, they soon reached the spot which was to give them liberty.

Ferdinand turned the key; the door unclosed, and, to their infinite joy, discovered to them the grey dawn. 'Now, my love,' said Hippolitus, 'you are safe, and I am happy.'— Immediately a loud voice from without exclaimed, 'Take, villain, the reward of your perfidy!' At the same instant Hippolitus received a sword in his body, and uttering a deep sigh, fell to the ground. Julia shrieked and fainted; Ferdinand drawing his sword, advanced towards the assassin, upon whose countenance the light of his lamp then shone, and discovered to him his father! The sword fell from his grasp, and he started back in an agony of horror. He was instantly surrounded, and seized by the servants of the marquis, while the marquis himself denounced vengeance upon his head, and ordered him to be thrown into the dungeon of the castle. At this instant the servants of the count, who were awaiting his arrival on the seashore, hearing the tumult, hastened to the scene, and there beheld their beloved master lifeless and weltering in his blood. They conveyed the bleeding body, with loud lamentations, on board the vessel which had been prepared for him, and immediately set sail for Italy.

Julia, on recovering her senses, found herself in a small room, of which she had no remembrance, with her maid weeping over her. Recollection, when it returned, brought to her mind an energy of grief, which exceeded even all former conceptions of sufferings. Yet her misery was heightened by the intelligence which she now received. She learned that Hippolitus had been borne away lifeless by his people, that Ferdinand was confined in a dungeon by order of the marquis, and that herself was a prisoner in a remote room, from which, on the day after the morrow, she was to be removed to the chapel of the castle, and there sacrificed to the ambition of her father, and the absurd love of the Duke de Luovo.

This accumulation of evil subdued each power of resistance, and reduced Julia to a state little short of distraction. No person was allowed to approach her but her maid, and the servant who brought her food. Emilia, who, though shocked by Julia's apparent want of confidence, severely sympathized in her distress, solicited to see her; but the pain of denial was so sharply aggravated by rebuke, that she dared not again to urge the request.

In the mean time Ferdinand, involved in the gloom of a dungeon, was resigned to the painful recollection of the past, and a horrid anticipation of the future. From the resentment of the marquis, whose passions were wild and terrible, and whose rank gave him an unlimited power of life and death in his own territories, Ferdinand had much to fear. Yet selfish apprehension soon yielded to a more noble sorrow. He mourned the fate of Hippolitus, and the sufferings of Julia. He could attribute the failure of their scheme only to the treachery of Robert, who had, however, met the wishes of Ferdinand with strong apparent sincerity, and generous interest in the cause of Julia. On the night of the intended elopement, he had consigned the keys to Ferdinand, who, immediately on receiving them, went to the apartment of Hippolitus. There they were detained till after the clock had struck one by a low noise, which returned at intervals, and convinced them that some part of the family was not yet retired to rest. This noise was undoubtedly occasioned by the people whom the marquis had employed to watch, and whose vigilance was too faithful to suffer the fugitives to escape. The very caution of Ferdinand defeated its purpose; for it is probable, that had he attempted to quit the castle by the common entrance, he might have escaped. The keys of the grand door, and those of the courts, remaining in the possession of Robert, the marquis was certain of the intended place of their departure; and was thus enabled to defeat their hopes at the very moment when they exulted in their success.

When the marchioness learned the fate of Hippolitus, the resentment of jealous passion yielded to emotions of pity. Revenge was satisfied, and she could now lament the sufferings of a youth whose personal charms had touched her heart as much as his virtues had disappointed her hopes. Still true to passion, and inaccessible to reason, she poured upon the defenceless Julia her anger for that calamity of which she herself was the unwilling cause. By a dextrous adaptation of her powers, she had worked upon the passions of the marquis so as to render him relentless in the pursuit of ambitious purposes, and insatiable in revenging his disappointment. But the effects of her artifices exceeded her intention in exerting them; and when she meant only to sacrifice a rival to her love, she found she had given up its object to revenge.

CHAPTER IV

The nuptial morn, so justly dreaded by Julia, and so impatiently awaited by the marquis, now arrived. The marriage was to be celebrated with a magnificence which demonstrated the joy it occasioned to the marquis. The castle was fitted up in a style of grandeur superior to any thing that had been before seen in it. The neighbouring nobility were invited to an entertainment which was to conclude with a splendid ball and supper, and the gates were to be thrown open to all who chose to partake of the bounty of the marquis. At an early hour the duke, attended by a numerous retinue, entered the castle. Ferdinand heard from his dungeon, where the rigour and the policy of the marquis still confined him, the loud clattering of hoofs in the courtyard above, the rolling of the carriage wheels, and all the tumultuous bustle which the entrance of the duke occasioned. He too well understood the cause of this uproar, and it awakened in him sensations resembling those which the condemned criminal feels, when his ears are assailed by the dreadful sounds that precede his execution. When he was able to think of himself, he wondered by what means the marquis would reconcile his absence to the guests. He, however, knew too well the dissipated character of the Sicilian nobility, to doubt that whatever story should be invented would be very readily believed by them; who, even if they knew the truth, would not suffer a discovery of their knowledge to interrupt the festivity which was offered them.

The marquis and marchioness received the duke in the outer hall, and conducted him to the saloon, where he partook of the refreshments prepared for him, and from thence retired to the chapel. The marquis now withdrew to lead Julia to the altar, and Emilia was ordered to attend at the door of the chapel, in which the priest and a numerous company were already assembled. The marchioness, a prey to the turbulence of succeeding passions, exulted in the near completion of her favorite scheme.—A disappointment, however, was prepared for her, which would at once crush the triumph of her malice and her pride. The marquis, on entering the prison of Julia, found it empty! His astonishment and indignation upon the discovery almost overpowered his reason. Of the servants of the castle, who were immediately summoned, he enquired concerning her escape, with a mixture of fury and sorrow which left them no opportunity to reply. They had, however, no information to give, but that her woman had not appeared during the whole morning. In the prison were found the bridal habiliments which the marchioness herself had sent on the preceding night, together with a letter addressed to Emilia, which contained the following words:

'Adieu, dear Emilia; never more will you see your wretched sister, who flies from the cruel fate now prepared for her, certain that she can never meet one more dreadful.— In happiness or misery—in hope or despair—whatever may be your situation—still remember me with pity and affection. Dear Emilia, adieu!—You will always be the sister of my heart—may you never be the partner of my misfortunes!'

While the marquis was reading this letter, the marchioness, who supposed the delay occasioned by some opposition from Julia, flew to the apartment. By her orders all the habitable parts of the castle were explored, and she herself assisted in the search. At length the intelligence was communicated to the chapel, and the confusion became universal. The priest quitted the altar, and the company returned to the saloon.

The letter, when it was given to Emilia, excited emotions which she found it impossible to disguise, but which did not, however, protect her from a suspicion that she was concerned in the transaction, her knowledge of which this letter appeared intended to conceal.

The marquis immediately dispatched servants upon the fleetest horses of his stables, with directions to take different routs, and to scour every corner of the island in pursuit of the fugitives. When these exertions had somewhat quieted his mind, he began to consider by what means Julia could have effected her escape. She had been confined in a small room in a remote part of the castle, to which no person had been admitted but her own woman and Robert, the confidential servant of the marquis. Even Lisette had not been suffered to enter, unless accompanied by Robert, in whose room, since the night of the fatal discovery, the keys had been regularly deposited. Without them it was impossible she could have escaped: the windows of the apartment being barred and grated, and opening into an inner court, at a prodigious height from the ground. Besides, who could she depend upon for protection—or whither could she intend to fly for concealment?—The associates of her former elopement were utterly unable to assist her even with advice. Ferdinand himself a prisoner, had been deprived of any means of intercourse with her, and Hippolitus had been carried lifeless on board a vessel, which had immediately sailed for Italy.

Robert, to whom the keys had been entrusted, was severely interrogated by the marquis. He persisted in a simple and uniform declaration of his innocence; but as the marquis believed it impossible that Julia could have escaped without his knowledge, he was ordered into imprisonment till he should confess the fact.

The pride of the duke was severely wounded by this elopement, which proved the excess of Julia's aversion, and compleated the disgraceful circumstances of his rejection. The marquis had carefully concealed from him her prior attempt at elopement, and her consequent confinement; but the truth now burst from disguise, and stood revealed with bitter aggravation. The duke, fired with indignation at the duplicity of the marquis, poured forth his resentment in terms of proud and bitter invective; and the marquis, galled by recent disappointment, was in no mood to restrain the impetuosity of his nature. He retorted with acrimony; and the consequence would have been serious, had not the friends of each party interposed for their preservation. The disputants were at length reconciled; it was agreed to pursue Julia with united, and indefatigable search; and that whenever she should be found, the nuptials should be solemnized without further delay. With the character of the duke, this conduct was consistent. His passions, inflamed by disappointment, and strengthened by repulse, now defied the power of obstacle; and those considerations which would have operated with a more delicate mind to overcome its original inclination, served only to encrease the violence of his.

Madame de Menon, who loved Julia with maternal affection, was an interested observer of all that passed at the castle. The cruel fate to which the marquis destined his daughter she had severely lamented, yet she could hardly rejoice to find that this had been avoided by elopement. She trembled for the future safety of her pupil; and her tranquillity, which was thus first disturbed for the welfare of others, she was not soon suffered to recover.

The marchioness had long nourished a secret dislike to Madame de Menon, whose virtues were a silent reproof to her vices. The contrariety of their disposition created in the marchioness an aversion which would have amounted to contempt, had not that dignity of virtue which strongly characterized the manners of madame, compelled the former to fear what she wished to despise. Her conscience whispered her that the dislike was mutual; and she now rejoiced in the opportunity which seemed to offer itself of lowering the proud integrity of madame's character. Pretending, therefore, to believe that she had encouraged Ferdinand to disobey his father's commands, and had been accessary to the elopement, she accused her of these offences, and stimulated the marquis to reprehend her conduct. But the integrity of Madame de Menon was not to be questioned with impunity. Without deigning to answer the imputation, she desired to resign an office of which she was no longer considered worthy, and to quit the castle immediately. This the policy of the marquis would not suffer; and he was compelled to make such ample concessions to madame, as induced her for the present to continue at the castle.

The news of Julia's elopement at length reached the ears of Ferdinand, whose joy at this event was equalled only by his surprize. He lost, for a moment, the sense of his own situation, and thought only of the escape of Julia. But his sorrow soon returned with accumulated force when he recollected that Julia might then perhaps want that assistance which his confinement alone could prevent his affording her.

The servants, who had been sent in pursuit, returned to the castle without any satisfactory information. Week after week elapsed in fruitless search, yet the duke was strenuous in continuing the pursuit. Emissaries were dispatched to Naples, and to the several estates of the Count Vereza, but they returned without any satisfactory information. The count had not been heard of since he quitted Naples for Sicily.

During these enquiries a new subject of disturbance broke out in the castle of Mazzini. On the night so fatal to the hopes of Hippolitus and Julia, when the tumult was subsided, and all was still, a light was observed by a servant as he passed by the window of the great stair-case in the way to his chamber, to glimmer through the casement before noticed in the southern buildings. While he stood observing it, it vanished, and presently reappeared. The former mysterious circumstances relative to these buildings rushed upon his mind; and fired with wonder, he roused some of his fellow servants to come and behold this phenomenon.

As they gazed in silent terror, the light disappeared, and soon after, they saw a small door belonging to the south tower open, and a figure bearing a light issue forth, which gliding along the castle walls, was quickly lost to their view. Overcome with fear they hurried back to their chambers, and revolved all the late wonderful occurrences. They doubted not, that this was the figure formerly seen by the lady Julia. The sudden change of Madame de Menon's apartments had not passed unobserved by the servants, but they now no longer hesitated to what to attribute the removal. They collected each various and uncommon circumstance attendant on this part of the fabric; and, comparing them with the present, their superstitious fears were confirmed, and their terror heightened to such a degree, that many of them resolved to quit the service of the marquis.

The marquis surprized at this sudden desertion, enquired into its cause, and learned the truth. Shocked by this discovery, he yet resolved to prevent, if possible, the ill effects which might be expected from a circulation of the report. To this end it was necessary to quiet the minds of his people, and to prevent their quitting his service. Having severely reprehended them for the idle apprehension they encouraged, he told them that, to prove the fallacy of their surmises, he would lead them over that part of the castle which was the subject of their fears, and ordered them to attend him at the return of night in the north hall. Emilia and Madame de Menon, surprised at this procedure, awaited the issue in silent expectation.

The servants, in obedience to the commands of the marquis, assembled at night in the north hall. The air of desolation which reigned through the south buildings, and the circumstance of their having been for so many years shut up, would naturally tend to inspire awe; but to these people, who firmly believed them to be the haunt of an unquiet spirit, terror was the predominant sentiment.

The marquis now appeared with the keys of these buildings in his hands, and every heart thrilled with wild expectation. He ordered Robert to precede him with a torch, and the rest of the servants following, he passed on. A pair of iron gates were unlocked, and they proceeded through a court, whose pavement was wildly overgrown with long grass, to the great door of the south fabric. Here they met with some difficulty, for the lock, which had not been turned for many years, was rusted.

During this interval, the silence of expectation sealed the lips of all present. At length the lock yielded. That door which had not been passed for so many years, creaked heavily upon its hinges, and disclosed the hall of black marble which Ferdinand had formerly crossed. 'Now,' cried the marquis, in a tone of irony as he entered, 'expect to encounter the ghosts of which you tell me; but if you fail to conquer them, prepare to quit my service. The people who live with me shall at least have courage and ability sufficient to defend me from these spiritual attacks. All I apprehend is, that the enemy will not appear, and in this case your valour will go untried.'

No one dared to answer, but all followed, in silent fear, the marquis, who ascended the great stair-case, and entered the gallery. 'Unlock that door,' said he, pointing to one on the left, 'and we will soon unhouse these ghosts.' Robert applied the key, but his hand shook so violently that he could not turn it. 'Here is a fellow,' cried the marquis, 'fit to encounter a whole legion of spirits. Do you, Anthony, take the key, and try your valour.'

'Please you, my lord,' replied Anthony, 'I never was a good one at unlocking a door in my life, but here is Gregory will do it.'—'No, my lord, an' please you,' said Gregory, 'here is Richard.'—'Stand off,' said the marquis, 'I will shame your cowardice, and do it myself.'

Saying this he turned the key, and was rushing on, but the door refused to yield; it shook under his hands, and seemed as if partially held by some person on the other side. The marquis was surprised, and made several efforts to move it, without effect. He then ordered his servants to burst it open, but, shrinking back with one accord, they cried, 'For God's sake, my lord, go no farther; we are satisfied here are no ghosts, only let us get back.'

'It is now then my turn to be satisfied,' replied the marquis, 'and till I am, not one of you shall stir. Open me that door.'—'My lord!'—'Nay,' said the marquis, assuming a look of stern authority—'dispute not my commands. I am not to be trifled with.'

They now stepped forward, and applied their strength to the door, when a loud and sudden noise burst from within, and resounded through the hollow chambers! The men started back in affright, and were rushing headlong down the stair-case, when the voice of the marquis arrested their flight. They returned, with hearts palpitating with terror. 'Observe what I say,' said the marquis, 'and behave like men. Yonder door,' pointing to one at some distance, 'will lead us through other rooms to this chamber—unlock it therefore, for I will know the cause of these sounds.' Shocked at this determination, the servants again supplicated the marquis to go no farther; and to be obeyed, he was obliged to exert all his authority. The door was opened, and discovered a long narrow passage, into which they descended by a few steps. It led to a gallery that terminated in a back stair-case, where several doors appeared, one of which the marquis unclosed. A spacious chamber appeared beyond, whose walls, decayed and discoloured by the damps, exhibited a melancholy proof of desertion.

They passed on through a long suite of lofty and noble apartments, which were in the same ruinous condition. At length they came to the chamber whence the noise had issued. 'Go first, Robert, with the light,' said the marquis, as they approached the door; 'this is the key.' Robert trembled—but obeyed, and the other servants followed in silence. They stopped a moment at the door to listen, but all was still within. The door was opened, and disclosed a large vaulted chamber, nearly resembling those they had passed, and on looking round, they discovered at once the cause of the alarm.—A part of the decayed roof was fallen in, and the stones and rubbish of the ruin falling against the gallery door, obstructed the passage. It was evident, too, whence the noise which occasioned their terror had arisen; the loose stones which were piled against the door being shook by the effort made to open it, had given way, and rolled to the floor.

After surveying the place, they returned to the back stairs, which they descended, and having pursued the several windings of a long passage, found themselves again in the marble hall. 'Now,' said the marquis, 'what think ye? What evil spirits infest these walls? Henceforth be cautious how ye credit the phantasms of idleness, for ye may not always meet with a master who will condescend to undeceive ye.'—They acknowledged the goodness of the marquis, and professing themselves perfectly conscious of the error of their former suspicions, desired they might search no farther. 'I chuse to leave nothing to your imagination,' replied the marquis, 'lest hereafter it should betray you into a similar error. Follow me, therefore; you shall see the whole of these buildings.' Saying this, he led them to the south tower. They remembered, that from a door of this tower the figure which caused their alarm had issued; and notwithstanding the late assertion of their suspicions being removed, fear still operated powerfully upon their minds, and they would willingly have been excused from farther research. 'Would any of you chuse to explore this tower?' said the marquis, pointing to the broken stair-case; 'for myself, I am mortal, and therefore fear to venture; but you, who hold communion with disembodied spirits, may partake something of their nature; if so, you may pass without apprehension where the ghost has probably passed before.' They shrunk at this reproof, and were silent.

The marquis turning to a door on his right hand, ordered it to be unlocked. It opened upon the country, and the servants knew it to be the same whence the figure had appeared. Having relocked it, 'Lift that trapdoor; we will desend into the vaults,' said the marquis. 'What trapdoor, my Lord?' said Robert, with encreased agitation; 'I see none.' The marquis pointed, and Robert, perceived a door, which lay almost concealed beneath the stones that had fallen from the stair-case above. He began to remove them, when the marquis suddenly turning—'I have already sufficiently indulged your folly,' said he, 'and am weary of this business. If you are capable of receiving conviction from truth, you must now be convinced that these buildings are not the haunt of a supernatural being; and if you are incapable, it would be entirely useless to proceed. You, Robert, may therefore spare yourself the trouble of removing the rubbish; we will quit this part of the fabric.'

The servants joyfully obeyed, and the marquis locking the several doors, returned with the keys to the habitable part of the castle.

Every enquiry after Julia had hitherto proved fruitless; and the imperious nature of the marquis, heightened by the present vexation, became intolerably oppressive to all around him. As the hope of recovering Julia declined, his opinion that Emilia had assisted her to escape strengthened, and he inflicted upon her the severity of his unjust suspicions. She was ordered to confine herself to her apartment till her innocence should be cleared, or her sister discovered. From Madame de Menon she received a faithful sympathy, which was the sole relief of her oppressed heart. Her anxiety concerning Julia daily encreased, and was heightened into the most terrifying apprehensions for her safety. She knew of no person in whom her sister could confide, or of any place where she could find protection; the most deplorable evils were therefore to be expected.

One day, as she was sitting at the window of her apartment, engaged in melancholy reflection, she saw a man riding towards the castle on full speed. Her heart beat with fear and expectation; for his haste made her suspect he brought intelligence of Julia; and she could scarcely refrain from breaking through the command of the marquis, and rushing into the hall to learn something of his errand. She was right in her conjecture; the person she had seen was a spy of the marquis's, and came to inform him that the lady Julia was at that time concealed in a cottage of the forest of Marentino. The marquis, rejoiced at this intelligence, gave the man a liberal reward. He learned also, that she was accompanied by a young cavalier; which circumstance surprized him exceedingly; for he knew of no person except the Count de Vereza with whom she could have entrusted herself, and the count had fallen by his sword! He immediately ordered a party of his people to accompany the messenger to the forest of Marentino, and to suffer neither Julia nor the cavalier to escape them, on pain of death.

When the Duke de Luovo was informed of this discovery, he entreated and obtained permission of the marquis to join in the pursuit. He immediately set out on the expedition, armed, and followed by a number of his servants. He resolved to encounter all hazards, and to practice the most desperate extremes, rather than fail in the object of his enterprize. In a short time he overtook the marquis's people, and they proceeded together with all possible speed. The forest lay several leagues distant from the castle of Mazzini, and the day was closing when they entered upon the borders. The thick foliage of the trees spread a deeper shade around; and they were obliged to proceed with caution. Darkness had long fallen upon the earth when they reached the cottage, to which they were directed by a light that glimmered from afar among the trees. The duke left his people at some distance; and dismounted, and accompanied only by one servant, approached the cottage. When he reached it he stopped, and looking through the window, observed a man and woman in the habit of peasants seated at their supper. They were conversing with earnestness, and the duke, hoping to obtain farther intelligence of Julia, endeavoured to listen to their discourse. They were praising the beauty of a lady, whom the duke did not doubt to be Julia, and the woman spoke much in praise of the cavalier. 'He has a noble heart,' said she; 'and I am sure, by his look, belongs to some great family.'—'Nay,' replied her companion, 'the lady is as good as he. I have been at Palermo, and ought to know what great folks are, and if she is not one of them, never take my word again. Poor thing, how she does take on! It made my heart ache to see her.'

They were some time silent. The duke knocked at the door, and enquired of the man who opened it concerning the lady and cavalier then in his cottage. He was assured there were no other persons in the cottage than those he then saw. The duke persisted in affirming that the persons he enquired for were there concealed; which the man being as resolute in denying, he gave the signal, and his people approached, and surrounded the cottage. The peasants, terrified by this circumstance, confessed that a lady and cavalier, such as the duke described, had been for some time concealed in the cottage; but that they were now departed.

Suspicious of the truth of the latter assertion, the duke ordered his people to search the cottage, and that part of the forest contiguous to it. The search ended in disappointment. The duke, however, resolved to obtain all possible information concerning the fugitives; and assuming, therefore, a stern air, bade the peasant, on pain of instant death, discover all he knew of them.

The man replied, that on a very dark and stormy night, about a week before, two persons had come to the cottage, and desired shelter. That they were unattended; but seemed to be persons of consequence in disguise. That they paid very liberally for what they had; and that they departed from the cottage a few hours before the arrival of the duke.

The duke enquired concerning the course they had taken, and having received information, remounted his horse, and set forward in pursuit. The road lay for several leagues through the forest, and the darkness, and the probability of encountering banditti, made the journey dangerous. About the break of day they quitted the forest, and entered upon a wild and mountainous country, in which they travelled some miles without perceiving a hut, or a human being. No vestige of cultivation appeared, and no sounds reached them but those of their horses feet, and the roaring of the winds through the deep forests that overhung the mountains. The pursuit was uncertain, but the duke resolved to persevere.

They came at length to a cottage, where he repeated his enquiries, and learned to his satisfaction that two persons, such as he described, had stopped there for refreshment about two hours before. He found it now necessary to stop for the same purpose. Bread and milk, the only provisions of the place, were set before him, and his attendants would have been well contented, had there been sufficient of this homely fare to have satisfied their hunger.

Having dispatched an hasty meal, they again set forward in the way pointed out to them as the route of the fugitives. The country assumed a more civilized aspect. Corn, vineyards, olives, and groves of mulberry-trees adorned the hills. The vallies, luxuriant in shade, were frequently embellished by the windings of a lucid stream, and diversified by clusters of half-seen cottages. Here the rising turrets of a monastery appeared above the thick trees with which they were surrounded; and there the savage wilds the travellers had passed, formed a bold and picturesque background to the scene.

To the questions put by the duke to the several persons he met, he received answers that encouraged him to proceed. At noon he halted at a village to refresh himself and his people. He could gain no intelligence of Julia, and was perplexed which way to chuse; but determined at length to pursue the road he was then in, and accordingly again set forward. He travelled several miles without meeting any person who could give the necessary information, and began to despair of success. The lengthened shadows of the mountains, and the fading light gave signals of declining day; when having gained the summit of a high hill, he observed two persons travelling on horseback in the plains below. On one of them he distinguished the habiliments of a woman; and in her air he thought he discovered that of Julia. While he stood attentively surveying them, they looked towards the hill, when, as if urged by a sudden impulse of terror, they set off on full speed over the plains. The duke had no doubt that these were the persons he sought; and he, therefore, ordered some of his people to pursue them, and pushed his horse into a full gallop. Before he reached the plains, the fugitives, winding round an abrupt hill, were lost to his view. The duke continued his course, and his people, who were a considerable way before him, at length reached the hill, behind which the two persons had disappeared. No traces of them were to be seen, and they entered a narrow defile between two ranges of high and savage mountains; on the right of which a rapid stream rolled along, and broke with its deep resounding murmurs the solemn silence of the place. The shades of evening now fell thick, and the scene was soon enveloped in darkness; but to the duke, who was animated by a strong and impetuous passion, these were unimportant circumstances. Although he knew that the wilds of Sicily were frequently infested with banditti, his numbers made him fearless of attack. Not so his attendants, many of whom, as the darkness increased, testified emotions not very honourable to their courage: starting at every bush, and believing it concealed a murderer. They endeavoured to dissuade the duke from proceeding, expressing uncertainty of their being in the right route, and recommending the open plains. But the duke, whose eye had been vigilant to mark the flight of the fugitives, and who was not to be dissuaded from his purpose, quickly repressed their arguments. They continued their course without meeting a single person.

The moon now rose, and afforded them a shadowy imperfect view of the surrounding objects. The prospect was gloomy and vast, and not a human habitation met their eyes. They had now lost every trace of the fugitives, and found themselves bewildered in a wild and savage country. Their only remaining care was to extricate themselves from so forlorn a situation, and they listened at every step with anxious attention for some sound that might discover to them the haunts of men. They listened in vain; the stillness of night was undisturbed but by the wind, which broke at intervals in low and hollow murmurs from among the mountains.

As they proceeded with silent caution, they perceived a light break from among the rocks at some distance. The duke hesitated whether to approach, since it might probably proceed from a party of the banditti with which these mountains were said to be infested. While he hesitated, it disappeared; but he had not advanced many steps when it returned. He now perceived it to issue from the mouth of a cavern, and cast a bright reflection upon the overhanging rocks and shrubs.

He dismounted, and followed by two of his people, leaving the rest at some distance, moved with slow and silent steps towards the cave. As he drew near, he heard the sound of many voices in high carousal. Suddenly the uproar ceased, and the following words were sung by a clear and manly voice:

SONG

Pour the rich libation high;
   The sparkling cup to Bacchus fill;
His joys shall dance in ev'ry eye,
   And chace the forms of future ill!

Quick the magic raptures steal
   O'er the fancy-kindling brain.
Warm the heart with social zeal,
   And song and laughter reign.

Then visions of pleasure shall float on our sight,
   While light bounding our spirits shall flow;
And the god shall impart a fine sense of delight
   Which in vain sober mortals would know.

The last verse was repeated in loud chorus. The duke listened with astonishment! Such social merriment amid a scene of such savage wildness, appeared more like enchantment than reality. He would not have hesitated to pronounce this a party of banditti, had not the delicacy of expression preserved in the song appeared unattainable by men of their class.

He had now a full view of the cave; and the moment which convinced him of his error served only to encrease his surprize. He beheld, by the light of a fire, a party of banditti seated within the deepest recess of the cave round a rude kind of table formed in the rock. The table was spread with provisions, and they were regaling themselves with great eagerness and joy. The countenances of the men exhibited a strange mixture of fierceness and sociality; and the duke could almost have imagined he beheld in these robbers a band of the early Romans before knowledge had civilized, or luxury had softened them. But he had not much time for meditation; a sense of his danger bade him fly while to fly was yet in his power. As he turned to depart, he observed two saddle-horses grazing upon the herbage near the mouth of the cave. It instantly occurred to him that they belonged to Julia and her companion. He hesitated, and at length determined to linger awhile, and listen to the conversation of the robbers, hoping from thence to have his doubts resolved. They talked for some time in a strain of high conviviality, and recounted in exultation many of their exploits. They described also the behaviour of several people whom they had robbed, with highly ludicrous allusions, and with much rude humour, while the cave re-echoed with loud bursts of laughter and applause. They were thus engaged in tumultuous merriment, till one of them cursing the scanty plunder of their late adventure, but praising the beauty of a lady, they all lowered their voices together, and seemed as if debating upon a point uncommonly interesting to them. The passions of the duke were roused, and he became certain that it was Julia of whom they had spoken. In the first impulse of feeling he drew his sword; but recollecting the number of his adversaries, restrained his fury. He was turning from the cave with a design of summoning his people, when the light of the fire glittering upon the bright blade of his weapon, caught the eye of one of the banditti. He started from his seat, and his comrades instantly rising in consternation, discovered the duke. They rushed with loud vociferation towards the mouth of the cave. He endeavoured to escape to his people; but two of the banditti mounting the horses which were grazing near, quickly overtook and seized him. His dress and air proclaimed him to be a person of distinction; and, rejoicing in their prospect of plunder, they forced him towards the cave. Here their comrades awaited them; but what were the emotions of the duke, when he discovered in the person of the principal robber his own son! who, to escape the galling severity of his father, had fled from his castle some years before, and had not been heard of since.

He had placed himself at the head of a party of banditti, and, pleased with the liberty which till then he had never tasted, and with the power which his new situation afforded him, he became so much attached to this wild and lawless mode of life, that he determined never to quit it till death should dissolve those ties which now made his rank only oppressive. This event seemed at so great a distance, that he seldom allowed himself to think of it. Whenever it should happen, he had no doubt that he might either resume his rank without danger of discovery, or might justify his present conduct as a frolic which a few acts of generosity would easily excuse. He knew his power would then place him beyond the reach of censure, in a country where the people are accustomed to implicit subordination, and seldom dare to scrutinize the actions of the nobility.

His sensations, however, on discovering his father, were not very pleasing; but proclaiming the duke, he protected him from farther outrage.

With the duke, whose heart was a stranger to the softer affections, indignation usurped the place of parental feeling. His pride was the only passion affected by the discovery; and he had the rashness to express the indignation, which the conduct of his son had excited, in terms of unrestrained invective. The banditti, inflamed by the opprobium with which he loaded their order, threatened instant punishment to his temerity; and the authority of Riccardo could hardly restrain them within the limits of forbearance.

The menaces, and at length entreaties of the duke, to prevail with his son to abandon his present way of life, were equally ineffectual. Secure in his own power, Riccardo laughed at the first, and was insensible to the latter; and his father was compelled to relinquish the attempt. The duke, however, boldly and passionately accused him of having plundered and secreted a lady and cavalier, his friends, at the same time describing Julia, for whose liberation he offered large rewards. Riccardo denied the fact, which so much exasperated the duke, that he drew his sword with an intention of plunging it in the breast of his son. His arm was arrested by the surrounding banditti, who half unsheathed their swords, and stood suspended in an attitude of menace. The fate of the father now hung upon the voice of the son. Riccardo raised his arm, but instantly dropped it, and turned away. The banditti sheathed their weapons, and stepped back.

Riccardo solemnly swearing that he knew nothing of the persons described, the duke at length became convinced of the truth of the assertion, and departing from the cave, rejoined his people. All the impetuous passions of his nature were roused and inflamed by the discovery of his son in a situation so wretchedly disgraceful. Yet it was his pride rather than his virtue that was hurt; and when he wished him dead, it was rather to save himself from disgrace, than his son from the real indignity of vice. He had no means of reclaiming him; to have attempted it by force, would have been at this time the excess of temerity, for his attendants, though numerous, were undisciplined, and would have fallen certain victims to the power of a savage and dexterous banditti.

With thoughts agitated in fierce and agonizing conflict, he pursued his journey; and having lost all trace of Julia, sought only for an habitation which might shelter him from the night, and afford necessary refreshment for himself and his people. With this, however, there appeared little hope of meeting.

CHAPTER V

The night grew stormy. The hollow winds swept over the mountains, and blew bleak and cold around; the clouds were driven swiftly over the face of the moon, and the duke and his people were frequently involved in total darkness. They had travelled on silently and dejectedly for some hours, and were bewildered in the wilds, when they suddenly heard the bell of a monastery chiming for midnight-prayer. Their hearts revived at the sound, which they endeavoured to follow, but they had not gone far, when the gale wafted it away, and they were abandoned to the uncertain guide of their own conjectures.

They had pursued for some time the way which they judged led to the monastery, when the note of the bell returned upon the wind, and discovered to them that they had mistaken their route. After much wandering and difficulty they arrived, overcome with weariness, at the gates of a large and gloomy fabric. The bell had ceased, and all was still. By the moonlight, which through broken clouds now streamed upon the building, they became convinced it was the monastery they had sought, and the duke himself struck loudly upon the gate.

Several minutes elapsed, no person appeared, and he repeated the stroke. A step was presently heard within, the gate was unbarred, and a thin shivering figure presented itself. The duke solicited admission, but was refused, and reprimanded for disturbing the convent at the hour sacred to prayer. He then made known his rank, and bade the friar inform the Superior that he requested shelter from the night. The friar, suspicious of deceit, and apprehensive of robbers, refused with much firmness, and repeated that the convent was engaged in prayer; he had almost closed the gate, when the duke, whom hunger and fatigue made desperate, rushed by him, and passed into the court. It was his intention to present himself to the Superior, and he had not proceeded far when the sound of laughter, and of many voices in loud and mirthful jollity, attracted his steps. It led him through several passages to a door, through the crevices of which light appeared. He paused a moment, and heard within a wild uproar of merriment and song. He was struck with astonishment, and could scarcely credit his senses!

He unclosed the door, and beheld in a large room, well lighted, a company of friars, dressed in the habit of their order, placed round a table, which was profusely spread with wines and fruits. The Superior, whose habit distinguished him from his associates, appeared at the head of the table. He was lifting a large goblet of wine to his lips, and was roaring out, 'Profusion and confusion,' at the moment when the duke entered. His appearance caused a general alarm; that part of the company who were not too much intoxicated, arose from their seats; and the Superior, dropping the goblet from his hands, endeavoured to assume a look of austerity, which his rosy countenance belied. The duke received a reprimand, delivered in the lisping accents of intoxication, and embellished with frequent interjections of hiccup. He made known his quality, his distress, and solicited a night's lodging for himself and his people. When the Superior understood the distinction of his guest, his features relaxed into a smile of joyous welcome; and taking him by the hand, he placed him by his side.

The table was quickly covered with luxurious provisions, and orders were given that the duke's people should be admitted, and taken care of. He was regaled with a variety of the finest wines, and at length, highly elevated by monastic hospitality, he retired to the apartment allotted him, leaving the Superior in a condition which precluded all ceremony.

He departed in the morning, very well pleased with the accommodating principles of monastic religion. He had been told that the enjoyment of the good things of this life was the surest sign of our gratitude to Heaven; and it appeared, that within the walls of a Sicilian monastery, the precept and the practice were equally enforced.

He was now at a loss what course to chuse, for he had no clue to direct him towards the object of his pursuit; but hope still invigorated, and urged him to perseverance. He was not many leagues from the coast; and it occurred to him that the fugitives might make towards it with a design of escaping into Italy. He therefore determined to travel towards the sea and proceed along the shore.

At the house where he stopped to dine, he learned that two persons, such as he described, had halted there about an hour before his arrival, and had set off again in much seeming haste. They had taken the road towards the coast, whence it was obvious to the duke they designed to embark. He stayed not to finish the repast set before him, but instantly remounted to continue the pursuit.

To the enquiries he made of the persons he chanced to meet, favorable answers were returned for a time, but he was at length bewildered in uncertainity, and travelled for some hours in a direction which chance, rather than judgment, prompted him to take.

The falling evening again confused his prospects, and unsettled his hopes. The shades were deepened by thick and heavy clouds that enveloped the horizon, and the deep sounding air foretold a tempest. The thunder now rolled at a distance, and the accumulated clouds grew darker. The duke and his people were on a wild and dreary heath, round which they looked in vain for shelter, the view being terminated on all sides by the same desolate scene. They rode, however, as hard as their horses would carry them; and at length one of the attendants spied on the skirts of the waste a large mansion, towards which they immediately directed their course.

They were overtaken by the storm, and at the moment when they reached the building, a peal of thunder, which seemed to shake the pile, burst over their heads. They now found themselves in a large and ancient mansion, which seemed totally deserted, and was falling to decay. The edifice was distinguished by an air of magnificence, which ill accorded with the surrounding scenery, and which excited some degree of surprize in the mind of the duke, who, however, fully justified the owner in forsaking a spot which presented to the eye only views of rude and desolated nature.

The storm increased with much violence, and threatened to detain the duke a prisoner in his present habitation for the night. The hall, of which he and his people had taken possession, exhibited in every feature marks of ruin and desolation. The marble pavement was in many places broken, the walls were mouldering in decay, and round the high and shattered windows the long grass waved to the lonely gale. Curiosity led him to explore the recesses of the mansion. He quitted the hall, and entered upon a passage which conducted him to a remote part of the edifice. He wandered through the wild and spacious apartments in gloomy meditation, and often paused in wonder at the remains of magnificence which he beheld.

The mansion was irregular and vast, and he was bewildered in its intricacies. In endeavouring to find his way back, he only perplexed himself more, till at length he arrived at a door, which he believed led into the hall he first quitted. On opening it he discovered, by the faint light of the moon, a large place which he scarcely knew whether to think a cloister, a chapel, or a hall. It retired in long perspective, in arches, and terminated in a large iron gate, through which appeared the open country.

The lighting flashed thick and blue around, which, together with the thunder that seemed to rend the wide arch of heaven, and the melancholy aspect of the place, so awed the duke, that he involuntarily called to his people. His voice was answered only by the deep echoes which ran in murmurs through the place, and died away at a distance; and the moon now sinking behind a cloud, left him in total darkness.

He repeated the call more loudly, and at length heard the approach of footsteps. A few moments relieved him from his anxiety, for his people appeared. The storm was yet loud, and the heavy and sulphureous appearance of the atmosphere promised no speedy abatement of it. The duke endeavoured to reconcile himself to pass the night in his present situation, and ordered a fire to be lighted in the place he was in. This with much difficulty was accomplished. He then threw himself on the pavement before it, and tried to endure the abstinence which he had so ill observed in the monastery on the preceding night. But to his great joy his attendants, more provident than himself, had not scrupled to accept a comfortable quantity of provisions which had been offered them at the monastery; and which they now drew forth from a wallet. They were spread upon the pavement; and the duke, after refreshing himself, delivered up the remains to his people. Having ordered them to watch by turns at the gate, he wrapt his cloak round him, and resigned himself to repose.

The night passed without any disturbance. The morning arose fresh and bright; the Heavens exhibited a clear and unclouded concave; even the wild heath, refreshed by the late rains, smiled around, and sent up with the morning gale a stream of fragrance.

The duke quitted the mansion, re-animated by the cheerfulness of morn, and pursued his journey. He could gain no intelligence of the fugitives. About noon he found himself in a beautiful romantic country; and having reached the summit of some wild cliffs, he rested, to view the picturesque imagery of the scene below. A shadowy sequestered dell appeared buried deep among the rocks, and in the bottom was seen a lake, whose clear bosom reflected the impending cliffs, and the beautiful luxuriance of the overhanging shades.

But his attention was quickly called from the beauties of inanimate nature, to objects more interesting; for he observed two persons, whom he instantly recollected to be the same that he had formerly pursued over the plains. They were seated on the margin of the lake, under the shade of some high trees at the foot of the rocks, and seemed partaking of a repast which was spread upon the grass. Two horses were grazing near. In the lady the duke saw the very air and shape of Julia, and his heart bounded at the sight. They were seated with their backs to the cliffs upon which the duke stood, and he therefore surveyed them unobserved. They were now almost within his power, but the difficulty was how to descend the rocks, whose stupendous heights and craggy steeps seemed to render them impassable. He examined them with a scrutinizing eye, and at length espied, where the rock receded, a narrow winding sort of path. He dismounted, and some of his attendants doing the same, followed their lord down the cliffs, treading lightly, lest their steps should betray them. Immediately upon their reaching the bottom, they were perceived by the lady, who fled among the rocks, and was presently pursued by the duke's people. The cavalier had no time to escape, but drew his sword, and defended himself against the furious assault of the duke.

The combat was sustained with much vigour and dexterity on both sides for some minutes, when the duke received the point of his adversary's sword, and fell. The cavalier, endeavouring to escape, was seized by the duke's people, who now appeared with the fair fugitive; but what was the disappointment—the rage of the duke, when in the person of the lady he discovered a stranger! The astonishment was mutual, but the accompanying feelings were, in the different persons, of a very opposite nature. In the duke, astonishment was heightened by vexation, and embittered by disappointment:— in the lady, it was softened by the joy of unexpected deliverance.

This lady was the younger daughter of a Sicilian nobleman, whose avarice, or necessities, had devoted her to a convent. To avoid the threatened fate, she fled with the lover to whom her affections had long been engaged, and whose only fault, even in the eye of her father, was inferiority of birth. They were now on their way to the coast, whence they designed to pass over to Italy, where the church would confirm the bonds which their hearts had already formed. There the friends of the cavalier resided, and with them they expected to find a secure retreat.

The duke, who was not materially wounded, after the first transport of his rage had subsided, suffered them to depart. Relieved from their fears, they joyfully set forward, leaving their late pursuer to the anguish of defeat, and fruitless endeavour. He was remounted on his horse; and having dispatched two of his people in search of a house where he might obtain some relief, he proceeded slowly on his return to the castle of Mazzini.

It was not long ere he recollected a circumstance which, in the first tumult of his disappointment, had escaped him, but which so essentially affected the whole tenour of his hopes, as to make him again irresolute how to proceed. He considered that, although these were the fugitives he had pursued over the plains, they might not be the same who had been secreted in the cottage, and it was therefore possible that Julia might have been the person whom they had for some time followed from thence. This suggestion awakened his hopes, which were however quickly destroyed; for he remembered that the only persons who could have satisfied his doubts, were now gone beyond the power of recall. To pursue Julia, when no traces of her flight remained, was absurd; and he was, therefore, compelled to return to the marquis, as ignorant and more hopeless than he had left him. With much pain he reached the village which his emissaries had discovered, when fortunately he obtained some medical assistance. Here he was obliged by indisposition to rest. The anguish of his mind equalled that of his body. Those impetuous passions which so strongly marked his nature, were roused and exasperated to a degree that operated powerfully upon his constitution, and threatened him with the most alarming consequences. The effect of his wound was heightened by the agitation of his mind; and a fever, which quickly assumed a very serious aspect, co-operated to endanger his life.

CHAPTER VI

The castle of Mazzini was still the scene of dissension and misery. The impatience and astonishment of the marquis being daily increased by the lengthened absence of the duke, he dispatched servants to the forest of Marentino, to enquire the occasion of this circumstance. They returned with intelligence that neither Julia, the duke, nor any of his people were there. He therefore concluded that his daughter had fled the cottage upon information of the approach of the duke, who, he believed, was still engaged in the pursuit. With respect to Ferdinand, who yet pined in sorrow and anxiety in his dungeon, the rigour of the marquis's conduct was unabated. He apprehended that his son, if liberated, would quickly discover the retreat of Julia, and by his advice and assistance confirm her in disobedience.

Ferdinand, in the stillness and solitude of his dungeon, brooded over the late calamity in gloomy ineffectual lamentation. The idea of Hippolitus—of Hippolitus murdered—arose to his imagination in busy intrusion, and subdued the strongest efforts of his fortitude. Julia too, his beloved sister—unprotected—unfriended—might, even at the moment he lamented her, be sinking under sufferings dreadful to humanity. The airy schemes he once formed of future felicity, resulting from the union of two persons so justly dear to him—with the gay visions of past happiness—floated upon his fancy, and the lustre they reflected served only to heighten, by contrast, the obscurity and gloom of his present views. He had, however, a new subject of astonishment, which often withdrew his thoughts from their accustomed object, and substituted a sensation less painful, though scarcely less powerful. One night as he lay ruminating on the past, in melancholy dejection, the stillness of the place was suddenly interrupted by a low and dismal sound. It returned at intervals in hollow sighings, and seemed to come from some person in deep distress. So much did fear operate upon his mind, that he was uncertain whether it arose from within or from without. He looked around his dungeon, but could distinguish no object through the impenetrable darkness. As he listened in deep amazement, the sound was repeated in moans more hollow. Terror now occupied his mind, and disturbed his reason; he started from his posture, and, determined to be satisfied whether any person beside himself was in the dungeon, groped, with arms extended, along the walls. The place was empty; but coming to a particular spot, the sound suddenly arose more distinctly to his ear. He called aloud, and asked who was there; but received no answer. Soon after all was still; and after listening for some time without hearing the sounds renewed, he laid himself down to sleep. On the following day he mentioned to the man who brought him food what he had heard, and enquired concerning the noise. The servant appeared very much terrified, but could give no information that might in the least account for the circumstance, till he mentioned the vicinity of the dungeon to the southern buildings. The dreadful relation formerly given by the marquis instantly recurred to the mind of Ferdinand, who did not hesitate to believe that the moans he heard came from the restless spirit of the murdered Della Campo. At this conviction, horror thrilled his nerves; but he remembered his oath, and was silent. His courage, however, yielded to the idea of passing another night alone in his prison, where, if the vengeful spirit of the murdered should appear, he might even die of the horror which its appearance would inspire.

The mind of Ferdinand was highly superior to the general influence of superstition;

but, in the present instance, such strong correlative circumstances appeared, as compelled even incredulity to yield. He had himself heard strange and awful sounds in the forsaken southern buildings; he received from his father a dreadful secret relative to them—a secret in which his honor, nay even his life, was bound up. His father had also confessed, that he had himself there seen appearances which he could never after remember without horror, and which had occasioned him to quit that part of the castle. All these recollections presented to Ferdinand a chain of evidence too powerful to be resisted; and he could not doubt that the spirit of the dead had for once been permitted to revisit the earth, and to call down vengeance on the descendants of the murderer.

This conviction occasioned him a degree of horror, such as no apprehension of mortal powers could have excited; and he determined, if possible, to prevail on Peter to pass the hours of midnight with him in his dungeon. The strictness of Peter's fidelity yielded to the persuasions of Ferdinand, though no bribe could tempt him to incur the resentment of the marquis, by permitting an escape. Ferdinand passed the day in lingering anxious expectation, and the return of night brought Peter to the dungeon. His kindness exposed him to a danger which he had not foreseen; for when seated in the dungeon alone with his prisoner, how easily might that prisoner have conquered him and left him to pay his life to the fury of the marquis. He was preserved by the humanity of Ferdinand, who instantly perceived his advantage, but disdained to involve an innocent man in destruction, and spurned the suggestion from his mind.

Peter, whose friendship was stronger than his courage, trembled with apprehension as the hour drew nigh in which the groans had been heard on the preceding night. He recounted to Ferdinand a variety of terrific circumstances, which existed only in the heated imaginations of his fellow-servants, but which were still admitted by them as facts. Among the rest, he did not omit to mention the light and the figure which had been seen to issue from the south tower on the night of Julia's intended elopement; a circumstance which he embellished with innumerable aggravations of fear and wonder. He concluded with describing the general consternation it had caused, and the consequent behaviour of the marquis, who laughed at the fears of his people, yet condescended to quiet them by a formal review of the buildings whence their terror had originated. He related the adventure of the door which refused to yield, the sounds which arose from within, and the discovery of the fallen roof; but declared that neither he, nor any of his fellow servants, believed the noise or the obstruction proceeded from that, 'because, my lord,' continued he, 'the door seemed to be held only in one place; and as for the noise—O! Lord! I never shall forget what a noise it was!—it was a thousand times louder than what any stones could make.'

Ferdinand listened to this narrative in silent wonder! wonder not occasioned by the adventure described, but by the hardihood and rashness of the marquis, who had thus exposed to the inspection of his people, that dreadful spot which he knew from experience to be the haunt of an injured spirit; a spot which he had hitherto scrupulously concealed from human eye, and human curiosity; and which, for so many years, he had not dared even himself to enter. Peter went on, but was presently interrupted by a hollow moan, which seemed to come from beneath the ground. 'Blessed virgin!' exclaimed he: Ferdinand listened in awful expectation. A groan longer and more dreadful was repeated, when Peter started from his seat, and snatching up the lamp, rushed out of the dungeon. Ferdinand, who was left in total darkness, followed to the door, which the affrighted Peter had not stopped to fasten, but which had closed, and seemed held by a lock that could be opened only on the outside. The sensations of Ferdinand, thus compelled to remain in the dungeon, are not to be imagined. The horrors of the night, whatever they were to be, he was to endure alone. By degrees, however, he seemed to acquire the valour of despair. The sounds were repeated, at intervals, for near an hour, when silence returned, and remained undisturbed during the rest of the night. Ferdinand was alarmed by no appearance, and at length, overcome with anxiety and watching, he sunk to repose.

On the following morning Peter returned to the dungeon, scarcely knowing what to expect, yet expecting something very strange, perhaps the murder, perhaps the supernatural disappearance of his young lord. Full of these wild apprehensions, he dared not venture thither alone, but persuaded some of the servants, to whom he had communicated his terrors, to accompany him to the door. As they passed along he recollected, that in the terror of the preceding night he had forgot to fasten the door, and he now feared that his prisoner had made his escape without a miracle. He hurried to the door; and his surprize was extreme to find it fastened. It instantly struck him that this was the work of a supernatural power, when on calling aloud, he was answered by a voice from within. His absurd fear did not suffer him to recognize the voice of Ferdinand, neither did he suppose that Ferdinand had failed to escape, he, therefore, attributed the voice to the being he had heard on the preceding night; and starting back from the door, fled with his companions to the great hall. There the uproar occasioned by their entrance called together a number of persons, amongst whom was the marquis, who was soon informed of the cause of alarm, with a long history of the circumstances of the foregoing night. At this information, the marquis assumed a very stern look, and severely reprimanded Peter for his imprudence, at the same time reproaching the other servants with their undutifulness in thus disturbing his peace. He reminded them of the condescension he had practised to dissipate their former terrors, and of the result of their examination. He then assured them, that since indulgence had only encouraged intrusion, he would for the future be severe; and concluded with declaring, that the first man who should disturb him with a repetition of such ridiculous apprehensions, or should attempt to disturb the peace of the castle by circulating these idle notions, should be rigorously punished, and banished his dominions. They shrunk back at his reproof, and were silent. 'Bring a torch,' said the marquis, 'and shew me to the dungeon. I will once more condescend to confute you.'

They obeyed, and descended with the marquis, who, arriving at the dungeon, instantly threw open the door, and discovered to the astonished eyes of his attendants—Ferdinand!—He started with surprize at the entrance of his father thus attended. The marquis darted upon him a severe look, which he perfectly comprehended.—'Now,' cried he, turning to his people, 'what do you see? My son, whom I myself placed here, and whose voice, which answered to your calls, you have transformed into unknown sounds. Speak, Ferdinand, and confirm what I say.' Ferdinand did so. 'What dreadful spectre appeared to you last night?' resumed the marquis, looking stedfastly upon him: 'gratify these fellows with a description of it, for they cannot exist without something of the marvellous.' 'None, my lord,' replied Ferdinand, who too well understood the manner of the marquis. ''Tis well,' cried the marquis, 'and this is the last time,' turning to his attendants, 'that your folly shall be treated with so much lenity.' He ceased to urge the subject, and forbore to ask Ferdinand even one question before his servants, concerning the nocturnal sounds described by Peter. He quitted the dungeon with eyes steadily bent in anger and suspicion upon Ferdinand. The marquis suspected that the fears of his son had inadvertently betrayed to Peter a part of the secret entrusted to him, and he artfully interrogated Peter with seeming carelessness, concerning the circumstances of the preceding night. From him he drew such answers as honorably acquitted Ferdinand of indiscretion, and relieved himself from tormenting apprehensions.

The following night passed quietly away; neither sound nor appearance disturbed the peace of Ferdinand. The marquis, on the next day, thought proper to soften the severity of his sufferings, and he was removed from his dungeon to a room strongly grated, but exposed to the light of day.

Meanwhile a circumstance occurred which increased the general discord, and threatened Emilia with the loss of her last remaining comfort—the advice and consolation of Madame de Menon. The marchioness, whose passion for the Count de Vereza had at length yielded to absence, and the pressure of present circumstances, now bestowed her smiles upon a young Italian cavalier, a visitor at the castle, who possessed too much of the spirit of gallantry to permit a lady to languish in vain. The marquis, whose mind was occupied with other passions, was insensible to the misconduct of his wife, who at all times had the address to disguise her vices beneath the gloss of virtue and innocent freedom. The intrigue was discovered by madame, who, having one day left a book in the oak parlour, returned thither in search of it. As she opened the door of the apartment, she heard the voice of the cavalier in passionate exclamation; and on entering, discovered him rising in some confusion from the feet of the marchioness, who, darting at madame a look of severity, arose from her seat. Madame, shocked at what she had seen, instantly retired, and buried in her own bosom that secret, the discovery of which would most essentially have poisoned the peace of the marquis. The marchioness, who was a stranger to the generosity of sentiment which actuated Madame de Menon, doubted not that she would seize the moment of retaliation, and expose her conduct where most she dreaded it should be known. The consciousness of guilt tortured her with incessant fear of discovery, and from this period her whole attention was employed to dislodge from the castle the person to whom her character was committed. In this it was not difficult to succeed; for the delicacy of madame's feelings made her quick to perceive, and to withdraw from a treatment unsuitable to the natural dignity of her character. She therefore resolved to depart from the castle; but disdaining to take an advantage even over a successful enemy, she determined to be silent on that subject which would instantly have transferred the triumph from her adversary to herself. When the marquis, on hearing her determination to retire, earnestly enquired for the motive of her conduct, she forbore to acquaint him with the real one, and left him to incertitude and disappointment.

To Emilia this design occasioned a distress which almost subdued the resolution of madame. Her tears and intreaties spoke the artless energy of sorrow. In madame she lost her only friend; and she too well understood the value of that friend, to see her depart without feeling and expressing the deepest distress. From a strong attachment to the memory of the mother, madame had been induced to undertake the education of her daughters, whose engaging dispositions had perpetuated a kind of hereditary affection. Regard for Emilia and Julia had alone for some time detained her at the castle; but this was now succeeded by the influence of considerations too powerful to be resisted. As her income was small, it was her plan to retire to her native place, which was situated in a distant part of the island, and there take up her residence in a convent.

Emilia saw the time of madame's departure approach with increased distress. They left each other with a mutual sorrow, which did honour to their hearts. When her last friend was gone, Emilia wandered through the forsaken apartments, where she had been accustomed to converse with Julia, and to receive consolation and sympathy from her dear instructress, with a kind of anguish known only to those who have experienced a similar situation. Madame pursued her journey with a heavy heart. Separated from the objects of her fondest affections, and from the scenes and occupations for which long habit had formed claims upon her heart, she seemed without interest and without motive for exertion. The world appeared a wide and gloomy desert, where no heart welcomed her with kindness—no countenance brightened into smiles at her approach. It was many years since she quitted Calini—and in the interval, death had swept away the few friends she left there. The future presented a melancholy scene; but she had the retrospect of years spent in honorable endeavour and strict integrity, to cheer her heart and encouraged her hopes.

But her utmost endeavours were unable to express the anxiety with which the uncertain fate of Julia overwhelmed her. Wild and terrific images arose to her imagination. Fancy drew the scene;—she deepened the shades; and the terrific aspect of the objects she presented was heightened by the obscurity which involved them.

[End of Vol. I]

CHAPTER VII

Towards the close of day Madame de Menon arrived at a small village situated among the mountains, where she purposed to pass the night. The evening was remarkably fine, and the romantic beauty of the surrounding scenery invited her to walk. She followed the windings of a stream, which was lost at some distance amongst luxuriant groves of chesnut. The rich colouring of evening glowed through the dark foliage, which spreading a pensive gloom around, offered a scene congenial to the present temper of her mind, and she entered the shades. Her thoughts, affected by the surrounding objects, gradually sunk into a pleasing and complacent melancholy, and she was insensibly led on. She still followed the course of the stream to where the deep shades retired, and the scene again opening to day, yielded to her a view so various and sublime, that she paused in thrilling and delightful wonder. A group of wild and grotesque rocks rose in a semicircular form, and their fantastic shapes exhibited Nature in her most sublime and striking attitudes. Here her vast magnificence elevated the mind of the beholder to enthusiasm. Fancy caught the thrilling sensation, and at her touch the towering steeps became shaded with unreal glooms; the caves more darkly frowned—the projecting cliffs assumed a more terrific aspect, and the wild overhanging shrubs waved to the gale in deeper murmurs. The scene inspired madame with reverential awe, and her thoughts involuntarily rose, 'from Nature up to Nature's God.' The last dying gleams of day tinted the rocks and shone upon the waters, which retired through a rugged channel and were lost afar among the receding cliffs. While she listened to their distant murmur, a voice of liquid and melodious sweetness arose from among the rocks; it sung an air, whose melancholy expression awakened all her attention, and captivated her heart. The tones swelled and died faintly away among the clear, yet languishing echoes which the rocks repeated with an effect like that of enchantment. Madame looked around in search of the sweet warbler, and observed at some distance a peasant girl seated on a small projection of the rock, overshadowed by drooping sycamores. She moved slowly towards the spot, which she had almost reached, when the sound of her steps startled and silenced the syren, who, on perceiving a stranger, arose in an attitude to depart. The voice of madame arrested her, and she approached. Language cannot paint the sensation of madame, when in the disguise of a peasant girl, she distinguished the features of Julia, whose eyes lighted up with sudden recollection, and who sunk into her arms overcome with joy. When their first emotions were subsided, and Julia had received answers to her enquiries concerning Ferdinand and Emilia, she led madame to the place of her concealment. This was a solitary cottage, in a close valley surrounded by mountains, whose cliffs appeared wholly inaccessible to mortal foot. The deep solitude of the scene dissipated at once madame's wonder that Julia had so long remained undiscovered, and excited surprize how she had been able to explore a spot thus deeply sequestered; but madame observed with extreme concern, that the countenance of Julia no longer wore the smile of health and gaiety. Her fine features had received the impressions not only of melancholy, but of grief. Madame sighed as she gazed, and read too plainly the cause of the change. Julia understood that sigh, and answered it with her tears. She pressed the hand of madame in mournful silence to her lips, and her cheeks were suffused with a crimson glow. At length, recovering herself, 'I have much, my dear madam, to tell,' said she, 'and much to explain, 'ere you will admit me again to that esteem of which I was once so justly proud. I had no resource from misery, but in flight; and of that I could not make you a confidant, without meanly involving you in its disgrace.'—'Say no more, my love, on the subject,' replied madame; 'with respect to myself, I admired your conduct, and felt severely for your situation. Rather let me hear by what means you effected your escape, and what has since be fallen you.'—Julia paused a moment, as if to stifle her rising emotion, and then commenced her narrative.

'You are already acquainted with the secret of that night, so fatal to my peace. I recall the remembrance of it with an anguish which I cannot conceal; and why should I wish its concealment, since I mourn for one, whose noble qualities justified all my admiration, and deserved more than my feeble praise can bestow; the idea of whom will be the last to linger in my mind till death shuts up this painful scene.' Her voice trembled, and she paused. After a few moments she resumed her tale. 'I will spare myself the pain of recurring to scenes with which you are not unacquainted, and proceed to those which more immediately attract your interest. Caterina, my faithful servant, you know, attended me in my confinement; to her kindness I owe my escape. She obtained from her lover, a servant in the castle, that assistance which gave me liberty. One night when Carlo, who had been appointed my guard, was asleep, Nicolo crept into his chamber, and stole from him the keys of my prison. He had previously procured a ladder of ropes. O! I can never forget my emotions, when in the dead hour of that night, which was meant to precede the day of my sacrifice, I heard the door of my prison unlock, and found myself half at liberty! My trembling limbs with difficulty supported me as I followed Caterina to the saloon, the windows of which being low and near to the terrace, suited our purpose. To the terrace we easily got, where Nicolo awaited us with the rope-ladder. He fastened it to the ground; and having climbed to the top of the parapet, quickly slided down on the other side. There he held it, while we ascended and descended; and I soon breathed the air of freedom again. But the apprehension of being retaken was still too powerful to permit a full enjoyment of my escape. It was my plan to proceed to the place of my faithful Caterina's nativity, where she had assured me I might find a safe asylum in the cottage of her parents, from whom, as they had never seen me, I might conceal my birth. This place, she said, was entirely unknown to the marquis, who had hired her at Naples only a few months before, without any enquiries concerning her family. She had informed me that the village was many leagues distant from the castle, but that she was very well acquainted with the road. At the foot of the walls we left Nicolo, who returned to the castle to prevent suspicion, but with an intention to leave it at a less dangerous time, and repair to Farrini to his good Caterina. I parted from him with many thanks, and gave him a small diamond cross, which, for that purpose, I had taken from the jewels sent to me for wedding ornaments.'

CHAPTER VIII

'About a quarter of a league from the walls we stopped, and I assumed the habit in which you now see me. My own dress was fastened to some heavy stones, and Caterina threw it into the stream, near the almond grove, whose murmurings you have so often admired. The fatigue and hardship I endured in this journey, performed almost wholly on foot, at any other time would have overcome me; but my mind was so occupied by the danger I was avoiding that these lesser evils were disregarded. We arrived in safety at the cottage, which stood at a little distance from the village of Ferrini, and were received by Caterina's parents with some surprise and more kindness. I soon perceived it would be useless, and even dangerous, to attempt to preserve the character I personated. In the eyes of Caterina's mother I read a degree of surprise and admiration which declared she believed me to be of superior rank; I, therefore, thought it more prudent to win her fidelity by entrusting her with my secret than, by endeavouring to conceal it, leave it to be discovered by her curiosity or discernment. Accordingly, I made known my quality and my distress, and received strong assurances of assistance and attachment. For further security, I removed to this sequestered spot. The cottage we are now in belongs to a sister of Caterina, upon whose faithfulness I have been hitherto fully justified in relying. But I am not even here secure from apprehension, since for several days past horsemen of a suspicious appearance have been observed near Marcy, which is only half a league from hence.'

Here Julia closed her narration, to which madame had listened with a mixture of surprise and pity, which her eyes sufficiently discovered. The last circumstance of the narrative seriously alarmed her. She acquainted Julia with the pursuit which the duke had undertaken; and she did not hesitate to believe it a party of his people whom Julia had described. Madame, therefore, earnestly advised her to quit her present situation, and to accompany her in disguise to the monastery of St Augustin, where she would find a secure retreat; because, even if her place of refuge should be discovered, the superior authority of the church would protect her. Julia accepted the proposal with much joy. As it was necessary that madame should sleep at the village where she had left her servants and horses, it was agreed that at break of day she should return to the cottage, where Julia would await her. Madame took all affectionate leave of Julia, whose heart, in spite of reason, sunk when she saw her depart, though but for the necessary interval of repose.

At the dawn of day madame arose. Her servants, who were hired for the journey, were strangers to Julia: from them, therefore, she had nothing to apprehend. She reached the cottage before sunrise, having left her people at some little distance. Her heart foreboded evil, when, on knocking at the door, no answer was returned. She knocked again, and still all was silent. Through the casement she could discover no object, amidst the grey obscurity of the dawn. She now opened the door, and, to her inexpressible surprise and distress, found the cottage empty. She proceeded to a small inner room, where lay a part of Julia's apparel. The bed had no appearance of having being slept in, and every moment served to heighten and confirm her apprehensions. While she pursued the search, she suddenly heard the trampling of feet at the cottage door, and presently after some people entered. Her fears for Julia now yielded to those for her own safety, and she was undetermined whether to discover herself, or remain in her present situation, when she was relieved from her irresolution by the appearance of Julia.

On the return of the good woman, who had accompanied madame to the village on the preceding night, Julia went to the cottage at Farrini. Her grateful heart would not suffer her to depart without taking leave of her faithful friends, thanking them for their kindness, and informing them of her future prospects. They had prevailed upon her to spend the few intervening hours at this cot, whence she had just risen to meet madame.

They now hastened to the spot where the horses were stationed, and commenced their journey. For some leagues they travelled in silence and thought, over a wild and picturesque country. The landscape was tinted with rich and variegated hues; and the autumnal lights, which streamed upon the hills, produced a spirited and beautiful effect upon the scenery. All the glories of the vintage rose to their view: the purple grapes flushed through the dark green of the surrounding foliage, and the prospect glowed with luxuriance.

They now descended into a deep valley, which appeared more like a scene of airy enchantment than reality. Along the bottom flowed a clear majestic stream, whose banks were adorned with thick groves of orange and citron trees. Julia surveyed the scene in silent complacency, but her eye quickly caught an object which changed with instantaneous shock the tone of her feelings. She observed a party of horsemen winding down the side of a hill behind her. Their uncommon speed alarmed her, and she pushed her horse into a gallop. On looking back Madame de Menon clearly perceived they were in pursuit. Soon after the men suddenly appeared from behind a dark grove within a small distance of them; and, upon their nearer approach, Julia, overcome with fatigue and fear, sunk breathless from her horse. She was saved from the ground by one of the pursuers, who caught her in his arms. Madame, with the rest of the party, were quickly overtaken; and as soon as Julia revived, they were bound, and reconducted to the hill from whence they had descended. Imagination only can paint the anguish of Julia's mind, when she saw herself thus delivered up to the power of her enemy. Madame, in the surrounding troop, discovered none of the marquis's people, and they were therefore evidently in the hands of the duke. After travelling for some hours, they quitted the main road, and turned into a narrow winding dell, overshadowed by high trees, which almost excluded the light. The gloom of the place inspired terrific images. Julia trembled as she entered; and her emotion was heightened, when she perceived at some distance, through the long perspective of the trees, a large ruinous mansion. The gloom of the surrounding shades partly concealed it from her view; but, as she drew near, each forlorn and decaying feature of the fabric was gradually disclosed, and struck upon her heart a horror such as she had never before experienced. The broken battlements, enwreathed with ivy, proclaimed the fallen grandeur of the place, while the shattered vacant window-frames exhibited its desolation, and the high grass that overgrew the threshold seemed to say how long it was since mortal foot had entered. The place appeared fit only for the purposes of violence and destruction: and the unfortunate captives, when they stopped at its gates, felt the full force of its horrors.

They were taken from their horses, and conveyed to an interior part of the building, which, if it had once been a chamber, no longer deserved the name. Here the guard said they were directed to detain them till the arrival of their lord, who had appointed this the place of rendezvous. He was expected to meet them in a few hours, and these were hours of indescribable torture to Julia and madame. From the furious passions of the duke, exasperated by frequent disappointment, Julia had every evil to apprehend; and the loneliness of the spot he had chosen, enabled him to perpetrate any designs, however violent. For the first time, she repented that she had left her father's house. Madame wept over her, but comfort she had none to give. The day closed—the duke did not appear, and the fate of Julia yet hung in perilous uncertainty. At length, from a window of the apartment she was in, she distinguished a glimmering of torches among the trees, and presently after the clattering of hoofs convinced her the duke was approaching. Her heart sunk at the sound; and throwing her arms round madame's neck, she resigned herself to despair. She was soon roused by some men, who came to announce the arrival of their lord. In a few moments the place, which had lately been so silent, echoed with tumult; and a sudden blaze of light illumining the fabric, served to exhibit more forcibly its striking horrors. Julia ran to the window; and, in a sort of court below, perceived a group of men dismounting from their horses. The torches shed a partial light; and while she anxiously looked round for the person of the duke, the whole party entered the mansion. She listened to a confused uproar of voices, which sounded from the room beneath, and soon after it sunk into a low murmur, as if some matter of importance was in agitation. For some moments she sat in lingering terror, when she heard footsteps advancing towards the chamber, and a sudden gleam of torchlight flashed upon the walls. 'Wretched girl! I have at least secured you!' said a cavalier, who now entered the room. He stopped as he perceived Julia; and turning to the men who stood without, 'Are these,' said he, 'the fugitives you have taken?'— 'Yes, my lord.'—'Then you have deceived yourselves, and misled me; this is not my daughter.' These words struck the sudden light of truth and joy upon the heart of Julia, whom terror had before rendered almost lifeless; and who had not perceived that the person entering was a stranger. Madame now stepped forward, and an explanation ensued, when it appeared that the stranger was the Marquis Murani, the father of the fair fugitive whom the duke had before mistaken for Julia.

The appearance and the evident flight of Julia had deceived the banditti employed by this nobleman, into a belief that she was the object of their search, and had occasioned her this unnecessary distress. But the joy she now felt, on finding herself thus unexpectedly at liberty, surpassed, if possible, her preceding terrors. The marquis made madame and Julia all the reparation in his power, by offering immediately to reconduct them to the main road, and to guard them to some place of safety for the night. This offer was eagerly and thankfully accepted; and though faint from distress, fatigue, and want of sustenance, they joyfully remounted their horses, and by torchlight quitted the mansion. After some hours travelling they arrived at a small town, where they procured the accommodation so necessary to their support and repose. Here their guides quitted them to continue their search.

They arose with the dawn, and continued their journey, continually terrified with the apprehension of encountering the duke's people. At noon they arrived at Azulia, from whence the monastery, or abbey of St Augustin, was distant only a few miles. Madame wrote to the Padre Abate, to whom she was somewhat related, and soon after received an answer very favourable to her wishes. The same evening they repaired to the abbey; where Julia, once more relieved from the fear of pursuit, offered up a prayer of gratitude to heaven, and endeavoured to calm her sorrows by devotion. She was received by the abbot with a sort of paternal affection, and by the nuns with officious kindness. Comforted by these circumstances, and by the tranquil appearance of every thing around her, she retired to rest, and passed the night in peaceful slumbers.

In her present situation she found much novelty to amuse, and much serious matter to interest her mind. Entendered by distress, she easily yielded to the pensive manners of her companions and to the serene uniformity of a monastic life. She loved to wander through the lonely cloisters, and high-arched aisles, whose long perspectives retired in simple grandeur, diffusing a holy calm around. She found much pleasure in the conversation of the nuns, many of whom were uncommonly amiable, and the dignified sweetness of whose manners formed a charm irresistibly attractive. The soft melancholy impressed upon their countenances, pourtrayed the situation of their minds, and excited in Julia a very interesting mixture of pity and esteem. The affectionate appellation of sister, and all that endearing tenderness which they so well know how to display, and of which they so well understand the effect, they bestowed on Julia, in the hope of winning her to become one of their order.

Soothed by the presence of madame, the assiduity of the nuns, and by the stillness and sanctity of the place, her mind gradually recovered a degree of complacency to which it had long been a stranger. But notwithstanding all her efforts, the idea of Hippolitus would at intervals return upon her memory with a force that at once subdued her fortitude, and sunk her in a temporary despair.

Among the holy sisters, Julia distinguished one, the singular fervor of whose devotion, and the pensive air of whose countenance, softened by the languor of illness, attracted her curiosity, and excited a strong degree of pity. The nun, by a sort of sympathy, seemed particularly inclined towards Julia, which she discovered by innumerable acts of kindness, such as the heart can quickly understand and acknowledge, although description can never reach them. In conversation with her, Julia endeavoured, as far as delicacy would permit, to prompt an explanation of that more than common dejection which shaded those features, where beauty, touched by resignation and sublimed by religion, shone forth with mild and lambent lustre.

The Duke de Luovo, after having been detained for some weeks by the fever which his wounds had produced, and his irritated passions had much prolonged, arrived at the castle of Mazzini.

When the marquis saw him return, and recollected the futility of those exertions, by which he had boastingly promised to recover Julia, the violence of his nature spurned the disguise of art, and burst forth in contemptuous impeachment of the valour and discernment of the duke, who soon retorted with equal fury. The consequence might have been fatal, had not the ambition of the marquis subdued the sudden irritation of his inferior passions, and induced him to soften the severity of his accusations, by subsequent concessions. The duke, whose passion for Julia was heightened by the difficulty which opposed it, admitted such concessions as in other circumstances he would have rejected; and thus each, conquered by the predominant passion of the moment, submitted to be the slave of his adversary.

Emilia was at length released from the confinement she had so unjustly suffered. She had now the use of her old apartments, where, solitary and dejected, her hours moved heavily along, embittered by incessant anxiety for Julia, by regret for the lost society of madame. The marchioness, whose pleasures suffered a temporary suspense during the present confusion at the castle, exercised the ill-humoured caprice, which disappointment and lassitude inspired, upon her remaining subject. Emilia was condemned to suffer, and to endure without the privilege of complaining. In reviewing the events of the last few weeks, she saw those most dear to her banished, or imprisoned by the secret influence of a woman, every feature of whose character was exactly opposite to that of the amiable mother she had been appointed to succeed.

The search after Julia still continued, and was still unsuccessful. The astonishment of the marquis increased with his disappointments; for where could Julia, ignorant of the country, and destitute of friends, have possibly found an asylum? He swore with a terrible oath to revenge on her head, whenever she should be found, the trouble and vexation she now caused him. But he agreed with the duke to relinquish for a while the search; till Julia, gaining confidence from the observation of this circumstance, might gradually suppose herself secure from molestation, and thus be induced to emerge from concealment.

CHAPTER IX

Meanwhile Julia, sheltered in the obscure recesses of St Augustin, endeavoured to attain a degree of that tranquillity which so strikingly characterized the scenes around her. The abbey of St Augustin was a large magnificent mass of Gothic architecture, whose gloomy battlements, and majestic towers arose in proud sublimity from amid the darkness of the surrounding shades. It was founded in the twelfth century, and stood a proud monument of monkish superstition and princely magnificence. In the times when Italy was agitated by internal commotions, and persecuted by foreign invaders, this edifice afforded an asylum to many noble Italian emigrants, who here consecrated the rest of their days to religion. At their death they enriched the monastery with the treasures which it had enabled them to secure.

The view of this building revived in the mind of the beholder the memory of past ages. The manners and characters which distinguished them arose to his fancy, and through the long lapse of years he discriminated those customs and manners which formed so striking a contrast to the modes of his own times. The rude manners, the boisterous passions, the daring ambition, and the gross indulgences which formerly characterized the priest, the nobleman, and the sovereign, had now begun to yield to learning—the charms of refined conversation—political intrigue and private artifices. Thus do the scenes of life vary with the predominant passions of mankind, and with the progress of civilization. The dark clouds of prejudice break away before the sun of science, and gradually dissolving, leave the brightening hemisphere to the influence of his beams. But through the present scene appeared only a few scattered rays, which served to shew more forcibly the vast and heavy masses that concealed the form of truth. Here prejudice, not reason, suspended the influence of the passions; and scholastic learning, mysterious philosophy, and crafty sanctity supplied the place of wisdom, simplicity, and pure devotion.

At the abbey, solitude and stillness conspired with the solemn aspect of the pile to impress the mind with religious awe. The dim glass of the high-arched windows, stained with the colouring of monkish fictions, and shaded by the thick trees that environed the edifice, spread around a sacred gloom, which inspired the beholder with congenial feelings.

As Julia mused through the walks, and surveyed this vast monument of barbarous superstition, it brought to her recollection an ode which she often repeated with melancholy pleasure, as the composition of Hippolitus.

SUPERSTITION

AN ODE

High mid Alverna's awful steeps,
   Eternal shades, and silence dwell.
Save, when the gale resounding sweeps,
   Sad strains are faintly heard to swell:

Enthron'd amid the wild impending rocks,

> Involved in clouds, and brooding future woe,
> The demon Superstition Nature shocks,
>   And waves her sceptre o'er the world below.
>
> Around her throne, amid the mingling glooms,
>   Wild—hideous forms are slowly seen to glide,
> She bids them fly to shade earth's brightest blooms,
>   And spread the blast of Desolation wide.
>
> See! in the darkened air their fiery course!
>   The sweeping ruin settles o'er the land,
> Terror leads on their steps with madd'ning force,
>   And Death and Vengeance close the ghastly band!
>
>   Mark the purple streams that flow!
>   Mark the deep empassioned woe!
>   Frantic Fury's dying groan!
>   Virtue's sigh, and Sorrow's moan!
>
> Wide—wide the phantoms swell the loaded air
> With shrieks of anguish—madness and despair!
>
> Cease your ruin! spectres dire!
>   Cease your wild terrific sway!
> Turn your steps—and check your ire,
>   Yield to peace the mourning day!

She wept to the memory of times past, and there was a romantic sadness in her feelings, luxurious and indefinable. Madame behaved to Julia with the tenderest attention, and endeavoured to withdraw her thoughts from their mournful subject by promoting that taste for literature and music, which was so suitable to the powers of her mind.

But an object seriously interesting now obtained that regard, which those of mere amusement failed to attract. Her favorite nun, for whom her love and esteem daily increased, seemed declining under the pressure of a secret grief. Julia was deeply affected with her situation, and though she was not empowered to administer consolation to her sorrows, she endeavoured to mitigate the sufferings of illness. She nursed her with unremitting care, and seemed to seize with avidity the temporary opportunity of escaping from herself. The nun appeared perfectly reconciled to her fate, and exhibited during her illness so much sweetness, patience, and resignation as affected all around her with pity and love. Her angelic mildness, and steady fortitude characterized the beatification of a saint, rather than the death of a mortal. Julia watched every turn of her disorder with the utmost solicitude, and her care was at length rewarded by the amendment of Cornelia. Her health gradually improved, and she attributed this circumstance to the assiduity and tenderness of her young friend, to whom her heart now expanded in warm and unreserved affection. At length Julia ventured to solicit what she had so long and so earnestly wished for, and Cornelia unfolded the history of her sorrows.

'Of the life which your care has prolonged,' said she, 'it is but just that you should know the events; though those events are neither new, or striking, and possess little power of interesting persons unconnected with them. To me they have, however, been unexpectedly dreadful in effect, and my heart assures me, that to you they will not be indifferent.

'I am the unfortunate descendant of an ancient and illustrious Italian family. In early childhood I was deprived of a mother's care, but the tenderness of my surviving parent made her loss, as to my welfare, almost unfelt. Suffer me here to do justice to the character of my noble father. He united in an eminent degree the mild virtues of social life, with the firm unbending qualities of the noble Romans, his ancestors, from whom he was proud to trace his descent. Their merit, indeed, continually dwelt on his tongue, and their actions he was always endeavouring to imitate, as far as was consistent with the character of his times, and with the limited sphere in which he moved. The recollection of his virtue elevates my mind, and fills my heart with a noble pride, which even the cold walls of a monastery have not been able to subdue.

'My father's fortune was unsuitable to his rank. That his son might hereafter be enabled to support the dignity of his family, it was necessary for me to assume the veil. Alas! that heart was unfit to be offered at an heavenly shrine, which was already devoted to an earthly object. My affections had long been engaged by the younger son of a neighbouring nobleman, whose character and accomplishments attracted my early love, and confirmed my latest esteem. Our families were intimate, and our youthful intercourse occasioned an attachment which strengthened and expanded with our years. He solicited me of my father, but there appeared an insuperable barrier to our union. The family of my lover laboured under a circumstance of similar distress with that of my own—it was noble—but poor! My father, who was ignorant of the strength of my affection, and who considered a marriage formed in poverty as destructive to happiness, prohibited his suit.

'Touched with chagrin and disappointment, he immediately entered into the service of his Neapolitan majesty, and sought in the tumultuous scenes of glory, a refuge from the pangs of disappointed passion.

'To me, whose hours moved in one round of full uniformity—who had no pursuit to interest—no variety to animate my drooping spirits—to me the effort of forgetfulness was ineffectual. The loved idea of Angelo still rose upon my fancy, and its powers of captivation, heightened by absence, and, perhaps even by despair, pursued me with incessant grief. I concealed in silence the anguish that preyed upon my heart, and resigned myself a willing victim to monastic austerity. But I was now threatened with a new evil, terrible and unexpected. I was so unfortunate as to attract the admiration of the Marquis Marinelli, and he applied to my father. He was illustrious at once in birth and fortune, and his visits could only be unwelcome to me. Dreadful was the moment in which my father disclosed to me the proposal. My distress, which I vainly endeavoured to command, discovered the exact situation of my heart, and my father was affected.

'After along and awful pause, he generously released me from my sufferings by leaving it to my choice to accept the marquis, or to assume the veil. I fell at his feet, overcome by the noble disinterestedness of his conduct, and instantly accepted the latter.

'This affair removed entirely the disguise with which I had hitherto guarded my heart;—my brother—my generous brother! learned the true state of its affections. He saw the grief which prayed upon my health; he observed it to my father, and he nobly—oh how nobly! to restore my happiness, desired to resign apart of the estate which had already descended to him in right of his mother. Alas! Hippolitus,' continued Cornelia, deeply sighing, 'thy virtues deserved a better fate.'

'Hippolitus!' said Julia, in a tremulous accent, 'Hippolitus, Count de Vereza!'—'The same,' replied the nun, in a tone of surprize. Julia was speechless; tears, however, came to her relief. The astonishment of Cornelia for some moment surpassed expression; at length a gleam of recollection crossed her mind, and she too well understood the scene before her. Julia, after some time revived, when Cornelia tenderly approaching her, 'Do I then embrace my sister!' said she. 'United in sentiment, are we also united in misfortune?' Julia answered with her sighs, and their tears flowed in mournful sympathy together. At length Cornelia resumed her narrative.

'My father, struck with the conduct of Hippolitus, paused upon the offer. The alteration in my health was too obvious to escape his notice; the conflict between pride and parental tenderness, held him for some time in indecision, but the latter finally subdued every opposing feeling, and he yielded his consent to my marriage with Angelo. The sudden transition from grief to joy was almost too much for my feeble frame; judge then what must have been the effect of the dreadful reverse, when the news arrived that Angelo had fallen in a foreign engagement! Let me obliterate, if possible, the impression of sensations so dreadful. The sufferings of my brother, whose generous heart could so finely feel for another's woe, were on this occasion inferior only to my own.

'After the first excess of my grief was subsided, I desired to retire from a world which had tempted me only with illusive visions of happiness, and to remove from those scenes which prompted recollection, and perpetuated my distress. My father applauded my resolution, and I immediately was admitted a noviciate into this monastery, with the Superior of which my father had in his youth been acquainted.

'At the expiration of the year I received the veil. Oh! I well remember with what perfect resignation, with what comfortable complacency I took those vows which bound me to a life of retirement, and religious rest.

'The high importance of the moment, the solemnity of the ceremony, the sacred glooms which surrounded me, and the chilling silence that prevailed when I uttered the irrevocable vow—all conspired to impress my imagination, and to raise my views to heaven. When I knelt at the altar, the sacred flame of pure devotion glowed in my heart, and elevated my soul to sublimity. The world and all its recollections faded from my mind, and left it to the influence of a serene and, holy enthusiasm which no words can describe.

'Soon after my noviciation, I had the misfortune to lose my dear father. In the tranquillity of this monastery, however, in the soothing kindness of my companions, and in devotional exercises, my sorrows found relief, and the sting of grief was blunted. My repose was of short continuance. A circumstance occurred that renewed the misery, which, can now never quit me but in the grave, to which I look with no fearful apprehension, but as a refuge from calamity, trusting that the power who has seen good to afflict me, will pardon the imperfectness of my devotion, and the too frequent wandering of my thoughts to the object once so dear to me.'

As she spoke she raised her eyes, which beamed with truth and meek assurance to heaven; and the fine devotional suffusion of her countenance seemed to characterize the beauty of an inspired saint.

'One day, Oh! never shall I forget it, I went as usual to the confessional to acknowledge my sins. I knelt before the father with eyes bent towards the earth, and in a low voice proceeded to confess. I had but one crime to deplore, and that was the too tender remembrance of him for whom I mourned, and whose idea, impressed upon my heart, made it a blemished offering to God.

'I was interrupted in my confession by a sound of deep sobs, and rising my eyes, Oh God, what were my sensations, when in the features of the holy father I discovered Angelo! His image faded like a vision from my sight, and I sunk at his feet. On recovering I found myself on my matrass, attended by a sister, who I discovered by her conversation had no suspicion of the occasion of my disorder. Indisposition confined me to my bed for several days; when I recovered, I saw Angelo no more, and could almost have doubted my senses, and believed that an illusion had crossed my sight, till one day I found in my cell a written paper. I distinguished at the first glance the handwriting of Angelo, that well-known hand which had so often awakened me to other emotions. I trembled at the sight; my beating heart acknowledged the beloved characters; a cold tremor shook my frame, and half breathless I seized the paper. But recollecting myself, I paused—I hesitated: duty at length yielded to the strong temptation, and I read the lines! Oh! those lines prompted by despair, and bathed in my tears! every word they offered gave a new pang to my heart, and swelled its anguish almost beyond endurance. I learned that Angelo, severely wounded in a foreign engagement, had been left for dead upon the field; that his life was saved by the humanity of a common soldier of the enemy, who perceiving signs of existence, conveyed him to a house. Assistance was soon procured, but his wounds exhibited the most alarming symptoms. During several months he languished between life and death, till at length his youth and constitution surmounted the conflict, and he returned to Naples. Here he saw my brother, whose distress and astonishment at beholding him occasioned a relation of past circumstances, and of the vows I had taken in consequence of the report of his death. It is unnecessary to mention the immediate effect of this narration; the final one exhibited a very singular proof of his attachment and despair;—he devoted himself to a monastic life, and chose this abbey for the place of his residence, because it contained the object most dear to his affections. His letter informed me that he had purposely avoided discovering himself, endeavouring to be contented with the opportunities which occurred of silently observing me, till chance had occasioned the foregoing interview.—But that since its effects had been so mutually painful, he would relieve me from the apprehension of a similar distress, by assuring me, that I should see him no more. He was faithful to his promise; from that day I have never seen him, and am even ignorant whether he yet inhabits this asylum; the efforts of religious fortitude, and the just fear of exciting curiosity, having withheld me from enquiry. But the moment of our last interview has been equally fatal to my peace and to my health, and I trust

I shall, ere very long, be released from the agonizing ineffectual struggles occasioned by the consciousness of sacred vows imperfectly performed, and by earthly affections not wholly subdued.'

Cornelia ceased, and Julia, who had listened to the narrative in deep attention, at once admired, loved, and pitied her. As the sister of Hippolitus, her heart expanded towards her, and it was now inviolably attached by the fine ties of sympathetic sorrow. Similarity of sentiment and suffering united them in the firmest bonds of friendship; and thus, from reciprocation of thought and feeling, flowed a pure and sweet consolation.

Julia loved to indulge in the mournful pleasure of conversing of Hippolitus, and when thus engaged, the hours crept unheeded by. A thousand questions she repeated concerning him, but to those most interesting to her, she received no consolatory answer. Cornelia, who had heard of the fatal transaction at the castle of Mazzini, deplored with her its too certain consequence.

CHAPTER X

Julia accustomed herself to walk in the fine evenings under the shade of the high trees that environed the abbey. The dewy coolness of the air refreshed her. The innumerable roseate tints which the parting sun-beams reflected on the rocks above, and the fine vermil glow diffused over the romantic scene beneath, softly fading from the eye, as the nightshades fell, excited sensations of a sweet and tranquil nature, and soothed her into a temporary forgetfulness of her sorrows.

The deep solitude of the place subdued her apprehension, and one evening she ventured with Madame de Menon to lengthen her walk. They returned to the abbey without having seen a human being, except a friar of the monastery, who had been to a neighbouring town to order provision. On the following evening they repeated their walk; and, engaged in conversation, rambled to a considerable distance from the abbey. The distant bell of the monastery sounding for vespers, reminded them of the hour, and looking round, they perceived the extremity of the wood. They were returning towards the abbey, when struck by the appearance of some majestic columns which were distinguishable between the trees, they paused. Curiosity tempted them to examine to what edifice pillars of such magnificent architecture could belong, in a scene so rude, and they went on.

There appeared on a point of rock impending over the valley the reliques of a palace, whose beauty time had impaired only to heighten its sublimity. An arch of singular magnificence remained almost entire, beyond which appeared wild cliffs retiring in grand perspective. The sun, which was now setting, threw a trembling lustre upon the ruins, and gave a finishing effect to the scene. They gazed in mute wonder upon the view; but the fast fading light, and the dewy chillness of the air, warned them to return. As Julia gave a last look to the scene, she perceived two men leaning upon a part of the ruin at some distance, in earnest conversation. As they spoke, their looks were so attentively bent on her, that she could have no doubt she was the subject of their discourse. Alarmed at this circumstance, madame and Julia immediately retreated towards the abbey. They walked swiftly through the woods, whose shades, deepened by the gloom of evening, prevented their distinguishing whether they were pursued. They were surprized to observe the distance to which they had strayed from the monastery, whose dark towers were now obscurely seen rising among the trees that closed the perspective. They had almost reached the gates, when on looking back, they perceived the same men slowly advancing, without any appearance of pursuit, but clearly as if observing the place of their retreat.

This incident occasioned Julia much alarm. She could not but believe that the men whom she had seen were spies of the marquis;—if so, her asylum was discovered, and she had every thing to apprehend. Madame now judged it necessary to the safety of Julia, that the Abate should be informed of her story, and of the sanctuary she had sought in his monastery, and also that he should be solicited to protect her from parental tyranny. This was a hazardous, but a necessary step, to provide against the certain danger which must ensue, should the marquis, if he demanded his daughter of the Abate, be the first to acquaint him with her story. If she acted otherwise, she feared that the Abate, in whose generosity she had not confided, and whose pity she had not solicited, would, in the pride of his resentment, deliver her up, and thus would she become a certain victim to the Duke de Luovo.

Julia approved of this communication, though she trembled for the event; and requested madame to plead her cause with the Abate. On the following morning, therefore, madame solicited a private audience of the Abate; she obtained permission to see him, and Julia, in trembling anxiety, watched her to the door of his apartment. This conference was long, and every moment seemed an hour to Julia, who, in fearful expectation, awaited with Cornelia the sentence which would decide her destiny. She was now the constant companion of Cornelia, whose declining health interested her pity, and strengthened her attachment.

Meanwhile madame developed to the Abate the distressful story of Julia. She praised her virtues, commended her accomplishments, and deplored her situation. She described the characters of the marquis and the duke, and concluded with pathetically representing, that Julia had sought in this monastery, a last asylum from injustice and misery, and with entreating that the Abate would grant her his pity and protection.

The Abate during this discourse preserved a sullen silence; his eyes were bent to the ground, and his aspect was thoughtful and solemn. When madame ceased to speak, a pause of profound silence ensued, and she sat in anxious expectation. She endeavoured to anticipate in his countenance the answer preparing, but she derived no comfort from thence. At length raising his head, and awakening from his deep reverie, he told her that her request required deliberation, and that the protection she solicited for Julia, might involve him in serious consequences, since, from a character so determined as the marquis's, much violence might reasonably be expected. 'Should his daughter be refused him,' concluded the Abate, 'he may even dare to violate the sanctuary.'

Madame, shocked by the stern indifference of this reply, was a moment silent. The Abate went on. 'Whatever I shall determine upon, the young lady has reason to rejoice that she is admitted into this holy house; for I will even now venture to assure her, that if the marquis fails to demand her, she shall be permitted to remain in this sanctuary unmolested. You, Madam, will be sensible of this indulgence, and of the value of the sacrifice I make in granting it; for, in thus concealing a child from her parent, I encourage her in disobedience, and consequently sacrifice my sense of duty, to what may be justly called a weak humanity.'

Madame listened to pompous declamation in silent sorrow and indignation. She made another effort to interest the Abate in favor of Julia, but he preserved his stern inflexibility, and repeating that he would deliberate upon the matter, and acquaint her with the result, he arose with great solemnity, and quitted the room.

She now half repented of the confidence she had reposed in him, and of the pity she had solicited, since he discovered a mind incapable of understanding the first, and a temper inaccessible to the influence of the latter. With an heavy heart she returned to Julia, who read in her countenance, at the moment she entered the room, news of no happy import. When madame related the particulars of the conference, Julia presaged from it only misery, and giving herself up for lost—she burst into tears. She severely deplored the confidence she had been induced to yield; for she now saw herself in the power of a man, stern and unfeeling in his nature: and from whom, if he thought it fit to betray her, she had no means of escaping. But she concealed the anguish of her heart; and to console madame, affected to hope where she could only despair.

Several days elapsed, and no answer was returned from the Abate. Julia too well understood this silence.

One morning Cornelia entering her room with a disturbed and impatient air, informed her that some emissaries from the marquis were then in the monastery, having enquired at the gate for the Abate, with whom, they said, they had business of importance to transact. The Abate had granted them immediate audience, and they were now in close conference.

At this intelligence the spirits of Julia forsook her; she trembled, grew pale, and stood fixed in mute despair. Madame, though scarcely less distressed, retained a presence of mind. She understood too justly the character of the Superior to doubt that he would hesitate in delivering Julia to the hands of the marquis. On this moment, therefore, turned the crisis of her fate!—this moment she might escape—the next she was a prisoner. She therefore advised Julia to seize the instant, and fly from the monastery before the conference was concluded, when the gates would most probably be closed upon her, assuring her, at the same time, she would accompany her in flight.

The generous conduct of madame called tears of gratitude into the eyes of Julia, who now awoke from the state of stupefaction which distress had caused. But before she could thank her faithful friend, a nun entered the room with a summons for madame to attend the Abate immediately. The distress which this message occasioned can not easily be conceived. Madame advised Julia to escape while she detained the Abate in conversation, as it was not probable that he had yet issued orders for her detention. Leaving her to this attempt, with an assurance of following her from the abbey as soon as possible, madame obeyed the summons. The coolness of her fortitude forsook her as she approached the Abate's apartment, and she became less certain as to the occasion of this summons.

The Abate was alone. His countenance was pale with anger, and he was pacing the room with slow but agitated steps. The stern authority of his look startled her. 'Read this letter,' said he, stretching forth his hand which held a letter, 'and tell me what that mortal deserves, who dares insult our holy order, and set our sacred prerogative at defiance.' Madame distinguished the handwriting of the marquis, and the words of the Superior threw her into the utmost astonishment. She took the letter. It was dictated by that spirit of proud vindictive rage, which so strongly marked the character of the marquis. Having discovered the retreat of Julia, and believing the monastery afforded her a willing sanctuary from his pursuit, he accused the Abate of encouraging his child in open rebellion to his will. He loaded him and his sacred order with opprobrium, and threatened, if she was not immediately resigned to the emissaries in waiting, he would in person lead on a force which should compel the church to yield to the superior authority of the father.

The spirit of the Abate was roused by this menace; and Julia obtained from his pride, that protection which neither his principle or his humanity would have granted. 'The man shall tremble,' cried he, 'who dares defy our power, or question our sacred authority. The lady Julia is safe. I will protect her from this proud invader of our rights, and teach him at least to venerate the power he cannot conquer. I have dispatched his emissaries with my answer.'

These words struck sudden joy upon the heart of Madame de Menon, but she instantly recollected, that ere this time Julia had quitted the abbey, and thus the very precaution which was meant to ensure her safety, had probably precipitated her into the hand of her enemy. This thought changed her joy to anguish; and she was hurrying from the apartment in a sort of wild hope, that Julia might not yet be gone, when the stern voice of the Abate arrested her. 'Is it thus,' cried he, 'that you receive the knowledge of our generous resolution to protect your friend? Does such condescending kindness merit no thanks—demand no gratitude?' Madame returned in an agony of fear, lest one moment of delay might prove fatal to Julia, if haply she had not yet quitted the monastery. She was conscious of her deficiency in apparent gratitude, and of the strange appearance of her abrupt departure from the Abate, for which it was impossible to apologize, without betraying the secret, which would kindle all his resentment. Yet some atonement his present anger demanded, and these circumstances caused her a very painful embarrassment. She formed a hasty excuse; and expressing her sense of his goodness, again attempted to retire, when the Abate frowning in deep resentment, his features inflamed with pride, arose from his seat. 'Stay,' said he; 'whence this impatience to fly from the presence of a benefactor?—If my generosity fails to excite gratitude, my resentment shall not fail to inspire awe.—Since the lady Julia is insensible of my condescension, she is unworthy of my protection, and I will resign her to the tyrant who demands her.'

To this speech, in which the offended pride of the Abate overcoming all sense of justice, accused and threatened to punish Julia for the fault of her friend, madame listened in dreadful impatience. Every word that detained her struck torture to her heart, but the concluding sentence occasioned new terror, and she started at its purpose. She fell at the feet of the Abate in an agony of grief. 'Holy father,' said she, 'punish not Julia for the offence which I only have committed; her heart will bless her generous protector, and for myself, suffer me to assure you that I am fully sensible of your goodness.'

'If this is true,' said the Abate, 'arise, and bid the lady Julia attend me.' This command increased the confusion of madame, who had no doubt that her detention had proved fatal to Julia. At length she was suffered to depart, and to her infinite joy found Julia in her own room. Her intention of escaping had yielded, immediately after the departure of madame, to the fear of being discovered by the marquis's people. This fear had been confirmed by the report of Cornelia, who informed her, that at that time several horsemen were waiting at the gates for the return of their companions. This was a dreadful circumstance to Julia, who perceived it was utterly impossible to quit the monastery, without rushing upon certain destruction. She was lamenting her destiny, when madame recited the particulars of the late interview, and delivered the summons of the Abate.

They had now to dread the effect of that tender anxiety, which had excited his resentment; and Julia, suddenly elated to joy by his first determination, was as suddenly sunk to despair by his last. She trembled with apprehension of the coming interview, though each moment of delay which her fear solicited, would, by heightening the resentment of the Abate, only increase the danger she dreaded.

At length, by a strong effort, she reanimated her spirits, and went to the Abate's closet to receive her sentence. He was seated in his chair, and his frowning aspect chilled her heart. 'Daughter,' said he, 'you have been guilty of heinous crimes. You have dared to dispute—nay openly to rebel, against the lawful authority of your father. You have disobeyed the will of him whose prerogative yields only to ours. You have questioned his right upon a point of all others the most decided—the right of a father to dispose of his child in marriage. You have even fled from his protection—and you have dared—insidiously, and meanly have dared, to screen your disobedience beneath this sacred roof. You have prophaned our sanctuary with your crime. You have brought insult upon our sacred order, and have caused bold and impious defiance of our high prerogative. What punishment is adequate to guilt like this?'

The father paused—his eyes sternly fixed on Julia, who, pale and trembling, could scarcely support herself, and who had no power to reply. 'I will be merciful, and not just,' resumed he,—'I will soften the punishment you deserve, and will only deliver you to your father.' At these dreadful words, Julia bursting into tears, sunk at the feet of the Abate, to whom she raised her eyes in supplicating expression, but was unable to speak. He suffered her to remain in this posture. 'Your duplicity,' he resumed, 'is not the least of your offences.—Had you relied upon our generosity for forgiveness and protection, an indulgence might have been granted;—but under the disguise of virtue you concealed your crimes, and your necessities were hid beneath the mask of devotion.'

These false aspersions roused in Julia the spirit of indignant virtue; she arose from her knees with an air of dignity, that struck even the Abate. 'Holy father,' said she, 'my heart abhors the crime you mention, and disclaims all union with it. Whatever are my offences, from the sin of hypocrisy I am at least free; and you will pardon me if I remind you, that my confidence has already been such, as fully justifies my claim to the protection I solicit. When I sheltered myself within these walls, it was to be presumed that they would protect me from injustice; and with what other term than injustice would you, Sir, distinguish the conduct of the marquis, if the fear of his power did not overcome the dictates of truth?'

The Abate felt the full force of this reproof; but disdaining to appear sensible to it, restrained his resentment. His wounded pride thus exasperated, and all the malignant passions of his nature thus called into action, he was prompted to that cruel surrender which he had never before seriously intended. The offence which Madame de Menon had unintentionally given his haughty spirit urged him to retaliate in punishment. He had, therefore, pleased himself with exciting a terror which he never meant to confirm, and he resolved to be further solicited for that protection which he had already determined to grant. But this reproof of Julia touched him where he was most conscious of defect; and the temporary triumph which he imagined it afforded her, kindled his resentment into flame. He mused in his chair, in a fixed attitude.—She saw in his countenance the deep workings of his mind—she revolved the fate preparing for her, and stood in trembling anxiety to receive her sentence. The Abate considered each aggravating circumstance of the marquis's menace, and each sentence of Julia's speech; and his mind experienced that vice is not only inconsistent with virtue, but with itself—for to gratify his malignity, he now discovered that it would be necessary to sacrifice his pride—since it would be impossible to punish the object of the first without denying himself the gratification of the latter. This reflection suspended his mind in a state of torture, and he sat wrapt in gloomy silence.

The spirit which lately animated Julia had vanished with her words—each moment of silence increased her apprehension; the deep brooding of his thoughts confirmed her in the apprehension of evil, and with all the artless eloquence of sorrow she endeavoured to soften him to pity. He listened to her pleadings in sullen stillness. But each instant now cooled the fervour of his resentment to her, and increased his desire of opposing the marquis. At length the predominant feature of his character resumed its original influence, and overcame the workings of subordinate passion. Proud of his religious authority, he determined never to yield the prerogative of the church to that of the father, and resolved to oppose the violence of the marquis with equal force.

He therefore condescended to relieve Julia from her terrors, by assuring her of his protection; but he did this in a manner so ungracious, as almost to destroy the gratitude which the promise demanded. She hastened with the joyful intelligence to Madame de Menon, who wept over her tears of thankfulness.

CHAPTER XI

Near a fortnight had elapsed without producing any appearance of hostility from the marquis, when one night, long after the hour of repose, Julia was awakened by the bell of the monastery. She knew it was not the hour customary for prayer, and she listened to the sounds, which rolled through the deep silence of the fabric, with strong surprise and terror. Presently she heard the doors of several cells creak on their hinges, and the sound of quick footsteps in the passages—and through the crevices of her door she distinguished passing lights. The whispering noise of steps increased, and every person of the monastery seemed to have awakened. Her terror heightened; it occurred to her that the marquis had surrounded the abbey with his people, in the design of forcing her from her retreat; and she arose in haste, with an intention of going to the chamber of Madame de Menon, when she heard a gentle tap at the door. Her enquiry of who was there, was answered in the voice of madame, and her fears were quickly dissipated, for she learned the bell was a summons to attend a dying nun, who was going to the high altar, there to receive extreme unction.

She quitted the chamber with madame. In her way to the church, the gleam of tapers on the walls, and the glimpse which her eye often caught of the friars in their long black habits, descending silently through the narrow winding passages, with the solemn toll of the bell, conspired to kindle imagination, and to impress her heart with sacred awe. But the church exhibited a scene of solemnity, such as she had never before witnessed. Its gloomy aisles were imperfectly seen by the rays of tapers from the high altar, which shed a solitary gleam over the remote parts of the fabric, and produced large masses of light and shade, striking and sublime in their effect.

While she gazed, she heard a distant chanting rise through the aisles; the sounds swelled in low murmurs on the ear, and drew nearer and nearer, till a sudden blaze of light issued from one of the portals, and the procession entered. The organ instantly sounded a high and solemn peal, and the voices rising altogether swelled the sacred strain. In front appeared the Padre Abate, with slow and measured steps, bearing the holy cross. Immediately followed a litter, on which lay the dying person covered with a white veil, borne along and surrounded by nuns veiled in white, each carrying in her hand a lighted taper. Last came the friars, two and two, cloathed in black, and each bearing a light.

When they reached the high altar, the bier was rested, and in a few moments the anthem ceased. 'The Abate now approached to perform the unction; the veil of the dying nun was lifted—and Julia discovered her beloved Cornelia! Her countenance was already impressed with the image of death, but her eyes brightened with a faint gleam of recollection, when they fixed upon Julia, who felt a cold thrill run through her frame, and leaned for support on madame. Julia now for the first time distinguished the unhappy lover of Cornelia, on whose features was depictured the anguish of his heart, and who hung pale and silent over the bier. The ceremony being finished, the anthem struck up; the bier was lifted, when Cornelia faintly moved her hand, and it was again rested upon the steps of the altar. In a few minutes the music ceased, when lifting her heavy eyes to her lover, with an expression of ineffable tenderness and grief, she attempted to speak, but the sounds died on her closing lips. A faint smile passed over her countenance, and was succeeded by a fine devotional glow; she folded her hands upon her bosom, and with a look of meek resignation, raising towards heaven her eyes, in which now sunk the last sparkles of expiring life—her soul departed in a short deep sigh.

Her lover sinking back, endeavoured to conceal his emotions, but the deep sobs which agitated his breast betrayed his anguish, and the tears of every spectator bedewed the sacred spot where beauty, sense, and innocence expired.

The organ now swelled in mournful harmony; and the voices of the assembly chanted in choral strain, a low and solemn requiem to the spirit of the departed.

Madame hurried Julia, who was almost as lifeless as her departed friend, from the church. A death so sudden heightened the grief which separation would otherwise have occasioned. It was the nature of Cornelia's disorder to wear a changeful but flattering aspect. Though she had long been declining, her decay was so gradual and imperceptible as to lull the apprehensions of her friends into security. It was otherwise with herself; she was conscious of the change, but forbore to afflict them with the knowledge of the truth. The hour of her dissolution was sudden, even to herself; but it was composed, and even happy. In the death of Cornelia, Julia seemed to mourn again that of Hippolitus. Her decease appeared to dissolve the last tie which connected her with his memory.

In one of the friars of the convent, madame was surprized to find the father who had confessed the dying Vincent. His appearance revived the remembrance of the scene she had witnessed at the castle of Mazzini; and the last words of Vincent, combined with the circumstances which had since occurred, renewed all her curiosity and astonishment. But his appearance excited more sensations than those of wonder. She dreaded lest he should be corrupted by the marquis, to whom he was known, and thus be induced to use his interest with the Abate for the restoration of Julia.

From the walls of the monastery, Julia now never ventured to stray. In the gloom of evening she sometimes stole into the cloisters, and often lingered at the grave of Cornelia, where she wept for Hippolitus, as well as for her friend. One evening, during vespers, the bell of the convent was suddenly rang out; the Abate, whose countenance expressed at once astonishment and displeasure, suspended the service, and quitted the altar. The whole congregation repaired to the hall, where they learned that a friar, retiring to the convent, had seen a troop of armed men advancing through the wood; and not doubting they were the people of the marquis, and were approaching with hostile intention, had thought it necessary to give the alarm. The Abate ascended a turret, and thence discovered through the trees a glittering of arms, and in the succeeding moment a band of men issued from a dark part of the wood, into a long avenue which immediately fronted the spot where he stood. The clattering of hoofs was now distinctly heard; and Julia, sinking with terror, distinguished the marquis heading the troops, which, soon after separating in two divisions, surrounded the monastery. The gates were immediately secured; and the Abate, descending from the turret, assembled the friars in the hall, where his voice was soon heard above every other part of the tumult. The terror of Julia made her utterly forgetful of the Padre's promise, and she wished to fly for concealment to the deep caverns belonging to the monastery, which wound under the woods. Madame, whose penetration furnished her with a just knowledge of the Abate's character, founded her security on his pride. She therefore dissuaded Julia from attempting to tamper with the honesty of a servant who had the keys of the vaults, and advised her to rely entirely on the effect of the Abate's resentment towards the marquis. While madame endeavoured to soothe her to composure, a message from the Abate required her immediate attendance. She obeyed, and he bade her follow him to a room which was directly over the gates of the monastery. From thence she saw her father, accompanied by the Duke de Luovo; and as her spirits died away at the sight, the marquis called furiously to the Abate to deliver her instantly into his hands, threatening, if she was detained, to force the gates of the monastery. At this threat the countenance of the Abate grew dark: and leading Julia forcibly to the window, from which she had shrunk back, 'Impious menacer!' said he, 'eternal vengeance be upon thee! From this moment we expel thee from all the rights and communities of our church. Arrogant and daring as you are, your threats I defy—Look here,' said he, pointing to Julia, 'and learn that you are in my power; for if you dare to violate these sacred walls, I will proclaim aloud, in the face of day, a secret which shall make your heart's blood run cold; a secret which involves your honour, nay, your very existence. Now triumph and exult in impious menace!' The marquis started involuntarily at this speech, and his features underwent a sudden change, but he endeavoured to recover himself, and to conceal his confusion. He hesitated for a few moments, uncertain how to act—to desist from violence was to confess himself conscious of the threatened secret; yet he dreaded to inflame the resentment of the Abate, whose menaces his own heart too surely seconded. At length—'All that you have uttered,' said he, 'I despise as the dastardly subterfuge of monkish cunning. Your new insults add to the desire of recovering my daughter, that of punishing you. I would proceed to instant violence, but that would now be an imperfect revenge. I shall, therefore, withdraw my forces, and appeal to a higher power. Thus shall you be compelled at once to restore my daughter and retract your scandalous impeachment of my honor.' Saying this, the turned his horse from the gates, and his people following him, quickly withdrew, leaving the Abate exulting in conquest, and Julia lost in astonishment and doubtful joy. When she recounted to madame the particulars of the conference, she dwelt with emphasis on the threats of the Abate; but madame, though her amazement was heightened at every word, very well understood how the secret, whatever it was, had been obtained. The confessor of Vincent she had already observed in the monastery, and there was no doubt that he had disclosed whatever could be collected from the dying words of Vincent. She knew, also, that the secret would never be published, unless as a punishment for immediate violence, it being one of the first principles of monastic duty, to observe a religious secrecy upon all matters entrusted to them in confession.

When the first tumult of Julia's emotions subsided, the joy which the sudden departure of the marquis occasioned yielded to apprehension. He had threatened to appeal to a higher power, who would compel the Abate to surrender her. This menace excited a just terror, and there remained no means of avoiding the tyranny of the marquis but by quitting the monastery. She therefore requested an audience of the Abate; and having represented the danger of her present situation, she intreated his permission to depart in quest of a safer retreat. The Abate, who well knew the marquis was wholly in his power, smiled at the repetition of his menaces, and denied her request, under pretence of his having now become responsible for her to the church. He bade her be comforted, and promised her his protection; but his assurances were given in so distant and haughty a manner, that Julia left him with fears rather increased than subdued. In crossing the hall, she observed a man hastily enter it, from an opposite door. He was not in the habit of the order, but was muffled up in a cloak, and seemed to wish concealment. As she passed he raised his head, and Julia discovered—her father! He darted at her a look of vengeance; but before she had time even to think, as if suddenly recollecting himself, he covered his face, and rushed by her. Her trembling frame could scarcely support her to the apartment of madame, where she sunk speechless upon a chair, and the terror of her look alone spoke the agony of her mind. When she was somewhat recovered, she related what she had seen, and her conversation with the Abate. But madame was lost in equal perplexity with herself, when she attempted to account for the marquis's appearance. Why, after his late daring menace, should he come secretly to visit the Abate, by whose connivance alone he could have gained admission to the monastery? And what could have influenced the Abate to such a conduct? These circumstances, though equally inexplicable, united to confirm a fear of treachery and surrender. To escape from the abbey was now inpracticable, for the gates were constantly guarded; and even was it possible to pass them, certain detection awaited Julia without from the marquis's people, who were stationed in the woods. Thus encompassed with danger, she could only await in the monastery the issue of her destiny.

While she was lamenting with madame her unhappy fate, she was summoned once more to attend the Abate. At this moment her spirits entirely forsook her; the crisis of her fate seemed arrived; for she did not doubt that the Abate intended to surrender her to the marquis, with whom she supposed he had negotiated the terms of accommodation. It was some time before she could recover composure sufficient to obey the summons; and when she did, every step that bore her towards the Abate's room increased her dread. She paused a moment at the door, 'ere she had courage to open it; the idea of her father's immediate resentment arose to her mind, and she was upon the point of retreating to her chamber, when a sudden step within, near the door, destroyed her hesitation, and she entered the closet. The marquis was not there, and her spirits revived. The flush of triumph was diffused over the features of the Abate, though a shade of unappeased resentment yet remained visible. 'Daughter,' said he, 'the intelligence we have to communicate may rejoice you. Your safety now depends solely on yourself. I give your fate into your own hands, and its issue be upon your head.' He paused, and she was suspended in wondering expectation of the coming sentence. 'I here solemnly assure you of my protection, but it is upon one condition only—that you renounce the world, and dedicate your days to God.' Julia listened with a mixture of grief and astonishment. 'Without this concession on your part, I possess not the power, had I even the inclination, to protect you. If you assume the veil, you are safe within the pale of the church from temporal violence. If you neglect or refuse to do this, the marquis may apply to a power from whom I have no appeal, and I shall be compelled at last to resign you.

'But to ensure your safety, should the veil be your choice, we will procure a dispensation from the usual forms of noviciation, and a few days shall confirm your vows.' He ceased to speak; but Julia, agitated with the most cruel distress, knew not what to reply.

'We grant you three days to decide upon this matter,' continued he, 'at the expiration of which, the veil, or the Duke de Luovo, awaits you.' Julia quitted the closet in mute despair, and repaired to madame, who could now scarcely offer her the humble benefit of consolation.

Meanwhile the Abate exulted in successful vengeance, and the marquis smarted beneath the stings of disappointment. The menace of the former was too seriously alarming to suffer the marquis to prosecute violent measures; and he had therefore resolved, by opposing avarice to pride, to soothe the power which he could not subdue. But he was unwilling to entrust the Abate with a proof of his compliance and his fears by offering a bribe in a letter, and preferred the more humiliating, but safer method, of a private interview. His magnificent offers created a temporary hesitation in the mind of the Abate, who, secure of his advantage, shewed at first no disposition to be reconciled, and suffered the marquis to depart in anxious uncertainty. After maturely deliberating upon the proposals, the pride of the Abate surmounted his avarice, and he determined to prevail upon Julia effectually to destroy the hopes of the marquis, by consecrating her life to religion. Julia passed the night and the next day in a state of mental torture exceeding all description. The gates of the monastery beset with guards, and the woods surrounded by the marquis's people, made escape impossible. From a marriage with the duke, whose late conduct had confirmed the odious idea which his character had formerly impressed, her heart recoiled in horror, and to be immured for life within the walls of a convent, was a fate little less dreadful. Yet such was the effect of that sacred love she bore the memory of Hippolitus, and such her aversion to the duke, that she soon resolved to adopt the veil. On the following evening she informed the Abate of her determination. His heart swelled with secret joy; and even the natural severity of his manner relaxed at the intelligence. He assured her of his approbation and protection, with a degree of kindness which he had never before manifested, and told her the ceremony should be performed on the second day from the present. Her emotion scarcely suffered her to hear his last words. Now that her fate was fixed beyond recall, she almost repented of her choice. Her fancy attached to it a horror not its own; and that evil, which, when offered to her decision, she had accepted with little hesitation, she now paused upon in dubious regret; so apt we are to imagine that the calamity most certain, is also the most intolerable!

When the marquis read the answer of the Abate, all the baleful passions of his nature were roused and inflamed to a degree which bordered upon distraction. In the first impulse of his rage, he would have forced the gates of the monastery, and defied the utmost malice of his enemy. But a moment's reflection revived his fear of the threatened secret, and he saw that he was still in the power of the Superior.

The Abate procured the necessary dispensation, and preparations were immediately began for the approaching ceremony. Julia watched the departure of those moments which led to her fate with the calm fortitude of despair. She had no means of escaping from the coming evil, without exposing herself to a worse; she surveyed it therefore with a steady eye, and no longer shrunk from its approach.

On the morning preceding the day of her consecration, she was informed that a stranger enquired for her at the grate. Her mind had been so long accustomed to the vicissitudes of apprehension, that fear was the emotion which now occurred; she suspected, yet scarcely knew why, that the marquis was below, and hesitated whether to descend. A little reflection determined her, and she went to the parlour—where, to her equal joy and surprise, she beheld—Ferdinand!

During the absence of the marquis from his castle, Ferdinand, who had been informed of the discovery of Julia, effected his escape from imprisonment, and had hastened to the monastery in the design of rescuing her. He had passed the woods in disguise, with much difficulty eluding the observation of the marquis's people, who were yet dispersed round the abbey. To the monastery, as he came alone, he had been admitted without difficulty.

When he learned the conditions of the Abate's protection, and that the following day was appointed for the consecration of Julia, he was shocked, and paused in deliberation. A period so short as was this interval, afforded little opportunity for contrivance, and less for hesitation. The night of the present day was the only time that remained for the attempt and execution of a plan of escape, which if it then failed of success, Julia would not only be condemned for life to the walls of a monastery, but would be subjected to whatever punishment the severity of the Abate, exasperated by the detection, should think fit to inflict. The danger was desperate, but the occasion was desperate also.

The nobly disinterested conduct of her brother, struck Julia with gratitude and admiration; but despair of success made her now hesitate whether she should accept his offer. She considered that his generosity would most probably involve him in destruction with herself; and she paused in deep deliberation, when Ferdinand informed her of a circumstance which, till now, he had purposely concealed, and which at once dissolved every doubt and every fear. 'Hippolitus,' said Ferdinand, 'yet lives.'—'Lives!' repeated Julia faintly,—'lives, Oh! tell me where—how.'—Her breath refused to aid her, and she sunk in her chair overcome with the strong and various sensations that pressed upon her heart. Ferdinand, whom the grate withheld from assisting her, observed her situation with extreme distress. When she recovered, he informed her that a servant of Hippolitus, sent no doubt by his lord to enquire concerning Julia, had been lately seen by one of the marquis's people in the neighbourhood of the castle. From him it was known that the Count de Vereza was living, but that his life had been despaired of; and he was still confined, by dangerous wounds, in an obscure town on the coast of Italy. The man had steadily refused to mention the place of his lord's abode. Learning that the marquis was then at the abbey of St Augustin, whither he pursued his daughter, the man disappeared from Mazzini, and had not since been heard of.

It was enough for Julia to know that Hippolitus lived; her fears of detection, and her scruples concerning Ferdinand, instantly vanished; she thought only of escape—and the means which had lately appeared so formidable—so difficult in contrivance, and so dangerous in execution, now seemed easy, certain, and almost accomplished.

They consulted on the plan to be adopted, and agreed, that in attempting to bribe a servant of the monastery to their interest, they should incur a danger too imminent, yet it appeared scarcely practicable to succeed in their scheme without risquing this. After much consideration, they determined to entrust their secret to no person but to madame. Ferdinand was to contrive to conceal himself till the dead of night in the church, between which and the monastery were several doors of communication.

When the inhabitants of the abbey were sunk in repose, Julia might without difficulty pass to the church, where Ferdinand awaiting her, they might perhaps escape either through an outer door of the fabric, or through a window, for which latter attempt Ferdinand was to provide ropes.

A couple of horses were to be stationed among the rocks beyond the woods, to convey the fugitives to a sea-port, whence they could easily pass over to Italy. Having arranged this plan, they separated in the anxious hope of meeting on the ensuing night.

Madame warmly sympathized with Julia in her present expectations, and was now somewhat relieved from the pressure of that self-reproach, with which the consideration of having withdrawn her young friend from a secure asylum, had long tormented her. In learning that Hippolitus lived, Julia experienced a sudden renovation of life and spirits. From the languid stupefaction which despair had occasioned she revived as from a dream, and her sensations resembled those of a person suddenly awakened from a frightful vision, whose thoughts are yet obscured in the fear and uncertainty which the passing images have impressed on his fancy. She emerged from despair; joy illumined her countenance; yet she doubted the reality of the scene which now opened to her view. The hours rolled heavily along till the evening, when expectation gave way to fear, for she was once more summoned by the Abate. He sent for her to administer the usual necessary exhortation on the approaching solemnity; and having detained her a considerable time in tedious and severe discourse, dismissed her with a formal benediction.

CHAPTER XII

The evening now sunk in darkness, and the hour was fast approaching which would decide the fate of Julia. Trembling anxiety subdued every other sensation; and as the minutes passed, her fears increased. At length she heard the gates of the monastery fastened for the night; the bell rang the signal for repose; and the passing footsteps of the nuns told her they were hastening to obey it. After some time, all was silent. Julia did not yet dare to venture forth; she employed the present interval in interesting and affectionate conversation with Madame de Menon, to whom, notwithstanding her situation, her heart bade a sorrowful adieu.

The clock struck twelve, when she arose to depart. Having embraced her faithful friend with tears of mingled grief and anxiety, she took a lamp in her hand, and with cautious, fearful steps, descended through the long winding passages to a private door, which opened into the church of the monastery. The church was gloomy and desolate; and the feeble rays of the lamp she bore, gave only light enough to discover its chilling grandeur. As she passed silently along the aisles, she cast a look of anxious examination around—but Ferdinand was no where to be seen. She paused in timid hesitation, fearful to penetrate the gloomy obscurity which lay before her, yet dreading to return.

As she stood examining the place, vainly looking for Ferdinand, yet fearing to call, lest her voice should betray her, a hollow groan arose from apart of the church very near her. It chilled her heart, and she remained fixed to the spot. She turned her eyes a little to the left, and saw light appear through the chinks of a sepulchre at some distance. The groan was repeated—a low murmuring succeeded, and while she yet gazed, an old man issued from the vault with a lighted taper in his hand. Terror now subdued her, and she utterred an involuntary shriek. In the succeeding moment, a noise was heard in a remote part of the fabric; and Ferdinand rushing forth from his concealment, ran to her assistance. The old man, who appeared to be a friar, and who had been doing penance at the monument of a saint, now approached. His countenance expressed a degree of surprise and terror almost equal to that of Julia's, who knew him to be the confessor of Vincent. Ferdinand seized the father; and laying his hand upon his sword, threatened him with death if he did not instantly swear to conceal for ever his knowledge of what he then saw, and also assist them to escape from the abbey.

'Ungracious boy!' replied the father, in a calm voice, 'desist from this language, nor add to the follies of youth the crime of murdering, or terrifying a defenceless old man. Your violence would urge me to become your enemy, did not previous inclination tempt me to be your friend. I pity the distresses of the lady Julia, to whom I am no stranger, and will cheerfully give her all the assistance in my power.'

At these words Julia revived, and Ferdinand, reproved by the generosity of the father, and conscious of his own inferiority, shrunk back. 'I have no words to thank you,' said he, 'or to entreat your pardon for the impetuosity of my conduct; your knowledge of my situation must plead my excuse.'—'It does,' replied the father, 'but we have no time to lose;—follow me.'

They followed him through the church to the cloisters, at the extremity of which was a small door, which the friar unlocked. It opened upon the woods.

'This path,' said he, 'leads thro' an intricate part of the woods, to the rocks that rise on the right of the abbey; in their recesses you may secrete yourselves till you are prepared for a longer journey. But extinguish your light; it may betray you to the marquis's people, who are dispersed about this spot. Farewell! my children, and God's blessing be upon ye.'

Julia's tears declared her gratitude; she had no time for words. They stepped into the path, and the father closed the door. They were now liberated from the monastery, but danger awaited them without, which it required all their caution to avoid. Ferdinand knew the path which the friar had pointed out to be the same that led to the rocks where his horses were stationed, and he pursued it with quick and silent steps. Julia, whose fears conspired with the gloom of night to magnify and transform every object around her, imagined at each step that she took, she perceived the figures of men, and fancied every whisper of the breeze the sound of pursuit.

They proceeded swiftly, till Julia, breathless and exhausted, could go no farther. They had not rested many minutes, when they heard a rustling among the bushes at some distance, and soon after distinguished a low sound of voices. Ferdinand and Julia instantly renewed their flight, and thought they still heard voices advance upon the wind. This thought was soon confirmed, for the sounds now gained fast upon them, and they distinguished words which served only to heighten their apprehensions, when they reached the extremity of the woods. The moon, which was now up, suddenly emerging from a dark cloud, discovered to them several man in pursuit; and also shewed to the pursuers the course of the fugitives. They endeavoured to gain the rocks where the horses were concealed, and which now appeared in view. These they reached when the pursuers had almost overtaken them—but their horses were gone! Their only remaining chance of escape was to fly into the deep recesses of the rock. They, therefore, entered a winding cave, from whence branched several subterraneous avenues, at the extremity of one of which they stopped. The voices of men now vibrated in tremendous echoes through the various and secret caverns of the place, and the sound of footsteps seemed fast approaching. Julia trembled with terror, and Ferdinand drew his sword, determined to protect her to the last. A confused volley of voices now sounded up that part of the cave were Ferdinand and Julia lay concealed. In a few moments the steps of the pursuers suddenly took a different direction, and the sounds sunk gradually away, and were heard no more. Ferdinand listened attentively for a considerable time, but the stillness of the place remained undisturbed. It was now evident that the men had quitted the rock, and he ventured forth to the mouth of the cave. He surveyed the wilds around, as far as his eye could penetrate, and distinguished no human being; but in the pauses of the wind he still thought he heard a sound of distant voices. As he listened in anxious silence, his eye caught the appearance of a shadow, which moved upon the ground near where he stood. He started back within the cave, but in a few minutes again ventured forth. The shadow remained stationary, but having watched it for some time, Ferdinand saw it glide along till it disappeared behind a point of rock. He had now no doubt that the cave was watched, and that it was one of his late pursuers whose shade he had seen. He returned, therefore, to Julia, and remained near an hour hid in the deepest recess of the rock; when, no sound having interrupted the profound silence of the place, he at length once more ventured to the mouth of the cave. Again he threw a fearful look around, but discerned no human form. The soft moon-beam slept upon the dewy landscape, and the solemn stillness of midnight wrapt the world. Fear heightened to the fugitives the sublimity of the hour. Ferdinand now led Julia forth, and they passed silently along the shelving foot of the rocks.

They continued their way without farther interruption; and among the cliffs, at some distance from the cave, discovered, to their inexpressible joy, their horses, who having broken their fastenings, had strayed thither, and had now laid themselves down to rest. Ferdinand and Julia immediately mounted; and descending to the plains, took the road that led to a small sea-port at some leagues distant, whence they could embark for Italy.

They travelled for some hours through gloomy forests of beech and chesnut; and their way was only faintly illuminated by the moon, which shed a trembling lustre through the dark foliage, and which was seen but at intervals, as the passing clouds yielded to the power of her rays. They reached at length the skirts of the forest. The grey dawn now appeared, and the chill morning air bit shrewdly. It was with inexpressible joy that Julia observed the kindling atmosphere; and soon after the rays of the rising sun touching the tops of the mountains, whose sides were yet involved in dark vapours.

Her fears dissipated with the darkness.—The sun now appeared amid clouds of inconceivable splendour; and unveiled a scene which in other circumstances Julia would have contemplated with rapture. From the side of the hill, down which they were winding, a vale appeared, from whence arose wild and lofty mountains, whose steeps were cloathed with hanging woods, except where here and there a precipice projected its bold and rugged front. Here, a few half-withered trees hung from the crevices of the rock, and gave a picturesque wildness to the object; there, clusters of half-seen cottages, rising from among tufted groves, embellished the green margin of a stream which meandered in the bottom, and bore its waves to the blue and distant main.

The freshness of morning breathed over the scene, and vivified each colour of the landscape. The bright dewdrops hung trembling from the branches of the trees, which at intervals overshadowed the road; and the sprightly music of the birds saluted the rising day. Notwithstanding her anxiety the scene diffused a soft complacency over the mind of Julia.

About noon they reached the port, where Ferdinand was fortunate enough to obtain a small vessel; but the wind was unfavourable, and it was past midnight before it was possible for them to embark.

When the dawn appeared, Julia returned to the deck; and viewed with a sigh of unaccountable regret, the receding coast of Sicily. But she observed, with high admiration, the light gradually spreading through the atmosphere, darting a feeble ray over the surface of the waters, which rolled in solemn soundings upon the distant shores. Fiery beams now marked the clouds, and the east glowed with increasing radiance, till the sun rose at once above the waves, and illuminating them with a flood of splendour, diffused gaiety and gladness around. The bold concave of the heavens, uniting with the vast expanse of the ocean, formed, a coup d'oeil, striking and sublime magnificence of the scenery inspired Julia with delight; and her heart dilating with high enthusiasm, she forgot the sorrows which had oppressed her.

The breeze wafted the ship gently along for some hours, when it gradually sunk into a calm. The glassy surface of the waters was not curled by the lightest air, and the vessel floated heavily on the bosom of the deep. Sicily was yet in view, and the present delay agitated Julia with wild apprehension. Towards the close of day a light breeze sprang up, but it blew from Italy, and a train of dark vapours emerged from the verge of the horizon, which gradually accumulating, the heavens became entirely overcast. The evening shut in suddenly; the rising wind, the heavy clouds that loaded the atmosphere, and the thunder which murmured afar off terrified Julia, and threatened a violent storm.

The tempest came on, and the captain vainly sounded for anchorage: it was deep sea, and the vessel drove furiously before the wind. The darkness was interrupted only at intervals, by the broad expanse of vivid lightnings, which quivered upon the waters, and disclosing the horrible gaspings of the waves, served to render the succeeding darkness more awful. The thunder, which burst in tremendous crashes above, the loud roar of the waves below, the noise of the sailors, and the sudden cracks and groanings of the vessel conspired to heighten the tremendous sublimity of the scene.

Far on the rocky shores the surges sound,
The lashing whirlwinds cleave the vast profound;
While high in air, amid the rising storm,
Driving the blast, sits Danger's black'ning form.

Julia lay fainting with terror and sickness in the cabin, and Ferdinand, though almost hopeless himself, was endeavouring to support her, when aloud and dreadful crash was heard from above. It seemed as if the whole vessel had parted. The voices of the sailors now rose together, and all was confusion and uproar. Ferdinand ran up to the deck, and learned that part of the main mast, borne away by the wind, had fallen upon the deck, whence it had rolled overboard.

It was now past midnight, and the storm continued with unabated fury. For four hours the vessel had been driven before the blast; and the captain now declared it was impossible she could weather the tempest much longer, ordered the long boat to be in readiness. His orders were scarcely executed, when the ship bulged upon a reef of rocks, and the impetuous waves rushed into the vessel:—a general groan ensued. Ferdinand flew to save his sister, whom he carried to the boat, which was nearly filled by the captain and most of the crew. The sea ran so high that it appeared impracticable to reach the shore: but the boat had not moved many yards, when the ship went to pieces. The captain now perceived, by the flashes of lightning, a high rocky coast at about the distance of half a mile. The men struggled hard at the oars; but almost as often as they gained the summit of a wave, it dashed them back again, and made their labour of little avail.

After much difficulty and fatigue they reached the coast, where a new danger presented itself. They beheld a wild rocky shore, whose cliffs appeared inaccessible, and which seemed to afford little possibility of landing. A landing, however, was at last affected; and the sailors, after much search, discovered a kind of pathway cut in the rock, which they all ascended in safety.

The dawn now faintly glimmered, and they surveyed the coast, but could discover no human habitation. They imagined they were on the shores of Sicily, but possessed no means of confirming this conjecture. Terror, sickness, and fatigue had subdued the strength and spirits of Julia, and she was obliged to rest upon the rocks.

The storm now suddenly subsided, and the total calm which succeeded to the wild tumult of the winds and waves, produced a striking and sublime effect. The air was hushed in a deathlike stillness, but the waves were yet violently agitated; and by the increasing light, parts of the wreck were seen floating wide upon the face of the deep. Some sailors, who had missed the boat, were also discovered clinging to pieces of the vessel, and making towards the shore. On observing this, their shipmates immediately descended to the boat; and, putting off to sea, rescued them from their perilous situation. When Julia was somewhat reanimated, they proceeded up the country in search of a dwelling.

They had travelled near half a league, when the savage features of the country began to soften, and gradually changed to the picturesque beauty of Sicilian scenery. They now discovered at some distance a villa, seated on a gentle eminence, crowned with woods. It was the first human habitation they had seen since they embarked for Italy; and Julia, who was almost sinking with fatigue, beheld it with delight. The captain and his men hastened towards it to make known their distress, while Ferdinand and Julia slowly followed. They observed the men enter the villa, one of whom quickly returned to acquaint them with the hospitable reception his comrades had received.

Julia with difficulty reached the edifice, at the door of which she was met by a young cavalier, whose pleasing and intelligent countenance immediately interested her in his favor. He welcomed the strangers with a benevolent politeness that dissolved at once every uncomfortable feeling which their situation had excited, and produced an instantaneous easy confidence. Through a light and elegant hall, rising into a dome, supported by pillars of white marble, and adorned with busts, he led them to a magnificent vestibule, which opened upon a lawn. Having seated them at a table spread with refreshments he left them, and they surveyed, with surprise, the beauty of the adjacent scene.

The lawn, which was on each side bounded by hanging woods, descended in gentle declivity to a fine lake, whose smooth surface reflected the surrounding shades. Beyond appeared the distant country, arising on the left into bold romantic mountains, and on the right exhibiting a soft and glowing landscape, whose tranquil beauty formed a striking contrast to the wild sublimity of the opposite craggy heights. The blue and distant ocean terminated the view.

In a short time the cavalier returned, conducting two ladies of a very engaging appearance, whom he presented as his wife and sister. They welcomed Julia with graceful kindness; but fatigue soon obliged her to retire to rest, and a consequent indisposition increased so rapidly, as to render it impracticable for her to quit her present abode on that day. The captain and his men proceeded on their way, leaving Ferdinand and Julia at the villa, where she experienced every kind and tender affection.

The day which was to have devoted Julia to a cloister, was ushered in at the abbey with the usual ceremonies. The church was ornamented, and all the inhabitants of the monastery prepared to attend. The Padre Abate now exulted in the success of his scheme, and anticipated, in imagination, the rage and vexation of the marquis, when he should discover that his daughter was lost to him for ever.

The hour of celebration arrived, and he entered the church with a proud firm step, and with a countenance which depictured his inward triumph; he was proceeding to the high altar, when he was told that Julia was no where to be found. Astonishment for awhile suspended other emotions—he yet believed it impossible that she could have effected an escape, and ordered every part of the abbey to be searched—not forgetting the secret caverns belonging to the monastery, which wound beneath the woods. When the search was over, and he became convinced she was fled, the deep workings of his disappointed passions fermented into rage which exceeded all bounds. He denounced the most terrible judgments upon Julia; and calling for Madame de Menon, charged her with having insulted her holy religion, in being accessary to the flight of Julia. Madame endured these reproaches with calm dignity, and preserved a steady silence, but she secretly determined to leave the monastery, and seek in another the repose which she could never hope to find in this.

The report of Julia's disappearance spread rapidly beyond the walls, and soon reached the ears of the marquis, who rejoiced in the circumstance, believing that she must now inevitably fall into his hands.

After his people, in obedience to his orders, had carefully searched the surrounding woods and rocks, he withdrew them from the abbey; and having dispersed them various ways in search of Julia, he returned to the castle of Mazzini. Here new vexation awaited him, for he now first learned that Ferdinand had escaped from confinement.

The mystery of Julia's flight was now dissolved; for it was evident by whose means she had effected it, and the marquis issued orders to his people to secure Ferdinand wherever he should be found.

CHAPTER XIII

Hippolitus, who had languished under a long and dangerous illness occasioned by his wounds, but heightened and prolonged by the distress of his mind, was detained in a small town in the coast of Calabria, and was yet ignorant of the death of Cornelia. He scarcely doubted that Julia was now devoted to the duke, and this thought was at times poison to his heart. After his arrival in Calabria, immediately on the recovery of his senses, he dispatched a servant back to the castle of Mazzini, to gain secret intelligence of what had passed after his departure. The eagerness with which we endeavour to escape from misery, taught him to encourage a remote and romantic hope that Julia yet lived for him. Yet even this hope at length languished into despair, as the time elapsed which should have brought his servant from Sicily. Days and weeks passed away in the utmost anxiety to Hippolitus, for still his emissary did not appear; and at last, concluding that he had been either seized by robbers, or discovered and detained by the marquis, the Count sent off a second emissary to the castle of Mazzini. By him he learned the news of Julia's flight, and his heart dilated with joy; but it was suddenly checked when he heard the marquis had discovered her retreat in the abbey of St Augustin. The wounds which still detained him in confinement, now became intolerable. Julia might yet be lost to him for ever. But even his present state of fear and uncertainty was bliss compared with the anguish of despair, which his mind had long endured.

As soon as he was sufficiently recovered, he quitted Italy for Sicily, in the design of visiting the monastery of St Augustin, where it was possible Julia might yet remain. That he might pass with the secrecy necessary to his plan, and escape the attacks of the marquis, he left his servants in Calabria, and embarked alone.

It was morning when he landed at a small port of Sicily, and proceeded towards the abbey of St Augustin. As he travelled, his imagination revolved the scenes of his early love, the distress of Julia, and the sufferings of Ferdinand, and his heart melted at the retrospect. He considered the probabilities of Julia having found protection from her father in the pity of the Padre Abate; and even ventured to indulge himself in a flattering, fond anticipation of the moment when Julia should again be restored to his sight.

He arrived at the monastery, and his grief may easily be imagined, when he was informed of the death of his beloved sister, and of the flight of Julia. He quitted St Augustin's immediately, without even knowing that Madame de Menon was there, and set out for a town at some leagues distance, where he designed to pass the night.

Absorbed in the melancholy reflections which the late intelligence excited, he gave the reins to his horse, and journeyed on unmindful of his way. The evening was far advanced when he discovered that he had taken a wrong direction, and that he was bewildered in a wild and solitary scene. He had wandered too far from the road to hope to regain it, and he had beside no recollection of the objects left behind him. A choice of errors, only, lay before him. The view on his right hand exhibited high and savage mountains, covered with heath and black fir; and the wild desolation of their aspect, together with the dangerous appearance of the path that wound up their sides, and which was the only apparent track they afforded, determined Hippolitus not to attempt their ascent. On his left lay a forest, to which the path he was then in led; its appearance was gloomy, but he preferred it to the mountains; and, since he was uncertain of its extent, there was a possibility that he might pass it, and reach a village before the night was set in. At the worst, the forest would afford him a shelter from the winds; and, however he might be bewildered in its labyrinths, he could ascend a tree, and rest in security till the return of light should afford him an opportunity of extricating himself. Among the mountains there was no possibility of meeting with other shelter than what the habitation of man afforded, and such a shelter there was little probability of finding. Innumerable dangers also threatened him here, from which he would be secure on level ground.

Having determined which way to pursue, he pushed his horse into a gallop, and entered the forest as the last rays of the sun trembled on the mountains. The thick foliage of the trees threw a gloom around, which was every moment deepened by the shades of evening. The path was uninterrupted, and the count continued to follow it till all distinction was confounded in the veil of night. Total darkness now made it impossible for him to pursue his way. He dismounted, and fastening his horse to a tree, climbed among the branches, purposing to remain there till morning.

He had not been long in this situation, when a confused sound of voices from a distance roused his attention. The sound returned at intervals for some time, but without seeming to approach. He descended from the tree, that he might the better judge of the direction whence it came; but before he reached the ground, the noise was ceased, and all was profoundly silent. He continued to listen, but the silence remaining undisturbed, he began to think he had been deceived by the singing of the wind among the leaves; and was preparing to reascend, when he perceived a faint light glimmer through the foliage from afar. The sight revived a hope that he was near some place of human habitation; he therefore unfastened his horse, and led him towards the spot whence the ray issued. The moon was now risen, and threw a checkered gleam over his path sufficient to direct him.

Before he had proceeded far the light disappeared. He continued, however, his way as nearly as he could guess, towards the place whence it had issued; and after much toil, found himself in a spot where the trees formed a circle round a kind of rude lawn. The moonlight discovered to him an edifice which appeared to have been formerly a monastery, but which now exhibited a pile of ruins, whose grandeur, heightened by decay, touched the beholder with reverential awe. Hippolitus paused to gaze upon the scene; the sacred stillness of night increased its effect, and a secret dread, he knew not wherefore, stole upon his heart.

The silence and the character of the place made him doubt whether this was the spot he had been seeking; and as he stood hesitating whether to proceed or to return, he observed a figure standing under an arch-way of the ruin; it carried a light in its hand, and passing silently along, disappeared in a remote part of the building. The courage of Hippolitus for a moment deserted him. An invincible curiosity, however, subdued his terror, and he determined to pursue, if possible, the way the figure had taken.

He passed over loose stones through a sort of court till he came to the archway; here he stopped, for fear returned upon him. Resuming his courage, however, he went on, still endeavouring to follow the way the figure had passed, and suddenly found himself in an enclosed part of the ruin, whose appearance was more wild and desolate than any he had yet seen. Seized with unconquerable apprehension, he was retiring, when the low voice of a distressed person struck his ear. His heart sunk at the sound, his limbs trembled, and he was utterly unable to move.

The sound which appeared to be the last groan of a dying person, was repeated. Hippolitus made a strong effort, and sprang forward, when a light burst upon him from a shattered casement of the building, and at the same instant he heard the voices of men!

He advanced softly to the window, and beheld in a small room, which was less decayed than the rest of the edifice, a group of men, who, from the savageness of their looks, and from their dress, appeared to be banditti. They surrounded a man who lay on the ground wounded, and bathed in blood, and who it was very evident had uttered the groans heard by the count.

The obscurity of the place prevented Hippolitus from distinguishing the features of the dying man. From the blood which covered him, and from the surrounding circumstances, he appeared to be murdered; and the count had no doubt that the men he beheld were the murderers. The horror of the scene entirely overcame him; he stood rooted to the spot, and saw the assassins rifle the pockets of the dying person, who, in a voice scarcely articulate, but which despair seemed to aid, supplicated for mercy. The ruffians answered him only with execrations, and continued their plunder. His groans and his sufferings served only to aggravate their cruelty. They were proceeding to take from him a miniature picture, which was fastened round his neck, and had been hitherto concealed in his bosom; when by a sudden effort he half raised himself from the ground, and attempted to save it from their hands. The effort availed him nothing; a blow from one of the villains laid the unfortunate man on the floor without motion. The horrid barbarity of the act seized the mind of Hippolitus so entirely, that, forgetful of his own situation, he groaned aloud, and started with an instantaneous design of avenging the deed. The noise he made alarmed the banditti, who looking whence it came, discovered the count through the casement. They instantly quitted their prize, and rushed towards the door of the room. He was now returned to a sense of his danger, and endeavoured to escape to the exterior part of the ruin; but terror bewildered his senses, and he mistook his way. Instead of regaining the arch-way, he perplexed himself with fruitless wanderings, and at length found himself only more deeply involved in the secret recesses of the pile.

The steps of his pursuers gained fast upon him, and he continued to perplex himself with vain efforts at escape, till at length, quite exhausted, he sunk on the ground, and endeavoured to resign himself to his fate. He listened with a kind of stern despair, and was surprised to find all silent. On looking round, he perceived by a ray of moonlight, which streamed through a part of the ruin from above, that he was in a sort of vault, which, from the small means he had of judging, he thought was extensive.

In this situation he remained for a considerable time, ruminating on the means of escape, yet scarcely believing escape was possible. If he continued in the vault, he might continue there only to be butchered; but by attempting to rescue himself from the place he was now in, he must rush into the hands of the banditti. Judging it, therefore, the safer way of the two to remain where he was, he endeavoured to await his fate with fortitude, when suddenly the loud voices of the murderers burst upon his ear, and he heard steps advancing quickly towards the spot where he lay.

Despair instantly renewed his vigour; he started from the ground, and throwing round him a look of eager desperation, his eye caught the glimpse of a small door, upon which the moon-beam now fell. He made towards it, and passed it just as the light of a torch gleamed upon the walls of the vault.

He groped his way along a winding passage, and at length came to a flight of steps. Notwithstanding the darkness, he reached the bottom in safety.

He now for the first time stopped to listen—the sounds of pursuit were ceased, and all was silent! Continuing to wander on in effectual endeavours to escape, his hands at length touched cold iron, and he quickly perceived it belonged to a door. The door, however, was fastened, and resisted all his efforts to open it. He was giving up the attempt in despair, when a loud scream from within, followed by a dead and heavy noise, roused all his attention. Silence ensued. He listened for a considerable time at the door, his imagination filled with images of horror, and expecting to hear the sound repeated. He then sought for a decayed part of the door, through which he might discover what was beyond; but he could find none; and after waiting some time without hearing any farther noise, he was quitting the spot, when in passing his arm over the door, it struck against something hard. On examination he perceived, to his extreme surprize, that the key was in the lock. For a moment he hesitated what to do; but curiosity overcame other considerations, and with a trembling hand he turned the key. The door opened into a large and desolate apartment, dimly lighted by a lamp that stood on a table, which was almost the only furniture of the place. The Count had advanced several steps before he perceived an object, which fixed all his attention. This was the figure of a young woman lying on the floor apparently dead. Her face was concealed in her robe; and the long auburn tresses which fell in beautiful luxuriance over her bosom, served to veil a part of the glowing beauty which the disorder of her dress would have revealed.

Pity, surprize, and admiration struggled in the breast of Hippolitus; and while he stood surveying the object which excited these different emotions, he heard a step advancing towards the room. He flew to the door by which he had entered, and was fortunate enough to reach it before the entrance of the persons whose steps he heard. Having turned the key, he stopped at the door to listen to their proceedings. He distinguished the voices of two men, and knew them to be those of the assassins. Presently he heard a piercing skriek, and at the same instant the voices of the ruffians grew loud and violent. One of them exclaimed that the lady was dying, and accused the other of having frightened her to death, swearing, with horrid imprecations, that she was his, and he would defend her to the last drop of his blood. The dispute grew higher; and neither of the ruffians would give up his claim to the unfortunate object of their altercation.

The clashing of swords was soon after heard, together with a violent noise. The screams were repeated, and the oaths and execrations of the disputants redoubled. They seemed to move towards the door, behind which Hippolitus was concealed; suddenly the door was shook with great force, a deep groan followed, and was instantly succeeded by a noise like that of a person whose whole weight falls at once to the ground. For a moment all was silent. Hippolitus had no doubt that one of the ruffians had destroyed the other, and was soon confirmed in the belief—for the survivor triumphed with brutal exultation over his fallen antagonist. The ruffian hastily quitted the room, and Hippolitus soon after heard the distant voices of several persons in loud dispute. The sounds seemed to come from a chamber over the place where he stood; he also heard a trampling of feet from above, and could even distinguish, at intervals, the words of the disputants. From these he gathered enough to learn that the affray which had just happened, and the lady who had been the occasion of it, were the subjects of discourse. The voices frequently rose together, and confounded all distinction.

At length the tumult began to subside, and Hippolitus could distinguish what was said. The ruffians agreed to give up the lady in question to him who had fought for her; and leaving him to his prize, they all went out in quest of farther prey. The situation of the unfortunate lady excited a mixture of pity and indignation in Hippolitus, which for some time entirely occupied him; he revolved the means of extricating her from so deplorable a situation, and in these thoughts almost forgot his own danger. He now heard her sighs; and while his heart melted to the sounds, the farther door of the apartment was thrown open, and the wretch to whom she had been allotted, rushed in. Her screams now redoubled, but they were of no avail with the ruffian who had seized her in his arms; when the count, who was unarmed, insensible to every pulse but that of a generous pity, burst into the room, but became fixed like a statue when he beheld his Julia struggling in the grasp of the ruffian. On discovering Hippolitus, she made a sudden spring, and liberated herself; when, running to him, she sunk lifeless in his arms.

Surprise and fury sparkled in the eyes of the ruffian, and he turned with a savage desperation upon the count; who, relinquishing Julia, snatched up the sword of the dead ruffian, which lay upon the floor, and defended himself. The combat was furious, but Hippolitus laid his antagonist senseless at his feet. He flew to Julia, who now revived, but who for some time could speak only by her tears. The transitions of various and rapid sensations, which her heart experienced, and the strangely mingled emotions of joy and terror that agitated Hippolitus, can only be understood by experience. He raised her from the floor, and endeavoured to soothe her to composure, when she called wildly upon Ferdinand. At his name the count started, and he instantly remembered the dying cavalier, whose countenance the glooms had concealed from his view. His heart thrilled with secret agony, yet he resolved to withhold his terrible conjectures from Julia, of whom he learned that Ferdinand, with herself, had been taken by banditti in the way from the villa which had offered them so hospitable a reception after the shipwreck. They were on the road to a port whence they designed again to embark for Italy, when this misfortune overtook them. Julia added, that Ferdinand had been immediately separated from her; and that, for some hours, she had been confined in the apartment where Hippolitus found her.

The Count with difficulty concealed his terrible apprehensions for Ferdinand, and vainly strove to soften Julia's distress. But there was no time to be lost—they had yet to find a way out of the edifice, and before they could accomplish this, the banditti might return. It was also possible that some of the party were left to watch this their abode during the absence of the rest, and this was another circumstance of reasonable alarm.

After some little consideration, Hippolitus judged it most prudent to seek an outlet through the passage by which he entered; he therefore took the lamp, and led Julia to the door. They entered the avenue, and locking the door after them, sought the flight of steps down which the count had before passed; but having pursued the windings of the avenue a considerable time without finding them, he became certain he had mistaken the way. They, however, found another flight, which they descended and entered upon a passage so very narrow and low, as not to admit of a person walking upright. This passage was closed by a door, which on examination was found to be chiefly of iron. Hippolitus was startled at the sight, but on applying his strength found it gradually yield, when the imprisoned air rushed out, and had nearly extinguished the light. They now entered upon a dark abyss; and the door which moved upon a spring, suddenly closed upon them. On looking round they beheld a large vault; and it is not easy to imagine their horror on discovering they were in a receptacle for the murdered bodies of the unfortunate people who had fallen into the hands of the banditti.

The count could scarcely support the fainting spirits of Julia; he ran to the door, which he endeavoured to open, but the lock was so constructed that it could be moved only on the other side, and all his efforts were useless. He was constrained, therefore, to seek for another door, but could find none. Their situation was the most deplorable that can be imagined; for they were now inclosed in a vault strewn with the dead bodies of the murdered, and must there become the victims of famine, or of the sword. The earth was in several places thrown up, and marked the boundaries of new-made graves. The bodies which remained unburied were probably left either from hurry or negligence, and exhibited a spectacle too shocking for humanity. The sufferings of Hippolitus were increased by those of Julia, who was sinking with horror, and who he endeavoured to support to apart of the vault which fell into a recess—where stood a bench.

They had not been long in this situation, when they heard a noise which approached gradually, and which did not appear to come from the avenue they had passed.

The noise increased, and they could distinguish voices. Hippolitus believed the murderers were returned; that they had traced his retreat, and were coming towards the vault by some way unknown to him. He prepared for the worst—and drawing his sword, resolved to defend Julia to the last. Their apprehension, however, was soon dissipated by a trampling of horses, which sound had occasioned his alarm, and which now seemed to come from a courtyard above, extremely near the vault. He distinctly heard the voices of the banditti, together with the moans and supplications of some person, whom it was evident they were about to plunder. The sound appeared so very near, that Hippolitus was both shocked and surprised; and looking round the vault, he perceived a small grated window placed very high in the wall, which he concluded overlooked the place where the robbers were assembled. He recollected that his light might betray him; and horrible as was the alternative, he was compelled to extinguish it. He now attempted to climb to the grate, through which he might obtain a view of what was passing without. This at length he effected, for the ruggedness of the wall afforded him a footing. He beheld in a ruinous court, which was partially illuminated by the glare of torches, a group of banditti surrounding two persons who were bound on horseback, and who were supplicating for mercy.

One of the robbers exclaiming with an oath that this was a golden night, bade his comrades dispatch, adding he would go to find Paulo and the lady.

The effect which the latter part of this sentence had upon the prisoners in the vault, may be more easily imagined than described. They were now in total darkness in this mansion of the murdered, without means of escape, and in momentary expectation of sharing a fate similar to that of the wretched objects around them. Julia, overcome with distress and terror, sunk on the ground; and Hippolitus, descending from the grate, became insensible of his own danger in his apprehension for her.

In a short time all without was confusion and uproar; the ruffian who had left the court returned with the alarm that the lady was fled, and that Paulo was murdered, The robbers quitting their booty to go in search of the fugitive, and to discover the murderer, dreadful vociferations resounded through every recess of the pile.

The tumult had continued a considerable time, which the prisoners had passed in a state of horrible suspence, when they heard the uproar advancing towards the vault, and soon after a number of voices shouted down the avenue. The sound of steps quickened. Hippolitus again drew his sword, and placed himself opposite the entrance, where he had not stood long, when a violent push was made against the door; it flew open, and a party of men rushed into the vault.

Hippolitus kept his position, protesting he would destroy the first who approached. At the sound of his voice they stopped; but presently advancing, commanded him in the king's name to surrender. He now discovered what his agitation had prevented him from observing sooner, that the men before him were not banditti, but the officers of justice. They had received information of this haunt of villainy from the son of a Sicilian nobleman, who had fallen into the hands of the banditti, and had afterwards escaped from their power.

The officers came attended by a guard, and were every way prepared to prosecute a strenuous search through these horrible recesses.

Hippolitus inquired for Ferdinand, and they all quitted the vault in search of him. In the court, to which they now ascended, the greater part of the banditti were secured by a number of the guard. The count accused the robbers of having secreted his friend, whom he described, and demanded to have liberated.

With one voice they denied the fact, and were resolute in persisting that they knew nothing of the person described. This denial confirmed Hippolitus in his former terrible surmise; that the dying cavalier, whom he had seen, was no other than Ferdinand, and he became furious. He bade the officers prosecute their search, who, leaving a guard over the banditti they had secured, followed him to the room where the late dreadful scene had been acted.

The room was dark and empty; but the traces of blood were visible on the floor; and Julia, though ignorant of the particular apprehension of Hippolitus, almost swooned at the sight. On quitting the room, they wandered for some time among the ruins, without discovering any thing extraordinary, till, in passing under the arch-way by which Hippolitus had first entered the building, their footsteps returned a deep sound, which convinced them that the ground beneath was hollow. On close examination, they perceived by the light of their torch, a trapdoor, which with some difficulty they lifted, and discovered beneath a narrow flight of steps. They all descended into a low winding passage, where they had not been long, when they heard a trampling of horses above, and a loud and sudden uproar.

The officers apprehending that the banditti had overcome the guard, rushed back to the trapdoor, which they had scarcely lifted, when they heard a clashing of swords, and a confusion of unknown voices. Looking onward, they beheld through the arch, in an inner sort of court, a large party of banditti who were just arrived, rescuing their comrades, and contending furiously with the guard.

On observing this, several of the officers sprang forward to the assistance of their friends; and the rest, subdued by cowardice, hurried down the steps, letting the trapdoor fall after them with a thundering noise. They gave notice to Hippolitus of what was passing above, who hurried Julia along the passage in search of some outlet or place of concealment. They could find neither, and had not long pursued the windings of the way, when they heard the trapdoor lifted, and the steps of persons descending. Despair gave strength to Julia, and winged her flight. But they were now stopped by a door which closed the passage, and the sound of distant voices murmured along the walls.

The door was fastened by strong iron bolts, which Hippolitus vainly endeavoured to draw. The voices drew near. After much labour and difficulty the bolts yielded—the door unclosed—and light dawned upon them through the mouth of a cave, into which they now entered. On quitting the cave they found themselves in the forest, and in a short time reached the borders. They now ventured to stop, and looking back perceived no person in pursuit.

CHAPTER XIV

When Julia had rested, they followed the track before them, and in a short time arrived at a village, where they obtained security and refreshment.

But Julia, whose mind was occupied with dreadful anxiety for Ferdinand, became indifferent to all around her. Even the presence of Hippolitus, which but lately would have raised her from misery to joy, failed to soothe her distress. The steady and noble attachment of her brother had sunk deep in her heart, and reflection only aggravated her affliction. Yet the banditti had steadily persisted in affirming that he was not concealed in their recesses; and this circumstance, which threw a deeper shade over the fears of Hippolitus, imparted a glimmering of hope to the mind of Julia.

A more immediate interest at length forced her mind from this sorrowful subject. It was necessary to determine upon some line of conduct, for she was now in an unknown spot, and ignorant of any place of refuge. The count, who trembled at the dangers which environed her, and at the probabilities he saw of her being torn from him for ever, suffered a consideration of them to overcome the dangerous delicacy which at this mournful period required his silence. He entreated her to destroy the possibility of separation, by consenting to become his immediately. He urged that a priest could be easily procured from a neighboring convent, who would confirm the bonds which had so long united their hearts, and who would thus at once arrest the destiny that so long had threatened his hopes.

This proposal, though similar to the one she had before accepted; and though the certain means of rescuing her from the fate she dreaded, she now turned from in sorrow and dejection. She loved Hippolitus with a steady and tender affection, which was still heightened by the gratitude he claimed as her deliverer; but she considered it a prophanation of the memory of that brother who had suffered so much for her sake, to mingle joy with the grief which her uncertainty concerning him occasioned. She softened her refusal with a tender grace, that quickly dissipated the jealous doubt arising in the mind of Hippolitus, and increased his fond admiration of her character.

She desired to retire for a time to some obscure convent, there to await the issue of the event, which at present involved her in perplexity and sorrow.

Hippolitus struggled with his feelings and forbore to press farther the suit on which his happiness, and almost his existence, now depended. He inquired at the village for a neighbouring convent, and was told, that there was none within twelve leagues, but that near the town of Palini, at about that distance, were two. He procured horses; and leaving the officers to return to Palermo for a stronger guard, he, accompanied by Julia, entered on the road to Palini.

Julia was silent and thoughtful; Hippolitus gradually sunk into the same mood, and he often cast a cautious look around as they travelled for some hours along the feet of the mountains. They stopped to dine under the shade of some beach-trees; for, fearful of discovery, Hippolitus had provided against the necessity of entering many inns. Having finished their repast, they pursued their journey; but Hippolitus now began to doubt whether he was in the right direction. Being destitute, however, of the means of certainty upon this point, he followed the road before him, which now wound up the side of a steep hill, whence they descended into a rich valley, where the shepherd's pipe sounded sweetly from afar among the hills. The evening sun shed a mild and mellow lustre over the landscape, and softened each feature with a vermil glow that would have inspired a mind less occupied than Julia's with sensations of congenial tranquillity.

The evening now closed in; and as they were doubtful of the road, and found it would be impossible to reach Palini that night, they took the way to a village, which they perceived at the extremity of the valley.

They had proceeded about half a mile, when they heard a sudden shout of voices echoed from among the hills behind them; and looking back perceived faintly through the dusk a party of men on horseback making towards them. As they drew nearer, the words they spoke were distinguishable, and Julia heard her own name sounded. Shocked at this circumstance, she had now no doubt that she was discovered by a party of her father's people, and she fled with Hippolitus along the valley. The pursuers, however, were almost come up with them, when they reached the mouth of a cavern, into which she ran for concealment. Hippolitus drew his sword; and awaiting his enemies, stood to defend the entrance.

In a few moments Julia heard the clashing of swords. Her heart trembled for Hippolitus; and she was upon the point of returning to resign herself at once to the power of her enemies, and thus avert the danger that threatened him, when she distinguished the loud voice of the duke.

She shrunk involuntarily at the sound, and pursuing the windings of the cavern, fled into its inmost recesses. Here she had not been long when the voices sounded through the cave, and drew near. It was now evident that Hippolitus was conquered, and that her enemies were in search of her. She threw round a look of unutterable anguish, and perceived very near, by a sudden gleam of torchlight, a low and deep recess in the rock. The light which belonged to her pursuers, grew stronger; and she entered the rock on her knees, for the overhanging craggs would not suffer her to pass otherwise; and having gone a few yards, perceived that it was terminated by a door. The door yielded to her touch, and she suddenly found herself in a highly vaulted cavern, which received a feeble light from the moon-beams that streamed through an opening in the rock above.

She closed the door, and paused to listen. The voices grew louder, and more distinct, and at last approached so near, that she distinguished what was said. Above the rest she heard the voice of the duke. 'It is impossible she can have quitted the cavern,' said he, 'and I will not leave it till I have found her. Seek to the left of that rock, while I examine beyond this point.'

These words were sufficient for Julia; she fled from the door across the cavern before her, and having ran a considerable way, without coming to a termination, stopped to breathe. All was now still, and as she looked around, the gloomy obscurity of the place struck upon her fancy all its horrors. She imperfectly surveyed the vastness of the cavern in wild amazement, and feared that she had precipitated herself again into the power of banditti, for whom along this place appeared a fit receptacle. Having listened a long time without hearing a return of voices, she thought to find the door by which she had entered, but the gloom, and vast extent of the cavern, made the endeavour hopeless, and the attempt unsuccessful. Having wandered a considerable time through the void, she gave up the effort, endeavoured to resign herself to her fate, and to compose her distracted thoughts. The remembrance of her former wonderful escape inspired her with confidence in the mercy of God. But Hippolitus and Ferdinand were now both lost to her—lost, perhaps, for ever—and the uncertainty of their fate gave force to fancy, and poignancy to sorrow.

Towards morning grief yielded to nature, and Julia sunk to repose. She was awakened by the sun, whose rays darting obliquely through the opening in the rock, threw a partial light across the cavern. Her senses were yet bewildered by sleep, and she started in affright on beholding her situation; as recollection gradually stole upon her mind, her sorrows returned, and she sickened at the fatal retrospect.

She arose, and renewed her search for an outlet. The light, imperfect as it was, now assisted her, and she found a door, which she perceived was not the one by which she had entered. It was firmly fastened; she discovered, however, the bolts and the lock that held it, and at length unclosed the door. It opened upon a dark passage, which she entered.

She groped along the winding walls for some time, when she perceived the way was obstructed. She now discovered that another door interrupted her progress, and sought for the bolts which might fasten it. These she found; and strengthened by desparation forced them back. The door opened, and she beheld in a small room, which received its feeble light from a window above, the pale and emaciated figure of a woman, seated, with half-closed eyes, in a kind of elbow-chair. On perceiving Julia, she started from her seat, and her countenance expressed a wild surprise. Her features, which were worn by sorrow, still retained the traces of beauty, and in her air was a mild dignity that excited in Julia an involuntary veneration.

She seemed as if about to speak, when fixing her eyes earnestly and steadily upon Julia, she stood for a moment in eager gaze, and suddenly exclaiming, 'My daughter!' fainted away.

The astonishment of Julia would scarcely suffer her to assist the lady who lay senseless on the floor. A multitude of strange imperfect ideas rushed upon her mind, and she was lost in perplexity; but as she examined the features of the stranger; which were now rekindling into life, she thought she discovered the resemblance of Emilia!

The lady breathing a deep sigh, unclosed her eyes; she raised them to Julia, who hung over her in speechless astonishment, and fixing them upon her with a tender earnest expression—they filled with tears. She pressed Julia to her heart, and a few moments of exquisite, unutterable emotion followed. When the lady became more composed, 'Thank heaven!' said she, 'my prayer is granted. I am permitted to embrace one of my children before I die. Tell me what brought you hither. Has the marquis at last relented, and allowed me once more to behold you, or has his death dissolved my wretched bondage?'

Truth now glimmered upon the mind of Julia, but so faintly, that instead of enlightening, it served only to increase her perplexity.

'Is the marquis Mazzini living?' continued the lady. These words were not to be doubted; Julia threw herself at the feet of her mother, and embracing her knees in an energy of joy, answered only in sobs.

The marchioness eagerly inquired after her children, 'Emilia is living,' answered Julia, 'but my dear brother—' 'Tell me,' cried the marchioness, with quickness. An explanation ensued; When she was informed concerning Ferdinand, she sighed deeply, and raising her eyes to heaven, endeavoured to assume a look of pious resignation; but the struggle of maternal feelings was visible in her countenance, and almost overcame her powers of resistance.

Julia gave a short account of the preceding adventures, and of her entrance into the cavern; and found, to her inexpressible surprize, that she was now in a subterranean abode belonging to the southern buildings of the castle of Mazzini! The marchioness was beginning her narrative, when a door was heard to unlock above, and the sound of a footstep followed.

'Fly!' cried the marchioness, 'secret yourself, if possible, for the marquis is coming.' Julia's heart sunk at these words; she paused not a moment, but retired through the door by which she had entered. This she had scarcely done, when another door of the cell was unlocked, and she heard the voice of her father. Its sounds thrilled her with a universal tremour; the dread of discovery so strongly operated upon her mind, that she stood in momentary expectation of seeing the door of the passage unclosed by the marquis; and she was deprived of all power of seeking refuge in the cavern.

At length the marquis, who came with food, quitted the cell, and relocked the door, when Julia stole forth from her hiding-place. The marchioness again embraced, and wept over her daughter. The narrative of her sufferings, upon which she now entered, entirely dissipated the mystery which had so long enveloped the southern buildings of the castle.

'Oh! why,' said the marchioness, 'is it my task to discover to my daughter the vices of her father? In relating my sufferings, I reveal his crimes! It is now about fifteen years, as near as I can guess from the small means I have of judging, since I entered this horrible abode. My sorrows, alas! began not here; they commenced at an earlier period. But it is sufficient to observe, that the passion whence originated all my misfortunes, was discovered by me long before I experienced its most baleful effects.

'Seven years had elapsed since my marriage, when the charms of Maria de Vellorno, a young lady singularly beautiful, inspired the marquis with a passion as violent as it was irregular. I observed, with deep and silent anguish, the cruel indifference of my lord towards me, and the rapid progress of his passion for another. I severely examined my past conduct, which I am thankful to say presented a retrospect of only blameless actions; and I endeavoured, by meek submission, and tender assiduities, to recall that affection which was, alas! gone for ever. My meek submission was considered as a mark of a servile and insensible mind; and my tender assiduities, to which his heart no longer responded, created only disgust, and exalted the proud spirit it was meant to conciliate.

'The secret grief which this change occasioned, consumed my spirits, and preyed upon my constitution, till at length a severe illness threatened my life. I beheld the approach of death with a steady eye, and even welcomed it as the passport to tranquillity; but it was destined that I should linger through new scenes of misery.

'One day, which it appears was the paroxysm of my disorder, I sunk in to a state of total torpidity, in which I lay for several hours. It is impossible to describe my feelings, when, on recovering, I found myself in this hideous abode. For some time I doubted my senses, and afterwards believed that I had quitted this world for another; but I was not long suffered to continue in my error, the appearance of the marquis bringing me to a perfect sense of my situation.

'I now understood that I had been conveyed by his direction to this recess of horror, where it was his will I should remain. My prayers, my supplications, were ineffectual; the hardness of his heart repelled my sorrows back upon myself; and as no entreaties could prevail upon him to inform me where I was, or of his reason for placing me here, I remained for many years ignorant of my vicinity to the castle, and of the motive of my confinement.

'From that fatal day, until very lately, I saw the marquis no more—but was attended by a person who had been for some years dependant upon his bounty, and whom necessity, united to an insensible heart, had doubtless induced to accept this office. He generally brought me a week's provision, at stated intervals, and I remarked that his visits were always in the night.

'Contrary to my expectation, or my wish, nature did that for me which medicine had refused, and I recovered as if to punish with disappointment and anxiety my cruel tyrant. I afterwards learned, that in obedience to the marquis's order, I had been carried to this spot by Vincent during the night, and that I had been buried in effigy at a neighbouring church, with all the pomp of funeral honor due to my rank.'

At the name of Vincent Julia started; the doubtful words he had uttered on his deathbed were now explained—the cloud of mystery which had so long involved the southern buildings broke at once away: and each particular circumstance that had excited her former terror, arose to her view entirely unveiled by the words of the marchioness.— The long and total desertion of this part of the fabric—the light that had appeared through the casement—the figure she had seen issue from the tower—the midnight noises she had heard—were circumstances evidently dependant on the imprisonment of the marchioness; the latter of which incidents were produced either by Vincent, or the marquis, in their attendance upon her.

When she considered the long and dreadful sufferings of her mother, and that she had for many years lived so near her, ignorant of her misery, and even of her existence— she was lost in astonishment and pity.

'My days,' continued the marchioness, 'passed in a dead uniformity, more dreadful than the most acute vicissitudes of misfortune, and which would certainly have subdued my reason, had not those firm principles of religious faith, which I imbibed in early youth, enabled me to withstand the still, but forceful pressure of my calamity.

'The insensible heart of Vincent at length began to soften to my misfortunes. He brought me several articles of comfort, of which I had hitherto been destitute, and answered some questions I put to him concerning my family. To release me from my present situation, however his inclination might befriend me, was not to be expected, since his life would have paid the forfeiture of what would be termed his duty.

'I now first discovered my vicinity to the castle. I learned also, that the marquis had married Maria de Vellorno, with whom he had resided at Naples, but that my daughters were left at Mazzini. This last intelligence awakened in my heart the throbs of warm maternal tenderness, and on my knees I supplicated to see them. So earnestly I entreated, and so solemnly I promised to return quietly to my prison, that, at length, prudence yielded to pity, and Vincent consented to my request.

'On the following day he came to the cell, and informed me my children were going into the woods, and that I might see them from a window near which they would pass. My nerves thrilled at these words, and I could scarcely support myself to the spot I so eagerly sought. He led me through long and intricate passages, as I guessed by the frequent turnings, for my eyes were bound, till I reached a hall of the south buildings. I followed to a room above, where the full light of day once more burst upon my sight, and almost overpowered me. Vincent placed me by a window, which looked towards the woods. Oh! what moments of painful impatience were those in which I awaited your arrival!

'At length you appeared. I saw you—I saw my children—and was neither permitted to clasp them to my heart, or to speak to them! You was leaning on the arm of your sister, and your countenances spoke the sprightly happy innocence of youth.—Alas! you knew not the wretched fate of your mother, who then gazed upon you! Although you were at too great a distance for my weak voice to reach you, with the utmost difficulty I avoided throwing open the window, and endeavouring to discover myself. The remembrance of my solemn promise, and that the life of Vincent would be sacrificed by the act, alone restrained me. I struggled for some time with emotions too powerful for my nature, and fainted away.

'On recovering I called wildly for my children, and went to the window—but you were gone! Not all the entreaties of Vincent could for some time remove me from this station, where I waited in the fond expectation of seeing you again—but you appeared no more! At last I returned to my cell in an ecstasy of grief which I tremble even to remember.

'This interview, so eagerly sought, and so reluctantly granted, proved a source of new misery—instead of calming, it agitated my mind with a restless, wild despair, which bore away my strongest powers of resistance. I raved incessantly of my children, and incessantly solicited to see them again—Vincent, however, had found but too much cause to repent of his first indulgence, to grant me a second.

'About this time a circumstance occurred which promised me a speedy release from calamity. About a week elapsed, and Vincent did not appear. My little stock of provision was exhausted, and I had been two days without food, when I again heard the doors that led to my prison creek on their hinges. An unknown step approached, and in a few minutes the marquis entered my cell! My blood was chilled at the sight, and I closed my eyes as I hoped for the last time. The sound of his voice recalled me. His countenance was dark and sullen, and I perceived that he trembled. He informed me that Vincent was no more, and that henceforward his office he should take upon himself. I forbore to reproach—where reproach would only have produced new sufferings, and withheld supplication where it would have exasperated conscience and inflamed revenge. My knowledge of the marquis's second marriage I concealed.

'He usually attended me when night might best conceal his visits; though these were irregular in their return. Lately, from what motive I cannot guess, he has ceased his nocturnal visits, and comes only in the day.

'Once when midnight increased the darkness of my prison, and seemed to render silence even more awful, touched by the sacred horrors of the hour, I poured forth my distress in loud lamentation. Oh! never can I forget what I felt, when I heard a distant voice answered to my moan! A wild surprize, which was strangely mingled with hope, seized me, and in my first emotion I should have answered the call, had not a recollection crossed me, which destroyed at once every half-raised sensation of joy. I remembered the dreadful vengeance which the marquis had sworn to execute upon me, if I ever, by any means, endeavoured to make known the place of my concealment; and though life had long been a burden to me, I dared not to incur the certainty of being murdered. I also well knew that no person who might discover my situation could effect my enlargement, for I had no relations to deliver me by force; and the marquis, you know, has not only power to imprison, but also the right of life and death in his own domains; I, therefore, forbore to answer the call, though I could not entirely repress my lamentation. I long perplexed myself with endeavouring to account for this strange circumstance, and am to this moment ignorant of its cause.'

Julia remembering that Ferdinand had been confined in a dungeon of the castle, it instantly occurred to her that his prison, and that of the marchioness, were not far distant; and she scrupled not to believe that it was his voice which her mother had heard. She was right in this belief, and it was indeed the marchioness whose groans had formerly caused Ferdinand so much alarm, both in the marble hall of the south buildings, and in his dungeon.

When Julia communicated her opinion, and the marchioness believed that she had heard the voice of her son—her emotion was extreme, and it was some time before she could resume her narration.

'A short time since,' continued the marchioness, 'the marquis brought me a fortnight's provision, and told me that I should probably see him no more till the expiration of that term. His absence at this period you have explained in your account of the transactions at the abbey of St Augustin. How can I ever sufficiently acknowledge the obligations I owe to my dear and invaluable friend Madame de Menon! Oh! that it might be permitted me to testify my gratitude.'

Julia attended to the narrative of her mother in silent astonishment, and gave all the sympathy which sorrow could demand. 'Surely,' cried she, 'the providence on whom you have so firmly relied, and whose inflictions you have supported with a fortitude so noble, has conducted me through a labyrinth of misfortunes to this spot, for the purpose of delivering you! Oh! let us hasten to fly this horrid abode—let us seek to escape through the cavern by which I entered.'

She paused in earnest expectation awaiting a reply. 'Whither can I fly?' said the marchioness, deeply sighing. This question, spoken with the emphasis of despair, affected Julia to tears, and she was for a while silent.

'The marquis,' resumed Julia, 'would not know where to seek you, or if he found you beyond his own domains, would fear to claim you. A convent may afford for the present a safe asylum; and whatever shall happen, surely no fate you may hereafter encounter can be more dreadful than the one you now experience.'

The marchioness assented to the truth of this, yet her broken spirits, the effect of long sorrow and confinement, made her hesitate how to act; and there was a kind of placid despair in her look, which too faithfully depicted her feelings. It was obvious to Julia that the cavern she had passed wound beneath the range of mountains on whose opposite side stood the castle of Mazzini. The hills thus rising formed a screen which must entirely conceal their emergence from the mouth of the cave, and their flight, from those in the castle. She represented these circumstances to her mother, and urged them so forcibly that the lethargy of despair yielded to hope, and the marchioness committed herself to the conduct of her daughter.

'Oh! let me lead you to light and life!' cried Julia with warm enthusiasm. 'Surely heaven can bless me with no greater good than by making me the deliverer of my mother.' They both knelt down; and the marchioness, with that affecting eloquence which true piety inspires, and with that confidence which had supported her through so many miseries, committed herself to the protection of God, and implored his favor on their attempt.

They arose, but as they conversed farther on their plan, Julia recollected that she was destitute of money—the banditti having robbed her of all! The sudden shock produced by this remembrance almost subdued her spirits; never till this moment had she understood the value of money. But she commanded her feelings, and resolved to conceal this circumstance from the marchioness, preferring the chance of any evil they might encounter from without, to the certain misery of this terrible imprisonment.

Having taken what provision the marquis had brought, they quitted the cell, and entered upon the dark passage, along which they passed with cautious steps. Julia came first to the door of the cavern, but who can paint her distress when she found it was fastened! All her efforts to open it were ineffectual.—The door which had closed after her, was held by a spring lock, and could be opened on this side only with a key. When she understood this circumstance, the marchioness, with a placid resignation which seemed to exalt her above humanity, addressed herself again to heaven, and turned back to her cell. Here Julia indulged without reserve, and without scruple, the excess of her grief. The marchioness wept over her. 'Not for myself,' said she, 'do I grieve. I have too long been inured to misfortune to sink under its pressure. This disappointment is intrinsically, perhaps, little—for I had no certain refuge from calamity—and had it even been otherwise, a few years only of suffering would have been spared me. It is for you, Julia, who so much lament my fate; and who in being thus delivered to the power of your father, are sacrificed to the Duke de Luovo—that my heart swells.'

Julia could make no reply, but by pressing to her lips the hand which was held forth to her, she saw all the wretchedness of her situation; and her fearful uncertainty concerning Hippolitus and Ferdinand, formed no inferior part of her affliction.

'If,' resumed the marchioness, 'you prefer imprisonment with your mother, to a marriage with the duke, you may still secret yourself in the passage we have just quitted, and partake of the provision which is brought me.'

'O! talk not, madam, of a marriage with the duke,' said Julia; 'surely any fate is preferable to that. But when I consider that in remaining here, I am condemned only to the sufferings which my mother has so long endured, and that this confinement will enable me to soften, by tender sympathy, the asperity of her misfortunes, I ought to submit to my present situation with complacency, even did a marriage with the duke appear less hateful to me.'

'Excellent girl!' exclaimed the marchioness, clasping Julia to her bosom; 'the sufferings you lament are almost repaid by this proof of your goodness and affection! Alas! that I should have been so long deprived of such a daughter!'

Julia now endeavoured to imitate the fortitude of her mother, and tenderly concealed her anxiety for Ferdinand and Hippolitus, the idea of whom incessantly haunted her imagination. When the marquis brought food to the cell, she retired to the avenue leading to the cavern, and escaped discovery.

CHAPTER XV

The marquis, meanwhile, whose indefatigable search after Julia failed of success, was successively the slave of alternate passions, and he poured forth the spleen of disappointment on his unhappy domestics.

The marchioness, who may now more properly be called Maria de Vellorno, inflamed, by artful insinuations, the passions already irritated, and heightened with cruel triumph his resentment towards Julia and Madame de Menon. She represented, what his feelings too acutely acknowledged,—that by the obstinate disobedience of the first, and the machinations of the last, a priest had been enabled to arrest his authority as a father—to insult the sacred honor of his nobility—and to overturn at once his proudest schemes of power and ambition. She declared it her opinion, that the Abate was acquainted with the place of Julia's present retreat, and upbraided the marquis with want of spirit in thus submitting to be outwitted by a priest, and forbearing an appeal to the pope, whose authority would compel the Abate to restore Julia.

This reproach stung the very soul of the marquis; he felt all its force, and was at the same time conscious of his inability to obviate it. The effect of his crimes now fell in severe punishment upon his own head. The threatened secret, which was no other than the imprisonment of the marchioness, arrested his arm of vengeance, and compelled him to submit to insult and disappointment. But the reproach of Maria sunk deep in his mind; it fomented his pride into redoubled fury, and he now repelled with disdain the idea of submission.

He revolved the means which might effect his purpose—he saw but one—this was the death of the marchioness.

The commission of one crime often requires the perpetration of another. When once we enter on the ladyrinth of vice, we can seldom return, but are led on, through correspondent mazes, to destruction. To obviate the effect of his first crime, it was now necessary the marquis should commit a second, and conceal the imprisonment of the marchioness by her murder. Himself the only living witness of her existence, when she was removed, the allegations of the Padre Abate would by this means be unsupported by any proof, and he might then boldly appeal to the pope for the restoration of his child.

He mused upon this scheme, and the more he accustomed his mind to contemplate it, the less scrupulous he became. The crime from which he would formerly have shrunk, he now surveyed with a steady eye. The fury of his passions, unaccustomed to resistance, uniting with the force of what ambition termed necessity—urged him to the deed, and he determined upon the murder of his wife. The means of effecting his purpose were easy and various; but as he was not yet so entirely hardened as to be able to view her dying pangs, and embrue his own hands in her blood, he chose to dispatch her by means of poison, which he resolved to mingle in her food.

But a new affliction was preparing for the marquis, which attacked him where he was most vulnerable; and the veil, which had so long overshadowed his reason, was now to be removed. He was informed by Baptista of the infidelity of Maria de Vellorno. In the first emotion of passion, he spurned the informer from his presence, and disdained to believe the circumstance. A little reflection changed the object of his resentment; he recalled the servant, whose faithfulness he had no reason to distrust, and condescended to interrogate him on the subject of his misfortune.

He learned that an intimacy had for some time subsisted between Maria and the Cavalier de Vincini; and that the assignation was usually held at the pavilion on the sea-shore, in an evening. Baptista farther declared, that if the marquis desired a confirmation of his words, he might obtain it by visiting this spot at the hour mentioned.

This information lighted up the wildest passions of his nature; his former sufferings faded away before the stronger influence of the present misfortune, and it seemed as if he had never tasted misery till now. To suspect the wife upon whom he doated with romantic fondness, on whom he had centered all his firmest hopes of happiness, and for whose sake he had committed the crime which embittered even his present moment, and which would involve him in still deeper guilt—to find her ungrateful to his love, and a traitoress to his honor—produced a misery more poignant than any his imagination had conceived. He was torn by contending passions, and opposite resolutions:—now he resolved to expiate her guilt with her blood—and now he melted in all the softness of love. Vengeance and honor bade him strike to the heart which had betrayed him, and urged him instantly to the deed—when the idea of her beauty—her winning smiles—her fond endearments stole upon his fancy, and subdued his heart; he almost wept to the idea of injuring her, and in spite of appearances, pronounced her faithful. The succeeding moment plunged him again into uncertainty; his tortures acquired new vigour from cessation, and again he experienced all the phrenzy of despair. He was now resolved to end his doubts by repairing to the pavilion; but again his heart wavered in irresolution how to proceed should his fears be confirmed. In the mean time he determined to watch the behaviour of Maria with severe vigilance.

They met at dinner, and he observed her closely, but discovered not the smallest impropriety in her conduct. Her smiles and her beauty again wound their fascinations round his heart, and in the excess of their influence he was almost tempted to repair the injury which his late suspicions had done her, by confessing them at her feet. The appearance of the Cavalier de Vincini, however, renewed his suspicions; his heart throbbed wildly, and with restless impatience he watched the return of evening, which would remove his suspence.

Night at length came. He repaired to the pavilion, and secreted himself among the trees that embowered it. Many minutes had not passed, when he heard a sound of low whispering voices steal from among the trees, and footsteps approaching down the alley. He stood almost petrified with terrible sensations, and presently heard some persons enter the pavilion. The marquis now emerged from his hiding-place; a faint light issued from the building. He stole to the window, and beheld within, Maria and the Cavalier de Vincini. Fired at the sight, he drew his sword, and sprang forward. The sound of his step alarmed the cavalier, who, on perceiving the marquis, rushed by him from the pavilion, and disappeared among the woods. The marquis pursued, but could not overtake him; and he returned to the pavilion with an intention of plunging his sword in the heart of Maria, when he discovered her senseless on the ground. Pity now suspended his vengeance; he paused in agonizing gaze upon her, and returned his sword into the scabbard.

She revived, but on observing the marquis, screamed and relapsed. He hastened to the castle for assistance, inventing, to conceal his disgrace, some pretence for her sudden illness, and she was conveyed to her chamber.

The marquis was now not suffered to doubt her infidelity, but the passion which her conduct abused, her faithlessness could not subdue; he still doated with absurd fondness, and even regretted that uncertainty could no longer flatter him with hope. It seemed as if his desire of her affection increased with his knowledge of the loss of it; and the very circumstance which should have roused his aversion, by a strange perversity of disposition, appeared to heighten his passion, and to make him think it impossible he could exist without her.

When the first energy of his indignation was subsided, he determined, therefore, to reprove and to punish, but hereafter to restore her to favor.

In this resolution he went to her apartment, and reprehended her falsehood in terms of just indignation.

Maria de Vellorno, in whom the late discovery had roused resentment, instead of awakening penitence; and exasperated pride without exciting shame—heard the upbraidings of the marquis with impatience, and replied to them with acrimonious violence.

She boldly asserted her innocence, and instantly invented a story, the plausibility of which might have deceived a man who had evidence less certain than his senses to contradict it. She behaved with a haughtiness the most insolent; and when she perceived that the marquis was no longer to be misled, and that her violence failed to accomplish its purpose, she had recourse to tears and supplications. But the artifice was too glaring to succeed; and the marquis quitted her apartment in an agony of resentment.

His former fascinations, however, quickly returned, and again held him in suspension between love and vengeance. That the vehemence of his passion, however, might not want an object, he ordered Baptista to discover the retreat of the Cavalier de Vincini on whom he meant to revenge his lost honor. Shame forbade him to employ others in the search.

This discovery suspended for a while the operations of the fatal scheme, which had before employed the thoughts of the marquis; but it had only suspended—not destroyed them. The late occurrence had annihilated his domestic happiness; but his pride now rose to rescue him from despair, and he centered all his future hopes upon ambition. In a moment of cool reflection, he considered that he had derived neither happiness or content from the pursuit of dissipated pleasures, to which he had hitherto sacrificed every opposing consideration. He resolved, therefore, to abandon the gay schemes of dissipation which had formerly allured him, and dedicate himself entirely to ambition, in the pursuits and delights of which he hoped to bury all his cares. He therefore became more earnest than ever for the marriage of Julia with the Duke de Luovo, through whose means he designed to involve himself in the interests of the state, and determined to recover her at whatever consequence. He resolved, without further delay, to appeal to the pope; but to do this with safety it was necessary that the marchioness should die; and he returned therefore to the consideration and execution of his diabolical purpose.

He mingled a poisonous drug with the food he designed for her; and when night arrived, carried it to the cell. As he unlocked the door, his hand trembled; and when he presented the food, and looked consciously for the last time upon the marchioness, who received it with humble thankfulness, his heart almost relented. His countenance, over which was diffused the paleness of death, expressed the secret movements of his soul, and he gazed upon her with eyes of stiffened horror. Alarmed by his looks, she fell upon her knees to supplicate his pity.

Her attitude recalled his bewildered senses; and endeavouring to assume a tranquil aspect, he bade her rise, and instantly quitted the cell, fearful of the instability of his purpose. His mind was not yet sufficiently hardened by guilt to repel the arrows of conscience, and his imagination responded to her power. As he passed through the long dreary passages from the prison, solemn and mysterious sounds seemed to speak in every murmur of the blast which crept along their windings, and he often started and looked back.

He reached his chamber, and having shut the door, surveyed the room in fearful examination. Ideal forms flitted before his fancy, and for the first time in his life he feared to be alone. Shame only withheld him from calling Baptista. The gloom of the hour, and the death-like silence that prevailed, assisted the horrors of his imagination. He half repented of the deed, yet deemed it now too late to obviate it; and he threw himself on his bed in terrible emotion. His head grew dizzy, and a sudden faintness overcame him; he hesitated, and at length arose to ring for assistance, but found himself unable to stand.

In a few moments he was somewhat revived, and rang his bell; but before any person appeared, he was seized with terrible pains, and staggering to his bed, sunk senseless upon it. Here Baptista, who was the first person that entered his room, found him struggling seemingly in the agonies of death. The whole castle was immediately roused, and the confusion may be more easily imagined than described. Emilia, amid the general alarm, came to her father's room, but the sight of him overcame her, and she was carried from his presence. By the help of proper applications the marquis recovered his senses and his pains had a short cessation.

'I am dying,' said he, in a faultering accent; 'send instantly for the marchioness and my son.'

Ferdinand, in escaping from the hands of the banditti, it was now seen, had fallen into the power of his father. He had been since confined in an apartment of the castle, and was now liberated to obey the summons. The countenance of the marquis exhibited a ghastly image; Ferdinand, when he drew near the bed, suddenly shrunk back, overcome with horror. The marquis now beckoned his attendants to quit the room, and they were preparing to obey, when a violent noise was heard from without; almost in the same instant the door of the apartment was thrown open, and the servant, who had been sent for the marchioness, rushed in. His look alone declared the horror of his mind, for words he had none to utter. He stared wildly, and pointed to the gallery he had quitted. Ferdinand, seized with new terror, rushed the way he pointed to the apartment of the marchioness. A spectacle of horror presented itself. Maria lay on a couch lifeless, and bathed in blood. A poignard, the instrument of her destruction, was on the floor; and it appeared from a letter which was found on the couch beside her, that she had died by her own hand. The paper contained these words:

TO THE MARQUIS DE MAZZINI

Your words have stabbed my heart. No power on earth could restore the peace you have destroyed. I will escape from my torture. When you read this, I shall be no more. But the triumph shall no longer be yours—the draught you have drank was given by the hand of the injured

MARIA DE MAZZINI.

It now appeared that the marquis was poisoned by the vengeance of the woman to whom he had resigned his conscience. The consternation and distress of Ferdinand cannot easily be conceived: he hastened back to his father's chamber, but determined to conceal the dreadful catastrophe of Maria de Vellorno. This precaution, however, was useless; for the servants, in the consternation of terror, had revealed it, and the marquis had fainted.

Returning pains recalled his senses, and the agonies he suffered were too shocking for the beholders. Medical endeavours were applied, but the poison was too powerful for antidote. The marquis's pains at length subsided; the poison had exhausted most of its rage, and he became tolerably easy. He waved his hand for the attendants to leave the room; and beckoning to Ferdinand, whose senses were almost stunned by this accumulation of horror, bade him sit down beside him. 'The hand of death is now upon me,' said he; 'I would employ these last moments in revealing a deed, which is more dreadful to me than all the bodily agonies I suffer. It will be some relief to me to discover it.' Ferdinand grasped the hand of the marquis in speechless terror. 'The retribution of heaven is upon me,' resumed the marquis. 'My punishment is the immediate consequence of my guilt. Heaven has made that woman the instrument of its justice, whom I made the instrument of my crimes;——that woman, for whose sake I forgot conscience, and braved vice—for whom I imprisoned an innocent wife, and afterwards murdered her.'

At these words every nerve of Ferdinand thrilled; he let go the marquis's hand and started back. 'Look not so fiercely on me,' said the marquis, in a hollow voice; 'your eyes strike death to my soul; my conscience needs not this additional pang.'—'My mother!' exclaimed Ferdinand—'my mother! Speak, tell me.'—'I have no breath,' said the marquis. 'Oh!—Take these keys—the south tower—the trapdoor.—'Tis possible—Oh!—'

The marquis made a sudden spring upwards, and fell lifeless on the bed; the attendants were called in, but he was gone for ever. His last words struck with the force of lightning upon the mind of Ferdinand; they seemed to say that his mother might yet exist. He took the keys, and ordering some of the servants to follow, hastened to the southern building; he proceeded to the tower, and the trapdoor beneath the stair-case was lifted. They all descended into a dark passage, which conducted them through several intricacies to the door of the cell. Ferdinand, in trembling horrible expectation, applied the key; the door opened, and he entered; but what was his surprize when he found no person in the cell! He concluded that he had mistaken the place, and quitted it for further search; but having followed the windings of the passage, by which he entered, without discovering any other door, he returned to a more exact examination of the cell. He now observed the door, which led to the cavern, and he entered upon the avenue, but no person was found there and no voice answered to his call. Having reached the door of the cavern, which was fastened, he returned lost in grief, and meditating upon the last words of the marquis. He now thought that he had mistaken their import, and that the words ''tis possible,' were not meant to apply to the life of the marchioness, he concluded, that the murder had been committed at a distant period; and he resolved, therefore, to have the ground of the cell dug up, and the remains of his mother sought for.

When the first violence of the emotions excited by the late scenes was subsided, he enquired concerning Maria de Vellorno.

It appeared that on the day preceding this horrid transaction, the marquis had passed some hours in her apartment; that they were heard in loud dispute;—that the passion of the marquis grew high;—that he upbraided her with her past conduct, and threatened her with a formal separation. When the marquis quitted her, she was heard walking quick through the room, in a passion of tears; she often suddenly stopped in vehement but incoherent exclamation; and at last threw herself on the floor, and was for some time entirely still. Here her woman found her, upon whose entrance she arose hastily, and reproved her for appearing uncalled. After this she remained silent and sullen.

She descended to supper, where the marquis met her alone at table. Little was said during the repast, at the conclusion of which the servants were dismissed; and it was believed that during the interval between supper, and the hour of repose, Maria de Vellorno contrived to mingle poison with the wine of the marquis. How she had procured this poison was never discovered.

She retired early to her chamber; and her woman observing that she appeared much agitated, inquired if she was ill? To this she returned a short answer in the negative, and her woman was soon afterwards dismissed. But she had hardly shut the door of the room when she heard her lady's voice recalling her. She returned, and received some trifling order, and observed that Maria looked uncommonly pale; there was besides a wildness in her eyes which frightened her, but she did not dare to ask any questions. She again quitted the room, and had only reached the extremity of the gallery when her mistress's bell rang. She hastened back, Maria enquired if the marquis was gone to bed, and if all was quiet? Being answered in the affirmative, she replied, 'This is a still hour and a dark one!—Good night!'

Her woman having once more left the room, stopped at the door to listen, but all within remaining silent, she retired to rest.

It is probable that Maria perpetrated the fatal act soon after the dismissal of her woman; for when she was found, two hours afterwards, she appeared to have been dead for some time. On examination a wound was discovered on her left side, which had doubtless penetrated to the heart, from the suddenness of her death, and from the effusion of blood which had followed.

These terrible events so deeply affected Emilia that she was confined to her bed by a dangerous illness. Ferdinand struggled against the shock with manly fortitude. But amid all the tumult of the present scenes, his uncertainty concerning Julia, whom he had left in the hands of banditti, and whom he had been withheld from seeking or rescuing, formed, perhaps, the most affecting part of his distress.

The late Marquis de Mazzini, and Maria de Vellorno, were interred with the honor due to their rank in the church of the convent of St Nicolo. Their lives exhibited a boundless indulgence of violent and luxurious passions, and their deaths marked the consequences of such indulgence, and held forth to mankind a singular instance of divine vengeance.

CHAPTER XVI

In turning up the ground of the cell, it was discovered that it communicated with the dungeon in which Ferdinand had been confined, and where he had heard those groans which had occasioned him so much terror.

The story which the marquis formerly related to his son, concerning the southern buildings, it was now evident was fabricated for the purpose of concealing the imprisonment of the marchioness. In the choice of his subject, he certainly discovered some art; for the circumstance related was calculated, by impressing terror, to prevent farther enquiry into the recesses of these buildings. It served, also, to explain, by supernatural evidence, the cause of those sounds, and of that appearance which had been there observed, but which were, in reality, occasioned only by the marquis.

The event of the examination in the cell threw Ferdinand into new perplexity. The marquis had confessed that he poisoned his wife—yet her remains were not to be found; and the place which he signified to be that of her confinement, bore no vestige of her having been there. There appeared no way by which she could have escaped from her prison; for both the door which opened upon the cell, and that which terminated the avenue beyond, were fastened when tried by Ferdinand.

But the young marquis had no time for useless speculation—serious duties called upon him. He believed that Julia was still in the power of banditti; and, on the conclusion of his father's funeral, he set forward himself to Palermo, to give information of the abode of the robbers, and to repair with the officers of justice, accompanied by a party of his own people, to the rescue of his sister. On his arrival at Palermo he was informed, that a banditti, whose retreat had been among the ruins of a monastery, situated in the forest of Marentino, was already discovered; that their abode had been searched, and themselves secured for examples of public justice—but that no captive lady had been found amongst them. This latter intelligence excited in Ferdinand a very serious distress, and he was wholly unable to conjecture her fate. He obtained leave, however, to interrogate those of the robbers, who were imprisoned at Palermo, but could draw from them no satisfactory or certain information.

At length he quitted Palermo for the forest of Marentino, thinking it possible that Julia might be heard of in its neighbourhood. He travelled on in melancholy and dejection, and evening overtook him long before he reached the place of his destination. The night came on heavily in clouds, and a violent storm of wind and rain arose. The road lay through a wild and rocky country, and Ferdinand could obtain no shelter. His attendants offered him their cloaks, but he refused to expose a servant to the hardship he would not himself endure. He travelled for some miles in a heavy rain; and the wind, which howled mournfully among the rocks, and whose solemn pauses were filled by the distant roarings of the sea, heightened the desolation of the scene. At length he discerned, amid the darkness from afar, a red light waving in the wind: it varied with the blast, but never totally disappeared. He pushed his horse into a gallop, and made towards it.

The flame continued to direct his course; and on a nearer approach, he perceived, by the red reflection of its fires, streaming a long radiance upon the waters beneath—a lighthouse situated upon a point of rock which overhung the sea. He knocked for admittance, and the door was opened by an old man, who bade him welcome.

Within appeared a cheerful blazing fire, round which were seated several persons, who seemed like himself to have sought shelter from the tempest of the night. The sight of the fire cheered him, and he advanced towards it, when a sudden scream seized his attention; the company rose up in confusion, and in the same instant he discovered Julia and Hippolitus. The joy of that moment is not to be described, but his attention was quickly called off from his own situation to that of a lady, who during the general transport had fainted. His sensations on learning she was his mother cannot be described.

She revived. 'My son!' said she, in a languid voice, as she pressed him to her heart. 'Great God, I am recompensed! Surely this moment may repay a life of misery!' He could only receive her caresses in silence; but the sudden tears which started in his eyes spoke a language too expressive to be misunderstood.

When the first emotion of the scene was passed, Julia enquired by what means Ferdinand had come to this spot. He answered her generally, and avoided for the present entering upon the affecting subject of the late events at the castle of Mazzini. Julia related the history of her adventures since she parted with her brother. In her narration, it appeared that Hippolitus, who was taken by the Duke de Luovo at the mouth of the cave, had afterwards escaped, and returned to the cavern in search of Julia. The low recess in the rock, through which Julia had passed, he perceived by the light of his flambeau. He penetrated to the cavern beyond, and from thence to the prison of the marchioness. No colour of language can paint the scene which followed; it is sufficient to say that the whole party agreed to quit the cell at the return of night. But this being a night on which it was known the marquis would visit the prison, they agreed to defer their departure till after his appearance, and thus elude the danger to be expected from an early discovery of the escape of the marchioness.

At the sound of footsteps above, Hippolitus and Julia had secreted themselves in the avenue; and immediately on the marquis's departure they all repaired to the cavern, leaving, in the hurry of their flight, untouched the poisonous food he had brought. Having escaped from thence they proceeded to a neighbouring village, where horses were procured to carry them towards Palermo. Here, after a tedious journey, they arrived, in the design of embarking for Italy. Contrary winds had detained them till the day on which Ferdinand left that city, when, apprehensive and weary of delay, they hired a small vessel, and determined to brave the winds. They had soon reason to repent their temerity; for the vessel had not been long at sea when the storm arose, which threw them back upon the shores of Sicily, and brought them to the lighthouse, where they were discovered by Ferdinand.

On the following morning Ferdinand returned with his friends to Palermo, where he first disclosed the late fatal events of the castle. They now settled their future plans; and Ferdinand hastened to the castle of Mazzini to fetch Emilia, and to give orders for the removal of his household to his palace at Naples, where he designed to fix his future residence. The distress of Emilia, whom he found recovered from her indisposition, yielded to joy and wonder, when she heard of the existence of her mother, and the safety of her sister. She departed with Ferdinand for Palermo, where her friends awaited her, and where the joy of the meeting was considerably heightened by the appearance of Madame de Menon, for whom the marchioness had dispatched a messenger to St Augustin's. Madame had quitted the abbey for another convent, to which, however, the messenger was directed. This happy party now embarked for Naples.

From this period the castle of Mazzini, which had been the theatre of a dreadful catastrophe; and whose scenes would have revived in the minds of the chief personages connected with it, painful and shocking reflections—was abandoned.

On their arrival at Naples, Ferdinand presented to the king a clear and satisfactory account of the late events at the castle, in consequence of which the marchioness was confirmed in her rank, and Ferdinand was received as the sixth Marquis de Mazzini.

The marchioness, thus restored to the world, and to happiness, resided with her children in the palace at Naples, where, after time had somewhat mellowed the remembrance of the late calamity, the nuptials of Hippolitus and Julia were celebrated. The recollection of the difficulties they had encountered, and of the distress they had endured for each other, now served only to heighten by contrast the happiness of the present period.

Ferdinand soon after accepted a command in the Neapolitan army; and amidst the many heroes of that warlike and turbulent age, distinguished himself for his valour and ability. The occupations of war engaged his mind, while his heart was solicitous in promoting the happiness of his family.

Madame de Menon, whose generous attachment to the marchioness had been fully proved, found in the restoration of her friend a living witness of her marriage, and thus recovered those estates which had been unjustly withheld from her. But the marchioness and her family, grateful to her friendship, and attached to her virtues, prevailed upon her to spend the remainder of her life at the palace of Mazzini.

Emilia, wholly attached to her family, continued to reside with the marchioness, who saw her race renewed in the children of Hippolitus and Julia. Thus surrounded by her children and friends, and engaged in forming the minds of the infant generation, she seemed to forget that she had ever been otherwise than happy.

* * * * *

Here the manuscript annals conclude. In reviewing this story, we perceive a singular and striking instance of moral retribution. We learn, also, that those who do only THAT WHICH IS RIGHT, endure nothing in misfortune but a trial of their virtue, and from trials well endured derive the surest claim to the protection of heaven.

FINIS

THE

ROMANCE OF THE FOREST:

INTERSPERSED

WITH SOME PIECES OF POETRY.

CHAPTER I

I am a man,So weary with disasters, tugg'd with fortune,That I would set my life on any chance,To mend it, or be rid ou't.

When once sordid interest seizes on the heart, it freezes up the source of every warm and liberal feeling; it is an enemy alike to virtue and to taste—this it perverts, and that it annihilates. The time may come, my friend, when death shall dissolve the sinews of avarice, and justice be permitted to resume her rights.

Such were the words of the Advocate Nemours to Pierre de la Motte, as the latter stept at midnight into the carriage which was to bear him far from Paris, from his creditors and the persecution of the laws. De la Motte thanked him for this last instance of his kindness; the assistance he had given him in escape; and, when the carriage drove away, uttered a sad adieu! The gloom of the hour, and the peculiar emergency of his circumstances, sunk him in silent reverie.

Whoever has read Gayot de Pitaval, the most faithful of those writers who record the proceedings in the Parliamentary Courts of Paris during the seventeenth century, must surely remember the striking story of Pierre de la Motte and the Marquess Philippe de Montalt: let all such, therefore, be informed, that the person here introduced to their notice was that individual Pierre de la Motte.

As Madame de la Motte leaned from the coach window, and gave a last look to the walls of Paris—Paris, the scene of her former happiness, and the residence of many dear friends—the fortitude, which had till now supported her, yielding to the force of grief—Farewell all! sighed she, this last look and we are separated for ever! Tears followed her words, and, sinking back, she resigned herself to the stillness of sorrow. The recollection of former times pressed heavily upon her heart; a few months before and she was surrounded by friends, fortune, and consequence; now she was deprived of all, a miserable exile from her native place, without home, without comfort—almost without hope. It was not the least of her afflictions that she had been obliged to quit Paris without bidding adieu to her only son, who was now on duty with his regiment in Germany; and such had been the precipitancy of this removal, that had she even known where he was stationed, she had no time to inform him of it, or of the alteration in his father's circumstances.

Pierre de la Motte was a gentleman, descended from an ancient house of France. He was a man whose passions often overcame his reason, and, for a time, silenced his conscience; but though the image of virtue, which nature had impressed upon his heart, was sometimes obscured by the passing influence of vice, it was never wholly obliterated. With strength of mind sufficient to have withstood temptation, he would have been a good man; as it was, he was always a weak, and sometimes a vicious member of society; yet his mind was active, and his imagination vivid, which co-operating with the force of passion, often dazzled his judgment and subdued principle. Thus he was a man, infirm in purpose and visionary in virtue:—in a word, his conduct was suggested by feeling, rather than principle; and his virtue, such as it was, could not stand the pressure of occasion.

Early in life he had married Constance Valentia, a beautiful and elegant woman, attached to her family and beloved by them. Her birth was equal, her fortune superior to his; and their nuptials had been celebrated under the auspices of an approving and flattering world. Her heart was devoted to La Motte, and, for some time, she found in him an affectionate husband; but, allured by the gaieties of Paris, he was soon devoted to its luxuries, and in a few years his fortune and affection were equally lost in dissipation. A false pride had still operated against his interest, and withheld him from honourable retreat while it was yet in his power: the habits which he had acquired, enchained him to the scene of his former pleasure; and thus he had continued an expensive style of life till the means of prolonging it were exhausted. He at length awoke from this lethargy of security; but it was only to plunge into new error, and to attempt schemes for the reparation of his fortune, which served to sink him deeper in destruction. The consequence of a transaction, in which he thus engaged, now drove him, with the small wreck of his property, into dangerous and ignominious exile.

It was his design to pass into one of the southern provinces, and there seek, near the borders of the kingdom, an asylum in some obscure village. His family consisted of a wife and two faithful domestics, a man and woman, who had followed the fortune of their master.

The night was dark and tempestuous, and at about the distance of three leagues from Paris, Peter, who now acted as postillion, having driven for some time over a wild heath where many ways crossed, stopped, and acquainted De la Motte with his perplexity. The sudden stopping of the carriage roused the latter from his reverie, and filled the whole party with the terror of pursuit; he was unable to supply the necessary direction, and the extreme darkness made it dangerous to proceed without one. During this period of distress, a light was perceived at some distance, and after much doubt and hesitation, La Motte, in the hope of obtaining assistance, alighted and advanced towards it; he proceeded slowly, from the fear of unknown pits. The light issued from the window of a small and ancient house, which stood alone on the heath, at the distance of half a mile.

Having reached the door, he stopped for some moments, listening in apprehensive anxiety—no sound was heard but that of the wind, which swept in hollow gusts over the waste. At length he ventured to knock, and having waited for some time, during which he indistinctly heard several voices in conversation, some one within inquired what he wanted? La Motte answered, that he was a traveller who had lost his way, and desired to be directed to the nearest town. That, said the person, is seven miles off, and the road bad enough, even if you could see it; if you only want a bed, you may have it here, and had better stay.

The "pitiless pelting" of the storm, which at this time beat with increasing fury upon La Motte, inclined him to give up the attempt of proceeding further till daylight; but, desirous of seeing the person with whom he conversed, before he ventured to expose his family by calling up the carriage, he asked to be admitted. The door was now opened by a tall figure with a light, who invited La Motte to enter. He followed the man through a passage into a room almost unfurnished, in one corner of which a bed was spread upon the floor. The forlorn and desolate aspect of this apartment made La Motte shrink involuntarily, and he was turning to go out when the man suddenly pushed him back, and he heard the door locked upon him; his heart failed, yet he made a desperate, though vain, effort to force the door, and called loudly for release. No answer was returned; but he distinguished the voices of men in the room above, and, not doubting but their intention was to rob and murder him, his agitation, at first, overcame his reason. By the light of some almost-expiring embers, he perceived a window, but the hope which this discovery revived was quickly lost, when he found the aperture guarded by strong iron bars. Such preparation for security surprised him, and confirmed his worst apprehensions. Alone, unarmed—beyond the chance of assistance, he saw himself in the power of people whose trade was apparently rapine!—murder their means!—After revolving every possibility of escape, he endeavoured to await the event with fortitude; but La Motte could boast of no such virtue.

The voices had ceased, and all remained still for a quarter of an hour, when, between the pauses of the wind, he thought he distinguished the sobs and moaning of a female; he listened attentively, and became confirmed in his conjecture; it was too evidently the accent of distress. At this conviction the remains of his courage forsook him, and a terrible surmise darted, with the rapidity of lightning, across his brain. It was probable that his carriage had been discovered by the people of the house, who, with a design of plunder, had secured his servant, and brought hither Madame de la Motte. He was the more inclined to believe this, by the stillness which had for some time reigned in the house, previous to the sounds he now heard. Or it was possible that the inhabitants were not robbers, but persons to whom he had been betrayed by his friend or servant, and who were appointed to deliver him into the hands of justice. Yet he hardly dared to doubt the integrity of his friend, who had been intrusted with the secret of his flight and the plan of his route, and had procured him the carriage in which he had escaped. Such depravity, exclaimed La Motte, cannot surely exist in human nature; much less in the heart of Nemours!

This ejaculation was interrupted by a noise in the passage leading to the room: it approached—the door was unlocked—and the man who had admitted La Motte into the house entered, leading, or rather forcibly dragging along, a beautiful girl, who appeared to be about eighteen. Her features were bathed in tears, and she seemed to suffer the utmost distress. The man fastened the lock and put the key in his pocket. He then advanced to La Motte, who had before observed other persons in the passage, and pointing a pistol to his breast, You are wholly in our power, said he, no assistance can reach you: if you wish to save your life, swear that you will convey this girl where I may never see her more; or rather consent to take her with you, for your oath I would not believe, and I can take care you shall not find me again.—Answer quickly, you have no time to lose.

He now seized the trembling hand of the girl, who shrunk aghast with terror, and hurried her towards La Motte, whom surprise still kept silent. She sunk at his feet, and with supplicating eyes, that streamed with tears, implored him to have pity on her. Notwithstanding his present agitation, he found it impossible to contemplate the beauty and distress of the object before him with indifference. Her youth, her apparent innocence—the artless energy of her manner forcibly assailed his heart, and he was going to speak, when the ruffian, who mistook the silence of astonishment for that of hesitation, prevented him, I have a horse ready to take you from hence, said he, and I will direct you over the heath. If you return within an hour, you die: after then, you are at liberty to come here when you please.

La Motte, without answering, raised the lovely girl from the floor, and was so much relieved from his own apprehensions, that he had leisure to attempt dissipating hers. Let us be gone, said the ruffian, and have no more of this nonsense; you may think yourself well off it's no worse. I'll go and get the horse ready.

The last words roused La Motte, and perplexed him with new fears; he dreaded to discover his carriage, lest its appearance might tempt the banditti to plunder; and to depart on horseback with this man might reduce a consequence yet more to be dreaded, Madame la Motte, wearied with apprehension, would, probably, send for her husband to the house, when all the former danger would be incurred, with the additional evil of being separated from his family, and the chance of being detected by the emissaries of justice in endeavouring to recover them. As these reflections passed over his mind in tumultuous rapidity, a noise was again heard in the passage, an uproar and scuffle ensued, and in the same moment he could distinguish the voice of his servant, who had been sent by Madame La Motte in search of him. Being now determined to disclose what could not long be concealed, he exclaimed aloud, that a horse was unnecessary, that he had a carriage at some distance, which would convey them from the heath, the man who was seized being his servant.

The ruffian, speaking through the door, bade him be patient a while and he should hear more from him. La Motte now turned his eyes upon his unfortunate companion, who, pale and exhausted, leaned for support against the wall. Her features, which were delicately beautiful, had gained from distress an expression of captivating sweetness: she had

An eyeAs when the blue sky trembles through a cloudOf purest white.

A habit of gray camlet, with short slashed sleeves, showed, but did not adorn, her figure: it was thrown open at the bosom, upon which part of her hair had fallen in disorder, while the light veil hastily thrown on, had, in her confusion, been suffered to fall back. Every moment of further observation heightened the surprise of La Motte, and interested him more warmly in her favour. Such elegance and apparent refinement, contrasted with the desolation of the house, and the savage manners of its inhabitants, seemed to him like a romance of imagination, rather than an occurrence of real life. He endeavoured to comfort her, and his sense of compassion was too sincere to be misunderstood. Her terror gradually subsided into gratitude and grief. Ah, Sir, said she, Heaven has sent you to my relief, and will surely reward you for your protection: I have no friend in the world, if do not find one in you.

La Motte assured her of his kindness, when he was interrupted by the entrance of the ruffian. He desired to be conducted to his family. All in good time, replied the latter; I have taken care of one of them, and will of you, please St. Peter; so be comforted. These comfortable words renewed the terror of La Motte, who now earnestly begged to know if his family were safe. O! as for that matter they are safe enough, and you will be with them presently; but don't stand parlying here all night. Do you choose to go or stay? you know the conditions. They now bound the eyes of La Motte and of the young lady, whom terror had hitherto kept silent, and then placing them on two horses, a man mounted behind each, and they immediately galloped off. They had proceeded in this way near half an hour, when La Motte entreated to know whither he was going? You will know that by and by, said the ruffian, so be at peace. Finding interrogatories useless, La Motte resumed silence till the horses stopped. His conductor then hallooed, and being answered by voices at some distance, in a few moments the sound of carriage wheels was heard, and, presently after, the words of a man directing Peter which way to drive. As the carriage approached, La Motte called, and, to his inexpressible joy, was answered by his wife.

You are now beyond the borders of the heath, and may go which way you will, said the ruffian; if you return within an hour, you will be welcomed by a brace of bullets. This was a very unnecessary caution to La Motte, whom they now released. The young stranger sighed deeply, as she entered the carriage; and the ruffian, having bestowed upon Peter some directions and more threats, waited to see him drive off. They did not wait long.

La Motte immediately gave a short relation of what passed at the house, including an account of the manner in which the young stranger had been introduced to him. During this narrative, her deep convulsive sighs frequently drew the attention of Madame La Motte, whose compassion became gradually interested in her behalf, and who now endeavoured to tranquillize her spirits. The unhappy girl answered her kindness in artless and simple expressions, and then relapsed into tears and silence. Madame forbore for the present to ask any questions that might lead to a discovery of her connexions, or seem to require an explanation of the late adventure, which now furnishing her with a new subject of reflection, the sense of her own misfortunes pressed less heavily upon her mind. The distress of La Motte was even for a while suspended; he ruminated on the late scene, and it appeared like a vision, or one of those improbable fictions that sometimes are exhibited in a romance: he could reduce it to no principles of probability, nor render it comprehensible by any endeavour to analyze it. The present charge, and the chance of future trouble brought upon him by this adventure, occasioned some dissatisfaction; but the beauty and seeming innocence of Adeline united with the pleadings of humanity in her favor, and he determined to protect her.

The tumult of emotions which had passed in the bosom of Adeline began now to subside; terror was softened into anxiety, and despair into grief. The sympathy so evident in the manners of her companions, particularly in those of Madame La Motte, soothed her heart, and encouraged her to hope for better days.

Dismally and silently the night passed on, for the minds of the travellers were too much occupied by their several sufferings to admit of conversation.

The dawn, so anxiously watched for, at length appeared, and introduced the strangers more fully to each other. Adeline derived comfort from the looks of Madame La Motte, who gazed frequently and attentively at her, and thought she had seldom seen a countenance so interesting, or a form so striking. The languor of sorrow threw a melancholy grace upon her features, that appealed immediately to the heart; and there was a penetrating sweetness in her blue eyes, which indicated an intelligent and amiable mind.

La Motte now looked anxiously from the coach window, that he might judge of their situation, and observe whether he was followed. The obscurity of the dawn confined his views, but no person appeared. The sun at length tinted the eastern clouds and the tops of the highest hills, and soon after burst in full splendour on the scene. The terrors of La Motte began to subside, and the griefs of Adeline to soften. They entered upon a lane confined by high banks and overarched by trees, on whose branches appeared the first green buds of spring glittering with dews. The fresh breeze of the morning animated the spirits of Adeline, whose mind was delicately sensible to the beauties of nature. As she viewed the flowery luxuriance of the turf, and the tender green of the trees, or caught, between the opening banks, a glimpse of the varied landscape, rich with wood, and fading into blue and distant mountains, her heart expanded in momentary joy. With Adeline the charms of external nature were heightened by those of novelty: she had seldom seen the grandeur of an extensive prospect, or the magnificence of a wide horizon—and not often the picturesque beauties of more confined scenery. Her mind had not lost by long oppression that elastic energy, which resists calamity; else, however, susceptible might have been her original taste, the beauties of nature would no longer have charmed her thus easily even to temporary repose.

The road, at length, wound down the side of a hill, and La Motte, again looking anxiously from the window, saw before him an open champaign country, through which the road, wholly unsheltered from observation, extended almost in a direct line. The danger of these circumstances alarmed him, for his flight might, without difficulty, be traced for many leagues from the hills he was now descending. Of the first peasant that passed, he inquired for a road among the hills, but heard of none. La Motte now sunk into his former terrors. Madame, notwithstanding her own apprehensions, endeavoured to reassure him; but finding her efforts ineffectual, she also retired to the contemplation of her misfortunes. Often, as they went on, did La Motte look back upon the country they had passed, and often did imagination suggest to him the sounds of distant pursuit.

The travellers stopped to breakfast in a village, where the road was at length obscured by woods, and La Motte's spirits again revived. Adeline appeared more tranquil than she had yet been, and La Motte now asked for an explanation of the scene he had witnessed on the preceding night. The inquiry renewed all her distress, and with tears she entreated for the present to be spared on the subject. La Motte pressed it no farther, but he observed that for the greater part of the day she seemed to remember it in melancholy and dejection. They now travelled among the hills, and were, therefore, in less danger of observation; but La Motte avoided the great towns, and stopped in obscure ones no longer than to refresh the horses. About two hours after noon, the road wound into a deep valley, watered by a rivulet and overhung with wood. La Motte called to Peter, and ordered him to drive to a thickly embowered spot, that appeared on the left. Here he alighted with his family; and Peter having spread the provisions on the turf, they seated themselves and partook of a repast, which, in other circumstances, would have been thought delicious. Adeline endeavoured to smile, but the languor of grief was now heightened by indisposition. The violent agitation of mind and fatigue of body which she had suffered for the last twenty-four hours, had overpowed her strength, and when La Motte led her back to the carriage, her whole frame trembled with illness. But she uttered no complaint, and, having long observed the dejection of her companions, she made a feeble effort to enliven them.

They continued to travel throughout the day without any accident or interruption, and about three hours after sunset arrived at Monville, a small town where La Motte determined to pass the night. Repose was, indeed, necessary to the whole party, whose pale and haggard looks, as they alighted from the carriage, were but too obvious to pass unobserved by the people of the inn. As soon as beds could be prepared, Adeline withdrew to her chamber, accompanied by Madame La Motte, whose concern for the fair stranger made her exert every effort to soothe and console her. Adeline wept in silence, and taking the hand of Madame, pressed it to her bosom. These were not merely tears of grief—they were mingled with those which flow from the grateful heart, when, unexpectedly, it meets with sympathy. Madame La Motte understood them. After some momentary silence, she renewed her assurances of kindness, and entreated Adeline to confide in her friendship; but she carefully avoided any mention of the subject which had before so much affected her. Adeline at length found words to express her sense of this goodness, which she did in a manner so natural and sincere, that Madame, finding herself much affected, took leave of her for the night.

In the morning, La Motte rose at an early hour, impatient to be gone. Every thing was prepared for his departure, and the breakfast had been waiting some time, but Adeline did not appear. Madame La Motte went to her chamber, and found her sunk in a disturbed slumber. Her breathing was short and irregular—she frequently started, or sighed, and sometimes she muttered an incoherent sentence. While Madame gazed with concern upon her languid countenance, she awoke, and, looking up, gave her hand to Madame La Motte, who found it burning with fever. She had passed a restless night, and, as she now attempted to rise, her head, which beat with intense pain, grew giddy, her strength failed, and she sunk back.

Madame was much alarmed, being at once convinced that it was impossible she could travel, and that a delay might prove fatal to her husband. She went to inform him of the truth, and his distress may be more easily imagined than described. He saw all the inconvenience and danger of delay, yet he could not so far divest himself of humanity as to abandon Adeline to the care, or rather to the neglect, of strangers. He sent immediately for a physician, who pronounced her to be in a high fever, and said a removal in her present state must be fatal. La Motte now determined to wait the event, and endeavour to calm the transports of terror which at times assailed him. In the mean while he took such precautions as his situation admitted of, passing the greater part of the day out of the village, in a spot from whence he had a view of the road for some distance; yet to be exposed to destruction by the illness of a girl whom he did not know, and who had actually been forced upon him, was a misfortune to which La Motte had not philosophy enough to submit with composure.

Adeline's fever continued to increase during the whole day, and at night, when the physician took his leave, he told La Motte the event would very soon be decided. La Motte received this intelligence with real concern. The beauty and innocence of Adeline had overcome the disadvantageous circumstances under which she had been introduced to him, and he now gave less consideration to the inconvenience she might hereafter occasion him, than to the hope of her recovery.

Madame La Motte watched over her with tender anxiety, and observed with admiration her patient sweetness and mild resignation. Adeline amply repaid her, though she thought she could not.—Young as I am, she would say, and deserted by those upon whom I have a claim for protection, I can remember no connexion to make me regret life so much, as that I hoped to form with you. If I live, my conduct will best express my sense of your goodness;—words are but feeble testimonies.

The sweetness of her manners so much attracted Madame La Motte, that she watched the crisis of her disorder with a solicitude which precluded every other interest. Adeline passed a very disturbed night, and, when the physician appeared in the morning, he gave orders that she should be indulged with whatever she liked, and answered the inquiries of La Motte with a frankness that left him nothing to hope.

In the mean time, his patient, after drinking profusely of some mild liquids, fell asleep, in which she continued for several hours, and so profound was her repose, that her breath alone gave sign of existence. She awoke free from fever, and with no other disorder than weakness, which in a few days she overcame so well as to be able to set out with La Motte for B——, a village out of the great road, which he thought it prudent to quit. There they passed the following night, and early the next morning commenced their journey upon a wild and woody tract of country. They stopped about noon at a solitary village, where they took refreshments, and obtained directions for passing the vast forest of Fontanville, upon the borders of which they now were. La Motte wished at first to take a guide, but he apprehended more evil from the discovery he might make of his route, than he hoped for benefit from assistance in the wilds of this uncultivated tract.

La Motte now designed to pass on to Lyons, where he could either seek concealment in its neighbourhood, or embark on the Rhone for Geneva, should the emergency of his circumstances hereafter require him to leave France. It was about twelve o'clock at noon, and he was desirous to hasten forward, that he might pass the forest of Fontanville, and reach the town on its opposite borders, before night-fall. Having deposited a fresh stock of provisions in the carriage, and received such directions as were necessary concerning the roads, they again set forward, and in a short time entered upon the forest. It was now the latter end of April, and the weather was remarkably temperate and fine. The balmy freshness of the air, which breathed the first pure essence of vegetation; and the gentle warmth of the sun, whose beams vivified every hue of nature, and opened every floweret of spring, revived Adeline and inspired her with life and health. As she inhaled the breeze, her strength seemed to return, and as her eyes wandered through the romantic glades that opened into the forest, her heart was gladdened with complacent delight: but when from these objects she turned her regard upon Monsieur and Madame La Motte, to whose tender attentions she owed her life, and in whose looks she now read esteem and kindness, her bosom glowed with sweet affections, and she experienced a force of gratitude which might be called sublime.

For the remainder of the day they continued to travel, without seeing a hut or meeting a human being. It was now near sunset, and the prospect being closed on all sides by the forest, La Motte began to have apprehensions that his servant had mistaken the way. The road, if a road it could be called, which afforded only a slight track upon the grass, was sometimes over-run by luxuriant vegetation, and sometimes obscured by the deep shades, and Peter at length stopped uncertain of the way. La Motte, who dreaded being benighted in a scene so wild and solitary as this forest, and whose apprehensions of banditti were very sanguine, ordered him to proceed at any rate, and, if he found no track, to endeavour to gain a more open part of the forest. With these orders Peter again set forwards; but having proceeded some way, and his views being still confined by woody glades and forest walks, he began to despair of extricating himself, and stopped for further orders. The sun was now set; but as La Motte looked anxiously from the window, he observed upon the vivid glow of the western horizon some dark towers rising from among the trees at a little distance, and ordered Peter to drive towards them.—If they belong to a monastery, said he, we may probably gain admittance for the night.

The carriage drove along under the shade of "melancholy boughs," through which the evening twilight, which yet coloured the air, diffused a solemnity that vibrated in thrilling sensations upon the hearts of the travellers. Expectation kept them silent. The present scene recalled to Adeline a remembrance of the late terrific circumstances, and her mind responded but too easily to the apprehension of new misfortunes. La Motte alighted at the foot of a green knoll, where the trees again opening to light, permitted a nearer though imperfect view of the edifice.

CHAPTER II

..........how these antique towersAnd vacant courts chill the suspended soul!Till expectation wears the face of fear:And fear, half ready to become devotion,Mutters a kind of mental orisonIt knows not wherefore! What a kind of beingIs circumstance!HORACE WALPOLE.

He approached, and perceived the Gothic remains of an abbey: it stood on a kind of rude lawn, overshadowed by high and spreading trees which seemed coeval with the building, and diffused a romantic gloom around. The greater part of the pile appeared to be sinking into ruins, and that which had withstood the ravages of time, showed the remaining features of the fabric more awful in decay. The lofty battlements, thickly enwreathed with ivy, were half demolished, and become the residence of birds of prey. Huge fragments of the eastern tower, which was almost demolished, lay scattered amid the high grass, that waved slowly to the breeze. "The thistle shook its lonely head; the moss whistled to the wind." A Gothic gate, richly ornamented with fret-work, which opened into the main body of the edifice, but which was now obstructed with brush-wood, remained entire. Above the vast and magnificent portal of this gate arose a window of the same order, whose pointed arches still exhibited fragments of stained glass, once the pride of monkish devotion. La Motte, thinking it possible it might yet shelter some human being, advanced to the gate and lifted a massy knocker. The hollow sounds rung through the emptiness of the place. After waiting a few minutes, he forced back the gate, which was heavy with iron work and creaked harshly on its hinges.

He entered what appeared to have been the chapel of the abbey, where the hymn of devotion had once been raised, and the tear of penitence had once been shed; sounds, which could now only be recalled by imagination—tears of penitence, which had been long since fixed in fate. La Motte paused a moment, for he felt a sensation of sublimity rising into terror—a suspension of mingled astonishment and awe! He surveyed the vastness of the place, and as he contemplated its ruins, fancy bore him back to past ages.—And these walls, said he, where once superstition lurked, and austerity anticipated an earthly purgatory, now tremble over the mortal remains of the beings who reared them!

The deepening gloom now reminded La Motte that he had no time to lose; but curiosity prompted him to explore further, and he obeyed the impulse. As he walked over the broken pavement, the sound of his steps ran in echoes through the place, and seemed like the mysterious accents of the dead reproving the sacrilegious mortal who thus dared to disturb their precincts.

From this chapel he passed into the nave of the great church, of which one window, more perfect than the rest, opened upon a long vista of the forest, through which was seen the rich colouring of evening, melting by imperceptible gradations into the solemn gray of upper air. Dark hills, whose outline appeared distinct upon the vivid glow of the horizon, closed the perspective. Several of the pillars, which had once supported the roof, remained the proud effigies of sinking greatness, and seemed to nod at every murmur of the blast over the fragments of those that had fallen a little before them. La Motte sighed. The comparison between himself and the gradation of decay which these columns exhibited, was but too obvious and affecting. A few years, said he, and I shall become like the mortals on whose relicks I now gaze, and, like them too, I may be the subject of meditation to a succeeding generation, which shall totter but a little while over the object they contemplate ere they also sink into the dust.

Retiring from the scene, he walked through the cloisters, till a door, which communicated with the lofty part of the building, attracted his curiosity. He opened this, and perceived across the foot of the staircase another door;—but now, partly checked by fear, and partly by the recollection of the surprise his family might feel in his absence, he returned with hasty steps to his carriage, having wasted some of the precious moments of twilight and gained no information.

Some slight answer to Madame La Motte's inquiries, and a general direction to Peter to drive carefully on and look for a road, was all that his anxiety would permit him to utter. The night shade fell thick around, which, deepened by the gloom of the forest, soon rendered it dangerous to proceed. Peter stopped; but La Motte, persisting in his first determination, ordered him to go on. Peter ventured to remonstrate, Madame La Motte entreated, but La Motte reproved—commanded, and at length repented; for the hind wheel rising upon the stump of an old tree, which the darkness had prevented Peter from observing, the carriage was in an instant overturned.

The party, as may be supposed, were much terrified, but no one was materially hurt; and having disengaged themselves from their perilous situation, La Motte and Peter endeavoured to raise the carriage. The extent of this misfortune was now discovered, for they perceived that the wheel was broke. Their distress was reasonably great, for not only was the coach disabled from proceeding, but it could not even afford a shelter from the cold dews of the night, it being impossible to preserve it in an upright situation. After a few moments' silence, La Motte proposed that they should return to the ruins which they had just quitted, which lay at a very short distance, and pass the night in the most habitable part of them: that, when morning dawned, Peter should take one of the coach horses, and endeavour to find a road and a town, from whence assistance could be procured for repairing the carriage. This proposal was opposed by Madame La Motte, who shuddered at the idea of passing so many hours of darkness in a place so forlorn as the monastery. Terrors, which she neither endeavoured to examine or combat, overcame her, and she told La Motte she had rather remain exposed to the unwholesome dews of night, than encounter the desolation of the ruins. La Motte had at first felt an equal reluctance to return to this spot; but having subdued his own feelings, he resolved not to yield to those of his wife.

The horses being now disengaged from the carriage, the party moved towards the edifice. As they proceeded, Peter, who followed them, struck a light, and they entered the ruins by the flame of sticks which he had collected. The partial gleams thrown across the fabric seemed to make its desolation more solemn, while the obscurity of the greater part of the pile heightened its sublimity, and led fancy on to scenes of horror. Adeline, who had hitherto remained in silence, now uttered an exclamation of mingled admiration and fear. A kind of pleasing dread thrilled her bosom, and filled all her soul. Tears started into her eyes:—she wished yet feared to go on;—she hung upon the arm of La Motte, and looked at him with a sort of hesitating interrogation.

He opened the door of the great hall, and they entered: its extent was lost in gloom.—Let us stay here, said Madame de La Motte, I will go no further. La Motte pointed to the broken roof, and was proceeding, when he was interrupted by an uncommon noise, which passed along the hall. They were all silent—it was the silence of terror. Madame La Motte spoke first. Let us quit this spot, said she, any evil is preferable to the feeling which now oppresses me. Let us retire instantly. The stillness had for some time remained undisturbed, and La Motte, ashamed of the fear he had involuntarily betrayed, now thought it necessary to affect a boldness which he did not feel. He therefore opposed ridicule to the terror of Madame, and insisted upon proceeding. Thus compelled to acquiesce, she traversed the hall with trembling steps. They came to a narrow passage, and Peter's sticks being nearly exhausted, they awaited here, while he went in search of more.

The almost expiring light flashed faintly upon the walls of the passage, showing the recess more horrible. Across the hall, the greater part of which was concealed in shadow, the feeble ray spread a tremulous gleam, exhibiting the chasm in the roof, while many nameless objects were seen imperfectly through the dusk. Adeline with a smile inquired of La Motte if he believed in spirits. The question was ill-timed; for the present scene impressed its terrors upon La Motte, and, in spite of endeavour, he felt a superstitious dread stealing upon him. He was now, perhaps, standing over the ashes of the dead. If spirits were ever permitted to revisit the earth, this seemed the hour and the place most suitable for their appearance. La Motte remaining silent, Adeline said, Were I inclined to superstition—she was interrupted by a return of the noise which had been lately heard. It sounded down the passage, at whose entrance they stood, and sunk gradually away. Every heart palpitated, and they remained listening in silence. A new subject of apprehension seized La Motte:—the noise might proceed from banditti, and he hesitated whether it would be safe to proceed. Peter now came with the light: Madame refused to enter the passage—La Motte was not much inclined to it; but Peter, in whom curiosity was more prevalent than fear, readily offered his services. La Motte, after some hesitation, suffered him to go, while he awaited at the entrance the result of the inquiry. The extent of the passage soon concealed Peter from view, and the echoes of his footsteps were lost in a sound which rushed along the avenue, and became fainter and fainter till it sunk into silence. La Motte now called aloud to Peter, but no answer was returned; at length, they heard the sound of a distant footstep, and Peter soon after appeared, breathless, and pale with fear.

When he came within hearing of La Motte, he called out, An please your honour, I've done for them, I believe, but I've had a hard bout. I thought I was fighting with the devil.—What are you speaking of? said La Motte.

They were nothing but owls and rooks after all, continued Peter; but the light brought them all about my ears, and they made such a confounded clapping with their wings, that I thought at first I had been beset with a legion of devils. But I have driven them all out, master, and you have nothing to fear now.

The latter part of the sentence, intimating a suspicion of his courage, La Motte, could have dispensed with, and to retrieve in some degree his reputation, he made a point of proceeding through the passage. They now moved on with alacrity, for, as Peter said, they had nothing to fear.

The passage led into a large area, on one side of which, over a range of cloisters, appeared the west tower, and a lofty part of the edifice; the other side was open to the woods. La Motte led the way to a door of the tower, which he now perceived was the same he had formerly entered; but he found some difficulty in advancing, for the area was overgrown with brambles and nettles, and the light which Peter carried afforded only an uncertain gleam. When he unclosed the door, the dismal aspect of the place revived the apprehensions of Madame La Motte, and extorted from Adeline an inquiry whither they were going. Peter held up the light to show the narrow staircase that wound round the tower; but La Motte, observing the second door, drew back the rusty bolts, and entered a spacious apartment, which, from its style and condition, was evidently of a much later date than the other part of the structure: though desolate and forlorn, it was very little impaired by time; the walls were damp, but not decayed; and the glass was yet firm in the windows.

They passed on to a suit of apartments resembling the first they had seen, and expressed their surprise at the incongruous appearance of this part of the edifice with the mouldering walls they had left behind. These apartments conducted them to a winding passage, that received light and air through narrow cavities placed high in the wall; and was at length closed by a door barred with iron, which being with some difficulty opened, they entered a vaulted room. La Motte surveyed it with a scrutinizing eye, and endeavoured to conjecture for what purpose it had been guarded by a door of such strength; but he saw little within to assist his curiosity. The room appeared to have been built in modern times upon a Gothic plan. Adeline approached a large window that formed a kind of recess raised by one step over the level of the floor; she observed to La Motte that the whole floor was inlaid with Mosaic work; which drew from him a remark, that the style of this apartment was not strictly Gothic. He passed on to a door which appeared on the opposite side of the apartment, and, unlocking it, found himself in the great hall by which he had entered the fabric.

He now perceived, what the gloom had before concealed, a spiral staircase which led to a gallery above, and which, from its present condition, seemed to have been built with the more modern part of the fabric, though this also affected the Gothic mode of architecture: La Motte had little doubt that these stairs led to apartments corresponding with those he had passed below, and hesitated whether to explore them; but the entreaties of Madame, who was much fatigued, prevailed with him to defer all further examination. After some deliberation in which of the rooms they should pass the night, they determined to return to that which opened from the tower.

A fire was kindled on a hearth, which it is probable had not for many years before afforded the warmth of hospitality; and Peter having spread the provision he had brought from the coach, La Motte and his family, encircled round the fire, partook of a repast which hunger and fatigue made delicious. Apprehension gradually gave way to confidence, for they now found themselves in something like a human habitation, and they had leisure to laugh at their late terrors; but, as the blasts shook the doors, Adeline often started, and threw a fearful glance around. They continued to laugh and talk cheerfully for a time; yet their merriment was transient, if not affected; for a sense of their peculiar and distressed circumstances pressed upon their recollection, and sunk each individual into languor and pensive silence. Adeline felt the forlornness of her condition with energy; she reflected upon the past with astonishment, and anticipated the future with fear. She found herself wholly dependent upon strangers, with no other claim than what distress demands from the common sympathy of kindred beings; sighs swelled her heart, and the frequent tear started to her eye; but she checked it, ere it betrayed on her check the sorrow which she thought it would be ungrateful to reveal.

La Motte at length broke this meditative silence, by directing the fire to be renewed for the night, and the door to be secured: this seemed a necessary precaution, even in this solitude, and was effected by means of large stones piled against it, for other fastening there was none. It had frequently occurred to La Motte, that this apparently forsaken edifice might be a place of refuge to banditti. Here was solitude to conceal them; and a wild and extensive forest to assist their schemes of rapine, and to perplex with its labyrinths those who might be bold enough to attempt pursuit. These apprehensions, however, he hid within his own bosom, saving his companions from a share of the uneasiness they occasioned. Peter was ordered to watch at the door; and having given the fire a rousing stir, our desolate party drew round it, and sought in sleep a short oblivion of care.

The night passed on without disturbance. Adeline slept, but uneasy dreams fleeted before her fancy, and she awoke at an early hour: the recollection of her sorrows arose upon her mind, and yielding to their pressure, her tears flowed silently and fast. That she might indulge them without restraint, she went to a window that looked upon an open part of the forest: all was gloom and silence; she stood for some time viewing the shadowy scene.

The first tender tints of morning now appeared on the verge of the horizon, stealing upon the darkness;—so pure, so fine, so ethereal! it seemed as if heaven was opening to the view. The dark mists were seen to roll off to the west, as the tints of light grew stronger, deepening the obscurity of that part of the hemisphere, and involving the features of the country below; meanwhile, in the east, the hues became more vivid, darting a trembling lustre far around, till a ruddy glow, which fired all that part of the heavens, announced the rising sun. At first, a small line of inconceivable splendour emerged on the horizon, which quickly expanding, the sun appeared in all his glory, unveiling the whole face of nature, vivifying every colour of the landscape, and sprinkling the dewy earth with glittering light. The low and gentle responses of birds, awakened by the morning ray, now broke the silence of the hour; their soft warblings rising by degrees till they swelled the chorus of universal gladness. Adeline's heart swelled too with gratitude and adoration.

The scene before her soothed her mind, and exalted her thoughts to the great Author of Nature; she uttered an involuntary prayer: Father of good, who made this glorious scene! I resign myself to thy hands: thou wilt support me under my present sorrows, and to protect me from future evil.

Thus confiding in the benevolence of God, she wiped the tears from her eyes, while the sweet union of conscience and reflection rewarded her trust; and her mind, losing the feelings which had lately oppressed it, became tranquil and composed.

La Motte awoke soon after, and Peter prepared to set out on his expedition. As he mounted his horse. An' please you, master, said he, I think we had as good look no further for a habitation till better times turn up; for nobody will think of looking for us here; and when one sees the place by daylight, it's none so bad, but what a little patching up would make it comfortable enough. La Motte made no reply, but he thought of Peter's words. During the intervals of the night, when anxiety had kept him waking, the same idea had occurred to him; concealment was his only security, and this place afforded it. The desolation of the spot was repulsive to his wishes; but he had only a choice of evils—a forest with liberty was not a bad home for one who had too much reason to expect a prison. As he walked through the apartments, and examined their condition more attentively, he perceived they might easily be made habitable; and now surveying them under the cheerfulness of morning, his design strengthened; and he mused upon the means of accomplishing it, which nothing seemed so much to obstruct as the apparent difficulty of procuring food.

He communicated his thoughts to Madame La Motte, who felt repugnance to the scheme. La Motte, however, seldom consulted his wife till he had determined how to act; and he had already resolved to be guided in this affair by the report of Peter. If he could discover a town in the neighbourhood of the forest, where provisions and other necessaries could be procured, he would seek no further for a place of rest.

In the mean time he spent the anxious interval of Peter's absence in examining the ruin, and walking over the environs; they were sweetly romantic, and the luxuriant woods with which they abounded, seemed to sequester this spot from the rest of the world. Frequently a natural vista would yield a view of the country, terminated by hills, which retiring in distance faded into the blue horizon. A stream, various and musical in its course, wound at the foot of the lawn on which stood the abbey; here it silently glided beneath the shades, feeding the flowers that bloomed on its banks, and diffusing dewy freshness around; there it spread in broad expanse to day, reflecting the sylvan scene, and the wild deer that tasted its waves. La Motte observed every where a profusion of game; the pheasants scarcely flew from his approach, and the deer gazed mildly at him as he passed. They were strangers to man!

On his return to the abbey, La Motte ascended the stairs that led to the tower. About half way up, a door appeared in the wall; it yielded, without resistance, to his hand; but a sudden noise within, accompanied by a cloud of dust, made him step back and close the door. After waiting a few minutes, he again opened it, and perceived a large room of the more modern building. The remains of tapestry hung in tatters upon the walls, which were become the residence of birds of prey, whose sudden flight on the opening of the door had brought down a quantity of dust, and occasioned the noise. The windows were shattered, and almost without glass; but he was surprised to observe some remains of furniture; chairs, whose fashion and condition bore the date of their antiquity; a broken table, and an iron grate almost consumed by rust.

On the opposite side of the room was a door which led to another apartment, proportioned like the first, but hung with arras somewhat less tattered. In one corner stood a small bedstead, and a few shattered chairs were placed round the walls. La Motte gazed with a mixture of wonder and curiosity. 'Tis strange, said he, that these rooms, and these alone, should bear the marks of inhabitation; perhaps, some wretched wanderer like myself, may have here sought refuge from a persecuting world; and here, perhaps, laid down the load of existence; perhaps, too, I have followed his footsteps, but to mingle my dust with his! He turned suddenly, and was about to quit the room, when he perceived a small door near the bed; it opened into a closet, which was lighted by one small window, and was in the same condition as the apartments he had passed, except that it was destitute even of the remains of furniture. As he walked over the floor, he thought he felt one part of it shake beneath his steps, and, examining, found a trap-door. Curiosity prompted him to explore further, and with some difficulty he opened it. It disclosed a staircase which terminated in darkness. La Motte descended a few steps, but was unwilling to trust the abyss; and, after wondering for what purpose it was so secretly constructed, he closed the trap, and quitted this suit of apartments.

The stairs in the tower above were so much decayed, that he did not attempt to ascend them: he returned to the hall, and by the spiral staircase which he had observed the evening before, reached the gallery, and found another suit of apartments entirely furnished, very much like those below.

He renewed with Madame La Motte his former conversation respecting the abbey, and she exerted all her endeavours to dissuade him from his purpose, acknowledging the solitary security of the spot, but pleading that other places might be found equally well adapted for concealment and more for comfort. This La Motte doubted: besides, the forest abounded with game, which would, at once, afford him amusement and food, a circumstance, considering his small stock of money, by no means to be overlooked; and he had suffered his mind to dwell so much upon the scheme, that it was become a favourite one. Adeline listened in anxiety to the discourse, and waited the issue of Peter's report.

The morning passed but Peter did not return. Our solitary party took their dinner of the provision they had fortunately brought with them, and afterwards walked forth into the woods. Adeline, who never suffered any good to pass unnoticed because it came attended with evil, forgot for a while the desolation of the abbey in the beauty of the adjacent scenery. The pleasantness of the shades soothed her heart, and the varied features of the landscape amused her fancy; she almost thought she could be contented to live here. Already she began to feel an interest in the concerns of her companions, and for Madame La Motte she felt more; it was the warm emotion of gratitude and affection.

The afternoon wore away, and they returned to the abbey. Peter was still absent, and his absence now began to excite surprise and apprehension. The approach of darkness also threw a gloom upon the hopes of the wanderers: another night must be passed under the same forlorn circumstances as the preceding one! and, what was still worse, with a very scanty stock of provisions. The fortitude of Madame La Motte now entirely forsook her, and she wept bitterly. Adeline's heart was as mournful as Madame's, but she rallied her drooping spirits, and gave the first instance of her kindness by endeavouring to revive those of her friend.

La Motte was restless and uneasy, and, leaving the abbey, he walked alone the way which Peter had taken. He had not gone far, when he perceived him between the trees, leading his horse.—What news, Peter? hallooed La Motte. Peter came on, panting for breath, and said not a word, till La Motte repeated the question in a tone of somewhat more authority. Ah, bless you, master! said he, when he had taken breath to answer, I am glad to see you; I thought I should never have got back again: I've met with a world of misfortunes.

Well, you may relate them hereafter; let me hear whether you have discovered—

Discovered? interrupted Peter, yes, I am discovered with a vengeance! if your honour will look at my arms, you'll see how I am discovered.

Discoloured! I suppose you mean, said La Motte. But how came you in this condition!

Why I tell you how it was, Sir; your honour knows I learnt a smack of boxing of that Englishman that used to come with his master to our house.

Well, well—tell me where you have been.

I scarcely know myself, master; I've been where I got a sound drubbing, but then it was in your business, and so I don't mind. But if ever I meet with that rascal again!—

You seem to like your first drubbing so well, that you want another, and unless you speak more to the purpose, you shall soon have one.

Peter was now frightened into method, and endeavoured to proceed: When I left the old abbey, said he, I followed the way you directed, and turning to the right of that grove of trees yonder, I looked this way and that to see if I could see a house or a cottage, or even a man, but not a soul of them was to be seen, and so I jogged on near the value of a league, I warrant, and then I came to a track; Oh! oh! says I, we have you now; this will do—paths can't be made without feet. However, I was out in my reckoning, for the devil a bit of a soul could I see, and after following the track this way and that way, for the third of a league, I lost it, and had to find out another.

Is it impossible for you to speak to the point? said La Motte; omit these foolish particulars, and tell whether you have succeeded.

Well, then, master, to be short, for that's the nearest way after all, I wandered a long while at random, I did not know where, all through a forest like this, and I took special care to note how the trees stood, that I might find my way back. At last I came to another path, and was sure I should find something now, though I had found nothing before, for I could not be mistaken twice; so, peeping between the trees, I spied a cottage, and I gave my horse a lash that sounded through the forest, and I was at the door in a minute. They told me there was a town about half a league off, and bade me follow the track and it would bring me there,—so it did; and my horse, I believe, smelt the corn in the manger by the rate he went at. I inquired for a wheel-wright, and was told there was but one in the place, and he could not be found. I waited and waited, for I knew it was in vain to think of returning without doing my business. The man at last came home from the country, and I told him how long I had waited; for, says I, I knew it was in vain to return without my business.

Do be less tedious, said La Motte, if it is in thy nature.

It is in my nature, answered Peter, and if it was more in my nature your honour should have it all. Would you think it, Sir, the fellow had the impudence to ask a louis-d'or for mending the coach-wheel! I believe in my conscience he saw I was in a hurry and could not do without him. A louis-d'or! says I, my master shall give no such price, he sha'n't be imposed upon by no such rascal as you. Whereupon, the fellow looked glum, and gave me a douse o'the chops: with this, I up with my fist and gave him another, and should have beat him presently, if another man had not come in, and then I was obliged to give up.

And so you are returned as wise as you went?

Why, master, I hope I have too much spirit to submit to a rascal, or let you submit, to one either: besides, I have bought some nails to try if I can't mend the wheel myself—I had always a hand at carpentry.

Well, I commend your zeal in my cause, but on this occasion it was rather ill-timed. And what have you got in that basket?

Why, master, I bethought me that we could not get away from this place till the carriage was ready to draw us, and in the mean time, says I, nobody can live without victuals, so I'll e'en lay out the little money I have and take a basket with me.

That's the only wise thing you have done yet, and this, indeed, redeems your blunders.

Why now, master, it does my heart good to hear you speak; I knew I was doing for the best all the while: but I've had a hard job to find my way back; and here's another piece of ill luck, for the horse has got a thorn in his foot.

La Motte made inquiries concerning the town, and found it was capable of supplying him with provision, and what little furniture was necessary to render the abbey habitable. This intelligence almost settled his plans, and he ordered Peter to return on the following morning and make inquiries concerning the abbey. If the answers were favourable to his wishes, he commissioned him to buy a cart and load it with some furniture, and some materials necessary for repairing the modern apartments. Peter stared: What, does your honour mean to live here?

Why, suppose I do?

Why, then your honour has made a wise determination, according to my hint; for your honour knows I said—

Well, Peter, it is not necessary to repeat what you said; perhaps I had determined on the subject before.

Egad, master, you're in the right, and I'm glad of it, for I believe we shall not quickly be disturbed here, except by the rooks and owls. Yes, yes—I warrant I'll make it a place fit for a king; and as for the town, one may get any thing, I'm sure of that; though they think no more about this place than they do about India or England, or any of those places.

They now reached the abbey; where Peter was received with great joy: but the hopes of his mistress and Adeline were repressed, when they learned that he returned without having executed his commission, and heard his account of the town. La Motte's orders to Peter were heard with almost equal concern by Madame and Adeline; but the latter concealed her uneasiness, and used all her efforts to overcome that of her friend. The sweetness of her behaviour, and the air of satisfaction she assumed, sensibly affected Madame, and discovered to her a source of comfort which she had hitherto overlooked. The affectionate attentions of her young friend promised to console her for the want of other society, and her conversation to enliven the hours which might otherwise be passed in painful regret.

The observations and general behaviour of Adeline already bespoke a good understanding and an amiable heart; but she had yet more—she had genius. She was now in her nineteenth year; her figure of the middling size, and turned to the most exquisite proportion; her hair was dark auburn, her eyes blue, and whether they sparkled with intelligence, or melted with tenderness, they were equally attractive: her form had the airy lightness of a nymph, and when she smiled, her countenance might have been drawn for the younger sister of Hebe: the captivations of her beauty were heightened by the grace and simplicity of her manners, and confirmed by the intrinsic value of a heart.

That might be shrined in chrystal,And have all its movements scann'd.

Annette now kindled the fire for the night: Peter's basket was opened, and supper prepared. Madame La Motte was still pensive and silent.—There is scarcely any condition so bad, said Adeline, but we may one time or the other wish we had not quitted it. Honest Peter, when he was bewildered in the forest, or had two enemies to encounter instead of one, confesses he wished himself at the abbey. And I am certain, there is no situation so destitute, but comfort may be extracted from it. The blaze of this fire shines yet more cheerfully from the contrasted dreariness of the place; and this plentiful repast is made yet more delicious from the temporary want we have suffered. Let us enjoy the good and forget the evil.

You speak, my dear, replied Madame La Motte, like one whose spirits have not been often depressed by misfortune (Adeline sighed), and whose hopes are therefore vigorous. Long suffering, said La Motte, has subdued in our minds that elastic energy which repels the pressure of evil and dances to the bound of joy. But I speak in raphsody, though only from the remembrance of such a time. I once, like you, Adeline, could extract comfort from most situations.

And may now, my dear Sir, said Adeline. Still believe it possible, and you will find it is so.

The illusion is gone—I can no longer deceive myself.

Pardon me, Sir, if I say, it is now only you deceive yourself, by suffering the cloud of sorrow to tinge every object you look upon.

It may be so, said La Motte, but let us leave the subject.

After supper, the doors were secured, as before, for the night, and the wanderers resigned themselves to repose.

On the following morning, Peter again set out for the little town of Auboine, and the hours of his absence were again spent by Madame La Motte and Adeline in much anxiety and some hope, for the intelligence he might bring concerning the abbey might yet release them from the plans of La Motte. Towards the close of the day he was descried coming slowly on; and the cart, which accompanied him, too certainly confirmed their fears. He brought materials for repairing the place, and some furniture.

Of the abbey he gave an account, of which the following is the substance:—It belonged, together with a large part of the adjacent forest, to a nobleman, who now resided with his family on a remote estate. He inherited it, in right of his wife, from his father-in-law, who had caused the more modern apartments to be erected, and had resided in them some part of every year, for the purpose of shooting and hunting. It was reported, that some person was, soon after it came to the present possessor, brought secretly to the abbey and confined in these apartments; who, or what he was, had never been conjectured, and what became of him nobody knew. The report died gradually away, and many persons entirely disbelieved the whole of it. But however this affair might be, certain it was, the present owner had visited the abbey only two summers since his succeeding to it; and the furniture after some time, was removed.

This circumstance had at first excited surprise, and various reports rose in consequence, but it was difficult to know what ought to be believed. Among the rest, it was said that strange appearances had been observed at the abbey, and uncommon noises heard; and though this report had been ridiculed by sensible persons as the idle superstition of ignorance, it had fastened so strongly upon the minds of the common people, that for the last seventeen years none of the peasantry had ventured to approach the spot. The abbey was now, therefore, abandoned to decay.

La Motte ruminated upon this account. At first it called up unpleasant ideas, but they were soon dismissed, and considerations more interesting to his welfare took place: he congratulated himself that he had now found a spot where he was not likely to be either discovered or disturbed; yet it could not escape him that there was a strange coincidence between one part of Peter's narrative, and the condition of the chambers that opened from the tower above stairs. The remains of furniture, of which the other apartments were void—the solitary bed—the number and connexion of the rooms, were circumstances that united to confirm his opinion. This, however, he concealed in his own breast, for he already perceived that Peter's account had not assisted in reconciling his family to the necessity of dwelling at the abbey.

But they had only to submit in silence, and whatever disagreeable apprehension might intrude upon them, they now appeared willing to suppress the expression of it. Peter, indeed, was exempt from any evil of this kind; he knew no fear, and his mind was now wholly occupied with his approaching business. Madame La Motte, with a placid kind of despair, endeavoured to reconcile herself to that which no effort of understanding could teach her to avoid, and which an indulgence in lamentation could only make more intolerable. Indeed, though a sense of the immediate inconveniences to be endured at the abbey had made her oppose the scheme of living there, she did not really know how their situation could be improved by removal: yet her thoughts often wandered towards Paris, and reflected the retrospect of past times, with the images of weeping friends left, perhaps, for ever. The affectionate endearments of her only son, whom, from the danger of his situation, and the obscurity of hers, she might reasonably fear never to see again, arose upon her memory and overcame her fortitude. Why—why was I reserved for this hour? would she say, and what will be my years to come?

Adeline had no retrospect of past delight to give emphasis to present calamity—no weeping friends—no dear regretted objects to point the edge of sorrow, and throw a sickly hue upon her future prospects: she knew not yet the pangs of disappointed hope, or the acuter sting of self-accusation; she had no misery but what patience could assuage, or fortitude overcome.

At the dawn of the following day Peter arose to his labour: he proceeded with alacrity, and in a few days two of the lower apartments were so much altered for the better that La Motte began to exult, and his family to perceive that their situation would not be so miserable as they had imagined. The furniture Peter had already brought was disposed in these rooms, one of which was the vaulted apartment. Madame La Motte furnished this as a sitting-room, preferring it for its large Gothic window, that descended almost to the floor, admitting a prospect of the lawn, and the picturesque scenery of the surrounding woods.

Peter having returned to Auboine for a further supply, all the lower apartments were in a few weeks not only habitable, but comfortable. These, however, being insufficient for the accommodation of the family, a room above stairs was prepared for Adeline: it was the chamber that opened immediately from the tower, and she preferred it to those beyond, because it was less distant from the family, and the windows fronting an avenue of the forest afforded a more extensive prospect. The tapestry, that was decayed, and hung loosely from the walls, was now nailed up, and made to look less desolate; and though the room had still a solemn aspect, from its spaciousness and the narrowness of the windows, it was not uncomfortable.

The first night that Adeline retired hither, she slept little: the solitary air of the place affected her spirits; the more so, perhaps, because she had, with friendly consideration, endeavoured to support them in the presence of Madame La Motte. She remembered the narrative of Peter, several circumstances of which had impressed her imagination in spite of her reason, and she found it difficult wholly to subdue apprehension. At one time, terror so strongly seized her mind, that she had even opened the door with an intention of calling Madame La Motte; but, listening for a moment on the stairs of the tower, every thing seemed still: at length, she heard the voice of La Motte speaking cheerfully, and the absurdity of her fears struck her forcibly; she blushed that she had for a moment submitted to them, and returned to her chamber wondering at herself.

CHAPTER III

*Are not these woods
More free from peril than the envious court?
Here feel we but the penalty of Adam,
The season's difference, as the icy fang
And churlish chiding of the winter's wind.*
SHAKSPEARE.

La Motte arranged his little plan of living. His mornings were usually spent in shooting or fishing, and the dinner, thus provided by his industry, he relished with a keener appetite than had ever attended him at the luxurious tables of Paris. The afternoons he passed with his family: sometimes he would select a book from the few he had brought with him, and endeavoured to fix his attention to the words his lips repeated:—but his mind suffered little abstraction from its own cares, and the sentiment he pronounced left no trace behind it. Sometimes he conversed, but oftener sat in gloomy silence, musing upon the past, or anticipating the future.

At these moments, Adeline, with a sweetness almost irresistible, endeavoured to enliven his spirits, and to withdraw him from himself. Seldom she succeeded; but when she did, the grateful looks of Madame La Motte, and the benevolent feelings of her own bosom, realized the cheerfulness she had at first only assumed. Adeline's mind had the happy art, or, perhaps, it were more just to say, the happy nature, of accommodating itself to her situation. Her present condition, though forlorn, was not devoid of comfort, and this comfort was confirmed by her virtues. So much she won upon the affections of her protectors, that Madame La Motte loved her as her child, and La Motte himself, though a man little susceptible of tenderness, could not be insensible to her solicitudes. Whenever he relaxed from the sullenness of misery, it was at the influence of Adeline.

Peter regularly brought a weekly supply of provisions from Auboine, and, on those occasions, always quitted the town by a route contrary to that leading to the abbey. Several weeks having passed without molestation, La Motte dismissed all apprehension of pursuit, and at length became tolerably reconciled to the complexion of his circumstances.

As habit and effort strengthened the fortitude of Madame La Motte, the features of misfortune appeared to soften. The forest, which at first seemed to her a frightful solitude, had lost its terrific aspect; and that edifice, whose half demolished walls and gloomy desolation had struck her mind with the force of melancholy and dismay, was now beheld as a domestic asylum, and a safe refuge from the storms of power.

She was a sensible and highly accomplished woman, and it became her chief delight to form the rising graces of Adeline, who had, as has been already shown, a sweetness of disposition, which made her quick to repay instruction with improvement, and indulgence with love. Never was Adeline so pleased as when she anticipated her wishes, and never so diligent as when she was employed in her business. The little affairs of the household she overlooked and managed with such admirable exactness, that Madame La Motte had neither anxiety nor care concerning them. And Adeline formed for herself in this barren situation, many amusements that occasionally banished the remembrance of her misfortunes. La Motte's books were her chief consolation. With one of these she would frequently ramble into the forest, where the river, winding through a glade, diffused coolness, and with its murmuring accents invited repose: there she would seat herself, and, resigned to the illusions of the page, pass many hours in oblivion of sorrow.

Here too, when her mind was tranquillized by the surrounding scenery, she wooed the gentle muse, and indulged in ideal happiness. The delight of these moments she commemorated in the following address:

TO THE VISIONS OF FANCY.

Dear, wild illusions of creative mind!Whose varying hues arise to Fancy's art,And by her magic force are swift combinedIn forms that please, and scenes that touch theheart:Oh! whether at her voice ye soft assumeThe pensive grace of sorrow drooping low;Or rise sublime on terror's lofty plume,And shake the soul with wildly thrilling woe;Or, sweetly bright, your gayer tints ye spread,Bid scenes of pleasures steal upon my view,Love wave his purple pinions o'er my head,And wake the tender thought to passion true.O! still——ye shadowy forms! attend my lonely hours,Still chase my real cares with your illusive powers!

Madame La Motte had frequently expressed curiosity concerning the events of Adeline's life, and by what circumstances she had been thrown into a situation so perilous and mysterious as that in which La Motte had found her. Adeline had given a brief account of the manner in which she had been brought thither, but had always with tears entreated to be spared for that time from a particular relation of her history. Her spirits were not then equal to retrospection; but now that they were soothed by quiet, and strengthened by confidence, she one day gave Madame La Motte the following narration.

* * * * * * * * * * * * * *

I am the only child, said Adeline, Of Louis de St. Pierre, a chevalier of reputable family, but of small fortune, who for many years resided at Paris. Of my mother I have a faint remembrance: I lost her when I was only seven years old, and this was my first misfortune. At her death, my father gave up housekeeping, boarded me in a convent, and quitted Paris. Thus was I, at this early period of my life, abandoned to strangers. My father came sometimes to Paris; he then visited me, and I well remember the grief I used to feel when he bade me farewell. On these occasions, which wrung my heart with grief, he appeared unmoved; so that I often thought he had little tenderness for me. But he was my father, and the only person to whom I could look up for protection and love.

In this convent I continued till I was twelve years old. A thousand times I had entreated my father to take me home; but at first, motives of prudence, and afterwards of avarice, prevented him. I was now removed from this convent, and placed in another, where I learned my father intended I should take the veil. I will not attempt to express my surprise and grief on this occasion. Too long I had been immured in the walls of a cloister, and too much had I seen of the sullen misery of its votaries, not to feel horror and disgust at the prospect of being added to their number.

The Lady Abbess was a woman of rigid decorum and severe devotion: exact in the observance of every detail of form, and never forgave an offence against ceremony. It was her method, when she wanted to make converts to her order, to denounce and terrify, rather than to persuade and allure. Hers were the arts of cunning practised upon fear, not those of sophistication upon reason. She employed numberless stratagems to gain me to her purpose, and they all wore the complexion of her character. But in the life to which she would have devoted me, I saw too many forms of real terror, to be overcome by the influence of her ideal host, and was resolute in rejecting the veil. Here I passed several years of miserable resistance against cruelty and superstition. My father I seldom saw; when I did, I entreated him to alter my destination; but he objected that his fortune was insufficient to support me in the world, and at length denounced vengeance on my head if I persisted in disobedience.

You, my dear Madam, can form little idea of the wretchedness of my situation, condemned to perpetual imprisonment, and imprisonment of the most dreadful kind, or to the vengeance of a father, from whom I had no appeal. My resolution relaxed—for some time I paused upon the choice of evils—but at length the horrors of the monastic life rose so fully to my view, that fortitude gave way before them. Excluded from the cheerful intercourse of society—from the pleasant view of nature—almost from the light of day—condemned to silence—rigid formality—abstinence and penance—condemned to forgo the delights of a world which imagination painted in the gayest and most alluring colours, and whose hues were, perhaps, not the less captivating because they were only ideal—such was the sate to which I was destined. Again my resolution was invigorated: my father's cruelty subdued tenderness, and roused indignation. Since he can forget, said I, the affection of a parent, and condemn his child without remorse to wretchedness and despair—the bond of filial and parental duty no longer subsists between us—he has himself dissolved it, and I will yet struggle for liberty and life.

Finding me unmoved by menace, the Lady Abbess had now recourse to more subtle measures: she condescended to smile, and even to flatter; but hers was the distorted smile of cunning, not the gracious emblem of kindness; it provoked disgust, instead of inspiring affection. She painted the character of a vestal in the most beautiful tints of art—its holy innocence—its mild dignity—its sublime devotion. I sighed as she spoke. This she regarded as a favourable symptom, and proceeded on her picture with more animation. She described the serenity of a monastic life—its security from the seductive charms, restless passions, and sorrowful vicissitudes of the world—the rapturous delights of religion, and the sweet reciprocal affection of the sisterhood.

So highly she finished the piece, that the lurking lines of cunning would, to an inexperienced eye, have escaped detection. Mine was too sorrowfully informed. Too often had I witnessed the secret tear and bursting sigh of vain regret, the sullen pinings of discontent, and the mute anguish of despair. My silence and my manner assured her of my incredulity, and it was with difficulty that she preserved a decent composure.

My father, as may be imagined, was highly incensed at my perseverance, which he called obstinacy; but, what will not be so easily believed, he soon after relented, and appointed a day to take me from the convent. O! judge of my feelings when I received this intelligence. The joy it occasioned awakened all my gratitude; I forgot the former cruelty of my father, and that the present indulgence was less the effect of his kindness than of my resolution. I wept that I could not indulge his every wish.

What days of blissful expectation were those that preceded my departure! The world, from which I had been hitherto secluded—the world, in which my fancy had been so often delighted to roam—whose paths were strewn with fadeless roses—whose every scene smiled in beauty and invited to delight—where all the people were good, and all the good happy—Ah! then that world was bursting upon my view. Let me catch the rapturous remembrance before it vanish! It is like the passing lights of autumn, that gleam for a moment on a hill, and then leave it to darkness. I counted the days and hours that withheld me from this fairy land. It was in the convent only that people were deceitful and cruel; it was there only that misery dwelt. I was quitting it all! How I pitied the poor nuns that were to be left behind! I would have given half that world I prized so much, had it been mine, to have taken them out with me.

The long wished for day at last arrived. My father came, and for a moment my joy was lost in the sorrow of bidding farewell to my poor companions, for whom I had never felt such warmth of kindness as at this instant. I was soon beyond the gates of the convent. I looked around me, and viewed the vast vault of heaven no longer bounded by monastic walls, and the green earth extended in hill and dale to the round verge of the horizon! My heart danced with delight, tears swelled in my eyes, and for some moments I was unable to speak. My thoughts rose to heaven in sentiments of gratitude to the Giver of all good!

At length I returned to my father: Dear Sir, said I, how I thank you for my deliverance, and how I wish I could do every thing to oblige you!

Return, then, to your convent, said he in a harsh accent. I shuddered: his look and manner jarred the tone of my feelings; they struck discord upon my heart! which had before responded only to harmony. The ardour of joy was in a moment repressed, and every object around me was saddened with the gloom of disappointment. It was not that I suspected my father would take me back to the convent; but that his feelings seemed so very dissonant to the joy and gratitude which I had but a moment before felt and expressed to him.—Pardon, Madam, a relation of these trivial circumstances; the strong vicissitudes of feeling which they impressed upon my heart, make me think them important, when they are, perhaps, only disgusting.

No, my dear, said Madame La Motte, they are interesting to me; they illustrate little traits of character, which I love to observe. You are worthy of all my regards, and from this moment I give my tenderest pity to your misfortunes, and my affection to your goodness.

These words melted the heart of Adeline; she kissed the hand which Madame held out, and remained a few minutes silent. At length she said, May I deserve this goodness! and may I ever be thankful to God, who, in giving me such a friend, has raised me to comfort and hope!

My father's house was situated a few leagues on the other side of Paris, and in our way to it we passed through that city. What a novel scene! Where were now the solemn faces, the demure manners I had been accustomed to see in the convent? Every countenance was here animated, either by business or pleasure; every step was airy, and every smile was gay. All the people appeared like friends; they looked and smiled at me; I smiled again, and wished to have told them how pleased I was. How delightful, said I, to live surrounded by friends!

What crowded streets! what magnificent hotels! what splendid equipages! I scarcely observed that the streets were narrow, or the way dangerous. What bustle, what tumult, what delight! I could never be sufficiently thankful that I was removed from the convent. Again I was going to express my gratitude to my father, but his looks forbad me, and I was silent. I am too diffuse; even the faint forms which memory reflects of passed delight are grateful to the heart. The shadow of pleasure is still gazed upon with a melancholy enjoyment, though the substance is fled beyond our reach.

Having quitted Paris, which I left with many sighs, and gazed upon till the towers of every church dissolved in distance from my view, we entered upon a gloomy and unfrequented road. It was evening when we reached a wild heath; I looked round in search of a human dwelling, but could find none; and not a human being was to be seen. I experienced something of what I used to feel in the convent; my heart had not been so sad since I left it. Of my father, who still sat in silence, I inquired if we were near home; he answered in the affirmative. Night came on, however, before we reached the place of our destination; it was a lone house on the waste; but I need not describe it to you, Madam. When the carriage stopped, two men appeared at the door, and assisted us to alight: so gloomy were their countenances, and so few their words, I almost fancied myself again in the convent; certain it is, I had not seen such melancholy faces since I quitted it. Is this a part of the world I have so fondly contemplated? said I.

The interior appearance of the house was desolate and mean; I was surprised that my father had chosen such a place for his habitation, and also that no woman was to be seen; but I knew that inquiry would only produce a reproof, and was therefore silent. At supper, the two men I had before seen sat down with us; they said little, but seemed to observe me much. I was confused and displeased; which my father noticing, frowned at them with a look which convinced me he meant more than I comprehended. When the cloth was drawn, my father took my hand and conducted me to the door of my chamber; having set down the candle, and wished me good night, he left me to my own solitary thoughts.

How different were they from those I had indulged a few hours before! then expectation, hope, delight, danced before me; now melancholy and disappointment chilled the ardour of my mind, and discoloured my future prospect. The appearance of every thing around conduced to depress me. On the floor lay a small bed without curtains or hangings; two old chairs and a table were all the remaining furniture in the room. I went to the window, with an intention of looking out upon the surrounding scene, and found it was grated. I was shocked at this circumstance, and comparing it with the lonely situation and the strange appearance of the house, together with the countenances and behaviour of the men who had supped with us, I was lost in a labyrinth of conjecture.

At length I lay down to sleep; but the anxiety of my mind prevented repose; gloomy unpleasing images flitted before my fancy, and I fell into a sort of waking dream: I thought that I was in a lonely forest with my father; his looks were severe, and his gestures menacing: he upbraided me for leaving the convent, and while he spoke, drew from his pocket a mirror, which he held before my face; I looked in it and saw, (my blood now thrills as I repeat it) I saw myself wounded, and bleeding profusely. Then I thought myself in the house again; and suddenly heard these words, in accents so distinct, that for some time after I awoke I could scarcely believe them ideal, Depart this house, destruction hovers here.

I was awakened by a footstep on the stairs; it was my father retiring to his chamber; the lateness of the hour surprised me, for it was past midnight.

On the following morning, the party of the preceding evening assembled at breakfast, and were as gloomy and silent as before. The table was spread by a boy of my father's; but the cook and the housemaid, whatever they might be, were invisible.

The next morning I was surprised, on attempting to leave my chamber, to find the door locked; I waited a considerable time before I ventured to call; when I did, no answer was returned; I then went to the window, and called more loudly, but my own voice was still the only sound I heard. Near an hour I passed in a state of surprise and terror not to be described: at length I heard a person coming up stairs, and I renewed the call; I was answered, that my father had that morning set off for Paris, whence he would return in a few days; in the meanwhile he had ordered me to be confined in my chamber. On my expressing surprise and apprehension at this circumstance, I was assured I had nothing to fear, and that I should live as well as if I was at liberty.

The latter part of this speech seemed to contain an odd kind of comfort; I made little reply, but submitted to necessity. Once more I was abandoned to sorrowful reflection: what a day was the one I now passed! alone, and agitated with grief and apprehension. I endeavoured to conjecture the cause of this harsh treatment; and at length concluded it was designed by my father, as a punishment for my former disobedience. But why abandon me to the power of strangers, to men, whose countenances bore the stamp of villainy so strongly as to impress even my inexperienced mind with terror! Surmise involved me only deeper in perplexity, yet I found it impossible to forbear pursuing the subject; and the day was divided between lamentation and conjecture. Night at length came, and such a night! Darkness brought new terrors: I looked round the chamber for some means of fastening my door on the inside, but could perceive none; at last I contrived to place the back of a chair in an oblique direction, so as to render it secure.

I had scarcely done this, and lain down upon my bed in my clothes, not to sleep, but to watch, when I heard a rap at the door of the house, which was opened and shut so quickly, that the person who had knocked, seemed only to deliver a letter or message. Soon after, I heard voices at intervals in a room below stairs, sometimes speaking very low, and sometimes rising all together, as if in dispute. Something more excusable than curiosity made me endeavour to distinguish what was said, but in vain; now and then a word or two reached me, and once I heard my name repeated, but no more.

Thus passed the hours till midnight, when all became still. I had lain for some time in a state between fear and hope, when I heard the lock of my door gently moved backward and forward; I started up and listened; for a moment it was still, then the noise returned, and I heard a whispering without; my spirits died away, but I was yet sensible. Presently an effort was made at the door, as if to force it; I shrieked aloud, and immediately heard the voices of the men I had seen at my father's table: they called loudly for the door to be opened, and on my returning no answer, uttered dreadful execrations. I had just strength sufficient to move to the window, in the desperate hope of escaping thence; but my feeble efforts could not even shake the bars. O! how can I recollect these moments of horror, and be sufficiently thankful that I am now in safety and comfort!

They remained some time at the door, then they quitted it, and went down stairs. How my heart revived at every step of their departure! I fell upon my knees, thanked God that he had preserved me this time, and implored his further protection. I was rising from this short prayer, when suddenly I heard a noise in a different part of the room, and on looking round, I perceived the door of a small closet open, and two men enter the chamber.

They seized me, and I sunk senseless in their arms; how long I remained in this condition I know not; but on reviving, I perceived myself again alone, and heard several voices from below stairs. I had presence of mind to run to the door of the closet, my only chance of escape; but it was locked! I then recollected it was possible that the ruffians might have forgot to turn the key of the chamber door, which was held by the chair; but here, also, I was disappointed. I clasped my hands in an agony of despair, and stood for some time immoveable.

A violent noise from below roused me, and soon after I heard people ascending the stairs: I now gave myself up for lost. The steps approached, the door of the closet was again unlocked. I stood calmly, and again saw the men enter the chamber; I neither spoke, nor resisted: the faculties of my soul were wrought up beyond the power of feeling; as a violent blow on the body stuns for awhile the sense of pain. They led me down stairs; the door of a room below was thrown open, and I beheld a stranger; it was then that my senses returned; I shrieked and resisted, but was forced along. It is unnecessary to say that this stranger was Monsieur La Motte, or to add, that I shall for ever bless him as my deliverer.

Adeline ceased to speak; Madame La Motte remained silent. There were some circumstances in Adeline's narrative, which raised all her curiosity. She asked if Adeline believed her father to be a party in this mysterious affair. Adeline, though it was impossible to doubt that he had been principally and materially concerned in some part of it, thought, or said she thought, he was innocent of any intention against her life. Yet, what motive, said Madame La Motte, could there be for a degree of cruelty so apparently unprofitable?—Here the inquiry ended; and Adeline confessed she had pursued it till her mind shrunk from all further research.

The sympathy which such uncommon misfortune excited, Madame La Motte now expressed without reserve, and this expression of it strengthened the tie of mutual friendship. Adeline felt her spirits relieved by the disclosure she had made to Madame La Motte; and the latter acknowledged the value of the confidence, by an increase of affectionate attentions.

CHAPTER IV

...... My May of lifeIs fall'n into the sear, the yellow leaf.MACBETH.

Full oft, unknowing and unknown,He wore his endless noons alone,Amid th' autumnal wood:Oft was he wont in hasty fit,Abrupt the social board to quit.WHARTON.

La Motte had now passed above a month in this seclusion; and his wife had the pleasure to see him recover tranquillity and even cheerfulness. In this pleasure Adeline warmly participated; and she might justly have congratulated herself as one cause of his restoration; her cheerfulness and delicate attention had effected what Madame La Motte's greater anxiety had failed to accomplish. La Motte did not seem regardless of her amiable disposition, and sometimes thanked her in a manner more earnest than was usual with him. She, in her turn, considered him as her only protector and now felt towards him the affection of a daughter.

The time she had spent in this peaceful retirement had softened the remembrance of past events, and restored her mind to its natural tone: and when memory brought back to her view the former short and romantic expectations of happiness, though she gave a sigh to the rapturous illusion, she less lamented the disappointment, than rejoiced in her present security and comfort.

But the satisfaction which La Motte's cheerfulness diffused around him was of short continuance; he became suddenly gloomy and reserved; the society of his family was no longer grateful to him; and he would spend whole hours in the most secluded parts of the forest, devoted to melancholy and secret grief. He did not, as formerly, indulge the humour of his sadness, without restraint, in the presence of others; he now evidently endeavoured to conceal it, and affected a cheerfulness that was too artificial to escape detection.

His servant Peter, either impelled by curiosity or kindness, sometimes followed him unseen, into the forest. He observed him frequently retire to one particular spot, in a remote part, which having gained, he always disappeared, before Peter, who was obliged to follow at a distance, could exactly notice where. All his endeavours, now prompted by wonder and invigorated by disappointment, were unsuccessful, and he was at length compelled to endure the tortures of unsatisfied curiosity.

This change in the manners and habits of her husband was too conspicuous to pass unobserved by Madame La Motte, who endeavoured, by all the stratagems which affection could suggest, or female invention supply, to win him to her confidence. He seemed insensible to the influence of the first, and withstood the wiles of the latter. Finding all her efforts insufficient to dissipate the glooms which overhung his mind, or to penetrate their secret cause, she desisted from further attempt, and endeavoured to submit to this mysterious distress.

Week after week elapsed, and the same unknown cause sealed the lips and corroded the heart of La Motte. The place of his visitation in the forest had not been traced. Peter had frequently examined round the spot where his master disappeared, but had never discovered any recess which could be supposed to conceal him. The astonishment of the servant was at length raised to an insupportable degree, and he communicated to his mistress the subject of it.

The emotion which this information excited, she disguised from Peter, and reproved him for the means he had taken to gratify his curiosity. But she revolved this circumstance in her thoughts, and comparing it with the late alteration in his temper, her uneasiness was renewed, and her perplexity considerably increased. After much consideration, being unable to assign any other motive for his conduct, she began to attribute it to the influence of illicit passion; and her heart, which now out-ran her judgment, confirmed the supposition, and roused all the torturing pangs of jealousy.

Comparatively speaking, she had never known affliction till now: she had abandoned her dearest friends and connexions—had relinquished the gaieties, the luxuries, and almost the necessaries of life;—fled with her family into exile, an exile the most dreary and comfortless; experiencing the evils of reality, and those of apprehension, united: all these she had patiently endured, supported by the affection of him for whose sake she suffered. Though that affection, indeed, had for some time appeared to be abated, she had borne its decrease with fortitude; but the last stroke of calamity, hitherto withheld, now came with irresistible force—the love, of which she lamented the loss, she now believed was transferred to another.

The operation of strong passion confuses the powers of reason, and warps them to its own particular direction. Her usual degree of judgment, unopposed by the influence of her heart, would probably have pointed out to Madame La Motte some circumstances upon the subject of her distress, equivocal, if not contradictory to her suspicions. No such circumstances appeared to her, and she did not long hesitate to decide, that Adeline was the object of her husband's attachment. Her beauty out of the question, who else, indeed, could it be in a spot thus secluded from the world?

The same cause destroyed, almost at the same moment, her only remaining comfort; and when she wept that she could no longer look for happiness in the affection of La Motte, she wept also, that she could no longer seek solace in the friendship of Adeline. She had too great an esteem for her, to doubt, at first, the integrity of her conduct; but, in spite of reason, her heart no longer expanded to her with its usual warmth of kindness. She shrunk from her confidence; and as the secret broodings of jealousy cherished her suspicions, she became less kind to her, even in manner.

Adeline, observing the change, at first attributed it to accident, and afterwards to a temporary displeasure arising from some little inadvertency in her conduct. She, therefore, increased her assiduities; but perceiving, contrary to all expectation, that her efforts to please failed of their usual consequence, and that the reserve of Madame's manner rather increased than abated, she became seriously uneasy, and resolved to seek an explanation. This Madame La Motte as sedulously avoided, and was for some time able to prevent. Adeline, however, too much interested in the event to yield to delicate scruples, pressed the subject so closely, that Madame, at first agitated and confused, at length invented some idle excuse, and laughed off the affair.

She now saw the necessity of subduing all appearance of reserve towards Adeline; and though her art could not conquer the prejudices of passion, it taught her to assume, with tolerable success, the aspect of kindness. Adeline was deceived, and was again at peace. Indeed, confidence in the sincerity and goodness of others was her weakness. But the pangs of stifled jealousy struck deeper to the heart of Madame La Motte, and she resolved, at all events, to obtain some certainty upon the subject of her suspicions.

She now condescended to a meanness which she had before despised, and ordered Peter to watch the steps of his master, in order to discover, if possible, the place of his visitation! So much did passion win upon her judgment, by time and indulgence, that she sometimes ventured even to doubt the integrity of Adeline, and afterwards proceeded to believe it possible that the object of La Motte's rambles might be an assignation with her. What suggested this conjecture was, that Adeline frequently took long walks alone in the forest, and sometimes was absent from the abbey for many hours. This circumstance, which Madame La Motte had at first attributed to Adeline's fondness for the picturesque beauties of nature, now operated forcibly upon her imagination, and she could view it in no other light, than as affording an opportunity for secret conversation with her husband.

Peter obeyed the orders of his mistress with alacrity, for they were warmly seconded by his own curiosity. All his endeavours were, however, fruitless; he never dared to follow La Motte near enough to observe the place of his last retreat. Her impatience thus heightened by delay, and her passion stimulated by difficulty, Madame La Motte now resolved to apply to her husband for an explanation of his conduct.

After some consideration concerning the manner most likely to succeed with him, she went to La Motte; but when she entered the room where he sat, forgetting all her concerted address, she fell at his feet, and was for some moments lost in tears. Surprised at her attitude and distress, he inquired the occasion of it, and was answered, that it was caused by his own conduct. My conduct! What part of it, pray? inquired he.

Your reserve, your secret sorrow, and frequent absence from the abbey.

Is it then so wonderful, that a man who has lost almost every thing should sometimes lament his misfortunes? or so criminal to attempt concealing his grief, that he must be blamed for it by those whom he would save from the pain of sharing it?

Having uttered these words, he quitted the room, leaving Madame La Motte lost in surprise, but somewhat relieved from the pressure of her former suspicions. Still however, she pursued Adeline with an eye of scrutiny; and the mask of kindness would sometimes fall off, and discover the features of distrust. Adeline, without exactly knowing why, felt less at ease and less happy in her presence than formerly; her spirits drooped, and she would often, when alone, weep at the forlornness of her condition. Formerly, her remembrance of past sufferings was lost in the friendship of Madame La Motte; now, though her behaviour was too guarded to betray any striking instances of unkindness, there was something in her manner which chilled the hopes of Adeline, unable as she was to analyze it. But a circumstance which soon occurred, suspended for a while the jealousy of Madame La Motte, and roused her husband from his state of gloomy stupefaction.

Peter, having been one day to Auboine for the weekly supply of provisions, returned with intelligence that awakened in La Motte new apprehension and anxiety.

Oh, Sir! I have heard something that has astonished me, as well it may, cried Peter, and so it will you when you come to know it. As I was standing in the blacksmith's shop, while the smith was driving a nail into the horse's shoe (by the by, the horse lost it in an odd way, I'll tell you, Sir, how it was)—

Nay, prithee leave it till another time, and go on with your story.

Why then, Sir, as I was standing in the blacksmith's shop, comes in a man with a pipe in his mouth, and a large pouch of tobacco in his hand—

Well—what has the pipe to do with the story?

Nay, Sir, you put me out; I can't go on, unless you let me tell it my own way. As I was saying—with a pipe in his mouth—I think I was there your honour!

Yes, yes.

He sets himself down on the bench, and, taking the pipe from his mouth, says to the blacksmith—Neighbour, do you know any body of the Name of La Motte hereabouts!—Bless your honour, I turned all of a cold sweat in a minute!—Is not your honour well! shall I fetch you any thing?

No—but be short in your narrative.

La Motte! La Motte! said the blacksmith, I think I've heard the name.—Have you? said I, you're cunning then, for there's no such person hereabouts, to my knowledge.

Fool!—why did you say that?

Because I did not want them to know your honour was here; and if I had not managed very cleverly, they would have found me out. There is no such person hereabouts, to my knowledge, says I.—Indeed! says the blacksmith, you know more of the neighbourhood than I do then.—Aye, says the man with the pipe, that's very true. How came you to know so much of the neighbourhood? I came here twenty-six years ago, come next St. Michael, and you know more than I do. How came you to know so much?

With that he put his pipe in his mouth, and gave a whiff full in my face. Lord! your honour, I trembled from head to foot. Nay, as for that matter says I, I don't know more than other people, but I'm sure I never heard of such a man as that.—Pray, says the blacksmith, staring me full in the face, an't you the man that was inquiring some time since about St. Clair's abbey?—Well, what of that? says I, what does that prove?—Why they say somebody lives in the abbey now, said the man, turning to the other; and, for aught I know, it may be this same La Motte.—Aye, or for aught I know either, says the man with the pipe, getting up from the bench, and you know more of this than you'll own. I'll lay my life on't, this Monsieur La Motte lives at the abbey.—Aye, says I, you are out there, for he does not live at the abbey now.

Confound your folly! cried La Motte; but be quick—how did the matter end?

My master does not live there now, said I.—Oh! oh! said the man with the pipe; he is your master then? And pray how long has he left the abbey—and where does he live now?—Hold, said I, not so fast—I know when to speak and when to hold my tongue—but who has been inquiring for him?

What! he expected somebody to inquire for him? says the man.—No, says I, he did not, but if he did, what does that prove?—that argues nothing. With that he looked at the blacksmith, and they went out of the shop together, leaving my horse's shoe undone. But I never minded that, for the moment they were gone, I mounted and rode away as fast as I could. But in my fright, your honour, I forgot to take the round about way, and so came straight home.

La Motte, extremely shocked at Peter's intelligence, made no other reply than by cursing his folly, and immediately went in search of Madame, who was walking with Adeline on the banks of the river. La Motte was too much agitated to soften his information by preface. We are discovered! said he, the king's officers have been inquiring for me at Auboine, and Peter has blundered upon my ruin. He then informed her of what Peter had related, and bade her prepare to quit the abbey.

But whither can we fly? said Madame La Motte, scarcely able to support herself. Any where! said he: to stay here is certain destruction. We must take refuge in Switzerland, I think. If any part of France would have concealed me, surely it had been this!

Alas, how are we persecuted! rejoined Madame. This spot is scarcely made comfortable, before we are obliged to leave it, and go we know not whither.

I wish we may not yet know whither, replied La Motte, that is the least evil that threatens us. Let us escape a prison, and I care not whither we go. But return to the abbey immediately, and pack up what moveables you can.—A flood of tears came to the relief of Madame La Motte, and she hung upon Adeline's arm, silent and trembling. Adeline, though she had no comfort to bestow, endeavoured to command her feelings and appear composed. Come, said La Motte, we waste time; let us lament hereafter, but at present prepare for flight; exert a little of that fortitude which is so necessary for our preservation. Adeline does not weep, yet her state is as wretched as your own, for I know not how long I shall be able to protect her.

Notwithstanding her terror, this reproof touched the pride of Madame La Motte, who dried her tears, but disdained to reply, and looked at Adeline with a strong expression of displeasure. As they moved silently toward the abbey, Adeline asked La Motte if he was sure they were the king's officers who inquired for him. I cannot doubt it, he replied, who else could possibly inquire for me? Besides, the behaviour of the man, who mentioned my name, puts the matter beyond a question.

Perhaps not, said Madame La Motte: let us wait till morning ere we set off. We may then find it will be unnecessary to go.

We may, indeed; the king's officers would probably by that time have told us as much. La Motte went to give orders to Peter. Set off in an hour! said Peter, Lord bless you, master! only consider the coach wheel; it would take me a day at least to mend it, for your honour knows I never mended one in my life.

This was a circumstance which La Motte had entirely overlooked. When they settled at the abbey, Peter had at first been too busy in repairing the apartments, to remember the carriage; and afterwards, believing it would not quickly be wanted, he had neglected to do it. La Motte's temper now entirely forsook him, and with many execrations he ordered Peter to go to work immediately: but on searching for the materials formerly bought, they were no where to be found; and Peter at length remembered, though he was prudent enough to conceal this circumstance, that he had used the nails in repairing the abbey.

It was now, therefore, impossible to quit the forest that night, and La Motte had only to consider the most probable plan of concealment, should the officers of justice visit the ruin before the morning; a circumstance which the thoughtlessness of Peter, in returning from Auboine by the straight way, made not unlikely.

At first, indeed, it occurred to him, that, though his family could not be removed, he might himself take one of the horses, and escape from the forest before night. But he thought there would still be some danger of detection in the towns through which he must pass, and he could not well bear the idea of leaving his family unprotected, without knowing when he could return to them, or whither he could direct them to follow him. La Motte was not a man of very vigorous resolution, and he was, perhaps, rather more willing to suffer in company than alone.

After much consideration, he recollected the trap-door of the closet belonging to the chambers above. It was invisible to the eye and whatever might be its direction, it would securely shelter him, at least, from discovery. Having deliberated further upon the subject he determined to explore the recess to which the stairs led, and thought it possible that for a short time his whole family might be concealed within it. There was little time between the suggestion of the plan and the execution of his purpose, for darkness was spreading around, and in every murmur of the wind he thought he heard the voices of his enemies.

He called for a light, and ascended alone to the chamber. When he came to the closet, it was some time before he could find the trap-door, so exactly did it correspond with the boards of the floor. At length, he found and raised it. The chill damps of long confined air rushed from the aperture, and he stood for a moment to let them pass, ere he descended. As he stood looking down the abyss, he recollected the report which Peter had brought concerning the abbey, and it gave him an uneasy sensation. But this soon yielded to more pressing interests.

The stairs were steep, and in many places trembled beneath his weight. Having continued to descend for some time, his feet touched the ground, and he found himself in a narrow passage; but as he turned to pursue it, the damp vapours curled round him and extinguished the light. He called aloud for Peter, but could make nobody hear, and after some time he endeavoured to find his way up the stairs. In this, with difficulty, he succeeded, and passing the chambers with cautious steps descended the tower.

The security which the place he had just quitted seemed to promise, was of too much importance to be slightly rejected, and he determined immediately to make another experiment with the light:—having now fixed it in a lantern, he descended a second time to the passage. The current of vapours occasioned by the opening of the trap-door was abated, and the fresh air thence admitted had begun to circulate: La Motte passed on unmolested.

The passage was of considerable length, and led him to a door which was fastened. He placed the lantern at some distance, to avoid the current of air, and applied his strength to the door. It shook under his hands, but did not yield. Upon examining it more closely, he perceived the wood round the lock was decayed, probably by the damps, and this encouraged him to proceed. After some time it gave way to his effort, and he found himself in a square stone room.

He stood for some time to survey it. The walls, which were dripping with unwholesome dews, were entirely bare, and afforded not even a window. A small iron grate alone admitted the air. At the further end, near a low recess, was another door. La Motte went towards it, and, as he passed, looked into the recess. Upon the ground within it stood a large chest, which he went forward to examine; and, lifting the lid, he saw the remains of a human skeleton. Horror struck upon his heart, and he involuntarily stepped back. During a pause of some moments, his first emotion subsided. That thrilling curiosity, which objects of terror often excite in the human mind, impelled him to take a second view of this dismal spectacle.

La Motte stood motionless as he gazed; the object before him seemed to confirm the report that some person had formerly been murdered in the abbey. At length he closed the chest, and advanced to the second door, which also was fastened, but the key was in the lock. He turned it with difficulty, and then found the door was held by two strong bolts. Having undrawn these, it disclosed a flight of steps, which he descended. They terminated in a chain of low vaults, or rather cells, that, from the manner of their construction and present condition, seemed to be coeval with the most ancient parts of the abbey. La Motte, in his then depressed state of mind, thought them the burial places of the monks, who formerly inhabited the pile above; but they were more calculated for places of penance for the living, than of rest for the dead.

Having reached the extremity of these cells, the way was again closed by a door. La Motte now hesitated whether he should attempt to proceed any further. The present spot seemed to afford the security he sought. Here he might pass the night unmolested by apprehension of discovery; and it was most probable, that if the officers arrived in the night, and found the abbey vacated, they would quit it before morning, or, at least, before he could have any occasion to emerge from concealment. These considerations restored his mind to a state of greater composure. His only immediate care was to bring his family, as soon as possible, to this place of security, lest the officers should come unawares upon them; and while he stood thus musing, he blamed himself for delay.

But an irresistible desire of knowing to what this door led, arrested his steps, and he turned to open it. The door, however, was fastened; and as he attempted to force it, he suddenly thought he heard a noice above. It now occurred to him that the officers might already have arrived, and he quitted the cells with precipitation, intending to listen at the trap-door.

There, said he, I may wait in security, and perhaps hear something of what passes. My family will not be known, or at least not hurt, and their uneasiness on my account they must learn to endure.

These were the arguments of La Motte, in which, it must be owned, selfish prudence was more conspicuous than tender anxiety for his wife. He had by this time reached the bottom of the stairs, when, on looking up, he perceived the trap-door was left open; and ascending in haste to close it, he heard footsteps advancing through the chambers above. Before he could descend entirely out of sight, he again looked up, and perceived through the aperture the face of a man looking down, upon him. Master, cried Peter.—La Motte was somewhat relieved at the sound of his voice, though angry that he had occasioned, him so much terror.

What brings you here, and what is the matter below?

Nothing, Sir, nothing's the matter, only my mistress sent me to see after your honour.

There's nobody there then? said La Motte, setting his foot upon the step.

Yes, Sir, there is my mistress and Mademoiselle Adeline, and—

Well—well—said La Motte briskly, go your ways, I am coming.

He informed Madame La Motte where he had been, and of his intention of secreting himself, and deliberated upon the means of convincing the officers, should they arrive, that he had quitted the abbey. For this purpose he ordered all the moveable furniture to be conveyed to the cells below. La Motte himself assisted in this business, and every hand was employed for dispatch. In a very short time the habitable part of the fabric was left almost as desolate as he had found it. He then bade Peter take the horses to a distance from the abbey and turn them loose. After further consideration, he thought it might contribute to mislead them, if he placed in some conspicuous part of the fabric an inscription, signifying his condition, and mentioning the date of his departure from the abbey. Over the door of the tower which led to the habitable part of the structure, he therefore cut the following lines:

O ye! whom misfortune may lead to this spot,
Learn that there are others as miserable as yourselves.

P——L—M——a wretched exile, sought within these walls a refuge from persecution on the 27th of April, 1658, and quitted them on the 12th of July in the same year, in search of a more convenient asylum.

After engraving these words with a knife, the small stock of provisions remaining from the week's supply (for Peter, in his fright, had returned unloaded from his last journey) was put into a basket; and La Motte having assembled his family, they all ascended the stairs of the tower, and passed through the chambers to the closet. Peter went first with a light, and with some difficulty found the trap-door. Madame La Motte shuddered as she surveyed the gloomy abyss; but they were all silent.

La Motte now took the light and led the way; Madame followed, and then Adeline. These old monks loved good wine as well as other people, said Peter, who brought up the rear; I warrant your honour, now, this was their cellar; I smell the casks already.

Peace, said La Motte, reserve your jokes for a proper occasion.

There is no harm in loving good wine, as your honour knows.

Have done with this buffoonery, said La Motte in a tone more authoritative, and go first. Peter obeyed.

They came to the vaulted room. The dismal spectacle he had seen here, deterred La Motte from passing a night in this chamber; and the furniture had, by his own order, been conveyed to the cells below. He was anxious that his family should not perceive the skeleton; an object which would probably excite a degree of horror not to be overcome during their stay. La Motte now passed the chest in haste; and Madame La Motte and Adeline were too much engrossed by their own thoughts, to give minute attention to external circumstances.

When they reached the cells, Madame La Motte wept at the necessity which condemned her to a spot so dismal. Alas, said she, are we indeed thus reduced! The apartments above formerly appeared to me a deplorable habitation; but they are a palace compared to these.

True, my dear, said La Motte, and let the remembrance of what you once thought them soothe your discontent now; these cells are also a palace compared to the Bicêtre, or the Bastille, and to the terrors of further punishment which would accompany them: let the apprehension of the greater evil teach you to endure the less: I am contented if we find here the refuge I seek.

Madame La Motte was silent, and Adeline, forgetting her late unkindness, endeavoured as much as she could to console her; while her heart was sinking with the misfortunes which she could not but anticipate, she appeared composed, and even cheerful. She attended Madame La Motte with the most watchful solicitude, and felt so thankful that La Motte was now secreted within this recess, that she almost lost her perception of its glooms and inconveniences.

This she artlessly expressed to him, who could not be insensible to the tenderness it discovered. Madame La Motte was also sensible of it, and it renewed a painful sensation. The effusions of gratitude she mistook for those of tenderness.

La Motte returned frequently to the trap-door to listen if any body was in the abbey; but no sound disturbed the stillness of night: at length they sat down to supper; the repast was a melancholy one. If the officers do not come hither to-night, said Madame La Motte, sighing, suppose, my dear, Peter returns to Auboine to-morrow? He may there learn something more of this affair; or, at least, he might procure a carriage to convey us hence.

To be sure he might, said La Motte peevishly, and people to attend it also. Peter would be an excellent person to show the officers the way to the abbey, and to inform them of what they might else be in doubt about, my concealment here.

How cruel is this irony! replied Madame La Motte. I proposed only what I thought would be for our mutual good; my judgment was, perhaps, wrong, but my intention was certainly right. Tears swelled into her eyes as she spoke these words. Adeline wished to relieve her; but delicacy kept her silent. La Motte observed the effect of his speech, and something like remorse touched his heart. He approached, and taking her hand, You must allow for the perturbation of my mind, said he, I did not mean to afflict you thus. The idea of sending Peter to Auboine, where he has already done so much harm by his blunders, teased me, and I could not let it pass unnoticed. No, my dear, our only chance of safety is to remain where we are while our provisions last. If the officers do not come here to-night, they probably will to-morrow, or, perhaps, the next day. When they have searched the abbey, without finding me, they will depart; we may then emerge from this recess, and take measures for removing to a distant country.

Madame La Motte acknowledged the justice of his words; and her mind being relieved by the little apology he had made, she became tolerably cheerful. Supper being ended, La Motte stationed the faithful though simple Peter at the foot of the steps that ascended to the closet, there to keep watch during the night. Having done this, he returned to the lower cells, where he had left his little family. The beds were spread; and having mournfully bidden each other good night, they lay down, and implored rest.

Adeline's thoughts were too busy to suffer her to repose, and when she believed her companions were sunk in slumbers, she indulged the sorrow which reflection brought. She also looked forward to the future with the most mournful apprehension. Should La Motte be seized, what was to become of her. She would then be a wanderer in the wide world; without friends to protect, or money to support her. The prospect was gloomy—was terrible! She surveyed it, and shuddered! The distresses too of Monsieur and Madame La Motte, whom she loved with the most lively affection, formed no inconsiderable part of hers.

Sometimes she looked back to her father; but in him she only saw an enemy from whom she must fly: this remembrance heightened her sorrow; yet it was not the recollection of the suffering he had occasioned her, by which she was so much afflicted, as by the sense of his unkindness: she wept bitterly. At length, with that artless piety which innocence only knows, she addressed the Supreme Being, and resigned herself to his care. Her mind then gradually became peaceful and reassured, and soon after she sunk to repose.

CHAPTER V

A SURPRISE—AN ADVENTURE—A MYSTERY.

The night passed without any alarm; Peter had remained upon his post, and heard nothing that prevented his sleeping. La Motte heard him, long before he saw him, most musically snoring; though it must be owned there was more of the bass than of any other part of the gamut in his performance. He was soon roused by the bravura of La Motte, whose notes sounded discord to his ears, and destroyed the torpor of his tranquillity.

God bless you, master! what's the matter? cried Peter, waking, are they come?

Yes, for aught you care, they might be come. Did I place you here to sleep, sirrah? Bless you, master, returned Peter, sleep is the only comfort to be had here; I'm sure I would not deny it to a dog in such a place as this.

La Motte sternly questioned him concerning any noise he might have heard in the night; and Peter full as solemnly protested he had heard none; an assertion which was strictly true, for he had enjoyed the comfort of being asleep the whole time.

La Motte ascended to the trap-door and listened attentively. No sounds were heard, and as he ventured to lift it, the full light of the sun burst upon his sight, the morning being now far advanced: he walked softly along the chambers, and looked through a window—no person was to be seen. Encouraged by this apparent security, he ventured down the stairs of the tower, and entered the first apartment. He was proceeding towards the second, when suddenly recollecting himself, he first peeped through the crevice of the door, which stood half open. He looked, and distinctly saw a person sitting near the window, upon which his arm rested.

The discovery so much shocked him, that for a moment he lost all presence of mind, and was utterly unable to move from the spot. The person, whose back was towards him, arose, and turned his head: La Motte now recovered himself, and quitting the apartment as quickly and at the same time as silently as possible, ascended to the closet. He raised the trap-door, but, before he closed it, heard the footsteps of a person entering the outward chamber. Bolts or other fastening to the trap there was none; and his security depended solely upon the exact correspondence of the boards. The outer door of the stone room had no means of defence, and the fastenings of the inner one were on the wrong side to afford security even till some means of escape could be found.

When he reached this room he paused, and heard distinctly persons walking in the closet above. While he was listening, he heard a voice call him by name, and he instantly fled to the cells below, expecting every moment to hear the trap lifted and the footsteps of pursuit; but he was fled beyond the reach of hearing either. Having thrown himself on the ground at the furthest extremity of the vaults, he lay for some time breathless with agitation. Madame La Motte and Adeline, in the utmost terror, inquired what had happened. It was some time before he could speak; when he did, it was almost unnecessary, for the distant noises which sounded from above, informed his family of a part of the truth.

The sounds did not seem to approach; but Madame La Motte, unable to command her terror, shrieked aloud: this redoubled the distress of La Motte. You have already destroyed me, cried he; that shriek has informed them where I am. He traversed the cells with clasped hands and quick steps. Adeline stood pale and still as death, supporting Madame La Motte, whom with difficulty she prevented from fainting. O! Dupras! Dupras! you are already avenged! said he in a voice that seemed to burst from his heart: there was a pause of silence. But why should I deceive myself with a hope of escaping? he resumed; why do I wait here for their coming? Let me rather end those torturing pangs by throwing myself into their hands at once.

As he spoke, he moved towards the door; but the distress of Madame La Motte arrested his steps. Stay, said she, for my sake, stay; do not leave me thus, nor throw yourself voluntarily into destruction!

Surely, Sir, said Adeline, you are too precipitate; this despair is useless, as it is ill-founded. We hear no person approaching; if the officers had discovered the trap-door, they would certainly have been here before now. The words of Adeline stilled the tumult of his mind: the agitation of terror subsided; and reason beamed a feeble ray upon his hopes. He listened attentively; and perceiving that all was silent, advanced with caution to the stone room, and thence to the foot of the stairs that led to the trap-door. It was closed: no sound was heard above.

He watched a long time, and the silence continuing, his hopes strengthened; and at length he began to believe that the officers had quitted the abbey; the day, however, was spent in anxious watchfulness. He did not dare to unclose the trap-door; and he frequently thought he heard distant noises. It was evident, however, that the secret of the closet had escaped discovery; and on this circumstance he justly founded his security. The following night was passed, like the day, in trembling hope and incessant watching.

But the necessities of hunger now threatened them. The provisions, which had been distributed with the nicest economy, were nearly exhausted, and the most deplorable consequences might be expected from their remaining longer in concealment. Thus circumstanced, La Motte deliberated upon the most prudent method of proceeding. There appeared no other alternative, than to send Peter to Auboine, the only town from which he could return within the time prescribed by their necessities. There was game, indeed, in the forest; but Peter could neither handle a gun nor use a fishing rod to any advantage.

It was therefore agreed he should go to Auboine for a supply of provisions, and at the same time bring materials for mending the coach-wheel, that they might have some ready conveyance from the forest. La Motte forbade Peter to ask any questions concerning the people who had inquired for him, or take any methods for discovering whether they had quitted the country, lest his blunders should again betray him. He ordered him to be entirely silent as to these subjects, and to finish his business and leave the place with all possible dispatch.

A difficulty yet remained to be overcome—Who should first venture abroad into the abbey, to learn whether it was vacated by the officers of justice? La Motte considered that if he was again seen, he should be effectually betrayed; which would not be so certain if one of his family was observed, for they were all unknown to the officers. It was necessary, however, that the person he sent should have courage enough to go through with the inquiry, and wit enough to conduct it with caution. Peter, perhaps, had the first; but was certainly destitute of the last. Annette had neither. La Motte looked at his wife, and asked her if, for his sake, she dared to venture. Her heart shrunk from the proposal, yet she was unwilling to refuse, or appear indifferent upon a point so essential to the safety of her husband. Adeline observed in her countenance the agitation of her mind, and, surmounting the fears which had hitherto kept her silent, she offered herself to go.

They will be less likely to offend me, said she, than a man—Shame would not suffer La Motte to accept her offer; and Madame, touched with the magnanimity of her conduct, felt a momentary renewal of all her former kindness. Adeline pressed her proposal so warmly, and seemed so much in earnest, that La Motte began to hesitate. You, Sir, said she, once preserved me from the most imminent danger, and your kindness has since protected me: do not refuse me the satisfaction of deserving your goodness by a grateful return of it. Let me go into the abbey; and if, by so doing, I should preserve you from evil, I shall be sufficiently rewarded for what little danger I may incur, for my pleasure will be at least equal to yours.

Madame La Motte could scarcely refrain from tears as Adeline spoke; and La Motte sighing deeply, said, Well, be it so; go, Adeline, and from this moment consider me as your debtor. Adeline staid not to reply, but taking a light, quitted the cells. La Motte following to raise the trap-door, and cautioning her to look, if possible, into every apartment before she entered it. If you should be seen, said he, you must account for your appearance so as not to discover me. Your own presence of mind may assist you, I cannot—God bless you!

When she was gone, Madame La Motte's admiration of her conduct began to yield to other emotions. Distrust gradually undermined kindness, and jealousy raised suspicions. It must be a sentiment more powerful than gratitude, thought she, that could teach Adeline to subdue her fears. What, but love, could influence her to a conduct so generous! Madame La Motte, when she found it impossible to account for Adeline's conduct without alleging some interested motives for it, however her suspicions might agree with the practice of the world, had surely forgotten how much she once admired the purity and disinterestedness of her young friend.

Adeline, mean while, ascended to the chambers: the cheerful beams of the sun played once more upon her sight, and reanimated her spirits; she walked lightly through the apartments, nor stopped till she came to the stairs of the tower. Here she stood for some time, but no sounds met her ear, save the sighing of the wind among the trees, and at length she descended. She passed the apartments below without seeing any person, and the little furniture that remained seemed to stand exactly as she had left it. She now ventured to look out from the tower: the only animate objects that appeared were the deer quietly grazing under the shade of the woods. Her favourite little fawn distinguished Adeline, and came bounding towards her with strong marks of joy. She was somewhat alarmed lest the animal, being observed, should betray her, and walked swiftly away through the cloisters.

She opened the door that lead to the great hall of the abbey, but the passage was so gloomy and dark that she feared to enter it, and started back. It was necessary, however, that she should examine further, particularly on the opposite side of the ruin, of which she had hitherto had no view: but her fears returned when she recollected how far it would lead her from her only place of refuge, and how difficult it would be to retreat. She hesitated what to do; but when she recollected her obligations to La Motte, and considered this as perhaps her only opportunity of doing him a service, she determined to proceed.

As these thoughts passed rapidly over her mind, she raised her innocent looks to heaven, and breathed a silent prayer. With trembling steps she proceeded over fragments of the ruin, looking anxiously around, and often starting as the breeze rustled among the trees, mistaking it for the whisperings of men. She came to the lawn which fronted the fabric, but no person was to be seen, and her spirits revived. The great door of the hall she now endeavoured to open; but suddenly remembering that it was fastened by La Motte's orders, she proceeded to the north end of the abbey, and, having surveyed the prospect around as far as the thick foliage of the trees would permit, without perceiving any person, she turned her steps to the tower from which she had issued.

Adeline was now light of heart, and returned with impatience to inform La Motte of his security. In the cloisters she was again met by her little favourite, and stopped for a moment to caress it. The fawn seemed sensible to the sound of her voice, and discovered new joy; but while she spoke, it suddenly started from her hand, and looking up, she perceived the door of the passage, leading to the great hall, open, and a man in the habit of a soldier issue forth.

With the swiftness of an arrow she fled along the cloisters, nor once ventured to look back; but a voice called to her to stop, and she heard steps advancing quick in pursuit. Before she could reach the tower, her breath failed her, and she leaned against a pillar of the ruin, pale and exhausted. The man came up, and gazing at her with a strong expression of surprise and curiosity, he assumed a gentle manner, assured her she had nothing to fear, and inquired if she belonged to La Motte. Observing that she still looked terrified and remained silent, he repeated his assurances and his question.

I know that he is concealed within the ruin, said the stranger; the occasion of his concealment I also know; but it is of the utmost importance I should see him, and he will then be convinced he has nothing to fear from me. Adeline trembled so excessively, that it was with difficulty she could support herself—she hesitated, and knew not what to reply. Her manner seemed to confirm the suspicions of the stranger, and her consciousness of this increased her embarrassment: he took advantage of it to press her further. Adeline at length, replied that La Motte had some time since resided at the abbey. And does still. Madam, said the stranger; lead me to where he may be found—I must see him, and—

Never, Sir, replied Adeline; and I solemnly assure you it will be in vain to search for him.

That I must try, resumed he, since you, Madam, will not assist me. I have already followed him to some chambers above, where I suddenly lost him; thereabouts he must be concealed, and it's plain therefore they afford some secret passage.

Without waiting Adeline's reply, he sprung to the door of the tower. She now thought it would betray a consciousness of the truth of his conjecture to follow him, and resolved to remain below. But upon further consideration, it occurred to her that he might steal silently into the closet, and possibly surprise La Motte at the door of the trap. She therefore hastened after him, that her voice might prevent the danger she apprehended. He was already in the second chamber when she overtook him: she immediately began to speak aloud.

This room he searched with the most scrupulous care; but finding no private door, or other outlet, he proceeded to the closet: then it was that it required all her fortitude to conceal her agitation. He continued the search. Within these chambers I know he is concealed, said he, though hitherto I have not been able to discover how. It was hither I followed a man, whom I believe to be him, and he could not escape without a passage; I shall not quit the place till I have found it.

He examined the walls and the boards, but without discovering the division of the floor, which indeed so exactly corresponded, that La Motte himself had not perceived it by the eye, but by the trembling of the floor beneath his feet. Here is some mystery, said the stranger, which I cannot comprehend, and perhaps never shall. He was turning to quit the closet, when, who can paint the distress of Adeline, upon seeing the trap-door gently raised, and La Motte himself appeared! Hah! cried the stranger, advancing eagerly to him. La Motte sprang forward, and they were locked in each other's arms.

The astonishment of Adeline, for a moment, surpassed even her former distress; but a remembrance darted across her mind, which explained the present scene, and before La Motte could exclaim My son! she knew the stranger as such. Peter, who stood at the foot of the stairs, and heard what passed above, flew to acquaint his mistress with the joyful discovery, and in a few moments she was folded in the embrace of her son. This spot, so lately the mansion of despair, seemed metamorphosed into the palace of pleasure, and the walls echoed only to the accents of joy and congratulation.

The joy of Peter on this occasion was beyond expression: he acted a perfect pantomime—he capered about, clasped his hands—ran to his young master—shook him by the hand, in spite of the frowns of La Motte; ran every where, without knowing for what, and gave no rational answer to any thing that was said to him.

After their first emotions were subsided, La Motte, as if suddenly recollecting himself, resumed his wanted solemnity: I am to blame, said he, thus to give way to joy, when I am still, perhaps surrounded by danger. Let us secure a retreat while it is yet in our power, continued he; in a few hours the king's officers may search for me again.

Louis comprehended his father's words, and immediately relieved his apprehensions by the following relation:—

A letter from Monsieur Nemours, containing an account of your flight from Paris, reached me at Peronne, where I was then upon duty with my regiment. He mentioned that you were gone towards the south of France, but as he had not since heard from you, he was ignorant of the place of your refuge. It was about this time that I was dispatched into Flanders; and being unable to obtain further intelligence of you, I passed some weeks of very painful solicitude. At the conclusion of the campaign I obtained leave of absence, and immediately set out for Paris, hoping to learn from Nemours where you had found an asylum.

Of this, however, he was equally ignorant with myself. He informed me that you had once before written to him from D——, upon your second day's journey from Paris, under an assumed name, as had been agreed upon; and that you then said the fear of discovery would prevent your hazarding another letter. He therefore remained ignorant of your abode, but said he had no doubt you had continued your journey to the southward. Upon this slender information I quitted Paris in search of you, and proceeded immediately to V——, where my inquiries concerning your further progress were successful as far as M——. There they told me you had staid some time, on account of the illness of a young lady; a circumstance which perplexed me much, as I could not imagine what young lady would accompany you. I proceeded, however, to L——; but there all traces of you seemed to be lost. As I sat musing at the window of the inn, I observed some scribbling on the glass, and the curiosity of idleness prompted me to read it. I thought I knew the characters, and the lines I read confirmed my conjectures, for I remembered to have heard you often repeat them.

Here I renewed my inquiries concerning your route, and at length I made the people of the inn recollect you, and traced you as far as Auboine. There I again lost you, till upon my return from a fruitless inquiry in the neighbourhood, the landlord of the little inn where I lodged, told me he believed he had heard news of you, and immediately recounted what had happened at a blacksmith's shop a few hours before.

His description of Peter was so exact, that I had not a doubt it was you who inhabited the abbey; and as I knew your necessity for concealment, Peter's denial did not shake my confidence. The next morning, with the assistance of my landlord, I found my way hither, and having searched every visible part of the fabric, I began to credit Peter's assertion: your appearance, however, destroyed this fear, by proving that the place was still inhabited, for you disappeared so instantaneously that I was not certain it was you whom I had seen. I continued seeking you till near the close of day, and till then scarcely quitted the chambers whence you had disappeared. I called on you repeatedly, believing that my voice might convince you of your mistake. At length I retired to pass the night at a cottage near the border of the forest.

I came early this morning to renew my inquiries, and hoped that, believing yourself safe, you would emerge from concealment. But how was I disappointed to find the abbey as silent and solitary as I had left it the preceding evening! I was returning once more from the great hall, when the voice of this young lady caught my ear, and effected the discovery I had so anxiously sought.

This little narrative entirely dissipated the late apprehensions of La Motte; but he now dreaded that the inquiries of his son, and his own obvious desire of concealment, might excite a curiosity amongst the people of Auboine, and lead to a discovery of his true circumstances. However, for the present he determined to dismiss all painful thoughts, and endeavour to enjoy the comfort which the presence of his son had brought him. The furniture was removed to a more habitable part of the abbey, and the cells were again abandoned to their own glooms.

The arrival of her son seemed to have animated Madame La Motte with new life, and all her afflictions were, for the present, absorbed in joy. She often gazed silently on him with a mother's fondness, and her partiality heightened every improvement which time had wrought in his person and manner. He was now in his twenty-third year; his person was manly and his air military; his manners were unaffected and graceful, rather than dignified; and though his features were irregular, they composed a countenance which, having seen it once, you would seek it again.

She made eager inquiries after the friends she had left at Paris, and learned that within the few months of her absence some had died and others quitted the place. La Motte also learned that a very strenuous search for him had been prosecuted at Paris; and, though this intelligence was only what he had before expected, it shocked him so much, that he now declared it would be expedient to remove to a distant country. Louis did not scruple to say that he thought he would be as safe at the abbey as at any other place; and repeated what Nemours had said, that the king's officers had been unable to trace any part of his route from Paris.

Besides, resumed Louis, this abbey is protected by a supernatural power, and none of the country people dare approach it.

Please you, my young master, said Peter, who was waiting in the room, we were frightened enough the first night we came here, and I myself, God forgive me! thought the place was inhabited by devils, but they were only owls, and such like, after all.

Your opinion was not asked, said La Motte, learn to be silent.

Peter was abashed. When he had quitted the room, La Motte asked his son with seeming carelessness, what were the reports circulated by the country people? O! Sir, replies Louis, I cannot recollect half of them: I remember, however, they said that, many years ago, a person (but nobody had ever seen him, so we may judge how far the report ought to be credited)—a person was privately brought to this abbey, and confined in some part of it, and that there was strong reasons to believe he came unfairly to his end.

La Motte sighed. They further said, continued Louis, that the spectre of the deceased had ever since watched nightly among the ruins: and to make the story more wonderful, for the marvellous is the delight of the vulgar, they added, that there was a certain part of the ruin from whence no person that had dared to explore it, had ever returned. Thus people, who have few objects of real interest to engage their thoughts, conjure up for themselves imaginary ones.

La Motte sat musing. And what were the reasons, said he, at length awaking from his reverie, they pretended to assign for believing the person confined here was murdered?

They did not use a term so positive as that, replied Louis.

True, said La Motte, recollecting himself, they only said he came unfairly to his end.

That is a nice distinction, said Adeline.

Why I could not well comprehend what these reasons were, resumed Louis; the people indeed say, that the person who was brought here, was never known to depart; but I do not find it certain that he ever arrived: that there was strange privacy and mystery observed, while he was here, and that the abbey has never since been inhabited by its owner. There seems, however, to be nothing in all this that deserves to be remembered.—La Motte raised his head, as if to reply, when the entrance of Madame turned the discourse upon a new subject, and it was not resumed that day.

Peter was now dispatched for provisions, while La Motte and Louis retired to consider how far it was safe for them to continue at the abbey. La Motte, notwithstanding the assurances lately given him, could not but think that Peter's blunders and his son's inquiries might lead to a discovery of his residence. He revolved this in his mind for some time; but at length a thought struck him, that the latter of these circumstances might considerably contribute to his security. If you, said he to Louis, return to the inn at Auboine, from whence you were directed here, and without seeming to intend giving intelligence, do give the landlord an account of your having found the abbey uninhabited, and then add, that you had discovered the residence of the person you sought in some distant town, it would suppress any reports that may at present exist, and prevent the belief of any in future. And if, after all this, you can trust yourself for presence of mind and command of countenance, so far as to describe some dreadful apparition, I think these circumstances, together with the distance of the abbey and the intricacies of the forest, could entitle me to consider this place as my castle.

Louis agreed to all that his father had proposed, and on the following day executed his commission with such success, that the tranquillity of the abbey might be then said to have been entirely restored.

Thus ended this adventure, the only one that had occurred to disturb the family during their residence in the forest. Adeline, removed from the apprehension of those evils with which the late situation of La Motte had threatened her, and from the depression which her interest in his occasioned her, now experienced a more than usual complacency of mind. She thought, too, that she observed in Madame La Motte a renewal of her former kindness; and this circumstance awakened all her gratitude, and imparted to her a pleasure as lively as it was innocent. The satisfaction with which the presence of her son inspired Madame La Motte, Adeline mistook for kindness to herself, and she exerted her whole attention in an endeavour to become worthy of it.

But the joy which his unexpected arrival had given to La Motte quickly began to evaporate, and the gloom of despondency again settled on his countenance. He returned frequently to his haunt in the forest—the same mysterious sadness tinctured his manner, and revived the anxiety of Madame La Motte, who was resolved to acquaint her son with this subject of distress, and solicit his assistance to penetrate its source.

Her jealousy of Adeline, however, she could not communicate, though it again tormented her, and taught her to misconstrue with wonderful ingenuity every look and word of La Motte, and often to mistake the artless expressions of Adeline's gratitude and regard for those of warmer tenderness. Adeline had formerly accustomed herself to long walks in the forest, and the design Madame had formed of watching her steps, had been frustrated by the late circumstances, and was now entirely overcome by her sense of its difficulty and danger. To employ Peter in the affair, would be to acquaint him with her fears; and to follow her herself, would most probably betray her scheme, by making Adeline aware of her jealousy. Being thus restrained by pride and delicacy, she was obliged to endure the pangs of uncertainty concerning the greatest part of her suspicions.

To Louis, however, she related the mysterious change in his father's temper. He listened to her account with very earnest attention, and the surprise and concern impressed upon his countenance spoke how much his heart was interested. He was, however, involved in equal perplexity with herself upon this subject, and readily undertook to observe the motions of La Motte, believing his interference likely to be of equal service, both to his father and his mother. He saw, in some degree, the suspicions of his mother; but as he thought she wished to disguise her feelings, he suffered her to believe that she succeeded.

He now inquired concerning Adeline; and listened to her little history, of which his mother gave a brief relation, with great apparent interest. So much pity did he express for her condition, and so much indignation at the unnatural conduct of her father, that the apprehensions which Madame La Motte began to form, of his having discovered her jealousy, yielded to those of a different kind. She perceived that the beauty of Adeline had already fascinated his imagination, and she feared that her amiable manners would soon impress his heart. Had her first fondness for Adeline continued, she would still have looked with displeasure upon their attachment, as an obstacle to the promotion and the fortune she hoped to see one day enjoyed by her son. On these she rested all her future hopes of prosperity, and regarded the matrimonial alliance which he might form as the only means of extricating his family from their present difficulties. She therefore touched lightly upon Adeline's merit, joined coolly with Louis, in compassionating her misfortunes, and with her censure of the father's conduct mixed an implied suspicion of that of Adeline's. The means she employed to repress the passions of her son had a contrary effect. The indifference which she repressed towards Adeline, increased his pity for her destitute condition; and the tenderness with which she affected to judge the father, heightened his honest indignation at his character.

As he quitted Madame La Motte, he saw his father cross the lawn and enter the deep shade of the forest on the left. He judged this to be a good opportunity of commencing his plan, and quitting the abbey, slowly followed at a distance. La Motte continued to walk straight forward, and seemed so deeply wrapt in thought, that he looked neither to the right nor left, and scarcely lifted his head from the ground. Louis had followed him near half a mile, when he saw him suddenly strike into an avenue of the forest, which took a different direction from the way he had hitherto gone. He quickened his steps that he might not lose sight of him, but, having reached the avenue, found the trees so thickly interwoven that La Motte was already hid from his view.

He continued, however, to pursue the way before him: it conducted him through the most gloomy part of the forest he had yet seen, till at length it terminated in an obscure recess, over-arched with high trees, whose interwoven branches secluded the direct rays of the sun, and admitted only a sort of solemn twilight. Louis looked around in search of La Motte, but he was no where to be seen. While he stood surveying the place, and considering what further should be done, he observed, through the gloom, an object at some distance, but the deep shadow that fell around prevented his distinguishing what it was.

In advancing, he perceived the ruins of a small building, which, from the traces that remained, appeared to have been a tomb. As he gazed upon it, Here, said he, are probably deposited the ashes of some ancient monk, once an inhabitant of the abbey; perhaps, of the founder, who, after having spent a life of abstinence and prayer, sought in heaven the reward of his forbearance upon earth. Peace be to his soul! but did he think a life of mere negative virtue deserved an eternal reward? Mistaken man! reason, had you trusted to its dictates, would have informed you, that the active virtues, the adherence to the golden rule, Do as you would be done unto, could alone deserve the favour of a Deity whose glory is benevolence.

He remained with his eyes fixed upon the spot, and presently saw a figure arise under the arch of the sepulchre. It started, as if on perceiving him, and immediately disappeared. Louis, though unused to fear, felt at that moment an uneasy sensation, but it almost immediately struck him that this was La Motte himself. He advanced to the ruin and called him. No answer was returned; and he repeated the call, but all was yet still as the grave. He then went up to the archway and endeavoured to examine the place where he had disappeared, but the shadowy obscurity rendered the attempt fruitless. He observed, however, a little to the right, an entrance to the ruin, and advanced some steps down a kind of dark passage, when, recollecting that this place might be the haunt of banditti, his danger alarmed him, and he retreated with precipitation.

He walked towards the abbey by the way he came; and finding no person followed him, and believing himself again in safety, his former surmise returned, and he thought it was La Motte he had seen. He mused upon this strange possibility, and endeavoured to assign a reason for so mysterious a conduct, but in vain. Notwithstanding this, his belief of it strengthened, and he entered the abbey under as full a conviction as the circumstances would admit of, that it was his father who had appeared in the sepulchre. On entering what was now used as a parlour, he was much surprised to find him quietly seated there with Madame La Motte and Adeline, and conversing as if he had been returned some time.

He took the first opportunity of acquainting his mother with his late adventure, and of inquiring how long La Motte had been returned before him; when, learning that it was near half an hour, his surprise increased, and he knew not what to conclude.

Meanwhile, a perception of the growing partiality of Louis co-operated with the canker of suspicion to destroy in Madame La Motte that affection which pity and esteem had formerly excited for Adeline. Her unkindness was now too obvious to escape the notice of her to whom it was directed, and, being noticed, it occasioned an anguish which Adeline found it very difficult to endure. With the warmth and candour of youth, she sought an explanation of this change of behaviour, and an opportunity of exculpating herself from any intention of provoking it. But this Madame La Motte artfully evaded; while at the same time she threw out hints that involved Adeline in deeper perplexity, and served to make her present affliction more intolerable.

I have lost that affection, she would say, which was my all. It was my only comfort—

yet I have lost it—and this without even knowing my offence. But I am thankful that I have not merited unkindness, and, though she has abandoned me, I shall always love her.

Thus distressed, she would frequently leave the parlour, and, retiring to her chamber, would yield to a despondency which she had never known till now.

One morning, being unable to sleep, she arose at a very early hour. The faint light of day now trembled through the clouds, and gradually spreading from the horizon, announced the rising sun. Every feature of the landscape was slowly unveiled, moist with the dews of night and brightening with the dawn, till at length the sun appeared and shed the full flood of day. The beauty of the hour invited her to walk, and she went forth into the forest to taste the sweets of morning. The carols of new-waked birds saluted her as she passed, and the fresh gale came scented with the breath of flowers, whose tints glowed more vivid through the dew drops that hung on their leaves.

She wandered on without noticing the distance, and, following the windings of the river, came to a dewy glade, whose woods, sweeping down to the very edge of the water, formed a scene so sweetly romantic, that she sealed herself at the foot of a tree, to contemplate its beauty. These images insensibly soothed her sorrow, and inspired her with that soft and pleasing melancholy so dear to the feeling mind. For some time she sat lost in a reverie, while the flowers that grew on the banks beside her seemed to smile in new life, and drew from her a comparison with her own condition. She mused and sighed, and then, in a voice whose charming melody was modulated by the tenderness of her heart, she sung the following words:

SONNET, TO THE LILY.

Soft silken flower! that in the dewy vale Unfold'st thy modest beauties to the morn, And breath'st thy fragrance on her wandering gale, O'er earth's green hills and shadowy valley borne.

When day has closed his dazzling eye, And dying gales sink soft away; When eve steals down the western sky, And mountains, woods, and vales decay.

Thy tender cups, that graceful swell, Droop sad beneath her chilly dew; Thy odours seek their silken cell, And twilight veils their languid hue.

But soon fair flower! the morn shall rise, And rear again thy pensive head; Again unveil thy snowy dyes, Again thy velvet foliage spread.

Sweet child of Spring! like thee, in sorrow's shade, Full oft I mourn in tears, and droop forlorn: And O! like thine, may light my glooms pervade, And Sorrow fly before Joy's living morn!

A distant echo lengthened out her tones, and she sat listening to the soft response, till repeating the last stanza of the sonnet she was answered by a voice almost as tender, and less distant. She looked round in surprise, and saw a young man in a hunter's dress leaning against a tree, and gazing on her with that deep attention which marks an enraptured mind.

A thousand apprehensions shot athwart her busy thought; and she now first remembered her distance from the abbey. She rose in haste to be gone, when the stranger respectfully advanced; but, observing her timid looks and retiring steps, he paused. She pursued her way towards the abbey; and though many reasons made her anxious to know whether she was followed, delicacy forbade her to look back. When she reached the abbey, finding the family was not yet assembled to breakfast, she retired to her chamber, where her whole thoughts were employed in conjectures concerning the stranger. Believing that she was interested on this point no further than as it concerned the safety of La Motte, she indulged without scruple the remembrance of that dignified air and manner which so much distinguished the youth she had seen. After revolving the circumstance more deeply, she believed it impossible that a person of his appearance should be engaged in a stratagem to betray a fellow-creature; and though she was destitute of a single circumstance that might assist her surmises of who he was, or what was his business in an unfrequented forest, she rejected, unconsciously, every suspicion injurious to his character. Upon further deliberation, therefore, she resolved not to mention this little circumstance to La Motte; well knowing, that though his danger might be imaginary, his apprehensions would be real, and would renew all the sufferings and perplexity from which he was but just released. She resolved, however, to refrain, for some time walking in the forest.

When she came down to breakfast, she observed Madame La Motte to be more than usually reserved. La Motte entered the room soon after her, and made some trifling observations on the weather; and, having endeavoured to support an effort at cheerfulness, sunk into his usual melancholy. Adeline watched the countenance of Madame with anxiety; and when there appeared in it a gleam of kindness, it was as sunshine to her soul: but she very seldom suffered Adeline thus to flatter herself. Her conversation was restrained, and often pointed at something more than could be understood. The entrance of Louis was a very seasonable relief to Adeline, who almost feared to trust her voice with a sentence, lest its trembling accents should betray her uneasiness.

This charming morning drew you early from your chamber? said Louis, addressing Adeline. You had, no doubt, a pleasant companion too? said Madame La Motte, a solitary walk is seldom agreeable.

I was alone, Madam, replied Adeline.

Indeed! your own thoughts must be highly pleasing then.

Alas! returned Adeline, a tear spite of her efforts starting to her eye, there are now few subjects of pleasure left for them.

That is very surprising, pursued Madame La Motte.

Is it, indeed, surprising, Madam, for those who have lost their last friend to be unhappy?

Madame La Motte's conscience acknowledged the rebuke, and she blushed.

Well, resumed she, after a short pause, that is not your situation, Adeline, looking earnestly at La Motte. Adeline, whose innocence protected her from suspicion, did not regard this circumstance; but, smiling through her tears, said, she rejoiced to hear her say so. During this conversation, La Motte had remained absorbed in his own thoughts; and Louis, unable to guess at what it pointed, looked alternately at his mother and Adeline for an explanation. The latter he regarded with an expression so full of tender compassion, that it revealed at once to Madame La Motte the sentiments of his soul; and she immediately replied to the last words of Adeline with a very serious air: A friend is only estimable when our conduct deserves one; the friendship that survives the merit of its object is a disgrace, instead of an honour, to both parties.

The manner and emphasis with which she delivered these words, again alarmed Adeline, who mildly said, she hoped she should never deserve such censure. Madame was silent; but Adeline was so much shocked by what had already passed, that tears sprung from her eyes, and she hid her face with her handkerchief.

Louis now rose with some emotion; and La Motte, roused from his reverie, inquired what was the matter: but before he could receive an answer he seemed to have forgotten that he had asked the question. Adeline may give you her own account, said Madame La Motte. I have not deserved this, said Adeline rising; but since my presence is displeasing, I will retire.

She moved towards the door; when Louis, who was pacing the room in apparent agitation, gently took her hand, saying, Here is some unhappy mistake—and would have led her to the seat: but her spirits were too much depressed to endure longer restraint; and, withdrawing her hand, Suffer me to go, said she; if there is any mistake, I am unable to explain it. Saying this, she quitted the room. Louis followed her with his eyes to the door; when turning to his mother, Surely, Madam, said he, you are to blame: my life on it she deserves your warmest tenderness.

You are very eloquent in her cause, Sir, said Madame, may I presume to ask what interested you thus in her favour.

Her own amiable manners, rejoined Louis, which no one can observe without esteeming them.

But you may presume too much on your own observations; it is possible these amiable manners may deceive you.

Your pardon Madam; I may, without presumption, affirm they cannot deceive me.

You have, no doubt, good reasons for this assertion, and I perceive, by your admiration of this artless innocence, she has succeeded in her design of entrapping your heart.

Without designing it, she has won my admiration, which would not have been the case, had she been capable of the conduct you mention.

Madame La Motte was going to reply, but was prevented by her husband, who, again roused from his reverie, inquired into the cause of dispute. Away with this ridiculous behaviour, said he in a voice of displeasure; Adeline has omitted some household duty, I suppose; and an offence so heinous deserves severe punishment, no doubt: but let me be no more disturbed with your petty quarrels; if you must be tyrannical, Madam, indulge your humour in private.

Saying this, he abruptly quitted the room; and Louis immediately following, Madame was left to her own unpleasant reflections. Her ill-humour proceeded from the usual cause. She had heard of Adeline's walk; and La Motte having gone forth into the forest at an early hour, her imagination, heated by the broodings of jealousy, suggested that they had appointed a meeting. This was confirmed to her by the entrance of Adeline, quickly followed by La Motte; and her perceptions thus jaundiced by passion, neither the presence of her son, nor her usual attention to good manners, had been able to restrain her emotions. The behaviour of Adeline in the late scene she considered as a refined piece of art, and the indifference of La Motte as affected. So true is it that:

...... Trifles, light as air,Are, to the jealous, confirmations strongAs proofs of Holy Writ;

and so ingenious was she 'to twist the true cause the wrong way.'

Adeline had retired to her chamber to weep. When her first agitations were subsided, she took an ample view of her conduct; and perceiving nothing of which she could accuse herself, she became more satisfied, deriving her best comfort from the integrity of her intentions. In the moment of accusation, innocence may sometimes be oppressed with the punishment due only to guilt; but reflection dissolves the illusion of terror, and brings to the aching bosom the consolations of virtue.

When La Motte quitted the room, he had gone into the forest; which Louis observing, he followed and joined him, with an intention of touching upon the subject of his melancholy. It is a fine morning, Sir, said Louis; if you will give me leave, I will walk with you. La Motte, though dissatisfied, did not object; and after they had proceeded some way, he changed the course of his walk, striking into a path contrary to that which Louis had observed him take on the foregoing day.

Louis remarked that the avenue they had quitted was more shady, and therefore more pleasant. La Motte not seeming to notice this remark, It leads to a singular spot, continued he, which I discovered yesterday. La Motte raised his head: Louis proceeded to describe the tomb, and the adventure he had met with. During this relation, La Motte regarded him with attention, while his own countenance suffered various changes. When he had concluded, You were very daring, said La Motte, to examine that place, particularly when you ventured down the passage: I would advise you to be more cautious how you penetrate the depths of this forest. I myself have not ventured beyond a certain boundary and am therefore uninformed what inhabitants it may harbour. Your account has alarmed me, continued he; for if banditti are in the neighbourhood, I am not safe from their depredations:—'tis true, I have but little to lose, except my life.

And the lives of your family, rejoined Louis.—Of course, said La Motte.

It would be well to have more certainty upon that head, rejoined Louis; I am considering how we may obtain it.

'Tis useless to consider that, said La Motte; the inquiry itself brings danger with it; your life would perhaps be paid for the indulgence of your curiosity; our only chance of safety is by endeavouring to remain undiscovered. Let us move towards the abbey.

Louis knew not what to think, but said no more upon the subject. La Motte soon after relapsed into a fit of musing; and his son now took occasion to lament that depression of spirits which he had lately observed in him. Rather lament the cause of it, said La Motte with a sigh. That I do most sincerely, whatever it may be. May I venture to inquire, Sir, what is this cause?

Are then my misfortunes so little known to you, rejoined La Motte, as to make that question necessary? Am I not driven from my home, from my friends, and almost from my country? And shall it be asked why I am afflicted? Louis felt the justice of this reproof, and was a moment silent. That you are afflicted, Sir, does not excite my surprise, resumed he; it would indeed be strange, were you not.

What then does excite your surprise?

The air of cheerfulness you wore when I first came hither.

You lately lamented that I was afflicted, said La Motte, and now seem not very well pleased that I once was cheerful. What is the meaning of this?

You much mistake me, said his son; nothing could give me so much satisfaction as to see that cheerfulness renewed; the same cause of sorrow existed at that time, yet you was then cheerful.

That I was then cheerful, said La Motte, you might, without flattery, have attributed to yourself; your presence revived me, and I was relieved at the same time from a load of apprehensions.

Why then, as the same cause exists, are you not still cheerful?

And why do you not recollect that it is your father you thus speak to?

I do, Sir, and nothing but anxiety for my father could have urged me thus far: it is with inexpressible concern I perceive you have some secret cause of uneasiness; reveal it, Sir, to those who claim a share in all your affliction, and suffer them, by participation to soften its severity. Louis looked up, and observed the countenance of his father pale as death: his lips trembled while he spoke. Your penetration, however, you may rely upon it, has, in the present instance, deceived you: I have no subject of distress, but what you are already acquainted with, and I desire this conversation may never be renewed.

If it is your desire, of course I obey, said Louis; but, pardon me, Sir, if—

I will not pardon you, Sir, interrupted La Motte; let the discourse end here. Saying this, he quickened his steps; and Louis, not daring to pursue, walked quietly on till he reached the abbey.

Adeline passed the greatest part of the day alone in her chamber, where, having examined her conduct, she endeavoured to fortify her heart against the unmerited displeasure of Madame La Motte. This was a task more difficult than that of self-acquittance. She loved her, and had relied on her friendship, which, notwithstanding the conduct of Madame, still appeared valuable to her. It was true, she had not deserved to lose it; but Madame was so averse to explanation, that there was little probability of recovering it, however ill-founded might be the cause of her dislike. At length she reasoned, or rather perhaps persuaded herself into tolerable composure; for to resign a real good with contentment is less an effort of reason than of temper.

For many hours she busied herself upon a piece of work which she had undertaken for Madame La Motte; and this she did without the least intention of conciliating her favour, but because she felt there was something in thus repaying unkindness, which was suitable to her own temper, her sentiments, and her pride. Self-love may be the centre round which the human affections move; for whatever motive conduces to self-gratification may be resolved into self-love; yet some of these affections are in their nature so refined, that though we cannot deny their origin, they almost deserve the name of virtue. Of this species was that of Adeline.

In this employment, and in reading, Adeline passed as much of the day as possible. From books, indeed, she had constantly derived her chief information and amusement: those belonging to La Motte were few, but well chosen; and Adeline could find pleasure in reading them more than once. When her mind was discomposed by the behaviour of Madame La Motte, or by a retrospection of her early misfortunes, a book was the opiate that lulled it to repose. La Motte had several of the best English poets, a language which Adeline had learned in the convent; their beauties, therefore, she was capable of tasting, and they often inspired her with enthusiastic delight.

At the decline of day she quitted her chamber to enjoy the sweet evening hour, but strayed no further than an avenue near the abbey, which fronted the west. She read a little; but finding it impossible any longer to abstract her attention from the scene around; she closed the book, and yielded to the sweet complacent melancholy which the hour inspired. The air was still; the sun sinking below the distant hill, spread a purple glow over the landscape, and touched the forest glades with softer light. A dewy freshness was diffused upon the air. As the sun descended, the dusk came silently on, and the scene assumed a solemn grandeur. As she mused, she recollected and repeated the following stanzas:

NIGHT.

Now Evening fades! her pensive step retires,And Night leads on the dews and shadowy hours:Her awful pomp of planetary fires,And all her train of visionary powers.

These paint with fleeting shapes the dream of sleep,These swell the waking soul with pleasing dread;These through the glooms in forms terrific sweep,And rouse the thrilling horrors of the dead!

Queen of the solemn thought—mysterious Night!Whose step is darkness, and whose voice is fear!Thy shades I welcome with severe delight,And hail thy hollow gales, that sigh so drear!

When wrapt in clouds, and riding in the blast,Thou roll'st the storm along the sounding shore,I love to watch the whelming billows castOn rocks below, and listen to the roar.

Thy milder terrors, Night, I frequent wooThy silent lightnings, and thy meteors' glare,Thy northern fires, bright with ensanguine hue,That light in heaven's high vault the fervid air.

But chief I love thee, when thy hold carSheds through the fleecy clouds a trembling gleam,And shows the misty mountain from afar,The nearer forest, and the valley's stream:

And nameless objects in the vale below,That, floating dimly to the musing eye,Assume, at Fancy's touch, fantastic show,And raise her sweet romantic visions high.

Then let me stand amidst thy glooms profound,On some wide woody steep, and hear the breezeThat swells in mournful melody around,And faintly dies upon the distant trees.

What melancholy charm steals o'er the mind!What hallow'd tears the rising rapture greet!While many a viewless spirit in the windSighs to the lonely hour in accents sweet!

Ah! who the dear illusions pleased would yield,Which Fancy wakes from silence and from shades,For all the sober forms of Truth reveal'd,For all the scenes that Day's bright eye pervades!

On her return to the abbey she was joined by Louis, who, after some conversation, said, I am much grieved by the scene to which I was witness this morning, and have longed for an opportunity of telling you so. My mother's behaviour is too mysterious to be accounted for, but it is not difficult to perceive she labours under some mistake. What I have to request is, that whenever I can be of service to you, you will command me.

Adeline thanked him for this friendly offer, which she felt more sensibly than she chose to express. I am unconscious, said she, of any offence that may have deserved Madame La Motte's displeasure, and am therefore totally unable to account for it. I have repeatedly sought an explanation, which she has as anxiously avoided; it is better, therefore, to press the subject no farther. At the same time, Sir, suffer me to assure you, I have a just sense of your goodness. Louis sighed, and was silent. At length, I wish you would permit me, resumed he, to speak with my mother upon this subject; I am sure I could convince her of her error.

By no means, replied Adeline: Madame La Motte's displeasure has given me inexpressible concern; but to compel her to an explanation, would only increase this displeasure, instead of removing it. Let me beg of you not to attempt it.

I submit to your judgment, said Louis, but, for once, it is with reluctance. I should esteem myself most happy if I could be of service to you. He spoke this with an accent so tender, that Adeline, for the first time, perceived the sentiments of his heart. A mind more fraught with vanity than hers would have taught her long ago to regard the attentions of Louis as the result of something more than well-bred gallantry. She did not appear to notice his last words, but remained silent, and involuntarily quickened her pace. Louis said no more, but seemed sunk in thought; and this silence remained uninterrupted till they entered the abbey.

CHAPTER VI

Hence, horrible shadow! Unreal mockery, hence! MACBETH.

Near a month elapsed without any remarkable occurrence: the melancholy of La Motte suffered little abatement; and the behaviour of Madame to Adeline, though somewhat softened, was still far from kind. Louis by numberless little attentions testified his growing affection for Adeline, who continued to treat them as passing civilities.

It happened, one stormy night, as they were preparing for rest, that they were alarmed by the trampling of horses near the abbey. The sound of several voices succeeded, and a loud knocking at the great gate of the hall soon after confirmed the alarm. La Motte had little doubt that the officers of justice had at length discovered his retreat, and the perturbation of fear almost confounded his senses: he, however, ordered the lights to be extinguished, and a profound silence to be observed, unwilling to neglect even the slightest possibility of security. There was a chance, he thought, that the persons might suppose the place uninhabited, and believe they had mistaken the object of their search. His orders were scarcely obeyed, when the knocking was renewed, and with increased violence. La Motte now repaired to a small grated window in the portal of the gate, that he might observe the number and appearance of the strangers.

The darkness of the night baffled his purpose, he could only perceive a group of men on horseback; but listening attentively, he distinguished part of their discourse. Several of the men contended that they had mistaken the place; till a person, who, from his authoritative voice, appeared to be their leader, affirmed that the lights had issued from this spot, and he was positive there were persons within. Having said this, he again knocked loudly at the gate, and was answered only by hollow echoes. La Motte's heart trembled at the sound, and he was unable to move.

After waiting some time, the strangers seemed as if in consultation; but their discourse was conducted in such a low tone of voice, that La Motte was unable to distinguish its purport. They withdrew from the gate, as if to depart; but he presently thought he heard them amongst the trees on the other side of the fabric, and soon became convinced they had not left the abbey. A few minutes held La Motte in a state of torturing suspense; he quitted the grate, where Louis now stationed himself, for that part of the edifice which overlooked the spot where he supposed them to be waiting.

The storm was now loud, and the hollow blasts which rushed among the trees prevented his distinguishing any other sound. Once, in the pauses of the wind, he thought he heard distinct voices; but he was not long left to conjecture, for the renewed knocking at the gate again appalled him; and regardless of the terrors of Madame La Motte and Adeline, he ran to try his last chance of concealment by means of the trap-door.

Soon after, the violence of the assailants seeming to increase with every gust of the tempest, the gate, which was old and decayed, burst from its hinges, and admitted them to the hall. At the moment of their entrance, a scream from Madame La Motte, who stood at the door of an adjoining apartment, confirmed the suspicions of the principal stranger, who continued to advance as fast as the darkness would permit him.

Adeline had fainted, and Madame La Motte was calling loudly for assistance, when Peter entered with lights, and discovered the hall filled with men, and his young mistress senseless upon the floor. A chevalier now advanced, and, soliciting pardon of Madame for the rudeness of his conduct, was attempting an apology, when, perceiving Adeline, he hastened to raise her from the ground; but Louis, who now returned, caught her in his arms, and desired the stranger not to interfere.

The person to whom he spoke this, wore the star of one of the first orders in France, and had an air of dignity which declared him to be of superior rank. He appeared to be about forty, but perhaps the spirit and fire of his countenance made the impression of time upon his features less perceptible. His softened aspect and insinuating manners, while, regardless of himself, he seemed attentive only to the condition of Adeline, gradually dissipated the apprehensions of Madame La Motte, and subdued the sudden resentment of Louis. Upon Adeline, who was yet insensible, he gazed with an eager admiration, which seemed to absorb all the faculties of his mind. She was indeed an object not to be contemplated with indifference.

Her beauty, touched with the languid delicacy of illness, gained from sentiment what it lost in bloom. The negligence of her dress, loosened for the purpose of freer respiration, discovered those glowing charms, which her auburn tresses, that fell in profusion over her bosom, shaded, but could not conceal.

There now entered another stranger, a young chevalier, who having spoke hastily to the elder, joined the general group that surrounded Adeline. He was of a person in which elegance was happily blended with strength, and had a countenance animated, but not haughty; noble, yet expressive of peculiar sweetness. What rendered it at present more interesting, was the compassion, he seemed to feel for Adeline, who now revived and saw him, the first object that met her eyes, bending over her in silent anxiety.

On perceiving him, a blush of quick surprise passed over her cheek, for she knew him to be the stranger she had seen in the forest. Her countenance instantly changed to the paleness of terror when she observed the room crowded with people. Louis now supported her into another apartment, where the two chevaliers, who followed her, again apologized for the alarm they had occasioned. The elder, turning to Madame La Motte, said, You are, no doubt, Madam, ignorant that I am the proprietor of this abbey. She started. Be not alarmed, Madam, you are safe and welcome. This ruinous spot has been long abandoned by me, and if it has afforded you a shelter I am happy. Madame La Motte expressed her gratitude for this condescension, and Louis declared his sense of the politeness of the Marquis de Montalt, for that was the name of the noble stranger.

My chief residence, said the Marquis, is in a distant province, but I have a chateau near the borders of the forest, and in returning from an excursion I have been benighted and lost my way. A light which gleamed through the trees attracted me hither; and such was the darkness without, that I did not know it proceeded from the abbey till I came to the door. The noble deportment of the strangers, the splendour of their apparel, and above all, this speech dissipated every remaining doubt of Madame's, and she was giving orders for refreshments to be set before them, when La Motte, who had listened, and was now convinced he had nothing to fear, entered the apartment.

He advanced towards the Marquis with a complacent air; but as he would have spoke, the words of welcome faltered on his lips, his limbs trembled, and a ghastly paleness overspread his countenance.

The Marquis was little less agitated, and in the first moment of surprise put his hand upon his sword; but recollecting himself, he withdrew it, and endeavoured to obtain a command of features. A pause of agonizing silence ensued. La Motte made some motion towards the door, but his agitated frame refused to support him, and he sunk into a chair, silent and exhausted. The horror of his countenance, together with his whole behaviour, excited the utmost surprise in Madame, whose eyes inquired of the Marquis more than he thought proper to answer: his look increased instead of explaining the mystery, and expressed a mixture of emotions which she could not analyze. Meanwhile she endeavoured to soothe and revive her husband; but he repressed her efforts, and, averting his face, covered it with his hands.

The Marquis seeming to recover his presence of mind, stepped to the door of the hall where his people were assembled, when La Motte, starting from his seat with a frantic air, called on him to return. The Marquis looked back and stopped: but still hesitating whether to proceed, the supplications of Adeline, who was now returned, added to those of La Motte, determined him, and he sat down. I request of you, my Lord, said La Motte, that we may converse for a few moments by ourselves.

The request is bold, and the indulgence perhaps dangerous, said the Marquis: it is more also than I will grant. You can have nothing to say with which your family are not acquainted—speak your purpose and be brief. La Motte's complexion varied to every sentence of this speech. Impossible, my Lord, said he; my lips shall close for ever, ere they pronounced before another human being the words reserved for you alone. I entreat—I supplicate of you a few moments' private discourse. As he pronounced these words, tears swelled into his eyes; and the Marquis, softened by his distress, consented, though with evident emotion and reluctance, to his request.

La Motte took a light and led the Marquis to a small room in a remote part of the edifice, where they remained near an hour. Madame, alarmed by the length of their absence, went in quest of them: as she drew near, a curiosity in such circumstances perhaps not unjustifiable, prompted her to listen. La Motte just then exclaimed—The phrensy of despair!—some words followed, delivered in a low tone, which she could not understand. I have suffered more than I can express, continued he; the same image has pursued me in my midnight dream and in my daily wanderings. There is no punishment, short of death, which I would not have endured to regain the state of mind with which I entered this forest. I again address myself to your compassion.

A loud gust of wind that burst along the passage where Madame La Motte stood, overpowered his voice and that of the Marquis, who spoke in reply: but she soon after distinguished these words,—To-morrow, my Lord, if you return to these ruins, I will lead you to the spot.

That is scarcely necessary, and may be dangerous, said the Marquis. From you, my Lord, I can excuse these doubts, resumed La Motte; but I will swear whatever you shall propose. Yes, continued he, whatever may be the consequence, I will swear to submit to your decree! The rising tempest again drowned the sound of their voices, and Madame La Motte vainly endeavoured to hear those words upon which probably hung the explanation of this mysterious conduct. They now moved towards the door, and she retreated with precipitation to the apartment where she had left Adeline with Louis and the young chevalier.

Hither the Marquis and La Motte soon followed, the first haughty and cool, the latter somewhat more composed than before, though the impression of horror was not yet faded from his countenance. The Marquis passed on to the hall where his retinue awaited; the storm was not yet subsided, but he seemed impatient to be gone, and ordered his people to be in readiness. La Motte observed a sullen silence, frequently pacing the room with hasty steps, and sometimes lost in reverie. Meanwhile the Marquis, seating himself by Adeline, directed to her his whole attention, except when sudden fits of absence came over his mind and suspended him in silence: at these times the young chevalier addressed Adeline, who with diffidence and some agitation shrunk from the observance of both.

The Marquis had been near two hours at the abbey, and the tempest still continuing, Madame La Motte offered him a bed. A look from her husband made her tremble for the consequence. Her offer was however politely declined, the Marquis being evidently as impatient to be gone, as his tenant appeared distressed by his presence. He often returned to the hall, and from the gates raised a look of impatience to the clouds. Nothing was to be seen through the darkness of night—nothing heard but the howlings of the storm.

The morning dawned before he departed. As he was preparing to leave the abbey, La Motte again drew him aside, and held him for a few moments in close conversation. His impassioned gestures, which Madame La Motte observed from a remote part of the room, added to her curiosity a degree of wild apprehension, derived from the obscurity of the subject. Her endeavour to distinguish the corresponding words was baffled by the low voice in which they were uttered.

The Marquis and his retinue at length departed; and La Motte, having himself fastened the gates, silently and dejectedly withdrew to his chamber. The moment they were alone, Madame seized the opportunity of entreating her husband to explain the scene she had witnessed. Ask me no questions, said La Motte sternly, for I will answer none. I have already forbidden your speaking to me on this subject.

What subject? said his wife. La Motte seemed to recollect himself—No matter—I was mistaken—I thought you had repeated these questions before.

Ah! said Madame La Motte, it is then as I suspected; your former melancholy and the distress of this night have the same cause.

And why should you either suspect or inquire? Am I always to be persecuted with conjectures?

Pardon me, I meant not to persecute you; but my anxiety for your welfare will not suffer me to rest under this dreadful uncertainty. Let me claim the privilege of a wife, and share the affliction which oppresses you. Deny me not.—La Motte interrupted her,

Whatever may be the cause of the emotions which you have witnessed, I swear that I will not now reveal it. A time may come when I shall no longer judge concealment necessary; till then be silent, and desist from importunity; above all, forbear to remark to any one what you may have seen uncommon in me, bury your surmise in your own bosom, as you would avoid my curse and my destruction. The determined air with which he spoke this, while his countenance was overspread with a livid hue, made his wife shudder; and she forbore all reply.

Madame La Motte retired to bed, but not to rest. She ruminated on the past occurrence; and her surprise and curiosity concerning the words and behaviour of her husband were but more strongly stimulated by reflection. One truth, however, appeared: she could not doubt but the mysterious conduct of La Motte, which had for so many months oppressed her with anxiety, and the late scene with the Marquis, originated from the same cause. This belief, which seemed to prove how unjustly she had suspected Adeline, brought with it a pang of self-accusation. She looked forward to the morrow, which would lead the Marquis again to the abbey, with impatience. Wearied nature at length resumed her rights, and yielded a short oblivion of care.

At a late hour the next day the family assembled to breakfast. Each individual of the party appeared silent and abstracted; but very different was the aspect of their features, and still more the complexion of their thoughts. La Motte seemed agitated by impatient fear, yet the sullenness of despair overspread his countenance; a certain wildness in his eye at times expressed the sudden start of horror, and again his features would sink into the gloom of despondency.

Madame La Motte seemed harassed with anxiety; she watched every turn of her husband's countenance, and impatiently awaited the arrival of the Marquis. Louis was composed and thoughtful. Adeline seemed to feel her full share of uneasiness; she had observed the behaviour of La Motte the preceding night with much surprise, and the happy confidence she had hitherto reposed in him was shaken. She feared also, lest the exigency of his circumstances should precipitate him again into the world, and that he would be either unable or unwilling to afford her a shelter beneath his roof.

During breakfast La Motte frequently rose to the window, from whence he cast many an anxious look. His wife understood too well the cause of his impatience, and endeavoured to repress her own. In these intervals Louis attempted by whispers to obtain some information from his father; but La Motte always returned to the table, where the presence of Adeline prevented further discourse.

After breakfast, as he walked upon the lawn, Louis would have joined him, but La Motte peremptorily declared he intended to be alone; and soon after, the Marquis having not yet arrived, proceeded to a greater distance from the abbey.

Adeline retired into their usual working room with Madame La Motte, who affected an air of cheerfulness and even of kindness. Feeling the necessity of offering some reason for the striking agitation of La Motte, and of preventing the surprise which the unexpected appearance of the Marquis would occasion Adeline, if she was left to connect it with his behaviour of the preceding night, she mentioned that the Marquis and La Motte had long been known to each other, and that this unexpected meeting, after an absence of many years, and under circumstances so altered and humiliating on the part of the latter, had occasioned him much painful emotion. This had been heightened by a consciousness that the Marquis had formerly misinterpreted some circumstances in his conduct towards him, which had caused a suspension of their intimacy.

This account did not bring conviction to the mind of Adeline, for it seemed inadequate to the degree of emotion which the Marquis and La Motte had mutually betrayed. Her surprise was excited, and her curiosity awakened by the words, which were meant to delude them both. But she forbore to express her thoughts.

Madame proceeding with her plan, said, the Marquis was now expected, and she hoped whatever differences remained would be perfectly adjusted. Adeline blushed, and endeavouring to reply, her lips faltered. Conscious of this agitation, and of the observance of Madame La Motte, her confusion increased, and her endeavours to suppress served only to heighten it. Still she tried to renew the discourse, and still she found it impossible to collect her thoughts. Shocked lest Madame should apprehend the sentiment which had till this moment been concealed almost from herself, her colour fled, she fixed her eyes on the ground, and for some time found it difficult to respire. Madame La Motte inquired if she was ill; when Adeline, glad of the excuse, withdrew to the indulgence of her own thoughts, which were now wholly engrossed by the expectation of seeing again the young chevalier who had accompanied the Marquis.

As she looked from her room, she saw the Marquis on horseback, with several attendants, advancing at a distance, and she hastened to apprize Madame La Motte of his approach. In a short time, he arrived at the gates, and Madame and Louis went out to receive him, La Motte being not yet returned. He entered the hall, followed by the young chevalier, and accosting Madame with a sort of stately politeness, inquired for La Motte, whom Louis now went to seek.

The Marquis remained for a few minutes silent, and then asked of Madame La Motte how her fair daughter did? Madame understood it was Adeline he meant; and having answered his inquiry, and slightly said that she was not related to them, Adeline, upon some indication of the Marquis's wish, was sent for. She entered the room with a modest blush and a timid air, which seemed to engage all his attention. His compliments she received with a sweet grace; but when the young chevalier approached, the warmth of his manner rendered hers involuntarily more reserved, and she scarcely dared to raise her eyes from the ground, lest they should encounter his.

La Motte now entered and apologized for his absence, which the Marquis noticed only by a slight inclination of his head, expressing at the same time by his looks both distrust and pride. They immediately quitted the abbey together, and the Marquis beckoned his attendants to follow at a distance. La Motte forbad his son to accompany him, but Louis observed he took the way into the thickest part of the forest. He was lost in a chaos of conjecture concerning this affair, but curiosity and anxiety for his father induced him to follow at some distance.

In the mean time the young stranger, whom the Marquis addressed by the name of Theodore, remained at the abbey with Madame La Motte and Adeline. The former, with all her address, could scarcely conceal her agitation during this interval. She moved involuntary to the door whenever she heard a footstep, and several times she went to the hall door, in order to look into the forest, but as often returned, checked by disappointment; no person appeared. Theodore seemed to address as much of his attention to Adeline as politeness would allow him to withdraw from Madame La Motte. His manners so gentle, yet dignified, insensibly subdued her timidity, and banished her reserve. Her conversation no longer suffered a painful constraint, but gradually disclosed the beauties of her mind, and seemed to produce a mutual confidence. A similarity of sentiment soon appeared; and Theodore, by the impatient pleasure which animated his countenance, seemed frequently to anticipate the thought of Adeline.

To them the absence of the Marquis was short, though long to Madame La Motte, whose countenance brightened when she heard the trampling of horses at the gate.

The Marquis appeared but for a moment, and passed on with La Motte to a private room, where they remained for some time in conference; immediately after which he departed. Theodore took leave of Adeline—who, as well as La Motte and Madame, attended them to the gates—with an expression of tender regret, and often, as he went, looked back upon the abbey, till the intervening branches entirely excluded it from his view.

The transient glow of pleasure diffused over the cheek of Adeline disappeared with the young stranger, and she sighed as she turned into the hall. The image of Theodore pursued her to her chamber; she recollected with exactness every particular of his late conversation—his sentiments so congenial with her own—his manners so engaging—his countenance so animated—so ingenious and so noble, in which manly dignity was blended with the sweetness of benevolence; these, and every other grace, she recollected, and a soft melancholy stole upon her heart. I shall see him no more, said she. A sigh that followed, told her more of her heart than she wished to know. She blushed, and sighed again; and then suddenly recollecting herself, she endeavoured to divert her thoughts to a different subject. La Motte's connection with the Marquis for sometime engaged her attention; but, unable to develop the mystery that attended it, she sought a refuge from her own reflections in the more pleasing ones to be derived from books.

During this time, Louis, shocked and surprised at the extreme distress which his father had manifested upon the first appearance of the Marquis, addressed him upon the subject. He had no doubt that the Marquis was intimately concerned in the event which made it necessary for La Motte to leave Paris, and he spoke his thoughts without disguise, lamenting at the same time the unlucky chance, which had brought him to seek refuge in a place, of all others, the least capable of affording it—the estate of his enemy. La Motte did not contradict this opinion of his son's, and joined in lamenting the evil fate which had conducted him thither.

The term of Louis's absence from his regiment was now nearly expired, and he took occasion to express his sorrow that he must soon be obliged to leave his father in circumstances so dangerous as the present. I should leave you, Sir, with less pain, continued he, was I sure I knew the full extent of your misfortunes; at present I am left to conjecture evils which perhaps do not exist. Relieve me, Sir, from this state of painful uncertainty, and suffer me to prove myself worthy of your confidence.

I have already answered you on this subject, said La Motte, and forbad you to renew it: I am now obliged to tell you, I care not how soon you depart, if I am to be subjected to these inquiries. La Motte walked abruptly away, and left his son to doubt and concern.

The arrival of the Marquis had dissipated the jealous fears of Madame La Motte, and she awoke to a sense of her cruelty towards Adeline. When she considered her orphan state—the uniform affection which had appeared in her behaviour—the mildness and patience with which she had borne her injurious treatment, she was shocked, and took an early opportunity of renewing her former kindness. But she could not explain this seeming inconsistency of conduct, without betraying her late suspicions, which she now blushed to remember, nor could she apologize for her former behaviour, without giving this explanation.

She contented herself, therefore, with expressing in her manner the regard which was thus revived. Adeline was at first surprised, but she felt too much pleasure at the change to be scrupulous in inquiring its cause.

But notwithstanding the satisfaction which Adeline received from the revival of Madame La Motte's kindness, her thoughts frequently recurred to the peculiar and forlorn circumstances of her condition. She could not help feeling less confidence than she had formerly done in the friendship of Madame La Motte, whose character now appeared less amiable than her imagination had represented it, and seemed strongly tinctured with caprice. Her thoughts often dwelt upon the strange introduction of the Marquis at the abbey, and on the mutual emotions and apparent dislike of La Motte and himself; and under these circumstances, it equally excited her surprise that La Motte should choose, and that the Marquis should permit him, to remain in his territory.

Her mind returned the oftener, perhaps, to this subject, because it was connected with Theodore; but it returned unconscious of the idea which attracted it. She attributed the interest she felt in the affair to her anxiety for the welfare of La Motte, and for her own future destination, which was now so deeply involved in his. Sometimes, indeed, she caught herself busy in conjecture as to the degree of relationship in which Theodore stood to the Marquis; but she immediately checked her thoughts, and severely blamed herself for having suffered them to stray to an object which she perceived was too dangerous to her peace.

CHAPTER VII

Present fearsAre less than horrible imaginings.

A few days after the occurrence related in the preceding chapter, as Adeline was alone in her chamber, she was roused from a reverie by a trampling of horses near the gate; and on looking from the casement she saw the Marquis de Montalt enter the abbey. This circumstance surprised her, and an emotion, whose cause she did not trouble herself to inquire for, made her instantly retreat from the window. The same cause, however, led her thither again as hastily; but the object of her search did not appear, and she was in no haste to retire.

As she stood musing and disappointed, the Marquis came out with La Motte, and immediately looking up, saw Adeline and bowed. She returned his compliment respectfully, and withdrew from the window, vexed at having been seen there. They went into the forest, but the Marquis's attendants did not, as before, follow them thither. When they returned, which was not till after a considerable time, the Marquis immediately mounted his horse and rode away.

For the remainder of the day La Motte appeared gloomy and silent, and was frequently lost in thought. Adeline observed him with particular attention and concern: she perceived that he was always more melancholy after an interview with the Marquis, and was now surprised to hear that the latter had appointed to dine the next day at the abbey.

When La Motte mentioned this, he added some high eulogiums on the character of the Marquis, and particularly praised his generosity and nobleness of soul. At this instant, Adeline recollected the anecdotes she had formerly heard concerning the abbey, and they threw a shadow over the brightness of that excellence which La Motte now celebrated. The account, however, did not appear to deserve much credit; a part of it, as far as a negative will admit of demonstration, having been already proved false; for it had been reported that the abbey was haunted, and no supernatural appearance had ever been observed by the present inhabitants.

Adeline, however, ventured to inquire whether it was the present Marquis of whom those injurious reports had been raised? La Motte answered her with a smile of ridicule: Stories of ghosts and hobgoblins have always been admired and cherished by the vulgar, said he: I am inclined to rely upon my own experience, at least as much as upon the accounts of these peasants; if you have seen any thing to corroborate these accounts, pray inform me of it, that I may establish my faith.

You mistake me, Sir, said she, it was not concerning supernatural agency that I would inquire; I alluded to a different part of the report, which hinted that some person had been confined here by order of the Marquis, who was said to have died unfairly; this was alleged as a reason for the Marquis's having abandoned the abbey.

All the mere coinage of idleness, said La Motte; a romantic tale to excite wonder: to see the Marquis is alone sufficient to refute this; and if we credit half the number of those stories that spring from the same source, we prove ourselves little superior to the simpletons who invent them. Your good sense, Adeline, I think, will teach you the merit of disbelief.

Adeline blushed and was silent; but La Motte's defence of the Marquis appeared much warmer and more diffuse than was consistent with his own disposition, or required by the occasion: his former conversation with Louis occurred to her, and she was the more surprised at what passed at present.

She looked forward to the morrow with a mixture of pain and pleasure: the expectation of seeing again the young chevalier occupying her thoughts, and agitating them with a various emotion:—now she feared his presence, and now she doubted whether he would come. At length she observed this, and blushed to find how much he engaged her attention. The morrow arrived—the Marquis came—but he came alone; and the sunshine of Adeline's mind was clouded, though she was able to wear her usual air of cheerfulness. The Marquis was polite, affable, and attentive: to manners the most easy and elegant, was added the last refinement of polished life. His conversation was lively, amusing, sometimes even witty, and discovered great knowledge of the world; or, what is often mistaken for it, an acquaintance with the higher circles, and with the topics of the day.

Here La Motte was also qualified to converse with him, and they entered into a discussion of the characters and manners of the age with great spirit and some humour. Madame La Motte had not seen her husband so cheerful since they left Paris, and sometimes she could almost fancy she was there. Adeline listened, till the cheerfulness which she had at first only assumed became real. The address of the Marquis was so insinuating and affable, that her reserve insensibly gave way before it, and her natural vivacity resumed its long-lost empire.

At parting, the Marquis told La Motte he rejoiced at having found so agreeable a neighbour. La Motte bowed. I shall sometimes visit you, continued he, and I lament that I cannot at present invite Madame La Motte and her fair friend to my chateau; but it is undergoing some repairs, which make it but an uncomfortable residence.

The vivacity of La Motte disappeared with his guest, and he soon relapsed into fits of silence and abstraction. The Marquis is a very agreeable man, said Madame La Motte. Very agreeable, replied he. And seems to have an excellent heart, she resumed. An excellent one, said La Motte.

You seem discomposed, my dear; what has disturbed you?

Not in the least—I was only thinking, that with such agreeable talents and such an excellent heart, it was a pity the Marquis should—

What? my dear, said Madame with impatience. That the Marquis should—should suffer this abbey to fall into ruins, replied La Motte.

Is that all? said Madame with disappointment.—That is all, upon my honour, said La Motte, and left the room.

Adeline's spirits, no longer supported by the animated conversation of the Marquis, sunk into languor, and when he departed she walked pensively into the forest. She followed a little romantic path that wound along the margin of the stream and was overhung with deep shades. The tranquillity of the scenes which autumn now touched with her sweetest tints, softened her mind to a tender kind of melancholy; and she suffered a tear, which she knew not wherefore had stolen into her eye, to tremble there unchecked. She came to a little lonely recess formed by high trees; the wind sighed mournfully among the branches, and as it waved their lofty heads scattered their leaves to the ground. She seated herself on a bank beneath, and indulged the melancholy reflections that pressed on her mind.

O! could I dive into futurity and behold the events which await me! said she; I should perhaps, by constant contemplation, be enabled to meet them with fortitude. An orphan in this wide world—thrown upon the friendship of strangers for comfort, and upon their bounty for the very means of existence, what but evil have I to expect? Alas, my father! how could you thus abandon your child—how leave her to the storms of life—to sink, perhaps, beneath them? alas, I have no friend!

She was interrupted by a rustling among the fallen leaves; she turned her head, and perceiving the Marquis's young friend, arose to depart. Pardon this intrusion, said he, your voice attracted me hither, and your words detained me: my offence, however, brings with it its own punishment; having learned your sorrows—how can I help feeling them myself? would that my sympathy or my suffering could rescue you from them!—He hesitated.—Would that I could deserve the title of your friend, and be thought worthy of it by yourself!

The confusion of Adeline's thoughts could scarcely permit her to reply; she trembled, and gently withdrew her hand, which he had taken while he spoke. You have perhaps heard, Sir, more than is true: I am indeed not happy; but a moment of dejection has made me unjust, and I am less unfortunate than I have represented. When I said I had no friend, I was ungrateful to the kindness of Monsieur and Madame La Motte, who have been more than friends—have been as parents to me.

If so, I honour them, cried Theodore with warmth; and if I did not feel it to be presumption, I would ask why you are unhappy?—But—he paused. Adeline, raising her eyes, saw him gazing upon her with intense and eager anxiety, and her looks were again fixed upon the ground. I have pained you, said Theodore, by an improper request. Can you forgive me, and also when I add, that it was an interest in your welfare which urged my inquiry?

Forgiveness, Sir, it is unnecessary to ask; I am certainly obliged by the compassion you express. But the evening is cold, if you please we will walk towards the abbey. As they moved on, Theodore was for some time silent. At length, It was but lately that I solicited your pardon, said he, and I shall now perhaps have need of it again; but you will do me the justice to believe that I have a strong and indeed a pressing reason to inquire how nearly you are related to Monsieur La Motte.

We are not at all related, said Adeline; but the service he has done me I can never repay, and I hope my gratitude will teach me never to forget it.

Indeed! said Theodore, surprised: and may I ask how long you have known him?

Rather, Sir, let me ask why these questions should be necessary.

You are just, said he, with an air of self-condemnation, my conduct has deserved this reproof; I should have been more explicit. He looked as if his mind was labouring with something which he was unwilling to express. But you know not how delicately I am circumstanced, continued he; yet I will aver that my questions are prompted by the tenderest interest in your happiness—and even by my fears for your safety. Adeline started. I fear you are deceived, said he, I fear there's danger near you.

Adeline stopped, and looking earnestly at him, begged he would explain himself. She suspected that some mischief threatened La Motte; and Theodore continuing silent, she repeated her request. If La Motte is concerned in this danger, said she, let me entreat you to acquaint him with it immediately; he has but too many misfortunes to apprehend.

Excellent Adeline! cried Theodore, that heart must be adamant that would injure you. How shall I hint what I fear is too true, and how forbear to warn you of your danger without—He was interrupted by a step among the trees, and presently after saw La Motte cross into the path they were in. Adeline felt confused at being thus seen with the chevalier, and was hastening to join La Motte; but Theodore detained her, and entreated a moment's attention. There is now no time to explain myself, said he; yet what I would say is of the utmost consequence to yourself.

Promise, therefore, to meet me in some part of the forest at about this time to-morrow evening; you will then, I hope, be convinced that my conduct is directed neither by common circumstances nor common regard. Adeline shuddered at the idea of making an appointment; she hesitated, and at length entreated Theodore not to delay till to-morrow an explanation which appeared to be so important, but to follow La Motte and inform him of his danger immediately. It is not with La Motte I would speak, replied Theodore; I know of no danger that threatens him—but he approaches, be quick, lovely Adeline, and promise to meet me.

I do promise, said Adeline, with a faltering voice; I will come to the spot where you found me this evening, an hour earlier to-morrow. Saying this, she withdrew her trembling hand, which Theodore had pressed to his lips in token of acknowledgement, and he immediately disappeared.

La Motte now approached Adeline, who, fearing that he had seen Theodore, was in some confusion. Whither is Louis gone so fast? said La Motte. She rejoiced to find his mistake, and suffered him to remain in it. They walked pensively towards the abbey, where Adeline, too much occupied by her own thoughts to bear company, retired to her chamber. She ruminated upon the words of Theodore; and the more she considered them, the more she was perplexed. Sometimes she blamed herself for having made an appointment, doubting whether he had not solicited it for the purpose of pleading a passion; and now delicacy checked this thought, and made her vexed that she had presumed upon having inspired one. She recollected the serious earnestness of his voice and manner when he entreated her to meet him; and as they convinced her of the importance of the subject, she shuddered at a danger which she could not comprehend, looking forward to the morrow with anxious impatience.

Sometimes too a remembrance of the tender interest he had expressed for her welfare, and of his correspondent look and air, would steal across her memory, awakening a pleasing emotion and a latent hope that she was not indifferent to him. From reflections like these she was roused by a summons to supper:—the repast was a melancholy one, it being the last evening of Louis's stay at the abbey. Adeline, who esteemed him, regretted his departure, while his eyes were often bent on her with a look which seemed to express that he was about to leave the object of his affection. She endeavoured by her cheerfulness to reanimate the whole party, and especially Madame La Motte, who frequently shed tears. We shall soon meet again, said Adeline, I trust in happier circumstances. La Motte sighed. The countenance of Louis brightened at her words. Do you wish it? said he with peculiar emphasis. Most certainly I do, she replied: can you doubt my regard for my best friends?

I cannot doubt any thing that is good of you, said he.

You forget you have left Paris, said La Motte to his son, while a faint smile crossed his face; such a compliment would there be in character with the place—in these solitary woods it is quite outre.

The language of admiration is not always that of compliment, Sir, said Louis. Adeline, willing to change the discourse, asked to what part of France he was going. He replied that his regiment was now at Peronne, and he should go immediately thither. After some mention of indifferent subjects, the family withdrew for the night to their several chambers.

The approaching departure of her son occupied the thoughts of Madame La Motte, and she appeared at breakfast with eyes swollen with weeping. The pale countenance of Louis seemed to indicate that he had rested no better than his mother. When breakfast was over, Adeline retired for a while, that she might not interrupt by her presence their last conversation. As she walked on the lawn before the abbey, she returned in thought to the occurrence of yesterday evening, and her impatience for the appointed interview increased. She was soon joined by Louis. It was unkind of you to leave us, said he, in the last moments of my stay. Could I hope that you would sometimes remember me when I am far away, I should depart with less sorrow. He then expressed his concern at leaving her: and though he had hitherto armed himself with resolution to forbear a direct avowal of an attachment, which must be fruitless, his heart now yielded to the force of passion, and he told what Adeline every moment feared to hear.

This declaration, said Adeline, endeavouring to overcome the agitation it excited, gives me inexpressible concern.

O, say not so! interrupted Louis, but give me some slender hope to support me in the miseries of absence. Say that you do not hate me—Say—

That I do most readily say, replied Adeline in a tremulous voice; if it will give you pleasure to be assured of my esteem and friendship—receive this assurance:—as the son of my best benefactors, you are entitled to——

Name not benefits, said Louis, your merits outrun them all: and suffer me to hope for a sentiment less cool than that of friendship, as well as to believe that I do not owe your approbation of me to the actions of others. I have long borne my passion in silence, because I foresaw the difficulties that would attend it; nay, I have even dared to endeavour to overcome it: I have dared to believe it possible—forgive the supposition, that I could forget you—and——

You distress me, interrupted Adeline; this is a conversation which I ought not to hear. I am above disguise, and therefore assure you that, though your virtues will always command my esteem, you have nothing to hope from my love. Were it even otherwise, our circumstances would effectually decide for us. If you are really my friend, you will rejoice that I am spared this struggle between affection and prudence. Let me hope, also, that time will teach you to reduce love within the limits of friendship.

Never, cried Louis vehemently: were this possible, my passion would be unworthy of its object. While he spoke, Adeline's favourite fawn came bounding towards her. This circumstance affected Louis even to tears. This little animal, said he, after a short pause, first conducted me to you: it was witness to that happy moment when I first saw you surrounded by attractions too powerful for my heart; that moment is now fresh in my memory, and the creature comes even to witness this sad one of my departure. Grief interrupted his utterance.

When he recovered his voice, he said, Adeline! when you look upon your little favourite and caress it, remember the unhappy Louis, who will then be far—far from you. Do not deny me the poor consolation of believing this!

I shall not require such a monitor to remind me of you, said Adeline with a smile; your excellent parents and your own merits have sufficient claim upon my remembrance. Could I see your natural good sense resume its influence over passion, my satisfaction would equal my esteem for you.

Do not hope it, said Louis, nor will I wish it; for passion here is virtue. As he spoke he saw La Motte turning round an angle of the abbey. The moments are precious, said he, I am interrupted. O! Adeline, farewell! and say that you will sometimes think of me.

Farewell, said Adeline, who was affected by his distress—farewell! and peace attend you. I will think of you with the affection of a sister.—He sighed deeply and pressed her hand; when La Motte, winding round another projection of the ruin, again appeared. Adeline left them together, and withdrew to her chamber, oppressed by the scene. Louis's passion and her esteem were too sincere not to inspire her with a strong degree of pity for his unhappy attachment. She remained in her chamber till he had quitted the abbey, unwilling to subject him or herself to the pain of a formal parting.

As evening and the hour of appointment drew nigh, Adeline's impatience increased; yet when the time arrived, her resolution failed, and she faltered from her purpose. There was something of indelicacy and dissimulation in an appointed interview on her part, that shocked her. She recollected the tenderness of Theodore's manner, and several little circumstances which seemed to indicate that his heart was not unconcerned in the event. Again she was inclined to doubt whether he had not obtained her consent to this meeting upon some groundless suspicion; and she almost determined not to go: yet it was possible Theodore's assertion might be sincere, and her danger real; the chance of this made her delicate scruples appear ridiculous; she wondered that she had for a moment suffered them to weigh against so serious an interest, and blaming herself for the delay they had occasioned, hastened to the place of appointment.

The little path which led to this spot, was silent and solitary, and when she reached the recess Theodore had not arrived. A transient pride made her unwilling he should find that she was more punctual to his appointment than himself; and she turned from the recess into a track which wound among the trees to the right. Having walked some way without seeing any person or hearing a footstep, she returned; but he was not come, and she again left the place. A second time she came back, and Theodore was still absent. Recollecting the time at which she had quitted the abbey, she grew uneasy, and calculated that the hour appointed was now much exceeded. She was offended and perplexed; but she seated herself on the turf, and was resolved to wait the event. After remaining here till the fall of twilight in fruitless expectation, her pride became more alarmed; she feared that he had discovered something of the partiality he had inspired; and believing that he now treated her with purposed neglect, she quitted the place with disgust and self-accusation.

When these emotions subsided, and reason resumed its influence, she blushed for what she termed this childish effervescence of self-love. She recollected, as if for the first time, these words of Theodore: I fear you are deceived, and that some danger is near you. Her judgment now acquitted the offender, and she saw only the friend. The import of these words, whose truth she no longer doubted, again alarmed her. Why did he trouble himself to come from the chateau, on purpose to hint her danger, if he did not wish to preserve her? And if he wished to preserve her, what but necessity could have withheld him from the appointment?

These reflections decided her at once. She resolved to repair on the following day at the same hour to the recess, whither the interest which she believed him to take in her fate would no doubt conduct him in the hope of meeting her. That some evil hovered over her she could not disbelieve, but what it might be she was unable to guess. Monsieur and Madame La Motte were her friends, and who else, removed as she now thought herself, beyond the reach of her father, could injure her? But why did Theodore say she was deceived? She found it impossible to extricate herself from the labyrinth of conjecture, but endeavoured to command her anxiety till the following evening. In the mean time she engaged herself in efforts to amuse Madame La Motte, who required some relief after the departure of her son.

Thus oppressed by her own cares and interested by those of Madame La Motte, Adeline retired to rest. She soon lost her recollection: but it was only to fall into harassed slumbers, such as but too often haunt the couch of the unhappy. At length her perturbed fancy suggested the following dream.

She thought she was in a large old chamber belonging to the abbey, more ancient and desolate, though in part furnished, than any she had yet seen. It was strongly barricadoed, yet no person appeared. While she stood musing and surveying the apartment, she heard a low voice call her; and looking towards the place whence it came, she perceived by the dim light of a lamp a figure stretched on a bed that lay on the floor. The Voice called again; and approaching the bed, she distinctly saw the features of a man who appeared to be dying. A ghastly paleness overspread his countenance, yet there was an expression of mildness and dignity in it, which strongly interested her.

While she looked on him his features changed, and seemed convulsed in the agonies of death. The spectacle shocked her, and she started back; but he suddenly stretched forth his hand, and seizing hers, grasped it with violence: she struggled in terror to disengage herself; and again looking on his face, saw a man who appeared to be about thirty, with the same features, but in full health, and of a most benign countenance. He smiled tenderly upon her, and moved his lips as if to speak, when the floor of the chamber suddenly opened and he sunk from her view. The effort she made to save herself from following awoke her.—This dream had so strongly impressed her fancy, that it was some time before she could overcome the terror it occasioned, or even be perfectly convinced she was in her own apartment. At length, however, she composed herself to sleep; again she fell into a dream.

She thought she was bewildered in some winding passages of the abbey; that it was almost dark, and that she wandered about a considerable time without being able to find a door. Suddenly she heard a bell toll from above, and soon after a confusion of distant voices. She redoubled her efforts to extricate herself. Presently all was still; and at length wearied with the search, she sat down on a step that crossed the passage. She had not been long here when she saw a light glimmer at a distance on the walls; but a turn in the passage, which was very long, prevented her seeing from what it proceeded. It continued to glimmer faintly for some time and then grew stronger, when she saw a man enter the passage habited in a long black cloak like those usually worn by attendants at funerals, and bearing a torch. He called to her to follow him, and led her through a long passage to the foot of a staircase. Here she feared to proceed, and was running back, when the man suddenly turned to pursue her, and with the terror which this occasioned she awoke.

Shocked by these visions, and more so by their seeming connection, which now struck her, she endeavoured to continue awake, lest their terrific images should again haunt her mind: after some time, however, her harassed spirits again sunk into slumber, though not to repose.

She now thought herself in a large old gallery, and saw at one end of it a chamber door standing a little open and a light within: she went towards it, and perceived the man she had before seen, standing at the door and beckoning her towards him. With the inconsistency so common in dreams, she no longer endeavoured to avoid him, but advancing, followed him into a suit of very ancient apartments hung with black and lighted up as if for a funeral. Still he led her on, till she found herself in the same chamber she remembered to have seen in her former dream: a coffin covered with a pall stood at the further end of the room; some lights and several persons surrounded it, who appeared to be in great distress.

Suddenly she thought these persons were all gone, and that she was left alone; that she went up to the coffin, and while she gazed upon it, she heard a voice speak, as if from within, but saw nobody. The man she had before seen, soon after stood by the coffin, and lifting the pall, she saw beneath it a dead person, whom she thought to be the dying chevalier she had seen in her former dream; his features were sunk in death, but they were yet serene. While she looked at him, a stream of blood gushed from his side, and descending to the floor the whole chamber was overflowed; at the same time some words were uttered in a voice she heard before; but the horror of the scene so entirely overcame her, that she started and awoke.

When she had recovered her recollection, she raised herself in the bed, to be convinced it was a dream she had witnessed; and the agitation of her spirits was so great, that she feared to be alone, and almost determined to call Annette. The features of the deceased person, and the chamber where he lay, were strongly impressed upon her memory, and she still thought she heard the voice and saw the countenance which her dream represented. The longer she considered these dreams, the more she was surprised; they were so very terrible, returned so often, and seemed to be so connected with each other, that she could scarcely think them accidental; yet why they should be supernatural, she could not tell. She slept no more that night.

CHAPTER VIII

...... When these prodigies Do so conjointly meet, let not men say, These are their reasons; they are natural; For I believe they are portentous things. JULIUS CÆSAR.

When Adeline appeared at breakfast, her harassed and languid countenance struck Madame La Motte, who inquired if she was ill. Adeline, forcing a smile upon her features, said she had not rested well, for that she had had very disturbed dreams: she was about to describe them, but a strong and involuntary impulse prevented her. At the same time La Motte ridiculed her concern so unmercifully, that she was almost ashamed to have mentioned it, and tried to overcome the remembrance of its cause.

After breakfast, she endeavoured to employ her thoughts by conversing with Madame La Motte; but they were really engaged by the incidents of the last two days, the circumstance of her dreams, and her conjectures concerning the information to be communicated to her by Theodore. They had thus sat for some time, when a sound of voices arose from the great gate of the abbey; and on going to the casement, Adeline saw the Marquis and his attendants on the lawn below. The portal of the abbey concealed several people from her view, and among these it was possible might be Theodore, who had not yet appeared: she continued to look for him with great anxiety, till the Marquis entered the hall with La Motte and some other persons, soon after which Madame went to receive him, and Adeline retired to her own apartment.

A message from La Motte, however, soon called her to join the party, where she vainly hoped to find Theodore. The Marquis arose as she approached, and, having paid her some general compliments, the conversation took a very lively turn. Adeline, finding it impossible to counterfeit cheerfulness while her heart was sinking with anxiety and disappointment, took little part in it: Theodore was not once named. She would have asked concerning him, had it been possible to inquire with propriety; but she was obliged to content herself with hoping, first, that he would arrive before dinner, and then before the departure of the Marquis.

Thus the day passed in expectation and disappointment. The evening was now approaching, and she was condemned to remain in the presence of the Marquis, apparently listening to a conversation which, in truth, she scarcely heard, while the opportunity was perhaps escaping that would decide her fate. She was suddenly relieved from this state of torture, and thrown into one, if possible, still more distressing.

The Marquis inquired for Louis, and being informed of his departure, mentioned that Theodore Peyrou had that morning set out for his regiment in a distant province. He lamented the loss he should sustain by his absence; and expressed some very flattering praise of his talents. The shock of this intelligence overpowered the long-agitated spirits of Adeline: the blood forsook her cheeks, and a sudden faintness came over her, from which she recovered only to a consciousness of having discovered her emotion, and the danger of relapsing into a second fit.

She retired to her chamber, where being once more alone, her oppressed heart found relief from tears, in which she freely indulged. Ideas crowded so fast upon her mind, that it was long ere she could arrange them so as to produce any thing like reasoning.

She endeavoured to account for the abrupt departure of Theodore. Is it possible, said she, that he should take an interest in my welfare, and yet leave me exposed to the full force of a danger which he himself foresaw? Or am I to believe that he has trifled with my simplicity for an idle frolic, and has now left me to the wondering apprehension he has raised? Impossible! a countenance so noble, and a manner so amiable, could never disguise a heart capable of forming so despicable a design. No!—whatever is reserved for me, let me not relinquish the pleasure of believing that he is worthy of my esteem.

She was awakened from thoughts like these by a peal of distant thunder, and now perceived that the gloominess of evening was deepened by the coming storm; it rolled onward, and soon after the lightning began to flash along the chamber. Adeline was superior to the affectation of fear, and was not apt to be terrified; but she now felt it unpleasant to be alone, and hoping that the Marquis might have left the abby, she went down to the sitting-room: but the threatening aspect of the heavens had hitherto detained him, and now the evening tempest made him rejoice that he had not quitted a shelter. The storm continued, and night came on. La Motte pressed his guest to take a bed at the abbey, and he at length consented; a circumstance which threw Madame La Motte into some perplexity as to the accommodation to be afforded him. After some time she arranged the affair to her satisfaction; resigning her own apartment to the Marquis, and that of Louis to two of his superior attendants; Adeline, it was further settled, should give up her room to Monsieur and Madame La Motte, and to remove to an inner chamber, where a small bed, usually occupied by Annette, was placed for her.

At supper the Marquis was less gay than usual; he frequently addressed Adeline, and his look and manner seemed to express the tender interest which her indisposition, for she still appeared pale and languid, had excited. Adeline, as usual, made an effort to forget her anxiety and appear happy: but the veil of assumed cheerfulness was too thin to conceal the features of sorrow; and her feeble smiles only added a peculiar softness to her air. The Marquis conversed with her on a variety of subjects, and displayed an elegant mind. The observations of Adeline, which, when called upon, she gave with reluctant modesty, in words at once simple and forceful, seemed to excite his admiration, which he sometimes betrayed by an inadvertent expression.

Adeline retired early to her room, which adjoined on one side to Madame La Motte's, and on the other to the closet formerly mentioned. It was spacious and lofty, and what little furniture it contained was falling to decay; but perhaps the present tone of her spirits might contribute more than these circumstances to give that air of melancholy which seemed to reign in it. She was unwilling to go to bed, lest the dreams that had lately pursued her should return; and determined to sit up till she found herself oppressed by sleep, when it was probable her rest would be profound. She placed the light on a small table, and taking a book, continued to read for above an hour, till her mind refused any longer to abstract itself from its own cares, and she sat for some time leaning pensively on her arm.

The wind was high, and as it whistled through the desolate apartment, and shook the feeble doors, she often started, and sometimes even thought she heard sighs between the pauses of the gust; but she checked these illusions, which the hour of the night and her own melancholy imagination conspired to raise. As she sat musing, her eyes fixed on the opposite wall, she perceived the arras, with which the room was hung, wave backwards and forwards; she continued to observe it for some minutes, and then rose to examine it further. It was moved by the wind; and she blushed at the momentary fear it had excited; but she observed that the tapestry was more strongly agitated in one particular place than elsewhere, and a noise that seemed something more than that of the wind issued thence. The old bedstead, which La Motte had found in this apartment, had been removed to accommodate Adeline, and it was behind the place where this had stood, that the wind seemed to rush with particular force: curiosity prompted her to examine still further; she felt about the tapestry, and perceiving the wall behind shake under her hand, she lifted the arras, and discovered a small door, whose loosened hinges admitted the wind, and occasioned the noise she had heard.

The door was held only by a bolt, having undrawn which, and brought the light, she descended by a few steps into another chamber; she instantly remembered her dreams. The chamber was not much like that in which she had seen the dying chevalier, and afterwards the bier; but it gave her a confused remembrance of one through which she had passed. Holding up the light to examine it more fully, she was convinced by its structure that it was part of the ancient foundation. A shattered casement, placed high from the floor, seemed to be the only opening to admit light. She observed a door on the opposite side of the apartment; and after some moments of hesitation gained courage, and determined to pursue the inquiry. A mystery seems to hang over these chambers, said she, which it is perhaps my lot to develop; I will at least see to what that door leads.

She stepped forward, and having unclosed it, proceeded with faltering steps along a suite of apartments, resembling the first in style and condition, and terminating in one exactly like that where her dream had represented the dying person; the remembrance struck so forcibly upon her imagination, that she was in danger of fainting; and looking round the room, almost expected to see the phantom of her dream.

Unable to quit the place, she sat down on some old lumber to recover herself, while her spirits were nearly overcome by a superstitious dread, such as she had never felt before. She wondered to what part of the abbey these chambers belonged, and that they had so long escaped detection. The casements were all too high to afford any information from without. When she was sufficiently composed to consider the direction of the rooms and the situation of the abbey, there appeared not a doubt that they formed an interior part of the original building.

As these reflections passed over her mind, a sudden gleam of moonlight fell upon some object without the casement. Being now sufficiently composed to wish to pursue the inquiry, and believing this object might afford her some means of learning the situation of these rooms, she combated her remaining terrors; and in order to distinguish it more clearly, removed the light to an outer chamber; but before she could return, a heavy cloud was driven over the face of the moon, and all without was perfectly dark; she stood for some moments waiting a returning gleam, but the obscurity continued. As she went softly back for the light, her foot stumbled over something on the floor; and while she stooped to examine it, the moon again shone, so that she could distinguish through the casement, the eastern towers of the abbey. This discovery confirmed her former conjectures concerning the interior situation of these apartments. The obscurity of the place prevented her discovering what it was that had impeded her steps, but having brought the light forward, she perceived on the floor an old dagger: with a trembling hand she took it up, and upon a closer view perceived that it was spotted and stained with rust.

Shocked and surprised, she looked round the room for some object that might confirm or destroy the dreadful suspicion which now rushed upon her mind; but she saw only a great chair with broken arms, that stood in one corner of the room, and a table in a condition equally shattered, except that in another part lay a confused heap of things, which appeared to be old lumber. She went up to it, and perceived a broken bedstead, with some decayed remnants of furniture, covered with dust and cobwebs, and which seemed indeed as if they had not been moved for many years. Desirous, however, of examining further, she attempted to raise what appeared to have been part of the bedstead; but it slipped from her hand, and, rolling to the floor, brought with it some of the remaining lumber. Adeline started aside and saved herself; and when the noise it made had ceased, she heard a small rustling sound, and as she was about to leave the chamber, saw something falling gently among the lumber.

It was a small roll of paper, tied with a string, and covered with dust. Adeline took it up, and on opening it perceived a hand writing. She attempted to read it, but the part of the manuscript she looked at was so much obliterated, that she found this difficult, though what few words were legible impressed her with curiosity and terror, and induced her to return with it immediately to her chamber.

Having reached her own room, she fastened the private door, and let the arras fall over it as before. It was now midnight. The stillness of the hour, interrupted only at intervals by the hollow sighings of the blast, heightened the solemnity of Adeline's feelings. She wished she was not alone, and before she proceeded to look into the manuscript, listened whether Madame La Motte was yet in her chamber:—not the least sound was heard, and she gently opened the door. The profound silence within almost convinced her that no person was there; but willing to be further satisfied, she brought the light and found the room empty. The lateness of the hour made her wonder that Madame La Motte was not in her chamber, and she proceeded to the top of the tower stairs, to hearken if any person was stirring.

She heard the sound of voices from below, and, amongst the rest, that of La Motte speaking in his usual tone. Being now satisfied that all was well, she turned towards her room, when she heard the Marquis pronounce her name with very unusual emphasis. She paused. I adore her, pursued he, and by Heaven—He was interrupted by La Motte, my Lord, remember your promise.

I do, replied the Marquis, and I will abide by it. But we trifle. To-morrow I will declare myself, and I shall then know both what to hope and how to act. Adeline trembled so excessively, that she could scarcely support herself: she wished to return to her chamber; yet she was too much interested in the words she had heard, not to be anxious to have them more fully explained. There was an interval of silence, after which they conversed in a lower tone. Adeline remembered the hints of Theodore, and determined, if possible, to be relieved from the terrible suspense she now suffered. She stole softly down a few steps, that she might catch the accents of the speakers, but they were so low that she could only now and then distinguish a few words. Her father, say you?

said the Marquis. Yes, my Lord, her father. I am well informed of what I say. Adeline shuddered at the mention of her father, a new terror seized her, and with increasing eagerness she endeavoured to distinguish their words, but for some time found this to be impossible. Here is no time to be lost, said the Marquis, to-morrow then.—She heard La Motte rise, and believing it was to leave the room, she hurried up the steps, and having reached her chamber, sunk almost lifeless in a chair.

It was her father only of whom she thought. She doubted not that he had pursued and discovered her retreat; and though this conduct appeared very inconsistent with his former behaviour in abandoning her to strangers, her fears suggested that it would terminate in some new cruelty. She did not hesitate to pronounce this the danger of which Theodore had warned her; but it was impossible to surmise how he had gained his knowledge of it, or how he had become sufficiently acquainted with her story, except through La Motte, her apparent friend and protector, whom she was thus, though unwillingly, led to suspect of treachery. Why, indeed, should La Motte conceal from her only his knowledge of her father's intention, unless he designed to deliver her into his hands? Yet it was long ere she could bring herself to believe this conclusion possible. To discover depravity in those whom we have loved, is one of the most exquisite tortures to a virtuous mind, and the conviction is often rejected before it is finally admitted.

The words of Theodore, which told her he was fearful she was deceived, confirmed this most painful apprehension of La Motte, with another yet more distressing, that Madame La Motte was also united against her. This thought, for a moment, subdued terror and left her only grief; she wept bitterly. Is this human nature? cried she. Am I doomed to find every body deceitful? An unexpected discovery of vice in those whom we have admired, inclines us to extend our censure of the individual to the species; we henceforth contemn appearances, and too hastily conclude that no person is to be trusted.

Adeline determined to throw herself at the feet of La Motte on the following morning, and implore his pity and protection. Her mind was now too much agitated by her own interests to permit her to examine the manuscripts, and she sat musing in her chair till she heard the steps of Madame La Motte, when she retired to bed. La Motte soon after came up to his chamber; and Adeline, the mild, persecuted Adeline, who had now passed two days of torturing anxiety, and one night of terrific visions, endeavoured to compose her mind to sleep. In the present state of her spirits she quickly caught alarm, and she had scarcely fallen into a slumber when she was roused by a loud and uncommon noise. She listened, and thought the sound came from the apartments below, but in a few minutes there was a hasty knocking at the door of La Motte's chamber.

La Motte, who had just fallen asleep, was not easily to be roused; but the knocking increased with such violence, that Adeline, extremely terrified, arose and went to the door that opened from her chamber into his, with a design to call him. She was stopped by the voice of the Marquis, which she now clearly distinguished at the door. He called to La Motte to rise immediately; and Madame La Motte endeavoured at the same time to rouse her husband, who at length awoke in much alarm, and soon after joining the Marquis, they went down stairs together. Adeline now dressed herself, as well as her trembling hands would permit, and went into the adjoining chamber, where she found Madame La Motte extremely surprised and terrified.

The Marquis in the mean time told La Motte, with great agitation, that he recollected having appointed some persons to meet him upon business of importance early in the morning, and it was therefore necessary for him to set off for his chateau immediately. As he said this, and desired that his servants might be called, La Motte could not help observing the ashy paleness of his countenance, or expressing some apprehension that his Lordship was ill. The Marquis assured him he was perfectly well, but desired that he might set out immediately. Peter was now ordered to call the other servants, and the Marquis having refused to take any refreshment, bade La Motte a hasty adieu, and as soon as his people were ready left the abbey.

La Motte returned to his chamber, musing on the abrupt departure of his guest, whose emotion appeared much too strong to proceed from the cause assigned. He appeased the anxiety of Madame La Motte, and at the same time excited her surprise by acquainting her with the occasion of the late disturbance. Adeline, who had retired from the chamber on the approach of La Motte, looked out from her window on hearing the trampling of horses. It was the Marquis and his people, who just then passed at a little distance. Unable to distinguish who the persons were, she was alarmed at observing such a party about the abbey at that hour, and calling to inform La Motte of the circumstance, was made acquainted with what had passed.

At length she retired to her bed, and her slumbers were this night undisturbed by dreams.

When she arose in the morning, she observed La Motte walking alone in the avenue below, and she hastened to seize the opportunity which now offered of pleading her cause. She approached him with faltering steps, while the paleness and timidity of her countenance discovered the disorder of her mind. Her first words, without entering upon any explanation, implored his compassion. La Motte stopped, and looking earnestly in her face, inquired whether any part of his conduct towards her merited the suspicion which her request implied. Adeline for a moment blushed that she had doubted his integrity, but the words she had overheard returned to her memory.

Your behaviour, Sir, said she, I acknowledge to have been kind and generous, beyond what I had a right to expect, but—and she paused. She knew not how to mention what she blushed to believe. La Motte continued to gaze on her in silent expectation, and at length desired her to proceed and explain her meaning. She entreated that he would protect her from her father. La Motte looked surprised and confused. Your father! said he. Yes, Sir, replied Adeline; I am not ignorant that he has discovered my retreat: I have every thing to dread from a parent who has treated me with such cruelty as you was witness of; and I again implore that you will save me from his hands.

La Motte stood fixed in thought, and Adeline continued her endeavours to interest his pity. What reason have you to suppose, or rather how have you learned, that your father pursues you? The question confused Adeline, who blushed to acknowledge that she had overheard his discourse, and disdained to invent or utter a falsity: at length she confessed the truth. The countenance of La Motte instantly changed to a savage fierceness, and, sharply rebuking her for a conduct to which she had been rather tempted by chance than prompted by design, he inquired what she had overheard that could so much alarm her. She faithfully repeated the substance of the incoherent sentences that had met her ear;—while she spoke, he regarded her with a fixed attention. And was this all you heard? Is it from these few words that you draw such a positive conclusion? Examine them, and you will find they do not justify it.

She now perceived, what the fervour of her fears had not permitted her to observe before, that the words, unconnectedly as she heard them, imported little, and that her imagination had filled up the void in the sentences, so as to suggest the evil apprehended. Notwithstanding this, her fears were little abated. Your apprehensions are, doubtless, now removed, resumed La Motte; but to give you a proof of the sincerity which you have ventured to question, I will tell you they were just. You seem alarmed, and with reason. Your father has discovered your residence, and has already demanded you. It is true, that from a motive of compassion I have refused to resign you, but I have neither authority to withhold nor means to defend you. When he comes to enforce his demand, you will perceive this. Prepare yourself, therefore, for the evil, which you see is inevitable.

Adeline for some time could speak only by her tears. At length, with a fortitude which despair had roused, she said, I resign myself to the will of Heaven! La Motte gazed on her in silence, and a strong emotion appeared in his countenance. He forbore, however, to renew the discourse, and withdrew to the abbey, leaving Adeline in the avenue, absorbed in grief.

A summons to breakfast hastened her to the parlour, where she passed the morning in conversation with Madame La Motte, to whom she told all her apprehensions, and expressed all her sorrow. Pity and superficial consolation were all that Madame La Motte could offer, though apparently much affected by Adeline's discourse. Thus the hours passed heavily away, while the anxiety of Adeline continued to increase, and the moment of her fate seemed fast approaching. Dinner was scarcely over, when Adeline was surprised to see the Marquis arrive. He entered the room with his usual ease, and apologizing for the disturbance he had occasioned on the preceding night, repeated what he had before told La Motte.

The remembrance of the conversation she had overheard at first gave Adeline some confusion, and withdrew her mind from a sense of the evils to be apprehended from her father. The Marquis, who was, as usual, attentive to Adeline, seemed affected by her apparent indisposition, and expressed much concern for that dejection of spirits which, notwithstanding every effort, her manner betrayed. When Madame La Motte withdrew, Adeline would have followed her; but the Marquis entreated a few moments' attention, and led her back to her seat. La Motte immediately disappeared.

Adeline knew too well what would be the purport of the Marquis's discourse, and his words soon increased the confusion which her fears had occasioned. While he was declaring the ardour of his passion in such terms as but too often make vehemence pass for sincerity, Adeline, to whom this declaration, if honourable, was distressing, and if dishonourable, was shocking, interrupted him and thanked him for the offer of a distinction which, with a modest but determined air, she said she must refuse. She rose to withdraw. Stay, too lovely Adeline! said he, and if compassion for my sufferings will not interest you in my favour, allow a consideration of your own dangers to do so. Monsieur La Motte has informed me of your misfortunes, and of the evil that now threatens you; accept from me the protection which he cannot afford.

Adeline continued to move towards the door, when the Marquis threw himself at her feet, and seizing her hand, impressed it with kisses. She struggled to disengage herself. Hear me, charming Adeline! hear me, cried the Marquis; I exist but for you. Listen to my entreaties, and my fortune shall be yours. Do not drive me to despair by ill-judged rigour, or, because—

My Lord, interrupted Adeline with an air of ineffable dignity, and still affecting to believe his proposal honourable, I am sensible of the generosity of your conduct, and also flattered by the distinction you offer me; I will therefore say something more than is necessary to a bare expression of the denial which I must continue to give. I can not bestow my heart. You can not obtain more than my esteem, to which, indeed, nothing can so much contribute as a forbearance from any similar offers in future.

She again attempted to go, but the Marquis prevented her; and, after some hesitation, again urged his suit, though in terms that would no longer allow her to misunderstand him. Tears swelled into her eyes, but she endeavoured to check them; and with a look in which grief and indignation seemed to struggle for pre-eminence, she said, My Lord, this is unworthy of reply; let me pass.

For a moment he was awed by the dignity of her manner, and he threw himself at her feet to implore forgiveness. But she waved her hand in silence, and hurried from the room. When she reached her chamber she locked the door, and, sinking into a chair, yielded to the sorrow that pressed at her heart. And it was not the least of her sorrow to suspect that La Motte was unworthy of her confidence; for it was almost impossible that he could be ignorant of the real designs of the Marquis. Madame La Motte, she believed, was imposed upon by a specious pretence of honourable attachment; and thus was she spared the pang which a doubt of her integrity would have added.

She threw a trembling glance upon the prospect around her. On one side was her father, whose cruelty had already been but too plainly manifested; and on the other, the Marquis pursuing her with insult and vicious passion. She resolved to acquaint Madame La Motte with the purport of the late conversation; and, in the hope of her protection and sympathy, she wiped away her tears, and was leaving the room just as Madame La Motte entered it. While Adeline related what had passed, her friend wept, and appeared to suffer great agitation. She endeavoured to comfort her, and promised to use her influence in persuading La Motte to prohibit the addressee of the Marquis. You know, my dear, added Madame, that our present circumstances oblige us to preserve terms with the Marquis, and you will therefore suffer as little resentment to appear in your manner towards him as possible; conduct yourself with your usual ease in his presence, and I doubt not this affair will pass over without subjecting you to further solicitation.

Ah, Madam! said Adeline, how hard is the task you assign me! I entreat you that I may never more be subjected to the humiliation of being in his presence,—that, whenever he visits the abbey, I may be suffered to remain in my chamber.

This, said Madame La Motte, I would most readily consent to, would our situation permit it. But you well know our asylum in this abbey depends upon the good-will of the Marquis, which we must not wantonly lose; and surely such a conduct as you propose would endanger this. Let us use milder measures, and we shall preserve his friendship without subjecting you to any serious evil. Appear with your usual complaisance: the task is not so difficult as you imagine.

Adeline sighed. I obey you, Madam, said she; it is my duty to do so: but I may be pardoned for saying—it is with extreme reluctance. Madame La Motte promised to go immediately to her husband; and Adeline departed, though not convinced of her safety, yet somewhat more at ease.

She soon after saw the Marquis depart; and as there now appeared to be no obstacle to the return of Madame La Motte, she expected her with extreme impatience. After thus waiting near an hour in her chamber, she was at length summoned to the parlour, and there found Monsieur La Motte alone. He arose upon her entrance, and for some minutes paced the room in silence. He then seated himself, and addressed her: What you have mentioned to Madame La Motte, said he, would give me much concern, did I consider the behaviour of the Marquis in a light so serious as she does. I know that young ladies are apt to misconstrue the unmeaning gallantry of fashionable manners; and you, Adeline, can never be too cautious in distinguishing between a levity of this kind and a more serious address.

Adeline was surprised and offended that La Motte should think so lightly both of her understanding and disposition as his speech implied. Is it possible, Sir, said she, that you have been apprized of the Marquis's conduct?

It is very possible, and very certain, replied La Motte with some asperity; and very possible, also, that I may see this affair with a judgment less discoloured by prejudice than you do. But, however, I shall not dispute this point; I shall only request that, since you are acquainted with the emergency of my circumstances, you will conform to them, and not, by an ill-timed resentment, expose me to the enmity of the Marquis. He is now my friend, and it is necessary to my safety that he should continue such; but if I suffer any part of my family to treat him with rudeness, I must expect to see him my enemy. You may surely treat him with complaisance. Adeline thought the term rudeness a harsh one as La Motte applied it, but she forbore from any expression of displeasure. I could have wished, Sir, said she, for the privilege of retiring whenever the Marquis appeared; but since you believe this conduct would affect your interest, I ought to submit.

This prudence and good-will delights me, said La Motte; and since you wish to serve me, know that you cannot more effectually do it than by treating the Marquis as a friend. The word friend, as it stood connected with the Marquis, sounded dissonantly to Adeline's ear; she hesitated, and looked at La Motte. As your friend, Sir, said she, I will endeavour to—treat him as mine, she would have said, but she found it impossible to finish the sentence. She entreated his protection from the power of her father.

What protection I can afford is yours, said La Motte; but you know how destitute I am both of the right and the means of resisting him, and also how much I require protection myself. Since he has discovered your retreat, he is probably not ignorant of the circumstances which detain me here; and if I oppose him, he may betray me to the officers of the law, as the surest method of obtaining possession of you. We are encompassed with dangers, continued La Motte; would I could see any method of extricating ourselves!

Quit this abbey, said Adeline, and seek an asylum in Switzerland or Germany; you will then be freed from further obligation to the Marquis, and from the persecution you dread. Pardon me for thus offering advice, which is certainly in some degree prompted by a sense of my own safety, but which, at the same time, seems to afford the only means of ensuring yours.

Your plan is reasonable, said La Motte, had I money to execute it. As it is, I must be contented to remain here as little known as possible, and defend myself by making those who know me my friends. Chiefly I must endeavour to preserve the favour of the Marquis: he may do much, should your father even pursue desperate measures. But why do I talk thus? your father may ere this have commenced these measures, and the effects of his vengeance may now be hanging over my head. My regard for you, Adeline, has exposed me to this; had I resigned you to his will, I should have remained secure.

Adeline was so much affected by this instance of La Motte's kindness, which she could not doubt, that she was unable to express her sense of it. When she could speak, she uttered her gratitude in the most lively terms.—Are you sincere in these expressions? said La Motte.

Is it possible I can be less than sincere? replied Adeline, weeping at the idea of ingratitude.—Sentiments are easily pronounced, said La Motte, though they may have no connection with the heart; I believe them to be sincere so far only as they influence our actions.

What mean you, Sir? said Adeline with surprise.

I mean to inquire whether, if an opportunity should ever offer of thus proving your gratitude, you would adhere to your sentiments?

Name one that I shall refuse, said Adeline with energy.

If, for instance, the Marquis should hereafter avow a serious passion for you, and offer you his hand, would no petty resentment, no lurking prepossession for some more happy lover prompt you to refuse it?

Adeline blushed, and fixed her eyes on the ground. You have, indeed, Sir, named the only means I should reject of evincing my sincerity. The Marquis I can never love, nor, to speak sincerely, ever esteem. I confess the peace of one's whole life is too much to sacrifice even to gratitude.—La Motte looked displeased. 'Tis as I thought, said he; these delicate sentiments make a fine appearance in speech, and render the person who utters them infinitely amiable; but bring them to the test of action, and they dissolve into air, leaving only the wreck of vanity behind.

This unjust sarcasm brought tears to her eyes. Since your safety, Sir, depends upon my conduct, said she, resign me to my father: I am willing to return to him, since my stay here must involve you in new misfortune: let me not prove myself unworthy of the protection I have hitherto experienced, by preferring my own welfare to yours. When I am gone, you will have no reason to apprehend the Marquis's displeasure, which you may probably incur if I stay here; for I feel it impossible that I could even consent to receive his addresses, however honourable were his views.

La Motte seemed hurt and alarmed. This must not be, said he; let us not harass ourselves by stating possible evils, and then, to avoid them, fly to those which are certain. No, Adeline, though you are ready to sacrifice yourself to my safety, I will not suffer you to do so;—I will not yield you to your father but upon compulsion. Be satisfied, therefore, upon this point. The only return I ask, is a civil deportment towards the Marquis.

I will endeavour to obey you, Sir, said Adeline.—Madame La Motte now entered the room, and this conversation ceased. Adeline passed the evening in melancholy thoughts, and retired as soon as possible to her chamber, eager to seek in sleep a refuge from sorrow.

CHAPTER IX

Full many a melancholy nightHe watch'd the slow return of light,And sought the powers of sleep;To spread a momentary calmO'er his sad couch, and in the balmOf bland oblivion's dews his burning eyes to steep.WARTON.

The MS. found by Adeline the preceding night had several times occurred to her recollection in the course of the day; but she had then been either too much interested by the events of the moment, or too apprehensive of interruption, to attempt a perusal of it. She now took it from the drawer in which it had been deposited, and, intending only to look cursorily over the few first pages, sat down with it by her bed-side.

She opened it with an eagerness of inquiry which the discoloured and almost obliterated ink but slowly gratified. The first words on the page were entirely lost, but those that appeared to commence the narrative were as follows:

O! ye, whoever ye are, whom chance or misfortune may hereafter conduct to this spot—to you I speak—to you reveal the story of my wrongs, and ask you to avenge them. Vain hope! yet it imparts some comfort to believe it possible that what I now write may one day meet the eye of a fellow-creature; that the words which tell my sufferings may one day draw pity from the feeling heart.

Yet stay your tears—your pity now is useless: lone since have the pangs of misery ceased; the voice of complaining is passed away. It is weakness to wish for compassion which cannot be felt till I shall sink in the repose of death, and taste, I hope, the happiness of eternity!

Know, then, that on the night of the twelfth of October, in the year 1642, I was arrested on the road to Caux,—and on the very spot where a column is erected to the memory of the immortal Henry,—by four ruffians, who, after disabling my servant, bore me through wilds and woods to this abbey. Their demeanour was not that of common banditti, and I soon perceived they were employed by a superior power to perpetrate some dreadful purpose. Entreaties and bribes were vainly offered them to discover their employer and abandon their design; they would not reveal even the least circumstance of their intentions.

But when, after a long journey, they arrived at this edifice, their base employer was at once revealed, and his horrid scheme but too well understood. What a moment was that! All the thunders of heaven seemed launched at this defenceless head! O! fortitude! nerve my heart to——

Adeline's light was now expiring in the socket, and the paleness of the ink, so feebly shone upon, baffled her efforts to discriminate the letters: it was impossible to procure a light from below, without discovering that she was yet up; a circumstance which would excite surprise, and lead to explanations such as she did not wish to enter upon. Thus compelled to suspend the inquiry, which so many attendant circumstances had rendered awfully interesting, she retired to her humble bed.

What she had read of the MS. awakened a dreadful interest in the fate of the writer, and called up terrific images to her mind. In these apartments!—said she; and she shuddered and closed her eyes. At length she heard Madame La Motte enter her chamber, and the phantoms of fear beginning to dissipate, left her to repose.

In the morning she was awakened by Madame La Motte, and found to her disappointment that she had slept so much beyond her usual time as to be unable to renew the perusal of the MS.—La Motte appeared uncommonly gloomy, and Madame wore an air of melancholy, which Adeline attributed to the concern she felt for her. Breakfast was scarcely over, when the sound of horses' feet announced the arrival of a stranger; and Adeline from the oriel recess of the hall saw the Marquis alight. She retreated with precipitation, and, forgetting the request of La Motte, was hastening to her chamber: but the Marquis was already in the hall; and seeing her leaving it, turned to La Motte with a look of inquiry. La Motte called her back, and by a frown too intelligent reminded her of her promise. She summoned all her spirits to her aid, but advanced, notwithstanding, in visible emotion; while the Marquis addressed her as usual, the same easy gaiety playing upon his countenance and directing his manner.

Adeline was surprised and shocked at this careless confidence; which, however, by awakening her pride, communicated to her an air of dignity that abashed him. He spoke with hesitation, and frequently appeared abstracted from the subject of discourse. At length arising, he begged Adeline would favour him with a few moments' conversation. Monsieur and Madame La Motte were now leaving the room, when Adeline, turning to the Marquis, told him she would not hear any conversation except in the presence of her friends. But she said it in vain, for they were gone; and La Motte, as he withdrew, expressed by his looks how much an attempt to follow would displease him.

She sat for some time in silence and trembling expectation. I am sensible, said the Marquis at length, that the conduct to which the ardour of my passion lately betrayed me, has injured me in your opinion, and that you will not easily restore me to your esteem; but I trust the offer which I now make you, both of my title and fortune, will sufficiently prove the sincerity of my attachment, and atone for the transgression which love only prompted.

After this specimen of common-place verbosity, which the Marquis seemed to consider as a prelude to triumph, he attempted to impress a kiss upon the hand of Adeline, who, withdrawing it hastily, said, You are already, my Lord, acquainted with my sentiments upon this subject, and it is almost unnecessary for me now to repeat that I cannot accept the honour you offer me.

Explain yourself, lovely Adeline! I am ignorant that till now I ever made you this offer.

Most true, Sir, said Adeline; and you do well to remind me of this, since, after having heard your former proposal, I cannot listen for a moment to any other. She rose to quit the room. Stay, Madam, said the Marquis, with a look in which offended pride struggled to conceal itself; do not suffer an extravagant resentment to operate against your true interests; recollect the dangers that surround you, and consider the value of an offer which may afford you at least an honourable asylum.

My misfortunes, my Lord, whatever they are, I have never obtruded upon you; you will, therefore, excuse my observing, that your present mention of them conveys a much greater appearance of insult than compassion. The Marquis, though with evident confusion, was going to reply; but Adeline would not be detained, and retired to her chamber. Destitute as she was, her heart revolted from the proposal of the Marquis, and she determined never to accept it. To her dislike of his general disposition, and the aversion excited by his late offer, was added, indeed, the influence of a prior attachment, and of a remembrance which she found it impossible to erase from her heart.

The Marquis staid to dine, and in consideration of La Motte, Adeline appeared at table, where the former gazed upon her with such frequent and silent earnestness, that her distress became insupportable; and when the cloth was drawn, she instantly retired. Madame La Motte soon followed, and it was not till evening that she had an opportunity of returning to the MS. When Monsieur and Madame La Motte were in their chamber, and all was still, she drew forth the narrative, and trimming her lamp, sat down to read as follows:

The ruffians unbound me from my horse, and led me through the hall up the spiral staircase of the abbey: resistance was useless; but I looked around in the hope of seeing some person less obdurate than the men who brought me hither; some one who might be sensible to pity, and capable at least of civil treatment. I looked in vain; no person appeared: and this circumstance confirmed my worst apprehensions. The secrecy of the business foretold a horrible conclusion. Having passed some chambers, they stopped in one hung with old tapestry. I inquired why we did not go on, and was told I should soon know.

At that moment I expected to see the instrument of death uplifted, and silently recommended myself to God. But death was not then designed for me; they raised the arras, and discovered a door, which they then opened. Seizing my arms, they led me through a suite of dismal chambers beyond. Having reached the furthest of these, they again stopped: the horrid gloom of the place seemed congenial to murder, and inspired deadly thoughts. Again I looked round for the instrument of destruction, and again I was respited. I supplicated to know what was designed me; it was now unnecessary to ask who was the author of the design. They were silent to my question, but at length told me this chamber was my prison. Having said this, and set down a jug of water, they left the room, and I heard the door barred upon me.

O sound of despair! O moment of unutterable anguish! The pang of death itself is surely not superior to that I then suffered. Shut out from day, from friends, from life—for such I must foretell it—in the prime of my years, in the height of my transgressions, and left to imagine horrors more terrible than any, perhaps, which certainty could give—I sink beneath the—

Here several pages of the manuscript were decayed with damp, and totally illegible. With much difficulty Adeline made out the following lines:

Three days have now passed in solitude and silence: the horrors of death are ever before my eyes, let me endeavour to prepare for the dreadful change! When I awake in the morning I think I shall not live to see another night; and when night returns, that I must never more unclose my eyes on morning. Why am I brought hither—why confined thus rigorously—but for death! Yet what action of my life has deserved this at the hand of a fellow-creature?—Of——

* * * * * * * * * * * * * * *
* * * * * * * * * * * * * * *
* * * * * * * * * * * *

O my children! O friends far distant! I shall never see you more—never more receive the parting look of kindness—never bestow a parting blessing!—Ye know not my wretched state—alas! ye cannot know it by human means. Ye believe me happy, or ye would fly to my relief. I know that what I now write cannot avail me, yet there is comfort in pouring forth my griefs; and I bless that man, less savage than his fellows, who has supplied me these means of recording them. Alas! he knows full well, that from this indulgence he has nothing to fear. My pen can call no friends to succour me, nor reveal my danger ere it is too late. O! ye, who may hereafter read what I now write, give a tear to my sufferings: I have wept often for the distresses of my fellow-creatures!

Adeline paused. Here the wretched writer appealed directly to her heart; he spoke in the energy of truth, and, by a strong illusion of fancy, it seemed as if his past suffering were at this moment present. She was for some time unable to proceed, and sat in musing sorrow. In these very apartments, said she, this poor sufferer was confined—here he—Adeline started, and thought she heard a sound; but the stillness of the night was undisturbed.—In these very chambers, said she, these lines were written—these lines, from which he then derived a comfort in believing they would hereafter be read by some pitying eye: this time is now come. Your miseries, O injured being! are lamented where they were endured. Here, where you suffered, I weep for your sufferings!

Her imagination was now strongly impressed, and to her distempered senses the suggestions of a bewildered mind appeared with the force of reality. Again she started and listened, and thought she heard Here distinctly repeated by a whisper immediately behind her. The terror of the thought, however, was but momentary, she knew it could not be; convinced that her fancy had deceived her, she took up the MS. and again began to read.

For what am I reserved? Why this delay? If I am to die—why not quickly? Three weeks have I now passed within these walls, during which time no look of pity has softened my afflictions; no voice, save my own, has met my ear. The countenances of the ruffians who attend me are stern and inflexible, and their silence is obstinate. This stillness is dreadful! O! ye, who have known what it is to live in the depths of solitude, who have passed your dreary days without one sound to cheer you; ye, and ye only, can tell what now I feel; and ye may know how much I would endure to hear the accents of a human voice.

O dire extremity! O state of living death! What dreadful stillness! All around me is dead; and do I really exist, or am I but a statue? Is this a vision? Are these things real? Alas, I am bewildered!—this death-like and perpetual silence—this dismal chamber—the dread of further sufferings have disturbed my fancy. O for some friendly breast to lay my weary head on! some cordial accents to revive my soul!

* * * * * * * * * * * * * * *
* * * * * * * * * * * * * * *

I write by stealth. He who furnished me with the means, I fear, has suffered for some symptoms of pity he may have discovered for me; I have not seen him for several days: perhaps he is inclined to help me, and for that reason is forbid to come. O that hope! but how vain! Never more must I quit these walls while life remains. Another day is gone, and yet I live; at this time to-morrow night my sufferings may be sealed in death. I will continue my journal nightly, till the hand that writes shall be stopped by death: when the journal ceases, the reader will know I am no more. Perhaps these are the last lines I shall ever write.

* * * * * * * * * * * * * * *
* * * * * * * * * * * * * * *
* * * * * * * * * * *

Adeline paused, while her tears fell fast. Unhappy man! she exclaimed: and was here no pitying soul to save thee! Great God! thy ways are wonderful! While she sat musing, her fancy, which now wandered in the regions of terror, gradually subdued reason. There was a glass before her upon the table, and she feared to raise her looks towards it, lest some other face than her own should meet her eyes: other dreadful ideas and strange images of fantastic thought now crossed her mind.

A hollow sigh seemed to pass near her. Holy Virgin, protect me! cried she, and threw a fearful glance round the room;—this is surely something more than fancy. Her fears so far overcame her, that she was several times upon the point of calling up a part of the family; but, unwillingness to disturb them, and a dread of ridicule, withheld her. She was also afraid to move, and almost to breathe. As she listened to the wind, that murmured at the casement of her lonely chamber, she again thought she heard a sigh. Her imagination refused any longer the control of reason, and, turning her eyes, a figure, whose exact form she could not distinguish, appeared to pass along an obscure part of the chamber: a dreadful chillness came over her, and she sat fixed in her chair. At length a deep sigh somewhat relieved her oppressed spirits, and her senses seemed to return.

All remaining quiet, after some time she began to question whether her fancy had not deceived her, and she so far conquered her terror as to desist from calling Madame La Motte: her mind was, however, so much disturbed, that she did not venture to trust herself that night again with the MS.; but having spent some time in prayer, and in endeavouring to compose her spirits, she retired to bed.

When she awoke in the morning, the cheerful sun-beams played upon the casements, and dispelled the illusions of darkness: her mind soothed and invigorated by sleep, rejected the mystic and turbulent promptings of imagination. She arose refreshed and thankful; but upon going down to breakfast, this transient gleam of peace fled upon the appearance of the Marquis, whose frequent visits at the abbey, after what had passed, not only displeased, but alarmed her. She saw that he was determined to persevere in addressing her: and the boldness and insensibility of this conduct, while it excited her indignation, increased her disgust. In pity to La Motte, she endeavoured to conceal these emotions, though she now thought that he required too much from her complaisance, and began seriously to consider how she might avoid the necessity of continuing it. The Marquis behaved to her with the most respectful attention; but

Adeline was silent and reserved, and seized the first opportunity of withdrawing.

As she passed up the spiral staircase, Peter entered the hall below, and seeing Adeline, he stopped and looked earnestly at her: she did not observe him, but he called her softly, and she then saw him make a signal, as if he had something to communicate. In the next instant, La Motte opened the door of the vaulted room, and Peter hastily disappeared. She proceeded to her chamber, ruminating upon this signal, and the cautious manner in which Peter had given it.

But her thoughts soon returned to their wonted subjects. Three days were now passed, and she heard no intelligence of her father; she began to hope that he had relented from the violent measures hinted at by La Motte, and that he meant to pursue a milder plan: but when she considered his character, this appeared improbable, and she relapsed into her former fears. Her residence at the abbey was now become painful, from the perseverance of the Marquis and the conduct which La Motte obliged her to adopt; yet she could not think without dread of quitting it to return to her father.

The image of Theodore often intruded upon her busy thoughts, and brought with it a pang which his strange departure occasioned. She had a confused notion that his fate was somehow connected with her own; and her struggles to prevent the remembrance of him served only to show how much her heart was his.

To divert her thoughts from these subjects, and gratify the curiosity so strongly excited on the preceding night, she now took up the MS. but was hindered from opening it by the entrance of Madame La Motte, who came to tell her the Marquis was gone. They passed their morning together in work and general conversation; La Motte not appearing till dinner, when he said little, and Adeline less. She asked him, however, if he had heard from her father? I have not heard from him, said La Motte; but there is good reason, as I am informed by the Marquis, to believe he is not far off.

Adeline was shocked, yet she was able to reply with becoming firmness. I have already, Sir, involved you too much in my distress, and now see that resistance will destroy you, without serving me; I am therefore contented to return to my father, and thus spare you further calamity.

This is a rash determination, replied La Motte; and if you pursue it, I fear you will severely repent. I speak to you as a friend, Adeline, and desire you will endeavour to listen to me without prejudice. The Marquis, I find, has offered you his hand. I know not which circumstance most excites my surprise, that a man of his rank and consequence should solicit a marriage with a person without fortune or ostensible connexions, or that a person so circumstanced should even for a moment reject the advantages just offered her. You weep, Adeline; let me hope that you are convinced of the absurdity of this conduct, and will no longer trifle with your good fortune. The kindness I have shown you must convince you of my regard, and that I have no motive for offering you this advice but your advantage. It is necessary, however, to say, that should your father not insist upon your removal, I know not how long my circumstances may enable me to afford even the humble pittance you receive here. Still you are silent.

The anguish which this speech excited, suppressed her utterance, and she continued to weep. At length she said, Suffer me, Sir, to go back to my father; I should indeed make an ill return for the kindness you mention, could I wish to stay after what you now tell me; and to accept the Marquis, I feel to be impossible. The remembrance of Theodore arose to her mind, and she wept aloud.

La Motte sat for some time musing. Strange infatuation! said he; is it possible that you can persist in this heroism of romance, and prefer a father so inhuman as yours, to the Marquis de Montalt! a destiny so full of danger, to a life of splendour and delight!

Pardon me, said Adeline; a marriage with the Marquis would be splendid, but never happy. His character excites my aversion, and I entreat, Sir, that he may no more be mentioned.

CHAPTER X

Nor are those empty hearted, whose low soundReverbs no hollowness.LEAR.

The conversation related in the last chapter was interrupted by the entrance of Peter, who, as he left the room, looked significantly at Adeline, and almost beckoned. She was anxious to know what he meant, and soon after went into the hall, where she found him loitering. The moment he saw her, he made a sign of silence, and beckoned her into the recess. Well, Peter, what is it you would say? said Adeline.

Hush, Ma'mselle; for heaven's sake speak lower; if we should be overheard, we are all blown up.—Adeline begged him to explain what he meant Yes, Ma'mselle, that is what I have wanted all day long: I have watched and watched for an opportunity, and looked and looked till I was afraid my master himself would see me; but all would not do, you would not understand.

Adeline entreated he would be quick. Yes Ma'm, but I'm so afraid we shall be seen; but I would do much to serve such a good young lady, for I could not bear to think of what threatened you, without telling you of it.

For God's sake, said Adeline, speak quickly, or we shall be interrupted.

Well then;—but you must first promise by the Holy Virgin never to say it was I that told you; my master would—

I do, I do, said Adeline.

Well, then—on Monday evening as I—hark! did not I hear a step? do, Ma'mselle, just step this way to the cloisters: I would not for the world we should be seen: I'll go out at the hall door, and you can go through the passage. I would not for the world we should be seen.—Adeline was much alarmed by Peter's words, and hurried to the cloisters. He quickly appeared, and, looking cautiously round, resumed his discourse. As I was saying, Ma'mselle, Monday night, when the Marquis slept here, you know he sat up very late, and I can guess, perhaps, the reason of that. Strange things came out, but it is not my business to tell all I think.

Pray do speak to the purpose, said Adeline impatiently; what is this danger which you say threatens me? Be quick, or we shall be observed.

Danger enough, Ma'mselle, replied Peter, if you knew all; and when you do, what will it signify? for you can't help yourself. But that's neither here nor there; I was resolved to tell you, though I may repent it.

Or rather, you are resolved not to tell me, said Adeline; for you have made no progress towards it. But what do you mean? You was speaking of the Marquis.

Hush, Ma'am, not so loud. The Marquis, as I said, sat up very late, and my master sat up with him. One of his men went to bed in the oak room, and the other staid to undress his lord. So as we were sitting together. Lord have mercy! it made my hair stand on end! I tremble yet. So as we were sitting together—but as sure as I live, yonder is my master: I caught a glimpse of him between the trees; if he sees me it is all over with us. I'll tell you another time. So saying, he hurried into the abbey, leaving Adeline in a state of alarm, curiosity, and vexation. She walked out into the forest ruminating upon Peter's words, and endeavouring to guess to what they alluded: there Madame La Motte joined her, and they conversed on various topics till they reached the abbey.

Adeline watched in vain through that day for an opportunity of speaking with Peter. While he waited at supper, she occasionally observed his countenance with great anxiety, hoping it might afford her some degree of intelligence on the subject of her fears. When she retired, Madame La Motte accompanied her to her chamber, and continued to converse with her for a considerable time, so that she had no means of obtaining an interview with Peter.—Madame La Motte appeared to labour under some great affliction; and when Adeline, noticing this, entreated to know the cause of her dejection, tears started into her eyes, and she abruptly left the room.

This behaviour of Madame La Motte concurred with Peter's discourse to alarm Adeline, who sat pensively upon her bed, giving up to reflection, till she was roused by the sound of a clock, which stood in the room below, and which now struck twelve. She was preparing for rest, when she recollected the MS. and was unable to conclude the night without reading it. The first words she could distinguish were the following:

Again I return to this poor consolation—again I have been permitted to see another day. It is now midnight! My solitary lamp burns beside me; the time is awful, but to me the silence of noon is as the silence of midnight; a deeper gloom is all in which they differ. The still, unvarying hours are numbered only by my sufferings; Great God! when shall I be released:

* * * * * * * * * * * * * * *
* * * * * * * * * * * *

But whence this strange confinement? I have never injured him. If death is designed me, why this delay; and for what but death am I brought hither? This abbey—alas!— Here the MS. was again illegible, and for several pages Adeline could only make out disjointed sentences.

O bitter draught! when, when shall I have rest? O my friends! will none of ye fly to aid me; will none of ye avenge my sufferings? Ah! when it is too late—when I am gone for ever, ye will endeavour to avenge them.

* * * * * * * * * * * * * * *
* * * * * * * * * * * *

Once more is night returned to me. Another day has passed in solitude and misery. I have climbed to the casement, thinking the view of nature would refresh my soul, and somewhat enable me to support these afflictions. Alas! even this small comfort is denied me, the windows open towards other parts of this abbey, and admit only a portion of that day which I must never more fully behold. Last night! last night! O scene of horror!

Adeline shuddered. She feared to read the coming sentence, yet curiosity prompted her to proceed. Still she paused: an unaccountable dread came over her. Some horrid deed has been done here, said she; the reports of the peasants are true: murder has been committed. The idea thrilled her with horror. She recollected the dagger which had impeded her steps in the secret chamber, and this circumstance served to confirm her most terrible conjectures. She wished to examine it, but it lay in one of these chambers, and she feared to go in quest of it.

Wretched, wretched victim! she exclaimed, could no friend rescue thee from destruction! O that I had been near! Yet what could I have done to save thee? Alas! nothing. I forget that even now, perhaps, I am, like thee, abandoned to dangers from which I have no friend to succour me. Too surely I guess the author of thy miseries! She stopped, and thought she heard a sigh, such as on the preceding night had passed along the chamber. Her blood was chilled, and she sat motionless. The lonely situation of her room, remote from the rest of the family, (for she was now in her old apartment, from which Madame La Motte had removed,) who were almost beyond call, struck so forcibly upon her imagination, that she with difficulty preserved herself from fainting. She sat for a considerable time, and all was still. When she was somewhat recovered, her first design was to alarm the family; but further reflection again withheld her.

She endeavoured to compose her spirits, and addressed a short prayer to that Being, who had hitherto protected her in every danger. While she was thus employed, her mind gradually became elevated and reassured; a sublime complacency filled her heart, and she sat down once more to pursue the narrative.

Several lines that immediately followed, were obliterated.—

* * * * * * * * * * * * * * *
* * * * * * * * * * * *

He had told me I should not be permitted to live long, not more than three days, and bade me choose whether I would die by poison or the sword. O the agonies of that moment! Great God! thou seest my sufferings! I often viewed, with a momentary hope of escaping, the high grated windows of my prison—all things within the compass of possibility I was resolved to try, and with an eager desperation I climbed towards the casements, but my foot slipped, and falling back to the floor, I was stunned by the blow. On recovering, the first sounds I heard, were the steps of a person entering my prison. A recollection of the past returned, and deplorable was my condition. I shuddered at what was to come. The same man approached; he looked at me at first with pity, but his countenance soon recovered its natural ferocity. Yet he did not then come to execute the purposes of his employer: I am reserved to another day—Great God, thy will be done!

Adeline could not go on. All the circumstances that seemed to corroborate the fate of this unhappy man, crowded upon her mind the reports concerning the abbey— the dreams which had forerun her discovery of the private apartments—the singular manner in which she had found the MS—and the apparition, which she now believed she had really seen. She blamed herself for not having yet mentioned the discovery of the manuscript and chambers to La Motte, and resolved to delay the disclosure no longer than the following morning. The immediate cares that had occupied her mind, and a fear of losing the manuscript before she had read it, had hitherto kept her silent.

Such a combination of circumstances, she believed, could only be produced by some supernatural power, operating for the retribution of the guilty. These reflections filled her mind with a degree of awe, which the loneliness of the large old chamber in which she sat, and the hour of the night, soon heightened into terror. She had never been superstitious, but circumstances so uncommon had hitherto conspired in this affair, that she could not believe them accidental. Her imagination, wrought upon by these reflections, again became sensible to every impression; she feared to look round, lest she should again see some dreadful phantom, and she almost fancied she heard voices swell in the storm which now shook the fabric.

Still she tried to command her feelings so as to avoid disturbing the family; but they became so painful, that even the dread of La Motte's ridicule had hardly power to prevent her quitting the chamber. Her mind was now in such a state, that she found it impossible to pursue the story in the MS. though, to avoid the tortures of suspense, she had attempted it. She laid it down again, and tried to argue herself into composure. What have I to fear? said she; I am at least innocent, and I shall not be punished for the crime of another.

The violent gust of wind that now rushed through the whole suite of apartments, shook the door that led from her late bedchamber to the private rooms so forcibly, that Adeline, unable to remain longer in doubt, ran to see from whence the noise issued. The arras which concealed the door was violently agitated, and she stood for a moment observing it in indescribable terror; till believing it was swayed by the wind, she made a sudden effort to overcome her feelings, and was stooping to raise it. At that instant she thought she heard a voice. She stopped and listened, but every thing was still; yet apprehension so far overcame her, that she had no power either to examine or to leave the chamber.

In a few moments the voice returned: she was now convinced she had not been deceived, for, though low, she heard it distinctly, and was almost sure it repeated her own name. So much was her fancy affected, that she even thought it was the same voice she had heard in her dreams. This conviction entirely subdued the small remains of her courage, and sinking into a chair she lost all recollection.

How long she remained in this state she knew not; but when she recovered, she exerted all her strength, and reached the winding staircase, where she called aloud. No one heard her; and she hastened, as fast as her feebleness would permit, to the chamber of Madame La Motte. She tapped gently at the door, and was answered by Madame, who was alarmed at being awakened at so unusual an hour, and believed that some danger threatened her husband. When she understood that it was Adeline, and that she was unwell, she quickly came to her relief. The terror that was yet visible in Adeline's countenance excited her inquiries, and the occasion of it was explained to her.

Madame was so much discomposed by the relation, that she called La Motte from his bed, who, more angry at being disturbed than interested for the agitation he witnessed, reproved Adeline for suffering her fancies to overcome her reason. She now mentioned the discovery she had made of the inner chamber and the manuscript, circumstances which roused the attention of La Motte so much, that he desired to see the MS. and resolved to go immediately to the apartments described by Adeline.

Madame La Motte endeavoured to dissuade him from his purpose; but La Motte, with whom opposition had always an effect contrary to the one designed, and who wished to throw further ridicule upon the terrors of Adeline, persisted in his intention. He called to Peter to attend with a light, and insisted that Madame La Motte and Adeline should accompany him. Madame La Motte desired to be excused, and Adeline at first declared she could not go; but he would be obeyed.

They ascended the tower, and entered the first chambers together, for each of the party was reluctant to be the last; in the second chamber all was quiet and in order. Adeline presented the MS. and pointed to the arras which concealed the door. La Motte lifted the arras, and opened the door; but Madame La Motte and Adeline entreated to go no further—again he called to them to follow. All was quiet in the first chamber: he expressed his surprise that the rooms should so long have remained undiscovered, and was proceeding to the second, but suddenly stopped. We will defer our examination till to-morrow, said he, the damps of these apartments are unwholesome at any time; but they strike one more sensibly at night. I am chilled. Peter, remember to throw open the windows early in the morning, that the air may circulate.

Lord bless your honour, said Peter, don't you see I can't reach them; besides, I don't believe they are made to open; see what strong iron bars there are; the room looks for all the world like a prison: I suppose this is the place the people meant, when they said nobody that had been in ever came out. La Motte, who during this speech had been looking attentively at the high windows, which if he had seen them at first he had certainly not observed, now interrupted the eloquence of Peter, and bade him carry the light before them. They all willingly quitted these chambers, and returned to the room below, where a fire was lighted, and the party remained together for some time.

La Motte for reasons best known to himself, attempted to ridicule the discovery and fears of Adeline, till she with a seriousness that checked him, entreated he would desist. He was silent; and soon after, Adeline, encouraged by the return of daylight, ventured to her chamber, and for some hours experienced the blessing of undisturbed repose.

On the following day, Adeline's first care was to obtain an interview with Peter, whom she had some hopes of seeing as she went downstairs: he, however, did not appear; and she proceeded to the sitting-room, where she found La Motte apparently much disturbed. Adeline asked him if he had looked at the MS. I have run my eye over it, said he, but it is so much obscured by time that it can scarcely be deciphered. It appears to exhibit a strange romantic story; and I do not wonder that after you had suffered its terrors to impress your imagination, you fancied you saw spectres and heard wondrous noises.

Adeline thought La Motte did not choose to be convinced, and she therefore forbore reply. During breakfast she often looked at Peter (who waited) with anxious inquiry; and from his countenance was still more assured that he had something of importance to communicate. In the hope of some conversation with him, she left the room as soon as possible, and repaired to her favourite avenue, where she had not long remained when he appeared.

God bless you! Ma'mselle, said he, I'm sorry I frighted you so last night.

Frighted me, said Adeline; how was you concerned in that?

He then informed her that when he thought Monsieur and Madame La Motte were asleep, he had stolen to her chamber door, with an intention of giving her the sequel of what he had begun in the morning; that he had called several times as loudly as he dared; but receiving no answer, he believed she was asleep, or did not choose to speak with him, and he had therefore left the door. This account of the voice she had heard, relieved Adeline's spirits; she was even surprised that she did not know it, till remembering the perturbation of her mind for some time preceding, this surprise disappeared.

She entreated Peter to be brief in explaining the danger with which she was threatened. If you'll let me go on my own way, Ma'am, you'll soon know it; but if you hurry me, and ask me questions here and there, out of their places, I don't know what I am saying.

Be it so, said Adeline; only, remember that we may be observed.

Yes. Ma'mselle, I'm as much afraid of that as you are, for I believe I should be almost as ill off; however, that is neither here nor there, but I'm sure if you stay in this old abbey another night it will be worse for you; for, as I said before, I know all about it.

What mean you, Peter?

Why, about this scheme that's going on.

What then, is my father——?—Your father! interrupted Peter; Lord bless you, that is all fudge, to frighten you: your father, nor nobody else has ever sent after you; I dare say he knows no more of you than the Pope does—not he. Adeline looked displeased. You trifle, said she; if you have any thing to tell, say it quickly; I am in haste.

Bless you, young lady, I meant no harm, I hope you're not angry; but I'm sure you can't deny that your father is cruel. But as I was saying, the Marquis de Montalt likes you; and he and my master (Peter looked round) have been laying their heads together about you. Adeline turned pale; she comprehended a part of the truth, and eagerly entreated him to proceed.

They have been laying their heads together about you. This is what Jaques the Marquis's man tells me: Says he, Peter, you little know what is going on: I could tell all if I chose it; but it is not for those who are trusted to tell again. I warrant now your master is close enough with you. Upon which I was piqued, and resolved to make him believe I could be trusted as well as he. Perhaps not says I; perhaps I know as much as you, though I do not choose to brag on't; and I winked.—Do you so? says he, then you are closer than I thought for. She is a fine girl, says he,—meaning you Ma'mselle; but she is nothing but a poor foundling after all, so it does not much signify. I had a mind to know further what he meant—so I did not knock him down. By seeming to know as much as he, I at last made him discover all; and he told me—but you look pale, Ma'mselle, are you ill?

No, said Adeline in a tremulous accent, and scarcely able to support herself; pray proceed.

And he told me that the Marquis had been courting you a good while, but you would not listen to him, and had even pretended he would marry you, and all would not do. As for marriage, says I, I suppose she knows the Marchioness is alive; and I'm sure she is not one for his turn upon other terms.

The Marchioness is really living then! said Adeline.

O yes, Ma'mselle! we all know that, and I thought you had known it too.—We shall see that, replies Jaques; at least, I believe that our master will outwit her.—I stared; I could not help it.—Aye, says he, you know your master has agreed to give her up to my Lord.

Good God! what will become of me? exclaimed Adeline.

Aye, Ma'mselle, I am sorry for you; but hear me out. When Jaques said this, I quite forgot myself: I'll never believe it, said I, I'll never believe my master would be guilty of such a base action; he'll not give her up, or I'm no Christian.—Oh! said, Jaques, for that matter, I thought you'd known all, else I should not have said a word about it. However, you may soon satisfy yourself by going to the parlour door, as I have done; they're in consultation about it now, I dare say.

You need not repeat any more of this conversation, said Adeline; but tell me the result of what you heard from the parlour.

Why, Ma'mselle, when he said this, I took him at his word, and went to the door, where, sure enough, I heard my master and the Marquis talking about you. They said a great deal which I could make nothing of; but, at last, I heard the Marquis say, You know the terms; on these terms only will I consent to bury the past in ob—ob—oblivion——that was the word. Monsieur La Motte then told the Marquis, if he would return to the abbey upon such a night, meaning this very night, Ma'mselle, every thing should be prepared according to his wishes;—Adeline shall then be yours, my Lord, said he—you are already acquainted with her chamber.

At these words Adeline clasped her hands, and raised her eyes to heaven in silent despair.—Peter went on. When I heard this, I could not doubt what Jaques had said.—Well, said he, what do you think of it now?—Why, that my master's a rascal, says I.—It's well you don't think mine one too, says he.—Why, as for that matter, says I——Adeline, interrupting him, inquired if he had heard any thing further. Just then, said Peter, we heard Madame La Motte come out from another room, and so we made haste back to the kitchen.

She was not present at this conversation then? said Adeline. No, Ma'mselle; but my master has told her of it, I warrant. Adeline was almost as much shocked by this apparent perfidy of Madame La Motte, as by a knowledge of the destruction that threatened her. After musing a few moments in extreme agitation, Peter, said she, you have a good heart, and feel a just indignation at your master's treachery—will you assist me to escape?

Ah, Ma'mselle! said he, how can I assist you? besides, where can we go? I have no friends about here, no more than yourself.

O! replied Adeline in extreme emotion, we fly from enemies; strangers may prove friends: assist me but to escape from this forest, and you will claim my eternal gratitude; I have no fears beyond it.

Why as for this forest, replied Peter, I am weary of it myself; though when we first came I thought it would be fine living here, at least, I thought it was very different from any life I had ever lived before. But these ghosts that haunt the abbey—I am no more a coward than other men, but I don't like them; and then there is so many strange reports abroad; and my master—I thought I could have served him to the end of the world, but now I care not how soon I leave him, for his behaviour to you, Ma'mselle.

You consent then to assist me in escaping? said Adeline with eagerness.

Why as to that, Ma'mselle, I would willingly, if I knew where to go. To be sure I have a sister lives in Savoy, but that is a great way off; and I have saved a little money out of my wages, but that won't carry us such a long journey.

Regard not that, said Adeline; if I was once beyond this forest, I would then endeavour to take care of myself, and repay you for your kindness.

O! as for that, Madam——Well, well, Peter, let us consider how we may escape. This night—say you this night—the Marquis is to return? Yes, Ma'mselle, to-night about dark. I have just thought of a scheme:—my master's horses are grazing in the forest; we may take one of them, and send it back from the first stage: but how shall we avoid being seen? besides if we go off in the daylight, he will soon pursue and overtake us; and if you stay till night, the Marquis will be come, and then there is no chance. If they miss us both at the same time too, they'll guess how it is, and set off directly. Could not you contrive to go first, and wait for me till the hurly-burly's over? Then, while they're searching in the place under ground for you, I can slip away, and we should be out of their reach before they thought of pursuing us.

Adeline agreed to the truth of all this, and was somewhat surprised at Peter's sagacity. She inquired if he knew of any place in the neighbourhood of the abbey, where she could remain concealed, till he came with a horse. Why yes, Madam, there is a place, now I think of it, where you may be safe enough, for nobody goes near; but they say it's haunted, and perhaps you would not like to go there. Adeline, remembering the last night, was somewhat startled at this intelligence; but a sense of her present danger pressed again upon her mind, and overcame every other apprehension. Where is this place? said she; if it will conceal me, I shall not hesitate to go.

It is an old tomb that stands in the thickest part of the forest, about a quarter of a mile off the nearest way and almost a mile the other. When my master used to hide himself so much in the forest, I have followed him somewhere thereabouts, but I did not find out the tomb till t'other day. However, that's neither here nor there; if you dare venture to it, Ma'mselle, I'll show you the nearest way. So saying he pointed to a winding path on the right. Adeline, having looked round without perceiving any person near, directed Peter to lead her to the tomb: they pursued the path, till turning into a gloomy romantic part of the forest, almost impervious to the rays of the sun, they came to the spot whither Louis had formerly traced his father.

The stillness and solemnity of the scene struck awe upon the heart of Adeline, who paused and surveyed it for some time in silence. At length Peter led her into the interior part of the ruin, to which they descended by several steps. Some old abbot, said he, was formerly buried here, as the Marquis's people say; and it's like enough that he belonged to the abbey yonder. But I don't see why he should take it in his head to walk; he was not murdered, surely!

I hope not, said Adeline.

That's more than can be said for all that lies buried at the abbey though, and—— Adeline interrupted him: Hark! surely I hear a noise, said she; Heaven protect us from discovery! They listened, but all was still; and they went on. Peter opened a low door, and they entered upon a dark passage, frequently obstructed by loose fragments of stone, and along which they moved with caution. Whither are we going? said Adeline.—I scarcely know myself, said Peter, for I never was so far before, but the place seems quiet enough. Something obstructed his way; it was a door which yielded to his hand, and discovered a kind of cell obscurely seen by the twilight admitted through a grate above. A partial gleam shot athwart the place, leaving the greatest part of it in shadow.

Adeline sighed as she surveyed it. This is a frightful spot, said she: but if it will afford me a shelter, it is a palace. Remember, Peter, that my peace and honour depend upon your faithfulness; be both discreet and resolute. In the dusk of the evening, I can pass from the abbey with least danger of being observed, and in this cell I will wait your arrival. As soon as Monsieur and Madame La Motte are engaged in searching the vaults, you will bring here a horse; three knocks upon the tomb shall inform me of your arrival. For Heaven's sake be cautious, and be punctual!

I will, Ma'mselle, let come what may.

They re-ascended to the forest; and Adeline fearful of observation, directed Peter, to run first to the abbey, and invent some excuse for his absence, if he had been missed. When she was again alone, she yielded to a flood of tears, and indulged the excess of her distress. She saw herself without friends, without relations, destitute, forlorn, and abandoned to the worst of evils; betrayed by the very persons to whose comfort she had so long administered, whom she had loved as her protectors, and revered as her parents! These reflections touched her heart with the most afflicting sensations, and the sense of her immediate danger was for a while absorbed in the grief occasioned by a discovery of such guilt in others.

At length she roused all her fortitude, and turning towards the abbey endeavoured to await with patience the hour of evening, and to sustain an appearance of composure in the presence of Monsieur and Madame La Motte. For the present she wished to avoid seeing either of them, doubting her ability to disguise her emotions: having reached the abbey, she therefore passed on to her chamber. Here she endeavoured to direct her attention to indifferent subjects, but in vain; the danger of her situation, and the severe disappointment she had received in the character of those whom she had so much esteemed and even loved, pressed hard upon her thoughts. To a generous mind few circumstances are more afflicting than a discovery of perfidy in those whom we have trusted, even though it may fail of any absolute inconvenience to ourselves. The behaviour of Madame La Motte in thus, by concealment, conspiring to her destruction, particularly shocked her.

How has my imagination deceived me! said she; what a picture did it draw of the goodness of the world! And must I then believe that every body is cruel and deceitful? No—let me still be deceived, and still suffer, rather than be condemned to a state of such wretched suspicion. She now endeavoured to extenuate the conduct of Madame La Motte, by attributing it to a fear of her husband. She dares not oppose his will, said she, else she would warn me of my danger, and assist me to escape from it. No—I will never believe her capable of conspiring my ruin; terror alone keeps her silent.

Adeline was somewhat comforted by this thought. The benevolence of her heart taught her, in this instance to sophisticate. She perceived not, that by ascribing the conduct of Madame La Motte to terror, she only softened the degree of her guilt, imputing it to a motive less depraved but not less selfish. She remained in her chamber till summoned to dinner, when, drying her tears, she descended with faltering steps and a palpitating heart to the parlour. When she saw La Motte, in spite of all her efforts she trembled and grew pale; she could not behold even with apparent indifference the man who she knew had destined her to destruction. He observed her emotion, and inquiring if she was ill, she saw the danger to which her agitation exposed her. Fearful lest La Motte should suspect its true cause, she rallied all her spirits, and with a look of complacency answered she was well.

During dinner she preserved a degree of composure that effectually concealed the varied anguish of her heart. When she looked at La Motte, terror and indignation were her predominant feelings; but when she regarded Madame La Motte, it was otherwise: gratitude for her former tenderness had long been confirmed into affection, and her heart now swelled with the bitterness of grief and disappointment. Madame La Motte appeared depressed and said little. La Motte seemed anxious to prevent thought, by assuming a fictitious and unnatural gaiety: he laughed and talked, and threw off frequent bumpers of wine: it was the mirth of desperation. Madame became alarmed, and would have restrained him; but he persisted in his libations to Bacchus till reflection seemed to be almost overcome.

Madame La Motte, fearful that in the carelessness of the present moment he might betray himself, withdrew with Adeline to another room. Adeline recollected the happy hours she once passed with her, when confidence banished reserve, and sympathy and esteem dictated the sentiments of friendship: now those hours were gone for ever; she could no longer unbosom her griefs to Madame La Motte, no longer even esteem her. Yet, notwithstanding all the danger to which she was exposed by the criminal silence of the latter, she could not converse with her, consciously for the last time, without feeling a degree of sorrow which wisdom may call weakness, but to which benevolence will allow a softer name.

Madame La Motte in her conversation appeared to labour under an almost equal oppression with Adeline: her thoughts were abstracted from the subject of discourse, and there were long and frequent intervals of silence. Adeline more than once caught her gazing with a look of tenderness upon her, and saw her eyes fill with tears. By this circumstance she was so much affected, that she was several times upon the point of throwing herself at her feet, and imploring her pity and protection. Cooler reflection showed her the extravagance and danger of this conduct: she suppressed her emotions, but they at length compelled her to withdraw from the presence of Madame La Motte.

CHAPTER XI

Thou! to whom the world unknownWith all its shadowy shapes is shown;Who seest appall'd th' unreal scene,While fancy lifts the veil between;Ah, Fear! ah, frantic Fear!I see, I see thee near!I know thy hurry'd step, thy haggard eyeLike thee I start, like thee disorder'd fly!COLLINS.

Adeline anxiously watched from her chamber window the sun set behind the distant hills, and the time of her departure draw nigh: it set with uncommon splendour, and threw a fiery gleam athwart the woods and upon some scattered fragments of the ruins, which she could not gaze upon with indifference. Never, probably, again shall I see the sun sink below those hills, said she, or illumine this scene! Where shall I be when next it sets—where this time to-morrow? sunk perhaps in misery! She wept at the thought. A few hours, resumed Adeline, and the Marquis will arrive—a few hours, and this abbey will be a scene of confusion and tumult: every eye will be in search of me, every recess will be explored. These reflections inspired her with new terror, and increased her impatience to be gone.

Twilight gradually came on, and she now thought it sufficiently dark to venture forth: but before she went, she kneeled down and addressed herself to Heaven. She implored support and protection, and committed herself to the care of the God of mercies. Having done this, she quitted her chamber, and passed with cautious steps down the winding staircase. No person appeared, and she proceeded through the door of the tower into the forest. She looked around; the gloom of the evening obscured every object.

With a trembling heart she sought the path pointed out by Peter, which led to the tomb: having found it, she passed along forlorn and terrified. Often did she start as the breeze shook the light leaves of the trees, or as the bat flitted by gamboling in the twilight; and often, as she looked back towards the abbey, thought she distinguished amid the deepening gloom the figures of men. Having proceeded some way, she suddenly heard the feet of horses, and soon after a sound of voices, among which she distinguished that of the Marquis; they seemed to come from the quarter she was approaching, and evidently advanced. Terror for some minutes arrested her steps; she stood in a state of dreadful hesitation: to proceed was to run into the hands of the Marquis; to return was to fall into the power of La Motte.

After remaining for some time uncertain whither to fly, the sounds suddenly took a different direction, and wheeled towards the abbey. Adeline had a short cessation of terror; she now understood that the Marquis had passed this spot only in his way to the abbey, and she hastened to secrete herself in the ruin. At length, after much difficulty, she reached it, the deep shades almost concealing it from her search. She paused at the entrance, awed by the solemnity that reigned within, and the utter darkness of the place; at length she determined to watch without till Peter should arrive. If any person approaches, said she, I can hear them before they can see me, and I can then secrete myself in the cell.

She leaned against a fragment of the tomb in trembling expectation, and as she listened, no sound broke the silence of the hour. The state of her mind can only be imagined by considering that upon the present time turned the crisis of her fate. They have now, thought she, discovered my flight; even now they are seeking me in every part of the abbey. I hear their dreadful voices call me; I see their eager looks. The power of imagination almost overcame her. While she yet looked around, she saw lights moving at a distance; sometimes they glimmered between the trees, and sometimes they totally disappeared.

They seemed to be in a direction with the abbey; and she now remembered that in the morning she had seen a part of the fabric through an opening in the forest. She had therefore no doubt that the lights she saw proceeded from people in search of her: who, she feared, not finding her at the abbey, might direct their steps towards the tomb. Her place of refuge now seemed too near her enemies to be safe, and she would have fled to a more distant part of the forest, but recollected that Peter would not know where to find her.

While these thoughts passed over her mind, she heard distant voices in the wind, and was hastening to conceal herself in the cell, when she observed the lights suddenly disappear. All was soon after hushed in silence and darkness, yet she endeavoured to find the way to the cell. She remembered the situation of the outward door and of the passage, and having passed these, she unclosed the door of the cell. Within it was utterly dark. She trembled violently, but entered; and having felt about the walls, at length seated herself on a projection of stone.

She here again addressed herself to Heaven, and endeavoured to reanimate her spirits till Peter should arrive. Above half an hour elapsed in this gloomy recess, and no sound foretold his approach. Her spirits sunk; she feared some part of their plan was discovered or interrupted, and that he was detained by La Motte. This conviction operated sometimes so strongly upon her fears, as to urge her to quit the cell alone, and seek in flight her only chance of escape.

While this design was fluctuating in her mind, she distinguished through the grate above a clattering of hoofs. The noise approached, and at length stopped at the tomb. In the succeeding moment she heard three strokes of a whip; her heart beat, and for some moments her agitation was such, that she made no effort to quit the cell. The strokes were repeated: she now roused her spirits, and stepping forward, ascended to the forest. She called Peter; for the deep gloom would not permit her to distinguish either man or horse. She was quickly answered, Hush! Ma'mselle, our voices will betray us.

They mounted and rode off as fast as the darkness would permit. Adeline's heart revived at every step they took. She inquired what had passed at the abbey, and how he had contrived to get away. Speak softly, Ma'mselle; you'll know all by and by, but I can't tell you now. He had scarcely spoke ere they saw lights move along at a distance; and coming now to a more open part of the forest, he set off on a full gallop, and continued the pace till the horse could hold it no longer. They looked back, and no lights appearing, Adeline's terror subsided. She inquired again what had passed at the abbey when her flight was discovered. You may speak without fear of being heard, said she, we are gone beyond their reach, I hope.

Why, Ma'mselle, said he, you had not been gone long before the Marquis arrived, and

Monsieur La Motte then found out you was fled. Upon this a great rout there was, and he talked a great deal with the Marquis.

Speak louder, said Adeline, I cannot hear you.

I will, Ma'mselle—

Oh! heavens! interrupted Adeline, What voice is this? It is not Peter's. For God's sake tell me who you are, and whither I am going?

You'll know that soon enough, young lady, answered the stranger, for it was indeed not Peter; I am taking you where my master ordered. Adeline, not doubting he was the Marquis's servant, attempted to leap to the ground; but the man, dismounting, bound her to the horse. One feeble ray of hope at length beamed upon her mind; she endeavoured to soften the man to pity, and pleaded with all the genuine eloquence of distress; but he understood his interest too well to yield even for a moment to the compassion which, in spite of himself, her artless supplication inspired.

She now resigned herself to despair, and in passive silence submitted to her fate. They continued thus to travel, till a storm of rain accompanied by thunder and lightning drove them to the covert of a thick grove. The man believed this a safe situation, and Adeline was now too careless of life to attempt convincing him of his error. The storm was violent and long, but as soon as it abated they set off on full gallop; and having continued to travel for about two hours, they came to the borders of the forest, and soon after to a high lonely wall, which Adeline could just distinguish by the moonlight, which now streamed through the parting clouds.

Here they stopped: the man dismounted, and having opened a small door in the wall, he unbound Adeline, who shrieked, though involuntarily and in vain, as he took her from the horse. The door opened upon a narrow passage, dimly lighted by a lamp, which hung at the further end. He led her on; they came to another door; it opened, and disclosed a magnificent saloon splendidly illuminated, and fitted up in the most airy and elegant taste.

The walls were painted in fresco, representing scenes from Ovid, and hung above with silk, drawn up in festoons, and richly fringed. The sofas were of a silk to suit the hangings. From the centre of the ceiling, which exhibited a scene from the Armida of Tasso, descended a silver lamp of Etruscan form; it diffused a blaze of light that, reflected from large pier glasses, completely illuminated the saloon. Busts of Horace, Ovid, Anacreon, Tibullus, and Petronius Arbiter, adorned the recesses, and stands of flowers placed in Etruscan vases breathed the most delicious perfume. In the middle of the apartment stood a small table spread with a collation of fruits, ices, and liqueurs. No person appeared. The whole seemed the works of enchantment, and rather resembled the palace of a fairy than any thing of human conformation.

Adeline was astonished, and inquired where she was; but the man refused to answer her questions; and having desired her to take some refreshment, left her. She walked to the windows, from which a gleam of moonlight discovered to her an extensive garden, where groves and lawns, and water glittering in the moonbeam, composed a scenery of varied and romantic beauty. What can this mean! said she: Is this a charm to lure me to destruction? She endeavoured, with a hope of escaping, to open the windows, but they were all fastened; she next attempted several doors, and found them also secured.

Perceiving all chance of escape was removed, she remained for some time given up to sorrow and reflection; but was at length drawn from her reverie by the notes of soft music, breathing such dulcet and entrancing sounds as suspended grief and awaked the soul to tenderness and pensive pleasure. Adeline listened in surprise, and insensibly became soothed and interested; a tender melancholy stole upon her heart, and subdued every harsher feeling: but the moment the strain ceased, the enchantment dissolved, and she returned to a sense of her situation.

Again the music sounded—music such as charmeth sleep—and again she gradually yielded to its sweet magic. A female voice, accompanied by a lute, a hautboy, and a few other instruments, now gradually swelled into a tone so exquisite as raised attention into ecstasy. It sunk by degrees, and touched a few simple notes with pathetic softness, when the measure was suddenly changed, and in a gay and airy melody Adeline distinguished the following words:

SONG.

Life's a varied, bright illusion,Joy and sorrow—light and shade;Turn from sorrow's dark suffusion,Catch the pleasures ere they fade.

Fancy paints with hues unreal,Smile of bliss, and sorrow's mood;If they both are but ideal,Why reject the seeming good?

Hence! no more! 'tis Wisdom calls ye,Bids ye court Time's present aid;The future trust not—Hope enthralls ye,"Catch the pleasures ere they fade."

The music ceased; but the sounds still vibrated on her imagination, and she was sunk in the pleasing languor they had inspired, when the door opened, and the Marquis de Montalt appeared. He approached the sofa where Adeline sat, and addressed her, but she heard not his voice—she had fainted. He endeavoured to recover her, and at length succeeded; but when she unclosed her eyes, and again beheld him, she relapsed into a state of insensibility; and having in vain tried various methods to restore her, he was obliged to call assistance. Two young women entered; and when she began to revive, he left them to prepare her for his reappearance. When Adeline perceived that the Marquis was gone, and that she was in the care of women, her spirits gradually returned; she looked at her attendants, and was surprised to see so much elegance and beauty.

Some endeavour she made to interest their pity; but they seemed wholly insensible to her distress, and began to talk of the Marquis in terms of the highest admiration. They assured her it would be her own fault if she was not happy, and advised her to appear so in his presence. It was with the utmost difficulty that Adeline forbore to express the disdain which was rising to her lips, and that she listened to their discourse in silence. But she saw the inconvenience and fruitlessness of opposition, and she commanded her feelings.

They were thus proceeding in their praises of the Marquis, when he himself appeared;

and waving his hand, they immediately quitted the apartment. Adeline beheld him with a kind of mute despair while he approached and took her hand, which she hastily withdrew; and turning from him with a look of unutterable distress, burst into tears. He was for some time silent, and appeared softened by her anguish: but again approaching and addressing her in a gentle voice, he entreated her pardon for the step which despair, and, as he called it, love had prompted. She was too much absorbed in grief to reply, till he solicited a return of his love; when her sorrow yielded to indignation, and she reproached him with his conduct. He pleaded that he had long loved and sought her upon honourable terms, and his offer of those terms he began to repeat; but raising his eyes towards Adeline, he saw in her looks the contempt which he was conscious he deserved.

For a moment he was confused, and seemed to understand both that his plan was discovered and his person despised; but soon resuming his usual command of feature, he again pressed his suit, and solicited her love. A little reflection showed Adeline the danger of exasperating his pride by an avowal of the contempt which his pretended offer of marriage excited; and she thought it not improper, upon an occasion in which the honour and peace of her life was concerned, to yield somewhat to the policy of dissimulation. She saw that her only chance of escaping his designs depended upon delaying them, and she now wished him to believe her ignorant that the Marchioness was living, and that his offers were delusive.

He observed her pause; and in the eagerness to turn her hesitation to his advantage, renewed his proposal with increased vehemence—To-morrow shall unite us, lovely Adeline; to-morrow you shall consent to become the Marchioness de Montalt. You will then return my love and——

You must first deserve my esteem, my Lord.

I will—I do deserve it. Are you not now in my power, and do I not forbear to take advantage of your situation? Do I not make you the most honourable proposals?— Adeline shuddered: If you wish I should esteem you, my Lord, endeavour, if possible, to make me forget by what means I came into your power; if your views are indeed honourable, prove them so by releasing me from my confinement.

Can you then wish, lovely Adeline, to fly from him who adores you? replied the Marquis with a studied air of tenderness. Why will you exact so severe a proof of my disinterestedness, a disinterestedness which is not consistent with love? No, charming Adeline! let me at least have the pleasure of beholding you till the bonds of the church shall remove every obstacle to my love. To-morrow——

Adeline saw the danger to which she was now exposed, and interrupted him. Deserve my esteem, Sir, and then you will obtain it: as a first step towards which, liberate me from a confinement that obliges me to look on you only with terror and aversion. How can I believe your professions of love, while you show that you have no interest in my happiness?—Thus did Adeline, to whom the arts and the practice of dissimulation were hitherto equally unknown, condescend to make use of them in disguising her indignation and contempt. But though these arts were adopted only for the purpose of self-preservation, she used them with reluctance, and almost with abhorrence; for her mind was habitually impregnated with the love of virtue, in thought, word, and action; and while her end in using them was certainly good, she scarcely thought that end could justify the means.

The Marquis persisted in his sophistry. Can you doubt the reality of that love, which to obtain you has urged me to risk your displeasure? But have I not consulted your happiness, even in the very conduct which you condemn? I have removed you from a solitary and desolate ruin to a gay and splendid villa, where every luxury is at your command, and where every person shall be obedient to your wishes.

My first wish is to go hence, said Adeline; I entreat, I conjure you, my Lord, no longer to detain me. I am a friendless and wretched orphan, exposed to many evils, and I fear abandoned to misfortune: I do not wish to be rude; but allow me to say, that no misery can exceed that I shall feel in remaining here, or indeed in being any where pursued by the offers you make me. Adeline had now forgot her policy: tears prevented her from proceeding, and she turned away her face to hide her emotion.

By Heaven! Adeline, you do me wrong, said the Marquis, rising from his seat and seizing her hand; I love, I adore you; yet you doubt my passion, and are insensible to my vows. Every pleasure possible to be enjoyed within these walls you shall partake,—but beyond them you shall not go. She disengaged her hand, and in silent anguish walked to a distant part of the saloon: deep sighs burst from her heart, and almost fainting she leaned on a window-frame for support.

The Marquis followed her: Why thus obstinately persist in refusing to be happy? said he: recollect the proposal I have made you, and accept it while it is yet in your power. To-morrow a priest shall join our hands—Surely, being, as you are, in my power, it must be your interest to consent to this? Adeline could answer only by tears; she despaired of softening his heart to pity, and feared to exasperate his pride by disdain. He now led her, and she suffered him, to a seat near the banquet, at which he pressed her to partake of a variety of confectionaries, particularly of some liqueurs of which he himself drank freely: Adeline accepted only of a peach.

And now the Marquis, who interrupted her silence into a secret compliance with his proposal, resumed all his gaiety and spirit, while the long and ardent regards he bestowed on Adeline overcame her with confusion and indignation. In the midst of the banquet, soft music again sounded the most tender and impassioned airs; but its effect on Adeline was now lost, her mind being too much embarrassed and distressed by the presence of the Marquis to admit even the soothings of harmony. A song was now heard, written with that sort of impotent art by which some voluptuous poets believe they can at once conceal and recommend the principles of vice. Adeline received it with contempt and displeasure; and the Marquis perceiving its effect, presently made a sign for another composition, which, adding the force of poetry to the charms of music, might withdraw her mind from the present scene, and enchant it in sweet delirium.

SONG OF A SPIRIT.

In the sightless air I dwell,On the sloping sun-beams play;Delve the cavern's inmost cell,Where never yet did daylight stray.

Dive beneath the green sea waves,And gambol in the briny deeps;Skim every shore that Neptune laves,From Lapland's plains to India's steeps.

Oft I mount with rapid forceAbove the wide earth's shadowy zone;Follow the day-star's flaming courseThrough realms of space to thought unknown:

And listen oft celestial soundsThat swell the air unheard of men,As I watch my nightly roundsO'er woody steep and silent glen.

Under the shade of waving trees,On the green bank of fountain clear,At pensive eve I sit at ease,While dying music murmurs near.

And oft on point of airy clift,That hangs upon the western main,I watch the gay tints passing swift,And twilight veil the liquid plain.

Then, when the breeze has sunk away,And ocean scarce is heard to lave,For me the sea-nymphs softly playTheir dulcet shells beneath the wave.

Their dulcet shells! I hear them now,Slow swells the strain upon mine earNow faintly falls—now warbles low,Till rapture melts into a tear.

The ray that silvers o'er the dew,And trembles through the leafy shade,And tints the scene with softer hue,Calls me to rove the lonely glade;

Or hie me to some ruin'd tower,Faintly shewn by moonlight gleam,Where the lone wanderer owns my powerIn shadows dire that substance seem.

In thrilling sounds that murmur woe,And pausing silence makes more dread;In music breathing from belowSad, solemn strains, that wake the dead.

Unseen I move—unknown am fear'd!Fancy's wildest dreams I weave;And oft by bards my voice is heardTo die along the gales of eve.

When the voice ceased, a mournful strain, played with exquisite expression, sounded from a distant horn; sometimes the notes floated on the air in soft undulations—now they swelled into full and sweeping melody, and now died faintly into silence, when again they rose and trembled in sounds so sweetly tender, as drew tears from Adeline, and exclamations of rapture from the Marquis: he threw his arm round her, and would have pressed her towards him; but she liberated herself from his embrace, and with a look, on which was impressed the firm dignity of virtue, yet touched with sorrow, she awed him to forbearance. Conscious of a superiority which he was ashamed to acknowledge, and endeavouring to despise the influence which he could not resist, he stood for a moment the slave of virtue, though the votary of vice. Soon, however, he recovered his confidence, and began to plead his love; when Adeline, no longer animated by the spirit she had lately shown, and sinking beneath the languor and fatigue which the various and violent agitations of her mind produced, entreated he would leave her to repose.

The paleness of her countenance and the tremulous tone of her voice were too expressive to be misunderstood; and the Marquis, bidding her remember to-morrow, with some hesitation withdrew. The moment she was alone she yielded to the bursting anguish of her heart; and was so absorbed in grief, that it was some time before she perceived she was in the presence of the young women who had lately attended her, and had entered the saloon soon after the Marquis quitted it; they came to conduct her to her chamber. She followed them for some time in silence, till, prompted by desperation, she again endeavoured to awaken their compassion: but again the praises of the Marquis were repeated: and perceiving that all attempts to interest them in her favour were in vain she dismissed them. She secured the door through which they had departed, and then, in the languid hope of discovering some means of escape, she surveyed her chamber. The airy elegance with which it was fitted up, and the luxurious accommodations with which it abounded, seemed designed to fascinate the imagination and to seduce the heart. The hangings were of straw-coloured silk, adorned with a variety of landscapes and historical paintings, the subjects of which partook of the voluptuous character of the owner; the chimney-piece, of Parian marble, was ornamented with several reposing figures from the antique. The bed was of silk, the colour of the hangings, richly fringed with purple and silver, and the head made in form of a canopy. The steps which were placed near the bed to assist in ascending it, were supported by cupids apparently of solid silver. China vases filled with perfume stood in several of the recesses, upon stands of the same structure as the toilet, which was magnificent, and ornamented with a variety of trinkets.

Adeline threw a transient look upon these various objects, and proceeded to examine the windows, which descended to the floor and opened into balconies towards the garden she had seen from the saloon. They were now fastened, and her efforts to move them were ineffectual: at length she gave up the attempt. A door next attracted her notice, which she found was not fastened; it opened upon a dressing-closet, to which she descended by a few steps: two windows appeared, she hastened towards them; one refused to yield, but her heart beat with sudden joy when the other opened to her touch.

In the transport of the moment, she forgot that its distance from the ground might yet deny the escape she meditated. She returned to lock the door of the closet, to prevent a surprise, which, however, was unnecessary, that of the bed-room being already secured. She now looked out from the window; the garden lay before her, and she perceived that the window, which descended to the floor, was so near the ground, that she might jump from it with ease: almost in the same moment she perceived this, she sprang forward and alighted safely in an extensive garden, resembling more an English pleasure ground, than a series of French parterres.

Thence she had little doubt of escaping, either by some broken fence, or low part of the wall; she tripped lightly along, for hope played round her heart. The clouds of the late storm were now dispersed, and the moonlight, which slept on the lawns and spangled the flowerets yet heavy with rain drops, afforded her a distinct view of the surrounding scenery; she followed the direction of the high wall that adjoined the chateau, till it was concealed from her sight by a thick wilderness, so entangled with boughs and obscured by darkness, that she feared to enter, and turned aside into a walk on the right; it conducted her to the margin of a lake overhung with lofty trees.

The moonbeams dancing upon the waters, that with gentle undulation played along the shore, exhibited a scene of tranquil beauty, which would have soothed a heart less agitated than was that of Adeline: she sighed as she transiently surveyed it, and passed hastily on in search of the garden wall, from which she had now strayed a considerable way. After wandering for some time through alleys and over lawns, without meeting with any thing like a boundary to the grounds, she again found herself at the lake, and now traversed its border with the footsteps of despair:—tears rolled down her cheeks. The scene around exhibited only images of peace and delight; every object seemed to repose; not a breath waved the foliage, not a sound stole through the air: it was in her bosom only that tumult and distress prevailed. She still pursued the windings of the shore, till an opening in the woods conducted her up a gentle ascent: the path now wound along the side of a hill where the gloom was so deep, that it was with some difficulty she found her way: suddenly, however, the avenue opened to a lofty grove, and she perceived a light issue from a recess at some distance.

She paused, and her first impulse was to retreat; but listening, and hearing no sound, a faint hope beamed upon her mind, that the person to whom the light belonged, might be won to favour her escape. She advanced, with trembling and cautious steps, towards the recess, that she might secretly observe the person, before she ventured to enter it. Her emotion increased as she approached; and, having reached the bower, she beheld, through an open window, the Marquis reclining on a sofa, near which stood a table, covered with fruit and wine. He was alone, and his countenance was flushed with drinking.

While she gazed, fixed to the spot by terror, he looked up towards the casement; the light gleamed full upon her face, but she stayed not to learn whether he had observed her, for, with the swiftness of sound, she left the place and ran, without knowing whether she was pursued. Having gone a considerable way, fatigue at length compelled her to stop, and she threw herself upon the turf, almost fainting with fear and languor. She knew, if the Marquis detected her in an attempt to escape, he would, probably, burst the bounds which she had hitherto prescribed to himself, and that she had the most dreadful evils to expect. The palpitations of terror were so strong, that she could with difficulty breathe.

She watched and listened in trembling expectation, but no form met her eye, no sound her ear; in this state she remained a considerable time. She wept, and the tears she shed relieved her oppressed heart. O my father! said she, why did you abandon your child? If you knew the dangers to which you have exposed her, you would, surely, pity and relieve her. Alas! shall I never find a friend! am I destined still to trust and be deceived?—Peter too, could he be treacherous? She wept again, and then returned to a sense of her present danger, and to a consideration of the means of escaping it—but no means appeared.

To her imagination the grounds were boundless; she had wandered from lawn to lawn, and from grove to grove, without perceiving any termination to the place; the garden-wall she could not find, but she resolved neither to return to the chateau, nor to relinquish her search. As she was rising to depart, she perceived a shadow move along at some distance: she stood still to observe it. It slowly advanced and then disappeared; but presently she saw a person emerge from the gloom, and approach the spot where she stood. She had no doubt that the Marquis had observed her, and she ran with all possible speed to the shade of some woods on the left. Footsteps pursued her, and she heard her name repeated, while she in vain endeavoured to quicken her pace.

Suddenly the sound of pursuit turned, and sunk away in a different direction: she paused to take breath; she looked around, and no person appeared. She now proceeded slowly along the avenue, and had almost reached its termination, when she saw the same figure emerge from the woods and dart across the avenue: it instantly pursued her and approached. A voice called her, but she was gone beyond its reach, for she had sunk senseless upon the ground: it was long before she revived: when she did, she found herself in the arms of a stranger, and made an effort to disengage herself.

Fear nothing, lovely Adeline, said he, fear nothing: you are in the arms of a friend, who will encounter any hazard for your sake; who will protect you with his life. He pressed her gently to his heart. Have you then forgot me? continued he. She looked earnestly at him, and was now convinced that it was Theodore who spoke. Joy was her first emotion; but, recollecting his former abrupt departure, at a time so critical to her safety and that he was the friend of the Marquis, a thousand mingled sensations struggled in her breast, and overwhelmed her with mistrust, apprehension, and disappointment.

Theodore raised her from the ground, and while he yet supported her, let us fly from this place, said he; a carriage waits to receive us; it shall go wherever you direct, and convey you to your friends. This last sentence touched her heart: Alas, I have no friends! said she, nor do I know whither to go. Theodore gently pressed her hand between his, and, in a voice of the softest compassion, said, My friends then shall be yours; suffer me to lead you to them. But I am in agony while you remain in this place; let us hasten to quit it. Adeline was going to reply, when voices were heard among the trees, and Theodore, supporting her with his arm, hurried her along the avenue; they continued their flight till Adeline, panting for breath, could go no further.

Having paused a while, and heard no footsteps in pursuit, they renewed their course: Theodore knew that they were now not far from the garden wall; but he was also aware, that in the intermediate space several paths wound from remote parts of the grounds into the walk he was to pass, from whence the Marquis's people might issue and intercept him. He, however, concealed his apprehensions from Adeline, and endeavoured to soothe and support her spirits.

At length they reached the wall, and Theodore was leading her towards a low part of it, near which stood the carriage, when again they heard voices in the air. Adeline's spirits and strength were nearly exhausted, but she made a last effort to proceed and she now saw the ladder at some distance by which Theodore had descended to the garden. Exert yourself yet a little longer, said he, and you will be in safety. He held the ladder while she ascended; the top of the wall was broad and level, and Adeline, having reached it, remained there till Theodore followed and drew the ladder to the other side.

When they had descended, the carriage appeared in waiting, but without the driver. Theodore feared to call, lest his voice should betray him; he, therefore, put Adeline into the carriage, and went in search of the postillion, whom he found asleep under a tree at some distance: having awakened him, they returned to the vehicle, which soon drove furiously away. Adeline did not yet dare to believe herself safe; but, after proceeding a considerable time without interruption, joy burst upon her heart, and she thanked her deliverer in terms of the warmest gratitude. The sympathy expressed in the tone of his voice and manner, proved that his happiness, on this occasion, almost equalled her own.

As reflection gradually stole upon her mind, anxiety superseded joy: in the tumult of the late moments, she thought only of escape; but the circumstances of her present situation now appeared to her, and she became silent and pensive: she had no friends to whom she could fly, and was going with a young chevalier, almost a stranger to her, she knew not whither. She remembered how often she had been deceived and betrayed where she trusted most, and her spirits sunk: she remembered also the former attention which Theodore had shown her, and dreaded lest his conduct might be prompted by a selfish passion. She saw this to be possible, but she disdained to believe it probable, and felt that nothing could give her greater pain than to doubt the integrity of Theodore.

He interrupted her reverie, by recurring to her late situation at the abbey. You would be much surprised, said he, and, I fear, offended that I did not attend my appointment at the abbey, after the alarming hints I had given you in our last interview. That circumstance has, perhaps, injured me in your esteem, if, indeed, I was ever so happy as to possess it: but my designs were overruled by those of the Marquis de Montalt; and I think I may venture to assert, that my distress upon this occasion was, at least, equal to your apprehensions.

Adeline said, she had been much alarmed by the hints he had given her, and by his failing to afford further information concerning the subject of her danger; and—She checked the sentence that hung upon her lips, for she perceived that she was unwarily betraying the interest he held in her heart. There were a few moments of silence, and neither party seemed perfectly at ease. Theodore, at length, renewed the conversation: Suffer me to acquaint you, said he, with the circumstances that withheld me from the interview I solicited; I am anxious to exculpate myself. Without waiting her reply, he proceeded to inform her, that the Marquis had, by some inexplicable means, learned or suspected the subject of their last conversation, and, perceiving his designs were in danger of being counteracted, had taken effectual means to prevent her obtaining further intelligence of them. Adeline immediately recollected that Theodore and herself had been seen in the forest by La Motte, who had, no doubt, suspected their growing intimacy, and had taken care to inform the Marquis how likely he was to find a rival in his friend.

On the day following that on which I last saw you, said Theodore, the Marquis, who is my colonel, commanded me to prepare to attend my regiment, and appointed the following morning for my journey. This sudden order gave me some surprise, but I was not long in doubt concerning the motive for it: a servant of the Marquis, who had been long attached to me, entered my room soon after I had left his lord, and expressing concern at my abrupt departure, dropped some hints respecting it, which excited my surprise. I inquired further, and was confirmed in the suspicions I had for some time entertained of the Marquis's designs upon you.

Jaques further informed me, that our late interview had been noticed and communicated to the Marquis. His information had been obtained from a fellow-servant, and it alarmed me so much, that I engaged him to send me intelligence from time to time, concerning the proceedings of the Marquis. I now looked forward to the evening which would bring me again to your presence with increased impatience: but the ingenuity of the Marquis effectually counteracted my endeavours and wishes; he had made an engagement to pass the day at the villa of a nobleman some leagues distant, and, notwithstanding all the excuses I could offer, I was obliged to attend him. Thus compelled to obey, I passed a day of more agitation and anxiety than I had ever before experienced. It was midnight before we returned to the Marquis's chateau. I arose early in the morning to commence my journey, and resolved to seek an interview with you before I left the province.

When I entered the breakfast room, I was much surprised to find the Marquis there already, who, commending the beauty of the morning, declared his intention of accompanying me as far as Chineau. Thus unexpectedly deprived of my last hope, my countenance, I believe, expressed what I felt, for the scrutinizing eye of the Marquis instantly changed from seeming carelessness to displeasure. The distance from Chineau to the abbey was at least twelve leagues; yet I had once some intention of returning from thence, when the Marquis should leave me, till I recollected the very remote chance there would even then be of seeing you alone, and also, that if I was observed by La Motte, it would awaken all his suspicions, and caution him against any future plan I might see it expedient to attempt; I therefore proceeded to join my regiment.

Jaques sent me frequent accounts of the operations of the Marquis; but his manner of relating them was so very confused, that they only served to perplex and distress me. His last letter, however, alarmed me so much, that my residence in quarters became intolerable; and, as I found it impossible to obtain leave of absence, I secretly left the regiment, and concealed myself in a cottage about a mile from the chateau, that I might obtain the earliest intelligence of the Marquis's plans. Jaques brought me daily information, and, at last, an account of the horrible plot which was laid for the following night.

I saw little probability of warning you of your danger. If I ventured near the abbey, La Motte might discover me, and frustrate every attempt on my part to save you; yet I determined to encounter this risk for the chance of seeing you, and towards evening I was preparing to set out for the forest, when Jaques arrived, and informed me that you was to be brought to the chateau. My plan was thus rendered less difficult. I learned also, that the Marquis, by means of those refinements in luxury, with which he is but too well acquainted, designed, now that his apprehension of losing you was no more, to seduce you to his wishes, and impose upon you by a fictitious marriage. Having obtained information concerning the situation of the room allotted you, I ordered a chaise to be in waiting, and with a design of scaling your window, and conducting you thence, I entered the garden at midnight.

Theodore having ceased to speak:—I know not how words can express my sense of the obligations I owe you, said Adeline, or my gratitude for your generosity.

Ah! call it not generosity, he replied, it was love. He paused. Adeline was silent. After some moments of expressive emotion, he resumed; But pardon this abrupt declaration; yet why do I call it abrupt, since my actions have already disclosed what my lips have never, till this instant, ventured to acknowledge. He paused again. Adeline was still silent. Yet do me the justice to believe, that I am sensible of the impropriety of pleading my love at present, and have been surprised into this confession. I promise also to forbear from a renewal of the subject, till you are placed in a situation where you may freely accept, or refuse, the sincere regards I offer you. If I could, however, now be certain that I possess your esteem, it would relieve me from much anxiety.

Adeline felt surprised that he should doubt her esteem for him, after the signal and generous service he had rendered her; but she was not yet acquainted with the timidity of love. Do you then, said she in a tremulous voice, believe me ungrateful? It is impossible I can consider your friendly interference in my behalf without esteeming you. Theodore immediately took her hand and pressed it to his lips in silence. They were both too much agitated to converse, and continued to travel for some miles without exchanging a word.

CHAPTER XII

*And hope enchanted smiled and waved her goldenhair,And longer had she sung—but, with a frown,Revenge impatient rose.*ODE TO THE PASSIONS.

The dawn of morning now trembled through the clouds, when the travellers stopped at a small town to change horses. Theodore entreated Adeline to alight and take some refreshment, and to this she at length consented. But the people of the inn were not yet up, and it was some time before the knocking and the roaring of the postillion could rouse them.

Having taken some slight refreshment, Theodore and Adeline returned to the carriage. The only subject upon which Theodore could have spoke with interest, delicacy forbade him at this time to notice; and after pointing out some beautiful scenery on the road, and making other efforts to support a conversation, he relapsed into silence. His mind, though still anxious, was now relieved from the apprehension that had long oppressed it. When he first saw Adeline, her loveliness made a deep impression on his heart: there was a sentiment in her beauty, which his mind immediately acknowledged, and the effect of which, her manners and conversation had afterwards confirmed. Her charms appeared to him like those since so finely described by an English poet:

Oh! have you seen, bathed in the morning dew,The budding rose its infant bloom display?When first its virgin tints unfold to view.It shrinks, and scarcely trusts the blaze of day.

So soft, so delicate, so sweet she came,Youth's damask glow just dawning on her cheek.I gaz'd, I sigh'd, I caught the tender flame,Felt the fond pang, and droop'd with passion weak.

A knowledge of her destitute condition and of the dangers with which she was environed, had awakened in his heart the tenderest touch of pity, and assisted the change of admiration into love. The distress he suffered, when compelled to leave her exposed to these dangers, without being able to warn her of them, can only be imagined. During his residence with his regiment, his mind was the constant prey of terrors, which he saw no means of combating but by returning to the neighbourhood of the abbey where he might obtain early intelligence of the Marquis's schemes, and be ready to give his assistance to Adeline.

Leave of absence he could not request, without betraying his design where most he dreaded it should be known; and at length with a generous rashness, which though it defied law was impelled by virtue, he secretly quitted his regiment. The progress of the Marquis's plan he had observed with trembling anxiety, till the night that was to decide the fate of Adeline and himself roused all his mind to action, and involved him in a tumult of hope and fear, horror and expectation.

Never till the present hour had he ventured to believe she was in safety. Now the distance they had gained from the chateau without perceiving any pursuit, increased his best hopes. It was impossible he could sit by the side of his beloved Adeline, and receive assurances of her gratitude and esteem, without venturing to hope for her love.

He congratulated himself as her preserver, and anticipated scenes of happiness when she should be under the protection of his family. The clouds of misery and apprehension disappeared from his mind, and left it to the sunshine of joy. When a shadow of fear would sometimes return, or when he recollected with compunction the circumstances under which he had left his regiment, stationed as it was upon the frontiers, and in a time of war, he looked at Adeline, and her countenance with instantaneous magic beamed peace upon his heart.

But Adeline had a subject of anxiety from which Theodore was exempt: the prospect of her future days was involved in darkness and uncertainty. Again she was going to claim the bounty of strangers—again going to encounter the uncertainty of their kindness; exposed to the hardships of dependance, or to the difficulty of earning a precarious livelihood. These anticipations obscured the joy occasioned by her escape, and by the affection which the conduct and avowal of Theodore had exhibited. The delicacy of his behaviour, in forbearing to take advantage of her present situation to plead his love, increased her esteem and flattered her pride.

Adeline was lost in meditation upon subjects like these, when the postillion stopped the carriage, and pointing to part of a road which wound down the side of a hill they had passed, said there were several horsemen in pursuit! Theodore immediately ordered him to proceed with all possible speed, and to strike out of the great road into the first obscure way that offered. The postillion cracked his whip in the air, and set off as if he was flying for life. In the meanwhile Theodore endeavoured to reanimate Adeline, who was sinking with terror, and who now thought, if she could only escape from the Marquis, she could defy the future.

Presently they struck into a by lane screened and overshadowed by thick trees. Theodore again looked from the window, but the closing boughs prevented his seeing far enough to determine whether the pursuit continued. For his sake Adeline endeavoured to disguise her emotions. This lane, said Theodore, will certainly lead to a town or village, and then we have nothing to apprehend: for, though my single arm could not defend you against the number of our pursuers, I nave no doubt of being able to interest some of the inhabitants in our behalf.

Adeline appeared to be comforted by the hope this reflection suggested: and Theodore again looked back: but the windings of the road closed his view, and the rattling of the wheels overcame every other sound. At length he called to the postillion to stop; and having listened attentively without perceiving any sound of horses, he began to hope they were now in safety. Do you know whither this road leads? said he. The postillion answered that he did not, but he saw some houses through the trees at a distance, and believed that it led to them. This was most welcome intelligence to Theodore, who looked forward and perceived the houses. The postillion set off. Fear nothing, my adored Adeline, said he, you are now safe; I will part with you but with life. Adeline sighed, not for herself only, but for the danger to which Theodore might be exposed.

They had continued to travel in this manner for near half an hour, when they arrived at a small village, and soon after stopped at an inn, the best the place afforded. As Theodore lifted Adeline from the chaise, he again entreated her to dismiss her apprehensions, and spoke with a tenderness to which she could reply only by a smile that ill concealed her anxiety. After ordering refreshments, he went out to speak with the landlord; but had scarcely left the room when Adeline observed a party of horsemen enter the inn yard, and she had no doubt these were the persons from whom they fled. The faces of two of them only were turned towards her, but she thought the figure of one of the others not unlike that of the Marquis.

Her heart was chilled, and for some moments the powers of reason forsook her. Her first design was to seek concealments but while she considered the means, one of the horsemen looked up to the window near, which she stood, and speaking to his companions they entered the inn. To quit the room without being observed was impossible; to remain there, alone and unprotected as she was, would almost be equally dangerous. She paced the room in an agony of terror, often secretly calling on Theodore, and often wondering he did not return. These were moments of indescribable suffering. A loud and tumultuous sound of voices now arose from a distant part of the house, and she soon, distinguished the words of the disputants. I arrest you in the king's name, said one; and bid you, at your peril, attempt to go from hence, except under a guard.

The next minute Adeline heard the voice of Theodore in reply. I do not mean to dispute the king's orders, said he, and give you my word of honour not to go without you; but first unhand me, that I may return to that room; I have a friend there whom I wish to speak with. To this proposal they at first objected, considering it merely as an excuse to obtain an opportunity of escaping; but after much altercation and entreaty his request was granted. He sprang forward towards the room where Adeline remained; and while a sergeant and corporal followed him to the door, the two soldiers went out into the yard of the inn to watch the windows of the apartment.

With an eager hand he unclosed the door; but Adeline hastened not to meet him, for she had fainted almost at the beginning of the dispute. Theodore called loudly for assistance; and the mistress of the inn soon appeared with her stock of remedies, which were administered in vain to Adeline, who remained insensible, and by breathing alone gave signs of her existence. The distress of Theodore was in the mean time heightened by the appearance of the officers, who, laughing at the discovery of his pretended friend, declared they could wait no longer. Saying this, they would have forced him from the inanimate form of Adeline, over whom he hung in unutterable anguish, when fiercely turning upon them he drew his sword, and swore no power on earth should force him away before the lady recovered.

The men, enraged by the action and the determined air of Theodore, exclaimed, Do you oppose the king's orders? and advanced to seize him: but he presented the point of his sword, and bade them at their peril approach. One of them immediately drew. Theodore kept his guard, but did not advance. I demand only to wait here till the lady recovers, said he;—you understand the alternative. The man already exasperated by the opposition of Theodore, regarded the latter part of his speech as a threat, and became determined not to give up the point: he pressed forward; and while his comrade called the men from the yard, Theodore wounded him slightly in the shoulder, and received himself the stroke of a sabre on his head.

The blood gushed furiously from the wound: Theodore, staggering to a chair, sunk into it, just as the remainder of the party entered the room; and Adeline unclosed her eyes to see him ghastly pale, and covered with blood. She uttered an involuntary scream, and exclaiming, They have murdered him, nearly relapsed. At the sound of her voice he raised his head, and smiling held out his hand to her. I am not much hurt said he faintly, and shall soon be better, if indeed you are recovered. She hastened towards him, and gave her hand. Is nobody gone for a surgeon? said she with a look of agony. Do not be alarmed, said Theodore, I am not so ill as you imagine. The room was now crowded with people, whom the report of the affray had now brought together; among these was a man who acted as physician, apothecary, and surgeon to the village, and who now stepped forward to the assistance of Theodore.

Having examined the wound, he declined giving his opinion, but ordered the patient to be immediately put to bed; to which the officers objected, alleging that it was their duty to carry him to the regiment. That cannot be done without great danger to his life, replied the doctor; and—

Oh; his life, said the sergeant; we have nothing to do with that, we must do our duty. Adeline, who had hitherto stood in trembling anxiety, could now no longer be silent. Since the surgeon, said she, has declared it his opinion that this gentleman cannot be removed in his present condition without endangering his life, you will remember that if he dies, yours will probably answer it.

Yes, rejoined the surgeon, who was unwilling to relinquish his patient; I declare before these witnesses, that he cannot be removed with safety: you will do well therefore to consider the consequences. He has received a very dangerous wound, which requires the most careful treatment, and the event is even then doubtful; but if he travels, a fever may ensue, and the wound will then be mortal. Theodore heard this sentence with composure, but Adeline could with difficulty conceal the anguish of her heart: she roused all her fortitude to suppress the tears that struggled in her eyes; and though she wished to interest the humanity or to awaken the fears of the men in behalf of their unfortunate prisoner, she dared not to trust her voice with utterance.

From this internal struggle she was relieved by the compassion of the people who filled the room, and becoming clamorous in the cause of Theodore, declared the officers would be guilty of murder if they removed him. Why he must die at any rate, said the sergeant, for quitting his post, and drawing upon me in the execution of the king's orders. A faint sickness seized the heart of Adeline, and she leaned for support against Theodore's chair, whose concern for himself was for a while suspended in his anxiety for her. He supported her with his arm, and forcing a smile, said in a low voice, which she only could hear. This is a misrepresentation; I doubt not, when the affair is inquired into, it will be settled without any serious consequences.

Adeline knew these words were uttered only to console her, and therefore did not give much credit to them, though Theodore continued to give her similar assurances of his safety. Meanwhile the mob, whose compassion for him had been gradually excited by the obduracy of the officer, were now roused to pity and indignation by the seeming certainty of his punishment, and the unfeeling manner in which it had been denounced. In a short time they became so much enraged that, partly from a dread of further consequences, and partly from the shame which their charges of cruelty occasioned, the sergeant consented that he should be put to bed, till his commanding officer might direct what was to be done. Adeline's joy at this circumstance overcame for a moment the sense of her misfortunes and of her situation.

She waited in an adjoining room the sentence of the surgeon, who was now engaged in examining the wound; and though the accident would in any other circumstances have severely afflicted her, she now lamented it the more, because she considered herself as the cause of it, and because the misfortune by illustrating more fully the affection of her lover, drew him closer to her heart, and seemed therefore to sharpen the poignancy of her affliction. The dreadful assertion that Theodore, should he recover, would be punished with death, she scarcely dared to consider, but endeavoured to believe that it was no more than a cruel exaggeration of his antagonist.

Upon the whole, Theodore's present danger, together with the attendant circumstances, awakened all her tenderness, and discovered to her the true state of her affections. The graceful form, the noble, intelligent, countenance, and the engaging manners which she had at first admired in Theodore, became afterwards more interesting by that strength of thought and elegance of sentiment exhibited in his conversation. His conduct, since her escape, had excited her warmest gratitude; and the danger which he had now encountered in her behalf, called forth her tenderness, and heightened it into love. The veil was removed from her heart, and she saw for the first time its genuine emotions.

The surgeon at length came out of Theodore's chamber into the room where Adeline was waiting to speak with him. She inquired concerning the state of his wound. You are a relation of the gentleman's, I presume, Madam; his sister, perhaps? The question vexed and embarrassed her, and without answering it she repeated her inquiry. Perhaps, Madam, you are more nearly related, pursued the surgeon, seeming also to disregard her question,—perhaps you are his wife? Adeline blushed, and was about to reply, but he continued his speech. The interest you take in his welfare is at least very flattering, and I would almost consent to exchange conditions with him, were I sure of receiving such tender compassion from so charming a lady. Saying this, he bowed to the ground. Adeline assuming a very reserved air, said, Now, Sir, that you have concluded your compliment, you will perhaps attend to my question; I have inquired how you have left your patient.

That, Madam, is perhaps a question very difficult to be resolved; and it is likewise a very disagreeable office to pronounce ill news—I fear he will die. The surgeon opened his snuff-box and presented it to Adeline. Die! she exclaimed in a faint voice, die!

Do not be alarmed, Madam, resumed the surgeon, observing her grow pale, do not be alarmed. It is possible that the wound may not have reached the——, he stammered, in that case the——, stammering again, is not affected; and if so, the interior membranes of the brain are not touched: in this case the wound may perhaps escape inflammation, and the patient may possibly recover. But if, on the other hand——

I beseech you, Sir, to speak intelligibly, interrupted Adeline, and not to trifle with my anxiety. Do you really believe him in danger?

In danger, Madam, exclaimed the surgeon, in danger! yes, certainly, in very great danger. Saying this, he walked away with an air of chagrin and displeasure. Adeline remained for some moments in the room, in an excess of sorrow, which she found it impossible to restrain; and then drying her tears, and endeavouring to compose her countenance, she went to inquire for the mistress of the inn, to whom she sent a waiter. After expecting her in vain for some time, she rang the bell, and sent another message somewhat more pressing. Still the hostess did not appear; and Adeline at length went herself down stairs, where she found her, surrounded by a number of people, relating, with a loud voice and various gesticulations, the particulars of the late accident. Perceiving Adeline, she called out, Oh! here is Mademoiselle herself; and the eyes of the assembly were immediately turned upon her. Adeline, whom the crowd prevented from approaching the hostess, now beckoned her, and was going to withdraw; but the landlady, eager in the pursuit of her story, disregarded the signal. In vain did Adeline endeavour to catch her eye; it glanced every where but upon her, who was unwilling to attract the further notice of the crowd by calling out.

It is a great pity, to be sure, that he should be shot, said the landlady, he's such a handsome man; but they say he certainly will if he recovers. Poor gentleman! he will very likely not suffer though, for the doctor says he will never go out of this house alive. Adeline now spoke to a man who stood near, and desiring he would tell the hostess she wished to speak with her, left the place.

In about ten minutes the landlady appeared. Alas! Mademoiselle, said she, your brother is in a sad condition; they fear he won't get over. Adeline inquired whether there was any other medical person in the town than the surgeon whom she had seen. Lord, Madam, this is a rare healthy place; we have little need of medicine people here; such an accident never happened in it before. The doctor has been here ten years, but there's very bad encouragement for his trade, and I believe he's poor enough himself. One of the sort's quite enough for us. Adeline interrupted her to ask some questions concerning Theodore, whom the hostess had attended to his chamber. She inquired how he had borne the dressing of the wound, and whether he appeared to be easier after the operation; questions to which the hostess gave no very satisfactory answers. She now inquired whether there was any surgeon in the neighbourhood of the town, and was told there was not.

The distress visible in Adeline's countenance seemed to excite the compassion of the landlady, who now endeavoured to console her in the best manner she was able. She advised her to send for her friends, and offered to procure a messenger. Adeline sighed, and said it was unnecessary. I don't know, Ma'mselle, what you may think necessary, continued the hostess; but I know I should think it very hard to die in a strange place, with no relations near me, and I dare say the poor gentleman thinks so himself; and besides, who is to pay for his funeral if he dies? Adeline begged she would be silent; and desiring that every proper attention might be given, she promised her a reward for her trouble, and requested pen and ink immediately. Ay, to be sure, Ma'mselle, that is the proper way; why your friends would never forgive you if you did not acquaint them; I know it by myself. And as for taking care of him, he shall have every thing the house affords; and I warrant there is never a better inn in the province, though the town is none of the biggest. Adeline was obliged to repeat her request for pen and ink, before the loquacious hostess would quit the room.

The thought of sending for Theodore's friends had, in the tumult of the late scenes, never occurred to her, and she was now somewhat consoled by the prospect of comfort which it opened for him. When the pen and ink were brought, she wrote the following note to Theodore:—

"In your present condition, you have need of every comfort that can be procured you; and surely there is no cordial more valuable in illness than the presence of a friend. Suffer me, therefore, to acquaint your family with your situation: it will be a satisfaction to me, and, I doubt not, a consolation to you."

In a short time after she had sent the note, she received a message from Theodore, entreating most respectfully, but earnestly, to see her for a few minutes. She immediately went to his chamber, and found her worst apprehensions confirmed, by the languor expressed in his countenance; while the shock she received, together with her struggle to disguise her emotions, almost overcame her. I thank you for this goodness, said he, extending his hand, which she received, and sitting down by the bed, burst into a flood of tears. When her agitation had somewhat subsided, and, removing her handkerchief from her eyes, she again looked on Theodore, a smile of the tenderest love expressed his sense of the interest she took in his welfare, and administered a temporary relief to her heart.

Forgive this weakness, said she; my spirits have of late been so variously agitated—Theodore interrupted her: These tears are more flattering to my heart. But for my sake endeavour to support yourself: I doubt not I shall soon be better; the surgeon—

I do not like him, said Adeline; but tell me how you find yourself? He assured her that he was now much easier than he had yet been; and mentioning her kind note, he led to the subject on account of which he had solicited to see her. My family, said he, reside at a great distance from hence, and I well know their affection is such, that, were they informed of my situation, no consideration, however reasonable, could prevent their coming to my assistance: but before they can arrive, their presence will probably be unnecessary (Adeline looked earnestly at him.) I should probably be well, pursued he, smiling, before a letter could reach them; it would, therefore, occasion them unnecessary pain, and moreover a fruitless journey. For your sake, Adeline, I could wish they were here; but a few days will more fully show the consequences of my wound: let us wait at least till then, and be directed by circumstances.

Adeline forbore to press the subject further, and turned to one more immediately interesting. I much wish, said she, that you had a more able surgeon; you know the geography of the province better than I do; are we in the neighbourhood of any town likely to afford you other advice?

I believe not, said he; and this is an affair of little consequence, for my wound is so inconsiderable that a very moderate share of skill may suffice to cure it. But why, my beloved Adeline, do you give way to this anxiety? why suffer yourself to be disturbed by this tendency to forebode the worst? I am willing, perhaps presumptuously so, to attribute it to your kindness; and suffer me to assure you, that while it excites my gratitude, it increases my tenderest esteem. O Adeline! since you wish my speedy recovery, let me see you composed: while I believe you to be unhappy I cannot be well.—She assured him she would endeavour to be at least tranquil; and fearing the conversation, if prolonged, would be prejudicial to him, she left him to repose.

As she turned out of the gallery she met the hostess, upon whom certain words of Adeline had operated as a talisman, transforming neglect and impertinence into officious civility. She came to inquire whether the gentleman above stairs had every thing that he liked, for she was sure it was her endeavour that he should. I have got him a nurse, Ma'mselle, to attend him, and I dare say she will do very well; but I will look to that, for I shall not mind helping him myself sometimes. Poor gentleman! how patiently he bears it! One would not think now that he believes he is going to die; yet the doctor told him so himself, or at least as good. Adeline was extremely shocked at this imprudent conduct of the surgeon, and dismissed the landlady, after ordering a slight dinner.

Towards evening the surgeon again made his appearance; and having passed some time with his patient, returned to the parlour, according to the desire of Adeline, to inform her of his condition. He answered Adeline's inquiries with great solemnity. It is impossible to determine positively at present. Madam, but I have reason to adhere to the opinion I gave you this morning. I am not apt indeed, to form opinions upon uncertain grounds—I will give you a singular instance of this:

It is not above a fortnight since I was sent for to a patient at some leagues distance: I was from home when the messenger arrived, and the case being urgent, before I could reach the patient another physician was consulted, who had ordered such medicines as he thought proper, and the patient had been apparently relieved by them. His friends were congratulating themselves upon his improvement when I arrived, and had agreed in opinion with the physician that there was no danger in his case. Depend upon it, said I, you are mistaken; these medicines cannot have relieved him; the patient is in the utmost danger. The patient groaned; but my brother physician persisted in affirming that the remedies he had prescribed would not only be certain, but speedy, some good effect having been already produced by them. Upon this I lost all patience; and adhering to my opinion, that these effects were fallacious and the case desperate, I assured the patient himself that his life was in the utmost danger. I am not one of those, Madam, who deceive their patients to the last moment;—but you shall hear the conclusion.

My brother physician was, I suppose, enraged by the firmness of my opposition, for he assumed a most angry look, which did not in the least affect me, and turning to the patient, desired he would decide upon which of our opinions to rely, for he must decline acting with me. The patient did me the honour, pursued the surgeon with a smile of complacency and smoothing his ruffles, to think more highly of me than, perhaps, I deserved, for he immediately dismissed my opponent. I could not have believed, said he, as the physician left the room—I could not have believed that a man who has been so many years in the profession could be so wholly ignorant of it.

I could not have believed it either, said I.—I am astonished that he was not aware of my danger, resumed the patient. I am astonished likewise, replied I. I was resolved to do what I could for the patient, for he was a man of understanding, as you perceive, and I had a regard for him. I therefore altered the prescriptions, and myself administered the medicines; but all would not do,—my opinion was verified, and he died even before the next morning.—Adeline, who had been compelled to listen to this long story, sighed at the conclusion of it. I don't wonder that you are affected, Madam, said the surgeon; the instance I have related is certainly a very affecting one. It distressed me so much, that it was some time before I could think or even speak concerning it. But you must allow, Madam, continued he, lowering his voice and bowing with a look of self-congratulation, that this was a striking instance of the infallibility of my judgment.

Adeline shuddered at the infallibility of his judgment, and made no reply. It was a shocking thing for the poor man, resumed the surgeon.—It was indeed, very shocking, said Adeline.—It affected me a good deal when it happened, continued he.—Undoubtedly, Sir, said Adeline.

But time wears away the most painful impressions.

I think you mention it was about a fortnight since this happened?

Somewhere thereabouts, replied the surgeon without seeming to understand the observation.—And will you permit me, Sir, to ask the name of the physician who so ignorantly opposed you?

Certainly, Madame; it is Lafance.

He lives in the obscurity he deserves, no doubt, said Adeline.

Why no, Madam, he lives in a town of some note, at about the distance of four leagues from hence; and affords one instance, among many others, that the public opinion, is generally erroneous. You will hardly believe it, but I assure you it is a fact, that this man comes into a great deal of practice, while I am suffered to remain here neglected, and, indeed very little known.

During his narrative Adeline had been considering by what means she could discover the name of the physician; for the instance that had been produced to prove his ignorance, and the infallibility of his opponent, had completely settled her opinion concerning them both. She now more than ever wished to deliver Theodore from the hands of the surgeon, and was musing on the possibility, when he with so much self-security, developed the means.

She asked him a few more questions concerning the state of Theodore's wound; and was told it was much as it had been, but that some degree of fever had come on. But I have ordered a fire to be made in the room, continued the surgeon, and some additional blankets to be laid on the bed; these, I doubt not, will have a proper effect. In the mean time they must be careful to keep from him every kind of liquid, except some cordial draughts which I shall send. He will naturally ask for drink, but it must on no account be given to him.

You do not approve then of the method which I have somewhere heard of, said Adeline, of attending to nature in these cases?

Nature, Madam! pursued he, nature is the most improper guide in the world: I always adopt a method directly contrary to what she would suggest; for what can be the use of art, if she is only to follow nature? This was my first opinion on setting out in life, and I have ever since strictly adhered to it. From what I have said, indeed, Madam, you may perhaps perceive that my opinions may be depended on; what they once are they always are, for my mind is not of that frivolous kind to be affected by circumstances.

Adeline was fatigued by this discourse, and impatient to impart to Theodore her discovery of a physician: but the surgeon seemed by no means disposed to leave her, and was expatiating upon various topics, with new instances of his surprising sagacity, when the waiter brought a message that some person desired to see him. He was, however, engaged upon too agreeable a topic to be easily prevailed upon to quit it, and it was not till after a second message was brought that he made his bow to Adeline and left the room. The moment he was gone she sent a note to Theodore, entreating his permission to call in the assistance of the physician.

The conceited manners of the surgeon had by this time given Theodore a very unfavourable opinion of his talents, and the last prescription had so fully confirmed it, that he now readily consented to have other advice. Adeline immediately inquired for a messenger; but recollecting that the residence of the physician was still a secret, she applied to the hostess, who being really ignorant of it, or pretending to be so, gave her no information. What further inquiries she made were equally ineffectual, and she passed some hours in extreme distress, while the disorder of Theodore rather increased than abated.

When supper appeared, she asked the boy who waited if he knew a physician of the name of Lafance in the neighbourhood. Not in the neighbourhood, Madame; but I know doctor Lafance of Chancy, for I come from the town.—Adeline inquired further, and received very satisfactory answers. But the town was at some leagues distance, and the delay this circumstance must occasion again alarmed her; she, however, ordered a messenger to be immediately dispatched, and having sent again to inquire concerning Theodore, retired to her chamber for the night.

The continued fatigue she had suffered for the last fourteen hours overcame anxiety, and her harassed spirits sunk to repose. She slept till late in the morning, and was then awakened by the landlady, who came to inform her that Theodore was much worse, and to inquire what should be done. Adeline, finding that the physician was not arrived, immediately arose, and hastened to inquire further concerning Theodore. The hostess informed her that he had passed a very disturbed night; that he had complained of being very hot, and desired that the fire in his room might be extinguished; but that the nurse knew her duty too well to obey him, and had strictly followed the doctor's orders.

She added, that he had taken the cordial draughts regularly, but had, notwithstanding, continued to grow worse, and at last became light-headed. In the mean time the boy who had been sent for the physician was still absent:—And no wonder, continued the hostess; why, only consider, it's eight leagues off, and the lad had to find the road, bad as it is, in the dark. But indeed, Ma'mselle, you might as well have trusted our doctor, for we never want any body else, not we, in the town here; and if I might speak my mind, Jaques had better have been sent off for the young gentleman's friends than for this strange doctor that nobody knows.

After asking some further questions concerning Theodore, the answers to which rather increased than diminished her alarm, Adeline endeavoured to compose her spirits, and await in patience the arrival of the physician. She was now more sensible than ever of the forlornness of her own condition, and of the danger of Theodore's, and earnestly wished that his friends could be informed of his situation; a wish which could not be gratified, for Theodore, who alone could acquaint her with their place of residence, was deprived of recollection.

When the surgeon arrived and perceived the situation of his patient, he expressed no surprise; but having asked some questions and given a few general directions, he went down to Adeline. After paying her his usual compliments, he suddenly assumed an air of importance,—I am sorry Madam, said he, that it is my office to communicate disagreeable intelligence, but I wish you to be prepared for the event, which I fear, is approaching. Adeline comprehended his meaning; and though she had hitherto given little faith to his judgment, she could not hear him hint at the immediate danger of Theodore without yielding to the influence of fear.

She entreated him to acquaint her with all he apprehended: and he then proceeded to say that Theodore was, as he had foreseen, much worse this morning than he had been the preceding night; and the disorder having now affected his head, there was every reason to fear it would prove fatal in a few hours. The worst consequences may ensue, continued he; if the wound becomes inflamed, there will be very little chance of his recovery.

Adeline listened to this sentence with a dreadful calmness, and gave no utterance to grief, either by words or tears. The gentleman, I suppose, Madam, has friends, and the sooner you inform them of his condition the better. If they reside at any distance, it is indeed too late; but there are other necessary—You are ill, Madam!

Adeline made an effort to speak, but in vain, and the surgeon now called loudly for a glass of water; she drank it, and a deep sigh that she uttered, seemed somewhat to relieve her oppressed heart: tears succeeded. In the mean time the surgeon perceiving she was better, though not well enough to listen to his conversation, took leave, and promised to return in an hour. The physician was not yet arrived, and Adeline awaited his appearance with a mixture of fear and anxious hope.

About noon he came; and having been informed of the accident by which the fever was produced, and of the treatment which the surgeon had given it, he ascended to Theodore's chamber. In a quarter of an hour he returned to the room where Adeline expected him: The gentleman is still delirious, said he, but I have ordered him a composing draught.——Is there any hope, Sir? inquired Adeline. Yes, Madam, certainly there is hope; the case at present is somewhat doubtful, but a few hours may enable me to judge with more certainty: in the mean time, I have directed that he shall be kept quiet, and be allowed to drink freely of some diluting liquids.

He had scarcely, at Adeline's request, recommended a surgeon, instead of the one at present employed, when the latter gentleman entered the room, and perceiving the physician, threw a glance of mingled surprise and anger at Adeline, who retired with him to another apartment, where she dismissed him with a politeness which he did not deign to return, and which he certainly did not deserve.

Early the following morning the surgeon arrived; but either the medicines or the crisis of the disorder had thrown Theodore into a deep sleep, in which he remained for several hours. The physician now gave Adeline reason to hope for a favourable issue, and every precaution was taken to prevent his being disturbed. He awoke perfectly sensible and free from fever; and his first words inquired for Adeline, who soon learned that he was out of danger.

In a few days he was sufficiently recovered to be removed from his chamber to a room adjoining, where Adeline met him with a joy which she found it impossible to repress; and the observance of this lighted up his countenance with pleasure: indeed Adeline, sensible to the attachment he had so nobly testified, and softened by the danger he had encountered, no longer attempted to disguise the tenderness of her esteem, and was at length brought to confess the interest his first appearance had impressed upon her heart.

After an hour of affecting conversation, in which the happiness of a young and mutual attachment totally occupied their minds, and excluded every idea not in unison with delight, they returned to a sense of their present embarrassments. Adeline recollected that Theodore was arrested for disobedience of orders, and deserting his post; and Theodore, that he must shortly be torn away from Adeline, who would be left exposed to all the evils from which he had so lately rescued her. This thought overwhelmed his heart with anguish; and after a long pause he ventured to propose what his wishes had often suggested—a marriage with Adeline before he departed from the village: this was the only means of preventing, perhaps, an eternal separation; and though he saw the many dangerous inconveniences to which she would be exposed by a marriage with a man circumstanced like himself, yet these appeared so unequal to those she would otherwise be left to encounter alone, that his reason could no longer scruple to adopt what his affection had suggested.

Adeline was for some time too much agitated to reply: and though she had little to oppose to the arguments and pleadings of Theodore; though she had no friends to control, and no contrariety of interests to perplex her, she could not bring herself to consent thus hastily to a marriage with a man of whom she had little knowledge, and to whose family and connexions she had no sort of introduction. At length she entreated he would drop the subject; and the conversation for the remainder of the day was more general, yet still interesting.

That similarity of taste and opinion which had at first attracted them, every moment now more fully disclosed. Their discourse was enriched by elegant literature, and endeared by mutual regard. Adeline had enjoyed few opportunities of reading; but the books to which she had access, operating upon a mind eager for knowledge, and upon a taste peculiarly sensible of the beautiful and the elegant, had impressed all their excellences upon her understanding. Theodore had received from nature many of the qualities of genius, and from education, all that it could bestow; to these were added a noble independency of spirit, a feeling heart, and manners which partook of a happy mixture of dignity and sweetness.

In the evening, one of the officers who, upon the representation of the sergeant, was sent by the person employed to prosecute military criminals, arrived at the village;

and entering the apartment of Theodore, from which Adeline immediately withdrew, informed him with an air of infinite importance that he should set out on the following day for head-quarters. Theodore answered that he was not able to bear the journey, and referred him to his physician: but the officer replied that he should take no such trouble, it being certain that the physician might be instructed what to say, and that he should begin his journey on the morrow. Here has been delay enough, said he, already; and you will have sufficient business on your hands when you reach head-quarters; for the sergeant whom you have severely wounded intends to appear against you; and this, with the offence you have committed by deserting your post——

Theodore's eyes flashed fire: Deserting! said he, rising from his seat and darting a look of menace at his accuser—who dares to brand me with the name of deserter? But instantly recollecting how much his conduct had appeared to justify the accusation, he endeavoured to stifle his emotions; and with a firm voice and composed manner said, that when he reached head-quarters he should be ready to answer whatever might be brought against him, but that till then he should be silent. The boldness of the officer was repressed by the spirit and dignity with which Theodore spoke these words, and muttering a reply that was scarcely audible, he left the room.

Theodore sat musing on the danger of his situation: he knew that he had much to apprehend from the peculiar circumstances attending his abrupt departure from his regiment, it having been stationed in a garrison town upon the Spanish frontiers, where the discipline was very severe, and from the power of his colonel, the Marquis de Montalt, whom pride and disappointment would now rouse to vengeance, and probably render indefatigable in the accomplishment of his destruction. But his thoughts soon fled from his own danger to that of Adeline; and in the consideration of this, all his fortitude forsook him: he could not support the idea of leaving her exposed to the evils he foreboded, nor, indeed, of a separation so sudden as that which now threatened him: and when she again entered the room, he renewed his solicitations for a speedy marriage, with all the arguments that tenderness and ingenuity could suggest.

Adeline, when she learned that he was to depart on the morrow, felt as if bereaved of her last comfort: all the horrors of his situation arose to her mind, and she turned from him in unutterable anguish. Considering her silence as a favourable presage, he repeated his entreaties that she would consent to be his, and thus give him a surety that their separation should not be eternal. Adeline sighed deeply to these words: And who can know that our separation will not be eternal, said she, even if I could consent to the marriage you propose? But while you hear my determination, forbear to accuse me of indifference; for indifference towards you would indeed be a crime, after the services you have rendered me.

And is a cold sentiment of gratitude all that I must expect from you? said Theodore. I know that you are going to distress me with a proof of your indifference, which you mistake for the suggestions of prudence; and that I shall be compelled to look without reluctance upon the evils that may shortly await me. Ah, Adeline! if you mean to reject this, perhaps the last proposal which I can ever make to you, cease at least to deceive yourself with an idea that you love me—that delirium is fading even from my mind.

Can you then so soon forget our conversation of this morning? replied Adeline; and can you think so lightly of me as to believe I would profess a regard which I do not feel? If indeed you can believe this, I shall do well to forget that I ever made such an acknowledgement, and you that you heard it.

Forgive me, Adeline, forgive the doubts and inconsistencies I have betrayed: let the anxieties of love, and the emergency of my circumstances, plead for me. Adeline; smiling faintly through her tears, held out her hand, which he seized and pressed to his lips. Yet do not drive me to despair by a rejection of my suit, continued Theodore; think what I must suffer to leave you here destitute of friends and protection.

I am thinking how I may avoid a situation so deplorable, said Adeline. They say there is a convent which receives boarders, within a few miles, and thither I wish to go.

A convent! rejoined Theodore; would you go to a convent? Do you know the persecutions you would be liable to; and that if the Marquis should discover you, there is little probability the superior would resist his authority, or at least his bribes?

All this I have considered, said Adeline, and am prepared to encounter it, rather than enter into an engagement which at this time can be productive only of misery to us both.

Ah, Adeline! could you think thus, if you truly loved? I see myself about to be separated, and that perhaps for ever, from the object of my tenderest affections; and I cannot but express all the anguish I feel—I cannot forbear to repeat every argument that may afford even the slightest possibility of altering your determination. But you, Adeline, you look with complacency upon a circumstance which tortures me with despair.

Adeline, who had long strove to support her spirits in his presence, while she adhered to a resolution which reason suggested, but which the pleadings of her heart powerfully opposed, was unable longer to command her distress, and burst into tears. Theodore was in the same moment convinced of his error, and shocked at the grief he had occasioned. He drew his chair towards her, and taking her hand, again entreated her pardon, and endeavoured in the tenderest accents to soothe and comfort her.—What a wretch was I to cause you this distress, by questioning that regard with which I can no longer doubt you honour me! Forgive me, Adeline; say but you forgive me, and whatever may be the pain of this separation, I will no longer oppose it.

You have given me some pain, said Adeline, but you have not offended me.—She then mentioned some further particulars concerning the convent. Theodore endeavoured to conceal the distress which the approaching separation occasioned him, and to consult with her on these plans with composure. His judgment by degrees prevailed over his passions, and he now perceived that the plan she suggested, would afford her best chance of security. He considered, what in the first agitation of his mind had escaped him, that he might be condemned upon the charges brought against him, and that his death, should they have been married, would not only deprive her of her protector, but leave her more immediately exposed to the designs of the Marquis, who would doubtless attend his trial. Astonished that he had not noticed this before, and shocked at the unwariness by which he might have betrayed her into so dangerous a situation, he became at once reconciled to the idea of leaving her in a convent. He could have wished to place her in the asylum of his own family: but the circumstances under which she must be introduced were so awkward and painful, and above all, the distance at which they resided would render a journey so highly dangerous for her, that he forbore to propose it. He entreated only that she would allow him to write to her; but recollecting that his letters might be a means of betraying the place of her residence to the Marquis, he checked himself: I must deny myself even this melancholy pleasure, said he, lest my letters should discover your abode; yet hew shall I be able to endure the impatience and uncertainty to which prudence condemns me! If you are in danger, I shall be ignorant of it; though, indeed, did I know it, said he with a look of despair, I could not fly to save you. O exquisite misery! 'tis now only I perceive all the horrors of confinement—'tis now only that I understand all the value of liberty.

His utterance was interrupted by the violent agitation of his mind; he arose from his chair, and walked with quick paces about the room. Adeline sat, overcome by the description which Theodore had given of his approaching situation, and by the consideration that she might remain in the most terrible suspense concerning his fate. She saw him in a prison—pale—emaciated, and in chains:—she saw all the vengeance of the Marquis descending upon him; and this for his noble exertions in her cause. Theodore, alarmed by the placid despair expressed in her countenance, threw himself into a chair by hers, and taking her hand, attempted to speak comfort to her; but the words faltered on his lips, and he could only bathe her hand with tears.

This mournful silence was interrupted by the arrival of the carriage at the inn, and Theodore, arising, went to the window that opened into the yard. The darkness of the night prevented his distinguishing the objects without, but a light now brought from the house showed him a carriage and four, attended by several servants. Presently he saw a gentleman, wrapped up in a roquelaure, alight and enter the inn, and in the next moment he heard the voice of the Marquis.

He had flown to support Adeline, who was sinking with terror, when the door opened, and the Marquis followed by the officers and several servants entered. Fury flashed from his eyes as they glanced upon Theodore, who hung over Adeline with a look of fearful solicitude—Seize that traitor, said he, turning to the officers; why have you suffered him to remain here so long?

I am no traitor, said Theodore with a firm voice and the dignity of conscious worth, but a defender of innocence, of one whom the treacherous Marquis de Montalt would destroy.

Obey your orders, said the Marquis to the officers. Adeline shrieked, held faster by Theodore's arm, and entreated the men not to part them. Force only can effect it, said Theodore, as he looked round for some instrument of defence; but he could see none, and in the same moment they surrounded and seized him. Dread every thing from my vengeance, said the Marquis to Theodore, as he caught the hand of Adeline, who had lost all power of resistance and was scarcely sensible of what passed; dread every thing from my vengeance; you know you have deserved it.

I defy your vengeance, cried Theodore, and dread only the pangs of conscience, which your power cannot inflict upon me, though your vices condemn you to its tortures.

Take him instantly from the room, and see that he is strongly fettered, said the Marquis;

he shall soon know what a criminal who adds insolence to guilt may suffer.—Theodore exclaiming, Oh, Adeline! farewell! was now forced out of the room; while Adeline, whose torpid senses were roused by his voice and his last looks, fell at the feet of the Marquis, and with tears of agony implored compassion for Theodore: but her pleadings for his rival served only to irritate the pride and exasperate the hatred of the Marquis. He denounced vengeance on his head, and imprecations too dreadful for the spirits of Adeline, whom he compelled to rise; and then endeavouring to stifle the emotions of rage, which the presence of Theodore had excited, he began to address her with his usual expressions of admiration.

The wretched Adeline, who, regardless of what he said, still endeavoured to plead for her unhappy lover, was at length alarmed by the returning rage which the countenance of the Marquis expressed; and exerting all her remaining strength, she sprung from his grasp towards the door of the room: but he seized her hand before she could reach it, and regardless of her shrieks, bringing her back to her chair, was going to speak, when voices were heard in the passage, and immediately the landlord and his wife, whom Adeline's cries had alarmed, entered the apartment. The Marquis, turning furiously at them, demanded what they wanted; but not waiting for an answer, he bade them attend him, and quitting the room, she heard the door locked upon her.

Adeline now ran to the windows, which were unfastened and opened into the inn-yard. All was dark and silent. She called aloud for help, but no person appeared; and the windows were so high that it was impossible to escape unassisted. She walked about the room in an agony of terror and distress, now stooping to listen, and fancying she heard voices disputing below and now quickening her steps, as suspense increased the agitation of her mind.

She had continued in this state for near half an hour, when she suddenly heard a violent noise in the lower part of the house, which increased till all was uproar and confusion. People passed quickly through the passages, and doors were frequently opened and shut. She called, but received no answer. It immediately occurred to her that Theodore, having heard her screams, had attempted to come to her assistance, and that the bustle had been occasioned by the opposition of the officers. Knowing their fierceness and cruelty, she was seized with dreadful apprehensions for the life of Theodore.

A confused uproar of voices now sounded from below, and the screams of women convinced her there was fighting; she even thought she heard the clashing of swords: the image of Theodore dying by the hands of the Marquis now rose to her imagination, and the terrors of suspense became almost insupportable. She made a desperate effort to force the door, and again called for help; but her trembling hands were powerless, and every person in the house seemed to be too much engaged even to hear her. A loud shriek now pierced her ears, and amidst the tumult that followed she clearly distinguished deep groans. This confirmation of her fears deprived her of all her remaining spirits, and growing faint, she sunk almost lifeless into a chair near the door. The uproar gradually subsided till all was still, but nobody returned to her. Soon after she heard voices in the yard, but she had no power to walk across the room, even to ask the questions she wished, yet feared, to have answered.

About a quarter of an hour elapsed, when the door was unlocked, and the hostess appeared with a countenance as pale as death. For God's sake, said Adeline, tell me what has happened? Is he wounded? Is he killed?

He is not dead, Ma'mselle, but—

He is dying then?—tell me where he is—let me go.

Stop, Ma'mselle, cried the hostess, you are to stay here, I only want the hartshorn out of that cupboard there. Adeline tried to escape by the door; but the hostess, pushing her aside, locked it, and went down stairs.

Adeline's distress now entirely overcame her, and she sat motionless and scarcely conscious that she existed, till roused by a sound of footsteps near the door, which was again opened, and three men, whom she knew to be the Marquis's servants entered. She had sufficient recollection to repeat the questions she had asked the landlady; but they answered only that she must come with them, and that a chaise was waiting for her at the door. Still she urged her questions. Tell me if he lives, cried she.—Yes, Ma'mselle, he is alive, but he is terribly wounded, and the surgeon is just come to him. As they spoke they hurried her along the passage: and without noticing her entreaties and supplications to know whither she was going, they had reached the foot of the stairs, when her cries brought several people to the door. To these the hostess related that the lady was the wife of a gentleman just arrived, who had overtaken her in her flight with a gallant; an account which the Marquis's servants corroborated. 'Tis the gentleman who has just fought the duel, added the hostess, and it was on her account.

Adeline, partly disdaining to take any notice of this artful story, and partly from her desire to know the particulars of what had happened, contented herself with repeating her inquiries; to which one of the spectators at last replied, that the gentleman was desperately wounded. The Marquis's people would now have hurried her into the chaise, but she sunk lifeless in their arms; and her condition so interested the humanity of the spectators, that, notwithstanding their belief of what had been said, they opposed the effort made to carry her, senseless as she was, into the carriage.

She was at length taken into a room, and by proper applications restored to her senses. There she so earnestly besought an explanation of what had happened, that the hostess acquainted her with some particulars of the late rencounter. When the gentleman that was ill heard your screams, Madam, said she, he became quite outrageous, as they tell me, and nothing could pacify him. The Marquis, for they say he is a Marquis, but you know best, was then in the room with my husband and I, and when he heard the uproar, he went down to see what was the matter; and when he came into the room where the Captain was, he found him struggling with the sergeant. Then the Captain was more outrageous than ever; and notwithstanding he had one leg chained, and no sword, he contrived to get the sergeant's cutlass out of the scabbard, and immediately flew at the Marquis, and wounded him desperately; upon which he was secured.—It is the Marquis then who is wounded, said Adeline; the other gentleman is not hurt?

No, not he, replied the hostess; but he will smart for it by and by, for the Marquis swears he will do for him. Adeline for a moment forgot all her misfortunes and all her danger in thankfulness for the immediate escape of Theodore; and she was proceeding to make some further inquiries concerning him, when the Marquis's servants entered the room, and declared they could wait no longer. Adeline, now awakened to a sense of the evils with which she was threatened, endeavoured to win the pity of the hostess, who however was, or affected to be, convinced of the truth of the Marquis's story, and therefore insensible to all she could urge. Again she addressed his servants, but in vain; they would neither suffer her to remain longer at the inn, nor inform her whither she was going; but in the presence of several persons, already prejudiced by the injurious assertions of the hostess, Adeline was hurried into the chaise, and her conductors mounting their horses, the whole party was very soon beyond the village.

Thus ended Adeline's share of an adventure, begun with a prospect not only of security, but of happiness—an adventure which had attached her more closely to Theodore, and shown him to be more worthy of her love; but which, at the same time, had distressed her by new disappointment, produced the imprisonment of her generous and now adored lover, and delivered both himself and her into the power of a rival irritated by delay, contempt, and opposition.

CHAPTER XIII

Nor sea, nor shade, nor shield, nor rock, nor cave,Nor silent deserts, nor the sullen grave,Where flame-eyed fury means to frown—can save.

The surgeon of the place, having examined the Marquis's wound, gave him an immediate opinion upon it, and ordered that he should be put to bed: but the Marquis, ill as he was, had scarcely any other apprehension than that of losing Adeline, and declared he should be able to begin his journey in a few hours. With this intention he had begun to give orders for keeping horses in readiness, when the surgeon persisting most seriously, and even passionately to exclaim that his life would be the sacrifice of his rashness, he was carried to a bedchamber, where his valet alone was permitted to attend him.

This man, the convenient confident of all his intrigues, had been the chief instrument in assisting his designs concerning Adeline, and was indeed the very person who had brought her to the Marquis's villa on the borders of the forest. To him the Marquis gave his further directions concerning her: and, foreseeing the inconvenience as well as the danger of detaining her at the inn, he had ordered him, with several other servants, to carry her away immediately in a hired carriage. The valet having gone to execute his orders, the Marquis was left to his own reflections, and to the violence of contending passions.

The reproaches and continued opposition of Theodore, the favoured lover of Adeline, exasperated his pride and roused all his malice. He could not for a moment consider this opposition, which was in some respects successful, without feeling an excess of indignation and inveteracy, such as the prospect of a speedy revenge could alone enable him to support.

When he had discovered Adeline's escape from the villa, his surprise at first equalled his disappointment; and, after exhausting the paroxysms of his rage upon his domestics, he dispatched them all different ways in pursuit of her, going himself to the abbey, in the faint hope that, destitute as she was of other succour, she might have fled thither. La Motte, however, being as much surprised as himself, and as ignorant of the route which Adeline had taken, he returned to the villa impatient of intelligence, and found some of his servants arrived, without any news of Adeline, and those who came afterwards were as successless as the first.

A few days after, a letter from the lieutenant-colonel of the regiment informed him, that Theodore had quitted his company, and had been for some time absent, nobody knew where. This information, confirming a suspicion which had frequently occurred to him, that Theodore had been by some means or other instrumental in the escape of Adeline, all his other passions became for a time subservient to his revenge, and he gave orders for the immediate pursuit and apprehension of Theodore: but Theodore, in the mean time, had been overtaken and secured.

It was in consequence of having formerly observed the growing partiality between him and Adeline, and of intelligence received from La Motte, who had noticed their interview in the forest, that the Marquis had resolved to remove a rival so dangerous to his love, and so likely to be informed of his designs. He had therefore told Theodore, in a manner as plausible as he could, that it would be necessary for him to join the regiment; a notice which affected him only as it related to Adeline, and which seemed the less extraordinary, as he had already been at the villa a much longer time than was usual with the officers invited by the Marquis. Theodore, indeed, very well knew the character of the Marquis, and had accepted his invitation rather from an unwillingness to show any disrespect to his colonel by a refusal, than from a sanguine expectation of pleasure.

From the men who had apprehended Theodore, the Marquis received the information, which had enabled him to pursue and recover Adeline; but though he had now effected this, he was internally a prey to the corrosive effects of disappointed passion and exasperated pride. The anguish of his wound was almost forgotten in that of his mind, and every pang he felt seemed to increase his thirst of revenge, and to recoil with new torture upon his heart. While he was in this state, he heard the voice of the innocent Adeline imploring protection; but her cries excited in him neither pity nor remorse: and when, soon after, the carriage drove away, and he was certain both that she was secured and Theodore was wretched, he seemed to feel some cessation of mental pain.

Theodore, indeed, did suffer all that a virtuous mind, labouring under oppression so severe, could feel; but he was at least free from those inveterate and malignant passions which tore the bosom of the Marquis, and which inflict upon the professor a punishment more severe than any they can prompt him to imagine for another. What indignation he might feel towards the Marquis, was at this time secondary to his anxiety for Adeline. His captivity was painful, as it prevented his seeking a just and honourable revenge; but it was dreadful, as it withheld him from attempting the rescue of her whom he loved more than life.

When he heard the wheels of the carriage that contained her drive off, he felt an agony of despair which almost overcame his reason. Even the stern hearts of the soldiers who attended him were not wholly insensible to his wretchedness, and by venturing to blame the conduct of the Marquis they endeavoured to console their prisoner. The physician, who was just arrived, entered the room during this paroxysm of his distress, and both feeling and expressing much concern at his condition, inquired with strong surprise why he had been thus precipitately removed to a room so very unfit for his reception?

Theodore explained to him the reason of this, of the distress he suffered, and of the chains by which he was disgraced; and perceiving the physician listened to him with attention and compassion, he became desirous of acquainting him with some further particulars, for which purpose he desired the soldiers to leave the room. The men, complying with his request, stationed themselves on the outside of the door.

He then related all the particulars of the late transaction, and of his connection with the Marquis. The physician attended to his narrative with deep concern, and his countenance frequently expressed strong agitation. When Theodore concluded, he remained for some time silent and lost in thought; at length, awaking from his reverie, he said, I fear your situation is desperate: the character of the Marquis is too well known to suffer him either to be loved or respected; from such a man you have nothing to hope, for he has scarcely any thing to fear: I wish it was in my power to serve you, but I see no possibility of it.

Alas! said Theodore, my situation is indeed desperate, and—for that suffering angel—deep sobs interrupted his voice, and the violence of his agitation would not allow him to proceed. The physician could only express the sympathy he felt for his distress, and entreat him to be more calm, when a servant entered the room from the Marquis, who desired to see the physician immediately. After some time, he said he would attend the Marquis; and having endeavoured to attain a degree of composure which he found it difficult to assume, he wrung the hand of Theodore and quitted the room, promising to return before he left the house.

He found the Marquis much agitated both in body and mind, and rather more apprehensive for the consequences of the wound than he had expected. His anxiety for Theodore now suggested a plan, by the execution of which he hoped he might be able to serve him. Having felt his patient's pulse, and asked some questions, he assumed a very serious look; when the Marquis, who watched every turn of his countenance, desired he would, without hesitation, speak his opinion.

I am sorry to alarm you, my Lord, but here is some reason for apprehension: how long is it since you received the wound.

Good God! there is danger then! cried the Marquis, adding some bitter execrations against Theodore.—There certainly is danger, replied the physician; a few hours may enable me to determine its degree.

A few hours, Sir! interrupted the Marquis; a few hours! The physician entreated him to be more calm. Confusion! cried the Marquis: a man in health may, with great composure, entreat a dying man to be calm. Theodore will be broke upon the wheel for it, however.

You mistake me, Sir, said the physician; if I believed you a dying man, or, indeed, very near death, I should not have spoken as I did. But it is of consequence I should know how long the wound has been inflicted.—The Marquis's terror now began to subside, and he gave a circumstantial account of the affray with Theodore, representing that he had been basely used in an affair where his own conduct had been perfectly just and humane. The physician heard this relation with great coolness, and when it concluded without making any comment upon it, told the Marquis he would prescribe a medicine which he wished him to take immediately.

The Marquis again alarmed by the gravity of his manner, entreated he would declare most seriously, whether he thought him in immediate danger. The physician hesitated, and the anxiety of the Marquis increased: It is of consequence, said he, that I should know my exact situation. The physician then said, that if he had any worldly affairs to settle, it would be as well to attend to them, for that it was impossible to say what might be the event.

He then turned the discourse, and said he had just been with the young officer under arrest, who, he hoped, would not be removed at present, as such a procedure must endanger his life. The Marquis uttered a dreadful oath, and, cursing Theodore for having brought him to his present condition, said he should depart with the guard that very night. Against the cruelty of this sentence the physician ventured to expostulate; and endeavouring to awaken the Marquis to a sense of humanity, pleaded earnestly for Theodore. But these entreaties and arguments seemed, by displaying to the Marquis a part of his own character, to rouse his resentment and rekindle all the violence of his passions.

The physician at length withdrew in despondency, after promising, at the Marquis's request, not to leave the inn. He had hoped, by aggravating his danger, to obtain some advantages both for Adeline and Theodore; but the plan had quite a contrary effect: for the apprehension of death, so dreadful to the guilty mind of the Marquis, instead of awakening penitence, increased his desire of vengeance against the man who had brought him to such a situation. He determined to have Adeline conveyed where Theodore, should he by any accident escape, could never obtain her; and thus to secure to himself at least some means of revenge. He knew, however, that when Theodore was once safely conveyed to his regiment, his destruction was certain; for should he even be acquitted of the intention of deserting, he would be condemned for having assaulted his superior officer.

The physician returned to the room where Theodore was confined. The violence of his distress was now subsided into a stern despair more dreadful than the vehemence which had lately possessed him. The guard, in compliance with his request, having left the room, the physician repeated to him some part of his conversation with the Marquis. Theodore, after expressing his thanks, said he had nothing more to hope. For himself he felt little; it was for his family and Adeline he suffered. He inquired what route she had taken; and though he had no prospect of deriving advantage from the information, desired the physician to assist him in obtaining it: but the landlord and his wife either were, or affected to be, ignorant of the matter, and it was in vain to apply to any other person.

The sergeant now entered with orders from the Marquis for the immediate departure of Theodore, who heard the message with composure, though the physician could not help expressing his indignation at this precipitate removal, and his dread of the consequences that might attend it. Theodore had scarcely time to declare his gratitude for the kindness of this valuable friend, before the soldiers entered the room to conduct him to the carriage in waiting. As he bade him farewell, Theodore slipped his purse into his hand, and turning abruptly away, told the soldiers to lead on: but the physician stopped him, and refused the present with such serious warmth that he was compelled to resume it. He wrung the hand of his new friend, and being unable to speak, hurried away. The whole party immediately set off; and the unhappy Theodore was left to the remembrance of his past hopes and sufferings, to his anxiety for the fate of Adeline, the contemplation of his present wretchedness, and the apprehension of what might be reserved for him in future. For himself, indeed, he saw nothing but destruction, and was only relieved from total despair by a feeble hope that she whom he loved better than himself might one time enjoy that happiness of which he did not venture to look for a participation.

CHAPTER XIV

Have you the heart? When your head did but ache,I knit my handkerchief about your brows,And with my hand at midnight held your head;And, like the watchful minutes to the hour.Still and anon cheer'd up the heavy time.KING JOHN.

If the midnight bellDid, with his iron tongue and brazen mouth,Sound one unto the drowsy race of night;If this same were a church-yard where we stand,And thou possessed with a thousand wrongs;Or if that surly spirit MelancholyHad baked thy blood and made it heavy, thick;Then, in despite of broad-eyed watchful day,I would into thy bosom pour my thoughts.KING JOHN.

Meanwhile the persecuted Adeline continued to travel, with little interruption, all night. Her mind suffered such a tumult of grief, regret, despair, and terror, that she could not be said to think. The Marquis's valet, who had placed himself in the chaise with her, at first seemed inclined to talk; but her inattention soon silenced him, and left her to the indulgence of her own misery.

They seemed to travel through obscure lanes and by-ways, along which the carriage drove as furiously as the darkness would permit. When the dawn appeared, she perceived herself on the borders of a forest, and renewed her entreaties to know whither she was going. The man replied he had no orders to tell, but she would soon see. Adeline, who had hitherto supposed they were carrying her to the villa, now began to doubt it; and as every place appeared less terrible to her imagination than that, her despair began to abate, and she thought only of the devoted Theodore, whom she knew to be the victim of malice and revenge.

They now entered upon the forest, and it occurred to her that she was going to the abbey; for though she had no remembrance of the scenery through which she passed, it was not the less probable that this was the forest of Fontanville, whose boundaries were by much too extensive to have come within the circle of her former walks. This conjecture revived a terror little inferior to that occasioned by the idea of going to the villa; for at the abbey she would be equally in the power of the Marquis, and also in that of her cruel enemy La Motte. Her mind revolted at the picture her fancy drew; and as the carriage moved under the shades, she threw from the window a look of eager inquiry for some object which might confirm or destroy her present surmise: she did not long look, before an opening in the forest showed her the distant towers of the abbey—I am, indeed, lost then, said she, bursting into tears.

They were soon at the foot of the lawn, and Peter was seen running to open the gate, at which the carriage stopped. When he saw Adeline, he looked surprised and made an effort to speak; but the chaise now drove up to the abbey, where, at the door of the hall, La Motte himself appeared. As he advanced to take her from the carriage, an universal trembling seized her; it was with the utmost difficulty she supported herself, and for some moments she neither observed his countenance nor heard his voice. He offered his arm to assist her into the abbey, which she at first refused, but having tottered a few paces was obliged to accept; they then entered the vaulted room, where, sinking into a chair, a flood of tears came to her relief. La Motte did not interrupt the silence, which continued for some time, but paced the room in seeming agitation. When Adeline was sufficiently recovered to notice external objects, she observed his countenance, and there read the tumult of his soul, while he was struggling to assume a firmness which his better feelings opposed.

La Motte now took her hand, and would have led her from the room; but she stopped, and with a kind of desperate courage made an effort to engage him to pity and to save her. He interrupted her; It is not in my power, said he in a voice of emotion; I am not master of myself or my conduct; inquire no further—it is sufficient for you to know that I pity you; more I cannot do. He gave her no time to reply, but taking her hand led her to the stairs of the tower, and from thence to the chamber she had formerly occupied.

Here you must remain for the present, said he, in a confinement which is, perhaps, almost as involuntary on my part as it can be on yours. I am willing to render it as easy as possible, and have therefore ordered some books to be brought you.

Adeline made an effort to speak; but he hurried from the room, seemingly ashamed of the part he had undertaken, and unwilling to trust himself with her tears. She heard the door of the chamber locked; and then looking towards the windows, perceived they were secured: the door that led to the other apartments was also fastened. Such preparation for security shocked her; and hopeless as she had long believed herself, she now perceived her mind sink deeper in despair. When the tears she shed had somewhat relieved her, and her thoughts could turn from the subjects of her immediate concern, she was thankful for the total seclusion allotted her, since it would spare her the pain she must feel in the presence of Monsieur and Madame La Motte, and allow the unrestrained indulgence of her own sorrow and reflection; reflection which, however distressing, was preferable to the agony inflicted on the mind when, agitated by care and fear, it is obliged to assume an appearance of tranquillity.

In about a quarter of an hour her chamber door was unlocked, and Annette appeared with refreshments and books: she expressed satisfaction at seeing Adeline again, but seemed fearful of speaking, knowing, probably, that it was contrary to the orders of La Motte, who, she said, was waiting at the bottom of the stairs. When Annette was gone, Adeline took some refreshment, which was indeed necessary, for she had tasted nothing since she left the inn. She was pleased, but not surprised, that Madame La Motte did not appear, who, it was evident, shunned her from a consciousness of her own ungenerous conduct,—a consciousness which offered some presumption that she was still not wholly unfriendly to her. She reflected upon the words of La Motte,—I am not master of myself or my conduct,—and though they afforded her no hope, she derived some comfort, poor as it was, from the belief that he pitied her. After some time spent in miserable reflection and various conjectures, her long-agitated spirits seemed to demand repose, and she lay down to sleep.

Adeline slept quietly for several hours, and awoke with a mind refreshed and tranquillized. To prolong this temporary peace, and to prevent therefore the intrusion of her own thoughts, she examined the books La Motte had sent her: among these she found some that in happier times had elevated her mind and interested her heart: their effect was now weakened; they were still, however, able to soften for a time the sense of her misfortunes.

But this Lethean medicine to a wounded mind was but a temporary blessing; the entrance of La Motte dissolved the illusions of the page, and awakened her to a sense of her own situation. He came with food, and having placed it on the table left the room without speaking. Again she endeavoured to read, but his appearance had broken the enchantment; bitter reflection returned to her mind, and brought with it the image of Theodore—of Theodore lost to her for ever!

La Motte meanwhile experienced all the terrors that could be inflicted by a conscience not wholly hardened to guilt. He had been led on by passion to dissipation, and from dissipation to vice; but having once touched the borders of infamy, the progressive steps followed each other fast, and he now saw himself the pander of a villain, and the betrayer of an innocent girl whom every plea of justice and humanity called upon him to protect. He contemplated his picture—he shrunk from it, but he could change its deformity only by an effort too nobly daring for a mind already effeminated by vice. He viewed the dangerous labyrinth into which he was led, and perceived, as if for the first time, the progression of his guilt: from this labyrinth he weakly imagined further guilt could alone extricate him. Instead of employing his mind upon the means of saving Adeline from destruction, and himself from being instrumental to it, he endeavoured only to lull the pangs of conscience, and to persuade himself into a belief that he must proceed in the course he had begun. He knew himself to be in the power of the Marquis, and he dreaded that power more than the sure though distant punishment that awaits upon guilt. The honour of Adeline, and the quiet of his own conscience, he consented to barter for a few years of existence.

He was ignorant of the present illness of the Marquis, or he would have perceived that there was a chance of escaping the threatened punishment at a price less enormous than infamy, and he would perhaps have endeavoured to save Adeline and himself by flight. But the Marquis, foreseeing the possibility of this, had ordered his servants carefully to conceal the circumstance which detained him, and to acquaint La Motte that he should be at the abbey in a few days, at the same time directing his valet to await him there. Adeline, as he expected, had neither inclination nor opportunity to mention it; and thus La Motte remained ignorant of the circumstance which might have preserved him from further guilt and Adeline from misery.

Most unwillingly had La Motte made his wife acquainted with the action which had made him absolutely dependent upon the will of the Marquis; but the perturbation of his mind partly betrayed him: frequently in his sleep he muttered incoherent sentences, and frequently would start from his slumber, and call in passionate exclamation upon Adeline. These instances of a disturbed mind had alarmed and terrified Madame La Motte, who watched while he slept, and soon gathered from his words a confused idea of the Marquis's designs.

She hinted her suspicions to La Motte, who reproved her for having entertained them; but his manner, instead of repressing, increased her fears for Adeline; fears, which the conduct of the Marquis soon confirmed. On the night that he slept at the abbey, it had occurred to her that whatever scheme was in agitation it would now most probably be discussed; and anxiety for Adeline made her stoop to a meanness which, in other circumstances, would have been despicable. She quitted her room, and concealing herself in an apartment adjoining that in which she had left the Marquis and her husband, listened to their discourse. It turned upon the subject she had expected, and disclosed to her the full extent of their designs. Terrified for Adeline, and shocked at the guilty weakness of La Motte, she was for some time incapable of thinking, or determining how to proceed. She knew her husband to be under great obligation to the Marquis, whose territory thus afforded him a shelter from the world, and that it was in the power of the former to betray him into the hands of his enemies. She believed also that the Marquis would do this, if provoked: yet she thought, upon such an occasion, La Motte might find some way of appeasing the Marquis without subjecting himself to dishonour. After some further reflection, her mind became more composed, and she returned to her chamber, where La Motte soon followed. Her spirits, however, were not now in a state to encounter either his displeasure or his opposition, which she had too much reason to expect whenever she should mention the subject of her concern, and she therefore resolved not to notice it till the morrow.

On the morrow she told La Motte all he had uttered in his dreams; and mentioned other circumstances, which convinced him it was in vain any longer to deny the truth of her apprehensions. His wife then represented to him how possible it was to avoid the infamy into which he was about to plunge, by quitting the territories of the Marquis; and pleaded so warmly for Adeline, that La Motte in sullen silence appeared to meditate upon the plan. His thoughts were however very differently engaged. He was conscious of having deserved from the Marquis a dreadful punishment, and knew that if he exasperated him by refusing to acquiesce with his wishes, he had little to expect from flight, for the eye of justice and revenge would pursue him with indefatigable research.

La Motte meditated how to break this to his wife, for he perceived that there was no other method of counteracting her virtuous compassion for Adeline, and the dangerous consequences to be expected from it, than by opposing it with terror for his safety; and this could be done only by showing her the full extent of the evils that must attend the resentment of the Marquis. Vice had not yet so entirely darkened his conscience, but that the blush of shame stained his cheek, and his tongue faltered when he would have told his guilt. At length, finding it impossible to mention particulars, he told her that on account of an affair which no entreaties should ever induce him to explain, his life was in the power of the Marquis. You see the alternative, said he, take your choice of evils; and, if you can, tell Adeline of her danger, and sacrifice my life to save her from a situation which many would be ambitious to obtain.—Madame La Motte, condemned to the horrible alternative of permitting the seduction of innocence, or of dooming her husband to destruction, suffered a distraction of thought which defied all control. Perceiving, however, that an opposition to the designs of the Marquis would ruin La Motte and avail Adeline little, she determined to yield and endure in silence.

At the time when Adeline was planning her escape from the abbey, the significant looks of Peter had led La Motte to suspect the truth and to observe them more closely. He had seen them separate in the hall with apparent confusion, and had afterwards observed them conversing together in the cloisters. Circumstances so unusual left him not a doubt that Adeline had discovered her danger, and was concerting with Peter some means of escape. Affecting, therefore, to be informed of the whole affair, he charged Peter with treachery towards himself, and threatened him with the vengeance of the Marquis if he did not disclose all he knew. The menace intimidated Peter, and supposing that all chance of assisting Adeline was gone, he made a circumstantial confession, and promised to forbear acquainting Adeline with the discovery of the scheme. In this promise he was seconded by inclination, for he feared to meet the displeasure which Adeline, believing he had betrayed her, might express.

On the evening of the day on which Adeline's intended escape was discovered, the Marquis designed to come to the abbey, and it had been agreed that he should then take Adeline to his villa. La Motte had immediately perceived the advantage of permitting Adeline to repair, in the belief of being undiscovered, to the tomb. It would prevent much disturbance and opposition, and spare himself the pain he must feel in her presence, when she should know that he had betrayed her. A servant of the Marquis might go at the appointed hour to the tomb, and wrapt in the disguise of night might take her quietly thence in the character of Peter. Thus, without resistance she would be carried to the villa, nor discover her mistake till it was too late to prevent its consequence.

When the Marquis did arrive, La Motte, who was not so much intoxicated by the wine he had drunk as to forget his prudence, informed him of what had happened and what he had planned; and the Marquis approving it, his servant was made acquainted with the signal, which afterwards betrayed Adeline to his power.

A deep consciousness of the unworthy neutrality she had observed in Adeline's concerns, made Madame La Motte anxiously avoid seeing her now that she was again in the abbey. Adeline understood this conduct; and she rejoiced that she was spared the anguish of meeting her as an enemy, whom she had once considered as a friend. Several days now passed in solitude, in miserable retrospection, and dreadful expectation. The perilous situation of Theodore was almost the constant subject of her thoughts. Often did she breathe an agonizing wish for his safety, and often look round the sphere of possibility in search of hope: but hope had almost left the horizon of her prospect, and when it did appear, it sprung only from the death of the Marquis, whose vengeance threatened most certain destruction.

The Marquis, meanwhile, lay at the inn at Caux, in a state of very doubtful recovery. The physician and surgeon, neither of whom he would dismiss nor suffer to leave the village, proceeded upon contrary principles; and the good effect of what the one prescribed, was frequently counteracted by the injudicious treatment of the other. Humanity alone prevailed on the physician to continue his attendance. The malady of the Marquis was also heightened by the impatience of his temper, the terrors of death, and the irritation of his passions. One moment he believed himself dying, another he could scarcely be prevented from attempting to follow Adeline to the abbey. So various were the fluctuations of his mind, and so rapid the schemes that succeeded each other, that his passions were in a continual state of conflict. The physician attempted to persuade him that his recovery greatly depended upon tranquillity, and to prevail upon him to attempt at least some command of his feelings; but he was soon silenced in hopeless disgust by the impatient answers of the Marquis.

At length the servant who had carried off Adeline returned; and the Marquis having ordered him into his chamber, asked so many questions in a breath, that the man knew not which to answer. At length he pulled a folded paper from his pocket, which he said had been dropped in the chaise by Mademoiselle Adeline, and as he thought his Lordship would like to see it, he had taken care of it. The Marquis stretched forth his hand with eagerness, and received a note addressed to Theodore. On perceiving the superscription, the agitation of jealous rage for a moment overcame him, and he held it in his hand unable to open it.

He, however, broke the seal, and found it to be a note of inquiry, written by Adeline to Theodore during his illness, and which from some accident she had been prevented from sending him. The tender solicitude it expressed for his recovery stung the soul of the Marquis, and drew from him a comparison of her feelings on the illness of his rival and that of himself. She could be solicitous for his recovery, said he, but for mine she only dreads it. As if willing to prolong the pain this little billet had excited, he then read it again. Again he cursed his fate and execrated his rival. Giving himself up, as usual, to the transports of his passion, he was going to throw it from him, when his eyes caught the seal, and he looked earnestly at it: his anger seemed now to have subsided, he deposited the note carefully in his pocket-book, and was for some time lost in thought.

After many days of hopes and fears, the strength of his constitution overcame his illness, and he was well enough to write several letters, one of which he immediately sent off to prepare La Motte for his reception. The same policy which had prompted him to conceal his illness from La Motte, now urged him to say what he knew would not happen, that he should reach the abbey on the day after his servant. He repeated this injunction, that Adeline should be strictly guarded, and renewed his promises of reward for the future services of La Motte.

La Motte, to whom each succeeding day had brought new surprise and perplexity concerning the absence of the Marquis, received this notice with uneasiness; for he had begun to hope that the Marquis had altered his intentions concerning Adeline, being either engaged in some new adventure, or obliged to visit his estates in some distant province: he would have been willing thus to have got rid of an affair, which was to reflect so much dishonour on himself.

This hope was now vanished, and he directed Madame to prepare for the reception of the Marquis. Adeline passed these days in a state of suspense which was now cheered by hope and now darkened by despair. The delay, so much exceeding her expectation, seemed to prove that the illness of the Marquis was dangerous; and when she looked forward to the consequences of his recovery, she could not be sorry that it was so. So odious was the idea of him to her mind, that she would not suffer her lips to pronounce his name, nor make the inquiry of Annette, which was of such consequence to her peace.

It was about a week after the receipt of the Marquis's letter that Adeline one day saw from her window a party of horsemen enter the avenue, and knew them to be the Marquis and his attendants. She retired from the window, in a state of mind not to be described, and sinking into a chair, was for some time scarcely conscious of the objects around her. When she had recovered from the first terror which his appearance excited, she again tottered to the window; the party was not in sight, but she heard the trampling of horses, and knew that the Marquis had wound round to the great gate of the abbey.

She addressed herself to Heaven for support and protection; and her mind being now somewhat composed, sat down to wait the event.

La Motte received the Marquis with expressions of surprise at his long absence; and the latter, merely saying he had been detained by illness, proceeded to inquire for Adeline. He was told she was in her chamber, from whence she might be summoned if he wished to see her. The Marquis hesitated, and at length excused himself, but desired she might be strictly watched. Perhaps, my Lord, said La Motte smiling, Adeline's obstinacy has been too powerful for your passion? you seem less interested concerning her than formerly.

O! by no means, replied the Marquis; she interests me if possible, more than ever; so much, indeed, that I cannot have her too closely guarded; and I therefore beg, La Motte, that you will suffer nobody to attend her but when you can observe them yourself. Is the room where she is confined sufficiently secure? La Motte assured him it was; but at the same time expressed his wish that she was removed to the villa. If by any means, said he, she should contrive to escape, I know what I must expect from your displeasure; and this reflection keeps my mind in continual anxiety.

This removal cannot be at present, said the Marquis; she is safer here, and you do wrong to disturb yourself with any apprehension of her escape, if her chamber is so secure as you represent it.

I can have no motive for deceiving you, my Lord, in this point.

I do not suspect you of any, said the Marquis; guard her carefully, and trust me she will not escape. I can rely upon my valet, and if you wish it he shall remain here. La Motte thought there could be no occasion for him, and it was agreed that the man should go home.

The Marquis, after remaining about half an hour in conversation with La Motte, left the abbey; and Adeline saw him depart with a mixture of surprise and thankfulness that almost overcame her. She had waited in momentary expectation of being summoned to appear, and had been endeavouring to arm herself with resolution to support his presence. She had listened to every voice that sounded from below; and at every step that crossed the passage her heart had palpitated with dread, lest it should be La Motte coming to lead her to the Marquis. This state of suffering had been prolonged almost beyond her power of enduring it, when she heard voices under her window, and rising, saw the Marquis ride away. After giving way to the joy and thankfulness that swelled her heart, she endeavoured to account for this circumstance, which, considering what had passed, was certainly very strange. It appeared, indeed, wholly inexplicable; and after much fruitless inquiry, she quitted the subject, endeavouring to persuade herself that it could only portend good.

The time of La Motte's usual visitation now drew near, and Adeline expected it in the trembling hope of hearing that the Marquis had ceased his persecution; but he was, as usual, sullen and silent, and it was not till he was about to quit the room that Adeline had the courage to inquire when the Marquis was expected again. La Motte, opening the door to depart, replied, on the following day; and Adeline, whom fear and delicacy embarrassed, saw she could obtain no intelligence of Theodore but by a direct question; she looked earnestly, as if she would have spoke, and he stopped; but she blushed and was still silent, till upon his again attempting to leave the room she faintly called him back.

I would ask, said she, after that unfortunate chevalier who has incurred the resentment of the Marquis, by endeavouring to serve me: Has the Marquis mentioned him?

He has, replied La Motte; and your indifference towards the Marquis is now fully explained.

Since I must feel resentment towards those who injure me, said Adeline, I may surely be allowed to be grateful towards those who serve me. Had the Marquis deserved my esteem, he would probably have possessed it.

Well, well, said La Motte, this young hero, who it seems has been brave enough to lift his arm against his Colonel, is taken care of, and I doubt not will soon be sensible of the value of his quixotism.—Indignation, grief, and fear, struggled in the bosom of Adeline; she disdained to give La Motte an opportunity of again pronouncing the name of Theodore; yet the uncertainty under which she laboured, urged her to inquire whether the Marquis had heard of him since he left Caux. Yes, said La Motte, he has been safely carried to his regiment, where he is confined till the Marquis can attend to appear against him.

Adeline had neither power nor inclination to inquire further; and La Motte quitting the chamber, she was left to the misery he had renewed. Though this information contained no new circumstance of misfortune, (for she now heard confirmed what she had always expected,) a weight of new sorrow seemed to fall upon her heart, and she perceived that she had unconsciously cherished a latent hope of Theodore's escape before he reached the place of his destination. All hope was now, however, gone; he was suffering the miseries of a prison, and the tortures of apprehension both for his own life and her safety. She pictured to herself the dark damp dungeon where he lay, loaded with chains and pale with sickness and grief; she heard him, in a voice that thrilled her heart, call upon her name, and raise his eyes to heaven in silent supplication: she saw the anguish of his countenance, the tears that fell slowly on his cheek; and remembering at the same time, the generous conduct that had brought him to this abyss of misery, and that it was for her sake he suffered, grief resolved itself into despair, her tears ceased to flow, and she sunk silently into a state of dreadful torpor.

On the morrow the Marquis arrived, and departed as before. Several days then elapsed, and he did not appear; till one evening, as La Motte and his wife were in their usual sitting-room, he entered, and conversed for some time upon general subjects, from which, however, he by degrees fell into a reverie, and after a pause of silence he rose and drew La Motte to the window. I would speak to you alone, said he, if you are at leisure; if not, another time will do. La Motte assuring him he was perfectly so, would have conducted him to another room, but the Marquis proposed a walk in the forest. They went out together; and when they had reached a solitary glade, where the spreading branches of the beech and oak deepened the shades of twilight and threw a solemn obscurity around, the Marquis turned to La Motte and addressed him:

Your condition, La Motte, is unhappy; this abbey is a melancholy residence for a man like you fond of society, and like you also qualified to adorn it. La Motte bowed. I wish it was in my power to restore you to the world, continued the Marquis; perhaps, if I knew the particulars of the affair which has driven you from it, I might perceive that my interest could effectually serve you:—I think I have heard you hint it was an affair of honour? La Motte was silent. I mean not to distress you, however; nor is it common curiosity that prompts this inquiry, but a sincere desire to befriend you. You have already informed me of some particulars of your misfortunes; I think the liberality of your temper led you into expenses which you afterwards endeavoured to retrieve by gaming?

Yes, my Lord, said La Motte, 'tis true that I dissipated the greater part of an affluent fortune in luxurious indulgencies, and that I afterwards took unworthy means to recover it: but I wish to be spared upon this subject. I would, if possible, lose the remembrance of a transaction which must for ever stain my character, and the rigorous effect of which, I fear, it is not in your power, my Lord, to soften.

You may be mistaken on this point, replied the Marquis; my interest at court is by no means inconsiderable. Fear not from me any severity of censure; I am not at all inclined to judge harshly of the faults of others: I well know how to allow for the emergency of circumstances; and I think La Motte, you have hitherto found me your friend.

I have, my Lord.

And when you recollect, that I have forgiven a certain transaction of late date——

It is true, my Lord; and allow me to say, I have a just sense of your generosity. The transaction you allude to is by far the worst of my life; and what I have to relate cannot therefore lower me in your opinion. When I had dissipated the greatest part of my property in habits of voluptuous pleasure, I had recourse to gaming to supply the means of continuing them. A run of good luck for some time enabled me to do this; and encouraging my most sanguine expectations, I continued in the same career of success.

Soon after this, a sudden turn of fortune destroyed my hopes, and reduced me to the most desperate extremity. In one night my money was lowered to the sum of two hundred louis. These I resolved to stake also, and with them my life; for it was my resolution not to survive their loss. Never shall I forget the horrors of that moment on which hung my fate, nor the deadly anguish that seized my heart when my last stake was gone. I stood for some time in a state of stupefaction, till, roused to a sense of my misfortune, my passion made me pour forth execrations on my more fortunate rivals, and act all the phrensy of despair. During this paroxysm of madness, a gentleman, who had been a silent observer of all that passed, approached me.—You are unfortunate, Sir, said he.—I need not be informed of that. Sir, I replied.

You have perhaps been ill used? resumed he.—Yes, Sir, I am ruined, and therefore it may be said I am ill used.

Do you know the people you have played with?

No; but I have met them in the first circles.

Then I am probably mistaken, said he, and walked away. His last words roused me, and raised a hope that my money had not been fairly lost. Wishing for further information, I went in search of the gentleman, but he had left the rooms. I however stifled my transports, returned to the table where I had lost my money, placed myself behind the chair of one of the persons who had won it, and closely watched the game. For some time I saw nothing that could confirm my suspicions, but was at length convinced they were just.

When the game was ended I called one of my adversaries out of the room, and telling him what I had observed, threatened instantly to expose him if he did not restore my property. The man was for some time as positive as myself; and assuming the bully, threatened me with chastisement for my scandalous assertions. I was not, however, in a state of mind to be frightened; and his manner served only to exasperate my temper, already sufficiently inflamed by misfortune. After retorting his threats, I was about to return to the apartment we had left, and expose what had passed, when, with an insidious smile and a softened voice, he begged I would favour him with a few moments' attention, and allow him to speak with the gentleman his partner. To the latter part of his request I hesitated, but in the mean time the gentleman himself entered the room. His partner related to him, in few words, what had passed between us, and the terror that appeared in his countenance sufficiently declared his consciousness of guilt.

They then drew aside, and remained a few minutes in conversation together, after which they approached me with an offer, as they phrased it, of a compromise. I declared, however, against any thing of this kind, and swore nothing less than the whole sum I had lost should content me.—Is it not possible, Monsieur, that you may be offered something as advantageous as the whole?—I did not understand their meaning; but after they had continued for some time to give distant hints of the same sort, they proceeded to explain.

Perceiving their characters wholly in my power, they wished to secure my interest to their party, and therefore informing me that they belonged to an association of persons who lived upon the folly and inexperience of others, they offered me a share in their concern. My fortunes were desperate; and the proposal now made me would not only produce an immediate supply, but enable me to return to those scenes of dissipated pleasure to which passion had at first, and long habit afterwards, attached me. I closed with the offer, and thus sunk from dissipation into infamy.

La Motte paused, as if the recollection of these times filled him with remorse. The Marquis understood his feelings. You judge too rigorously of yourself, said he; there are few persons, let their appearance of honesty be what it may, who in such circumstances would have acted better than you have done. Had I been in your situation, I know not how I might have acted. That rigid virtue which shall condemn you, may dignify itself with the appellation of wisdom, but I wish not to possess it; let it still reside where it generally is to be found, in the cold bosoms of those who, wanting feeling to be men, dignify themselves with the title of philosophers. But pray proceed.

Our success was for some time unlimited, for we held the wheel of fortune, and trusted not to her caprice. Thoughtless and voluptuous by nature, my expenses fully kept pace with my income. An unlucky discovery of the practices of our party was at length made by a young nobleman, which obliged us to act for some time with the utmost circumspection. It would be tedious to relate the particulars, which made us at length so suspected, that the distant civility and cold reserve of our acquaintance rendered the frequenting public assemblies both painful and unprofitable. We turned our thoughts to other modes of obtaining money; and a swindling transaction, in which I engaged to a very large amount, soon compelled me to leave Paris. You know the rest my Lord.

La Motte was now silent, and the Marquis continued for some time musing. You perceive, my Lord, at length resumed La Motte, you perceive that my case is hopeless.

It is bad indeed, but not entirely hopeless. From my soul I pity you: yet, if you should return to the world, and incur the danger of prosecution, I think my interest with the minister might save you from any severe punishment. You seem, however, to have lost your relish for society, and perhaps do not wish to return to it.

Oh! my Lord can you doubt this?—But I am overcome with the excess of your goodness; would to heaven it were in my power to prove the gratitude it inspires!

Talk not of goodness, said the Marquis; I will not pretend that my desire of serving you is unalloyed by any degree of self-interest: I will not affect to be more than man, and trust me those who do are less. It is in your power to testify your gratitude, and bind me to your interest for ever. He paused. Name but the means, cried La Motte,—name but the means, and if they are within the compass of possibility they shall be executed. The Marquis was still silent. Do you doubt my sincerity, my Lord, that you are yet silent? Do you fear to repose a confidence in the man whom you have already loaded with obligation? who lives by your mercy, and almost by your means! The Marquis looked earnestly at him, but did not speak. I have not deserved this of you, my Lord; speak, I entreat you.

There are certain prejudices attached to the human mind, said the Marquis in a slow and solemn voice, which it requires all our wisdom to keep from interfering with our happiness; certain set notions, acquired in infancy, and cherished involuntarily by age, which grow up and assume a gloss so plausible, that few minds, in what is called a civilized country, can afterwards overcome them. Truth is often perverted by education. While the refined Europeans boast a standard of honour and a sublimity of virtue which often leads them from pleasure to misery, and from nature to error, the simple uninformed American follows the impulse of his heart, and obeys the inspiration of wisdom. The Marquis paused, and La Motte continued to listen in eager expectation.

Nature, uncontaminated by false refinement, resumed the Marquis, every where acts alike in the great occurrences of life. The Indian discovers his friend to be perfidious, and he kills him; the wild Asiatic does the same: the Turk, when ambition fires or revenge provokes, gratifies his passion at the expense of life, and does not call it murder. Even the polished Italian, distracted by jealousy, or tempted by a strong circumstance of advantage, draws his stiletto, and accomplishes his purpose. It is the first proof of a superior mind to liberate itself from prejudices of country or of education. You are silent, La Motte: are you not of my opinion?

I am attending, my Lord, to your reasoning.

There are, I repeat it, said the Marquis, people of minds so weak, as to shrink from acts they have been accustomed to hold wrong, however advantageous; they never suffer themselves to be guided by circumstances, but fix for life upon a certain standard, from which they will on no account depart. Self-preservation is the great law of nature; when a reptile hurts us, or an animal of prey threatens us, we think no further, but endeavour to annihilate it. When my life, or what may be essential to my life, requires the sacrifice of another,—or even if some passion, wholly unconquerable, requires it,—I should be a madman to hesitate. La Motte, I think I may confide in you—there are ways of doing certain things—you understand me? There are times, and circumstances, and opportunities—you comprehend my meaning?

Explain yourself, my Lord.

Kind services that—in short, there are services which excite all our gratitude, and which we can never think repaid. It is in your power to place me in such a situation.

Indeed! my Lord, name the means.

I have already named them. This abbey well suits the purpose; it is shut up from the eye of observation; any transaction may be concealed within its walls; the hour of midnight may witness the deed, and the morn shall not dawn to disclose it; these woods tell no tales. Ah! La Motte am I right in trusting this business with you? may I believe you are desirous of serving me, and of preserving yourself? The Marquis paused, and looked steadfastly at La Motte, whose countenance was almost concealed by the gloom of evening.

My Lord, you may trust me in any thing; explain yourself more fully.

What security will you give me of your faithfulness?

My life, my Lord; is it not already in your power? The Marquis hesitated, and then said, To-morrow about this time I shall return to the abbey, and will then explain my meaning, if indeed you shall not already have understood it. You in the mean time will consider your own powers of resolution, and be prepared either to adopt the purpose I shall suggest, or to declare you will not. La Motte made some confused reply. Farewell till to-morrow, said the Marquis; remember that freedom and affluence are now before you. He moved towards the abbey, and, mounting his horse, rode off with his attendants. La Motte walked slowly home, musing on the late conversation.

CHAPTER XV

Danger, whose limbs of giant mould/What mortal eye can fixed behold?/Who stalks his round, an hideous form!/Howling amidst the midnight storm!——And with him thousand phantoms join'd,/Who prompt to deeds accurst the mind!/On whom that rav'ning brood of Fate/Who lap the blood of Sorrow wait;/Who, Fear! this ghastly train can see,/And look not madly wild like thee!/COLLINS.

The Marquis was punctual to the hour. La Motte received him at the gate; but he declined entering, and said he preferred a walk in the forest. Thither, therefore, La Motte attended him. After some general conversation, Well, said the Marquis, have you considered what I said, and are you prepared to decide?

I have, my Lord, and will quickly decide, when you shall further explain yourself: till then I can form no resolution. The Marquis appeared dissatisfied, and was a moment silent. Is it then possible, he at length resumed, that you do not understand? This ignorance is surely affected. La Motte, I expect sincerity. Tell me, therefore, is it necessary I should say more?

It is, my Lord, said La Motte immediately. If you fear to confide in me freely, how can I fully accomplish your purpose?

Before I proceed further, said the Marquis, let me administer some oath which shall bind you to secrecy. But this is scarcely necessary; for, could I even doubt your word of honour, the remembrance of a certain transaction would point out to you the necessity of being as silent yourself as you must wish me to be. There was now a pause of silence, during which both the Marquis and La Motte betrayed some confusion. I think, La Motte, said he, I have given you sufficient proof that I can be grateful: the services you have already rendered me with respect to Adeline have not been unrewarded.

True, my Lord; I am ever willing to acknowledge this; and am sorry it has not been in my power to serve you more effectually. Your further views respecting her I am ready to assist.

I thank you.—Adeline——the Marquis hesitated—Adeline, rejoined La Motte, eager to anticipate his wishes, has beauty worthy of your pursuit: she has inspired a passion of which she ought to be proud, and at any rate she shall soon be yours. Her charms are worthy of——

Yes, yes, interrupted the Marquis; but—he paused. But they have given you too much trouble in the pursuit, said La Motte; and to be sure, my Lord, it must be confessed they have; but this trouble is all over—you may now consider her as your own.

I would do so, said the Marquis, fixing an eye of earnest regard upon La Motte—I would do so.

Name your hour, my Lord; you shall not be interrupted. Beauty such as Adeline's—

Watch her closely, interrupted the Marquis, and on no account suffer her to leave her apartment. Where is she now?

Confined in her chamber.

Very well. But I am impatient.

Name your time, my Lord—to-morrow night.

To-morrow night, said the Marquis, to-morrow night. Do you understand me now?

Yes, my Lord, this night if you wish it so. But had you not better dismiss your servants, and remain yourself in the forest? You know the door that opens upon the woods from the west tower. Come thither about twelve—I will be there to conduct you to her chamber. Remember then, my Lord, that to-night—

Adeline dies! interrupted the Marquis in a low voice scarcely human. Do you understand me now?

——La Motte shrunk aghast—My Lord!

La Motte! said the Marquis.—There was a silence of several minutes, in which La Motte endeavoured to recover himself. Let me ask, my Lord, the meaning of this? said he, when he had breath to speak. Why should you wish the death of Adeline—of Adeline, whom so lately you loved?

Make no inquiries for my motive, said the Marquis; but it is as certain as that I live that she you name must die. This is sufficient. The surprise of La Motte equalled his horror. The means are various, resumed the Marquis. I could have wished that no blood might be spilt; and there are drugs sure and speedy in their effect, but they cannot be soon or safely procured. I also wish it over—it must be done quickly—this night.

This night, my Lord!

Aye, this night, La Motte; if it is to be, why not soon? Have you no convenient drug at hand?

None, my Lord.

I feared to trust a third person, or I should have been provided, said the Marquis. As it is, take this poniard! use it as occasion offers, but be resolute. La Motte received the poniard with a trembling hand, and continued to gaze upon it for some time, scarcely knowing what he did. Put it up, said the Marquis, and endeavour to recollect yourself. La Motte obeyed, but continued to muse in silence.

He saw himself entangled in the web which his own crimes had woven. Being in the power of the Marquis, he knew he must either consent to the commission of a deed, from the enormity of which, depraved as he was, he shrunk in horror, or sacrifice fortune, freedom, probably life itself, to the refusal. He had been led on by slow gradations from folly to vice, till he now saw before him an abyss of guilt which startled even the conscience that so long had slumbered. The means of retreating were desperate—to proceed was equally so.

When he considered the innocence and the helplessness of Adeline, her orphan state, her former affectionate conduct, and her confidence in his protection, his heart melted with compassion for the distress he had already occasioned her, and shrunk in terror from the deed he was urged to commit. But when, on the other hand, he contemplated the destruction that threatened him from the vengeance of the Marquis, and then considered the advantages that were offered him of favour, freedom, and probably fortune,—terror and temptation contributed to overcome the pleadings of humanity, and silence the voice of conscience. In this state of tumultuous uncertainty he continued for some time silent, until the voice of the Marquis roused him to a conviction of the necessity of at least appearing to acquiesce in his designs.

Do you hesitate? said the Marquis.—No, my Lord, my resolution is fixed—I will obey you. But methinks it would be better to avoid bloodshed. Strange secrets have been revealed by——

Aye, but how avoid it? interrupted the Marquis.—Poison I will not venture to procure. I have given you one sure instrument of death. You also may find it dangerous to inquire for a drug. La Motte perceived that he could not purchase poison without incurring a discovery much greater than that he wished to avoid. You are right, my Lord, and I will follow your orders implicitly. The Marquis now proceeded, in broken sentences, to give further directions concerning this dreadful scheme.

In her sleep, said he, at midnight; the family will then be at rest. Afterwards they planned a story which was to account for her disappearance, and by which it was to seem that she had sought an escape in consequence of her aversion to the addresses of the Marquis. The doors of her chamber and of the west tower were to be left open to corroborate this account, and many other circumstances were to be contrived to confirm the suspicion. They further consulted how the Marquis was to be informed of the event; and it was agreed that he should come as usual to the abbey on the following day.—To-night then, said the Marquis, I may rely upon your resolution?

You may, my Lord.

Farewell, then. When we meet again——

When we meet again said La Motte, it will be done. He followed the Marquis to the abbey; and having seen him mount his horse and wished him a good night, he retired to his chamber, where he shut himself up.

Adeline, meanwhile, in the solitude of her prison gave way to the despair which her condition inspired. She tried to arrange her thoughts, and to argue herself into some degree of resignation; but reflection, by representing the past, and reason, by anticipating the future, brought before her mind the full picture, of her misfortunes, and she sunk in despondency. Of Theodore, who, by a conduct so noble, had testified his attachment and involved himself in ruin, she thought with a degree of anguish infinitely superior to any she had felt upon any other occasion.

That the very exertions which had deserved all her gratitude, and awakened all her tenderness, should be the cause of his destruction, was a circumstance so much beyond the ordinary bounds of misery, that her fortitude sunk at once before it. The idea of Theodore suffering—Theodore dying—was for ever present to her imagination;

and frequently excluding the sense of her own danger, made her conscious only of his. Sometimes the hope he had given her of being able to vindicate his conduct, or at least to obtain a pardon, would return; but it was like the faint beam of an April morn, transient and cheerless. She knew that the Marquis, stung with jealousy and exasperated to revenge, would pursue him with unrelenting malice.

Against such an enemy what could Theodore oppose? Conscious rectitude would not avail him to ward off the blow which disappointed passion and powerful pride directed. Her distress was considerably heightened by reflecting that no intelligence of him could reach her at the abbey, and that she must remain she knew not how long in the most dreadful suspense concerning his fate. From the abbey she saw no possibility of escaping. She was a prisoner in a chamber inclosed at every avenue; she had no opportunity of conversing with any person who could afford her even a chance of relief; and she saw herself condemned to await in passive silence the impending destiny, infinitely more dreadful to her imagination than death itself.

Thus circumstanced, she yielded to the pressure of her misfortunes, and would sit for hours motionless and given up to thought. Theodore! she would frequently exclaim, you cannot hear my voice, you cannot fly to help me; yourself a prisoner and in chains. The picture was too horrid: the swelling anguish of her heart would subdue her utterance—tears bathed her cheeks—and she became insensible to every thing but the misery of Theodore.

On this evening her mind had been remarkably tranquil; and as she watched from her window, with a still and melancholy pleasure, the setting sun, the fading splendour of the western horizon, and the gradual approach of twilight, her thoughts bore her back to the time when in happier circumstances she had watched the same appearances. She recollected also the evening of her temporary escape from the abbey, when from this same window she had viewed the declining sun—how anxiously she had awaited the fall of twilight—how much she had endeavoured to anticipate the events of her future life—with what trembling fear she had descended from the tower and ventured into the forest. These reflections produced others that filled her heart with anguish and her eyes with tears.

While she was lost in her melancholy reverie she saw the Marquis mount his horse and depart from the gate. The sight of him revived in all its force a sense of the misery he inflicted on her beloved Theodore, and a consciousness of the evils which more immediately threatened herself. She withdrew from the window in an agony of tears, which continuing for a considerable time, her frame was at length quite exhausted, and she retired early to rest.

La Motte remained in his chamber till supper obliged him to descend. At table his wild and haggard countenance, which, in spite of all his endeavours, betrayed the disorder of his mind, and his long and frequent fits of abstraction, surprised as well as alarmed Madame La Motte. When Peter left the room she tenderly inquired what had disturbed him, and he with a distorted smile tried to be gay; but the effort was beyond his art, and he quickly relapsed into silence; or when Madame La Motte spoke, and he strove to conceal the absence of his thoughts, he answered so entirely from the purpose that his abstraction became still more apparent. Observing this, Madame La Motte appeared to take no notice of his present temper; and they continued to sit in uninterrupted silence till the hour of rest, when they retired to their chamber.

La Motte lay in a state of disturbed watchfulness for some time, and his frequent starts awoke Madame, who however, being pacified by some trifling excuse, soon went to sleep again. This agitation continued till near midnight, when recollecting that the time was now passing in idle reflection which ought to be devoted to action, he stole silently from his bed, wrapped himself in his night-gown, and taking the lamp which burned nightly in his chamber, passed up the spiral staircase. As he went he frequently looked back, and often started and listened to the hollow sighings of the blast.

His hand shook so violently when he attempted to unlock the door of Adeline's chamber, that he was obliged to set the lamp on the ground, and apply both his hands. The noise he made with the key induced him to suppose he must have awakened her; but when he opened the door, and perceived the stillness that reigned within, he was convinced she was asleep. When he approached the bed he heard her gently breathe, and soon after sigh—and he stopped: but silence returning he again advanced, and then heard her sing in her deep. As he listened he distinguished some notes of a melancholy little air, which in her happier days she had often sung to him. The low and mournful accent in which she now uttered them expressed too well the tone of her mind.

La Motte now stepped hastily towards the bed, when breathing a deep sigh she was again silent. He undrew the curtain and saw her lying in a profound sleep, her cheek, yet wet with tears, resting upon her arm. He stood a moment looking at her; and as he viewed her innocent and lovely countenance, pale in grief, the light of the lamp, which shone strong upon her eyes, awoke her, and perceiving a man, she uttered a scream. Her recollection returning, she knew him to be La Motte; and it instantly occurring to her that the Marquis was at hand, she raised herself in bed, and implored pity and protection. La Motte stood looking eagerly at her, but without replying.

The wildness of his looks and the gloomy silence he preserved increased her alarm, and with tears of terror she renewed her supplication. You once saved me from destruction, cried she; O save me now! have pity upon me—I have no protector but you.

What is it you fear? said La Motte in a tone scarcely articulate.—O save me—save me from the Marquis!

Rise then, said he, and dress yourself quickly: I shall be back again in a few minutes. He lighted a candle that stood on the table, and left the chamber; Adeline immediately arose and endeavoured to dress; but her thoughts were so bewildered that she scarcely knew what she did, and her whole frame so violently agitated, that it was with the utmost difficulty she preserved herself from fainting. She threw her clothes hastily on, and then sat down to await the return of La Motte. A considerable time elapsed, yet he did not appear; and having in vain endeavoured to compose her spirits, the pain of suspense became at length so insupportable, that she opened the door of her chamber, and went to the top of the staircase to listen. She thought she heard voices below; but considering that if the Marquis was there, her appearance could only increase her danger, she checked the step she had almost involuntarily taken to descend. Still she listened, and still thought she distinguished voices. Soon after, she heard a door shut, and then footsteps, and she hastened back to her chamber.

Near a quarter of an hour had elapsed and La Motte did not appear; when again she thought she heard a murmur of voices below and also passing steps: and at length, her anxiety not suffering her to remain in her room, she moved through the passage that communicated with the spiral staircase; but all was now still. In a few moments, however, a light flashed across the hall, and La Motte appeared at the door of the vaulted room. He looked up, and seeing Adeline in the gallery, beckoned her to descend.

She hesitated, and looked towards her chamber; but La Motte now approached the stairs, and with faltering steps she went to meet him. I fear the Marquis may see me, said she, whispering; where is he? La Motte took her hand and led her on, assuring her she had nothing to fear from the Marquis. The wildness of his looks, however, and the trembling of his hand, seemed to contradict this assurance, and she inquired whether he was leading her. To the forest, said La Motte, that you may escape from the abbey—a horse waits for you without: I can save you by no other means. New terror seized her. She could scarcely believe that La Motte, who had hitherto conspired with the Marquis, and had so closely confined her, should now himself undertake her escape; and she at this moment felt a dreadful presentiment which it was impossible to account for, that he was leading her out to murder her in the forest. Again shrinking back, she supplicated his mercy. He assured her he meant only to protect her, and desired she would not waste time.

There was something in his manner that spoke sincerity, and she suffered him to conduct her to a side door that opened into the forest, where she could just distinguish through the gloom a man on horseback. This brought to her remembrance the night in which she had quitted the tomb, when, trusting to the person who appeared, she had been carried to the Marquis's villa. La Motte called, and was answered by Peter, whose voice somewhat reassured Adeline.

He then told her that the Marquis would return to the abbey on the following morning and that this could be her only opportunity of escaping his designs; that she might rely upon his (La Motte's) word, that Peter had orders to carry her wherever she choose; but as he knew the Marquis would be indefatigable in search of her, he advised her by all means to leave the kingdom, which she might do with Peter, who was a native of Savoy, and would convey her to the house of his sister. There she might remain till La Motte himself, who did not now think it would be safe to continue much longer in France, should join her. He entreated her, whatever might happen, never to mention the events which had passed at the abbey. To save you, Adeline, I have risked my life; do not increase my danger and your own by any unnecessary discoveries. We may never meet again, but I hope you will be happy; and remember, when you think of me, that I am not quite so bad as I have been tempted to be.

Having said this, he gave her some money, which he told her would be necessary to defray the expenses of her journey. Adeline could no longer doubt his sincerity, and her transports of joy and gratitude would scarcely permit her to thank him. She wished to have bid Madame La Motte farewell, and indeed earnestly requested it; but he again told her she had no time to lose; and having wrapped her in a large cloak, he lifted her upon the horse. She bade him adieu with tears of gratitude, and Peter set off as fast as the darkness would permit.

When they were got some way,—I am glad with all my heart, Mam'selle, said he, to see you again. Who would have thought, after all, that my master himself would have bid me take you away! Well, to be sure, strange things come to pass; but I hope we shall have better luck this time. Adeline, not choosing to reproach him with the treachery of which she feared he had been formerly guilty, thanked him for his good wishes, and said she hoped they should be more fortunate: but Peter, in his usual strain of eloquence, proceeded to undeceive her in this point, and to acquaint her with every circumstance which his memory, and it was naturally a strong one could furnish.

Peter expressed such an artless interest in her welfare, and such a concern for her disappointment, that she could no longer doubt his faithfulness; and this conviction not only strengthened her confidence in the present undertaking, but made her listen to his conversation with kindness and pleasure. I should never have staid at the abbey till this time, said he, if I could have got away; but my master frighted me so much about the Marquis, and I had not money enough to carry me into my own country, so that I was forced to stay. It's well we have got some solid louis d'ors now; for I question, Ma'mselle, whether the people on the road would have taken those trinkets you formerly talked of for money.

Possibly not, said Adeline: I am thankful to Monsieur La Motte that we have more certain means of procuring conveniences. What route shall you take when we leave the forest, Peter?—Peter mentioned very correctly a great part of the road to Lyons; And then, said he, we can easily get to Savoy, and that will be nothing. My sister, God bless her! I hope, is living; I have not seen her many a year: but if she is not all the people will be glad to see me, and you will easily get a lodging, Ma'mselle, and every thing you want.

Adeline resolved to go with him to Savoy. La Motte, who knew the character and designs of the Marquis, had advised her to leave the kingdom, and had told her, what her fears would have suggested, that the Marquis would be indefatigable in search of her. His motive for this advice must be a desire of serving her; why else, when she was already in his power, should he remove her to another place, and even furnish her with money for the expenses of a journey?

At Leloncourt, where Peter said he was well known, she would be most likely to meet with protection and comfort, even should his sister be dead; and its distance and solitary situation pleased her. These reflections would have pointed out to her the prudence of proceeding to Savoy, had she been less destitute of resources in France; in her present situation they proved it to be necessary.

She inquired further concerning the route they were to take, and whether Peter was sufficiently acquainted with the road. When once I get to Thiers, I know it well enough, said Peter; for I have gone it many a time in my younger days, and any body will tell us the way there. They travelled for several hours in darkness and silence; and it was not till they emerged from the forest that Adeline saw the morning light streak the eastern clouds. The sight cheered and revived her; and as she travelled silently along, her mind revolved the events of the past night, and meditated plans for the future. The present kindness of La Motte appeared so very different from his former conduct, that it astonished and perplexed her; and she could only account for it by attributing it to one of those sudden impulses of humanity which sometimes operate even upon the most depraved hearts.

But when she recollected his former words—that he was not master of himself—she could scarcely believe that mere pity could induce him to break the bonds which had hitherto so strongly held him; and then, considering the altered conduct of the Marquis, she was inclined to think that she owed her liberty to some change in his sentiments towards her: yet the advice La Motte had given her to quit the kingdom, and the money with which he had supplied her for that purpose, seemed to contradict this opinion, and involved her again in doubt.

Peter now got directions to Thiers, which place they reached without any accident, and there stopped to refresh themselves. As soon as Peter thought the horse sufficiently rested, they again set forward, and from the rich plains of the Lyonnois, Adeline for the first time caught a view of the distant Alps, whose majestic heads, seeming to prop the vault of heaven, filled her mind with sublime emotions.

In a few hours they reached the vale in which stands the city of Lyons, whose beautiful environs, studded with villas and rich with cultivation, withdrew Adeline from the melancholy contemplation of her own circumstances, and her more painful anxiety for Theodore.

When they reached that busy city, her first care was to inquire concerning the passage of the Rhone; but she forbore to make these inquiries of the people of the inn, considering that if the Marquis should trace her thither, they might enable him to pursue her route. She, therefore, sent Peter to the quays to hire a boat, while she herself took a slight repast, it being her intention to embark immediately. Peter presently returned, having engaged a boat and men to take them up the Rhone to the nearest part of Savoy, from whence they were to proceed by land to the village of Leloncourt.

Having taken some refreshment, she ordered him to conduct her to the vessel. A new and striking scene presented itself to Adeline, who looked with surprise upon the river, gay with vessels, and the quay crowded with busy faces, and felt the contrast which the cheerful objects around bore to herself—to her, an orphan, desolate, helpless, and flying from persecution and her country. She spoke with the master of the boat; and having sent Peter back to the inn for the horse, (La Motte's gift to Peter in lieu of some arrears of wages,) they embarked.

As they slowly passed up the Rhone, whose steep banks, crowned with mountains, exhibited the most various, wild, and romantic scenery, Adeline sat in pensive reverie. The novelty of the scene through which she floated, now frowning with savage grandeur, and now smiling in fertility and gay with towns and villages, soothed her mind, and her sorrow gradually softened into a gentle and not unpleasing melancholy. She had seated herself at the head of the boat, where she watched its sides cleave the swift stream, and listened to the dashing of the waters.

The boat, slowly opposing the current, passed along for some hours, and at length the veil of evening was stretched over the landscape. The weather was fine, and Adeline, regardless of the dews that now fell, remained in the open air, observing the objects darken round her, the gay tints of the horizon fade away, and the stars gradually appear trembling upon the lucid mirror of the waters. The scene was now sunk in deep shadow, and the silence of the hour was broken only by the measured dashing of the oars, and now and then by the voice of Peter speaking to the boatmen. Adeline sat lost in thought—the forlornness of her circumstances came heightened to her imagination.

She saw herself surrounded by the darkness and stillness of night, in a strange place, far distant from any friends, going she scarcely knew whither, under the guidance of strangers, and pursued, perhaps, by an inveterate enemy. She pictured to herself the rage of the Marquis now that he had discovered her flight; and though she knew it very unlikely he should follow her by water, for which reason she had chosen that manner of travelling, she trembled at the portrait her fancy drew. Her thoughts then wandered to the plan she should adopt after reaching Savoy; and much as her experience had prejudiced her against the manners of a convent, she saw no place more likely to afford her a proper asylum. At length she retired to the little cabin for a few hours repose.

She awoke with the dawn: and her mind being too much disturbed to sleep again, she rose and watched the gradual approach of day. As she mused, she expressed the feelings of the moment in the following:

SONNETMorn's beaming eyes at length unclose,And wake the blushes of the rose,That all night oppress'd with dews,And veil'd in chilly shade its hues,Reclined, forlorn, the languid head,And sadly sought its parent bed;Warmth from her ray the trembling flower derives,And, sweetly blushing, through its tears revives.

Morn's beaming eyes at length unclose,And melt the tears that bend the rose;But can their charms suppress the sigh,Or chase the tear from Sorrow's eye?Can all their lustrous light impartOne ray of peace to Sorrow's heart?Ah! no; their fires her fainting soul oppress——Eve's pensive shades more soothe her meek distress!

When Adeline left the abbey, La Motte had remained for some time at the gate, listening to the steps of the horse that carried her, till the sound was lost in distance: he then turned into the hall with a lightness of heart to which he had long been a stranger. The satisfaction of having thus preserved her, as he hoped, from the designs of the Marquis, overcame for a while all sense of the danger in which this step must involve him. But when he returned entirely to his own situation, the terrors of the Marquis's resentment struck their full force upon his mind, and he considered how he might best escape it.

It was now past midnight—the Marquis was expected early on the following day; and in this interval it at first appeared probable to him that he might quit the forest. There was only one horse; but he considered whether it would be best to set off immediately for Auboine, where a carriage might be procured to convey his family and his moveables from the abbey, or quietly await the arrival of the Marquis, and endeavour to impose upon him by a forged story of Adeline's escape.

The time which must elapse before a carriage could reach the abbey would leave him scarcely sufficient to escape from the forest; what money he had remaining from the Marquis's bounty would not carry him far; and when it was expended he must probably be at a loss for subsistence, should he not before then be detected. By remaining at the abbey it would appear that he was unconscious of deserving the Marquis's resentment; and though he could not expect to impress a belief upon him that his orders had been executed, he might make it appear that Peter only had been accessary to the escape of Adeline; an account which would seem the more probable, from Peter's having been formerly detected in a similar scheme. He believed, also, that if the Marquis should threaten to deliver him into the hands of justice he might save himself by a menace of disclosing the crime he had commissioned him to perpetrate.

Thus arguing, La Motte resolved to remain at the abbey, and await the event of the Marquis's disappointment.

When the Marquis did arrive, and was informed of Adeline's flight, the strong workings of his soul, which appeared in his countenance, for a while alarmed and terrified La Motte. He cursed himself and her in terms of such coarseness and vehemence, as La Motte was astonished to hear from a man whose manners were generally amiable, whatever might be the violence and criminality of his passions. To invent and express these terms seemed to give him not only relief, but delight; yet he appeared more shocked at the circumstance of her escape than exasperated at the carelessness of La Motte; and recollecting at length that he wasted time, he left the abbey, and dispatched several of his servants in pursuit of her.

When he was gone, La Motte, believing that his story had succeeded, returned to the pleasure of considering that he had done his duty, and to the hope that Adeline was now beyond the reach of pursuit. This calm was of short continuance. In a few hours the Marquis returned, accompanied by the officers of justice. The affrighted La Motte, perceiving him approach, endeavoured to conceal himself, but was seized and carried to the Marquis, who drew him aside.

I am not to be imposed upon, said he, by such a superficial story as you have invented; you know your life is in my hands; tell me instantly where you have secreted Adeline, or I will charge you with the crime you have committed against me; but upon your disclosing the place of her concealment I will dismiss the officers and, if you wish it, assist you to leave the kingdom. You have no time to hesitate, and may know that I will not be trifled with. La Motte attempted to appease the Marquis, and affirmed that Adeline was really fled he knew not whither. You will remember, my Lord, that your character is also in my power; and that, if you proceed to extremities, you will compel me to reveal in the face of day that you would have made me a murderer.

And who will believe you? said the Marquis. The crimes that banished you from society will be no testimony of your veracity, and that with which I now charge you will bring with it a sufficient presumption that your accusation is malicious. Officers, do your duty.

They then entered the room and seized La Motte, whom terror now deprived of all power of resistance, could resistance have availed him; and in the perturbation of his mind he informed the Marquis that Adeline had taken the road to Lyons. This discovery, however, was made too late to serve himself; the Marquis seized the advantage it offered: but the charge had been given; and with the anguish of knowing that he had exposed Adeline to danger without benefiting himself, La Motte submitted in silence to his fate. Scarcely allowing him time to collect what little effects might easily be carried with him, the officers conveyed him from the abbey: but the Marquis, in consideration of the extreme distress of Madame La Motte, directed one of his servants to procure a carriage from Auboine, that she might follow her husband.

The Marquis in the mean time, now acquainted with the route Adeline had taken, sent forward his faithful valet to trace her to her place of concealment, and return immediately with intelligence to the villa.

Abandoned to despair, La Motte and his wife quitted the forest of Fontanville, which had for so many months afforded them an asylum, and embarked once more upon the tumultuous world, where justice would meet La Motte in the form of destruction. They had entered the forest as a refuge, rendered necessary by the former crimes of La Motte, and for sometime found in it the security they sought: but other offences, for even in that sequestered spot there happened to be temptation, soon succeeded; and his life, already sufficiently marked by the punishment of vice, now afforded him another instance of this great truth, "That where guilt is, there peace cannot enter."

CHAPTER XVI

Hail awful scenes, that calm the troubled breast,And woo the weary to profound repose!BEATTIE.

Adeline meanwhile, and Peter, proceeded on their voyage without any accident, and landed in Savoy, where Peter placed her upon the horse, and himself walked beside her. When he came within sight of his native mountains, his extravagant joy burst forth into frequent exclamations, and he would often ask Adeline if she had ever seen such hills in France. No, no, said he, the hills there are very well for French hills, but they are not to be named on the same day with ours. Adeline, lost in admiration of the astonishing and tremendous scenery around her, assented very warmly to the truth of Peter's assertion, which encouraged him to expatiate more largely upon the advantages of his country; its disadvantages he totally forgot; and though he gave away his last sous to the children of the peasantry that ran barefooted by the side of the horse, he spoke of nothing but the happiness and content of the inhabitants.

His native village, indeed, was an exception to the general character of the country, and to the usual effects of an arbitrary government; it was flourishing, healthy, and happy; and these advantages it chiefly owed to the activity and attention of the benevolent clergyman whose cure it was.

Adeline, who now began to feel the effects of long anxiety and fatigue, much wished to arrive at the end of her journey, and inquired impatiently of Peter concerning it. Her spirits thus weakened, the gloomy grandeur of the scenes which had so lately awakened emotions of delightful sublimity, now awed her into terror; she trembled at the sound of the torrents rolling among the cliffs and thundering in the vale below, and shrunk from the view of the precipices, which sometimes overhung the road and at others appeared beneath it. Fatigued as she was, she frequently dismounted to climb on foot the steep flinty road, which she feared to travel on horseback.

The day was closing when they drew near a small village at the foot of the Savoy Alps; and the sun, in all his evening splendour, now sinking behind their summits, threw a farewell gleam athwart the landscape so soft and glowing as drew from Adeline, languid as she was, an exclamation of rapture.

The romantic situation of the village next attracted her notice. It stood at the foot of several stupendous mountains, which formed a chain round a lake at some little distance, and the woods that swept from their summits almost embosomed the village. The lake, unruffled by the lightest air, reflected the vermeil tints of the horizon with the sublime on its borders, darkening every instant with the falling twilight.

When Peter perceived the village, he burst into a shout of joy. Thank God, said he, we are near home; there is my dear native place: it looks just as it did twenty years ago: and there are the same old trees growing round our cottage yonder, and the huge rock that rises above it. My poor father died there, Ma'mselle. Pray Heaven my sister be alive! it is a long while since I saw her. Adeline listened with a melancholy pleasure to these artless expressions of Peter, who in retracing the scenes of his former days seemed to live them over again. As they approached the village, he continued to point out various objects of his remembrance. And there too is the good pastor's chateau; look, Ma'mselle, that white house with the smoke curling, that stands on the edge of the lake yonder. I wonder whether he is alive yet: he was not old when I left the place, and as much beloved as ever man was; but death spares nobody!

They had by this time reached the village, which was extremely neat, though it did not promise much accommodation. Peter had hardly advanced ten steps before he was accosted by some of his old acquaintance, who shook hands, and seemed not to know how to part with him. He inquired for his sister, and was told she was alive and well. As they passed on, so many of his old friends flocked round him, that Adeline became quite weary of the delay. Many whom he had left in the vigour of life were now tottering under the infirmities of age, while their sons and daughters, whom he had known only in the playfulness of infancy, were grown from his remembrance, and in the pride of youth. At length they approached the cottage, and were met by his sister, who having heard of his arrival, came and welcomed him with unfeigned joy.

On seeing Adeline, she seemed surprised, but assisted her to alight; and conducting her into a small but neat cottage, received her with a warmth of ready kindness which would have graced a better situation. Adeline desired to speak with her alone, for the room was now crowded with Peter's friends; and then acquainting her with such particulars of her circumstances as it was necessary to communicate, desired to know if she could be accommodated with lodging in the cottage. Yes, Ma'mselle, said the good woman, such as it is, you are heartily welcome: I am only sorry it is not better. But you seem ill Ma'mselle; what shall I get you?

Adeline, who had been long struggling with fatigue and indisposition, now yielded to their pressure. She said she was indeed ill; but hoped that rest would restore her, and desired a bed might be immediately prepared. The good woman went out to obey her, and soon returning showed her to a little cabin, where she retired to a bed whose cleanliness was its only recommendation.

But notwithstanding her fatigue, she could not sleep; and her mind, in spite of all her efforts, returned to the scenes that were passed, or presented gloomy and imperfect visions of the future.

The difference between her own condition and that of other persons, educated as she had been, struck her forcibly, and she wept. They, said she, have friends and relations, all striving to save them not only from what may hurt, but what may displease them; watching not only for their present safety, but for their future advantage, and preventing them even from injuring themselves. But during my whole life I have never known a friend; have been in general surrounded by enemies, and very seldom exempt from some circumstance either of danger or calamity. Yet surely I am not born to be for ever wretched; the time will come when——She began to think she might one time be happy; but recollecting the desperate situation of Theodore,—No, said she, I can never hope even for peace!

Early the following morning the good woman of the house came to inquire how she had rested; and found she had slept little, and was much worse than on the preceding night. The uneasiness of her mind contributed to heighten the feverish symptoms that attended her, and in the course of the day her disorder began to assume a serious aspect. She observed its progress with composure, resigning herself to the will of God, and feeling little to regret in life. Her kind hostess did every thing in her power to relieve her, and there was neither physician nor apothecary in the village, so that nature was deprived of none of her advantages. Notwithstanding this, the disorder rapidly increased, and on the third day from its first attack she became delirious, after which she sunk into a state of stupefaction.

How long she remained in this deplorable condition she knew not; but on recovering her senses she found herself in an apartment very different from any she remembered. It was spacious and almost beautiful, the bed and every thing around being in one style of elegant simplicity. For some minutes she lay in a trance of surprise, endeavouring to recollect her scattered ideas of the past, and almost fearing to move lest the pleasing vision should vanish from her eyes.

At length she ventured to raise herself, when she presently heard a soft voice speaking near her, and the bed curtain on one side was gently undrawn by a beautiful girl. As she leaned forward over the bed, and with a smile of mingled tenderness and joy inquired of her patient how she did. Adeline gazed in silent admiration upon the most interesting female countenance she had ever seen, in which the expression of sweetness, united with lively sense and refinement, was chastened by simplicity.

Adeline at length recollected herself sufficiently to thank her kind inquirer, and begged to know to whom she was obliged, and where she was? The lovely girl pressed her hand, 'Tis we who are obliged, said she. Oh! how I rejoice to find that you have recovered your recollection! She said no more, but flew to the door of the apartment, and disappeared. In a few minutes she returned with an elderly lady, who approaching the bed with an air of tender interest, asked concerning the state of Adeline; to which the latter replied as well as the agitation of her spirits would permit, and repeated her desire of knowing to whom she was so greatly obliged. You shall know that hereafter, said the lady; at present be assured that you are with those who will think their care much overpaid by your recovery; submit, therefore, to every thing that may conduce to it, and consent to be kept as quiet as possible.

Adeline gratefully smiled and bowed her head in silent assent. The lady now quitted the room for a medicine; having given which to Adeline, the curtain was closed and she was left to repose. But her thoughts were too busy to suffer her to profit by the opportunity:—she contemplated the past and viewed the present; and when she compared them, the contrast struck her with astonishment: the whole appeared like one of those sudden transitions so frequent in dreams, in which we pass from grief and despair, we know not how, to comfort and delight.

Yet she looked forward to the future with a trembling anxiety that threatened to retard her recovery, and which when she remembered the words of her generous benefactress, she endeavoured to suppress. Had she better known the disposition of the persons in whose house she now was, her anxiety, as far as it regarded herself, must in a great measure have been done away; for La Luc, its owner, was one of those rare characters to whom misfortune seldom looks in vain, and whose native goodness, confirmed by principle, is uniform and unassuming in its acts. The following little picture of his domestic life, his family, and his manners, will more fully illustrate his character. It was drawn from the life, and its exactness will, it is hoped, compensate for its length.

THE FAMILY OF LA LUC. But half mankind, like Handel's fool, destroy, Through rage and ignorance, the strain of joy; Irregularly wild, the passions roll Through Nature's finest instrument, the soul:—While men of sense, with Handel's happier skill, Correct the taste and harmonize the will; Teach their affections like his notes to flow, Nor raised too high, nor ever sunk too low; Till every virtue, measured and refined, As fits the concert of the master mind, Melts in its kindred sounds, and pours along Th' according music of the moral song. CAWTHORNE.

In the village of Leloncourt, celebrated for its picturesque situation at the foot of the Savoy Alps, lived Arnaud La Luc, a clergyman descended from an ancient family of France, whose decayed fortunes occasioned them to seek a retreat in Switzerland, in an age when the violence of civil commotion seldom spared the conquered. He was minister of the village, and equally loved for the piety and benevolence of the Christian, as respected for the dignity and elevation of the philosopher. His was the philosophy of nature, directed by common sense. He despised the jargon of the modern schools, and the brilliant absurdities of systems which dazzled without enlightening, and guided without convincing their disciples.

His mind was penetrating; his views extensive; and his systems, like his religion, were simple, rational, and sublime. The people of his parish looked up to him as to a father; for while his precepts directed their minds, his example touched their hearts.

In early youth La Luc lost a wife whom he tenderly loved. This event threw a tincture of soft and interesting melancholy over his character, which remained when time had mellowed the remembrance that occasioned it. Philosophy had strengthened, not hardened, his heart; it enabled him to resist the pressure of affliction, rather than to overcome it.

Calamity taught him to feel with peculiar sympathy the distresses of others. His income from the parish was small, and what remained from the divided and reduced estates of his ancestors did not much increase it; but though he could not always relieve the necessities of the indigent, his tender pity and holy conversation seldom failed in administering consolation to the mental sufferer. On these occasions the sweet and exquisite emotions of his heart have often induced him to say, that could the voluptuary be once sensible of these feelings, he would never after forego the luxury of doing good. Ignorance of true pleasure, he would say, more frequently than temptation to that which is false, leads to vice.

La Luc had one son and a daughter, who were too young when their mother died to lament their loss. He loved them with peculiar tenderness, as the children of her whom he never ceased to deplore; and it was for some time his sole amusement to observe the gradual unfolding of their infant minds, and to bend them to virtue. His was the deep and silent sorrow of the heart: his complaints he never obtruded upon others, and very seldom did he even mention his wife. His grief was too sacred for the eye of the vulgar. Often he retired to the deep solitude of the mountains, and amid their solemn and tremendous scenery would brood over the remembrance of times past, and resign himself to the luxury of grief. On his return from these little excursions he was always more placid and contented. A sweet tranquillity, which arose almost to happiness, was diffused over his mind, and his manners were more than usually benevolent. As he gazed on his children, and fondly kissed them, a tear would sometimes steal into his eye: but it was a tear of tender regret, unmingled with the darker qualities of sorrow, and was most precious to his heart.

On the death of his wife he received into his house a maiden sister, a sensible, worthy woman, who was deeply interested in the happiness of her brother. Her affectionate attention and judicious conduct anticipated the effect of time in softening the poignancy of his distress; and her unremitted care of his children, while it proved the goodness of her own heart, attracted her more closely to his.

It was with inexpressible pleasure that he traced in the infant features of Clara the resemblance of her mother. The same gentleness of manner and the same sweetness of disposition soon displayed themselves; and as she grew up, her actions frequently reminded him so strongly of his lost wife as to fix him in reveries, which absorbed all his soul.

Engaged in the duties of his parish, the education of his children, and in philosophic research, his years passed in tranquillity. The tender melancholy with which affliction had tinctured his mind, was by long indulgence become dear to him, and he would not have relinquished it for the brightest dream of airy happiness. When any passing incident disturbed him, he retired for consolation to the idea of her he so faithfully loved, and yielding to a gentle, and what the world would call a romantic, sadness, gradually reassumed his composure. This was the secret luxury to which he withdrew from temporary disappointment—the solitary enjoyment which dissipated the cloud of care, and blunted the sting of vexation—which elevated his mind above this world, and opened to his view the sublimity of another.

The spot he now inhabited, the surrounding scenery, the romantic beauties of the neighbouring walks, were dear to La Luc, for they had once been loved by Clara; they had been the scenes of her tenderness, and of his happiness.

His chateau stood on the borders of a small lake that was almost environed by mountains of stupendous height, which, shooting into a variety of grotesque forms, composed a scenery singularly solemn and sublime. Dark woods intermingled with bold projections of rock, sometimes barren and sometimes covered with the purple bloom of wild flowers, impended over the lake, and were seen in the clear mirror of its waters. The wild and alpine heights which rose above, were either crowned with perpetual snows, or exhibited tremendous crags and masses of solid rock, whose appearance was continually changing as the rays of light were variously reflected on their surface, and whose summits were often wrapt in impenetrable mists. Some cottages and hamlets, scattered on the margin of the lake or seated in picturesque points of view on the rocks above, were the only objects that reminded the beholder of humanity.

On the side of the lake, nearly opposite to the chateau, the mountains receded, and a long chain of Alps was seen stretching in perspective. Their innumerable tints and shades, some veiled in blue mists, some tinged with rich purple, and others glittering in partial light, gave luxurious and magical colouring to the scene.

The chateau was not large, but it was convenient, and was characterized by an air of elegant simplicity and good order. The entrance was a small hall, which opening by a glass door into the garden, afforded a view of the lake, with the magnificent scenery exhibited on its borders. On the left of the hall was La Luc's study, where he usually passed his mornings; and adjoining was a small room fitted up with chemical apparatus, astronomical instruments, and other implements of science. On the right hand was the family parlour, and behind it a room which belonged exclusively to Madame La Luc. Here were deposited various medicines and botanical distillations, together with the apparatus for preparing them. From this room the whole village was liberally supplied with medicinal comfort; for it was the pride of Madame to believe herself skilful in relieving the disorders of her neighbours.

Behind the chateau rose a tuft of pines, and in front a gentle declivity, covered with verdure and flowers, extended to the lake, whose waters flowed even with the grass, and gave freshness to the acacias that waved over its surface. Flowering shrubs, intermingled with mountain-ash, cypress, and ever-green oak, marked the boundary of the garden.

At the return of spring it was Clara's care to direct the young shoots of the plants, to nurse the budding flowers, and to shelter them with the luxuriant branches of the shrubs from the cold blasts that descended from the mountains. In summer she usually rose with the sun, and visited her favourite flowers while the dew yet hung glittering on their leaves. The freshness of early day, with the glowing colouring which then touched the scenery, gave a pure and exquisite delight to her innocent heart. Born amid scenes of grandeur and sublimity, she had quickly imbibed a taste for their charms, which taste was heightened by the influence of a warm imagination. To view the sun rising above the Alps, tinging their snowy heads with light, and suddenly darting his rays over the whole face of nature—to see the fiery splendour of the clouds reflected in the lake below, and the roseate tints first steal upon the rocks above—were among the earliest pleasures of which Clara was susceptible. From being delighted with the observance of nature, she grew pleased with seeing her finely imitated, and soon displayed a taste for poetry and painting. When she was about sixteen she often selected from her father's library those of the Italian poets most celebrated for picturesque beauty, and would spend the first hours of morning in reading them under the shade of the acacias that bordered the lake. Here too she would often attempt rude sketches of the surrounding scenery; and at length by repeated efforts, assisted by some instruction from her brother she succeeded so well as to produce twelve drawings in crayon, which were judged worthy of decorating the parlour of the chateau.

Young La Luc played the flute, and she listened to him with exquisite delight, particularly when he stood on the margin of the lake, under her beloved acacias. Her voice was sweet and flexible, though not strong, and she soon learned to modulate it to the instrument. She knew nothing of the intricacies of execution; her airs were simple, and her style equally so; but she soon gave them a touching expression, inspired by the sensibility of her heart, which seldom left those of her hearers unaffected.

It was the happiness of La Luc to see his children happy; and in one of his excursions to Geneva, whither he went to visit some relations of his late wife, he bought Clara a lute. She received it with more gratitude than she could express; and having learned one air, she hastened to her favourite acacias, and played it again and again till she forgot every thing besides. Her little domestic duties, her books, her drawing, even the hour which her father dedicated to her improvement, when she met her brother in the library, and with him partook of knowledge, even this hour passed unheeded by. La Luc suffered it to pass. Madame was displeased that her niece neglected her domestic duties, and wished to reprove her, but La Luc begged she would be silent. Let experience teach her her error, said he, precept seldom brings conviction to young minds.

Madame objected that experience was a slow teacher. It is a sure one, replied La Luc, and is not unfrequently the quickest of all teachers: when it cannot lead us into serious evil, it is well to trust to it.

The second day passed with Clara as the first, and the third as the second. She could now play several tunes; she came to her father and repeated what she had learnt.

At supper the cream was not dressed, and there was no fruit on the table. La Luc inquired the reason; Clara recollected it, and blushed. She observed that her brother was absent, but nothing was said. Toward the conclusion of the repast he appeared; his countenance expressed unusual satisfaction, but he seated himself in silence. Clara inquired what had detained him from supper, and learnt that he had been to a sick family in the neighbourhood with the weekly allowance which her father gave them. La Luc had intrusted the care of this family to his daughter, and it was her duty to have carried them their little allowance on the preceding day, but she had forgotten every thing but music.

How did you find the woman? said La Luc to his son. Worse, Sir, he replied; for her medicines had not been regularly given and the children had had little or no food to-day.

Clara was shocked. No food to-day! said she to herself; and I have been playing all day on my lute, under the acacias by the lake! Her father did not seem to observe her emotion, but turned to his son. I left her better, said the latter; the medicines I carried eased her pain, and I had the pleasure to see her children make a joyful supper.

Clara, perhaps, for the first time in her life, envied him his pleasure; her heart was full, and she sat silent. No food to-day! thought she.

She retired pensively to her chamber. The sweet serenity with which she usually went to rest was vanished, for she could no longer reflect on the past day with satisfaction.

What a pity, said she, that what is so pleasing should be the cause of so much pain! This lute is my delight, and my torment! This reflection occasioned her much internal debate; but before she could come to any resolution upon the point in question, she fell asleep.

She awoke very early the next morning, and impatiently watched the progress of the dawn. The sun at length appearing, she arose, and determined to make all the atonement in her power for her former neglect, hastened to the cottage.

Here she remained a considerable time, and when she returned to the chateau, her countenance had recovered all its usual serenity. She resolved, however, not to touch her lute that day.

Till the hour of breakfast she busied herself in binding up the flowers and pruning the shoots that were too luxuriant, and she at length found herself, she scarcely knew how, beneath her beloved acacias by the side of the lake. Ah! said she with a sigh, how sweetly would the song I learned yesterday sound now over the waters! But she remembered her determination, and checked the step she was involuntarily taking towards the chateau.

She attended her father in the library at the usual hour, and learned from his discourse with her brother on what had been read the two preceding days, that she had lost much entertaining knowledge. She requested her father would inform her to what this conversation alluded; but he calmly replied, that she had preferred another amusement at the time when the subject was discussed, and must therefore content herself with ignorance. You would reap the rewards of study from the amusements of idleness, said he; learn to be reasonable—do not expect to unite inconsistencies.

Clara felt the justness of this rebuke, and remembered her lute. What mischief has it occasioned! sighed she. Yes, I am determined not to touch it at all this day. I will prove that I am able to control my inclinations when I see it is necessary so to do. Thus resolving, she applied herself to study with more than usual assiduity.

She adhered to her resolution, and towards the close of the day went into the garden to amuse herself. The evening was still and uncommonly beautiful. Nothing was heard but the faint shivering of the leaves, which returned but at intervals, making silence more solemn, and the distant murmurs of the torrents that rolled among the cliffs. As she stood by the lake, and watched the sun slowly sinking below the Alps, whose summits were tinged with gold and purple; as she saw the last rays of light gleam upon the waters, whose surface was not curled by the slightest air, she sighed, oh! how enchanting would be the sound of my lute at this moment, on this spot, and when every thing is so still around me!

The temptation was too powerful for the resolution of Clara: she ran to the chateau, returned with the instrument to her dear acacias, and beneath their shade continued to play till the surrounding objects faded in darkness from her sight. But the moon rose, and shedding a trembling lustre on the lake, made the scene more captivating than ever.

It was impossible to quit so delightful a spot; Clara repeated her favourite airs again and again. The beauty of the hour awakened all her genius; she never played with such expression before, and she listened with increasing rapture to the tones as they languished over the waters and died away on the distant air. She was perfectly enchanted—no! nothing was ever so delightful as to play on the lute beneath her acacias, on the margin of the lake, by moonlight!

When she returned to the chateau, supper was over. La Luc had observed Clara, and would not suffer her to be interrupted.

When the enthusiasm of the hour was passed, she recollected that she had broken her resolution, and the reflection gave her pain. I prided myself on controlling my inclinations, said she, and I have weakly yielded to their direction. But what evil have I incurred by indulging them this evening? I have neglected no duty, for I had none to perform. Of what then have I to accuse myself? It would have been absurd to have kept my resolution, and denied myself a pleasure when there appeared no reason for this self-denial.

She paused, not quite satisfied with this reasoning. Suddenly resuming her inquiry, But how, said she, am I certain that I should have resisted my inclinations if there had been a reason for opposing them? If the poor family whom I neglected yesterday had been unsupplied to-day, I fear I should again have forgotten them while I played on my lute on the banks of the lake.

She then recollected all that her father had at different times said on the subject of self-command, and she felt some pain.

No, said she, if I do not consider that to preserve a resolution, which I have once solemnly formed, is a sufficient reason to control my inclinations, I fear no other motive would long restrain me. I seriously determined not to touch my lute this whole day, and I have broken my resolution. To-morrow perhaps I may be tempted to neglect some duty, for I have discovered that I cannot rely on my own prudence. Since I cannot conquer temptation, I will fly from it.

On the following morning she brought her lute to La Luc, and begged he would receive it again, and at least keep it till she had taught her inclinations to submit to control.

The heart of La Luc swelled as she spoke. No, Clara, said he, it is unnecessary that I should receive your lute; the sacrifice you would make proves you worthy of my confidence. Take back the instrument; since you have sufficient resolution to resign it when it leads you from duty, I doubt not that you will be able to control its influence now that it is restored to you.

Clara felt a degree of pleasure and pride at these words, such as she had never before experienced; but she thought, that to deserve the commendation they bestowed, it was necessary to complete the sacrifice she had begun. In the virtuous enthusiasm of the moment the delights of music were forgotten in those of aspiring to well-earned praise; and when she refused the lute thus offered, she was conscious only of exquisite sensations. Dear Sir, said she, tears of pleasure, swelling in her eyes, allow me to deserve the praises you bestow, and then I shall indeed be happy.

La Luc thought she had never resembled her mother so much as at this instant, and tenderly kissing her, he for some moments wept in silence. When he was able to speak, You do already deserve my praises, said he, and I restore your lute as a reward for the conduct which excites them. This scene called back recollections too tender for the heart of La Luc, and giving Clara the instrument, he abruptly quitted the room.

La Luc's son, a youth of much promise, was designed by his father for the church, and had received from him an excellent education, which, however, it was thought necessary he should finish at an university. That of Geneva was fixed upon by La

Luc. His scheme had been to make his son not a scholar only; he was ambitious that he should also be enviable as a man. From early infancy he had accustomed him to hardihood and endurance, and as he advanced in youth, he encouraged him in manly exercises, and acquainted him with the useful arts as well as with abstract science.

He was high-spirited and ardent in his temper, but his heart was generous and affectionate. He looked forward to Geneva, and to the new world it would disclose, with the sanguine expectations of youth; and in the delight of these expectations was absorbed the regret he would otherways have felt at a separation from his family.

A brother of the late Madame La Luc, who was by birth an Englishman, resided at Geneva with his family. To have been related to his wife was a sufficient claim upon the heart of La Luc, and he had therefore always kept up an intercourse with Mr. Audley, though the difference in their characters and manner of thinking would never permit this association to advance into friendship. La Luc now wrote to him, signifying an intention of sending his son to Geneva, and recommending him to his care. To this letter Mr. Audley returned a friendly answer; and a short time after, an acquaintance of La Luc's being called to Geneva, he determined that his son should accompany him. The separation was painful to La Luc, and almost insupportable to Clara. Madame was grieved, and took care that he should have a sufficient quantity of medicines put up in his travelling trunk; she was also at some pains to point out their virtues, and the different complaints for which they were requisite; but she was careful to deliver her lecture during the absence of her brother.

La Luc, with his daughter, accompanied his son on horseback to the next town, which was about eight miles from Leloncourt; and there again enforcing all the advice he had formerly given him respecting his conduct and pursuits, and again yielding to the tender weakness of the father, he bade him farewell. Clara wept, and felt more sorrow at this parting than the occasion could justify; but this was almost the first time she had known grief, and she artlessly yielded to its influence.

La Luc and Clara travelled pensively back, and the day was closing when they came within view of the lake, and soon after of the chateau. Never had it appeared gloomy till now; but now Clara wandered forlornly through every deserted apartment where she had been accustomed to see her brother, and recollected a thousand little circumstances which, had he been present, she would have thought immaterial, but on which imagination now stamped a value. The garden, the scenes around, all wore a melancholy aspect, and it was long ere they resumed their natural character and Clara recovered her vivacity.

Near four years had elapsed since this separation, when one evening, as Madame La Luc and her niece were sitting at work together in the parlour, a good woman in the neighbourhood desired to be admitted. She came to ask for some medicines, and the advice of Madame La Luc. Here is a sad accident happened at our house, Madame, said she; I am sure my heart aches for the poor young creature.—Madame La Luc desired she would explain herself, and the woman proceeded to say that her brother Peter, whom she had not seen for so many years, was arrived, and had brought a young lady to her cottage, who she verily believed was dying. She described her disorder, and acquainted Madame with what particulars of her mournful story Peter had related, failing not to exaggerate such as her compassion for the unhappy stranger and her love of the marvellous prompted.

The account appeared a very extraordinary one to Madame; but pity for the forlorn condition of the young sufferer induced her to inquire further into the affair. Do let me go to her, Madame, said Clara, who had been listening with ready compassion to the poor woman's narrative: Do suffer me to go—she must want comforts, and I wish much to see how she is. Madame asked some further questions concerning her disorder, and then, taking off her spectacles, she rose from her chair, and said she would go herself. Clara desired to accompany her. They put on their hats and followed the good woman to the cottage, where, in a very small close room, on a miserable bed, lay Adeline, pale, emaciated, and unconscious of all around her. Madame turned to the woman, and asked how long she had been in this way, while Clara went up to the bed, and taking the almost lifeless hand that lay on the quilt, looked anxiously in her face. She observes nothing, said she, poor creature! I wish she was at the chateau, she would be better accommodated, and I could nurse her there. The woman told Madame La Luc that the young lady had lain in that state for several hours. Madame examined her pulse, and shook her head. This room is very close, said she.—Very close indeed, cried Clara eagerly; surely she would be better at the chateau, if she could be moved.

We will see about that, said her aunt. In the mean time let me speak to Peter; it is some years since I saw him. She went to the outer room, and the woman ran out of the cottage to look for him. When she was gone, This is a miserable habitation for the poor stranger, said Clara; she will never be well here: do, Madame, let her be carried to our house; I am sure my father would wish it. Besides, there is something in her features, even inanimate as they now are, that prejudices me in her favour.

Shall I never persuade you to give up that romantic notion of judging people by their faces? said her aunt. What sort of a face she has is of very little consequence—her condition is lamentable, and I am desirous of altering it; but I wish first to ask Peter a few questions concerning her.

Thank you, my dear aunt, said Clara; she will be removed then. Madame La Luc was going to reply; but Peter now entered, and expressing great joy at seeing her again, inquired how Monsieur La Luc and Clara did. Clara immediately welcomed honest Peter to his native place, and he returned her salutation with many expressions of surprise at finding her so much grown. Though I have so often dandled you in my arms, Ma'mselle, I should never have known you again: Young twigs shoot fast, as they say.

Madame La Luc now inquired into the particulars of Adeline's story; and heard as much as Peter knew of it, being only that his late master found her in a very distressed situation, and that he had himself brought her from the abbey to save her from a French Marquis. The simplicity of Peter's manner would not suffer her to question his veracity, though some of the circumstances he related excited all her surprise and awakened all her pity. Tears frequently stood in Clara's eyes during the course of his narrative; and when he concluded, she said, Dear Madame, I am sure when my father learns the history of this unhappy young woman he will not refuse to be a parent to her, and I will be her sister.

She deserves it all, said Peter, for she is very good indeed. He then proceeded in a strain of praise which was very unusual with him.—I will go home and consult with my brother about her, said Madame La Luc, rising: she certainly ought to be removed to a more airy room. The chateau is so near, that I think she may be carried thither without much risk.

Heaven bless you! Madam, cried Peter, rubbing his hands, for your goodness to my poor young lady.

La Luc had just returned from his evening walk when they reached the chateau. Madame told him where she had been, and related the history of Adeline and her present condition.—By all means have her removed hither, said La Luc, whose eyes bore testimony to the tenderness of his heart: she can be better attended to here than in Susan's cottage.

I knew you would say so, my dear father, said Clara: I will go and order the green bed to be prepared for her.

Be patient, niece, said Madame La Luc; there is no occasion for such haste: some things are to be considered first; but you are young and romantic.—La Luc smiled.—The evening is now closed, resumed Madame; it will therefore be dangerous to remove her before morning. Early to-morrow a room shall be got ready, and she shall be brought here; in the mean time I will go and make up a medicine which I hope may be of service to her.—Clara reluctantly assented to this delay, and Madame La Luc retired to her closet.

On the following morning Adeline, wrapped in blankets and sheltered as much as possible from the air, was brought to the chateau, where the good La Luc desired she might have every attention paid her, and where Clara watched over her with unceasing anxiety and tenderness. She remained in a state of torpor during the greater part of the day, but towards evening she breathed more freely; and Clara, who still watched by her bed, had at length the pleasure of perceiving that her senses were restored. It was at this moment that she found herself in the situation from which we have digressed to give this account of the venerable La Luc and his family. The reader will find that his virtues and his friendship to Adeline deserved this notice.

CHAPTER XVII

Still Fancy, to herself unkind,Awakes to grief the soften'd mind.And points the bleeding friend.COLLINS.

Adeline, assisted by a fine constitution, and the kind attentions of her new friends, was in a little more than a week so much recovered as to leave her chamber. She was introduced to La Luc, whom she met with tears of gratitude, and thanked for his goodness in a manner so warm, yet so artless, as interested him still more in her favour. During the progress of her recovery, the sweetness of her behaviour had entirely won the heart of Clara, and greatly interested that of her aunt, whose reports of Adeline, together with the praises bestowed by Clara, had excited both esteem and curiosity in the breast of La Luc; and he now met her with an expression of benignity which spoke peace and comfort to her heart. She had acquainted Madame La Luc with such particulars of her story as Peter, either through ignorance or inattention, had not communicated, suppressing only, through a false delicacy perhaps, an acknowledgment of her attachment to Theodore. These circumstances were repeated to La Luc, who, ever sensible to the sufferings of others, was particularly interested by the singular misfortunes of Adeline.

Near a fortnight had elapsed since her removal to the chateau, when one morning La Luc desired to speak with her alone. She followed him into his study, and then in a manner the most delicate he told her, that as he found she was so unfortunate in her father, he desired she would henceforth consider him as her parent, and his house as her home. You and Clara shall be equally my daughters, continued he; I am rich in having such children. The strong emotions of surprise and gratitude for some time kept Adeline silent. Do not thank me, said La Luc; I know all you would say, and I know also that I am but doing my duty: I thank God that my duty and my pleasures are generally in unison. Adeline wiped away the tears which his goodness had excited, and was going to speak; but La Luc pressed her hand, and turning away to conceal his emotion, walked out of the room.

Adeline was now considered as a part of the family; and in the parental kindness of La Luc, the sisterly affection of Clara, and the steady and uniform regard of Madame, she would have been happy as she was thankful, had not unceasing anxiety for the fate of Theodore, of whom in this solitude she was less likely than ever to hear, corroded her heart, and embittered every moment of reflection. Even when sleep obliterated for awhile the memory of the past, his image frequently arose to her fancy, accompanied by all the exaggerations of terror. She saw him in chains, and struggling in the grasp of ruffians, or saw him led, amidst the dreadful preparations for execution, into the field: she saw the agony of his look, and heard him repeat her name in frantic accents, till the horrors of the scene overcame her and she awoke.

A similarity of taste and character attached her to Clara; yet the misery that preyed upon her heart was of a nature too delicate to be spoken of, and she never mentioned Theodore even to her friend. Her illness had yet left her weak and languid, and the perpetual anxiety of her mind contributed to prolong this state. She endeavoured by strong and almost continual efforts to abstract her thoughts from their mournful subject, and was often successful. La Luc had an excellent library, and the instruction it offered at once gratified her love of knowledge, and withdrew her mind from painful recollections. His conversation too afforded her another refuge from misery.

But her chief amusement was to wander among the sublime scenery of the adjacent country, sometimes with Clara, though often with no other companion than a book. There were indeed times when the conversation of her friend imposed a painful restraint, and, when, given up to reflection, she would ramble alone through scenes whose solitary grandeur assisted and soothed the melancholy of her heart. Here she would retrace all the conduct of her beloved Theodore, and endeavour to recollect his exact countenance, his air and manner. Now she would weep at the remembrance, and then, suddenly considering that he had perhaps already suffered an ignominious death for her sake, even in consequence of the very action which had proved his love, a dreadful despair would seize her, and, arresting her tears, would threaten to bear down every barrier that fortitude and reason could oppose.

Fearing longer to trust her own thoughts, she would hurry home, and by a desperate effort would try to lose, in the conversation of La Luc, the remembrance of the past. Her melancholy, when he observed it, La Luc attributed to a sense of the cruel treatment she had received from her father; a circumstance which, by exciting his compassion, endeared her more strongly to his heart; while that love of rational conversation, which in her calmer hours so frequently appeared, opened to him a new source of amusement in the cultivation of a mind eager for knowledge, and susceptible of all the energies of genius. She found a melancholy pleasure in listening to the soft tones of Clara's lute, and would often soothe her mind by attempting to repeat the airs she heard.

The gentleness of her manners, partaking so much of that pensive character which marked La Luc's, was soothing to his heart, and tinctured his behaviour with a degree of tenderness that imparted comfort to her, and gradually won her entire confidence and affection. She saw with extreme concern the declining state of his health, and united her efforts with those of the family to amuse and revive him.

The pleasing society of which she partook, and the quietness of the country, at length restored her mind to a state of tolerable composure. She was now acquainted with all the wild walks of the neighbouring mountains; and never tired of viewing their astonishing scenery, she often indulged herself in traversing alone their unfrequented paths, where now and then a peasant from a neighbouring village was all that interrupted the profound solitude. She generally took with her a book, that if she perceived her thought inclined to fix on the one object of her grief, she might force them to a subject less dangerous to her peace. She had become a tolerable proficient in English while at the convent where she received her education, and the instruction of La Luc, who was well acquainted with the language, now served to perfect her. He was partial to the English; he admired their character, and the constitution of their laws, and his library contained a collection of their best authors, particularly of their philosophers and poets. Adeline found that no species of writing had power so effectually to withdraw her mind from the contemplation of its own misery as the higher kinds of poetry, and in these her taste soon taught her to distinguish the superiority of the English from that of the French. The genius of the language, more perhaps than the genius of the people, if indeed the distinction may be allowed, occasioned this.

She frequently took a volume of Shakespeare or of Milton, and, having gained some wild eminence, would seat herself beneath the pines, whose low murmurs soothed her heart, and conspired with the visions of the poet to lull her to forgetfulness of grief.

One evening, when Clara was engaged at home, Adeline wandered alone to a favourite spot among the rocks that bordered the lake. It was an eminence which commanded an entire view of the lake, and of the stupendous mountains that environed it. A few ragged thorns grew from the precipice beneath, which descended perpendicularly to the water's edge; and above rose a thick wood of larch, pine, and fir, intermingled with some chesnut and mountain ash. The evening was fine, and the air so still that it scarcely waved the light leaves of the trees around, or rippled the broad expanse of the waters below. Adeline gazed on the scene with a kind of still rapture, and watched the sun sinking amid a crimson glow, which tinted the bosom of the lake and the snowy heads of the distant Alps. The delight which the scenery inspired:

Soothing each gust of passion into peace,All but the swellings of the soften'd heart,That waken, not disturb, the tranquil mind;

was now heightened by the tones of a French horn, and, looking on the lake, she perceived at some distance a pleasure-boat. As it was a spectacle rather uncommon in this solitude, she concluded the boat contained a party of foreigners come to view the wonderful scenery of the country, or perhaps of Genevois, who choose to amuse themselves on a lake as grand, though much less extensive, than their own; and the latter conjecture was probably just.

As she listened to the mellow and enchanting tones of the horn, which gradually sunk away in distance, the scene appeared more lovely than before; and finding it impossible to forbear attempting to paint in language what was so beautiful in reality, she composed the following:

STANZASHow smooth that lake expands its ample breast!Where smiles in soften'd glow the summer sky:How vast the rocks that o'er its surface rest!How wild the scenes its winding shores supply!

Now down the western steep slow sinks the sun,And paints with yellow gleam the tufted woods;While here the mountain-shadows, broad and dun,Sweep o'er the crystal mirror of the floods.

Mark how his splendour tips with partial lightThose shatter'd battlements! that on the browOf yon bold promontory burst to sightFrom o'er the woods that darkly spread below.

In the soft blush of light's reflected power,The ridgy rock, the woods that crown its steep,Th' illumin'd battlement, and darker tower,On the smooth wave in trembling beauty sleep.

But, lo! the sun recalls his fervid ray,And cold and dim the watery visions fail;While o'er yon cliff, whose pointed crags decay,Mild evening draws her thin empurpled veil!

How sweet that strain of melancholy horn!That floats along the slowly-ebbing wave,And up the far-receding mountains borne,Returns a dying close from Echo's cave!

Hail! shadowy forms of still, expressive Eve!Your pensive graces stealing on my heart,Bid all the fine-attun'd emotions live,And Fancy all her loveliest dreams impart.

La Luc observing how much Adeline was charmed with the features of the country, and desirous of amusing her melancholy, which, notwithstanding her efforts, was often too apparent, wished to show her other scenes than those to which her walks were circumscribed. He proposed a party on horseback to take a nearer view of the Glaciers; to attempt their ascent was a difficulty and fatigue to which neither La Luc, in his present state of health, nor Adeline were equal. She had not been accustomed to ride single, and the mountainous road they were to pass made the experiment rather dangerous; but she concealed her fears, and they were not sufficient to make her wish to forego an enjoyment such as was now offered her.

The following day was fixed for this excursion. La Luc and his party arose at an early hour, and having taken a slight breakfast, they set out towards the Glacier of Montanvert, which lay at a few leagues distance. Peter carried a small basket of provisions; and it was their plan to dine on some pleasant spot in the open air.

It is unnecessary to describe the high enthusiasm of Adeline, the more complacent pleasure of La Luc, and the transports of Clara, as the scenes of this romantic country shifted to their eyes. Now frowning in dark and gloomy grandeur, it exhibited only tremendous rocks and cataracts rolling from the heights into some deep and narrow valley, along which their united waters roared and foamed, and burst away to regions inaccessible to mortal foot: and now the scene arose less fiercely wild:

The pomp of groves and garniture of fields

were intermingled with the ruder features of nature; and while the snow froze on the summit of the mountain, the vine blushed at its foot.

Engaged in interesting conversation, and by the admiration which the country excited, they travelled on till noon, when they looked round for a pleasant spot where they might rest and take refreshment. At some little distance they perceived the ruins of a fabric which had once been a castle; it stood almost on a point of rock that overhung a deep valley; and its broken turrets rising from among the woods that embosomed it, heightened the picturesque beauty of the object.

The edifice invited curiosity, and the shades repose—La Luc and his party advanced.

Deep struck with awe they mark'd the dome o'erthrown,Where once the beauty bloom'd, the warrior shone:They saw the castle's mouldering towers decay'd,The loose stone tottering o'er the trembling shade.

They seated themselves on the grass under the shade of some high trees near the ruins. An opening in the woods afforded a view of the distant Alps—the deep silence of solitude reigned. For some time they were lost in meditation. Adeline felt a sweet complacency, such as she had long been a stranger to. Looking at La Luc, she perceived a tear stealing down his cheek, while the elevation of his mind was strongly expressed on his countenance. He turned on Clara his eyes, which were now filled with tenderness, and made an effort to recover himself.

The stillness and total seclusion of this scene, said Adeline, those stupendous mountains, the gloomy grandeur of these woods, together with that monument of faded glory on which the hand of time is so emphatically impressed, diffuse a sacred enthusiasm over the mind, and awaken sensations truly sublime.

La Luc was going to speak; but Peter coming forward, desired to know whether he had not better open the wallet, as he fancied his honour and the young ladies must be main hungry, jogging on so far up hill and down before dinner. They acknowledged the truth of honest Peter's suspicion, and accepted his hint.

Refreshments were spread on the grass; and having seated themselves under the canopy of waving woods, surrounded by the sweets of wild flowers, they inhaled the pure breeze of the Alps, which might be called spirit of air, and partook of a repast which these circumstances rendered delicious.

When they arose to depart,—I am unwilling, said Clara, to quit this charming spot. How delightful would it be to pass one's life beneath these shades with the friends who are dear to one!—La Luc smiled at the romantic simplicity of the idea: but Adeline sighed deeply to the image of felicity and of Theodore which it recalled, and turned away to conceal her tears.

They now mounted their horses, and soon after arrived at the foot of Montanvert. The emotions of Adeline, as she contemplated in various points of view the astonishing objects around her, surpassed all expression; and the feelings of the whole party were too strong to admit of conversation. The profound stillness which reigned in these regions of solitude inspired awe, and heightened the sublimity of the scenery to an exquisite degree.

It seems, said Adeline, as if we were walking over the ruins of the world, and were the only persons who had survived the wreck. I can scarcely persuade myself that we are not left alone on the globe.

The view of these objects, said La Luc, lift the soul to their Great Author, and we contemplate with a feeling almost too vast for humanity—the sublimity of his nature in the grandeur of his works.—La Luc raised his eyes, filled with tears, to heaven, and was for some moments lost in silent adoration.

They quitted these scenes with extreme reluctance; but the hour of the day, and the appearance of the clouds, which seemed gathering for a storm, made them hasten their departure. Could she have been sheltered from its fury, Adeline almost wished to have witnessed the tremendous effect of a thunder storm in these regions.

They returned to Leloncourt by a different route, and the shade of the overhanging precipices was deepened by the gloom of the atmosphere. It was evening when they came within view of the lake, which the travelers rejoiced to see, for the storm so long threatened was now fast approaching; the thunder murmured among the Alps; and the dark vapours that rolled heavily along their sides heightened their dreadful sublimity. La Luc would have quickened his pace, but the road winding down the steep side of a mountain made caution necessary. The darkening air and the lightnings that now flashed along the horizon terrified Clara, but she withheld the expression of her fear in consideration of her father. A peal of thunder, which seemed to shake the earth to its foundations, and was reverberated in tremendous echoes from the cliffs, burst over their heads. Clara's horse took fright at the sound, and setting off, hurried her with amazing velocity down the mountain towards the lake, which washed its foot. The agony of La Luc, who viewed her progress in the horrible expectation of seeing her dashed down the precipice that bordered the road, is not to be described.

Clara kept her seat, but terror had almost deprived her of sense. Her efforts to preserve herself were mechanical, for she scarcely knew what she did. The horse, however, carried her safely almost to the foot of the mountain, but was making towards the lake, when a gentleman who travelled along the road caught the bridle as the animal endeavoured to pass. The sudden stopping of the horse threw Clara to the ground, and, impatient of restraint, the animal burst from the hand of the stranger, and plunged into the lake. The violence of the fall deprived her of recollection; but while the stranger endeavoured to support her, his servant ran to fetch water.

She soon recovered, and unclosing her eyes found herself in the arms of a chevalier, who appeared to support her with difficulty. The compassion expressed in his countenance while he inquired how she did, revived her spirits; and she was endeavouring to thank him for his kindness, when La Luc and Adeline came up. The terror impressed on her father's features was perceived by Clara; languid as she was, she tried to raise herself, and said with a faint smile, which betrayed instead of disguising her sufferings, Dear Sir, I am not hurt. Her pale countenance and the blood that trickled down her cheek contradicted her words. But La Luc, to whom terror had suggested the utmost possible evil, now rejoiced to hear her speak; he recalled some presence of mind, and while Adeline applied her salts, he chafed her temples.

When she revived, she told him how much she was obliged to the stranger. La Luc endeavoured to express his gratitude; but the former interrupting him, begged he might be spared the pain of receiving thanks for having followed only an impulse of common humanity.

They were now not far from Leloncourt; but the evening was almost shut in, and the thunder murmured deeply among the hills. La Luc was distressed how to convey Clara home.

In endeavouring to raise her from the ground, the stranger betrayed such evident symptoms of pain, that La Luc inquired concerning it. The sudden jerk which the horse had given the arm of the chevalier, in escaping from his hold, had violently sprained his shoulder, and rendered his arm almost useless. The pain was exquisite; and La Luc, whose fears for his daughter were now subsiding, was shocked at the circumstance, and pressed the stranger to accompany him to the village, where relief might be obtained. He accepted the invitation; and Clara, being at length placed on a horse led by her father, was conducted to the chateau.

When Madame, who had been looking out for La Luc some time, perceived the cavalcade approaching, she was alarmed, and her apprehensions were confirmed when she saw the situation of her niece. Clara was carried into the house, and La Luc would have sent for a surgeon, but there was none within several leagues of the village, neither were there any of the physical profession within the same distance. Clara was assisted to her chamber by Adeline, and Madame La Luc undertook to examine the wounds. The result restored peace to the family, for though she was much bruised, she had escaped material injury; a slight contusion on the forehead had occasioned the bloodshed which at first alarmed La Luc. Madame undertook to restore her niece in a few days with the assistance of a balsam composed by herself, on the virtues of which she descanted with great eloquence, till La Luc interrupted her by reminding her of the condition of her patient.

Madame having bathed Clara's bruises, and given her a cordial of incomparable efficacy, left her; and Adeline watched in the chamber of her friend till she retired to her own for the night.

La Luc, whose spirits had suffered much perturbation, was now tranquillized by the report his sister made of Clara. He introduced the stranger; and having mentioned the accident he had met with, desired that he might have immediate assistance. Madame hastened to her closet; and it is perhaps difficult to determine whether she felt most concern for the sufferings of her guest, or pleasure at the opportunity thus offered of displaying her medical skill. However this might be, she quitted the room with great alacrity, and very quickly returned with a phial containing her inestimable balsam; and having given the necessary directions for the application of it, she left the stranger to the care of his servant.

La Luc insisted that the chevalier, M. Verneuil, should not leave the chateau that night, and he very readily submitted to be detained. His manners during the evening were as frank and engaging as the hospitality and gratitude of La Luc were sincere, and they soon entered into interesting conversation. M. Verneuil conversed like a man who had seen much, and thought more; and if he discovered any prejudice in his opinions, it was evidently the prejudice of a mind which, seeing objects through the medium of his own goodness, tinges them with the hue of its predominant quality. La Luc was much pleased, for in his retired situation he had not often an opportunity of receiving the pleasure which results from a communion of intelligent minds. He found that M. Verneuil had travelled. La Luc having asked some questions relative to England, they fell into discourse concerning the national characters of the French and English.

If it is the privilege of wisdom, said M. Verneuil, to look beyond happiness, I own I had rather be without it. When we observe the English, their laws, writings, and conversations, and at the same time mark their countenances, manners, and the frequency of suicide among them, we are apt to believe that wisdom and happiness are incompatible. If, on the other hand, we turn to their neighbours, the French, and see[1] their wretched policy, their sparkling but sophistical discourse, frivolous occupations, and, withal, their gay animated air, we shall be compelled to acknowledge that happiness and folly too often dwell together.

It is the end of wisdom, said La Luc, to attain happiness, and I can hardly dignify that conduct or course of thinking which tends to misery with the name of wisdom. By this rule, perhaps, the folly, as we term it, of the French deserves, since its effect is happiness, to be called wisdom. That airy thoughtlessness, which alike to contemn reflection and anticipation, produces all the effect of it without reducing its subjects to the mortification of philosophy. But in truth wisdom is an exertion of mind to subdue folly; and as the happiness of the French is less the consequence of mind than of constitution, it deserves not the honours of wisdom.

Discoursing on the variety of opinions that are daily formed on the same conduct, La Luc observed how much that which is commonly called opinion is the result of passion and temper.

True, said M. Vernueil, there is a tone of thought, as there is a key note in music, that leads all its weaker affections. Thus, where the powers of judging may be equal, the disposition to judge is different; and the actions of men are but too often arraigned by whim and caprice, by partial vanity, and the humour of the moment.

Here La Luc took occasion to reprobate the conduct of those writers, who, by showing the dark side only of human nature, and by dwelling on the evils only which are incident to humanity, have sought to degrade man in his own eyes, and to make him discontented with life. What should we say of a painter, continued La Luc, who collected in his piece objects of a black hue only, who presents you with a black man, a black horse, a black dog, &c. &c., and tells you that his is a picture of nature, and that nature is black?—'Tis true, you would reply, the objects you exhibit do exist in nature, but they form a very small part of her works. You say that nature is black, and, to prove it, you have collected on your canvass all the animals of this hue that exist. But you have forgot to paint the green earth, the blue sky, the white man, and objects of all those various hues with which creation abounds, and of which black is a very inconsiderable part.

The countenance of M. Verneuil lightened with peculiar animation during the discourse of La Luc.—To think well of his nature, said he, is necessary to the dignity and the happiness of man. There is a decent pride which becomes every mind, and is congenial to virtue. That consciousness of innate dignity, which shows him the glory of his nature, will be his best protection from the meanness of vice. Where this consciousness is wanting, continued M. Verneuil, there can be no sense of moral honour, and consequently none of the higher principles of action. What can be expected of him who says it is his nature to be mean and selfish? Or who can doubt that he who thinks thus, thinks from the experience of his own heart, from the tendency of his own inclinations? Let it always be remembered, that he who would persuade men to be good, ought to show them that they are great.

You speak, said La Luc, with the honest enthusiasm of a virtuous mind; and in obeying the impulse of your heart, you utter the truths of philosophy: and, trust me, a bad heart and a truly philosophic head have never yet been united in the same individual. Vicious inclinations not only corrupt the heart, but the understanding, and thus lead to false reasoning. Virtue only is on the side of truth.

La Luc and his guest, mutually pleased with each other, entered upon the discussion of subjects so interesting to them both, that it was late before they parted for the night.

CHAPTER XVIII

'Twas such a scene as gave a kind relief To memory, in sweetly pensive grief. VIRGIL'S TOMB.

Mine be the breezy hill, that skirts the down, Where a green grassy turf is all I crave, With here and there a violet bestrown, And many an evening sun shine sweetly on my grave. THE MINSTREL.

Repose had so much restored Clara, that when Adeline, anxious to know how she did, went early in the morning to her chamber, she found her already risen, and ready to attend the family at breakfast. Monsieur Verneuil appeared also; but his looks betrayed a want of rest, and indeed he had suffered during the night a degree of anguish from his arm which it was an effort of some resolution to endure in silence. It was now swelled and somewhat inflamed, and this might in some degree be attributed to the effect of Madame La Luc's balsam, the restorative qualities of which for once had failed. The whole family sympathized with his sufferings, and Madame at the request of M. Verneuil, abandoned her balsam, and substituted an emollient fomentation.

From an application of this, he in a short time found an abatement of the pain, and returned to the breakfast table with greater composure. The happiness which La Luc felt at seeing his daughter in safety was very apparent; but the warmth of his gratitude towards her preserver he found it difficult to express. Clara spoke the genuine emotions of her heart with artless but modest energy, and testified sincere concern for the sufferings which she had occasioned M. Verneuil.

The pleasure received from the company of his guest, and the consideration of the essential services he had rendered him, co-operated with the natural hospitality of La Luc, and he pressed M. Verneuil to remain some time at the chateau.—I can never repay the services you have done me, said La Luc; yet I seek to increase my obligations to you by requesting you will prolong your visit, and thus allow me an opportunity of cultivating your acquaintance.

M. Verneuil, who at the time he met La Luc was travelling from Geneva to a distant part of Savoy, merely for the purpose of viewing the country, being now delighted with his host and with every thing around him, willingly accepted the invitation. In this circumstance prudence concurred with inclination, for to have pursued his journey on horseback, in his present situation, would have been dangerous, if not impracticable.

The morning was spent in conversation, in which M. Verneuil displayed a mind enriched with taste, enlightened by science, and enlarged by observation. The situation of the chateau and the features of the surrounding scenery charmed him, and in the evening he found himself able to walk with La Luc and explore the beauties of this romantic region. As they passed through the village, the salutations of the peasants, in whom love and respect were equally blended, and their eager inquiries after Clara, bore testimony to the character of La Luc; while his countenance expressed a serene satisfaction, arising from the consciousness of deserving and possessing their love.—I live surrounded by my children, said he, turning to M. Verneuil, who had noticed their eagerness; for such I consider my parishioners. In discharging the duties of my office,

I am repaid not only by my own conscience, but by their gratitude. There is a luxury in observing their simple and honest love, which I would not exchange for any thing the world calls blessings.

Yet the world, Sir, would call the pleasures of which you speak romantic, said M. Verneuil; for to be sensible of this pure and exquisite delight requires a heart untainted with the vicious pleasures of society—pleasures that deaden its finest feelings and poison the source of its truest enjoyments.—They pursued their way along the borders of the lake, sometimes under the shade of hanging woods, and sometimes over hillocks of turf, where the scene opened in all its wild magnificence. M. Verneuil often stopped in raptures to observe and point out the singular beauties it exhibited, while La Luc, pleased with the delight his friend expressed, surveyed with more than usual satisfaction the objects which had so often charmed him before. But there was a tender melancholy in the tone of his voice and his countenance, which arose from the recollection of having often traced those scenes, and partaken of the pleasure they inspired, with her who had long since bade them an eternal farewell.

They presently quitted the lake, and, winding up a steep ascent between the woods, came after a hour's walk to a green summit, which appeared, among the savage rocks that environed it, like the blossom on the thorn. It was a spot formed for solitary delight, inspiring that soothing tenderness so dear to the feeling mind, and which calls back to memory the images of past regret, softened by distance and endeared by frequent recollection. Wild shrubs grew from the crevices of the rocks beneath, and the high trees of pine and cedar that waved above, afforded a melancholy and romantic shade. The silence of the scene was interrupted only by the breeze as it rolled over the woods, and by the solitary notes of the birds that inhabited the cliffs.

From this point the eye commanded an entire view of those majestic and sublime Alps whose aspect fills the soul with emotions of indescribable awe, and seems to lift it to a nobler nature. The village and the chateau of La Luc appeared in the bosom of the mountains, a peaceful retreat from the storms that gathered on their tops. All the faculties of M. Verneuil were absorbed in admiration, and he was for some time quite silent; at length, bursting into a rhapsody, he turned, and would have addressed La Luc, when he perceived him at a distance leaning against a rustic urn, over which drooped in beautiful luxuriance the weeping willow.

As he approached, La Luc quitted his position, and advanced to meet him, while M. Verneuil inquired upon what occasion the urn had been erected. La Luc, unable to answer, pointed to it, and walked silently away, and M. Verneuil approaching the urn, read the following inscription:

TO
THE MEMORY OF CLARA LA LUC,
THIS URN

IS ERECTED ON THE SPOT WHICH SHE
LOVED, IN TESTIMONY OF
THE AFFECTION OF

A HUSBAND.

M. Verneuil now comprehended the whole, and, feeling for his friend, was hurt that he had noticed this monument of his grief. He rejoined La Luc, who was standing on the point of the eminence contemplating the landscape below with an air more placid, and touched with the sweetness of piety and resignation. He perceived that M. Verneuil was somewhat disconcerted, and he sought to remove his uneasiness. You will consider it, said he, as a mark of my esteem that I have brought you to this spot: it is never profaned by the presence of the unfeeling; they would deride the faithfulness of an attachment which has so long survived its object, and which, in their own breasts, would quickly have been lost amidst the dissipation of general society. I have cherished in my heart the remembrance of a woman whose virtues claimed all my love: I have cherished it as a treasure to which I could withdraw from temporary cares and vexations, in the certainty of finding a soothing, though melancholy comfort.

La Luc paused. M. Verneuil expressed the sympathy he felt, but he knew the sacredness of sorrow, and soon relapsed into silence. One of the brightest hopes of a future state, resumed La Luc, is, that we shall meet again those whom we have loved upon earth. And perhaps our happiness may be permitted to consist very much in the society of our friends, purified from the frailties of mortality, with the finer affections more sweetly attuned, and with the faculties of mind infinitely more elevated and enlarged. We shall then be enabled to comprehend subjects which are too vast for human conception; to comprehend, perhaps, the sublimity of that Deity who first called us into being. These views of futurity, my friend, elevate us above the evils of this world, and seem to communicate to us a portion of the nature we contemplate.

Call them not the illusions of a visionary brain, proceeded La Luc: I trust in their reality. Of this I am certain, that whether they are illusions or not, a faith in them ought to be cherished for the comfort it brings to the heart, and reverenced for the dignity it imparts to the mind. Such feelings make a happy and an important part of our belief in a future existence: they give energy to virtue, and stability to principle.

This, said M. Verneuil, is what I have often felt, and what every ingenuous mind must acknowledge.

La Luc and M. Verneuil continued in conversation till the sun had left the scene. The mountains, darkened by twilight, assumed a sublimer aspect, while the tops of some of the highest Alps were yet illuminated by the sun's rays, and formed a striking contrast to the shadowy obscurity of the world below. As they descended through the woods, and traversed the margin of the lake, the stillness and solemnity of the hour diffused a pensive sweetness over their minds, and sunk them into silence.

They found supper spread, as was usual, in the hall, of which the windows opened upon a garden, where the flowers might be said to yield their fragrance in gratitude to the refreshing dews. The windows were embowered with eglantine and other sweet shrubs, which hung in wild luxuriance around, and formed a beautiful and simple decoration. Clara and Adeline loved to pass their evenings in this hall, where they had acquired the first rudiments of astronomy, and from which they had a wide view of the heavens. La Luc pointed out to them the planets and the fixed stars, explained their laws, and from thence taking occasion to mingle moral with scientific instruction, would often ascend towards that great First Cause, whose nature soars beyond the grasp of human comprehension.

No study, he would sometimes say, so much enlarges the mind, or impresses it with so sublime an idea of the Deity, as that of astronomy. When the imagination launches into the regions of space, and contemplates the innumerable worlds which are scattered through it, we are lost in astonishment and awe. This globe appears as a mass of atoms in the immensity of the universe, and man a mere insect. Yet how wonderful! that man, whose frame is so diminutive in the scale of being, should have powers which spurn the narrow boundaries of time and place, soar beyond the sphere of his existence, penetrate the secret laws of nature, and calculate their progressive effects.

O! how expressively does this prove the spirituality of our being! Let the materialist consider it, and blush that he has ever doubted.

In this hall the whole family now met at supper; and during the remainder of the evening the conversation turned upon general subjects, in which Clara joined in modest and judicious remark. La Luc had taught her to familiarize her mind to reasoning, and had accustomed her to deliver her sentiments freely: she spoke them with a simplicity extremely engaging, and which convinced her hearers that the love of knowledge, not the vanity of talking, induced her to converse. M. Verneuil evidently endeavoured to draw forth her sentiments; and Clara, interested by the subjects he introduced, a stranger to affectation, and pleased with the opinions he expressed, answered them with frankness and animation. They retired mutually pleased with each other.

M. Verneuil was about six-and-thirty; his figure manly, his countenance frank and engaging. A quick penetrating eye, whose fire was softened by benevolence, disclosed the chief traits of his character; he was quick to discern, but generous to excuse, the follies of mankind; and while no one more sensibly felt an injury, none more readily accepted the concession of an enemy.

He was by birth a Frenchman. A fortune lately devolved to him, had enabled him to execute the plan which his active and inquisitive mind had suggested, of viewing the most remarkable parts of the continent. He was peculiarly susceptible of the beautiful and sublime in nature. To such a taste, Switzerland and the adjacent country was, of all others, the most interesting; and he found the scenery it exhibited infinitely surpassing all that his glowing imagination had painted; he saw with the eye of a painter, and felt with the rapture of a poet.

In the habitation of La Luc he met with the hospitality, the frankness, and the simplicity so characteristic of the country; in his venerable host he saw the strength of philosophy united with the finest tenderness of humanity—a philosophy which taught him to correct his feelings, not to annihilate them; in Clara, the bloom of beauty with the most perfect simplicity of heart; and in Adeline, all the charms of elegance and grace, with a genius deserving of the highest culture. In this family picture the goodness of Madame La Luc was not unperceived or forgotten. The cheerfulness and harmony that reigned within the chateau was delightful; but the philanthropy which, flowing from the heart of the pastor, was diffused through the whole village, and united the inhabitants in the sweet and firm bonds of social compact, was divine. The beauty of its situation conspired with these circumstances to make Leloncourt seem almost a paradise. M. Verneuil sighed that he must soon quit it. I ought to seek no further, said he, for here wisdom and happiness dwell together.

The admiration was reciprocal: La Luc and his family found themselves much interested in M. Verneuil, and looked forward to the time of his departure with regret. So warmly they pressed him to prolong his visit, and so powerfully his own inclinations seconded theirs, that he accepted the invitation. La Luc admitted no circumstance which might contribute to the amusement of his guest, who having in a few days recovered the use of his arm, they made several excursions among the mountains. Adeline and Clara, whom the care of Madame had restored to her usual health, were generally of the party.

After spending a week at the chateau, M. Verneuil bade adieu to La Luc and his family. They parted with mutual regret; and the former promised that when he returned to Geneva, he would take Leloncourt in his way. As he said this, Adeline, who had for some time observed with much alarm La Luc's declining health, looked mournfully on his languid countenance, and uttered a secret prayer that he might live to receive the visit of M. Verneuil.

Madame was the only person who did not lament his departure; she saw that the efforts of her brother to entertain his guest were more than his present state of health would admit of, and she rejoiced in the quiet that would now return to him.

But this quiet brought La Luc no respite from illness; the fatigue he had suffered in his late excursions seemed to have increased his disorder, which in a short time assumed the aspect of a consumption. Yielding to the solicitations of his family, he went to Geneva for advice, and was there recommended to try the air of Nice.

The journey thither, however, was of considerable length; and believing his life to be very precarious, he hesitated whether to go. He was also unwilling to leave the duty of his parish unperformed for so long a period as his health might require; but this was an objection which would not have withheld him from Nice, had his faith in the climate been equal to that of his physicians.

His parishioners felt the life of their pastor to be of the utmost consequence to them: it was a general cause, and they testified at once his worth, and their sense of it, by going in a body to solicit him to leave them. He was much affected by this instance of their attachment. Such a proof of regard, joined with the entreaties of his own family, and a consideration that for their sakes it was a duty to endeavour to prolong his life, was too powerful to be withstood, and he determined to set out for Italy.

It was settled that Clara and Adeline, whose health La Luc thought required change of air and scene, should accompany him, attended by the faithful Peter.

On the morning of his departure, a large body of his parishioners assembled round the door to bid him farewell. It was an affecting scene;—they might meet no more. At length, wiping the tears from his eyes, La Luc said, Let us trust in God, my friends; he has power to heal all disorders both of body and mind. We shall meet again, if not in this world, I hope in a better;—let our conduct be such as to ensure that better.

The sobs of his people prevented any reply. There was scarcely a dry eye in the village; for there was scarcely an inhabitant of it that was not now assembled in the presence of La Luc. He shook hands with them all; Farewell, my friends, said he, we shall meet again.—God grant we may! said they, with one voice of fervent petition.

Having mounted his horse, and Clara and Adeline being ready, they took a last leave of Madame La Luc, and quitted the chateau. The people unwilling to leave La Luc, the greater part of them accompanied him to some distance from the village. As he moved slowly on, he cast a last lingering look at his little home, where he had spent so many peaceful years, and which he now gazed on perhaps for the last time, and tears rose to his eyes; but he checked them. Every scene of the adjacent country called up, as he passed, some tender remembrance. He looked towards the spot consecrated to the memory of his deceased wife; the dewy vapours of the morning veiled it. La Luc felt the disappointment more deeply, perhaps, than reason could justify; but those who know from experience how much the imagination loves to dwell on any object, however remotely connected with that of our tenderness, will feel with him. This was an object round which the affections of La Luc had settled themselves; it was a memorial to the eye, and the view of it awakened more forcibly in the memory every tender idea that could associate with the primary subject of his regard. In such cases fancy gives to the illusions of strong affection the stamp of reality, and they are cherished by the heart with romantic fondness.

His people accompanied him for near a mile from the village, and could scarcely then be prevailed on to leave him: at length he once more bade them farewell, and went on his way, followed by their prayers and blessings.

La Luc and his little party travelled slowly on, sunk in pensive silence—a silence too pleasingly sad to be soon relinquished, and which they indulged without fear of interruption. The solitary grandeur of the scenes through which they passed, and the soothing murmur of the pines that waved above, aided this soft luxury of meditation.

They proceeded by easy stages; and after travelling for some days among the romantic mountains and green valleys of Piedmont, they entered the rich country of Nice. The gay and luxuriant views which now opened upon the travellers as they wound among the hills, appeared like scenes of fairy enchantment, or those produced by the lonely visions of the poets. While the spiral summits of the mountains exhibited the snowy severity of winter, the pine, the cypress, the olive, and the myrtle shaded their sides with the green tints of spring, and groves of orange, lemon, and citron, spread over their feet the full glow of autumn. As they advanced, the scenery became still more diversified; and at length, between the receding heights, Adeline caught a glimpse of the distant waters of the Mediterranean fading into the blue and cloudless horizon. She had never till now seen the ocean; and this transient view of it roused her imagination, and made her watch impatiently for a nearer prospect.

It was towards the close of day when the travellers, winding round an abrupt projection of that range of Alps which crowns the amphitheatre that environs Nice, looked down upon the green hills that stretch to the shores, on the city, and its ancient castle, and on the wide waters of the Mediterranean; with the mountains of Corsica in the furthest distance. Such a sweep of sea and land, so varied with the gay, the magnificent, and the awful, would have fixed any eye in admiration. For Adeline and Clara novelty and enthusiasm added their charms to the prospect. The soft and salubrious air seemed to welcome La Luc to this smiling region, and the serene atmosphere to promise invariable summer. They at length descended upon the little plain where stands the city of Nice, and which was the most extensive piece of level ground they had passed since they entered the country. Here, in the bosom of the mountains, sheltered from the north and the east, where the western gales alone seemed to breathe, all the blooms of spring and the riches of autumn were united. Trees of myrtle bordered the road, which wound among groves of orange, lemon, and bergamot, whose delicious fragrance came to the sense mingled with the breath of roses and carnations that blossomed in their shade. The gently swelling hills that rose from the plain were covered with vines, and crowned with cypresses, olives, and date trees; beyond, there appeared the sweep of lofty mountains whence the travellers had descended, and whence rose the little river Paglion, swollen by the snows that melt on their summits, and which, after meandering through the plain, washes the walls of Nice, where it falls into the Mediterranean. In this blooming region Adeline observed that the countenances of the peasants, meagre and discontented, formed a melancholy contrast to the face of the country; and she lamented again the effects of an arbitrary government, where the bounties of nature, which were designed for all, are monopolized by a few, and the many are suffered to starve, tantalized by surrounding plenty.

The city lost much of its enchantment on a nearer approach; its narrow streets and shabby houses but ill answered the expectation which a distant view of its ramparts and its harbour, gay with vessels, seemed to authorize. The appearance of the inn at which La Luc now alighted did not contribute to soften his disappointment: but if he was surprised to find such indifferent accommodation at the inn of a town celebrated as the resort of valetudinarians, he was still more so when he learned the difficulty of procuring furnished lodgings.

After much search, he procured apartments in a small but pleasant house situated a little way out of the town; it had a garden, and a terrace which overlooked the sea, and was distinguished by an air of neatness very unusual in the houses of Nice. He agreed to board with the family, whose table likewise accommodated a gentleman and lady, their lodgers; and thus he became a temporary inhabitant of this charming climate.

On the following morning Adeline rose at an early hour, eager to indulge the new and sublime emotion with which a view of the ocean inspired her, and walked with Clara toward the hills that afforded a more extensive prospect. They pursued their way for some time between high embowering banks, till they arrived at an eminence, whence:

Heaven, earth, ocean, smiled!

They sat down on a point of rock overshadowed by lofty palm-trees, to contemplate at leisure the magnificent scene. The sun was just emerged from the sea, over which his rays shed a flood of light, and darted a thousand brilliant tints on the vapours that ascend the horizon, and floated there in light clouds, leaving the bosom of the waters below clear as crystal, except where the white surges were seen to beat upon the rocks; and discovering the distant sails of the fishing-boats, and the far distant highlands of Corsica tinted with ethereal blue. Clara, after some time, drew forth her pencil, but threw it aside in despair. Adeline, as they returned home through a romantic glen, when her senses were no longer absorbed in the contemplation of this grand scenery, and when its images floated on her memory only in softened colours, repeated the following lines:

SUNRISE: A SONNETOft let me wander, at the break of day,Through the cool vale o'erhung with waving woods,Drink the rich fragrance of the budding May,And catch the murmur of the distant floods;Or rest on the fresh bank of limpid rill,Where sleeps the violet in the dewy shade,Where opening lilies balmy sweets distil,And the wild musk-rose weeps along the glade:Or climb the eastern cliff, whose airy headHangs rudely o'er the blue and misty main;Watch the fine hues of morn through ether spread,And paint with roseate glow the crystal plain.Oh! who can speak the rapture of the soulWhen o'er the waves the sun first steals to sight,And all the world of waters, as they roll,And Heaven's vast vault unveils in living light!So life's young hour to man enchanting smiles,With sparkling health, and joy, and fancy's fairy wiles!

La Luc in his walks met with some sensible and agreeable companions, who like himself came to Nice in search of health. Of these he soon formed a small but pleasant society, among whom was a Frenchman, whose mild manners, marked with a deep and interesting melancholy, had particularly attracted La Luc. He very seldom mentioned himself, or any circumstance that might lead to a knowledge of his family, but on other subjects conversed with frankness and much intelligence. La Luc had frequently invited him to his lodgings, but he had always declined the invitation; and this in a manner so gentle as to disarm displeasure, and convince La Luc that his refusal was the consequence of a certain dejection of mind which made him reluctant to meet other strangers.

The description which La Luc had given of this foreigner had excited the curiosity of Clara; and the sympathy which the unfortunate feel for each other called forth the commiseration of Adeline; for that he was unfortunate she could not doubt. On their return from an evening walk La Luc pointed out the chevalier, and quickened his pace to overtake him. Adeline was for a moment impelled to follow; but delicacy checked her steps, she knew how painful the presence of a stranger often is to a wounded mind, and forbore to intrude herself on his notice for the sake of only satisfying an idle curiosity. She turned therefore into another path: but the delicacy which now prevented the meeting, accident in a few days defeated, and La Luc introduced the stranger. Adeline received him with a soft smile, but endeavoured to restrain the expression of pity which her features had involuntarily assumed; she wished him not to know that she observed he was unhappy.

After this interview he no longer rejected the invitations of La Luc, but made him frequent visits, and often accompanied Adeline and Clara in their rambles. The mild and sensible conversation of the former seemed to soothe his mind, and in her presence he frequently conversed with a degree of animation which La Luc till then had not observed in him. Adeline too derived from the similarity of their taste, and his intelligent conversation, a degree of satisfaction which contributed, with the compassion his dejection inspired, to win her confidence, and she conversed with an easy frankness rather unusual to her.

His visits soon became more frequent. He walked with La Luc and his family; he attended them on their little excursions to view those magnificent remains of Roman antiquity which enrich the neighbourhood of Nice. When the ladies sat at home and worked, he enlivened the hours by reading to them, and they had the pleasure to observe his spirits somewhat relieved from the heavy melancholy that had oppressed him.

M. Amand was passionately fond of music. Clara had not forgot to bring her beloved lute: he would sometimes strike the chords in the most sweet and mournful symphonies, but never could be prevailed on to play. When Adeline or Clara played, he would sit in deep reverie, and lost to every object around him, except when he fixed his eyes in mournful gaze on Adeline, and a sigh would sometimes escape him.

One evening, Adeline having excused herself from accompanying La Luc and Clara in a visit to a neighbouring family, she retired to the terrace of the garden which overlooked the sea; and as she viewed the tranquil splendour of the setting sun, and his glories reflected on the polished surface of the waves, she touched the strings of the lute in softest harmony, her voice accompanying it with words which she had one day written after having read that rich effusion of Shakespeare's genius, "A Midsummer Night's Dream."

TITANIA TO HER LOVE.O! fly with me through distant airTo isles that gem the western deep!For laughing Summer revels there,And hangs her wreath on every steep.

As through the green transparent seaLight floating on the waves we go,The nymphs shall gaily welcome me,Far in their coral caves below.

For oft upon their margin sands,When twilight leads the freshening hours,I come with all my jocund bandsTo charm them from their sea-green bowers.

And well they love our sports to view,And on the ocean's breast to lave;And oft as we the dance renew,They call up music from the wave.

Swift hie we to that splendid clime,Where gay Jamaica spreads her scene,Lifts the blue mountain—wild—sublime!And smooths her vales of vivid green.

Where throned high, in pomp of shade,The power of vegetation reigns,Expanding wide, o'er hill and glade,Shrubs of all growth—fruit of all stains:

She steals the sun-beam's fervid glow,To paint her flowers of mingling hue;And o'er the grape the purple throw,Breaking from verdant leaves to view.

There myrtle bowers, and citron grove,O'er canopy our airy dance;And there the sea-breeze loves to rove,When trembles day's departing glance.

And when the false moon steals away,Or ere the chasing morn doth rise,Oft, fearless, we our gambols playBy the fire-worm's radiant eyes.

And suck the honey'd reeds that swellIn tufted plumes of silver white;Or pierce the cocoa's milky cell,To sip the nectar of delight!

And when the shaking thunders roll,And lightnings strike athwart the gloom,We shelter in the cedar's bole,And revel 'mid the rich perfume!

But chief we love beneath the palm,Or verdant plantain's spreading leaf,To hear, upon the midnight calm,Sweet Philomela pour her grief.

To mortal sprite such dulcet sound,Such blissful hours, were never known!O fly with me my airy round,And I will make them all thine own!

Adeline ceased to sing—when she immediately heard repeated in a low voice:

To mortal sprite such dulcet sound,Such blissful hours, were never known! and turning her eyes whence it came, she saw M. Amand. She blushed and laid down the lute, which he instantly took up, and with a tremulous hand drew forth tones

That might create a soul,Under the ribs of death:

In a melodious voice, that trembled with sensibility, he sang the following

SONNETHow sweet is Love's first gentle sway,When crown'd with flowers he softly smiles!His blue eyes fraught with tearful wiles,Where beams of tender transport play:Hope leads him on his airy way,And faith and fancy still beguiles——Faith quickly tangled in her toils——Fancy, whose magic forms so sayThe fair deceiver's self deceive——How sweet is love's first gentle sway!Ne'er would that heart he bids to grieveFrom sorrow's soft enchantments stray——Ne'er—till the God exulting in his art,Relentless frowns and wings th' envenom'd dart.

Monsieur Amand paused: he seemed much oppressed, and at length, bursting into tears, laid down the instrument and walked abruptly away to the further end of the terrace. Adeline, without seeming to observe his agitation, arose and leaned upon the wall, below which a group of fishermen were busily employed in drawing a net. In a few moments he returned with a composed and softened countenance. Forgive this abrupt conduct, said he; I know not how to apologize for it but by owning its cause. When I tell you, Madame, that my tears flow to the memory of a lady who strongly resembled you, and who is lost to me for ever, you will know how to pity me.— His voice faltered, and he paused. Adeline was silent. The lute he resumed, was her favourite instrument, and when you touched it with such a melancholy expression, I saw her very image before me. But, alas! why do I distress you with a knowledge of my sorrows! she is gone, and never to return! And you, Adeline,—you——He checked his speech; and Adeline turning on him a look of mournful regard, observed a wildness in his eyes which alarmed her. These recollections are too painful, said she in a gentle voice: let us return to the house; M. La Luc is probably come home. O no! replied M. Amand;—No—this breeze refreshes me. How often at this hour have I talked with her, as I now talk with you!—such were the soft tones of her voice—such the ineffable expression of her countenance.—Adeline interrupted him. Let me beg of you to consider your health—this dewy air cannot be good for invalids. He stood with his hands clasped, and seemed not to hear her. She took up the lute to go, and passed her fingers lightly over the chords. The sounds recalled his scattered senses: he raised his eyes, and fixed them in long unsettled gaze upon hers. Must I leave you here? said she smiling, and standing in an attitude to depart—I entreat you to play again the air I heard just now, said M. Amand in a hurried voice.—Certainly; and she immediately began to play. He leaned against a palm tree in an attitude of deep attention, and as the sounds languished on the air, his features gradually lost their wild expression, and he melted into tears. He continued to weep silently till the song concluded, and it was some time before he recovered voice enough to say, Adeline, I cannot thank you for this goodness: my mind has recovered its bias; you have soothed a broken heart. Increase the kindness you have shown me, by promising never to mention what you have witnessed this evening, and I will endeavour never again to wound your sensibility by a similar offence.—Adeline gave the required promise; and M. Amand, pressing her hand, with a melancholy smile hurried from the garden, and she saw him no more that night.

La Luc had been near a fortnight at Nice, and his health, instead of amending seemed rather to decline, yet he wished to make a longer experiment of the climate. The air which failed to restore her venerable friend revived Adeline, and the variety and novelty of the surrounding scenes amused her mind, though, since they could not obliterate the memory of past, or suppress the pang of present affection, they were ineffectual to dissipate the sick languor of melancholy. Company, by compelling her to withdraw her attention from the subject of her sorrow, afforded her a transient relief, but the violence of the exertion generally left her more depressed. It was in the stillness of solitude, in the tranquil observance of beautiful nature, that her mind recovered its tone, and, indulging the pensive inclination now become habitual to it, was soothed and fortified. Of all the grand objects which nature had exhibited, the ocean inspired her with the most sublime admiration. She loved to wander alone on its shores; and when she could escape so long from the duties or forms of society, she would sit for hours on the beach watching the rolling waves, and listening to their dying murmur, till her softened fancy recalled long-lost scenes, and restored the image of Theodore; when tears of despondency too often followed those of pity and regret. But these visions of memory, painful as they were, no longer excited that phrensy of grief they formerly awakened in Savoy; the sharpness of misery was passed, though its heavy influence was not perhaps less powerful. To these solitary indulgences generally succeeded calmness, and what Adeline endeavoured to believe was resignation.

She usually rose early, and walked down to the shore to enjoy, in the cool and silent hours of the morning, the cheering beauty of nature, and inhale the pure sea-breeze. Every object then smiled in fresh and lively colours. The blue sea, the brilliant sky, the distant fishing-boats with their white sails, and the voices of the fishermen borne at intervals on the air, were circumstances which reanimated her spirits; and in one of her rambles, yielding to that taste for poetry which had seldom forsaken her, she repeated the following lines:—

MORNING, ON THE SEA SHORE

What print of fairy feet is hereOn Neptune's smooth and yellow sands?What midnight revel's airy dance,Beneath the moonbeam's trembling glanceHas blest these shores?—What sprightly bandsHave chased the waves uncheck'd by fear?Whoe'er they were they fled from morn,For now, all silent and forlorn,These tide-forsaken sands appear—Return, sweet sprites! the scene to cheer!

In vain the call!—Till moonlight's hourAgain diffuse its softer power,Titania, nor her fairy loves,Emerge from India's spicy groves.Then, when the shadowy hour returns,When silence reigns o'er air and earth,And every star in ether burns,They come to celebrate their mirth;In frolic ringlet trip the ground,Bid music's voice on silence win,Till magic echoes answer round—Thus do their festive rites begin.

O fairy forms so coy to mortal ken,Your mystic steps to poets only shown;O! lead me to the brook, or hollow'd glen,Retiring far, with winding woods o'ergrownWhere'er ye best delight to rule;If in some forest's lone retreat,Thither conduct my willing feetTo the light brink of fountain cool,Where, sleeping in the midnight dew,Lie spring's young buds of every hue,Yielding their sweet breath to the air;To fold their silken leaves from harm,And their chill heads in moonshine warm,Is bright Titania's tender care.

There, to the night-birds's plaintive chauntYour carols sweet ye love to raise,With oaten reed and pastoral lays;And guard with forceful spell her haunt,Who, when your antic sports are done,Oft lulls ye in the lily's cell,Sweet flower! that suits your slumbers well,And shields ye from the rising sun.When not to India's steeps ye flyAfter twilight and the moon,In honey buds ye love to lie,While reigns supreme light's fervid noon;Nor quit the cell where peace pervades.Till night leads on the dews and shades.

E'en now your scenes enchanted meet my sight!I see the earth unclose, the palace rise,The high dome swell, and long arcades of lightGlitter among the deep embowering woods,And glance reflecting from the trembling floods!While to soft lutes the portals wide unfold,And fairy forms, of fine ethereal dyes,Advance with frolic step and laughing eyes,Their hair with pearl, their garments deck'd with gold;Pearls that in Neptune's briny waves they sought,And gold from India's deepest caverns brought. Thus your light visions to my eyes unveil,Ye sportive pleasures, sweet illusion, hail!But ah! at morn's first blush again ye fade!So from youth's ardent gaze life's landscape gay,And forms in fancy's summer hues array'd,Dissolve at once in air at truth's resplendent day!

During several days succeeding that on which M. Amand had disclosed the cause of his melancholy, he did not visit La Luc. At length Adeline met him in one of her solitary rambles on the shore. He was pale, and dejected, and seemed much agitated when he observed her; she therefore endeavoured to avoid him, but he advanced with quickened steps and accosted her. He said it was his intention to leave Nice in a few days. I have found no benefit from the climate, added M. Amand; alas! what climate can relieve the sickness of the heart! I go to lose in the varieties of new scenes the remembrance of past happiness; yet the effort is vain; I am every where equally restless and unhappy. Adeline tried to encourage him to hope much from time and change of place. Time will blunt the sharpest edge of sorrow, said she; I know it from experience.

Yet while she spoke, the tears in her eyes contradicted the assertions of her lips.—You have been unhappy, Adeline!—Yes—I knew it from the first. The smile of pity which you gave me, assured me that you knew what it was to suffer. The desponding air with which he spoke renewed her apprehension of a scene similar to the one she had lately witnessed, and she changed the subject; but he soon returned to it. You bid me hope much from time!—My wife!—My dear wife!——his tongue faltered—It is now many months since I lost her—yet the moment of her death seems but as yesterday. Adeline faintly smiled. You can scarcely judge of the effect of time, yet you have much to hope for. He shook his head. But I am again intruding my misfortunes on your notice; forgive this perpetual egotism. There is a comfort in the pity of the good, such as nothing else can impart; this must plead my excuse; may you, Adeline, never want it! Ah! those tears——Adeline hastily dried them. M. Amand forbore to press the subject, and immediately began to converse on indifferent topics. They returned towards the chateau; but La Luc being from home, M. Amand took leave at the door. Adeline retired to her chamber, oppressed by her own sorrows, and those of her amiable friend.

Near three weeks had now elapsed at Nice, during which the disorder of La Luc seemed rather to increase than abate, when his physician very honestly confessed the little hope he entertained from the climate, and advised him to try the effect of a sea voyage, adding that if the experiment failed, even the air of Montpellier appeared to him more likely to afford relief than that of Nice. La Luc received this disinterested advice with a mixture of gratitude and disappointment. The circumstances which had made him reluctant to quit Savoy, rendered him yet more so to protract his absence and increase his expenses; but the ties of affection that bound him to his family, and the love of life, which so seldom leaves us, again prevailed over inferior considerations; and he determined to coast the Mediterranean as far as Languedoc, where if the voyage did not answer his expectation he would land and proceed to Montpellier.

When M. Amand learned that La Luc designed to quit Nice in a few days, he determined not to leave it before him. During this interval he had not sufficient resolution to deny himself the frequent conversation of Adeline, though her presence, by reminding him of his lost wife, gave him more pain than comfort. He was the second son of a French gentleman of family, and had been married about a year to a lady to whom he had long been attached, when she died in her lying-in. The infant soon followed its mother, and left the disconsolate father abandoned to grief, which had preyed so heavily on his health, that his physician thought it necessary to send him to Nice. From the air of Nice, however, he had derived no benefit; and he now determined to travel further into Italy, though he no longer felt any interest in those charming scenes which in happier days and with her whom he never ceased to lament, would have afforded him the highest degree of mental luxury—now he sought only to escape from himself, or rather from the image of her who had once constituted his truest happiness.

La Luc having laid his plan, hired a small vessel, and in a few days embarked, with a sick hope, bidding adieu to the shores of Italy and the towering Alps, and seeking on a new element the health which had hitherto mocked his pursuit.

M. Amand took a melancholy leave of his new friends, whom he attended to the seaside. When he assisted Adeline on board, his heart was too full to suffer him to say farewell; but he stood long on the beach pursuing with his eyes her course over the waters, and waving his hand, till tears dimmed his sight. The breeze wafted the vessel gently from the coast, and Adeline saw herself surrounded by the undulating waves of the ocean. The shore appeared to recede, its mountains to lessen, the gay colours of its landscape to melt into each other, and in a short time the figure of M. Amand was seen no more: the town of Nice, with its castle and harbour next faded away in distance, and the purple tint of the mountains was at length all that remained on the verge of the horizon. She sighed as she gazed, and her eyes filled with tears. So vanished my prospect of happiness, said she; and my future view is like the waste of waters that surround me. Her heart was full, and she retired from observation to a remote part of the deck, where she indulged her tears as she watched the vessel cut its way through the liquid glass. The water was so transparent that she saw the sun-beams playing at a considerable depth, and fish of various colours glance athwart the current. Innumerable marine plants spread their vigorous leaves on the rocks below, and the richness of their verdure formed a beautiful contrast to the glowing scarlet of the coral that branched beside them.

The distant coast at length entirely disappeared. Adeline gazed with an emotion the most sublime, on the boundless expanse of waters that spread on all sides: she seemed as if launched into a new world: the grandeur and immensity of the view astonished and overpowered her: for a moment she doubted the truth of the compass, and believed it to be almost impossible for the vessel to find its way over the pathless waters to any shore. And when she considered that a plank alone separated her from death, a sensation of unmixed terror superseded that of sublimity, and she hastily turned her eyes from the prospect, and her thoughts from the subject.

CHAPTER XIX

Is there a heart that music cannot melt?Alas! how is that rugged heart forlorn!Is there who ne'er the mystic transports feltOf solitude and melancholy born?He need not woo the Muse—he is her scorn.BEATTIE.

Towards evening the captain, to avoid the danger of encountering a Barbary corsair steered for the French coast, and Adeline distinguished in the gleam of the setting sun the shores of Provence, feathered with wood and green with pasturage. La Luc, languid and ill, had retired to the cabin, whither Clara attended him. The pilot at the helm guiding the tall vessel through the sounding waters, and one solitary sailor leaning with crossed arms against the mast, and now and then singing parts of a mournful ditty, were all of the crew, except Adeline, that remained upon deck—and Adeline silently watched the declining sun, which threw a saffron glow upon the waves and on the sails gently swelling in the breeze that was now dying away. The sun at length sunk below the ocean, and twilight stole over the scene, leaving the shadowy shores yet visible, and touching with a solemn tint the waters that stretched wide around. She sketched the picture, but it was with a faint pencil.

NIGHT

O'er the dim breast of Ocean's waveNight spreads afar her gloomy wings,And pensive thought, and silence brings,Save when the distant waters lave;Or when the mariner's lone voiceSwells faintly in the passing gale,Or when the screaming sea-gulls poiseO'er the tall mast and swelling sail.Bounding the grey gleam of the deep,Where fancied forms arouse the mind,Dark sweep the shores, on whose rude steepSighs the sad spirit of the wind.Sweet is its voice upon the air,At Evening's melancholy close,When the smooth wave in silence flows!Sweet, sweet the peace its stealing accents bear!Blest be thy shades, O Night! and blest the songThy low winds breathe the distant shores along!

As the shadows thickened, the scene sunk into deeper repose. Even the sailor's song had ceased; no sound was heard but that of the waters dashing beneath the vessel, and their fainter murmur on the pebbly coast. Adeline's mind was in unison with the tranquillity of the hour; lulled by the waves, she resigned herself to a still melancholy and sat lost in reverie. The present moment brought to her recollection her voyage up the Rhone, when seeking refuge from the terrors of the Marquis de Montalt, she so anxiously endeavoured to anticipate her future destiny. She then, as now, had watched the fall of evening and the fading prospect, and she remembered what a desolate feeling had accompanied the impression which those objects made. She had then no friends— no asylum—no certainty of escaping the pursuit of her enemy. Now she had found affectionate friends—a secure retreat—and was delivered from the terrors she then suffered—but still she was unhappy. The remembrance of Theodore—of Theodore who had loved her so truly, who had encountered and suffered so much for her sake, and of whose fate she was now as ignorant as when she traversed the Rhone, was an incessant pang to her heart. She seemed to be more remote than ever from the possibility of hearing of him. Sometimes a faint hope crossed her that he had escaped the malice of his persecutor; but when she considered the inveteracy and power of the latter, and the heinous light in which the law regards an assault upon a superior officer, even this poor hope vanished, and left her to tears and anguish, such as this reverie, which began with a sensation of only gentle melancholy, now led to. She continued to muse till the moon arose from the bosom of the ocean, and shed her trembling lustre upon the waves, diffusing peace, and making silence more solemn; beaming a soft light on the white sails, and throwing upon the waters the tall shadow of the vessel which now seemed to glide along unopposed by any current. Her tears had somewhat relieved the anguish of her mind, and she again reposed in placid melancholy, when a strain of such tender and entrancing sweetness stole on the silence of the hour, that it seemed more like celestial than mortal music—so soft, so soothing, it sunk upon her ear, that it recalled her from misery to hope and love. She wept again—but these were tears which she would not have exchanged for mirth and joy. She looked round, but perceived neither ship nor boat; and as the undulating sounds swelled on the distant air, she thought they came from the shore. Sometimes the breeze wafted them away, and again returned them in tones of the most languishing softness. The links of the air thus broken, it was music rather than melody that she caught, till, the pilot gradually steering nearer the coast, she distinguished the notes of a song familiar to her ear. She endeavoured to recollect where she had heard it, but in vain; yet her heart beat almost unconsciously with a something resembling hope. Still she listened, till the breeze again stole the sounds. With regret she now perceived that the vessel was moving from them, and at length they trembled faintly on the waves, sunk away at distance, and were heard no more. She remained upon deck a considerable time, unwilling to relinquish the expectation of hearing them again, and their sweetness still vibrating on her fancy, and at length retired to the cabin oppressed by a degree of disappointment which the occasion did not appear to justify.

La Luc grew better during the voyage, his spirits revived, and when the vessel entered that part of the Mediterranean called the Gulf of Lyons, he was sufficiently animated to enjoy from the deck the noble prospect which the sweeping shores of Provence, terminating in the far distant ones of Languedoc, exhibited. Adeline and Clara, who anxiously watched his looks, rejoiced in their amendment; and the fond wishes of the latter already anticipated his perfect recovery. The expectations of Adeline had been too often checked by disappointment permit her now to indulge an equal degree of hope with that of her friend, yet she confided much in the effect of this voyage.

La Luc amused himself at intervals with discoursing, and pointing out the situations of considerable ports on the coast, and the mouths of the rivers that, after wandering through Provence, disembogue themselves into the Mediterranean. The Rhone, however, was the only one of much consequence which he passed. On this object, though it was so distant that fancy perhaps, rather than the sense, beheld it, Clara gazed with peculiar pleasure, for it came from the banks of Savoy; and the wave which she thought she perceived, had washed the feet of her dear native mountains. The time passed with mingled pleasure and improvement as La Luc described to his attentive pupils the manners and commerce of the different inhabitants of the coast, and the natural history of the country: or as he traced in imagination the remote wanderings of rivers to their source, and delineated the characteristic beauties of their scenery.

After a pleasant voyage of a few days, the shores of Provence receded, and that of Languedoc, which had long bounded the distance, became the grand object of the scene, and the sailors drew near their port. They landed in the afternoon at a small town, situated at the foot of a woody eminence, on the right overlooking the sea, and on the left the rich plains of Languedoc gay with the purple vine. La Luc determined to defer his journey till the following day, and was directed to a small inn at the extremity of the town, where the accommodation, such as it was, he endeavoured to be contented with.

In the evening, the beauty of the hour and the desire of exploring new scenes, invited Adeline to walk. La Lac was fatigued, and did not go out, and Clara remained with him. Adeline took her way to the woods that rose from the margin of the sea, and climbed the wild eminence on which they hung. Often as she went she turned her eyes to catch between the dark foliage the blue waters of the bay, the white sail that flitted by, and the trembling gleam of the setting sun. When she reached the summit, and looked down over the dark tops of the woods on the wide and various prospect, she was seized with a kind of still rapture impossible to be expressed, and stood unconscious of the flight of time, till the sun had left the scene, and twilight threw its solemn shade upon the mountains. The sea alone reflected the fading splendour of the west; its tranquil surface was partially disturbed by the low wind that crept in tremulous lines along the waters, whence rising to the woods, it shivered their light leaves, and died away. Adeline, resigning herself to the luxury of sweet and tender emotions, repeated the following lines:—

SUNSET

Soft o'er the mountain's purple browMeek Twilight draws her shadows gray;From tufted woods and valleys low,Light's magic colours steal away.Yet still, amid the spreading gloom,Resplendent glow the western waves,That roll o'er Neptune's coral caves,A zone of light on Evening's dome.On this lone summit let me rest,And view the forms to Fancy dear,Till on the Ocean's darken'd breastThe stars of Evening tremble clear;Or the moon's pale orb appear,Throwing her line of radiance wide,Far o'er the lightly-curling tide,That seems the yellow sands to chide.No sounds o'er silence now prevail,Save of the dying wave below,Or sailor's song borne on the gale,Or oar at distance striking slow.So sweet! so tranquil! may my evening raySet to this world—and rise in future day!

Adeline quitted the heights, and followed a narrow path that wound to the beach below: her mind was now particularly sensible to fine impressions, and the sweet notes of the nightingale amid the stillness of the woods again awakened her enthusiasm.

TO THE NIGHTINGALE

Child of the melancholy song!O yet that tender strain prolong!

Her lengthen'd shade when Evening flings,From mountain-cliffs, and forests green,And sailing slow on silent wings,Along the glimmering West is seen;I love o'er pathless hills to stray,Or trace the winding vale remote,And pause, sweet Bird! to hear thy layWhile moonbeams on the thin clouds float,Till o'er the Mountain's dewy headPale Midnight steals to wake the dead.

Far through the heaven's ethereal blue,Wafted on Spring's light airs you come,With blooms, and flowers, and genial dew,From climes where Summer joys to roam;O! welcome to your long-lost home!"Child of the melancholy song!"Who lov'st the lonely woodland gladeTo mourn, unseen, the boughs among,When Twilight spreads her pensive shade,Again thy dulcet voice I hail!O pour again the liquid noteThat dies upon the evening gale!For Fancy loves the kindred tone;Her griefs the plaintive accents own.She loves to hear thy music floatAt solemn Midnight's stillest hour,And think on friends for ever lost,On joys by disappointment crost,And weep anew Love's charmful power!

Then Memory wakes the magic smile,Th' impassion'd voice, the melting eye,That wont the trusting heart beguile,And wakes again the hopeless sigh.Her skill the glowing tints reviveOf scenes that Time had bade decay;She bids the soften'd Passions live—The Passions urge again their sway.Yet o'er the long-regretted sceneThy song the grace of sorrow throws;A melancholy charm serene,More rare than all that mirth bestows,Then hail, sweet Bird, and hail thy pensive tear!To Taste, to Fancy, and to Virtue dear!

The spreading dusk at length reminded Adeline of her distance from the inn, and that she had her way to find through a wild and lonely wood: she bade adieu to the syren that had so long detained her, and pursued the path with quick steps. Having followed it for some time, she became bewildered among the thickets, and the increasing darkness did not allow her to judge of the direction she was in. Her apprehensions heightened her difficulties: she thought she distinguished the voices of men at some little distance, and she increased her speed till she found herself on the sea-sands over which the woods impended. Her breath was now exhausted—she paused a moment to recover herself, and fearfully listened: but instead of the voices of men, she heard faintly swelling in the breeze the notes of mournful music.—Her heart, ever sensible to the impressions of melody, melted with the tones, and her fears were for a moment lulled in sweet enchantment. Surprise was soon mingled with delight when, as the sound advanced, she distinguished the tone of that instrument, and the melody of that well-known air, she had heard a few preceding evenings from the shores of Provence. But she had no time for conjecture—footsteps approached, and she renewed her speed. She was now emerged from the darkness of the woods, and the moon, which shone bright, exhibited along the level sands the town and port in the distance. The steps that had followed now came up with her, and she perceived two men; but they passed in conversation without noticing her, and as they passed she was certain she recollected the voice of him who was then speaking. Its tones were so familiar to her ear, that she was surprised at the imperfect memory which did not suffer her to be assured by whom they were uttered. Another step now followed, and a rude voice called to her to stop. As she hastily turned her eyes she saw imperfectly by the moonlight a man in sailor's habit pursuing, while he renewed the call. Impelled by terror, she fled along the sands; but her steps were short and trembling—those of her pursuer strong and quick.

She had just strength sufficient to reach the men who had before passed her, and to implore their protection, when her pursuer came up with them, but suddenly turned into the woods on the left, and disappeared.

She had no breath to answer the inquiries of the strangers who supported her, till a sudden exclamation, and the sound of her own name, drew her eyes attentively upon the person who uttered them, and in the rays which shone strong from his features she distinguished M. Verneuil! Mutual satisfaction and explanation ensued; and when he learned that La Luc and his daughter were at the inn, he felt an increased pleasure in conducting her thither. He said that he had accidentally met with an old friend in Savoy, whom he now introduced by the name of Mauron, and who had prevailed on him to change his route and accompany him to the shores of the Mediterranean. They had embarked from the coast of Provence only a few preceding days, and had that evening landed in Languedoc on the estate of M. Mauron. Adeline had now no doubt that it was the flute of M. Verneuil, and which had so often delighted her at Leloncourt, that she had heard on the sea.

When they reached the inn, they found La Luc under great anxiety for Adeline, in search of whom he had sent several people. Anxiety yielded to surprise and pleasure, when he perceived her with M. Verneuil, whose eyes beamed with unusual animation on seeing Clara. After mutual congratulations, M. Verneuil observed, and lamented, the very indifferent accommodation which the inn afforded his friends, and M. Mauron immediately invited them to his chateau with a warmth of hospitality that overcame every scruple which delicacy or pride could oppose. The woods that Adeline had traversed formed a part of his domain, which extended almost to the inn; but he insisted that his carriage should take his guests to the chateau, and departed to give orders for their reception. The presence of M. Verneuil, and the kindness of his friend, gave to La Luc an unusual flow of spirits; he conversed with a degree of vigour and liveliness to which he had long been unaccustomed, and the smile of satisfaction that Clara gave to Adeline expressed how much she thought he was already benefited by the voyage. Adeline answered her look with a smile of less confidence, for she attributed his present animation to a more temporary cause.

About half an hour after the departure of M. Mauron, a boy who served as waiter brought a message from a chevalier then at the inn, requesting permission to speak with Adeline. The man who had pursued her along the sands instantly occurred to her, and she scarcely doubted that the stranger was some person belonging to the Marquis de Montalt, perhaps the Marquis himself, though that he should have discovered her accidentally, in so obscure a place, and so immediately upon her arrival, seemed very improbable. With trembling lips and a countenance pale as death she inquired the name of the chevalier. The boy was not acquainted with it. La Luc asked what sort of a person he was; but the boy, who understood little of the art of describing, gave such a confused account of him, that Adeline could only learn he was not large, but of a middle stature. This circumstance, however, convincing her it was not the Marquis de Montalt who desired to see her, she asked whether it would be agreeable to La Luc to have the stranger admitted. La Luc said, By all means; and the waiter withdrew. Adeline sat in trembling expectation till the door opened, and Louis de la Motte entered the room. He advanced with an embarrassed and melancholy air, though his countenance had been enlightened with a momentary pleasure when he first beheld Adeline—Adeline, who was still the idol of his heart. After the first salutations were over, all apprehensions of the Marquis being now dissipated, she inquired when Louis had seen Monsieur and Madame La Motte.

I ought rather to ask you that question, said Louis in some confusion, for I believe you have seen them since I have; and the pleasure of meeting you thus is equalled by my surprise. I have not heard from my father for some time, owing probably to my regiment being removed to new quarters.

He looked as if he wished to be informed with whom Adeline now was; but as this was a subject upon which it was impossible she could speak in the presence of La Luc, she led the conversation to general topics, after having said that Monsieur and Madame La Motte were well when she left them. Louis spoke little, and often looked anxiously at Adeline, while his mind seemed labouring under strong oppression. She observed this, and recollecting the declaration he had made her on the morning of his departure from the abbey, she attributed his present embarrassment to the effect of a passion yet unsubdued, and did not appear to notice it. After he had sat near a quarter of an hour, under a struggle of feelings which he could neither conquer nor conceal, he rose to leave the room; and as he passed Adeline, said, in a low voice, Do permit me to speak with you alone for five minutes. She hesitated in some confusion, and then, saying there were none but friends present, begged he would be seated.—Excuse me, said he, in the same low accent; what I would say nearly concerns you, and you only. Do favour me with a few moments' attention. He said this with a look that surprised her; and having ordered candles in another room, she went thither.

Louis sat for some moments silent, and seemingly in great perturbation of mind. At length he said, I know not whether to rejoice or to lament at this unexpected meeting, though, if you are in safe hands, I ought certainly to rejoice, however hard the task that now falls to my lot. I am not ignorant of the dangers and persecutions you have suffered, and cannot forbear expressing my anxiety to know how you are now circumstanced. Are you indeed with friends?—I am, said Adeline; M. La Motte has informed you——No, replied Louis with a deep sigh, not my father.—He paused.—But I do indeed rejoice, resumed he, O! how sincerely rejoice! that you are in safety. Could you know, lovely Adeline, what I have suffered!—He checked himself.—I understood you had something of importance to say, Sir, said Adeline; you must excuse me if I remind you that I have not many moments to spare.

It is indeed of importance, replied Louis; yet I know not how to mention it—how to soften——This task is too severe. Alas! my poor friend!

Whom is it you speak of, Sir? said Adeline with quickness. Louis rose from his chair and walked about the room. I would prepare you for what I have to say, he resumed, but upon my soul I am not equal to it.

I entreat you to keep me no longer in suspense, said Adeline, who had a wild idea that it was Theodore he would speak of. Louis still hesitated. Is it—O! is it?—I conjure you tell me the worst at once, said she in a voice of agony. I can bear it,—indeed I can.

My unhappy friend! exclaimed Louis. O! Theodore!—Theodore! faintly articulated Adeline; he lives then!—He does, said Louis, but—He stopped.—But what? cried Adeline, trembling violently; if he is living, you cannot tell me worse than my fears suggest; I entreat you therefore not to hesitate.—Louis resumed his seat and, endeavouring to assume a collected air, said, He is living, Madame, but he is a prisoner; and—for why should I deceive you? I fear he has little to hope in this world.

I have long feared so, Sir, said Adeline in a voice of forced composure; you have something more terrible than this to relate, and I again entreat you will explain yourself.

He has every thing to apprehend from the Marquis de Montalt, said Louis. Alas! why do I say to apprehend? His judgment is already fixed—he is condemned to die.

At this confirmation of her fears, a death-like paleness diffused itself over the countenance of Adeline; she sat motionless, and attempted to sigh, but seemed almost suffocated. Terrified at her situation, and expecting to see her faint, Louis would have supported her, but with her hand she waved him from her, and was unable to speak. He now called for assistance, and La Luc and Clara, with M. Verneuil, informed of Adeline's indisposition, were quickly by her side.

At the sound of their voices she looked up, and seemed to recollect herself, when uttering a heavy sigh she burst into tears. La Luc, rejoiced to see her weep, encouraged her tears, which after some time relieved her; and when she was able to speak, she desired to go back to La Luc's parlour. Louis attended her thither; when she was better he would have withdrawn, but La Luc begged he would stay.

You are perhaps a relation of this young lady, Sir, said he, and may have brought news of her father?—Not so, Sir, replied Louis, hesitating—This gentleman, said Adeline, who had now recollected her dissipated thoughts, is the son of the M. La Motte whom you may have heard me mention.—Louis seemed shocked to be declared the son of a man that had once acted so unworthily towards Adeline, who, instantly perceiving the pain her words occasioned, endeavoured to soften their effect by saying that La Motte had saved her from imminent danger, and had afforded her an asylum for many months.—Adeline sat in a state of dreadful solicitude to know the particulars of Theodore's situation, yet could not acquire courage to renew the subject in the presence of La Luc; she ventured, however, to ask Louis if his own regiment was quartered in the town.

He replied that his regiment lay at Vaceau, a French town on the frontiers of Spain; that he had just crossed a part of the Gulf of Lyons, and was on his way to Savoy, whither he should set out early in the morning.

We are lately come from thence, said Adeline; may I ask to what part of Savoy you are going?—To Leloncourt, he replied.—To Leloncourt! said Adeline, in some surprise.—I am a stranger to the country, resumed Louis; but I go to serve my friend. You seem to know Leloncourt.—I do indeed, said Adeline.—You probably know then that M. La Luc lives there, and will guess the motive of my journey?

O Heavens! is it possible? exclaimed Adeline—is it possible that Theodore Peyrou is a relation of M. La Luc?

Theodore! what of my son? asked La Luc in surprise and apprehension—Your son! said Adeline, in a trembling voice—your son!—The astonishment and anguish depicted on her countenance increased the apprehensions of this unfortunate father, and he renewed his question. But Adeline was totally unable to answer him; and the distress of Louis, on thus unexpectedly discovering the father of his unhappy friend, and knowing that it was his task to disclose the fate of his son, deprived him for some time of all power of utterance; and La Luc and Clara, whose fears were every instant heightened by this dreadful silence, continued to repeat their questions.

At length a sense of the approaching sufferings of the good La Luc overcoming every other feeling, Adeline recovered strength of mind sufficient to try to soften the intelligence Louis had to communicate, and to conduct Clara to another room. Here she collected resolution to tell her, and with much tender consideration, the circumstances of her brother's situation, concealing only her knowledge of his sentence being already pronounced. This relation necessarily included the mention of their attachment, and in the friend of her heart Clara discovered the innocent cause of her brother's destruction. Adeline also learned the occasion of that circumstance which had contributed to keep her ignorant of Theodore's relationship to La Luc; she was told the former had taken the name of Peyrou, with an estate which had been left him about a year before by a relation of his mother's upon that condition. Theodore had been designed for the church, but his disposition inclined him to a more active life than the clerical habit would admit of; and on his accession to this estate he had entered into the service of the French king.

In the few and interrupted interviews which had been allowed them at Caux, Theodore had mentioned his family to Adeline only in general terms; and thus, when they were so suddenly separated, had, without designing it, left her in ignorance of his father's name and place of residence.

The sacredness and delicacy of Adeline's grief, which had never permitted her to mention the subject of it even to Clara, had since contributed to deceive her.

The distress of Clara, on learning the situation of her brother, could endure no restraint; Adeline, who had commanded her feelings so as to impart this intelligence with tolerable composure, only by a strong effort of mind, was now almost overwhelmed by her own and Clara's accumulated suffering. While they wept forth the anguish of their hearts; a scene if possible, more affecting passed between La Luc and Louis; who perceived it was necessary to inform him, though cautiously and by degrees, of the full extent of his calamity. He, therefore, told La Luc, that though Theodore had been first tried for the offence of having quitted his post, he was now condemned on a charge of assault made upon his general officer the Marquis de Montalt, who had brought witnesses to prove that his life had been endangered by the circumstance; and who, having pursued the prosecution with the most bitter rancour, had at length obtained the sentence which the law could not withhold, but which every other officer in the regiment deplored.

Louis added, that the sentence was to be executed in less than a fortnight, and that Theodore being very unhappy at receiving no answers to the letters he had sent his father, wishing to see him once more, and knowing that there was now no time to be lost, had requested him to go to Leloncourt and acquaint his father with his situation.

La Luc received the account of his son's condition with a distress that admitted neither of tears nor complaint. He asked where Theodore was; and desiring to be conducted to him, he thanked Louis for all his kindness, and ordered post horses immediately.

A carriage was soon ready; and this unhappy father, after taking a mournful leave of M. Verneuil, and sending a compliment to M. Mauron, attended by his family set out for the prison of his son. The journey was a silent one; each individual of the party endeavoured, in consideration of each other, to suppress the expression of grief, but was unable to do more. La Luc appeared calm and complacent; he seemed frequently to be engaged in prayer; but a struggle for resignation and composure was sometimes visible upon his countenance, notwithstanding the efforts of his mind.

CHAPTER XX

And venom'd with disgrace the dart of Death.SEWARD.

We now return to the Marquis de Montalt, who having seen La Motte safely lodged in the prison of D——y, and learning the trial would not come on immediately, had returned to his villa on the borders of the forest, where he expected to hear news of Adeline. It had been his intention to follow his servants to Lyons; but he now determined to wait a few days for letters, and he had little doubt that Adeline, since her flight had been so quickly pursued, would be overtaken, and probably before she could reach that city. In this expectation he had been miserably disappointed; for his servants informed him, that though they traced her thither, they had neither been able to follow her route beyond, nor to discover her at Lyons. This escape she probably owed to having embarked on the Rhone, for it does not appear that the Marquis's people thought of seeking her on the course of that river.

His presence was soon after required at Vaceau, where the court-martial was then sitting; thither therefore he went, with passions still more exasperated by his late disappointment, and procured the condemnation of Theodore. The sentence was universally lamented, for Theodore was much beloved in his regiment; and the occasion of the Marquis's personal resentment towards him being known, every heart was interested in his cause.

Louis de La Motte happening at this time to be stationed in the same town, heard an imperfect account of his story; and being convinced that the prisoner was the young chevalier whom he had formerly seen with the Marquis at the abbey, he was induced partly from compassion, and partly with a hope of hearing of his parents, to visit him. The compassionate sympathy which Louis expressed, and the zeal with which he tendered his services, affected Theodore, and excited in him a warm return of friendship; Louis made him frequent visits, did every thing that kindness could suggest to alleviate his sufferings, and a mutual esteem and confidence ensued.

Theodore at length communicated the chief subject of his concern to Louis; who discovered with inexpressible grief that it was Adeline whom the Marquis had thus cruelly persecuted, and Adeline for whose sake the generous Theodore was about to suffer. He soon perceived also that Theodore was his favoured rival; but he generously suppressed the jealous pang this discovery occasioned, and determined that no prejudice of passion should withdraw him from the duties of humanity and friendship. He eagerly inquired where Adeline then resided. She is yet, I fear, in the power of the Marquis, said Theodore, sighing deeply. O God!—these chains!—and he threw an agonizing glance upon them. Louis sat silent and thoughtful; at length starting from his reverie, he said he would go to the Marquis, and immediately quitted the prison. The Marquis, was, however, already set off for Paris, where he had been summoned to appear at the approaching trial of La Motte; and Louis, yet ignorant of the late transactions at the abbey, returned to the prison; where he endeavoured to forget that Theodore was the favoured rival of his love, and to remember him only as the defender of Adeline. So earnestly he pressed his offers of service, that Theodore, whom the silence of his father equally surprised and afflicted, and who was very anxious to see him once again, accepted his proposal of going himself to Savoy. My letters I strongly suspect to have been intercepted by the Marquis, said Theodore; if so, my poor father will have the whole weight of this calamity to sustain at once, unless I avail myself of your kindness, and I shall neither see him nor hear from him before I die. Louis! there are moments when my fortitude shrinks from the conflict, and my senses threaten to desert me.

No time was to be lost; the warrant for his execution had already received the king's signature, and Louis immediately set forward for Savoy. The letters of Theodore had indeed been intercepted by order of the Marquis, who, in the hope of discovering the asylum of Adeline, had opened and afterwards destroyed them.

But to return to La Luc, who now drew near Vaceau, and whom his family observed to be greatly changed in his looks since he had heard the late calamitous intelligence; he uttered no complaint; but it was too obvious that his disorder had made a rapid progress. Louis, who during the journey proved the goodness of his disposition by the delicate attentions he paid this unhappy party, concealed his observation of the decline of La Luc, and to support Adeline's spirits, endeavoured to convince her that her apprehensions on this subject were groundless. Her spirits did indeed require support, for she was now within a few miles of the town that contained Theodore; and while her increasing perturbation almost overcame her, she yet tried to appear composed. When the carriage entered the town, she cast a timid and anxious glance from the window in search of the prison; but having passed through several streets without perceiving any building which corresponded with her idea of that she looked for, the coach stopped at the inn. The frequent changes in La Luc's countenance betrayed the violent agitation of his mind; and when he attempted to alight, feeble and exhausted, he was compelled to accept the support of Louis, to whom he faintly said as he passed to the parlour, I am indeed sick at heart, but I trust the pain will not be long. Louis pressed his hand without speaking, and hastened back for Adeline and Clara, who were already in the passage. La Luc wiped the tears from his eyes (they were the first he had shed) as they entered the room. I would go immediately to my poor boy, said he to Louis; yours, Sir, is a mournful office—be so good as to conduct me to him. He rose to go, but, feeble and overcome with grief, again sat down. Adeline and Clara united in entreating that he would compose himself, and take some refreshment; and Louis urging the necessity of preparing Theodore for the interview, prevailed with him to delay it till his son should be informed of his arrival, and immediately quitted the inn for the prison of his friend. When he was gone, La Luc, as a duty he owed those he loved, tried to take some support; but the convulsions of his throat would not suffer him to swallow the wine he held to his parched lips, and he was now so much disordered, that he desired to retire to his chamber, where alone, and in prayer, he passed the dreadful interval of Louis's absence.

Clara on the bosom of Adeline, who sat in calm but deep distress, yielded to the violence of her grief. I shall lose my dear father too, said she; I see it; I shall lose my father and my brother together. Adeline wept with her friend for some time in silence; and then attempted to persuade her that La Luc was not so ill as she apprehended.

Do not mislead me with hope, she replied that will not survive the shock of this calamity—I saw it from the first. Adeline knowing that La Luc's distress would be heightened by the observance of his daughter's, and that indulgence would only increase its poignancy, endeavoured to rouse her to an exertion of fortitude by urging the necessity of commanding her emotion in the presence of her father. This is possible, added she, however painful may be the effort. You must know, my dear, that my grief is not inferior to your own, yet I have hitherto been enabled to support my sufferings in silence; for M. La Luc I do, indeed, love and reverence as a parent.

Louis meanwhile reached the prison of Theodore, who received him with an air of mingled surprise and impatience. What brings you back so soon? said he, have you heard news of my father? Louis now gradually unfolded the circumstances of their meetings and La Luc's arrival at Vaceau. A various emotion agitated the countenance of Theodore on receiving this intelligence. My poor father! said he, he has then followed his son to this ignominious place! Little did I think when last we parted he would meet me in a prison under condemnation! This reflection roused an impetuosity of grief which deprived him for some time of speech? But where is he? said Theodore, recovering himself; now he is come I shrink from the interview I have so much wished for. The sight of his distress will be dreadful to me. Louis! when I am gone, comfort my poor father. His voice was again interrupted by sobs; and Louis, who had been fearful of acquainting him at the same time of the arrival of La Luc and the discovery of Adeline, now judged it proper to administer the cordial of this latter intelligence.

The glooms of a prison and of calamity vanished for a transient moment; those who had seen Theodore would have believed this to be the instant which gave him life and liberty. When his first emotions subsided, I will not repine, said he, since I know that Adeline is preserved, and that I shall once more see my father, I will endeavour to die with resignation. He inquired if La Luc was then in the prison, and was told he was at the inn with Clara and Adeline. Adeline! Is Adeline there too?—This is beyond my hopes. Yet why do I rejoice? I must never see her more: this is no place for Adeline. Again he relapsed into an agony of distress—and again repeated a thousand questions concerning Adeline, till he was reminded by Louis that his father was impatient to see him—when, shocked that he had so long detained his friend, he entreated him to conduct La Luc to the prison, and endeavoured to recollect fortitude for the approaching interview.

When Louis returned to the inn, La Luc was still in his chamber; and Clara quitting the room to call him, Adeline seized with trembling impatience the opportunity to inquire more particularly concerning Theodore, than she chose to do in the presence of his unhappy sister. Louis represented him to be much more tranquil than he really was. Adeline was somewhat soothed by the account; and her tears, hitherto restrained, flowed silently and fast till La Luc appeared. His countenance had recovered its serenity, but was impressed with a deep and steady sorrow, which excited in the beholder a mingled emotion of pity and reverence. How is my son, Sir? said he as he entered the room. We will go to him immediately.

Clara renewed the entreaties that had been already rejected, to accompany her father, who persisted in a refusal. To-morrow you shall see him, added he; but our first meeting must be alone. Stay with your friend, my dear; she has need of consolation. When La Luc was gone, Adeline, unable longer to struggle against the force of grief, retired to her chamber and her bed.

La Luc walked silently towards the prison, resting on the arm of Louis. It was now night: a dim lamp that hung above showed them the gates, and Louis rang a bell: La Luc, almost overcome with agitation, leaned against the postern till the porter appeared. He inquired for Theodore, and followed the man; but when he reached the second courtyard he seemed ready to faint, and again stopped. Louis desired the porter would fetch some water; but La Luc, recovering his voice, said he should soon be better, and would not suffer him to go. In a few minutes he was able to follow Louis, who led him through several dark passages, and up a flight of steps to a door which, being unbarred, disclosed to him the prison of his son. He was seated at a small table, on which stood a lamp that threw a feeble light across the place, sufficient only to show its desolation and wretchedness. When he perceived La Luc he sprung from his chair, and in the next moment was in his arms. My father! said he in a tremulous voice. My son! exclaimed La Luc; and they were for some time silent, and locked in each other's embrace. At length Theodore led him to the only chair the room afforded, and seating himself with Louis at the foot of the bed, had leisure to observe the ravages which illness and calamity had made on the features of his parent. La Luc made several efforts to speak; but, unable to articulate, laid his hand upon his breast and sighed deeply. Fearful of the consequence of so affecting a scene on his shattered frame, Louis endeavoured to call off his attention from the immediate object of his distress, and interrupted the silence; but La Luc shuddering, and complaining he was very cold, sunk back in his chair. His condition roused Theodore from the stupor of despair; and while he flew to support his father, Louis ran out for other assistance.—I shall soon be better, Theodore, said La Luc, unclosing his eyes, the faintness is already going off. I have not been well of late; and this sad meeting!—Unable any longer to command himself, Theodore wrung his hand, and the distress which had long struggled for utterance burst in convulsive throbs from his breast. La Lac gradually revived, and exerted himself to calm the transports of his son; but the fortitude of the latter had now entirely forsaken him, and he could only utter exclamation and complaint. Ah! little did I think we should ever meet under circumstances so dreadful as the present! But I have not deserved them, my father! the motives of my conduct have still been just.

That is my supreme consolation, said La Luc, and ought to support you in this hour of trial. The Almighty God, who is the judge of hearts, will reward you hereafter. Trust in him, my son; I look to him with no feeble hope, but with a firm reliance on his justice! La Luc's voice faltered; he raised his eyes to heaven with an expression of meek devotion, while the tears of humanity fell slowly on his cheek.

Still more affected by his last words, Theodore turned from him, and paced the room with quick steps: the entrance of Louis was a very seasonable relief to La Luc, who, taking a cordial he had brought, was soon sufficiently restored to discourse on the subject most interesting to him. Theodore tried to attain a command of his feelings, and succeeded. He conversed with tolerable composure for above an hour, during which La Luc endeavoured to elevate, by religious hope, the mind of his son, and to enable him to meet with fortitude the awful hour that approached. But the appearance of resignation which Theodore attained always vanished when he reflected that he was going to leave his father a prey to grief, and his beloved Adeline for ever. When La Luc was about to depart he again mentioned her. Afflicting as an interview must be in our present circumstances, said he, I cannot bear the thought of quitting the world without seeing her once more; yet I know not how to ask her to encounter, for my sake, the misery of a parting scene. Tell her that my thoughts never, for a moment, leave her; that——La Luc interrupted, and assured him, that since he so much wished it, he should see her, though a meeting could serve only to heighten the mutual anguish of a final separation.

I know it—I know it too well, said Theodore; yet I cannot resolve to see her no more, and thus spare her the pain this interview must inflict. O my father! when I think of those whom I must soon leave for ever, my heart breaks. But I will, indeed, try to profit by your precept and example, and show that your paternal care has not been in vain. My good Louis, go with my father—he has need of support. How much I owe this generous friend, added Theodore, you well know, Sir.—I do, in truth, replied La Luc, and can never repay his kindness to you. He has contributed to support us all; but you require comfort more than myself—he shall remain with you—I will go alone.

This Theodore would not suffer; and La Luc no longer opposing him, they affectionately embraced, and separated for the night.

When they reached the inn, La Luc consulted with Louis on the possibility of addressing a petition to the sovereign time enough to save Theodore. His distance from Paris, and the short interval before the period fixed for this execution of the sentence, made this design difficult: but believing it was practicable, La Luc, incapable as he appeared of performing so long a journey, determined to attempt it. Louis, thinking that the undertaking would prove fatal to the father, without benefiting the son, endeavoured, though faintly, to dissuade him from it—but his resolution was fixed—If I sacrifice the small remains of my life in the service of my child, said he, I shall lose little: if I save him, I shall gain every thing. There is no time to be lost—I will set off immediately.

He would have ordered post-horses, but Louis and Clara, who were now come from the bed-side of her friend, urged the necessity of his taking a few hours' repose: he was at length compelled to acknowledge himself unequal to the immediate exertion which parental anxiety prompted, and consented to seek rest.

When he had retired to his chamber, Clara lamented the condition of her father.—He will not bear the journey, said she; he is greatly changed within these few days.— Louis was so entirely of her opinion, that he could not disguise it, even to flatter her with a hope. She added, what did not contribute to raise his spirits, that Adeline was so much indisposed by her grief for the situation of Theodore and the sufferings of La Luc that she dreaded the consequence.

It has been seen that the passion of young La Motte had suffered no abatement from time or absence; on the contrary, the persecution and the dangers which had pursued Adeline awakened all his tenderness, and drew her nearer to his heart. When he had discovered that Theodore loved her, and was beloved again, he experienced all the anguish of jealousy and disappointment; for, though she had forbidden him to hope, he found it too painful an effort to obey her, and had secretly cherished the flame which he ought to have stifled. His heart was, however, too noble to suffer his zeal for Theodore to abate because he was his favoured rival, and his mind too strong not to conceal the anguish this certainty occasioned. The attachment which Theodore had testified towards Adeline even endeared him to Louis, when he had recovered from the first shock of disappointment, and that conquest over jealousy which originated in principle, and was pursued with difficulty, became afterwards his pride and his glory. When, however, he again saw Adeline—saw her in the mild dignity of sorrow more interesting than ever—saw her, though sinking beneath its pressure, yet tender and solicitous to soften the afflictions of those around her—it was with the utmost difficulty he preserved his resolution, and forebore to express the sentiments she inspired. When he further considered that her acute sufferings arose from the strength of her affection, he more than ever wished himself the object of a heart capable of so tender a regard—and Thedore in prison and in chains was a momentary object of envy.

In the morning, when La Luc arose from short and disturbed slumbers, he found Louis, Clara, and Adeline, whom indisposition could not prevent from paying him this testimony of respect and affection, assembled in the parlour of the inn to see him depart. After a slight breakfast, during which his feelings permitted him to say little, he bade his friends a sad farewell, and stepped into the carriage, followed by their tears and prayers.—Adeline immediately retired to her chamber, which she was too ill to quit that day. In the evening Clara left her friend, and, conducted by Louis, went to visit her brother, whose emotions, on hearing of his father's departure, were various and strong.

CHAPTER XXI

'Tis only when with inbred horror smoteAt some base act, or done, or to be done,That the recoiling soul, with conscious dread.Shrinks back into itself.MASON.

We return now to Pierre de la Motte, who, after remaining some weeks in the prison of D——y, was removed to take his trial in the courts of Paris, whether the Marquis de Montalt followed to prosecute the charge. Madame de la Motte accompanied her husband to the prison of the Chatelet. His mind sunk under the weight of his misfortunes; nor could all the efforts of his wife rouse him from the torpidity of despair which a consideration of his circumstances occasioned. Should he be even acquitted of the charge brought against him by the Marquis, (which was very unlikely,) he was now in the scene of his former crimes, and the moment that should liberate him from the walls of his prison would probably deliver him again into the hands of offended justice.

The prosecution of the Marquis was too well founded, and its object of a nature too serious, not to justify the terror of La Motte. Soon after the latter had settled at the abbey of St. Clair, the small stock of money which the emergency of his circumstances had left him being nearly exhausted, his mind became corroded with the most cruel anxiety concerning the means of his future subsistence. As he was one evening riding alone in a remote part of the forest, musing on his distressed circumstances, and meditating plans to relieve the exigencies which he saw approaching, he perceived among the trees at some distance a chevalier on horseback, who was riding deliberately along, and seemed wholly unattended. A thought darted across the mind of La Motte, that he might be spared the evils which threatened him by robbing this stranger. His former practices had passed the boundary of honesty—fraud was in some degree familiar to him—and the thought was not dismissed. He hesitated——every moment of hesitation increased the power of temptation—the opportunity was such as might never occur again. He looked round, and as far as the trees opened saw no person but the chevalier, who seemed by his air to be a man of distinction. Summoning all his courage, La Motte rode forward and attacked him. The Marquis de Montalt, for it was he, was unarmed; but knowing that his attendants were not far off, he refused to yield. While they were struggling for victory, La Motte saw several horsemen enter the extremity of the avenue, and rendered desperate by opposition and delay, he drew from his pocket a pistol, (which an apprehension of banditti made him usually carry when he rode to a distance from the abbey) and fired at the Marquis, who staggered and fell senseless to the ground. La Motte had time to tear from his coat a brilliant star, some diamond rings from his fingers, and to rifle his pockets before his attendants came up. Instead of pursuing the robber, they all, in their first confusion, flew to assist their Lord, and La Motte escaped.

He stopped before he reached the abbey at a little ruin, the tomb formerly mentioned, to examine his booty. It consisted of a purse containing seventy louis d'ors; of a diamond star, three rings of great value, and a miniature set with brilliants of the Marquis himself, which he had intended as a present for his favourite mistress. To La Motte, who but a few hours before had seen himself nearly destitute, the view of this treasure excited an almost ungovernable transport; but it was soon checked when he remembered the means he had employed to obtain it, and that he had paid for the wealth he contemplated, the price of blood. Naturally violent in his passions, this reflection sunk him from the summit of exultation to the abyss of despondency. He considered himself a murderer, and, startled as one awakened from a dream, would have given half the world, had it been his, to have been as poor, and comparatively as guiltless, as a few preceding hours had seen him. On examining the portrait he discovered the resemblance; and believing that his hand had deprived the original of life, he gazed upon the picture with unutterable anguish. To the horrors of remorse succeeded the perplexities of fear. Apprehensive of he knew not what, he lingered at the tomb, where he at length deposited his treasure, believing that if his offence should awaken justice, the abbey might be searched, and these jewels betray him. From Madame La Motte it was easy to conceal his increase of wealth; for as he had never made her acquainted with the exact state of his finances, she had not suspected the extreme poverty which menaced him; and as they continued to live as usual, she believed that their expenses were drawn from the usual supply. But it was not so easy to disguise the workings of remorse and horror: his manner became gloomy and reserved, and his frequent visits to the tomb, where he went partly to examine his treasure, but chiefly to indulge in the dreadful pleasure of contemplating the picture of the Marquis, excited curiosity. In the solitude of the forest, where no variety of objects occurred to renovate his ideas, the horrible one of having committed murder was ever present to him.—When the Marquis arrived at the abbey, the astonishment and terror of La Motte (for at first he scarce knew whether he held the shadow or the substance of a human form) were quickly succeeded by apprehension of the punishment due to the crime he had really committed. When his distress had prevailed on the Marquis to retire, he informed him that he was by birth a chevalier: he then touched upon such parts of his misfortunes as he thought would excite pity, expressed such abhorrence of his guilt, and voluntarily uttered such a solemn promise of returning the jewels he had yet in his possession, (for he had ventured to dispose only of a small part,) that the Marquis at length listened to him with some degree of compassion. This favourable sentiment, seconded by a selfish motive, induced the Marquis to compromise with La Motte. Of quick and inflammable passions, he had observed the beauty of Adeline with an eye of no common regard, and he resolved to spare the life of La Motte upon no other condition than the sacrifice of this unfortunate girl. La Motte had neither resolution nor virtue sufficient to reject the terms—the jewels were restored, and he consented to betray the innocent Adeline. But as he was too well acquainted with her heart to believe that she would easily be won to the practice of vice, and as he still felt a degree of pity and tenderness for her, he endeavoured to prevail on the Marquis to forbear precipitate measures, and to attempt gradually to undermine her principles by seducing her affections. He approved and adopted this plan: the failure of his first scheme induced him to employ the stratagems he afterwards pursued, and thus to multiply the misfortunes of Adeline.

Such were the circumstances which had brought La Motte to his present deplorable situation. The day of trial was now come, and he was led from prison into the court, where the Marquis appeared as his accuser. When the charge was delivered, La Motte, as is usual, pleaded Not guilty, and the Advocate Nemours, who had undertaken to plead for him, afterwards endeavoured to make it appear that the accusation, on the part of the Marquis de Montalt, was false and malicious. To this purpose he mentioned the circumstance of the latter having attempted to persuade his client to the murder of Adeline: he further urged that the Marquis had lived in habits of intimacy with La

Motte for several months immediately preceding his arrest, and that it was not till he had disappointed the designs of his accuser, by conveying beyond his reach the unhappy object of his vengeance, that the Marquis had thought proper to charge La Motte with the crime for which he stood indicted. Nemours urged the improbability of one man's keeping up a friendly intercourse with another from whom he had suffered the double injury of assault and robbery; yet it was certain that the Marquis had observed a frequent intercourse with La Motte for some months following the time specified for the commission of the crime. If the Marquis intended to prosecute, why was it not immediately after his discovery of La Motte? and if not then, what had influenced him to prosecute at so distant a period?

To this nothing was replied on the part of the Marquis; for, as his conduct on this point had been subservient to his designs on Adeline, he could not justify it but by exposing schemes which would betray the darkness of his character, and invalidate his cause. He, therefore, contented himself with producing several of his servants as witnesses of the assault and robbery, who swore without scruple to the person of La Motte, though not one of them had seen him otherwise than through the gloom of evening and riding off at full speed. On a cross-examination most of them contradicted each other; their evidence was of course rejected: but as the Marquis had yet two other witnesses to produce, whose arrival at Paris had been hourly expected, the event of the trial was postponed, and the court adjourned.

La Motte was re-conducted to his prison under the same pressure of despondency with which he had quitted it. As he walked through one of the avenues he passed a man who stood by to let him proceed, and who regarded him with a fixed and earnest eye. La Motte thought he had seen him before; but the imperfect view he caught of his features through the darkness of the place made him uncertain as to this, and his mind was in too perturbed a state to suffer him to feel an interest on the subject. When he was gone, the stranger inquired of the keeper of the prison who La Motte was: on being told, and receiving answers to some further questions he put, he desired he might be admitted to speak with him. The request, as the man was only a debtor, was granted; but as the doors were now shut for the night, the interview was deferred till the morrow.

La Motte found Madame in his room, where she had been waiting for some hours to hear the event of the trial. They now wished more earnestly than ever to see their son; but they were, as he had suspected, ignorant of his change of quarters, owing to the letters which he had as usual, addressed to them under an assumed name, remaining at the post-house of Auboine. This circumstance occasioned Madame La Motte to address her letters to the place of her son's late residence, and he had thus continued ignorant of his father's misfortunes and removal. Madame La Motte, surprised at receiving no answers to her letters, sent off another, containing an account of the trial as far as it had proceeded, and a request that her son would obtain leave of absence, and set out for Paris instantly. As she was still ignorant, of the failure of her letters, and, had it been otherwise, would not have known whither to have sent them, she directed this as usual.

Meanwhile his approaching fate was never absent for a moment from the mind of La Motte, which, feeble by nature, and still more enervated by habits of indulgence, refused to support him at this dreadful period.

While these scenes were passing at Paris, La Luc arrived there without any accident, after performing a journey, during which he had been supported almost entirely by the spirit of his resolution. He hastened to throw himself at the feet of the sovereign; and such was the excess of his feeling on presenting the petition which was to decide the fate of his son, that he could only look silently up, and then fainted. The king received the paper, and giving orders for the unhappy father to be taken care of, passed on. He was carried back to his hotel, where he awaited the event of this his final effort.

Adeline, meanwhile, continued at Vaceau in a state of anxiety too powerful for her long-agitated frame, and the illness in consequence of this, confined her almost wholly to her chamber. Sometimes she ventured to flatter herself with a hope that the journey of La Luc would be successful: but these short and illusive intervals of comfort served only to heighten, by contrast, the despondency that succeeded; and in the alternate extremes of feeling she experienced a state more torturing than that produced either by the sharp sting of unexpected calamity, or the sullen pain of settled despair.

When she was well enough she came down to the parlour to converse with Louis, who brought her frequent accounts of Theodore, and who passed every moment he could snatch from the duty of his profession in endeavours to support and console his afflicted friends. Adeline and Theodore, both looked to him for the little comfort allotted them, for he brought them intelligence of each other, and whenever he appeared a transient melancholy kind of pleasure played round their hearts. He could not conceal from Theodore Adeline's indisposition, since it was necessary to account for her not indulging the earnest wish he repeatedly expressed to see her again. To Adeline he spoke chiefly of the fortitude and resignation of his friend, not however forgetting to mention the tender affection he constantly expressed for her. Accustomed to derive her sole consolation from the presence of Louis, and to observe his unwearied friendship towards him whom she so truly loved, she found her esteem for him ripen into gratitude, and her regard daily increase.

The fortitude with which he had said Theodore supported his calamities was somewhat exaggerated. He could not forget those ties which bound him to life sufficiently to meet his fate with firmness; but though the paroxysms of grief were acute and frequent, he sought, and often attained in the presence of his friends, a manly composure. From the event of his father's journey he hoped little, yet that little was sufficient to keep his mind in the torture of suspense till the issue should appear.

On the day preceding that fixed for the execution of the sentence, La Luc reached Vaceau. Adeline was at her chamber window when the carriage drew up to the inn; she saw him alight, and with feeble steps, supported by Peter, enter the house. From the languor of his air she drew no favourable omen, and, almost sinking under the violence of her emotion, she went to meet him. Clara was already with her father when Adeline entered the room. She approached him, but, dreading to receive from his lips a confirmation of the misfortune his countenance seemed to indicate, she looked expressively at him and sat down, unable to speak the question she would have asked. He held out his hand to her in silence, sunk back in his chair, and seemed to be fainting under oppression of heart. His manner confirmed all her fears; at this dreadful conviction her senses failed her, and she sat motionless and stupefied.

La Luc and Clara were too much occupied by their own distress to observe her situation; after some time she breathed a heavy sigh, and burst into tears. Relieved by weeping, her spirits gradually returned, and she at length said to La Luc, It is unnecessary, Sir, to ask the success of your journey; yet, when you can bear to mention the subject, I wish—

La Luc waved his hand—Alas! said he, I have nothing to tell but what you already guess too well. My poor Theodore!—His voice was convulsed with sorrow, and some moments of unutterable anguish followed.

Adeline was the first who recovered sufficient recollection to notice the extreme languor of La Luc, and attend to his support. She ordered him refreshments, and entreated he would retire to his bed and suffer her to send for a physician; adding, that the fatigue he had suffered made repose absolutely necessary. Would that I could find it, my dear child! said he; it is not in this world that I must look for it, but in a better, and that better, I trust, I shall soon attain. But where is our good friend, Louis La Motte? He must lead me to my son.—Grief again interrupted his utterance, and the entrance of Louis was a very seasonable relief to them all. Their tears explained the question he would have asked. La Luc immediately inquired for his son; and thanking Louis for all his kindness to him, desired to be conducted to the prison. Louis endeavoured to persuade him to defer his visit till the morning, and Adeline and Clara joined their entreaties with his, but La Luc determined to go that night.—His time is short, said he; a few hours and I shall see him no more, at least in this world; let me not neglect these precious moments. Adeline! I had promised my poor boy that he should see you once more; you are not now equal to the meeting; I will try to reconcile him to the disappointment: but if I fail, and you are better in the morning, I know you will exert yourself to sustain the interview.—Adeline looked impatient, and attempted to speak. La Luc rose to depart, but could only reach the door of the room, where, faint and feeble, he sat down in a chair. I must submit to necessity, said he; I find I am not able to go further to-night. Go to him, La Motte, and tell him I am somewhat disordered by my journey, but that I will be with him early in the morning. Do not flatter him with a hope; prepare him for the worst.—There was a pause of silence. La Luc at length recovering himself, desired Clara would order his bed to be got ready, and she willingly obeyed. When he withdrew, Adeline told Louis, what was indeed unnecessary, the event of La Luc's journey. I own, continued she, that I had sometimes suffered myself to hope, and I now feel this calamity with double force: I fear too that M. La Luc will sink under its pressure; he is much altered for the worse since he set out for Paris. Tell me your opinion sincerely.

The change was so obvious that Louis could not deny it; but he endeavoured to soothe her apprehension by ascribing this alteration, in a great measure, to the temporary fatigue of travelling. Adeline declared her resolution of accompanying La Luc to take leave of Theodore in the morning. I know not how I shall support the interview, said she; but to see him once more is a duty I owe both to him and myself. The remembrance of having neglected to give him this last proof of affection would pursue me with incessant remorse.

After some further conversation on this subject Louis withdrew to the prison, ruminating on the best means of imparting to his friend the fatal intelligence he had to communicate. Theodore received it with more composure than he had expected; but he asked with impatience why he did not see his father and Adeline; and on being informed that indisposition withheld them, his imagination seized on the worst possibility, and suggested that his father was dead. It was a considerable time before Louis could convince him of the contrary, and that Adeline was not dangerously ill: when, however, he was assured that he should see them in the morning, he became more tranquil. He desired his friend would not leave him that night. These are the last hours we can pass together, added he; I cannot sleep! Stay with me and lighten their heavy moments. I have need of comfort, Louis. Young as I am, and held by such strong attachments, I cannot quit the world with resignation. I know not how to credit those stories we hear of philosophic fortitude; wisdom cannot teach us cheerfully to resign a good, and life in my circumstances is surely such.

The night was passed in embarrassed conversation; sometimes interrupted by long fits of silence, and sometimes by the paroxysms of despair; and the morning of that day which was to lead Theodore to death, at length dawned through the grates of his prison.

La Luc meanwhile passed a sleepless and dreadful night. He prayed for fortitude and resignation both for himself and Theodore; but the pangs of nature were powerful in his heart, and not to be subdued. The idea of his lamented wife, and of what she would have suffered had she lived to witness the ignominious death which awaited her son, frequently occurred to him.

It seemed as if a destiny had hung over the life of Theodore; for it is probable that the king might have granted the petition of the unhappy father, had it not happened that the Marquis de Montalt was present at court when the paper was presented. The appearance and singular distress of the petitioner had interested the monarch, and, instead of putting by the paper, he opened it. As he threw his eyes over it, observing that the criminal was of the Marquis de Montalt's regiment, he turned to him and inquired the nature of the offence for which the culprit was about to suffer. The answer was such as might have been expected from the Marquis, and the king was convinced that Theodore was not a proper object of mercy.

But to return to La Luc, who was called, according to his order, at a very early hour. Having passed some time in prayer, he went down to the parlour, where Louis, punctual to the moment, already waited to conduct him to the prison. He appeared calm and collected, but his countenance was impressed with a fixed despair that sensibly affected his young friend. While they waited for Adeline he spoke little, and seemed struggling to attain the fortitude necessary to support him through the approaching scene. Adeline not appearing, he at length sent to hasten her, and was told she had been ill, but was recovering. She had indeed passed a night of such agitation, that her frame had sunk under it, and she was now endeavouring to recover strength and composure sufficient to sustain her in this dreadful hour. Every moment that brought her nearer to it had increased her emotion, and the apprehension of being prevented seeing Theodore had alone enabled her to struggle against the united pressure of illness and grief.

She now, with Clara, joined La Luc, who advanced as they entered the room, and took a hand of each in silence. After some moments he proposed to go, and they stepped into a carriage which conveyed them to the gates of the prison. The crowd had already begun to assemble there, and a confused murmur arose as the carriage moved forward; it was a grievous sight to the friends of Theodore. Louis supported Adeline when she alighted, she was scarcely able to walk, and with trembling steps she followed La Luc, whom the keeper led towards that part of the prison where his son was confined. It was now eight o'clock, the sentence was not to be executed till twelve, but a guard of soldiers was already placed in the court; and as this unhappy party passed along the narrow avenues, they were met by several officers who had been to take a last farewell of Theodore. As they ascended the stairs that led to his apartment. La Luc's ear caught the clink of chains, and heard him walking above with a quick irregular step. The unhappy father, overcome by the moment which now pressed upon him, stopped, and was obliged to support himself by the bannister. Louis fearing the consequence of his grief might be fatal, shattered as his frame already was, would have gone for assistance, but he made a sign to him to stay, I am better, said La Luc; O God! support me through this hour!—and in a few minutes he was able to proceed.

As the warder unlocked the door, the harsh grating of the key shocked Adeline, but in the next moment she was in the presence of Theodore, who sprung to meet her, and caught her in his arms before she sunk to the ground. As her head reclined on his shoulder, he again viewed that countenance so dear to him, which had so often lighted rapture in his heart, and which, though pale and inanimate as it now was, awakened him to momentary delight. When at length she unclosed her eyes, she fixed them in long and mournful gaze upon Theodore, who pressing her to his heart could answer her only with a smile of mingled tenderness and despair; the tears he endeavoured to restrain trembled in his eyes, and he forgot for a time every thing but Adeline. La Luc, who had seated himself at the foot of the bed, seemed unconscious of what passed around him, and entirely absorbed in his own grief; but Clara, as she clasped the hand of her brother and hung weeping on his arm, expressed aloud all the anguish of her heart, and at length recalled the attention of Adeline, who in a voice scarcely audible entreated she would spare her father. Her words roused Theodore, and supporting Adeline to a chair, he turned to La Luc. My dear child! said La Luc, grasping his hand and bursting into tears, my dear child! They wept together. After a long interval of silence, he said, I thought I could have supported this hour, but I am old and feeble. God knows my efforts for resignation, my faith in his goodness.

Theodore by a strong and sudden exertion assumed a composed and firm countenance, and endeavoured by every gentle argument to soothe and comfort his weeping friends. La Luc at length seemed to conquer his sufferings; drying his eyes, he said, My son, I ought to have set you a better example, and have practised the precepts of fortitude I have so often given you. But it is over; I know and will perform my duty. Adeline breathed a heavy sigh, and continued to weep. Be comforted, my love, we part but for a time, said Theodore as he kissed the tears from her cheek; and uniting her hand with that of his father's, he earnestly recommended her to his protection. Receive her, added he, as the most precious legacy I can bequeath; consider her as your child: she will console you when I am gone, she will more than supply the loss of your son.

La Luc assured him that he did now, and should continue to regard Adeline as his daughter. During those afflicting hours he endeavoured to dissipate the terrors of approaching death by inspiring his son with religious confidence. His conversation was pious, rational, and consolatory; he spoke not from the cold dictates of the head, but from the feelings of a heart which had long loved and practised the pure precepts of Christianity, and which now drew from them a comfort such as nothing earthly could bestow.

You are young, my son, said he, and are yet innocent of any great crime; you may therefore look on death without terror, for to the guilty only is his approach dreadful. I feel that I shall not long survive you, and I trust in a merciful God that we shall meet in a state where sorrow never comes; where the Sun of Righteousness shall arise with healing on his wings! As he spoke he looked up; the tears still trembled in his eyes, which beamed with meek yet fervent devotion, and his countenance glowed with the dignity of a superior being.

Let us not neglect the awful moments, said La Luc rising, let our united prayers ascend to Him who alone can comfort and support us! They all knelt down, and he prayed with that simple and sublime eloquence which true piety inspires. When he arose he embraced his children separately, and when he came to Theodore he paused, gazed upon him with an earnest, mournful expression, and was for some time unable to speak. Theodore could not bear this; he drew his hand before his eyes, and vainly endeavoured to stifle the deep sobs which convulsed his frame. At length recovering his voice, he entreated his father would leave him. This misery is too much for us all, said he, let us not prolong it. The time is now drawing on—leave me to compose myself; the sharpness of death consists in parting with those who are dear to us; when that is passed death is disarmed.

I will not leave you, my son, replied La Luc; my poor girls shall go, but for me, I will be with you in your last moments. Theodore felt that this would be too much for them both, and urged every argument which reason could suggest to prevail with his father to relinquish his design: but he remained firm in his determination. I will not suffer a selfish consideration of the pain I may endure, said La Luc, to tempt me to desert my child when he will most require my support. It is my duty to attend you, and nothing shall withhold me.

Theodore seized on the words of La Luc—As you would that I should be supported in my last hour, said he, I entreat that you will not be witness of it. Your presence, my dear father, would subdue all my fortitude—would destroy what little composure I may otherwise be able to attain. Add not to my sufferings the view of your distress, but leave me to forget, if possible, the dear parent I must quit for ever. His tears flowed anew. La Luc continued to gaze on him in silent agony. At length he said, Well, be it so. If indeed my presence would distress you, I will not go. His voice was broken and interrupted. After a pause of some moments he again embraced Theodore—We must part, said he, we must part, but it is only for a time—we shall soon be reunited in a higher world!—O God! thou seest my heart—thou seest all its feelings in this bitter hour!—Grief again overcame him. He pressed Theodore in his arms: and at length seeming to summon all his fortitude, he again said, We must part—Oh! my son, farewell for ever in this world!—The mercy of Almighty God support and bless you!

He turned away to leave the prison, but quite worn out with grief, sunk into a chair near the door he would have opened. Theodore gazed, with a distracted countenance, alternately on his father, on Clara, and on Adeline, whom he pressed to his throbbing heart, and their tears flowed together. And do I then, cried he, for the last time look upon that countenance!—Shall I never—never more behold it?—O! exquisite misery! Yet once again—once more, continued he, pressing her cheek; but it was insensible and cold as marble.

Louis, who had left the room soon after La Luc arrived, that his presence might not interrupt their farewell grief, now returned. Adeline raised her head, and perceiving who entered, it again sunk on the bosom of Theodore.

Louis appeared much agitated. La Luc arose. We must go, said he; Adeline, my love, exert yourself—Clara—my children, let us depart.—Yet one last—last embrace, and then!——Louis advanced and took his hand; My dear Sir, I have something to say; yet I fear to tell it.—What do you mean? said La Luc with quickness: no new misfortune can have power to afflict me at this moment; do not fear to speak.—I rejoice that I cannot put you to the proof, replied Louis; I have seen you sustain the most trying affliction with fortitude. Can you support the transports of hope?—La Luc gazed eagerly on Louis—Speak! said he, in a faint voice. Adeline raised her head, and, trembling between hope and fear, looked as if she would have searched his soul. He smiled cheerfully upon her. Is it—O! is it possible! she exclaimed, suddenly reanimated—He lives! He lives!—She said no more, but ran to La Luc, who sunk fainting in his chair, while Theodore and Clara with one voice called on Louis to relieve them from the tortures of suspense.

He proceeded to inform them that he had obtained from the commanding officer a respite for Theodore till the king's further pleasure could be known, and this in consequence of a letter received that morning from his mother, Madame de La Motte, in which she mentioned some very extraordinary circumstances that had appeared in the course of a trial lately conducted at Paris, and which so materially affected the character of the Marquis de Montalt as to render it possible a pardon might be obtained for Theodore.

These words darted with the rapidity of lightning upon the hearts of his hearers. La Luc revived, and that prison so lately the scene of despair now echoed only to the voices of gratitude and gladness. La Luc, raising his clasped hands to heaven, said, Great God! support me in this moment as thou hast already supported me!—If my son lives, I die in peace.

He embraced Theodore, and remembering the anguish of his last embrace, tears of thankfulness and joy flowed to the contrast. So powerful indeed was the effect of this temporary reprieve, and of the hope it introduced, that if an absolute pardon had been obtained, it could scarcely for the moment have diffused a more lively joy. But when the first emotions were subsided, the uncertainty of Theodore's fate once more appeared. Adeline forbore to express this; but Clara without scruple lamented the possibility that her brother might yet be taken from them, and all their joy be turned to sorrow. A look from Adeline checked her. Joy was, however, so much the predominant feeling of the present moment, that the shade which reflection threw upon their hopes passed away like the cloud that is dispelled by the strength of the sunbeam; and Louis alone was pensive and abstracted.

When they were sufficiently composed, he informed them that the contents of Madame de La Motte's letter obliged him to set out for Paris immediately; and that the intelligence he had to communicate intimately concerned Adeline, who would undoubtedly judge it necessary to go thither also as soon as her health would permit. He then read to his impatient auditors such passages in the letter as were necessary to explain his meaning; but as Madame de La Motte had omitted to mention some circumstances of importance to be understood, the following is a relation of the occurrences that had lately happened at Paris.

It may be remembered that on the first day of his trial, La Motte, in passing from the courts to his prison, saw a person whose features, though imperfectly seen through the dusk, he thought he recollected; and that this same person, after inquiring the name of La Motte, desired to be admitted to him. On the following day the warder complied with his request, and the surprise of La Motte may be imagined when in the stronger light of his apartment, he distinguished the countenance of the man, from whose hands he had formerly received Adeline.

On observing Madame de La Motte in the room, he said he had something of consequence to impart, and desired to be left alone with the prisoner. When she was gone, he told De La Motte that he understood he was confined at the suit of the Marquis de Montalt. La Motte assented.—I know him for a villain, said the stranger boldly. Your case is desperate. Do you wish for life?

Need the question be asked?

Your trial, I understand proceeds to-morrow. I am now under confinement in this place for debt; but if you can obtain leave for me to go with you into the courts, and a condition from the judge that what I reveal shall not criminate myself, I will make discoveries that shall confound that same Marquis; I will prove him a villain; and it shall then be judged how far his word ought to be taken against you.

La Motte, whose interest was now strongly excited, desired he would explain himself; and the man proceeded to relate a long history of the misfortunes and consequent poverty which had tempted him to become subservient to the schemes of the Marquis, till he suddenly checked himself, and said. When I obtain from the court the promise I require, I will explain myself fully; till then, I cannot say more on the subject.

La Motte could not forbear expressing a doubt of his sincerity, and a curiosity concerning the motive that had induced him to become the Marquis's accuser.—As to my motive, it is a very natural one, replied the man: it is no easy matter to receive ill usage without resenting it, particularly from a villain whom you have served.— La Motte, for his own sake, endeavoured to check the vehemence with which this was uttered. I care not who hears me continued the stranger, but at the same time he lowered his voice; I repeat it—the Marquis has used me ill—I have kept his secret long enough: he does not think it worth while to secure my silence, or he would relieve my necessities. I am in prison for debt, and have applied to him for relief; since he does not choose to give it, let him take the consequence. I warrant he shall soon repent that he has provoked me, and 'tis fit he should.

The doubts of La Motte were now dissipated; the prospect of life again opened upon him, and he assured Du Bosse (which was the stranger's name) with much warmth, that he would commission his advocate to do all in his power to obtain leave for his appearance on the trial, and to procure the necessary condition. After some further conversation they parted.

CHAPTER XXII

Drag forth the legal monster into light, Wrench from his hand oppression's iron rod, And bid the cruel feel the pains they give.

Leave was at length granted for the appearance of Du Bosse, with a promise that his words should not criminate him, and he accompanied La Motte into court.

The confusion of the Marquis de Montalt on perceiving this man was observed by many persons present, and particularly by La Motte, who drew from this circumstance a favourable presage for himself.

When Du Bosse was called upon, he informed the court, that on the night of the twenty-first of April, in the preceding year, one Jean D'Aunoy, a man he had known many years, came to his lodging. After they had discoursed for some time on their circumstances, D'Aunoy said he knew a way by which Du Bosse might change all his poverty to riches, but that he would not say more till he was certain he would be willing to follow it. The distressed state in which Du Bosse then was, made him anxious to learn the means which would bring him relief; he eagerly inquired what his friend meant, and after some time D'Aunoy explained himself. He said he was employed by a nobleman (who he afterwards told Du Bosse was the Marquis de Montalt) to carry off a young girl from a convent, and that she was to be taken to a house a few leagues distant from Paris. I knew the house he described well, said Du Bosse, for I had been there many times with D'Aunoy, who lived there to avoid his creditors, though he often passed his nights at Paris. He would not tell me more of the scheme, but said he should want assistants, and if I and my brother, who is since dead, would join him, his employer would grudge no money, and we should be well rewarded. I desired him again to tell me more of the plan, but he was obstinate; and after I had told him I would consider of what he said, and speak to my brother, he went away.

When he called the next night for his answer, my brother and I agreed to engage, and accordingly we went home with him. He then told us that the young lady he was to bring thither was a natural daughter of the Marquis de Montalt and of a nun belonging to a convent of Ursulines; that his wife had received the child immediately on its birth, and had been allowed a handsome annuity to bring it up as her own, which she had done till her death. The child was then placed in a convent and designed for the veil; but when she was of an age to receive the vows, she had steadily persisted in refusing them. This circumstance had so much exasperated the Marquis, that in his rage he ordered that if she persisted in her obstinacy she should be removed from the convent, and got rid of any way; since if she lived in the world her birth might be discovered, and in consequence of this, her mother, for whom he had yet a regard, would be condemned to expiate her crime by a terrible death.

Du Bosse was interrupted in his narrative by the counsel of the Marquis, who contended that the circumstances alleged tending to criminate his client, the proceeding was both irrelevant and illegal. He was answered that it was not irrelevant, and therefore not illegal; for that the circumstances which threw light upon the character of the Marquis, affected his evidence against La Motte. Du Bosse was suffered to proceed.

D'Aunoy then said that the Marquis had ordered him to dispatch her, but that, as he had been used to see her from her infancy, he could not find in his heart to do it, and wrote to tell him so. The Marquis then commanded him to find those who would, and this was the business for which he wanted us. My brother and I were not so wicked as this came to, and so we told D'Aunoy; and I could not help asking why the Marquis resolved to murder his own child rather than expose her mother to the risque of suffering death. He said the Marquis had never seen his child and that, therefore, it could not be supposed he felt much kindness towards it, and still less that he could love it better than he loved its mother.

Du Bosse proceeded to relate how much he and his brother had endeavoured to soften the heart of D'Aunoy towards the Marquis's daughter, and that they prevailed with him to write again and plead for her. D'Aunoy went to Paris to await the answer, leaving them and the young girl at the house on the heath, where the former had consented to remain, seemingly for the purpose of executing the orders they might receive, but really with a design to save the unhappy victim from the sacrifice.

It is probable that Du Bosse, in this instance, gave a false account of his motive; since, if he was really guilty of an intention so atrocious as that of murder, he would naturally endeavour to conceal it. However this might be, he affirmed, that on the night of the twenty-sixth of April, he received an order from D'Aunoy for the destruction of the girl, whom he had afterwards delivered into the hands of La Motte.

La Motte listened to this relation in astonishment; when he knew that Adeline was the daughter of the Marquis, and remembered the crime to which he had once devoted her, his frame thrilled with horror. He now took up the story, and added an account of what had passed at the abbey between the Marquis and himself, concerning a design of the former upon the life of Adeline, and urged, as a proof of the present prosecution originating in malice, that it had commenced immediately after he had effected her escape from the Marquis. He concluded, however, with saying, that as the Marquis had immediately sent his people in pursuit of her, it was possible she might yet have fallen a victim to his vengeance.

Here the Marquis's counsel again interfered, and their objections were again overruled by the court. The uncommon degree of emotion which his countenance betrayed during the narrations of Du Bosse and De La Motte was generally observed. The court suspended the sentence of the latter, ordered that the Marquis should be put under immediate arrest, and that Adeline (the name given by her fostermother) and Jean D'Aunoy should be sought for.

The Marquis was accordingly seized at the suit of the crown, and put under confinement till Adeline should appear, or proof could be obtained that she died by his order; and till D'Aunoy should confirm or destroy the evidence of De La Motte.

Madame, who at length obtained intelligence of her son's residence from the town where he was formerly stationed, had acquainted him with his father's situation, and the proceedings of the trial; and as she believed that Adeline, if she had been so fortunate as to escape the Marquis's pursuit, was still in Savoy, she desired Louis would obtain leave of absence, and bring her to Paris, where her immediate presence was requisite to substantiate the evidence, and probably to save the life of La Motte.

On the receipt of her letter, which happened on the morning appointed for the execution of Theodore, Louis went immediately to the commanding officer to petition for a respite till the king's further pleasure should be known. He founded his plea on the arrest of the Marquis, and showed the letter he had just received. The commanding officer readily granted a reprieve; and Louis, who, on the arrival of this letter had forborne to communicate its contents to Theodore, lest it should torture him with false hope, now hastened to him with this comfortable news.

CHAPTER XXIII

Low on his funeral couch he lies!No pitying heart, no eye, affordA tear lo grace his obsequies.GRAY.

On learning the purport of Madame de La Motte's letter, Adeline saw the necessity of her immediate departure for Paris. The life of La Motte, who had more than saved hers, the life perhaps of her beloved Theodore, depended on the testimony she should give. And she who had so lately been sinking under the influence of illness and despair, who could scarcely raise her languid head, or speak but in the faintest accents, now reanimated with hope, and invigorated by a sense of the importance of the business before her, prepared to perform a rapid journey of some hundred miles.

Theodore tenderly entreated that she would so far consider her health as to delay this journey for a few days: but with a smile of enchanting tenderness she assured him, that she was now too happy to be ill, and that the same cause which would confirm her happiness would confirm her health. So strong was the effect of hope upon her mind, now that it succeeded to the misery of despair, that it overcame the shock she suffered on believing herself a daughter of the Marquis, and every other painful reflection. She did not even foresee the obstacle that circumstance might produce to her union with Theodore, should he at last be permitted to live.

It was settled that she should set off for Paris in a few hours with Louis, and attended by Peter. These hours were passed by La Luc and his family in the prison.

When the time of her departure arrived, the spirits of Adeline again forsook her, and the illusions of joy disappeared. She no longer beheld Theodore as one respited from death, but took leave of him with a mournful presentiment that she should see him no more. So strongly was this presage impressed upon her mind, that it was long before she could summon resolution to bid him farewell; and when she had done so, and even left the apartment, she returned to take of him a last look. As she was once more quitting the room, her melancholy imagination represented Theodore at the place of execution, pale, and convulsed in death; she again turned her lingering eyes upon him; but fancy affected her sense, for she thought as she now gazed that his countenance changed, and assumed a ghastly hue. All her resolution vanished; and such was the anguish of her heart, that she resolved to defer her journey till the morrow, though she must by this means lose the protection of Louis, whose impatience to meet his father would not suffer the delay. The triumph of passion, however, was transient; soothed by the indulgence she promised herself, her grief subsided; reason resumed its influence; she again saw the necessity of her immediate departure, and recollected sufficient resolution to submit. La Luc would have accompanied her for the purpose of again soliciting the king in behalf of his son, had not the extreme weakness and lassitude to which he was reduced made travelling impracticable.

At length, Adeline with a heavy heart quitted Theodore, notwithstanding his entreaties that she would not undertake the journey in her present weak state, and was accompanied by Clara and La Luc to the inn. The former parted from her friend with many tears, and much anxiety for her welfare, but under a hope of soon meeting again. Should a pardon be granted to Theodore, La Luc designed to fetch Adeline from Paris; but should this be refused, she was to return with Peter. He bade her adieu with a father's kindness, which she repaid with a filial affection, and in her last words conjured him to attend to the recovery of his health: the languid smile he assumed seemed to express that her solicitude was vain, and that he thought his health past recovery.

Thus Adeline quitted the friends so justly dear to her, and so lately found, for Paris, where she was a stranger, almost without protection, and compelled to meet a father, who had pursued her with the utmost cruelty, in a public court of justice. The carriage in leaving Vaceau passed by the prison; she threw an eager look towards it as she passed; its heavy black walls, and narrow-grated windows, seemed to frown upon her hopes—but Theodore was there, and leaning from the window: she continued to gaze upon it till an abrupt turning in the street concealed it from her view. She then sunk back in the carriage, and yielding to the melancholy of her heart, wept in silence. Louis was not disposed to interrupt it; his thoughts were anxiously employed on his father's situation, and the travellers proceeded many miles without exchanging a word.

At Paris, whither we shall now return, the search after Jean D'Aunoy was prosecuted without success. The house on the heath, described by Du Bosse, was found uninhabited, and to the places of his usual resort in the city, where the officers of the police awaited him, he no longer came. It even appeared doubtful whether he was living, for he had absented himself from the houses of his customary rendezvous sometime before the trial of La Motte; it was therefore certain that his absence was not occasioned by any thing which had passed in the courts.

In the solitude of his confinement the Marquis de Montalt had leisure to reflect on the past, and to repent of his crimes; but reflection and repentance formed as yet no part of his disposition. He turned with impatience from recollections which produced only pain, and looked forward to the future with an endeavour to avert the disgrace and punishment which he saw impending. The elegance of his manners had so effectually veiled the depravity of his heart, that he was a favourite with his sovereign; and on this circumstance he rested his hope of security. He, however, severely repented that he had indulged the hasty spirit of revenge which had urged him to the prosecution of La Motte, and had thus unexpectedly involved him in a situation dangerous—if not fatal—since if Adeline could not be found he would be concluded guilty of her death. But the appearance of D'Aunoy was the circumstance he most dreaded; and to oppose the possibility of this, he employed secret emissaries to discover his retreat, and to bribe him to his interest. These were, however as unsuccessful in their research as the officers of police, and the Marquis at length began to hope that the man was really dead.

La Motte meanwhile awaited with trembling impatience the arrival of his son, when he should be relieved in some degree from his uncertainty concerning Adeline. On this appearance he rested his only hope of life, since the evidence against him would lose much of its validity from the confirmation she would give of the bad character of his prosecutor; and if the Parliament even condemned La Motte, the clemency of the king might yet operate in his favour.

Adeline arrived at Paris after a journey of several days, during which she was chiefly supported by the delicate attentions of Louis, whom she pitied and esteemed, though she could not love. She was immediately visited at the hotel by Madame La Motte: the meeting was affecting on both sides. A sense of her past conduct excited in the latter an embarrassment which the delicacy and goodness of Adeline would willingly have spared her; but the pardon solicited was given with so much sincerity, that Madame gradually became composed and reassured. This forgiveness, however, could not have been thus easily granted, had Adeline believed her former conduct was voluntary; a conviction of the restraint and terror under which Madame had acted, alone induced her to excuse the past. In this first meeting they forbore dwelling on particular subjects; Madame La Motte proposed that Adeline should remove from the hotel to her lodgings near the Chatelet; and Adeline, for whom a residence at a public hotel was very improper, gladly accepted the offer.

Madame there gave her a circumstantial account of La Motte's situation, and concluded with saying, that as the sentence of her husband had been suspended till some certainty could be obtained concerning the late criminal designs of the Marquis, and as Adeline could confirm the chief part of La Motte's testimony, it was probable that now she was arrived the court would proceed immediately. She now learnt the full extent of her obligation to La Motte; for she was till now ignorant that when he sent her from the forest he saved her from death. Her horror of the Marquis, whom she could not bear to consider as her father, and her gratitude to her deliverer, redoubled, and she became impatient to give the testimony so necessary to the hopes of her preserver. Madame then said, she believed it was not too late to gain admittance that night to the Chatelet; and as she knew how anxiously her husband wished to see Adeline, she entreated her consent to go thither. Adeline, though much harassed and fatigued, complied. When Louis returned from M. Nemours, his father's advocate, whom he had hastened to inform of her arrival, they all set out for the Chatelet. The view of the prison into which they were now admitted, so forcibly recalled to Adeline's mind the situation of Theodore, that she with difficulty supported herself to the apartment of La Motte. When he saw her, a gleam of joy passed over his countenance; but again relapsing into despondency, he looked mournfully at her, and then at Louis, and groaned deeply. Adeline, in whom all remembrance of his former cruelty was lost in his subsequent kindness, expressed her thankfulness for the life he had preserved, and her anxiety to serve him, in warm and repeated terms. But her gratitude evidently distressed him; instead of reconciling him to himself, it seemed to awaken a remembrance of the guilty designs he had once assisted, and to strike the pangs of conscience deeper in his heart. Endeavouring to conceal his emotions, he entered on the subject of his present danger, and informed Adeline what testimony would be required of her on the trial. After above an hour's conversation with La Motte, she returned to the lodgings of Madame, where, languid and ill, she withdrew to her chamber, and tried to obliviate her anxieties in sleep.

The Parliament which conducted the trial re-assembled in a few days after the arrival of Adeline, and the two remaining witnesses of the Marquis, on whom he now rested his cause against La Motte, appeared. She was led trembling into the court, where almost the first object that met her eyes was the Marquis de Montalt, whom she now beheld with an emotion entirely new to her, and which was strongly tinctured with horror. When Du Bosse saw her he immediately swore to her identity; his testimony was confirmed by her manner; for, on perceiving him she grew pale, and an universal tremor seized her. Jean D'Aunoy could no where be found, and La Motte was thus deprived of an evidence which essentially affected his interest. Adeline, when called upon, gave her little narrative with clearness and precision; and Peter, who had conveyed her from the abbey, supported the testimony she offered. The evidence produced was sufficient to criminate the Marquis of the intention of murder, in the minds of most people present; but it was not sufficient to affect the testimony of his two last witnesses, who positively swore to the commission of the robbery, and to the person of La Motte, on whom sentence of death was accordingly pronounced. On receiving the sentence the unhappy criminal fainted, and the compassion of the assembly, whose feelings had been unusually interested in the decision, was expressed in a general groan.

Their attention was quickly called to a new object—it was Jean D'Aunoy, who now entered the court. But his evidence, if it could ever, indeed, have been the means of saving La Motte, came too late. He was reconducted to prison; but Adeline, who, extremely shocked by his sentence, was much indisposed, received orders to remain in the court during the examination of D'Aunoy. This man had been at length found in the prison of a provincial town, where some of his creditors had thrown him, and from which even the money which the Marquis had remitted to him for the purpose of satisfying the craving importunities of Du Bosse, had been insufficient to release him. Meanwhile the revenge of the latter had been roused against the Marquis by an imaginary neglect, and the money which was designed to relieve his necessities, was spent by D'Aunoy in riotous luxury.

He was confronted with Adeline and with Du Bosse, and ordered to confess all he knew concerning this mysterious affair, or to undergo the torture. D'Aunoy, who was ignorant how far the suspicions concerning the Marquis extended, and who was conscious that his own words might condemn him, remained for some time obstinately silent; but when the question was administered, his resolution gave way, and he confessed a crime of which he had not even been suspected.

It appeared, that, in the year 1642, D'Aunoy, together with one Jaques Martigny, and Francis Balliere, had way-laid and seized Henri, Marquis de Montalt, half-brother to Philippe; and after having robbed him, and bound his servant to a tree, according to the orders they had received, they conveyed him to the abbey of St. Clair, in the distant forest of Fontanville. Here he was confined for some time, till further directions were received from Philippe de Montalt, the present Marquis, who was then on his estates in a northern province of France. These orders were for death, and the unfortunate Henri was assassinated in his chamber in the third week of his confinement at the abbey.

On hearing this, Adeline grew faint: she remembered the MS. she had found, together with the extraordinary circumstances that had attended the discovery; every nerve thrilled with horror, and, raising her eyes, she saw the countenance of the Marquis overspread with the livid paleness of guilt. She endeavoured, however, to arrest her fleeting spirits while the man proceeded in his confession.

When the murder was perpetrated, D'Aunoy had returned to his employer, who gave him the reward agreed upon, and in a few months after delivered into his hands the infant daughter of the late Marquis, whom he conveyed to a distant part of the kingdom, where, assuming the name of St. Pierre, he brought her up as his own child, receiving from the present Marquis a considerable annuity for his secrecy.

Adeline, no longer able to struggle with the tumult of emotions that now rushed upon her heart, uttered a deep sigh and fainted away. She was carried from the court; and when the confusion occasioned by this circumstance subsided, Jean D'Aunoy went on. He related, that on the death of his wife, Adeline was placed in a convent, from whence she was afterwards removed to another, where the Marquis had destined her to receive the vows. That her determined rejection of them had occasioned him to resolve upon her death, and that she had accordingly been removed to the house on the heath. D'Aunoy added, that by the Marquis's order he had misled Du Bosse with a false story of her birth. Having, after some time, discovered that his comrades had deceived him concerning her death, D'Aunoy separated from them in enmity; but they unanimously determined to conceal her escape from the Marquis, that they might enjoy the recompense of their supposed crime. Some months subsequent to this period, however, D'Aunoy received a letter from the Marquis, charging him with the truth, and promising him a large reward if he would confess where he had placed Adeline. In consequence of this letter, he acknowledged that she had been given into the hands of a stranger; but, who he was, or where he lived, was not known.

Upon these depositions Philippe de Montalt was committed to take his trial for the murder of Henri, his brother; D'Aunoy was thrown into a dungeon of the Chatelet, and Du Bosse was bound to appear as evidence.

The feelings of the Marquis, who, in a prosecution stimulated by revenge, had thus unexpectedly exposed his crimes to the public eye, and betrayed himself to justice, can only be imagined. The passions which had tempted him to the commission of a crime so horrid as that of murder,—and what, if possible, heightened its atrocity, the murder of one connected with him by the ties of blood, and by habits of even infantine association—the passions which had stimulated him to so monstrous a deed, were ambition and the love of pleasure. The first was more immediately gratified by the title of his brother; the latter, by the riches which would enable him to indulge his voluptuous inclinations.

The late Marquis de Montalt, the father of Adeline, received from his ancestors a patrimony very inadequate to support the splendour of his rank; but he had married the heiress of an illustrious family, whose fortune amply supplied the deficiency of his own. He had the misfortune to lose her, for she was amiable and beautiful, soon after the birth of a daughter, and it was then that the present Marquis formed the diabolical design of destroying his brother. The contrast of their characters prevented that cordial regard between them which their near relationship seemed to demand. Henri was benevolent, mild, and contemplative. In his heart reigned the love of virtue; in his manners the strictness of justice was tempered, not weakened, by mercy; his mind was enlarged by science, and adorned by elegant literature. The character of Philippe has been already delineated in his actions; its nicer shades were blended with some shining tints; but these served only to render more striking by contrast the general darkness of the portrait.

He had married a lady, who, by the death of her brother, inherited considerable estates, of which the abbey of St. Clair, and the villa on the borders of the forest of Fontanville, were the chief. His passion for magnificence and dissipation, however, soon involved him in difficulties, and pointed out to him the conveniency of possessing his brother's wealth. His brother and his infant daughter only stood between him and his wishes; how he removed the father has been already related; why he did not employ the same means to secure the child, seems somewhat surprising, unless we admit that a destiny hung over him on this occasion, and that she was suffered to live as an instrument to punish the murderer of her parent. When a retrospect is taken of the vicissitudes and dangers to which she had been exposed from her earliest infancy, it appears as if her preservation was the effect of something more than human policy, and affords a striking instance, that justice, however long delayed, will overtake the guilty.

While the late unhappy Marquis was suffering at the abbey, his brother, who, to avoid suspicion, remained in the north of France, delayed the execution of his horrid purpose from a timidity natural to a mind not yet inured to enormous guilt. Before he dared to deliver his final orders, he waited to know whether the story he contrived to propagate of his brother's death would veil his crime from suspicion. It succeeded but too well; for the servant, whose life had been spared that he might relate the tale, naturally enough concluded that his lord had been murdered by banditti; and the peasant, who, a few hours after, found the servant wounded, bleeding, and bound to a tree, and knew also that this spot was infested by robbers, as naturally believed him, and spread the report accordingly.

From this period the Marquis, to whom the abbey of St. Clair belonged in right of his wife, visited it only twice, and that at distant times, till, after an interval of several years, he accidentally found La Motte its inhabitant. He resided at Paris and on his estate in the north, except that once a year he usually passed a month at his delightful villa on the borders of the forest. In the busy scenes of the court, and in the dissipations of pleasure, he tried to lose the remembrance of his guilt; but there were times when the voice of conscience would be heard, though it was soon again lost in the tumult of the world.

It is probable, that on the night of his abrupt departure from the abbey, the solitary silence and gloom of the hour, in a place which had been the scene of his former crime, called up the remembrance of his brother with a force too powerful for fancy, and awakened horrors which compelled him to quit the polluted spot. If it was so, it is however certain that the spectres of conscience vanished with the darkness; for on the following day he returned to the abbey, though, it may be observed, he never attempted to pass another night there. But though terror was roused for a transient moment, neither pity nor repentance succeeded; since, when the discovery of Adeline's birth excited apprehension for his own life, he did not hesitate to repeat the crime, and would again have stained his soul with human blood. This discovery was effected by means of a seal bearing the arms of her mother's family, which was impressed on the note his servant had found, and had delivered to him at Caux. It may be remembered, that having read this note, he was throwing it from him in the fury of jealousy; but, that after examining it again, it was carefully deposited in his pocket-book. The violent agitation which a suspicion of this terrible truth occasioned, deprived him for awhile of all power to act. When he was well enough to write, he dispatched a letter to D'Aunoy, the purport of which has been already mentioned. From D'Aunoy he received the confirmation of his fears. Knowing that his life must pay the forfeiture of his crime, should Adeline ever obtain a knowledge of her birth, and not daring again to confide in the secrecy of a man who had once deceived him, he resolved, after some deliberation, on her death. He immediately set out for the abbey, and gave those directions concerning her which terror for his own safety, still more than a desire of retaining her estates, suggested.

As the history of the seal which revealed the birth of Adeline is rather remarkable, it may not be amiss to mention, that it was stolen from the Marquis, together with a gold watch, by Jean D'Aunoy: the watch was soon disposed of, but the seal had been kept as a pretty trinket by his wife, and at her death went with Adeline among her clothes to the convent. Adeline had carefully preserved it, because it had once belonged to the woman whom she believed to have been her mother.

CHAPTER XXIV

While anxious doubt distracts the tortured heart.

We now return to the course of the narrative, and to Adeline, who was carried from the court to the lodging of Madame de La Motte. Madame was, however, at the Chatelet with her husband, suffering all the distress which the sentence pronounced against him might be supposed to inflict. The feeble frame of Adeline, so long harassed by grief and fatigue, almost sunk under the agitation which the discovery of her birth excited. Her feelings on this occasion were too complex to be analysed. From an orphan, subsisting on the bounty of others, without family, with few friends, and pursued by a cruel and powerful enemy, she saw herself suddenly transformed to the daughter of an illustrious house, and the heiress of immense wealth. But she learned also that her father had been murdered—murdered in the prime of his days—murdered by means of his brother, against whom she must now appear, and in punishing the destroyer of her parent, doom her uncle to death.

When she remembered the manuscript so singularly found, and considered that when she wept to the sufferings it described, her tears had flowed for those of her father, her emotion cannot easily be imagined. The circumstances attending the discovery of these papers no longer appeared to be a work of chance, but of a Power whose designs are great and just. O, my father! she would exclaim, your last wish is fulfilled—the pitying heart you wished might trace your sufferings shall avenge them.

On the return of Madame La Motte, Adeline endeavoured, as usual, to suppress her own emotions, that she might soothe the affliction of her friend. She related what had passed in the courts after the departure of La Motte, and thus excited, even in the sorrowful heart of Madame, a momentary gleam of satisfaction. Adeline determined to recover, if possible, the manuscript. On inquiry she learned that La Motte, in the confusion of his departure, had left it among other things at the abbey. This circumstance much distressed her, the more so because she believed its appearance might be of importance on the approaching trial; she determined, however, if she could recover her rights, to have the manuscript sought for.

In the evening Louis joined this mournful party: he came immediately from his father, whom he left more tranquil than he had been since the fatal sentence was pronounced. After a silent and melancholy supper they separated for the night; and Adeline, in the solitude of her chamber, had leisure to meditate on the discoveries of this eventful day. The sufferings of her dead father, such as she had read them recorded by his own hand, pressed most forcibly to her thoughts. The narrative had formerly so much affected her heart, and interested her imagination, that her memory now faithfully reflected each particular circumstance there disclosed. But when she considered that she had been in the very chamber where her parent had suffered, where even his life had been sacrificed, and that she had probably seen the very dagger, seen it stained with rust, the rust of blood! by which he had fallen, the anguish and horror of her mind defied all control.

On the following day Adeline received orders to prepare for the prosecution of the Marquis de Montalt, which was to commence as soon as the requisite witnesses could be collected. Among these were the abbess of the convent, who had received her from the hands of D'Aunoy; Madame La Motte, who was present when Du Bosse compelled her husband to receive Adeline; and Peter, who had not only been witness to this circumstance, but who had conveyed her from the abbey that she might escape the designs of the Marquis. La Motte and Theodore La Luc were incapacitated by the sentence of the law from appearing on the trial.

When La Motte was informed of the discovery of Adeline's birth, and that her father had been murdered at the abbey of St. Clair, he instantly remembered, and mentioned to his wife, the skeleton he found in the stone room leading to the subterranean cells. Neither of them doubted, from the situation in which it lay, hid in a chest in an obscure room strongly guarded, that La Motte had seen the remains of the late Marquis. Madame, however, determined not to shock Adeline with the mention of this circumstance till it should be necessary to declare it on the trial.

As the time of this trial drew near, the distress and agitation of Adeline increased. Though justice demanded the life of the murderer, and though the tenderness and pity which the idea of her father called forth, urged her to revenge his death, she could not without horror consider herself as the instrument of dispensing that justice which would deprive a fellow-being of existence; and there were times when she wished the secret of her birth had never been revealed. If this sensibility was, in her peculiar circumstances, a weakness, it was at least an amiable one, and as such deserves to be reverenced.

The accounts she received from Vaceau of the health of M. La Luc did not contribute to tranquillize her mind. The symptoms described by Clara seemed to say that he was in the last stage of a consumption, and the grief of Theodore and herself on this occasion was expressed in her letters with the lively eloquence so natural to her. Adeline loved and revered La Luc for his own worth, and for the parental tenderness he had shown her; but he was still dearer to her as the father of Theodore and her concern for his declining state was not inferior to that of his children. It was increased by the reflection that she had probably been the means of shortening his life; for she too well knew that the distress occasioned him by the situation in which it had been her misfortune to involve Theodore, had shattered his frame to its present infirmity. The same cause also withheld him from seeking in the climate of Montpellier the relief he had formerly been taught to expect there. When she looked around on the condition of her friends, her heart was almost overwhelmed with the prospect; it seemed as if she was destined to involve all those most dear to her in calamity. With respect to La Motte, whatever were his vices, and whatever the designs in which he had formerly engaged against her, she forgot them all in the service he had finally rendered her; and considered it to be as much her duty, as she felt it to be her inclination, to intercede in his behalf. This, however, in her present situation, she could not do with any hope of success; but if the suit, upon which depended the establishment of her rank, her fortune, and consequently her influence, should be decided in her favour, she determined to throw herself at the king's feet, and when she pleaded the cause of Theodore, ask the life of La Motte.

A few days preceding that of the trial, Adeline was informed a stranger desired to speak with her; and on going to the room where he was, she found M. Verneuil. Her countenance expressed both surprise and satisfaction at this unexpected meeting, and she inquired, though with little expectation of an affirmative, if he had heard of M. La Luc. I have seen him, said M. Verneuil; I am just come from Vaceau: but, I am sorry I cannot give you a better account of his health; he is greatly altered since I saw him before.

Adeline could scarcely refrain from tears at the recollection these words revived of the calamities which had occasioned this lamented change. M. Verneuil delivered her a packet from Clara. As he presented it, he said, besides this introduction to your notice, I have a claim of a different kind, which I am proud to assert, and which will perhaps justify the permission I ask of speaking upon your affairs.—Adeline bowed; and M. Verneuil, with a countenance expressive of the most tender solicitude, added, that he had heard of the late proceedings of the Parliament of Paris, and of the discoveries that so intimately concerned her. I know not, continued he, whether I ought to congratulate or condole with you on this trying occasion. That I sincerely sympathize in all that concerns you I hope you will believe, and I cannot deny myself the pleasure of telling you that I am related, though distantly, to the late Marchioness your mother—for that she was your mother I cannot doubt.

Adeline rose hastily and advanced towards M. Verneuil; surprise and satisfaction reanimated her features. Do I indeed see a relation? said she in a sweet and tremulous voice; and one whom I can welcome as a friend? Tears trembled in her eyes; and she received M. Verneuil's embrace in silence. It was some time before her emotion would permit her to speak.

To Adeline, who from her earliest infancy had been abandoned to strangers, a forlorn and helpless orphan; who had never till lately known a relation, and who then found one in the person of an inveterate enemy; to her this discovery was as delightful as unexpected. But, after struggling for some time with the various emotions that pressed upon her heart, she begged of M. Verneuil permission to withdraw till she could recover composure. He would have taken leave, but she entreated him not to go.

The interest which M. Verneuil took in the concerns of La Luc, which was strengthened by his increasing regard for Clara, had drawn him to Vaceau, where he was informed of the family and peculiar circumstances of Adeline. On receiving this intelligence he immediately set out for Paris, to offer his protection and assistance to his newly-discovered relation, and to aid, if possible, the cause of Theodore.

Adeline in a short time returned, and could then bear to converse on the subject of her family. M. Verneuil offered her his support and assistance, if they should be found necessary. But I trust, added he, to the justice of your cause, and hope it will not require any adventitious aid. To those who remember the late Marchioness, your features bring sufficient evidence of your birth. As a proof that my judgment in this instance is not biassed by prejudice, the resemblance struck me when I was in Savoy, though I knew the Marchioness only by her portrait; and I believe I mentioned to M. La Luc that you often reminded me of a deceased relation. You may form some judgment of this yourself, added M. Verneuil, taking a miniature from his pocket. This was your amiable mother.

Adeline's countenance changed; she received the picture eagerly, gazed on it for a long time in silence, and her eyes filled with tears. It was not the resemblance she studied; but the countenance—the mild and beautiful countenance of her parent, whose blue eyes, full of tender sweetness, seemed bent upon hers, while a soft smile played on her lips; Adeline pressed the picture to hers, and again gazed in silent reverie. At length, with a deep sigh, she said. This surely was my mother. Had she but lived—O, my poor father! you had been spared. This reflection quite overcame her, and she burst into tears. M. Verneuil did not interrupt her grief, but took her hand and sat by her without speaking, till she became more composed. Again kissing the picture, she held it out to him with a hesitating look. No, said he, it is already with its true owner. She thanked him with a smile of ineffable sweetness; and after some conversation on the subject of the approaching trial, on which occasion she requested M. Verneuil would support her by his presence, he withdrew, having begged leave to repeat his visit on the following day.

Adeline now opened her packet, and saw once more the well known characters of Theodore: for a moment She felt as if in his presence, and the conscious blush overspread her cheek. With a trembling hand she broke the seal, and read the tenderest assurances and solicitates of his love. She often paused that she might prolong the sweet emotions which these assurances awakened; but while tears of tenderness stood trembling on her eyelids, the bitter recollection of his situation would return, and they fell in anguish on her bosom.

He congratulated her, and with peculiar delicacy, on the prospects of life which were opening to her; said, every thing that might tend to animate and support her, but avoided dwelling on his own circumstances, except by expressing his sense of the zeal and kindness of his commanding officer, and adding that he did not despair of finally obtaining a pardon.

This hope, though but faintly expressed, and written evidently for the purpose of consoling Adeline, did not entirely fail of the desired effect. She yielded to its enchanting influence, and forgot for awhile the many subjects of care and anxiety which surrounded her. Theodore said little of his father's health; what he did say was by no means so discouraging as the accounts of Clara, who, less anxious to conceal a truth that must give pain to Adeline, expressed without reserve all her apprehension and concern.

CHAPTER XXV

...... Heaven is just! And, when the measure of his crimes is full, Will bare its red right arm, and launch its lightnings. MASON.

The day of the trial so anxiously awaited, and on which the fate of so many persons depended, at length arrived. Adeline, accompanied by M. Verneuil and Madame La Motte, appeared as the prosecutor of the Marquis de Montalt; and D'Aunoy, Du Bosse, Louis de La Motte, and several other persons, as witnesses in her cause. The judges were some of the most distinguished in France, and the advocates on both sides men of eminent abilities. On a trial of such importance the court, as may be imagined, was crowded with persons of distinction, and the spectacle it presented was strikingly solemn, yet magnificent.

When she appeared before the tribunal, Adeline's emotion surpassed all the arts of disguise; but, adding to the natural dignity of her air an expression of soft timidity, and to her downcast eyes a sweet confusion, it rendered her an object still more interesting; and she attracted the universal pity and admiration of the assembly. When she ventured to raise her eyes, she perceived that the Marquis was not yet in the court; and while she awaited his appearance in trembling expectation, a confused murmuring rose in a distant part of the hall. Her spirits now almost forsook her; the certainty of seeing immediately, and consciously, the murderer of her father, chilled her with horror, and she was with difficulty preserved from fainting. A low sound now ran through the court, and an air of confusion appeared, which was soon communicated to the tribunal itself. Several of the members arose, some left the hall, the whole place exhibited a scene of disorder, and a report at length reached Adeline that the Marquis de Montalt was dying. A considerable time elapsed in uncertainty: but the confusion continued; the Marquis did not appear, and at Adeline's request M. Verneuil went in quest of more positive information.

He followed a crowd which was hurrying towards the Chatelet, and with some difficulty gained admittance into the prison; but the porter at the gate, whom he had bribed for a passport, could give him no certain information on the subject of his inquiry, and not being at liberty to quit his post, furnished M. Verneuil with only a vague direction to the Marquis's apartment. The courts were silent and deserted; but as he advanced, a distant hum of voices led him on, till, perceiving several persons running towards a staircase which appeared beyond the archway of a long passage, he followed thither, and learned that the Marquis was certainly dying. The staircase was filled with people; he endeavoured to press through the crowd, and after much struggle and difficulty he reached the door of an ante-room which communicated with the apartment where the Marquis lay, and whence several persons now issued. Here he learned that the object of his inquiry was already dead. M. Verneuil, however, pressed through the ante-room to the chamber where lay the Marquis on a bed surrounded by officers of the law, and two notaries, who appeared to have been taking down depositions. His countenance was suffused with a black and deadly hue, and impressed with the horrors of death. M. Verneuil turned away, shocked by the spectacle; and on inquiry heard that the Marquis had died by poison.

It appeared that, convinced he had nothing to hope from his trial, he had taken this method of avoiding an ignominious death. In the last hours of life, while tortured with the remembrance of his crime, he resolved to make all the atonement that remained for him; and having swallowed the potion, he immediately sent for a confessor to take a full confession of his guilt, and two notaries, and thus establish Adeline beyond dispute in the rights of her birth: and also bequeathed her a considerable legacy.

In consequence of these depositions she was soon after formally acknowledged as the daughter and heiress of Henri, Marquis de Montalt, and the rich estates of her father were restored to her. She immediately threw herself at the feet of the king in behalf of Theodore and of La Motte. The character of the former, the cause in which he had risked his life, the occasion of the late Marquis's enmity towards him, were circumstances so notorious and so forcible, that it is more than probable the monarch would have granted his pardon to a pleader less irresistible than was Adeline de Montalt. Theodore La Luc not only received an ample pardon, but, in consideration of his gallant conduct towards Adeline, he was soon after raised to a post of considerable rank in the army.

For La Motte, who had been condemned for the robbery on full evidence, and who had been also charged with the crime which had formerly compelled him to quit Paris, a pardon could not be obtained; but, at the earnest supplication of Adeline, and in consideration of the service he had finally rendered her, his sentence was softened from death to banishment. This indulgence, however, would have availed him little, had not the noble generosity of Adeline silenced other prosecutions that were preparing against him, and bestowed on him a sum more than sufficient to support his family in a foreign country. This kindness operated so powerfully upon his heart, which had been betrayed through weakness rather than natural depravity, and awakened so keen a remorse for the injuries he had once meditated against a benefactress so noble, that his former habits became odious to him, and his character gradually recovered the hue which it would probably always have worn had he never been exposed to the tempting dissipations of Paris.

The passion which Louis had so long owned for Adeline was raised almost to adoration by her late conduct; but he now relinquished even the faint hope which he had hitherto almost unconsciously cherished; and since the life which was granted to Theodore rendered this sacrifice necessary, he could not repine. He resolved, however, to seek in absence the tranquillity he had lost, and to place his future happiness on that of two persons so deservedly dear to him.

On the eve of his departure, La Motte and his family took a very affecting leave of Adeline; he left Paris for England, where it was his design to settle; and Louis, who was eager to fly from her enchantments, set out on the same day for his regiment.

Adeline remained some time at Paris to settle her affairs, where she was introduced by M. Verneuil to the few and distant relations that remained of her family. Among these were the Count and Countess D——, and the Monsieur Amand who had so much engaged her pity and esteem at Nice. The lady whose death he lamented was of the family of De Montalt; and the resemblance which he had traced between her features and those of Adeline, her cousin, was something more than the effect of fancy. The death of his elder brother had abruptly recalled him from Italy; but Adeline had the satisfaction to observe, that the heavy melancholy which formerly oppressed him, had yielded to a sort of placid resignation, and that his countenance was often enlivened by a transient gleam of cheerfulness.

The Count and Countess D——, who were much interested by her goodness and beauty, invited her to make their hotel her residence while she remained at Paris.

Her first care was to have the remains of her parent removed from the abbey of St. Clair, and deposited in the vault of his ancestors. D'Aunoy was tried, condemned, and hanged, for the murder. At the place of execution he had described the spot where the remains of the Marquis were concealed, which was in the stone room already mentioned belonging to the abbey. M. Verneuil accompanied the officers appointed for the search, and attended the ashes of the Marquis to St. Maur, an estate in one of the northern provinces. There they were deposited with the solemn funeral pomp becoming his rank; Adeline attended as chief mourner; and this last duty paid to the memory of her parent, she became more tranquil and resigned. The MS. that recorded his sufferings had been found at the abbey, and delivered to her by M. Verneuil, and she preserved it with the pious enthusiasm so sacred a relique deserved.

On her return to Paris, Theodore La Luc, who was come from Montpellier, awaited her arrival. The happiness of this meeting was clouded by the account he brought of his father, whose extreme danger had alone withheld him from hastening the moment he obtained his liberty to thank Adeline for the life she had preserved. She now received him as the friend to whom she was indebted for her preservation, and as the lover who deserved and possessed her tenderest affection. The remembrance of the circumstances under which they had last met, and of their mutual anguish, rendered more exquisite the happiness of the present moments, when, no longer oppressed by the horrid prospect of ignominious death and final separation, they looked forward only to the smiling days that awaited them, when hand in hand they should tread the flowery scenes of life. The contrast which memory drew of the past with the present, frequently drew tears of tenderness and gratitude to their eyes; and the sweet smile which seemed struggling to dispel from the countenance of Adeline those gems of sorrow, penetrated the heart of Theodore, and brought to his recollection a little song which in other circumstances he had formerly sung to her. He took up a lute that lay on the table, and touching the dulcet chords, accompanied it with the following words:—

SONG

The rose that weeps with morning dew,And glitters in the sunny ray,In tears and smiles resembles you,When Love breaks sorrow's cloud away.

The dews that bend the blushing flowerEnrich the scent—renew the glow;So Love's sweet tears exalt his power,So bliss more brightly shines by woe!

Her affection for Theodore had induced Adeline to reject several suitors whom her goodness, beauty, and wealth, had already attracted, and who, though infinitely his superiors in point of fortune, were many of them inferior to him in family, and all of them in merit.

The various and tumultuous emotions which the late events had called forth in the bosom of Adeline were now subsided; but the memory of her father still tinctured her mind with a melancholy that time only could subdue; and she refused to listen to the supplications of Theodore, till the period she had prescribed for her mourning should be expired. The necessity of rejoining his regiment obliged him to leave Paris within the fortnight after his arrival; but he carried with him assurance of receiving her hand soon after she should lay aside her sable habit, and departed therefore with tolerable composure.

M. La Luc's very precarious state was a source of incessant disquietude to Adeline, and she determined to accompany M. Verneuil, who was now the declared lover of Clara, to Montpellier, whither La Luc had immediately gone on the liberation of his son. For this journey she was preparing, when she received from her friend a flattering account of his amendment; and as some further settlement of her affairs required her presence at Paris, she deferred her design, and M. Verneuil departed alone.

When Theodore's affairs assumed a more favourable aspect, M. Verneuil had written to La Luc, and communicated to him the secret of his heart respecting Clara. La Luc, who admired and esteemed M. Verneuil, and who was not ignorant of his family connexions, was pleased with the proposed alliance. Clara thought she had never seen any person whom she was so much inclined to love; and M. Verneuil received an answer favourable to his wishes, and which encouraged him to undertake the present journey to Montpellier.

The restoration of his happiness and the climate of Montpellier did all for the health of La Luc that his most anxious friends could wish, and he was at length so far recovered as to visit Adeline at her estate of St. Maur. Clara and M. Verneuil accompanied him, and a cessation of hostilities between France and Spain soon after permitted Theodore to join this happy party. When La Luc, thus restored to those most dear to him, looked back on the miseries he had escaped, and forward to the blessings that awaited him, his heart dilated with emotions of exquisite joy and gratitude; and his venerable countenance, softened by an expression of complacent delight, exhibited a perfect picture of happy age.

CHAPTER XXVI

Last came Joy's ecstatic trial:—

They would have thought who heard the strain,They saw in Tempe's vale her native maidsAmidst the festal sounding shades,To some unwearied minstrel dancing,While as his flying fingers kiss'd the strings,Love framed with mirth a gay fantastic round.
ODE TO THE PASSIONS.

Adeline, in the society of friends so beloved, lost the impression of that melancholy which the fate of her parent had occasioned: she recovered all her natural vivacity; and when she threw off the mourning habit which filial piety had required her to assume, she gave her hand to Theodore. The nuptials, which were celebrated at St. Maur, were graced by the presence of the Count and Countess D——; and La Luc had the supreme felicity of confirming on the same day the flattering destinies of both his children. When the ceremony was over, he blessed and embraced them all with tears of fatherly affection. I thank thee, O God! that I have been permitted to see this hour, said he; whenever it shall please thee to call me hence, I shall depart in peace.

Long, very long, may you be spared to bless your children! replied Adeline. Clara kissed her father's hand and wept: Long, very long! she repeated in a voice scarcely audible. La Luc smiled cheerfully, and turned the conversation to a subject less affecting.

But the time now drew nigh when La Luc thought it necessary to return to the duties of his parish, from which he had so long been absent. Madame La Luc too, who had attended him during the period of his danger at Montpellier, and hence returned to Savoy, complained much of the solitude of her life; and this was with her brother an additional motive for his speedy departure. Theodore and Adeline, who could not support the thought of a separation, endeavoured to persuade him to give up his chateau, and to reside with them in France; but he was held by many ties to Leloncourt. For many years he had constituted the comfort and happiness of his parishioners; they revered and loved him as a father—he regarded them with an affection little short of parental. The attachment they discovered towards him on his departure was not forgotten either; it had made a deep impression on his mind, and he could not bear the thought of forsaking them now that Heaven had showered on him its abundance. It is sweet to live for them, said he, and I will also die amongst them. A sentiment also of a more tender nature,—(and let not the stoic profane it with the name of weakness, or the man of the world scorn it as unnatural)—a sentiment still more tender attached him to Leloncourt,—the remains of his wife reposed there.

Since La Luc would not reside in France, Theodore and Adeline, to whom the splendid gaieties that courted them at Paris, were very inferior temptations to the sweet domestic pleasures and refined society which Leloncourt would afford, determined to accompany La Luc and Monsieur and Madame Verneuil abroad. Adeline arranged her affairs so as to render her residence in France unnecessary; and having bid an affectionate adieu to the Count and Countess D——, and to M. Amand, who had recovered a tolerable degree of cheerfulness, she departed with her friends for Savoy.

They travelled leisurely, and frequently turned out of their way to view whatever was worthy of observation. After a long and pleasant journey they came once more within view of the Swiss mountains, the sight of which revived a thousand interesting recollections in the mind of Adeline. She remembered the circumstances and the sensations under which she had first seen them—when an orphan, flying from persecution to seek shelter among strangers, and lost to the only person on earth whom she loved—she remembered this, and the contrast of the present moment struck with all its force upon her heart.

The countenance of Clara brightened into smiles of the most animated delight as she drew near the beloved scenes of her infant pleasures; and Theodore, often looking from the windows, caught with patriotic enthusiasm the magnificent and changing scenery which the receding mountains successively disclosed.

It was evening when they approached within a few miles of Leloncourt, and the road winding round the foot of a stupendous crag, presented them a full view of the lake, and of the peaceful dwelling of La Luc. An exclamation of joy from the whole party announced the discovery, and the glance of pleasure was reflected from every eye. The sun's last light gleamed upon the waters that reposed in "crystal purity" below, mellowed every feature of the landscape, and touched with purple splendour the clouds that rolled along the mountain tops.

La Luc welcomed his family to his happy home, and sent up a silent thanksgiving that he was permitted thus to return to it. Adeline continued to gaze upon each well known object; and again reflecting on the vicissitudes of grief and joy, and the surprising change of fortune which she had experienced since last she saw them, her heart dilated with gratitude and complacent delight. She looked at Theodore, whom in these very scenes she had lamented as lost to her for ever; who, when found again, was about to be torn from her by an ignominious death; but, who now sat by her side her secure and happy husband, the pride of his family and herself; and while the sensibility of her heart flowed in tears from her eyes, a smile of ineffable tenderness told him all she felt. He gently pressed her hand, and answered her with a look of love.

Peter, who now rode up to the carriage with a face fall of joy and of importance, interrupted a course of sentiment which was become almost too interesting. Ah! my dear master! cried he, welcome home again. Here is the village, God bless it! It is worth a million such places as Paris. Thank St. Jaques, we are all come safe back again.

This effusion of honest Peter's joy was received and answered with the kindness it deserved. As they drew near the lake, music sounded over the water, and they presently saw a large party of the villagers assembled on a green spot that sloped to the very margin of the waves, and dancing in all their holiday finery. It was the evening of a festival. The elder peasants sat under the shade of the trees that crowned this little eminence, eating milk and fruits, and watching their sons and daughters frisk it away to the sprightly notes of the tabor and pipe, which was joined by the softer tones of a mandolin.

The scene was highly interesting; and what added to its picturesque beauty was a group of cattle that stood, some on the brink, some half in the water, and others reposing on the green bank, while several peasant girls, dressed in the neat simplicity of their country, were dispensing the milky feast. Peter now rode on first, and a crowd soon collected round him, who, learning that their beloved master was at hand, went forth to meet and welcome him. Their warm and honest expressions of joy diffused an exquisite satisfaction over the heart of the good La Luc, who met them with the kindness of a father, and could scarcely forbear shedding tears to this testimony of their attachment. When the younger part of the peasants heard the news of his arrival, the general joy was such, that, led by the tabor and pipe, they danced before his carriage to the chateau, where they again welcomed him and his family with the enlivening strains of music. At the gate of the chateau they were received by Madame La Luc,—and a happier party never met.

As the evening was uncommonly mild and beautiful, supper was spread in the garden. When the repast was over, Clara, whose heart was all glee, proposed a dance by moonlight. It will be delicious, said she; the moonbeams are already dancing on the waters. See what a stream of radiance they throw across the lake, and how they sparkle round that little promontory on the left. The freshness of the hour too invites to dancing.

They all agreed to the proposal.—And let the good people who have so heartily welcomed us home be called in too, said La Luc: they shall all partake our happiness: there is devotion in making others happy, and gratitude ought to make us devout. Peter, bring more wine, and set some tables under the trees. Peter flew; and while chairs and tables were placing, Clara ran for her favourite lute, the lute which had formerly afforded her such delight, and which Adeline had often touched with a melancholy expression. Clara's light hand now ran over the chords, and drew forth tones of tender sweetness, her voice accompanying the following:

AIR

Now at Moonlight's fairy hoar,When faintly gleams each dewy steep,And vale and mountain, lake and bower,In solitary grandeur sleep;

When slowly sinks the evening breeze,That lulls the mind in pensive care,And Fancy loftier visions sees,Bid music wake the silent air:

Bid the merry merry tabor sound,And with the Fays of lawn or gladeIn tripping circlet beat the groundUnder the high trees' trembling shade.

"Now at Moonlight's fairy hour"Shall Music breathe her dulcet voice,And o'er the waves, with magic power,Call on Echo to rejoice!

Peter, who could not move in a sober step, had already spread refreshments under the trees, and in a short time the lawn was encircled with peasantry. The rural pipe and tabor were placed, at Clara's request, under the shade of her beloved acacias on the margin of the lake; the merry notes of music sounded, Adeline led off the dance, and the mountains answered only to the strains of mirth and melody.

The venerable La Luc, as he sat among the elder peasants, surveyed the scene—his children and people thus assembled round him in one grand compact of harmony and joy—the frequent tear bedewed his cheek, and he seemed to taste the fulness of an exalted delight.

So much was every heart roused to gladness, that the morning dawn began to peep upon the scene of their festivity, when every cottager returned to his home, blessing the benevolence of La Luc.

After passing some weeks with La Luc, M. Verneuil bought a chateau in the village of Leloncourt; and as it was the only one not already occupied, Theodore looked out for a residence in the neighbourhood. At the distance of a few leagues, on the beautiful banks of the lake of Geneva, where the waters retire into a small bay, he purchased a villa. The chateau was characterized by an air of simplicity and taste rather than of magnificence, which, however, was the chief trait in the surrounding scene. The chateau was almost encircled with woods, which formed a grand amphitheatre, swept down to the water's edge, and abounded with wild and romantic walks. Here nature was suffered to sport in all her beautiful luxuriance, except where, here and there, the hand of art formed the foliage to admit a view of the blue waters of the lake, with the white sail that glided by, or of the distant mountains. In front of the chateau the woods opened to a lawn, and the eye was suffered to wander over the lake, whose bosom presented an ever-moving picture, while its varied margin sprinkled with villas, woods, and towns, and crowned beyond with the snowy and sublime Alps, rising point behind point in awful confusion, exhibited a scenery of almost unequalled magnificence.

Here, contemning the splendour of false happiness, and possessing the pure and rational delights of love refined into the most tender friendship, surrounded by the friends so dear to them, and visited by a select and enlightened society—here, in the very bosom of felicity, lived Theodore and Adeline La Luc.

The passion of Louis de La Motte yielded at length to the powers of absence and necessity. He still loved Adeline, but it was with the placid tenderness of friendship; and when, at the earnest invitation of Theodore, he visited the villa, he beheld their happiness with a satisfaction unalloyed by any emotions of envy. He afterwards married a lady of some fortune at Geneva; and resigning his commission in the French service, settled on the borders of the lake, and increased the social delights of Theodore and Adeline.

Their former lives afforded an example of trials well endured—and their present, of virtues greatly rewarded; and this reward they continued to deserve—for, not to themselves was their happiness contracted, but diffused to all who came within the sphere of their influence. The indigent and unhappy rejoiced in their benevolence, the virtuous and enlightened in their friendship, and their children in parents whose example impressed upon their hearts, the precepts offered to their understandings.

THE CASTLES

OF ATHLIN

AND DUNBAYNE,

History arrived in the Highlands of Scotland.

CHAPTER I.

Situation of Athlin Castle.—Sorrow of those who dwell there, caused by the death of the Earl, formerly slain by Malcolm, chief of the tribe of Dunbayne—Retired life of Maltida, widow of the Earl.—First years of his two children, Osbert and Marie.—Young Alleyn.—Beginning of the friendship of Osbert and Alleyn.

Sn the east coast of Scotland, approaching north, in the middle of the site, the most romantic of the mountains, is the castle of Athlin, built on the top of a rock, whose base is in the sea This building is venerable by its antiquity and its Gothic structure, but even more by the virtues which it contains. There reside the widow, still beautiful, and the children of the Earl of Athlin, who perishes by the hand of Malcolm, one of the neighboring chiefs, proud, oppressive, vindictive, and living amidst all the pomp of feudal power, not far from Athlin. Usurpations on the domain of Athlin gave birth to the animosity which broke out between the two chiefs. Their tribes often came to blows, and those of Athlin almost always emerged victorious in these battles. Malcolm, whose pride was wounded by the defeats of his vassals, and whose ambition was restrained by the power of the count, conceived for him that mortal hatred which resistance to favorite passions naturally excites in a soul like his, dominated by arrogance. and little accustomed to contradiction; he solved the death of Athlin. His project was carried out with the cunning which forms the principal trait of his character. In a fight involving the two chiefs in person, he succeeded in surrounding the count, accompanied only by a small part of his troops, and killed him. The death of Athlin was soon followed by the general rout of his tribe, which suffered a terrible carnage, and of which a small number, barely escaping, came to inform Maltida of this horrible event. Maltida, overwhelmed by this story, and deprived, by the loss of her family, from the hope of succeeding in his revenge, refrained from sacrificing the lives of the rest of his vassals; she resigned herself to bearing her misfortunes in silence.

Inconsolable at the death of her husband, Maltida hid herself from the public gaze, and decided to confine herself to her ancient mansion. There, in the midst of her family and her vassals, she devoted herself entirely to the education of her children. A son and a daughter remained to him to share his cares; and their virtues, which showed themselves more every day, promised to reward her for her tenderness. Osbert was in his nineteenth year; he inherited from nature an ardent spirit, susceptible of all kinds of knowledge; education had added to this advantage, that of giving breadth and delicacy to his ideas. His imagination was lively, brilliant; and his heart, which had not yet been cooled by misfortune, was open to warm benevolence.

When we enter the theater of the world, the imagination of youth embellishes every scene, and our soul spreads over all that surrounds us. A feeling of benevolence leads us to believe that every being we meet is good, and to wonder that not every good being is happy. Outrage grips us at the story of injustice and the sight of callousness. The spectacle of misfortune makes our tears flow, sweet tribute of our pity; a virtuous action expands our heart: we bless him who has done it, and we believe ourselves capable of it. But as we go through life, our imagination is forced to abandon some of these sweet chimeras; the sad path of experience leads us to truth, and the objects on which we wear do not sometimes a benevolent gaze, are examined with a stern eye. Then an entirely different scene presents itself. Where was the sweet smile, there is mood and sorrow; heavy shadow has replaced brilliant light, and wretched passions, or repulsive apathy, degrade the features of the principal characters. We turn away in horror from such a sad picture, and try to recall the illusions of our early years; but unfortunately! they disappeared forever. Constrained to see objects as they really are, their deformity becomes less painful to us by degrees. Frequent irritation destroys moral susceptibility, and soon confounded in the world, we swell the number of those who worship him. Then an entirely different scene presents itself. Where was the sweet smile, there is mood and sorrow; heavy shadow has replaced brilliant light, and wretched passions, or repulsive apathy, degrade the features of the principal characters. We turn away in horror from such a sad picture, and try to recall the illusions of our early years; but unfortunately! they disappeared forever. Constrained to see objects as they really are, their deformity becomes less painful to us by degrees. Frequent irritation destroys moral susceptibility, and soon confounded in the world, we swell the number of those who worship him. Then an entirely different scene presents itself. Where was the sweet smile, there is mood and sorrow; heavy shadow has replaced brilliant light, and wretched passions, or repulsive apathy, degrade the features of the principal characters. We turn away in horror from such a sad picture, and try to recall the illusions of our early years; but unfortunately! they disappeared forever. Constrained to see objects as they really are, their deformity becomes less painful to us by degrees. Frequent irritation destroys moral susceptibility, and soon confounded in the world, we swell the number of those who worship him. and miserable passions, or a repulsive apathy, degrade the features of the principal personages. We turn away in horror from such a sad picture, and try to recall the illusions of our early years; but unfortunately! they disappeared forever. Constrained to see objects as they really are, their deformity becomes less painful to us by degrees. Frequent irritation destroys moral susceptibility, and soon confounded in the world, we swell the number of those who worship him. and miserable passions, or a repulsive apathy, degrade the features of the principal personages. We turn away in horror from such a sad picture, and try to recall the illusions of our early years; but unfortunately! they disappeared forever. Constrained to see objects as they really are, their deformity becomes less painful to us by degrees. Frequent irritation destroys moral susceptibility, and soon confounded in the world, we swell the number of those who worship him. they truly are, their deformity becomes less painful to us by degrees. Frequent irritation destroys moral susceptibility, and soon confounded in the world, we swell the number of those who worship him. they truly are, their deformity becomes less painful to us by degrees. Frequent irritation destroys moral susceptibility, and soon confounded in the world, we swell the number of those who worship him.

Marie was seventeen; she joined to the perfections, which are commonly the prerogative of mature age, the touching simplicity of youth. The graces of her face were inferior only to those of her mind, which gave her whole person an inimitable expression.

Twelve years had passed since the count's death. Time, the effect of which is to blunt the sharp point of pain, had changed Maltida's into a gentle melancholy which gave something touching to the natural dignity of her character. Up to this day she had occupied herself only with cultivating those virtues, with which nature had so liberally endowed her children, and which had been further increased by her care; but her heart had just been opened to entirely new solicites. These beloved children had arrived at a dangerous age, both by her tender susceptibility and by the empire which imagination allows the passions to take hold of. We see too often that the impressions received at this time of life can no longer be erased. He was, moreover, for this tender mother, who

From the moment Osbert had been informed of the details of his father's death, he had been burning to avenge it. The count, by his wise government, had made himself adored by his tribe. Everyone wanted to punish Malcolm. Chained by the generous compassion of the Countess, they silenced their murmurs, but they flattered themselves that their young leader would one day lead them to victory and revenge. The time seemed to them to approach when they would be permitted to console themselves for their long sufferings. Maltida's maternal heart would not allow her to think of exposing her son and his vassals; so she forbade Osbert to attempt the chances of combat. He submitted in silence to what was required of him, and strove, by giving himself up to his favorite studies, to repress his fondness for arms. Osbert possessed all the talents befitting a man of his rank, but he especially excelled in military exercises. His noble soul seemed to take particular delight in it; and he tasted a secret pleasure in thinking that the skill he had acquired there might one day serve him in his design to obtain justice for the death of his father. His burning imagination made him cherish poetry, and he practiced it himself. He loved to wander amidst the great scenes which the mountains present at every step, and which, by the wild variety which nature displays there, are calculated to inspire enthusiasm. Seeking large and terrible paintings, he neglected those which were only soft, and often carried away by the need which his imagination felt to be strongly struck,

One day, in one of his races, after having made several miles over mountains covered with heather, whence his eye discovered only the confines of cultivated nature, rocks piled on rocks, high cataracts and vast deserts, he no longer recognized the path he had just cleared for himself. It was in vain that he cast his eyes on all the objects he could discover. For the first time his heart felt fear. Nowhere did he see traces of men; the awful silence of this place was interrupted only by the sound of the falling torrents and the cry of the birds of prey which crossed the air above his head. He began to shout himself, and the deep echoes of the mountains alone answered his voice. For some time he remained motionless and silent. This state had its charm at first, but soon it became so painful that he could no longer bear it. Dejected and almost hopeless, he sought to retrace his steps: nothing he encountered seemed to him to have already struck his sight. Finally, after having wandered for a long time, he came to a narrow path which he entered, succumbing to the fatigue of his useless searches. Scarcely had he taken a few steps when an opening which pierced a rock let him see a site full of beauties. It was a valley surrounded by huge rocks, the base of which was shaded by thick fir trees. A torrent rushed from their summit, and rolling with impetuosity through these majestic woods, was going to throw itself into a vast lake which occupied the middle of the valley, and which we saw lost in the distant gorges of the mountains. Many flocks of sheep wandered over a rich lawn. Osbert's eye was deliciously affected by discovering human habitations: a few well-kept cottages were scattered here and there, not far from the lake. His heart experienced a sensation of joy so vivid that he forgot at first that he had to seek the road by which one could arrive at this Elisha. He was beginning to occupy himself with it when his attention was attracted by a young inhabitant of the mountains, who advanced towards him with an air of benevolence and offered to lead him to his dwelling, as soon as he had learned of his pain. . Osbert accepted this invitation; they descended the mountain together, taking long circuits, by a rough and covered path. Arrived at one of the cottages which Osbert had seen from the height, they entered, and the young mountaineer introduced his guest to his father, who was a venerable old man. Refreshments were brought by a young girl of a graceful face; Osbert, after taking some of them, and staying a few moments in this house, set out accompanied by Alleyn, this young peasant who had wanted to be his guide. Both sought to deceive the length of the march by conversation. Osbert took a keen interest in his companion, in whom he discovered an elevated soul and feelings entirely analogous to his own. On their way they passed a short distance from Dunbayne Castle; this sight threw Osbert into bitter thoughts, and a sudden and involuntary movement escaped him. Alleyn made some observations on the bad policy of an oppressive leader, and cited, as an example, Baron Malcolm. "These lands," he said, "belong to him, and they are scarcely enough to feed his wretched vassals who, groaning under the cruellest extortion, neglect to cultivate them, and thus deprive their lord of much wealth: the tribe threatens to to rise up and to take justice into its own hands. The Baron, full of arrogant confidence, laughs at their complaints, and ignores his danger. If an insurrection breaks out, other tribes will hasten to unite with it to bring about its ruin and strike at the same time the tyrant and the assassin. Astonished by the spirit of independence that reigned in this speech, delivered with unusual energy, Osbert felt his heart beating, and the word, O my father! came out of his lips without him being able to hold it back. Alleyn paused, unsure of the effect of what he had said, but after a moment the full truth dawned on his mind. He recognized the son of this chief, whom he had been taught to love from his earliest childhood, and whose story was engraved in his heart; he wanted to throw himself at her feet and embrace her knees: Osbert restrained him. The astonishment in which the young count was plunged soon ceased when he heard these words, which filled his eyes at once with tears of joy and sadness. "There are other tribes ready, like yours, to avenge the offenses of the noble Earl of Athlin; the Fitz-Henrys will always be the friends of virtue". I' The air of the young mountaineer, while he spoke, was full of a deeply felt dignity, and his eyes animated with the pride that befits virtue. Osbert's soul kindled at these generous remarks; but the image of his mother in tears suddenly tempered his ardor. "O my friend! he resumed, perhaps one day your zeal will be accepted with all the warmth of recognition it deserves. Particular circumstances do not allow me to say more at present". And Alleyn's attachment to his father penetrated to the bottom of his heart. the image of his mother in tears suddenly tempered his ardor. "O my friend! he resumed, perhaps one day your zeal will be accepted with all the warmth of recognition it deserves. Particular circumstances do not allow me to say more at present". And Alleyn's attachment to his father penetrated to the bottom of his heart. the image of his mother in tears suddenly tempered his ardor. "O my friend! he resumed, perhaps one day your zeal will be accepted with all the warmth of recognition it deserves. Particular circumstances do not allow me to say more at present". And Alleyn's attachment to his father penetrated to the bottom of his heart.

The day was already advanced when they arrived at the castle; it was decided that Alleyn would stay there the night.

CHAPTER II.

Annual festival of Athlin Castle: its origin.—The tribe desires to avenge the death of the Earl, and second the plan of Osbert.—Alarms of Maltida and Marie concerning Osbert.—Alleyn falls in love with Marie.— Osbert and Alleyn attack Dunbayne Castle, residence of Malcolm.—They are taken prisoner.—Grief of Maltida and Mary; her tender pity for Alleyn.

The following day was destined to celebrate the annual feast which the count gave to his vassals; he would not consent to Alleyn's departure. The great hall of the castle was filled with tables, and dancing and joy were everywhere. It was the custom for the tribe to assemble in arms, because, two centuries previously, it had been surprised on such a day by an enemy tribe, and it was thus desired to perpetuate the memory of this event.

The morning was devoted to military exercises, in which honorable prizes, intended for those who distinguished themselves the most, excited emulation. From the ramparts of the castle, the Countess and her lovely daughter watched the exploits taking place on the plain. Their attention was aroused, and their curiosity keenly piqued by the appearance of a stranger who wielded the bow and spear with great dexterity, and emerged victorious from all combats. This stranger was Alleyn; he received from the hands of the count, according to custom, the palm of victory, and all the spectators were charmed by his demeanor full of modest dignity.

Le comte assista à la fête. Comme elle finissait, chacun des hôtes, saisissant son verre de la main gauche, tandis que de la droite il tirait son épée, but à la mémoire de son défunt chef. La salle retentit d'un cri général, et ce cri parut à Osbert le tocsin de la guerre. Tous les membres de la tribu se prirent par la main et burent à l'honneur du fils de leur dernier chef. Le jeune Thane comprit ce signal, et bientôt toute espèce de considération eut cédé chez lui au désir de venger son père. Il se leva et adressa à sa tribu un discours rempli du feu de la jeunesse et de l'indignation de la vertu. Pendant qu'il parlait, la contenance de ses vassaux annonçait toute l'impatience de la joie; et dès qu'il eut cessé, un long murmure d'applaudissement se fit entendre dans l'assemblée. Alors chaque homme, croisant son épée avec celle de son voisin, jura, par ce gage sacré, de ne point abandonner la cause dans laquelle il s'engageait, jusqu'à ce que la vie de l'ennemi commun eût acquitté la dette qu'il devait à la justice et à la vengeance.

In the evening, the wives and daughters of the peasants came to the castle and took part in the feast. It was the custom for the Countess and her wives to watch from a gallery the various circles which met for dancing and singing, and the castle girl was to perform a highland dance with the winner of the matinee. Soon Alleyn saw the charming Marie, led by the Count, who had come to present her to him; she received Alleyn's homage with amiable grace. Her dress was that worn by young mountain girls, and her hair, falling in braids over her collar, had, for its only ornament, a simple garland of roses: she danced with the lightness that poets give to graces. The admiration of the spectators was divided between her and the victorious foreigner. Marie, after having danced, retired to the gallery; and everyone, except the earl and Alleyn, spent the rest of the evening in transports of joy. Both had different reasons for concern. Osbert recalled in his mind the events of that day; he yearned to accomplish the designs which filial piety had imposed on him, but he dreaded the effect their revelation would have on Maltida's tender heart. However, he decided to teach them to him the next day, and to attempt, in a few days, the fate of arms. fulfill the purposes which filial piety had imposed on him, but he dreaded the effect their revelation would have on Maltida's tender heart. However, he decided to teach them to him the next day, and to attempt, in a few days, the fate of arms. fulfill the purposes which filial piety had imposed on him, but he dreaded the effect their revelation would have on Maltida's tender heart. However, he decided to teach them to him the next day, and to attempt, in a few days, the fate of arms.

Alleyn, whose heart up to that moment had only been touched by the sorrows of others, began to feel those of his own. His agitated mind offered him the image of Mary: he tried to banish her; but her efforts were so feeble that she constantly represented herself. Satisfied and sad at the same time, he did not want to admit to himself that he loved (so ingenious are we sometimes in deceiving ourselves.) He got up at daybreak and left the a chateau full of lively gratitude and secret love, to go and rouse his friends at the approaching war.

The Count fell into a very restless sleep. As soon as he woke up, he had to think of going to brave his mother's tender resistance; he entered her room with an uncertain step, and showing in his countenance the emotion of his soul. Maltida soon learned from him what his heart had presaged; Overwhelmed by this terrible blow, she fell unconscious in her chair. Osbert ran for help, and Marie and the servants called her back to life and pain.

Osbert's spirit was engaged in the most cruel combat: the duty of a son, honor, revenge commanded him to march; filial tenderness, regret, pity dictated the opposite. Marie was at his feet, and clasping his knees with all the energy of pain, she begged him to abandon his fatal design and thus save the life of that of the authors of his days who had survived. Her tears, her sighs, and the touching abandonment of her bearing spoke louder than her tongue. The silent pain of the Countess was even more eloquent. Osbert, casting his eyes on her, was once ready to yield, when the image of his dying father presented itself to his mind, and restored him to his project. The tender Maltida, given over to all maternal anxiety, already saw his son in the midst of the fray, and the death of his lord recalled at this moment to his memory, awakened the sensations of pain excited by this cruel event, which the consoling time had scarcely diminished. Pity is so amiable in all its developments that we persuade ourselves that it can never go too far; but it becomes a vice when it destroys the resolutions of a stronger virtue. Austere principles guarded the heart of Osbert against its influence and impelled him to take up arms. He called around him those of his tribe who seemed to him the most prudent, and held a council of war. It was decided that Malcolm would be attacked with all the forces that could be mustered and all the promptness that the importance of an expedition of this nature would allow.

At the same time Alleyn busied himself with ardor in joining his friends at Osbert; in a few days he had collected a considerable number of them. Another motive was confused in his heart with the enthusiasm of virtue. It was no longer the simple attachment to the cause of justice that led him to act; the hope of distinguishing himself in the eyes of his mistress, of obtaining her esteem by his eager services, added a new force to the impression given by benevolence. The sweet idea of meriting Marie's gratitude secretly inflamed his soul; for he was still ignorant of the impression he had made on his heart. It was in this state that he returned to the chateau to tell the count that his friends were prepared to follow him whenever he gave the signal.

A few days sufficed for all arrangements: Alleyn and his friends were warned, and the armed tribe, having the young earl at their head, set out.

The separation of Osbert and his family is easy to conceive; but all the pride of an expected victory did not prevent Alleyn from heaving a sigh, when his eyes separated from Marie, who, on the terrace of the castle with the countess, followed with her eyes the progress of her well-to-do brother. loved, until distance had concealed him entirely from his sight. Marie returned to the castle, weeping, and presaging some great calamity; she tried, however, to put on a calm air to deceive Maltida's fears and distract her from her pain. The Countess, whose mind was as strong as her heart was tender, having been unable to prevent this perilous expedition, had gathered all her courage to combat the impressions of fruitless pain, and to seek the advantages that current opportunity offered. His efforts were not in vain; she understood that this enterprise should honor the memory of her murdered lord and bring the punishment on the head of the murderer.

It was one afternoon that the Count left the chateau. At first he followed an opposite route, until night having fallen he marched towards that of Dunbayne. The profound darkness of the weather favored his plan, which consisted in scaling the walls, surprising the sentries, and entering the inner court, sword in hand. Already, with a hurried step, we had made several miles, through arid heather, without being helped by the least ray of light, when suddenly the lugubrious sound of the bell of a clock, which marked the hour of the night, was heard. Everyone's heart beat; they understood that they were near the baron's residence. A halt was ordered to deliberate, and it was decided that the Earl, accompanied by Alleyn and some choice men, should reconnoitre the castle, while the rest of the troop would remain at a slight distance where they would wait for a signal. The count and his small detachment executed their march in silence. A faint light they saw guided them from the clock tower to the castle; they thus arrived at the foot of its walls, and stopped a moment to assure themselves that they heard no movement. Night covered all objects with a thick veil, and the silence of death reigned everywhere. The situation of the castle was examined as much as the darkness would permit. It was an edifice built with Gothic magnificence on high and dangerous rock. The height of its towers, and its vast expanse betrayed the power of its ancient owners. The rock was surrounded by a wide but shallow ditch, on which lay two drawbridges, one on the north side and the other on the east; both were separated about the middle, and had one half lowered on the country side. The bridge placed to the north led to the main gate of the castle, and that of the east to the clock tower. These were the only entrances to the castle. The rock was almost perpendicular with the walls which were high and strong. After considering this situation, Osbert, and his troop, climbed on a mound from which the rock seemed more accessible and was contiguous to the main gate: there they gave the signal to the rest of the tribe. The latter approached noiselessly, and throwing into the ditch the fascines which she had collected, she built a bridge over which she passed, and made his preparations to climb the rock. It had been resolved that a party, commanded by Alleyn, would scale the walls, surprise the sentries, and open the gate to the tribe who were to wait outside with the earl. Alleyn placed his ladder first and climbed: he was soon followed by his companions who, with great difficulty and some danger, managed to reach the top of the ramparts. This troop crossed a part of the platform without hearing the sound of any voice or any step. Everything seemed buried in a deep sleep. A party approached several sentries who were asleep and grabbed them. Alleyn and a few others moved forward to open the nearest door and lower the bridge. This operation was finished, when suddenly the signal of surprise was given; the alarm bell rang, and the chateau resounded with the sound of arms. There was tumult and confusion everywhere. The count and some of his people had passed through the door, when suddenly they saw the portcullis fall; the bridge rose immediately, and the count and his companions found themselves surrounded by an armed multitude which descended in torrents from all the remote places of the castle. Surprised, but not intimidated, Osbert rushed forward, sword in hand, and fought with desperate valour. Alleyn's soul seemed to acquire new vigor in the midst of this disorder; he fought like a man breathing glory and certain of victory: wherever he went the crowd dispersed before him. Reunited with the Count, he had reached the inner courts, where they were looking for the Baron. Both were burning to satisfy a just revenge and end this fight with the death of Malcolm. Once they entered the courtyards, the doors closed behind them; a large troop of guards pressed them on all sides, and, after a short resistance in which Alleyn received a slight wound, they were seized and made prisoners of war. The carnage became terrible; the baron's vassals, filled with fury, were insatiable with blood. Many of those who had followed the count were killed in the courtyards or on the platform; many, trying to escape, rushed from the ramparts, and a large number had perished in the sudden raising of the bridge. A very small part of this brave and generous troop, devoted to the cause of justice, succeeded in getting away from the walls, and survived to bring this terrible news to the Countess. The Earl's fate was entirely unknown to his friends. A particular cause combined to further increase their consternation: it was the astonishing manner in which the victory had just been won; for it was known that Malcolm, save in cases of necessity, never had more soldiers at Dunbayne than feudal pomp required; able to withstand an entire tribe. The secret intelligences of the Baron were unknown: an alarmed conscience kept him in arms for his own safety, and for some years spies, placed by him in the neighborhood of Athlin Castle, had been watching what was going on. went there and gave him an immediate account of all the preparations for war which they noticed. It was unlikely that so public an event as that which took place on the day of the feast, when all the vassals swore to avenge the death of their leader, could escape the watchful eye of Malcolm's hired men. . They had in fact hastened to tell him, accompanying their story with all the exaggerations of fear and astonishment. This news warns him to put himself in defense. What was told him of the Count's military preparations convinced him that he must make haste; and, smiling at these false rumors of a distant war, he brought men and arms into his castle, and held himself ready to receive the assailants. The baron's plan, conducted with great art and secrecy, consisted in letting the enemy scale the walls, to then put them to the sword. But it was nearly aborted, as a result of the sleep to which the sentinels responsible for giving the alarm had given themselves up.

Maltida's courage gave way to such a great calamity; she was attacked by a violent illness which almost ended her sufferings and her life, and made all the tender care of her daughter useless. However, these cares did not remain without effect; Maltida came back to life, and they helped her to bear the hours of affliction which she owed to her uncertainty of the Count's fate. Marie, imbued with all the lamentability of these last events, was unsuited to the role of comforter; but her generous heart, suffering from the deep sorrows of Maltida, endeavored to forget her own sorrows to concern herself only with those of her mother. Often, however, she imagined her brother delivered to the horrors of prison and death, and this frightful image bewildered her reason.

CHAPTER III.

Captivity of Osbert and Alleyn.—Malcolm's scheme of revenge;—He attempts to have Mary kidnapped;—She is rescued by Alleyn who had escaped from his prison.—Record of how Alleyn came to s 'escape: his first attempts are fruitless: two soldiers, in charge of guarding him, flee with him: strange encounter which they have in an underground passage of Dunbayne Castle.—Alleyn plans to deliver his friend Osbert.

O sbert, after having been put in irons, was led into the principal prison of the chateau, and left alone to the most cruel reflections. But the misfortune which shook his firmness could not overcome it, and hope was not yet entirely lost for him. It is the characteristic of great souls to find against the blows of fate a strength which increases unceasingly; the resistance among them becomes vigorous in proportion to the attack; and it may be said that this species of men triumphs over adversity with the weapons it furnishes.

After a while it occurred to Osbert to examine his prison. It was a square chamber, which was at the top of a tower adjoining the eastern side of the castle, from which the mournful roar of the winds could be heard incessantly. The interior walls were dilapidated and threatened with ruin. A mattress placed in one of the corners of the room, a broken mat chair and a shaky table made up all the furniture. Light and air barely penetrated through two narrow windows fitted with large iron bars, one of which gave a glimpse of an inner courtyard, and the other a range of barren and wild mountains.

Alleyn was dragged, through dark conduits, into a remote part of the castle, at the end of which a small iron door opened to show him a dungeon from which light and hope alike were banished. He shivered as he entered, and immediately the door closed behind him.

The spirit of the baron was agitated at the same time by the dark passions of hatred, revenge and irritated pride; he tormented his imagination to invent tortures equal to the violence of his feelings. After long reflections, he persuaded himself that the torture of waiting in uncertainty caused more suffering than the greatest evils against which, as soon as they are known, strong souls stiffen up. He decided, therefore, that the count should remain in the tower, uncertain of the fate reserved for him, and that he should be given enough food to put him in a condition to feel his deplorable situation.

Osbert was buried in his thoughts when he heard the door of his dreadful living room groaning on its hinges; and suddenly Malcolm appeared before him. Osbert's heart swelled with indignation, and defiance flashed in his eyes. "I come," said the insolent conqueror, "to congratulate the Earl of Athlin on his arrival in my castle, and to show him how I know how to exercise hospitality towards my friends; but I admit it I have not yet decided on the party I should give him».

"Cowardly tyrant," replied Osbert, "with all the dignity of virtue, it is for an assassin to insult a vanquished; I do not expect the one who immolated the father to spare the son: but know that the son despises your anger, and that the fear of your cruelty will never be able to shake him».

"Téméraire young man, answered the baron, your words are only wind; your vaunted strength has given way under my power, and it is for me to decide your fate". After these words he left the prison, quivering and furious at the count's unshakable courage.

The sight of Malcolm excited in the soul of Osbert the opposing movements of violent indignation, and tender pity which the memory of his father inspired in him; for a while he was reduced to a most miserable state. The terrible energy of his sensations threw him into a kind of delirium; the firmness he had just shown had entirely disappeared, and he was on the point of renouncing virtue and life, with the help of a short dagger which he kept hidden under his jacket: Suddenly the melodious sound of a lute caught his attention; this instrument was accompanied by a soft and tender voice, which was for the heart of Osbert like a salutary beauty; it seemed to him that heaven was using it to stop him in his designs and change his destiny. The turmoil subsided, and was soon dissolved in tears of pity and repentance. The languor which reigned in the song, seemed to announce that it was that of a being suffering and undoubtedly also prisoner. When he had ceased, Osbert, still full of astonishment, approached the bars of the window to try to discover where these enchanting sounds had come from; but no one presented themselves to his eyes, and he could not judge whether it was from inside or outside the castle. Vainly did he try to get from the guard, who came to bring him a small portion of food, some information about what he had heard; the obstinate silence of Malcolm's satellite left him in his ignorance. a suffering being and no doubt also a prisoner. When he had ceased, Osbert, still full of astonishment, approached the bars of the window to try to discover where these enchanting sounds had come from; but no one presented themselves to his eyes, and he could not judge whether it was from inside or outside the castle. Vainly did he try to get from the guard, who came to bring him a small portion of food, some information about what he had heard; the obstinate silence of Malcolm's satellite left him in his ignorance. a suffering being and no doubt also a prisoner. When he had ceased, Osbert, still full of astonishment, approached the bars of the window to try to discover where these enchanting sounds had come from; but no one presented themselves to his eyes, and he could not judge whether it was from inside or outside the castle. Vainly did he try to get from the guard, who came to bring him a small portion of food, some information about what he had heard; the obstinate silence of Malcolm's satellite left him in his ignorance. and he could not judge whether it was from inside or outside the castle. Vainly did he try to get from the guard, who came to bring him a small portion of food, some information about what he had heard; the obstinate silence of Malcolm's satellite left him in his ignorance. and he could not judge whether it was from inside or outside the castle. Vainly did he try to get from the guard, who came to bring him a small portion of food, some information about what he had heard; the obstinate silence of Malcolm's satellite left him in his ignorance.

Sorrow filled Athlin Castle and its surroundings. The news of the count's imprisonment had finally reached Maltida's ears, and her soul had lost all hope. She immediately sent to offer the baron a large ransom for the freedom of her son and the other prisoners; but the ferocity of Malcolm's soul disdained an incomplete triumph. Vengeance prevailed over his avarice, and the offers were rejected with contempt. Another motive acted on his mind, and confirmed him in his designs. He had often been told of Marie's beauty in such a way as to excite his curiosity; he had succeeded in procuring the means of meeting her; and this sight had kindled in his bosom a passion which the violence of his character prevented from extinguishing. Already he had formed, to obtain it, various projects which had all remained unimplemented; the captivity of the count appeared to him a favorable occasion for his love; he therefore resolved to ask Mary's hand in exchange for his brother's freedom; but he determined not to let his views appear at first, so that the pangs of anxiety and despair acting on Maltida, she might resolve to sacrifice her daughter to her enemy.

The weak remnants of the tribe, resisting the horrible reverse they had just suffered, still had the courage to assemble: and dangerous as was the project of snatching their chief from prison, they stopped. Hope sustained Maltida again; but soon a new source of sorrow was opened for her. Marie's health was noticeably declining: she was silent and pensive: her delicate complexion could not withstand the pains of her mind, and these pains were increased by the effort she made to hide them. She imposed on herself amusement and pleasant exercise, as a means of restoring peace and health more easily to her. One day when, in search of these treasures, she was riding on horseback, she was tempted by the beauty of the evening to prolong her course beyond her ordinary bounds. The sun was setting as she entered a wood whose dark, sad darkness suited the melancholy of her heart perfectly. The peaceful serenity of the weather and the majestic aspect of the place combined to make her fall imperceptibly into a sweet oblivion of her sorrows: she abandoned herself to it with delight, when suddenly she was drawn from it by the sound of the steps of advancing horses. close to her. The thick foliage obstructed her view, but she thought she saw weapons gleaming a short distance away. She turned her horse away and tried to gain the entrance to the wood. His heart, agitated by fear, made him hasten his retreat. Looking behind her, she clearly distinguished three armed and disguised men running after her. Ready to lose consciousness, in vain the dread gave her wings; all her efforts were useless, and the brigands soon overtook her. One of them seized his horse's bridle, and the others fell on the two servants who accompanied him. There was a sharp fight: the strength of his servants was forced to yield to the arms of their adversaries. Overwhelmed, they saw themselves dragged into the woods and tied to trees. Marie, fainting in the arms of the one who had seized her, was carried through dark and silent paths: it is easy to imagine her terror when, opening her eyes, she found herself in the midst of unknown men. Her cries, her tears, her prayers had no effect. These wretches, insensitive to pity and its demands, kept a fierce silence. They led her towards the entrance of a horrible cave: then the most frightful despair seized her, and soon she gave no more sign of life: this state lasted a long time; but it is impossible to express what she felt, when, coming to herself by degrees, she saw Alleyn himself, who, in the liveliest anxiety, awaited his return to life, and whose eyes filled with joy and of tenderness when she began to revive. Astonishment, a joy mingled with fear, and all the symptoms of a host of confused sensations quickly appeared on Marie's face. Her surprise increased still more at the sight of her servants who were ranged beside her. She hardly dared to believe the testimony of her eyes, but Alleyn's voice, trembling with tenderness, dissipated, in a moment, the prestige of her uncertainty, and no longer allowed her to doubt the astonishing reality of the objects whose she was surrounded. No sooner had she regained sufficient strength than they hastened to leave this place of terror; the road was continued at a slow pace, and night had long since fallen when the procession arrived at the chateau. Pain and confusion reigned there. The Countess, filled with the saddest fears, had sent servants on different roads to meet her daughter. In her first transport, she paid no attention when she saw her arrive, that she was accompanied by Alleyn. Soon, however, her joy equaled her astonishment when she recognized the companion of Osbert; and in the midst of the various impressions she experienced, she hardly knew which of the two she should question first. When she had been informed of the perils her daughter had run, and had known him who had torn her from it, she prepared with eager solicitude to hear the news of her beloved son, and how the brave and young mountain dweller had escaped the baron's vigilance. Alleyn could say nothing of the Earl at Maltida, except that he had been taken prisoner with him, within the fortress courts, as they fought side by side; and that, without having received any injury, her son had been conducted to a tower situated at the eastern corner of the castle, where he was still detained. He added that he himself, having been locked up in a remote part of the building, had been unable to obtain any other information on the account of Osbert; then he gave a succinct account of the particular circumstances which concerned them.

He had been in his horrible dungeon for a few weeks, awaiting death every day; his desperate situation made him inventive, and he devised the following plan to escape. He had noticed that the guard, in charge of bringing him his food, took care, on leaving the dungeon, to strike the area near the door with his sword; his curiosity was excited by this circumstance, and a ray of hope shone in the depths of his prison. He examined the ground there as well as the darkness would permit, and found that it was lined, like the rest of his dungeon, with large stones everywhere equally solid. However, he remained none the less certain, according to the usual precautions of the guard, that he must find under this place some way by which he could save himself. and prepared for more exact research when he had no fear of being observed. One day, immediately after the guard had left, Alleyn began to lift the stones that formed the pavement. This work required a great deal of patience and industry, and was executed with a knife which he had withdrawn from the vigilance of the soldiers. At first, under the pavement, the earth seemed firm to him, and in no way indicated that it had been freshly disturbed. After digging a few feet, he discovered a trap; joy and anxiety made him tremble in all his limbs. Night then began to approach; and as he was overwhelmed with fatigue, he feared that he would not be able, before daybreak, to penetrate as far as the trap, and overcome the other obstacles which he still had to encounter; he hastened to throw the earth back into the hole he had made. He had already succeeded, not without great difficulty, in filling it, but it was not possible for him to replace the pavement exactly in its first state. The darkness made it impossible to choose the stones, and he saw that when he succeeded, this new floor would have no solidity. In the overwhelm of his body and his mind, he threw himself on the ground, and gave himself up to the deepest despair. The night was far advanced when the return of his strength and his reason led him to new efforts; he promptly pushed aside the earth and broke the lock of the trapdoor: then raising it, without hesitating or wanting to consider anything, he rushed through the opening. The vault was deep, and he was first knocked down by the violence of his fall. A dull and trembling echo which seemed to propagate in the distance, taught him that this place must have had a considerable extent. No light guided him; he walked with his arms outstretched, in silence, and anxiously seeking to examine the place he was traversing. After wandering for a long time in the void, he came to a wall, which he followed gropingly; he made a fairly long walk in this way, at the end of which he felt that the wall was turning; he did not abandon it, and soon his hand touched the cold bar of a window: a gentle ripple of air struck his face, and it was for him, coming out of the damp vapors of a dungeon, a moment of voluptuousness. The air gave Alleyn new strength; the means of flight which seemed to present themselves revived his courage. He placed his foot against the wall, and seizing with his hand one of the bars of the window, he succeeded in shaking it and tearing it entirely out after repeated efforts. He soon turned to a second, but this one was more firmly fixed; he could not untie it: then he perceived that this bar was sealed in a large stone, and that he had no other means to take than to lift the stone itself. His knife served him again on this occasion; and with much patience he loosened enough mortar to effect his design. After several hours spent in an occupation which the darkness rendered painful and often pointless, he had removed several bars and made an opening which enabled him to escape, when the first rays of day began to appear. It was with inexpressible anguish that he discovered that this window overlooked the inner courtyard of the chateau; soon he noticed soldiers descending slowly into the yard by the narrow steps adjoining their quarters. His heart failed him at the sight: overwhelmed, he leaned against the wall, and was about to enter the yard, and make a desperate effort to save himself, or die in the attempt, when, with the aid of the light, which was becoming more considerable, a thick door, placed in an opposite side of the wall, attracted his eyes; he went to it immediately, and tried to open it, but it was stopped by a latch and several external bolts. He knocked against this door with his foot; a dull noise, which was then heard, indicated that there was a long arch on the other side; and he was assured, by his direction, that it must extend to the outer walls of the castle. He understood that, if he could penetrate beyond this vault the following night, it would be easy for him to scale the wall, and to cross the ditch. There was not enough time left for him to force the latch before the arrival of the guard, who came at daybreak to visit his prison; After a few moments of reflection, he decided to hide in a dark part of the vault, and thus to wait for the guard who, perceiving that the bars of the window had been disturbed, was to conclude that he had escaped through the opening. Hardly, in accordance with this plan, had he placed himself, than the door of the dungeon opened: a loud voice was heard; and the name "Alleyn" was pronounced with the accent of despair and consternation. This cry having been repeated, a man rushed through the opening of the trapdoor. Alleyn, though hidden himself in the darkness, discovered, by the aid of a dim light which fell upon the threshing-floor, a soldier armed with a drawn sword; this one approached the bars of the window, the curse in the mouth: he then went towards the door, and finding it closed, he returned to the window; after which he began to walk along the walls, against which he rested the point of his sword, and thus arrived at the place where Alleyn stood. Alleyn, feeling the sword touch his arm, quickly grabbed the hand that held it, and knocked the weapon to the ground. The fight began; Alleyn knocked down his adversary, and throwing himself on him, he seized his sword, which he presented it to her on the heart: but soon the soldier begged for mercy. Alleyn had always been reluctant to take a man's life: he felt, moreover, at this moment that if he were to kill the soldier, his comrades would soon descend under the vault. So he turned away the sword; "receive life," he said; your death would be of no use to me; if you want, go tell Malcolm that an innocent man tried to escape death." The guard, struck by this behavior, got up in silence; after receiving his sword he followed Alleyn to the trapdoor through which they entered the dungeon together. Alleyn was soon left alone: the soldier, uncertain of what he should do, was about to rejoin his comrades, when on his way he met Malcolm who, always worried and vigilant, often walked the rampart at daybreak. The baron inquired if everything was in good order, and the guard, who feared being discovered, and was not in the habit of concealing, hesitated on this question. Then a terrible look compelled him to declare what had just happened. The baron reproached him for his negligence with great bitterness, and followed him at once to the keep, where he charged Alleyn with outrages. He examined the interior of the chamber, went down himself under the vault, and returned to the keep, he stopped there until he saw fixed in the wall a chain which he had sent to fetch in a place away from the castle. When Alleyn was attached to it: 'We won't leave you here long,' said Malcolm, leaving the room; in a few days you will be returned to the freedom you are so in love with: but as a conqueror must have spectators at his triumph, it is necessary to wait until I have been able to gather a sufficient number of them to witness the death of such a great hero". I despise your insults, resumed Alleyn; I am equally capable of bearing misfortune, and of defying a tyrant." Malcolm withdrew with rage in his heart, seeing the fearlessness of his prisoner, and made the most terrible threats to the guard who sought in vain to justify himself. "You answer on your head, he shouted at her, furious. The wounded soldier retraced his steps in sorrowful silence: the fear that his prisoner might not manage to escape seized his mind, and the memory of the expressions which Malcolm had used filled him with vexation; his gratitude for Alleyn, whose life he had received, joining in these sentiments, he hesitated whether he would obey the baron or free Alleyn, and flee with him. At noon he brought her his usual food. Alleyn was not so overwhelmed as to observe the shadows of sadness that enveloped his features; he foresaw in his soul what threatened him, and the soldier announced to him his sentence of death. The next day was to be the day of the execution; already the vassals were summoned to witness it. We may have tried to familiarize ourselves with death, it always seems terrible when it arrives. Alleyn had been waiting for him for a long time; he had practiced looking at her without fear, but his strength left him when she was present, and his whole body quivered. "Don't worry," said the soldier to him, in an affectionate voice, "I am far from insensitive to your miserable fate, and if you are of opinion to run the danger of tortures, compared to which those which one prepares for you at this moment are nothing, I will try all to return you to freedom, and to follow you far from a ferocious tyrant". At these words Alleyn, who was stretched out on the ground, was transported with surprise and joy; and rising hastily, 'what are you talking about tortures,' he cried; all are equal if death should end them; but I may still live. Lead me out of these walls, and the little I have will be yours". I need nothing, resumed the generous soldier; my only goal is to save the life of my fellow man." These words sunk deep into Alleyn's heart, his eyes filling with tears of gratitude. Edric then informed Alleyn that the door discovered by him, led to a vault, which extended beyond the walls of the castle, communicated with an underground way, dug formerly to facilitate the retreat of the castle, and that this way ended in a cavern in the medium of the close forest. He added that if they could manage to open this door, nothing would prevent them from fleeing. The two then deliberated upon the measures which necessity prescribed of them. The soldier handed Alleyn a knife stronger than his own, which was to be used to make a cut in the door around the lock. It was decided that Edric would keep watch, and that at midnight both would descend into the vault. Edric, after having untied the chain from Alleyn, came out of the prison, and the latter occupied himself, again, to raise the paving stones which had been replaced by order of the baron. The hope of his speedy deliverance had doubled his strength: his new knife was fitter for his purpose; and he worked with ardor and joy. He soon reached the trapdoor, and rushed once more into the vault. The door was extremely thick; it was not without great difficulty that he succeeded in removing the lock: then with his trembling hands he pushed the bolts open; the door opened, and he saw the new vault the soldier had told him about. It was not until evening approached that he had finished his work. He had already entered the dungeon, and had stretched out on the ground to rest, when he heard distant footsteps. Both filled with fear and hope, he listened to this sound which seemed to approach: finally the door opened. Alleyn, barely breathing, got up, looked that way, and saw not Edric, but another soldier; he thought that the overture he had made was about to be discovered, and believed himself lost forever. The soldier placed a pitcher of water on the ground, and after casting his eyes with somber curiosity around the prison, he left without saying a single word. All that human strength could bear was exhausted; Alleyn fell into a deep numbness; when he had come to himself, he found himself delivered again to the horrors of the night, of silence and of despair: nevertheless in the midst of his sufferings he blushed to raise suspicions of Edric's good faith. We are naturally inclined to repel painful sentiments; etc' doubting the sincerity of those in whom it has placed its trust is one of the greatest tortures that an honest soul can experience. Alleyn concluded that his conversation of the morning had been overheard, and that the new guard had been sent to examine his prison, and watch his movements: he believed that Edric, in consequence of his generosity, was like himself destined to perish; this idea overwhelmed him so much that it made him, for a few moments, lose sight of his own situation.

It was midnight, and Edric had not appeared; Alleyn's doubts then assumed in his mind the character of certainty; he abandoned himself to this frightful tranquility of mute despair. The castle clock having struck one o'clock, he took this sound for that of the funeral bell announcing his death. Called back to him by this terrible sensation, he rose from the ground, in the anguish of the keenest pain. Soon he distinguished the sound of the footsteps of two people advancing towards his prison: Malcolm and the assassination then presented themselves to his mind: he had no doubt that the people he heard were coming to carry out the baron's final orders; they were about to enter when he suddenly remembered the vault door. Until then occupied with his only despair, the The idea of running away had never occurred to him. In the midst of the violence of his pain, he had not even thought of this last resource. But at that moment she was like a flash that shone in his eyes; he rushed through the trapdoor, and his foot had scarcely touched the floor of the vault, when the bolts of his prison were drawn. A voice which he recognized to be Edric's, was soon heard; fear was so masterful of his mind that he hesitated for some time to uncover himself; but a moment's reflection sufficed to drive away all suspicion of Edric's fidelity, and he answered her voice. Edric came down immediately, followed by the soldier, whose appearance that morning had filled Alleyn with despair; he introduced him to him as his best friend, his comrade, and like a victim of Malcolm's tyranny, determined to follow them. It was a moment of happiness too vivid to describe. Alleyn, drunk with joy and impatient to flee, was barely listening to what Edric was saying to him; the latter went back up to close the door of the dungeon; precaution, the object of which was to arrest for a time those who might be tempted to pursue them; after placing in the hands of Alleyn a sword which he had brought with him, he marched at the head of his two companions, and advanced along the arch. The vast silence of the place was disturbed only by the sound of their footsteps, which, repeated by deep echoes, brought terror to their minds: often, while crossing these dark and sad recesses, they happened to stop to listen, and their fear made them hear the distant march of men who pursued them. On leaving the vault they entered a winding path of extreme length, and cut by various passages pierced in the living rock; it was closed by a low, narrow door opening near the underground path which went, by a fairly steep slope, to go under the ditch of the castle. Edric knew the place perfectly. They passed the door, and after having closed it on them, they began to descend. Suddenly the lamp that Edric held in his hand was extinguished by a gust of wind, and left them in complete darkness. It is easier to imagine what they felt than to render it; deprived of seeing the path they were to follow, hardly daring to put one foot in front of the other, and carrying a restless hand forward, they advanced into this deep abyss. When they had continued to descend for some time, they once again felt themselves on the earth. Edric warned them that there was another staircase before reaching the underground path, and recommended that they search for it with great care. They were walking slowly and cautiously, when Alleyn's foot struck against something that made a sound not unlike that of smashed armor; he bent down to recognize what he had touched, and seized the cold hand of a dead man. A sudden horror seized him, and he recoiled in fear. All three remained silent for some time; they dared not retrace their steps and were afraid to advance. A faint light, which seemed to come from the bottom of the second staircase, throwing some light around them, showed them at their feet a pale and disfigured body, covered with armor; and not far from them, three men whose movements they could distinguish. The first idea which struck their minds was that these men could only be assassins belonging to the baron, and engaged in the pursuit of some fugitive. There was no hope for them to hide except by staying where they were. But the light seemed to advance, and the three men to move towards them. In their fright they returned to the first staircase, which they climbed hastily; arrived at the door, they wanted to open it, hoping to be able to gain the breakthroughs of the rock: but all their efforts were in vain; the door was closed by the bolt of the lock, and the key was on the other side. Forced thus not to yield to their fear, they ventured to look behind them, and found themselves a second time in darkness. For a rather considerable time, all three remained motionless on the steps; they listened, and all was in silence: no ray of light no longer struck their eyes; finally they decided to march forward once more; they had found the place where they believed they had left the dead body, and were seeking to avoid its horrible meeting, when the light showed itself a second time in the same place where it had first been discovered; despair petrified them. However, the light made slow movements, and was hidden by the windings of the path. They remained in suspense for a long time, and without uttering a word; but having no longer any obstacle in front of them, they continued on their way. The light had made known to them the place where they were, as well as the staircase which they could descend with safety. Having reached the bottom without any alarming encounter, they listened again, and heard no sound; Edric announced that now they should be under the ditch. The path before them was level, and they believed that the light and the men seen by them had turned in another direction: for Edric knew that the main path had several outlets in the rock. Joy gave them wings: their deliverance seemed imminent, and Edric repeated that the cave was near. The issue they were looking for presented itself to them; but at the same time their hope was destroyed. Suddenly the light of a lamp struck them, and showed to their weak and dazzled eyes four men in a menacing attitude, and ready to receive them sword in hand. Alleyn drew his. "We will die, he cried, but as brave men." At the sound of his voice, the weapons fell from the hands of those who were before him, and he saw them come forward full of joy. Alleyn recognized with astonishment, three of these strangers, loyal friends and companions, and Edric, a soldier of his comrades in the fourth. It was the same purpose that brought them all together in this place; they left the cave together; and Alleyn, delighted to have recovered a liberty of which he had been deprived for so long, resolved never again to close his soul to hope. All were persuaded that the body found by them was that of a person whom hunger or

They walked together and came within a few miles of Athlin Castle. There Alleyn stated his intention of going to collect his friends, and undertake, with the tribe, to deliver the earl. Edric, as well as the soldier his comrade, solemnly enlisted for this cause, and we separated. Alleyn and Edric continued on their way to the castle, and the others went to different parts of the country. Alleyn and Edric had come but a short way, when the moans of Maltida's wounded servants drew them into the wood, where the horrible scene had taken place. Alleyn's surprise was extreme on seeing men attached to the Earl in this state; but this feeling gave way to another more poignant one, as soon as he was informed that Marie had been abducted by armed men. He barely gave himself time to untie the two servants, and springing on one of the horses which were grazing at a short distance, he ordered everyone to follow him, and took the road by which he was told that the kidnappers had passed. Alleyn and the soldier reached them, just as they were about to arrive at the mouth of the cave, the horrible aspect of which had given Marie momentary death. The brigands made vain efforts to flee; one of them was wounded, and nevertheless managed to save himself. His companions, seeing the servants of the count come running, abandoned their prey, and escaped through the dark detours of the cave. Mary looked lifeless, and Alleyn's eyes fixed in horror on this object: at last she opened her eyes herself amid eager efforts, by which he sought to restore her feeling; and joy seized Alleyn's soul.

Throughout Alleyn's story, where the greatest modesty reigned, Marie's heart was given over to various emotions, all of which sympathized with the vicissitudes of the young mountaineer's situation. She would have liked to hide from herself the interest she took in his adventures; but his efforts were so out of proportion with his emotion, that when Alleyn related the scene which had happened in Dunbayne's cave, pallor covered his quivering cheeks; and we saw her faint. This circumstance at first alarmed the penetrating Countess; the knowledge she had of her daughter's weak complexion soon seemed to her the only cause of this state, and was enough to repress her fears. Alleyn felt a delicious mixture of hope and anxiety that he did not yet know.

The Countess lavished on him all the outpourings of a soul filled with gratitude, and Marie's blushes told him more than her mouth could have done. All three sought the name and rank of the author of such a detestable plot. Their suspicions finally rested on Baron Malcolm, and this supposition acquired a great degree of probability, when they remembered that the brigands were on horseback; circumstance which was to make them considered as the agents of someone above them. Their conjectures turned out to be true. Malcolm was the author of the plan; he had charged with its execution several of his vassals, who had not been able to find the occasion to act before the surprise of the castle; and from that moment the too agitated baron had forgotten to withdraw his orders.

Alleyn was not long without making known his plan to reunite the feeble remnant of his friends with the tribe, and march against Dunbayne Castle. 'Good young man,' cried the Countess, unable to contain her admiration any longer, 'how can I ever pay for your generous services? Am I then destined to receive my two children from your hands? The tribe rises once more, and goes to attack the walls which defend Malcolm: lead it to the conquest and return my son to me. At these words the languid eyes of Marie resumed their brilliancy: she was intoxicated with the sweet hope of pressing to her bosom a brother from whom she had been separated for so long; but she soon passed from hope to fear; it was Alleyn who was to command the company, and Alleyn could perish in the fight. These opposing sentiments revealed to her the state of her heart, and her imagination was not long in showing her a long series of anxieties and sorrows which were preparing for her. She tried to banish from her mind the memory of the past and that of the fatal discovery she had just made; but her efforts were in vain: continually the image of Alleyn, adorned with all that strong and manly virtue which had guided her conduct, presented itself to her: the peasant disappeared, and she saw only the man endowed with the most noble character.

Alleyn spent the night at the castle: the next morning after having greeted the Countess and her daughter, to whom his eye bade a sad and respectful farewell. He left with Edric to go to his father's cottage. The ardent young man was impatient to assure himself of the health of this first object of his affections, and to embrace his friends. The breath of love had changed into an active flame the sparks of ambition which had kindled, with so much difficulty, in his heart. Now he was no longer animated by the sole desire to avenge oppressed virtue, and to snatch from misery and death the son of a chief whom he was accustomed to respect: he still burned to punish outrage. done to his mistress, and to signalize himself by some brilliant action worthy of his admiration and his gratitude.

Alleyn found her father taking lunch beside his niece: the old man, whose face was clouded with sadness, did not at first see Alleyn; but soon he almost succumbed to the excess of his joy on seeing that this son, his consolation and his hope, had been restored to him: Edric was received with as much cordiality as if he had been an old friend.

CHAPTER IV.

Continuation of Osbert's captivity;—He discovers two female prisoners like himself in Dunbayne Castle.—Malcolm condemns Osbert to death, and soon afterwards decides to postpone his execution.—Maltida and Mary believe Osbert dead; he sends them a letter.—Alleyn sets off with the tribe of Athlin, with the design of delivering Osbert.—Mary's love for Alleyn: her efforts to forget him.—Osbert tries to make himself noticed by the two prisoners.

Ihe count, prisoner in the tower and delivered to a frightful solitude, did not know the fate which was reserved for him: but the magnanimity of his character defied the cruel efforts of the hatred of the baron. As a result of his habit of preparing for the worst his enemy might imagine, he had come to regard death with a calm eye. The violent transports with which he had been agitated at the sight of Malcolm had subsided since he was no longer exposed to seeing him; he avoided with the greatest care to remember the fate of his father, on which he had never been able to set his mind, without feeling a horrible torment. But when he thought of the sufferings of the Countess and her sister, all his strength left him: often he wished to know how they bore the misfortune of his loss, and to let them know the state he was in: sometimes he took the resolution to endeavor not to concern himself with his present situation, and to procure help artificial against the sad objects with which it was surrounded. His main amusement consisted in observing the habits of the birds of prey which had come to lodge in the battlements of his tower; and their inclination to robbery furnished him with the occasion of a too just parallel with the habits of men. His main amusement consisted in observing the habits of the birds of prey which had come to lodge in the battlements of his tower; and their inclination to robbery furnished him with the occasion of a too just parallel with the habits of men. His main amusement consisted in observing the habits of the birds of prey which had come to lodge in the battlements of his tower; and their inclination to robbery furnished him with the occasion of a too just parallel with the habits of men.

As he was one day, in front of the gate that overlooked the castle, busy watching the races of the birds, his ear was again struck by the lute whose chords had already saved him from death. The melodious voice he had heard still accompanied him, and sang the verses that follow to a tender tune.

"When my eye was opened to the first morning rays of life, I saw around me only an enchanting scene; then the storms of the night did not present themselves to my eyes:»

"The brilliant illusions of hope seduced my soul, and misled the thoughts of my youth: imagination came to embellish everything with its bright colors, and revealed to me in the distance a future of happiness:"

"The void of my simple and pure heart was filled with filial tenderness: and the love of a father sufficed for his needs, for his ardor:"

"But oh cruel and rapid reverse! everything I loved is gone; the pale and dark misfortune has dispersed the trembling rays of hope, and the sweet reveries of the imagination have fled forever.

In the midst of his deep surprise, Osbert cast his gaze into the inner courtyard of the castle from which the voice seemed to issue: a moment later he saw a young person enter the part of the courtyard which holds the tower: another woman more aged, but still retaining traces of beauty, leaned on her arm. It was easy to recognize from the melancholy that darkened her features that the hand of pain had preceded the ravages of time. She was dressed in a widow's habit; a black veil, fastened on her forehead, gave a noble grace to her face; he was thrown back, and falling to the ground where he trailed himself in long folds, he seemed to add still more to the natural majesty of his bearing. This woman advanced slowly, supported by her companion, whose veil, half raised, showed the features. Sadness gave the beauty of the young person the most touching expression, and the dignity of her step announced that she was born in a high rank. From his arm hung the lute whose chords had so deliciously touched the Count. Osbert's astonishment at this sight was equaled only by his admiration. The two women withdrew by a door which was located towards the extremity of the opposite side of the courtyard, and it was no longer possible to see them. Osbert sought to follow them with his eyes, and for some time kept his eyes fixed on the door through which they had disappeared. Returning to himself, he thought, for the first time, that he experienced the horror of solitude; he conjectured that these women were foreigners detained by the unjust power of the baron, and her eyes filled with tears of pity. But the idea that so much beauty and so much dignity were victims of a tyrant soon filled his heart with indignation, and made his captivity more unbearable than ever. He burned to become the defender of virtue, and the liberator of oppressed innocence; the hatred he bore to Malcolm increased still further; and his soul received new strength from the persuasion in which he was that he would succeed in avenging himself. His guard entered at this moment: Osbert wanted to obtain from him some information relative to the two strangers; but it was in vain. The soldier was charged with bringing him sad news: he announced to the count that he must prepare for death, and that his execution was fixed for the following day. Osbert heard him calmly, and without deigning to let out the slightest murmur. He hastily pushed away the tender memory of his mother and his sister, too capable of weakening his courage. His guard told him that Alleyn had escaped. Then he had no doubt that this generous young man would do everything to punish the tyrant who was killing him.

When the baron had been informed of Alleyn's escape, rage had seized his heart; he had sent for the keep guards; but after long and painful searches, it was certain that they had accompanied their prisoner, and that several other captives had also escaped. Malcolm ordered that a sentry who remained be punished for the treachery of his comrades and his own negligence; and remembering the earl whom he had forgotten in the first heat of his resentment, he was glad that he had afforded him the opportunity of a complete revenge. In the midst of transports of joy he retracted the sentencing of the guard. No sooner had he sent the count the fatal message announcing his death than he took a new resolution. Such is the effect of guilty passions: they do not allow us to act with continuity: we can only satisfy one by sacrificing the other, and the moment when we believe we have grasped happiness is the very moment that destroys the hope of it . The baron felt the truth of this observation; he seemed to have arrived at the excess of felicity when he contemplated the approaches of his revenge; but suddenly the idea of Marie came to fill his heart with another passion. He had learned that she had been in the power of her emissaries and delivered on the spot. The very pain he felt at seeing his desires crossed, increased their violence, he could not make up his mind to give up his pursuit; and the only means of obtaining the one which was the object of it seemed to him to be to renounce his favorite passion. He had no doubt that they would not give him Marie, when he had declared that he wanted no other ransom for the count's life. These two passions, love and revenge, swayed so much in his heart that it would have been difficult to judge which was to prevail. Finally vengeance yielded to love; but he resolved to deliver the count to all the torments which the prospect of approaching death must produce, and to conceal from him his intention of staying his execution.

The Count awaited death with the firmness he had shown on learning of his sentence; he was led from the tower to the platform of the chateau without uttering a word or showing the slightest emotion. There he saw with a fixed eye all the preparations for his execution, the instruments of death, and the soldiers arrayed in file; the very aspect of eternity had little effect on his imagination. Among the objects which surrounded him, only one could bring him out of the profound indifference in which he seemed immersed; it was his murderer who showed himself with all the pomp displayed in triumphal pomp. At the sight of her Osbert paused for a moment, and felt his heart leap; but not wishing to appear troubled, he was striving to regain his dignity, when the memory of his mother presented itself to him.

When he came to himself, he found himself in his prison; he learned that the baron had granted him a respite: Malcolm, mistaking the earl's pain, had flattered himself that he had carried his sufferings to the last degree, and had ordered that he be taken back to the tower.

A scene so atrocious and so public as that which had just taken place at Dunbayne Castle was soon, in the neighborhood, the subject of all conversation. The Countess learned of it with a strange variety of circumstances which had been added to it; he was even assured that his son had really perished. At this overwhelming news, she relapsed into her first languor. Marie was too weak to give him care similar to that which she had already lavished on him with so much zeal. The doctor declared that the Countess' illness had its seat in the soul, and was beyond the reach of human science. One day she received a letter whose address was from the hand of Osbert: her eye recognized the characters, and breaking the seal, with eagerness, she learned that her son was still alive, and that he did not despair of throwing himself once more at her feet. He demanded that the rest of the tribe unite to attempt his deliverance; and learned in which part of the castle was his prison. Osbert believed that with the help of ropes and long ladders placed in the way he indicated, he could manage to save himself. This letter was an excellent cordial for the Countess and for Marie.

Cependant Alleyn mettait un zèle infatigable à rassembler les compagnons qui devaient l'aider dans son entreprise. Dès qu'il fut informé que le comte avait démenti le bruit de sa mort, il se rendit au milieu de la tribu, et la pressa de ne point différer d'agir. Aucun des vassaux n'avait besoin d'être sollicité: c'était une cause chérie par eux, qu'il s'agissait de défendre, et la main de tous était prête. Les préparatifs furent bientôt terminés, et Alleyn, à la tête de ses amis, vint se joindre à la tribu.

The Countess watched, a second time from the top of the walls, the departure of her vassals who were going to seek perils as certain as those to which they had exposed themselves the first time. This scene reminded her of the one she had already witnessed. She experienced the same fears, made the same wishes; and when the distance had concealed the troop from her sight, she returned to the chateau bursting into tears. Mary's heart was a prey to many kinds of pain. Unable to hide any longer from herself the tender interest she took in Alleyn's departure, her trouble became more visible. In vain the Countess tried to restore her some peace of mind. Marie, filled with gratitude, and moreover impelled by the natural frankness of her character, sometimes wished she could take it upon herself to confide her weakness to her mother (if one must call weakness a feeling which had its origin in the admiration aroused by noble and generous qualities). But his delicacy and his timidity always stopped him in the middle of his resolutions, and held on his lips the confession ready to escape him. The sorrows of his soul deteriorated little by little his health; her doctor recognized that her illness was due to a grief that she was trying to suppress; he indicated as the best remedy a friend in whose bosom she could deposit all the secrets of her soul. Maltida then had no difficulty in guessing the cause of her daughter's illness: she remembered her observations; and what she had at first suspected seemed certain to her. They' occupied in gaining her confidence by gentle and considerate caresses. Marie, finding his silence ungenerous, finally decided not to conceal anything more from her mother.

One day when the latter pressed her tenderly against her bosom, she declared to him her passion for Alleyn. The Countess had nothing more at heart than to ensure her daughter's happiness; the generosity and other virtues of the young mountaineer filled her with admiration. But the pride of his soul made him reject any idea of alliance with a man of such undistinguished birth. Her daughter's attachment seemed to her to be only a passing impression, born of a lively and exalted imagination, and she had no doubt that her advice and time would succeed in triumphing over it. Marie listened to her mother calmly: her reason applauded while her heart groaned; and she made up her mind to combat a feeling which was to cause so much grief to her and her family.

But the generous qualities of Alleyn continually reappeared in his memory with all their brilliance. It was impossible for him not to notice that he was in love with her; she appreciated all his struggles, and felt how great was the delicacy which had led him to distance himself, in respectful silence, from the object of his passion. She again turned to her mother to help her banish an image destructive of her happiness; the Countess employed all sorts of means to make him forget Alleyn; every hour, except those reserved for the exercises necessary for Marie's health, was employed in cultivating her mind and perfecting her talents. Maltida's efforts were not without fruit; she noticed that her daughter was beginning to recover peace of mind and health; Mary believed herself, sometimes, having learned to forget the one who was so dear to him. The precautions of the mother and the efforts of the daughter served at least to overcome the boredom of the moments which were passed in waiting for news of Alleyn and his company.

Dunbayne Castle was always the abode of misfortune: virtues groaned there under the sway of crime; and the baron, torn by conflicting passions, was himself a victim of their power.

The count had been forced to recognize that his days depended on the whim of a tyrant. His soul was prepared for the most cruel blows; but nevertheless he conceived some hope of escaping when he thought of this letter which one of his guards, touched with compassion, had undertaken to deliver to the Countess. While waiting, he passed every hour by the grating of his window; given over to the liveliest uneasiness, he cast his sight on the distant mountains, to assure himself whether he should not discover the march of his tribe. While he was thus deprived of real relief, these mountains became for him the source of an ideal pleasure. Often, in the beautiful summer evenings, he saw, from his window, walking on the terrace located at the bottom of the tower, these women whose appearance had excited his admiration and his pity. One day when he was filled with hope for himself and with compassion for them, his sufferings seemed to him to have eased. He conceived the idea of letting the two prisoners know that they had a companion, and of exciting their interest. The sun was hiding behind the summits of the mountains, and the shadow had already descended into the valleys. The tranquility of the evening inspired him with a sweet melancholy: he composed the stanzas that were to be read, and the following evening, came and threw them on the terrace. arouse their interest. The sun was hiding behind the summits of the mountains, and the shadow had already descended into the valleys. The tranquility of the evening inspired him with a sweet melancholy: he composed the stanzas that were to be read, and the following evening, came and threw them on the terrace. arouse their interest. The sun was hiding behind the summits of the mountains, and the shadow had already descended into the valleys. The tranquility of the evening inspired him with a sweet melancholy: he composed the stanzas that were to be read, and the following evening, came and threw them on the terrace.

"Hail, O sacred mountains; your peaks are cooled by the winds, and springs of water spring from between your rocks. The high pine that shades you receives the first rays of day, and its proud head is still the last object struck by the setting sun.

"Hail, O distant mountains! hello, valleys formed by them. Often the imagination reveals to me your beauties hidden by the damp mists. While the shepherd puffs up his blowtorch, or the poet yields to the pleasure of singing, my suffering heart laments the sad destiny that overwhelms me.

"Thrice happy the hour when the evening twilight comes to envelop these beloved woods in its shadow. Peaceful chords are then heard along the clearing: the imagination picks them up through the murmur of the winds; and the lovers of this powerful divinity lend a charmed ear."

"O how penetrating are these sounds! they are prolonged in the distant mountains, and the echo of the caves, which repeats them, disturbs the silence of the deserts.

Osbert was pleased to see that the paper was picked up by the two women, who retired immediately afterwards to the castle.

CHAPTER V.

Alleyn and the tribe of Athlin present themselves before Dunbayne Castle. Malcolm has Osbert brought to the ramparts, and threatens to kill him if Alleyn and his people do not withdraw; he offers to set Osbert free, on condition that he will obtain Marie in marriage.—Alleyn goes to Athlin Castle to carry Malcolm's proposals.—Pain of Maltida and Marie.—Marie decides to marry Malcolm to save the life to her brother.—Alleyn is instructed by Maltida to ask Malcolm for a few days' delay, at the end of which she must give her answer.

IThe next day, at daybreak, the Count saw a flag rising in the distance; his heart opened to a hope which the event confirmed. It was his loyal vassals, led by Alleyn, who advanced to surround and attack the castle. Their small number did not allow them to dare flatter themselves with reducing it; but they believed, that in the midst of the tumult of the combat, they would succeed in delivering the count. The sentries shouted at them as soon as they were within a certain distance, and the alarm was given from all sides. At the same moment the walls were covered with soldiers. The baron was present and himself directed the defense preparations; he had secretly decided on his plan. The tribe, surrounding the ditch, into which they threw fascines, prepared for the attack, and high ladders jutted out to facilitate climbing; the count, to whom joy and hope had given new strength, found the means of tearing off one of the bars of the grid: he already had his foot resting on the window, and was ready to escape, when he was seized by Malcolm's guards, and rushed out of the prison. While he gave way to despair and indignation, he was led to the highest part of the ramparts, whence he could see Alleyn and the tribe, and be seen himself. At his appearance his vassals were happy; but they were so only for a moment, for they noticed that their chief was loaded with chains, surrounded by guards, and followed by the instruments of death. Animated by a last hope, they pushed the attack with redoubled fury, when the baron's trumpets demanded a parley. So they suspended the fight; Malcolm appeared on the rampart, and Alleyn approached to hear him. "The moment of the attack, cried the baron, will be that of the death of your leader: if you want his life to be preserved, cease this assault; retire in peace, and take the following message to the Countess: "Baron Malcolm will accept no other ransom than the beautiful Marie, whom he burns to make his wife. If Maltida accepts this proposal, Osbert is free on the spot; if she refuses it, he is dead." The emotion of the Count and of Alleyn was inexpressible: the Count, full of haughty courage, hastened to reject this vile bargain. "Give me death," he cried, "the house of Athlin cannot dishonor himself by an alliance with a murderer. Recommend your attack, O my brave vassals! you can no longer save my life, at least you will avenge my death; I prefer her to the dishonor of my family." Osbert had not yet ceased speaking when a double hedge of guards surrounded him, and hid him from the gaze of the tribe.

Alleyn, whose heart was torn by conflicting sentiments, listened only to the voice of honour; he disobeys Osbert's orders; and laying down his arms, he declared that he was going to Athlin Castle to carry the baron's proposals. The tribe followed Alleyn's example, and some of its members prepared to accompany him: such loyal vassals could not yield to the earl's exhortations. For him, he felt a sharp pain when the news of Alleyn's departure reached his prison.

His situation was dreadful; all the energy of his soul was barely enough to support it. He was charged with a message whose result was to plunge into despair a woman he adored, or to kill the friend who was dearest to him.

When the Countess was informed of Alleyn's arrival, joy and impatience seized her heart; she had no doubt that Malcolm would send her to offer an accommodation; and there was no ransom she was not willing to give to buy her son's freedom. At the sound of Alleyn's voice, the turmoil that had begun to subside in Marie's womb awoke, it was impossible for her not to recognize a love that should not allow her any hope: in vain, at the moment of to see again the one who was the object of it, she tried to repress her emotion; her blushes indicated the state of her soul; and all his efforts to hide his feelings only served to make them appear still more.

When Alleyn appeared before the Countess, his strength was exhausted by a result of the violent agitation he had experienced. The gloomy sadness spread over his face, the pallor which his fear gave him, betrayed his interior torments; Maltida conceived at her sight keen alarms on account of her son, and in a trembling voice inquired of his destiny. Alleyn hastened to reassure her; he was careful to employ the greatest precautions, when he came to fulfill his message, and to relate the scene which he had witnessed. The baron's resolution seemed such a terrible blow to Marie's heart that she fainted on learning of it. Alleyn ran to support her, and the Countess, busy giving assistance to her daughter, found herself for a moment distracted from the pain that this news must naturally arouse in her. It was only with great difficulty that Marie was called back to life, or rather to the feeling of her misfortune; but it is impossible to imagine, in all its extent, the painful situation of Maltida. His heart, divided between two interests so powerful, had become the seat of disorder and terror. Whichever way she looked, she saw only misfortune and destruction. The murderer of her husband demanded the sacrifice of his daughter, and on the arrest of a mother depended the fatal blow which threatened her son; she killed him, rejecting Malcolm's proposal; in accepting it, she outraged the memory of her cowardly slaughtered husband, and exposed herself to the reproaches of indignant virtue. Such an alliance destroyed the happiness of his daughter and the honor of his house. It was no longer permissible to think of freeing Osbert by force of arms, since the baron had declared that the moment of the attack would be that of his death. Honor, humanity, maternal tenderness commanded Maltida to save her son, and by a strange opposition of interests, these same virtues united to prevent him from making the sacrifice Malcolm demanded. Up to this day a feeble ray of hope had not ceased to show itself to this unfortunate mother. Now despair shrouded her in thick darkness, through which she saw only the altar on which one of her children was to be slain. She shuddered at the mere idea of uniting her daughter to her father's murderer, and also knew that the ferocity of Malcolm's character was enough alone to corrupt the happiness of the woman who would share his destiny. In her grief she forcefully rejected the baron's proposed exchange; but the sight of her son, pale and losing all his blood in the midst of the convulsions of death, suddenly presented itself to his imagination, and caused him a kind of delirium.

There was a combat no less violent at Marie's; nature had given him a heart susceptible to all tender and delicate affections; her mind easily grasped all the reports of the most rigorous morality, and she constantly conducted herself according to the principles she had formed. All these advantages were not necessary to make him know the rigor of his fate, which would have been felt by a common soul; but they served to make his grief more acute; and to show him, in a brighter light, the horror of his situation. The memory of his father, the duty imposed by virtue, and the love which made his trembling but strong voice heard, spoke alone to his heart; the idea of uniting with Malcolm filled her with dread. Could she receive a hand still smoldering with her father's blood? could she consent to spend her life with a man who had severed the days of the one whose existence she had received, a man who would always be before her eyes a monument of her misfortune and of the dishonor of her family, and whose aspect banish forever from his heart all gentle and generous affections? She could not cherish noble and elevated sentiments without cherishing the memory of her father and that of her lover. How unhappy she must have been if she were forced to erase from her memory the image of virtue in the hope of obtaining a dreadful tranquillity! Wherever his sad eyes sought relief they met only despair. On the one hand she saw herself buried in the arms of an assassin: another was her brother, laden with irons and awaiting death, who offered himself to her. It was impossible for him to bear this picture to which the imagination lent all the horrors of reality. However, in the midst of her sufferings, she considered that it was possible for her to save her brother: then she clung strongly to this idea; since she must be unhappy, she resolved at least to be so nobly, and to offer herself as a victim, when horrible conjunctures demanded this sacrifice. it was possible for her to save her brother: then she clung strongly to this idea; since she must be unhappy, she resolved at least to be so nobly, and to offer herself as a victim, when horrible conjunctures demanded this sacrifice. it was possible for her to save her brother: then she clung strongly to this idea; since she must be unhappy, she resolved at least to be so nobly, and to offer herself as a victim, when horrible conjunctures demanded this sacrifice.

Filled with these ideas, she entered the room of the Countess; she hastened to announce her resolution to him, and waited, trembling, what her mother was about to decide.

Maltida felt at that moment a pain beyond that which she had felt up to that day; at the death of her husband, whom she loved with tenderness, she had suffered greatly: the manner in which he had perished had contributed to making her grief more acute; but this event, although terrible, had not been accompanied by circumstances similar to those in which she found herself; a superior force had brought him, when she had learned it, it was no longer in her power to save her husband; she hadn't had to make a frightening choice between horrors, ratify her misfortune with her own mouth, and poison the rest of her days with dreadful memories. Although it was the power of a tyrant that imposed this choice on her, she attributed it to herself in part,

When Marie presented herself before her, her soul, exhausted by the excess of her pain, had fallen into a dull and silent despair. Insensitive to the objects around her, she was, so to speak, to her own ills, and she hardly heard her daughter. "He will live, exclaimed Marie in a weak and broken voice, I will sacrifice myself." At these words "he will live," the Countess, raising her eyes, cast a gloomy look around her which suddenly took on an expression of tenderness when it was fixed on Marie. A few tears ran down her cheeks, and were like dew from heaven, which, falling on a withered plant, revives its dying leaf. These tears were the first she had shed since the arrival of the fatal message. She sent for Alleyn, with whom she wanted to examine whether he there was no way of snatching the count from his prison. Often, in great afflictions, when death has not yet given sad certainty to events, the spirit soars beyond the sphere of the possible to run after hope, until the frightful reality shows him the nothingness of his illusions. So it was with Maltida; the violence of her grief, caused by the first news of her misfortune, was beginning to lessen, and she was inclined to believe that her situation was not as desperate as it had seemed to her at first. His heart opened to the hope that Osbert might be given an opportunity to escape. Alleyn came in trembling; he dreaded what was going to be announced to him, and proposed to offer to brave all dangers to free the count. The idea that Marie would become Malcolm's wife was horrible to him, and he repelled her like a poison capable of stopping the movement of life in his heart. He wanted at all costs to snatch Marie from this calamity, and draw the Count from his prison. The spectacle which struck him at the moment when he approached the Countess increased his torment; she was stretched out on a pale, mute sofa. Her unseeing eyes were fixed on a window in front of her. Her whole countenance announced the disorder of her mind, and she was for some time without seeing Alleyn. Such was the fluctuation of his thoughts that if a ray of hope sometimes crossed the darkness which enveloped him, soon a return to himself would make him faint. Mary, seated near her, held her hand pressed to her bosom. Pain had spread an enchanting languor throughout his person; she tried to express again the painful decision she had taken, but her voice trembled, and half her sentence expired on her lips: her eyes seemed to seek to avoid Alleyn, like an object capable of making her give up his purpose. He came forward to ask the Countess what she wanted to order. "I am ready," said Marie at this moment, "to devote myself like a victim to the baron's revenge: at least I will have saved my brother." As she spoke thus, a deadly chill seized Alleyn's heart; and she herself struggled to finish, her whole body shuddered; her eyes were covered with a thick cloud, and she fell fainting on the sofa where she was sitting.

Alleyn, a prey to all the pangs of despair, his gaze fixed and motionless, awaited in the silence of anxiety the moment of his return to life; the help lavished on her soon brought her back, and the joy he felt at it made him forget his situation for a moment; he pressed Marie's hand ardently to his bosom. This unfortunate girl, who had barely recovered the use of her senses, yielded, without realizing it, to the first movement of her heart, and an expressive smile of the liveliest tenderness gave Alleyn the certainty of being loved. Hitherto despair had chained his passion; there was too great a distance between him and the sister of Osbert, and his modesty had not allowed him to imagine that he had enough merit to attract the attention of the lovely Mary. Perhaps also this self-distrust, so natural to true love, had contributed to deceiving him. It was only then that this certainty gave him the most delicious sensation he had yet experienced. He forgot for a moment the distress of his hosts and his own condition; all his ideas vanished to give way to the new knowledge he had just acquired, and for a few minutes he tasted the most perfect bliss. Thought was not long in bringing back the dark thoughts and their dark aftermath and plunging him back into the depths of the abyss. he would still have experienced. He forgot for a moment the distress of his hosts and his own condition; all his ideas vanished to give way to the new knowledge he had just acquired, and for a few minutes he tasted the most perfect bliss. Thought was not long in bringing back the dark thoughts and their dark aftermath and plunging him back into the depths of the abyss. he would still have experienced. He forgot for a moment the distress of his hosts and his own condition; all his ideas vanished to give way to the new knowledge he had just acquired, and for a few minutes he tasted the most perfect bliss. Thought was not long in bringing back the dark thoughts and their dark aftermath and plunging him back into the depths of the abyss.

The Countess had then regained enough strength to talk about the subject she had most at heart. The idea of a new attempt to deliver his son had not escaped Alleyn; he said that he was ready to face all dangers to achieve this goal, and he spoke in such a confident tone of the probability of success, that he once again revived hope in Maltida's bosom; she nevertheless feared to give way too hastily to such a dubious hope. It was resolved that Alleyn should consult with the ablest and most faithful men of the tribe, whom age or infirmity had hitherto kept out of the fight, upon the means best suited to the success of the enterprise, and that he would then march, without delay, at the head of the combatants; that

Alleyn therefore formed a council of the ablest people of the tribe. Various projects were proposed, the success of which seemed very uncertain. At last someone observed that it was possible that Osbert was no longer in the tower, and that the place of his detention was changed: a thing which must first be known in order to form a suitable plan. It was therefore resolved to suspend the deliberations until Alleyn had procured the necessary information, and in the meantime he was instructed to deliver the Countess's message to Malcolm. That is why he immediately set out for the castle.

CHAPTER VI.

Transfer of Osbert to another prison.—Message from Maltida to Malcolm.—Discovery of a moving panel by which one enters several vast apartments.—Osbert reaches that of the two prisoners.—Their surprise at the sight of the Count.—The latter's tender interest in their sufferings. He asks and obtains permission to renew his visit.—Alleyn's steps to discover the count's prison, and to try to get him out of it.—Desertion of two soldiers from Malcolm's castle who come to enlist under the banners of 'Alleyn.

During that time Dunbayne Castle had become the scene of triumph and distress. Proud of his project, Malcolm already saw Marie at his feet, while Osbert was experiencing torments more cruel than death. The baron was surprised that his invention had not yet suggested this means of torture. For the first time love had attractions for him, because it became the instrument of his revenge, and because, moreover, the violence of his passion had represented to him the charms of Marie under the most flattering colors. He therefore resolved never to release the earl except on the terms he had offered, and by that means to render the house of Athlin an everlasting monument to his triumph.

For greater safety, Osbert had been transferred to the center of the castle in a vast and dark apartment, and whose Gothic windows let in only enough light to perceive the horror. That wasn't what tormented him the most; his heart felt much sharper pains. A misfortune as terrible as that which threatened him had never presented itself to his imagination. Long familiar with the idea of death, he regarded it only as a passing illness; but to see her family in ignominy, to see her contract an alliance with her father's assassin, the thought tore her soul.

He feared that maternal tenderness would induce Maltida to accept the baron's offers, and he had no doubt that his sister had enough nobility of soul to sacrifice herself in order to save his life. He is said to have written to the Countess to forbid her to accept these conditions, and to declare to her his firm resolution to die; but he had no means of getting his letter to her; the guard, who had had the generosity to pass his first, no longer appeared. The courage which had sustained him thus far did not abandon him at this critical moment. Accustomed for a long time to experiencing numberless contradictions, he had acquired the art of surmounting them; the greatest reverses were not capable of overthrowing it; resistance only served

Alleyn had just joined the tribe, and was doing all he could to get the necessary information. He learned that the Count was no longer in the tower, but he could not discover to what part of the castle he was relegated; on this point we had only vague and implausible conjectures. What led to the belief that he had not been put to death was the policy of the baron, whose violent love for Marie was no longer a mystery. Alleyn vainly employed all the stratagems that invention could suggest to him to discover the earl's prison. Finally, forced to deliver to Malcolm the message with which he was charged, he requested as a preliminary that Osbert be brought to the ramparts, in order to show his vassals that he was still alive.

The Count appeared safe and sound on the ramparts. At the sight of him his vassals made the air resound with their cries to testify their joy; the baron was at his side, and looked at them with an air of contempt. Alleyn approached the walls and delivered

Maltida's message. Osbert shudders at its content; he foresaw that a deliberation announced a submission. Torn by this thought, he swore aloud that he would never survive such infamy; then addressing himself to Alleyn, he commanded her to return immediately to the Countess, and to tell her not to submit to such humiliating conditions, unless she wished to sacrifice her two children to the murderer of their father. These words brought a smile of triumph to the baron's face, and he turned in a disdainful silence. The guards escorted Osbert back to his prison; but all the efforts of his friend to discover the road they were taking were useless; the height of the walls soon made them disappear from his eyes.

Alleyn furnishes us with an example of the firmness and constancy with which an energetic soul pursues a favorite object; untoward circumstances may come in the way, lack of success may momentarily arrest one's progress; but it rises above all obstacles, and to achieve its ends it goes even beyond the bounds of possibility. This young man did not yet despair; but he did not know how he should act.

Passing near a window, Osbert was surprised to see two ladies there: despite the agitation of his mind, he recognized them as the same people whom he had observed from the gates of the tower with so much emotion, and which had aroused both his compassion and his curiosity. In the midst of his distress, the gentleness and graces of the youngest had often occupied his thoughts, and he ardently desired to know the subject of her grief; for the melancholy painted on her face announced that she was unhappy. They watched Osbert as he passed, and their eyes expressed their pity at his situation. He stared at them tenderly, and back in his prison, he asked new questions about them; but they continued to maintain an inflexible silence in this respect.

One day when he was buried in his thoughts, his eyes involuntarily fixed on a panel of the paneling of his prison: he noticed that he was differently made than the others and that his projection was ever so slightly greater; a glimmer of hope seized his mind, and he rose to examine it. He saw that it was surrounded by a cleft, and pushing it with his hands, he moved. Certain there was something more than a panel, he put all his strength into it; but it produced no other effect. After futilely trying to remove it in various ways, he gave up the business, and returned to sit sad and desperate. Several days passed without his giving any further thought to the panelling. However, not wanting to give up this last hope, he made a new examination, and in trying to shake the panel, his foot accidentally fell against a place which caused it to open instantly. There was a hidden spring inside which held it fastened, and by pressing a certain part of the panel it opened by itself; it was this part that the Count's foot had touched.

This discovery gave him inexpressible joy. He then saw in front of him a vast apartment similar to that which formed his prison; its tall, arched windows were adorned with painted glass; its pavement was of marble, and this place appeared to be the remains of an abandoned church. Osbert hesitantly crossed its long nave, and came to a large double-leafed oak door which terminated this gloomy room: he opened it and saw a long and spacious gallery; its windows, as gothic as those of the church, were covered with thick ivy which, so to speak, kept out the light. He stopped for a while at the entrance, uncertain if he should go any further; he listened, and hearing no sound in his prison, he continued. The gallery ended on the left by turning, to a grand staircase, very ancient and apparently very neglected, which led to a room below; to the right was a low, dimly lit door.

Osbert, afraid of being discovered, went up the stairs and opened the door. Then a line of superb, magnificently furnished apartments presented itself to his astonished eyes. He followed without seeing anyone; but, after crossing the second room, he heard the sobs of a weeping person. He paused for a moment, not knowing whether to continue; an irresistible curiosity carried him further, and he entered an apartment where were seated the beautiful strangers, the sight of whom had made such an impression on him.

The eldest of the ladies was bursting into tears, and on a table beside her were a cassette tape and some open papers. The youngest was so busy with a drawing that she paid no attention to the entrance of the count. As soon as the first saw him, she got up in disorder, and the surprise which broke out in her games seemed to demand an explanation for such an extraordinary visit. Osbert, astonished at what he had just seen, took a few steps back, intending to retire; but remembering that this intrusion required an apology, he returned. The grace with which he excused himself confirmed the impression his face had made on the mind of Laure (such was the name of the young lady) who, raising her head, revealed a face in which the one discovered a happy mixture of dignity and gentleness. She was about twenty years old, of medium height, extremely delicate, and very well made. The coloring of her youth had a tint of soft and reflective melancholy which gave a very interesting expression to her large blue eyes; her features were partly hidden by her beautiful brown hair which, after forming a number of curls around her face, descended on her bosom: all the graces of an amiable sex were united in her person, and the natural majesty of her bearing demonstrated the purity and nobility of his soul. When she caught sight of the Count, a faint blush spread over her cheeks, and she involuntarily left the drawing in which she was occupied. extremely delicate and very well made. The coloring of her youth had a tint of soft and reflective melancholy which gave a very interesting expression to her large blue eyes; her features were partly hidden by her beautiful brown hair which, after forming a number of curls around her face, descended on her bosom: all the graces of an amiable sex were united in her person, and the natural majesty of her bearing demonstrated the purity and nobility of his soul. When she caught sight of the Count, a faint blush spread over her cheeks, and she involuntarily left the drawing in which she was occupied. extremely delicate and very well made. The coloring of her youth had a tint of soft and reflective melancholy which gave a very interesting expression to her large blue eyes; her features were partly hidden by her beautiful brown hair which, after forming a number of curls around her face, descended on her bosom: all the graces of an amiable sex were united in her person, and the natural majesty of her bearing demonstrated the purity and nobility of his soul. When she caught sight of the Count, a faint blush spread over her cheeks, and she involuntarily left the drawing in which she was occupied. her features were partly hidden by her beautiful brown hair which, after forming a number of curls around her face, descended on her bosom: all the graces of an amiable sex were united in her person, and the natural majesty of her bearing demonstrated the purity and nobility of his soul. When she caught sight of the Count, a faint blush spread over her cheeks, and she involuntarily left the drawing in which she was occupied. her features were partly hidden by her beautiful brown hair which, after forming a number of curls around her face, descended on her bosom: all the graces of an amiable sex were united in her person, and the natural majesty of her bearing demonstrated the purity and nobility of his soul. When she caught sight of the Count, a faint blush spread over her cheeks, and she involuntarily left the drawing in which she was occupied.

If the mere sight of Laure was able to make an impression on Osbert's heart, he became much more strongly in love with her when he could contemplate her beauty. He imagined that the Baron, charmed by her charms, had made her fall into some of his traps and was keeping her in the chateau in spite of herself. The sadness painted on his face and the mystery that seemed to surround him, confirmed him in this conjecture. Full of this idea, his sufferings inspired him with the greatest compassion, and the love which then burned in his heart soon came to unite with this feeling. At that moment he forgot the danger of his situation; he even forgot that he was a prisoner, and, thinking only of the means of alleviating the sorrows of this unfortunate woman, he did not allow himself to be deterred by a false delicacy, and he resolved,

Addressing himself therefore to the baroness: "Madame," he said, "if I could in any way lighten the sorrows which I cannot affect not to see and which have touched me so deeply, I would regard this moment as the happiest of my life; of a lifetime, alas! which has already been only too marked at the corner of misfortune. But misfortune has not been useless to me, since it has made me know sympathy. The baroness was not unaware of the count's character and misfortunes. A victim of oppression herself, she knew how to pity the sufferings of others. She had always felt a tender compassion for Osbert's misfortunes, and she could not help expressing to him all her gratitude for the interest he was willing to take in her sorrows. She showed him her surprise at seeing him thus at liberty;

He told her about the discovery of the sign that had led him to find the way to his apartment. The idea of facilitating his escape first occurred to the Baroness; but her own situation soon made her see the uselessness of it, and she was compelled to abandon a thought which had inspired in her the veneration she had for the character of the late Count, and the interest she took to his son; she showed him the deepest chagrin at not being able to serve him, and informed him that she and her daughter were also prisoners; that their liberty did not extend beyond the walls of the castle, and that they had been under the rod of tyranny for fifteen years.

The count expressed his indignation at this story, assured the baroness that she could count on her discretion, and begged her, if this relationship was not too painful to her, to inform him at least how she had had the misfortune. to fall into the power of Malcolm. The baroness, fearing for the safety of Osbert, reminded him of the danger of being discovered by staying any longer outside his prison; and, thanking him once more for the interest he had kindly taken in his sufferings, assured him of his most sincere wishes for his deliverance, and promised him that, if ever the occasion presented itself, she would let him know the sad peculiarities of her adventures. The earl's eyes expressed his gratitude more expressively than his tongue could have done. He asked, trembling, permission to renew his visits, which would afford him some intervals of consolation during the sad captivity to which he was condemned. The baroness, out of pity for his sufferings, consented to his request. Osbert left, casting a tender and sorrowful look at Laure; he was nevertheless satisfied with what had passed, and retired to his prison, experiencing one of those moments of calm which are not even foreign to the unfortunate.

He found everything quiet, and after carefully closing the panel, he sat down to reflect on the past and think about the future. He flattered himself that the discovery of the panel might facilitate his escape; the shadows of despair with which his mind had so recently been enveloped gradually dissipated, and gave him a glimpse of a more flattering horizon; but unfortunately! these brilliant hopes vanished like a dream. He remembered that this castle was surrounded by guards whose vigilance was ensured by the severity of the baron; that the beautiful foreigners who had taken such a tender interest in his fate were like him prisoners, and that he did not know a generous soldier who would teach him the secret passages of the chateau and accompany him in his flight. His imagination was full of the image of Laure; in vain did he endeavor to hide the truth from himself, his heart constantly betraying the sophisms of his arguments. He had, without knowing it, drunk from the cup of love, and he was forced to confess his indiscretion. He could not, however, bring himself to remove this delicious poison from his heart; he couldn't bring himself to stop seeing her. The painful apprehensions for his safety which the Baroness would feel if he did not take advantage of the permission he had so earnestly solicited; the lack of respect such conduct would show; the violent curiosity to know the story of his misfortunes; the lively interest with which he would learn about the relations of Laure and the baron, and the extravagant and deceptive hope of being able to be of use to them, determined him to renew his visit.

Alleyn, however, was back at Athlin Castle where he had communicated Osbert's resolution, which had only served to aggravate the distress of the unfortunate people who dwelt there. But in order not to make them lose all hope, he had hidden from them that the count was no longer in the tower; he meditated in silence and almost without hope on the means of discovering his prison, and he tried to give the Countess and Marie a consolation in which he himself could not take part. He went, without wasting time, to find the old men whom he had assembled on his departure, and informed them of the count's change of prison: a circumstance which was to suspend their deliberations for the present. That is why he left them and immediately went to the tribe to continue his research.

The time fixed for the Countess' reply was approaching; despair was painted on all faces, all hearts were torn with the greatest anguish; when one evening the sentries of the camp were alarmed by the approach of some men whose voices were unknown to them; fearing a surprise, they surrounded them and led them to Alleyn. These prisoners said that to escape the tyranny of Malcolm they had come to take refuge in the camp of his enemies whose misfortunes they deplored and whose cause they wanted to defend. Charmed by this circumstance, without however absolutely believing in it, Alleyn questioned the soldiers approaching the count's prison. He learned that Osbert had been transferred to a very difficult part of the castle, and that any plan of escape was impracticable.

Alleyn then had a prospect of success which his most exaggerated hopes had not yet presented to him. The soldiers solemnly promised to help him with all their power; they also informed him that there was a general discontent among the baron's vassals who were only waiting for a favorable moment to shake off the yoke of tyranny and resume the rights of nature; that Malcolm's suspicions urged him to punish with the utmost rigor the slightest appearance of inattention, and that being themselves condemned to a very severe punishment for a slight fault, they had tried to avoid it, thus than to the future oppression of their leader, by desertion.

Alleyn immediately summoned a council before which the soldiers brought in repeated their first assertions, and one of them added that he had a brother who would have deserted with them if he had not been on guard that day. with the count: which had made him fear of being discovered; he added that his brother would be on guard the next day at the door of the little drawbridge where there were only a few sentinels; that he would run the risk of going to him, and that he was persuaded that he would not refuse to favor the deliverance of the count. At these words Alleyn's heart throbbed with joy. He promised this brave soldier a great reward for him and for his brother, if they would both undertake the enterprise. His companion knew perfectly the subterranean passages of the rock; he also offered his services. Alleyn's hopes became every moment more founded, and he would have liked at that moment to be able to communicate to the unhappy family of Osbert the joy which dilated his heart.

The next day was fixed for beginning the enterprise, and Jacques instructed to make every effort to win over his brother. These preliminaries settled, they parted to go and rest, but Alleyn could not sleep a wink all night: the anxiety of expectation seized his mind and filled his imagination with the most pleasant visions; he pictured to himself the count's reunion with his family; he anticipated the thanks he was about to receive from the amiable Marie, and he sighed as he reflected that mere thanks were all he had reason to hope for.

At the end the day appeared and offered the tribe a very different perspective than that of the day before. Alleyn, impatient to know the result of the meeting which was to take place between the two brothers, found the hours too long. The night finally came to second his desires. The darkness was interrupted only by the faint moonlight that peeked from time to time through the dark clouds that surrounded the horizon. The wind broke the silence of the darkness at intervals. Alleyn watched all the movements of the chateau; the lights disappeared successively, the tower clock struck one; everything seemed quiet inside, and Jacques walked towards the drawbridge. This bridge was cut in the middle, and the part on the side of the plain was lowered; Jacques stepped on it and called in a low voice, but firm, Edmund. No answer: he began to fear that his brother had already left the castle. He paused for some time before repeating his call, and he heard the bolts of the drawbridge door being gently drawn; then Edmund appeared.

He was surprised to find Jacques and ordered him to flee at once to avoid the danger which threatened him. The baron, angered by the frequent desertion of his soldiers, had sent people after them and promised considerable rewards to those who arrested the deserters. This speech had no effect on Jacques' mind; he remained, resolved to achieve his ends. Fortunately the sentries on duty with Edmund were all buried in a deep sleep, by the effect of a drink which he had administered to them to facilitate his escape: which caused the two brothers to continue, in low voices, their conversation, without being interrupted.

Edmund would not delay his flight any longer, and had not enough firmness to run the dangers of the enterprise. The lure of the reward, however, awakened his courage, and he allowed himself to be persuaded; he was well acquainted with all the underground avenues of the chateau; the only difficulty that remained to be surmounted was to deceive the vigilance of the other sentries, and he did not think it possible for the count to leave his prison without being seen. The soldiers who were to stand guard with him the following night were in other parts of the castle, which they were not to leave until they were placed in prison: it was therefore difficult to administer this same potion that had dulled the senses of his comrades. Trusting their integrity and striving to seduce them, would have been putting his life at their disposal and probably aggravating the count's ills. This project was surrounded by too many dangers to hazard it, and their imagination offered them none more probable.

It was nevertheless agreed that, the following night, Edmund should seize a favorable moment to inform the earl of the designs of his friends, and to consult him on the means of putting them into execution. In accordance with this resolution, Jacques returned safe and sound to Alleyn's tent, where the chiefs of the tribe were assembled, awaiting his return with the greatest anxiety. The soldier's report considerably weakens the hopes of this young man; the vigilance with which the prison was guarded seemed to render any escape impracticable. He was, however, condemned to remain in this cruel uncertainty for nearly three days, until Edmund was again at the post of the drawbridge and could communicate with his brother. But Alleyn did not suspect a circumstance which would have absolutely annihilated all his hopes, and the consequences of which might ruin all their plans. A sentinel posted on the part of the rampart which overlooked the drawbridge had been alarmed by the noise of the bolts, and, having approached the walls, had seen a man on the half of the bridge which was beyond the ditch, conversing with someone inside. She had come forward as far as the walls would allow, and had done her best to hear what they were saying. The darkness of the night had prevented her from recognizing the person who was on deck; but she had distinguished Edmund's voice very well. Surprised at what was happening, she gave her full attention to discovering the subject of their conversation. The distance which half the raised bridge left between the two brothers obliged them to speak louder than they would otherwise have done, and the sentry heard enough to be informed that they were concerting for the escape of the county; that this enterprise was to take place on the night that Edmund would be on guard at the prison, and that some of the Earl's friends would be waiting for him in the neighborhood of the castle. This man kept all this in his memory, and the next morning he shared it with his comrades. and that some of the Count's friends were waiting for him near the chateau. This man kept all this in his memory, and the next morning he shared it with his comrades. and that some of the Count's friends were waiting for him near the chateau. This man kept all this in his memory, and the next morning he shared it with his comrades.

The next day, towards evening, the count, yielding to the impulse of his heart, opened his hatch again, and advanced towards the apartments of the baroness. She received it with signs of satisfaction, while the pleasure of innocence, painted on Laure's face, testified that her heart, hitherto a prey to pain, experienced at this moment a delicious sensation. Osbert reminded him of his promise, which the desire to arouse the compassion of those one esteems and the melancholy pleasure one finds in retracing the picture of a past happiness, had made him give. Having endeavored to compose her minds, which the memory of her past sufferings had shaken, she related to him the following.